Y0-BCP-057

THE MODERN LIBRARY
OF THE WORLD'S BEST BOOKS

PETER AND ALEXIS

Turn to the end of this volume
for a complete list of titles
in the Modern Library

PETER AND ALEXIS

BY
DMITRI MEREJKOWSKI

TRANSLATED BY
BERNARD GUILBERT GUERNEY

BENNETT A. CERF · DONALD S. KLOPFER

THE MODERN LIBRARY

NEW YORK

PG
3467
M4
A23
1931

This volume completes MEREJOWSKI'S
famous trilogy, consisting of

THE ROMANCE OF LEONARDO DA VINCI 138
THE DEATH OF THE GODS 153
PETER AND ALEXIS 175

20599

Alfred F. Goldsmith, Esq.,
At the Sign of the Sparrow,
New York City.

My dear Mr. Goldsmith:

I have repeatedly asserted in conversations with clients and fellow book-sellers (but always behind your back) that, had I one-tenth of your unbelievable knowledge of books, or one-twentieth of your unequaled graciousness, I would consider myself the second-best bookman in this by no means small city. I now take this opportunity in dedicating my translation of this Russian classic to you (as a small token of my great esteem and admiration for you), to state the same consideration right out in public, in all the comparative immortality and irretrievability of cold type.

Believe me,

Faithfully yours,

B. G. G.

At the Sign of the Blue Faun,
New York City,
Autumn of 1930.

FOREWORD

Those who already have my translation of *The Romance of Leonardo da Vinci* [1] are referred to the able biographical sketch of the author contained therein; those who have *The Death of the Gods* [2] are referred to the critical note which serves as a preface thereto; those who possess only one of the foregoing (or neither,—which, after all, may be possible) are referred to the nearest bookshop. . . . In the preface to this, the concluding volume of the *Trilogy of Christ and Antichrist*, there remains but to pick up and knot whatever loose strands may have remained from the preceding prefaces.

As I have previously pointed out, the theme of this Trilogy is the eternal struggle between Man the God and Men the Lice. I am not unaware that the accepted critical cant would be 'the eternal struggle between Good and Evil'; nevertheless, I shall stick to my guns. The careful reader of the Trilogy cannot but have perceived by this time that the author, as an artist, regards Good and Evil as but the two sides of a single coin; that to him the Prince of Darkness is also identical with the Lightbearer, and that Peter the Filicide is also the Great Helmsman of Russia.

And, even as with the artist, so with the man; Merejkowski presents a paradox: the last of the authentic Pagans at heart, and the first of the exceedingly few Christians (using the word carefully) of to-day. That is why he is an intense misanthrope of Man-in-the-Mob, Man-the-Herd-Animal,—Man the Louse, and as intense a philanthrope of Man-Alone, Man the Individual,—Man the God. I do not believe there is a more ardent practicing Christian than Merejkowski since Tolstoi; yet it is Christ he is in love with, and never Christianity,—either as

[1] No. 138 in The Modern Library.
[2] No. 153 in The Modern Library.

practiced in the fourth century, under Julian, or in the sixteenth, in da Vinci's time, or in the eighteenth, during Peter the Great's reign. And his very Christ is different from that of Tolstoi; Tolstoi loved the Christ Who preached to multitudes, Who cherished the lowly, the meek, the oppressed,—in simple English, man in his seething, stinking mass: the mob; Merejkowski loves the Christ Who sought solitude in deserts, Who agonized alone at Gethsemane,—the lone sacrifice to the Eternal Mob that lynched and tortured Him, and is crucifying Him anew each day. . . .

Of the not inconsiderable number of translations I have done to date, I do not hesitate to pronounce the present the most difficult. I therefore hope that the public will be indulgent over the unavoidable delay in the publication of *Peter and Alexis*. In addition to my endeavor to carry over the eighteenth-century flavor of the original, there have been well-nigh insuperable terminological difficulties: architectural, ecclesiastical, legalistic, mechanical, military, technical, theological, and so forth. Any corrections, criticisms or suggestions sent to the subjoined address will be appreciated. I also avail myself of this opportunity to thank all those who have been kind enough to write me in connection with the two previous volumes.

I have but to add that the Englishing of this Trilogy has been a marvelous and memorable experience; with that I leave the patient reader to enjoy in this book an aspect of Merejkowski which may be new to him: that of a Prophet.

BERNARD GUILBERT GUERNEY.

The Blue Faun Bookshop,
136 West 23rd Street,
New York City.
Autumn of 1931.

CONTENTS

PETER AND ALEXIS

BOOK ONE

THE VENUS OF PETERBURGH

I

"ANTICHRIST would fain be. He himself, the last of the devils, has not yet been, but there has been a great litter of his whelps,—all the earth under the heavens is filled with them. The children are beating a path for their father. They arrange all things in the image of Antichrist. But when they shall have arranged everything, and cleared and smoothed everything, then he shall e'en put in his appearance,—e'en in his own good time. He is already at the portals,—he will be here soon!"

This was spoken by an old man of some fifty years, in the tattered *kaftan* of a pettifogger, to a young man seated at a table, in a nankeen dressing gown and with his bare feet in house-slippers.

"And whence do ye know all this?" queried the young man.

" 'Tis writ: Neither the Son, nor the angels know. And yet ye know. . . ."

He was silent for a while, then yawned and asked:

"Art thou one of the Raskolniki heretics, now?"

"I am of the Orthodox faith."

"Wherefore hast thou journeyed to Peterburgh?"

"Out of Moscow was I taken, from my poor dwelling, with my account books, because of information lodged by some informer as to my taking bribes."

"Didst take any?"

"I did. Not because I was forced to, or because of any thievish nature; but according to love and conscience, as much as any one would give for my official efforts."

1

He spoke with such simplicity that it was evident he really did not deem it a sin to take bribes.

"And as for exposing my guilt, he, this informer, did not lodge any information at all leading thereto. It was only through the records of the contractors who, during the course of many years had been giving me small sums, that they counted up two hundred and fifteen rubles of such offerings, —yet I have naught to repay this with. For I be beggared, and old, and full of sorrows, and lowly, and maimed, and most miserable, and unable to carry on official matters,—I knock my forehead on the ground before thee and implore to be retired. Your Most Merciful Highness, deign to look upon me from the fullness of your benevolent generosity, intercede for an old man that hath none to intercede for him, that he may be freed from this unrighteous impost. Have compassion, be gracious, My Lord Czarevich, Alexei Petrovich!"

Czarevich Alexei had come upon this old man several months ago in Peterburgh, in the Church of St. Simeon the Hospitaler and St. Anna the Prophetess, which is near the small river of Fontannaya and Sheremetevsky Court on the Liteinaya Street. Having been struck by his beard (a thing unusual among government clerks),—long untrimmed and grizzled,—and by his assiduous reading of the Psalter in the choir, the Czarevich had asked who he was, where he was from, and what his position was. The old man had described himself as a clerk in the Moscow Artillery Bureau, one Larion Dokukin; he had come from Moscow and was stopping at the house of a woman who baked wafers for this same Church of St. Simeon. He had brought up his poverty, and the sneaky accusation made against him,—and also, almost from the very first words, had spoken of the Antichrist. This old man seemed pitiful to the Czarevich. He bade this man to come to him at his quarters, that he might help him with advice and moneys.

Now Dokukin was standing before him, in his ragged, wretched *kaftan*, looking like a beggar. He was the most ordinary of clerks, one of those who are called quill-drivers and pettifoggers. He had uncouth, seemingly petrified wrinkles; an uncouth, chill look in his small dull eyes; an

uncouth and neglected gray beard; his face was drab, wearisome, like those papers which he transcribed; he must have
puttered and puttered around with them in his department
probably for some thirty years; had taken bribes from contractors, "according to love and conscience"; and, perhaps,
may even have indulged in sneaky intrigues,—and now, look
ye, what he has thought up: "Antichrist would fain be!"

"Come, but isn't he a knave?" the Czarevich thought dubiously, bestowing a closer look upon him. But nothing of the
knavish or the crafty could be found in this face,—rather,
something simple-hearted and helpless, glum and stubborn,—
as in the face of people who are possessed by a single fixed
idea.

"I have come from Moscow also on another matter," added
the old man, and seemed to hesitate. The fixed idea was, with
a slow effort, coming to the surface of his uncouth features.
He cast down his eyes, rummaged with his hand in his bosom,
dragged out some papers which had fallen within the lining
through a hole in his pocket, and handed them to the Czarevich.

These were two slim, greasy little notebooks, made of
sheets folded in four, written in a large clear hand,—a copyist's hand.

Alexei at first read them absent-mindedly, but, as he read
on, his interest became greater and greater. At first he came
upon excerpts from the Holy Fathers, the Prophets, and the
Apocalypse anent Antichrist and the end of the world. Then,
—a call to the "Arch-Pastors of great Russia and of all
creation," with a prayer that they forgive his, Dokukin's,
"liberty and rudeness, in having, without their paternal blessing, written this because of his so great sorrow and pity, and
zeal for the church," and also going on to ask them to intercede for him before the Czar, and to use their best efforts to
placate him, so that he might have mercy upon him, and hear
him out to the end. Further there followed what was apparently Dokukin's main idea:

"Man is ordained by God to be self-ruled."

And finally there was an indictment of the Sovereign, Peter
Alexeievich:

"But now we are all cut off from the said divine gift of

a self-ruled and free life, as well as from our houses and our trafficking, our tilling of the soil and our handicrafts, and all our former industries and anciently established laws,—also are we deprived of all Christian devoutness. From house to house, from place to place, from city to city, are we driven, insulted and infuriated. All our ways, and speech, and our dress have we changed; our heads and our beards have we clipped; our persons have we in mockery dishonored. There is no longer in us any kindness, or dignity, or any distinction from those of other faiths; instead we have completely merged with them; their affairs have become a matter of habit to us, whereas our own Christian ways we have cast down and have left our sacred churches desolate. We have narrowed our eyes against the East, we have turned our feet in flight toward the West; in strange and unknown ways have we set our steps, and have perished in the land of oblivion. We have taken strangers to be our sons this day, have showered them with blessings in every way, while our own flesh and blood we through hunger did slay, spurning their rights, ruining them with tributes they could not pay. There be other things 'tis not even expedient to talk about,—'tis more expedient to put a guard upon one's lips. Yet the heart doth ache greatly, beholding the desolation of the New Jerusalem, and the people in their misfortunes are wounded with most grievous wounds!

"Yet all this," the conclusion ran, "is wrought upon us in the name of our Lord Jesus Christ. Oh, ye mystical martyrs, be ye not horrified and despair ye not; wax greater in goodness and arm yourselves, with the Cross of our Lord for a weapon, against the might of Antichrist! Suffer ye for the sake of the Lord,—suffer ye but a little while longer! For we shall not be forsaken by Christ,—to Whom be glory now and forever and for ages without end. Amen."

"Wherefore didst thou write this?" asked the Czarevich, having finished reading the notebooks.

"I dropped just such a letter only the other day at the Church of St. Simeon, at the portals thereof," answered Dokukin. "But then, when they found that letter, they did burn it and made no report thereof to the Sovereign, nor did they look into the matter. But as for this petition, I want to nail it at the Church of the Trinity, near our Sovereign's palace, so that all may read what is written thereon, and know of it, and tell of it to His Imperial Majesty. As for the writing of it, 'twas done for the sake of reform, so that, when he has come to his proper senses, His Imperial Majesty might mend his ways."

"A knave!" again flashed through Alexei's mind. "Or perhaps he is an informer to boot! It must be the devil himself that prompted me to take up with him!"

"But do you know, Larion," said he, looking him straight in the eyes, "do you know that I, in duty bound, as a citizen and a son, am supposed to tell my sovereign father about thy inciting and seditious writing? 'Tis in the Military Statutes, Article 20: He that shall offend against His Majesty with words or utterances of dispraise, the same shall be deprived of his life and be punished by having his head lopped off."

"As thou wilt, Czarevich. I was thinking myself of coming here that I might suffer for the word of Christ."

He said this with the same simplicity that he had but now used in speaking of bribes. The Czarevich looked at him still more intently. Before him stood the very same ordinary clerk, a governmental quill-driver,—the very same chill, dull gaze and weary face. Only in the very depths of his eyes something again stirred with a slow effort.

"Art thou in thy right mind, old man? Think of what thou art doing. Thou wilt find thyself within the walls of a garrison,—'tis no jesting matter there: they shall hang thee up by one rib,—and then smoke thee thoroughly, even as they did Grishka Talitzky."

Talitzky was one of the prophets who preached the end of the world and the second coming of Christ; he had affirmed that the Sovereign, Peter Alexeievich, was the Antichrist, and who several years ago had been executed by the fearful punishment of being smoked over a slow fire.

"With God's help I am ready to give up e'en my life's breath," answered the old man; "it may not be now, yet each one of us is bound to die, one way or another. One must have some good deed to one's credit wherewith to arise before the Lord; but as for death,—none can escape it."

He spoke as simply as ever, but there was something in

his calm face, in his quiet voice, which inspired the conviction that this retired Artillery copyist, accused of taking bribes, would actually go to his death with never a qualm of fear, like one of those mystical martyrs whom he had mentioned in his appeal.

"No," the Czarevich suddenly decided, "he is neither a knave nor an informer,—but either one out of his mind or a downright martyr!"

The old man cast down his head and added still more quietly, as though he were talking to himself and had forgot all about his companion:

" 'Tis ordained from God that man be self-ruled."

Alexei got up in silence, tore a leaf out of the notebook, lit it at a little holy lamp burning before the images in a corner, took out the damper and, opening the door of the stove, thrust the papers therein, stirring them with a poker as he waited until they were entirely consumed, and then, when nothing but ashes were left, he approached Dokukin who was standing on one spot, with his eyes fixed on the Czarevich, and placed his hand on the clerk's shoulder:

"Hearken, old man,—I shan't inform upon thee to anybody. I can see that thou art a truth-loving man. I trust thee. Tell me: dost thou wish me well?"

Dokukin made no answer, but the glance he bestowed upon the Czarevich obviated the necessity of any.

"But thou canst, if thou wouldst, throw this silly stuff out of thy head! As for these obstreperous letters, durst not even think of them,—these be not the times for such things. If thou dost slip up, and 'tis found out that thou hast been to see me, evil shall befall me also. Go thy ways and God be with thee, and come no more. Speak with none about me. Should they ask thee,—keep thy peace. And do thou go as speedily as thy legs will carry thee from Peterburgh. Look thou, Larion,—wilt thou remember my will?"

"Where are we to escape to from thy will?" Dokukin let drop. "God is my witness, I am thy faithful servant unto death."

"As for the informer's complaint,—have no concern over it," continued Alexei. "I shall put in a word where it will be needed. Be assured thou shalt be exonerated from everything. Well, go. . . . Or, no, stay,—let me have thy kerchief."

Dokukin handed him a large, blue, checkered handkerchief, faded and full of holes, just as "miserable" as its owner. The Czarevich pulled out a box from his small desk of walnut, which stood alongside of the table, took out of it, without counting, some twenty rubles in silver and coppers, —a whole treasure trove for the beggarly Dokukin,—knotted all this wealth in one corner of the kerchief, and gave it to him with a kindly smile.

"Take that to tide thee over on the road. When thou shalt return to Moscow order a mass in the Cathedral of the Archangel, and take thou out a bit of a wafer for the health of Alexei, humble servant of God. Only look thou, blab not that it is for the Czarevich."

The old man took the money, but neither thanked him nor took his leave. He still stood with his head cast down. Finally he lifted up his eyes and solemnly launched into what was probably a carefully prepared speech:

"Even as of old God did slake the thirst of Samson through the jaw-bone of an ass, will not the same God, even now, work through my folly, Sire, something beneficent and refreshing to thee?"

But suddenly he broke down. His voice broke, his solemn speech came to an abrupt close, his lips quivered,—he shook all over and slumped at the feet of the Czarevich.

"Have compassion upon us, father, hearken unto us poor folk, us who are raising up our voices,—us, your least slaves! Do thou work for the Christian faith, rear up and look after and give to the Church peace and single-mindedness. Verily, Sovereign Czarevich, our dear, beautiful little one, our churchly one, our little sun, thou hope of all the Russias! The whole universe is fain to be enlightened through thee. The exhausted people of God rejoice over thee! If thou art not for our Lord God, who, then, shall succor us? We are perished, we are all perished without thee, our own one. Have compassion upon us!"

He was embracing and kissing the Czarevich's feet. racked with sobs. The Czarevich heard him, and it seemed to him that, in this despairing supplication, there was reaching him the supplication of all the perishing, "the insulted and the infuriated,"—the outcry of all the nation for help.

"That will do, now, that will do, old man," he managed to say at last, bending over him and attempting to lift him up. "Do I not know,—do I not see? Doth not my heart ache for ye? We all share the same grief. Wherever ye are, there am I also. If God wills it, and I shall rule, I shall do everything to lighten the lot of the people. Nor shall I forget thee, I have need of faithful servants. But in the meanwhile, endure ye and pray that God may grant the consummation soon,—may His will be sacred in all things!"

He helped him to get up on his feet. Now the old man seemed very decrepit, weak, and piteous. His eyes alone shone with such joy as though he were already beholding the salvation of Russia. Alexei embraced him and kissed him on the forehead.

"Farewell, Larion. If God grants it we shall see each other again. God be with thee!"

When Dokukin went away the Czarevich once more seated himself in his leather armchair,—old, torn, with its stuffing of hair sticking out of the holes, but very restful and soft— and became plunged into something between a doze and a coma.

He was twenty-five, tall of stature, thin, and narrow shouldered, with a sunken chest; his face, too, was narrow,— so lantern-jawed as to be peculiar, just as though it were drawn out and sharpened at the chin, like an ancient image and super-sensitive, with a swarthily xanthochroous color, as in those who suffer from liver complaint; his mouth was very small and piteously childlike; his disproportionately large, beetling, round forehead, which made him seem bald, was framed with scandent strands of long, lanky, black hair. Such faces are to be found among novices in monasteries and rural deacons. But when he smiled his eyes glowed with intellect and kindness,—his face immediately becoming younger and better looking, as though it were illumined by a calm, inner light. At these moments he recalled his grandfather, the Most Pacific Czar Alexei Mikhailovich, in his youth.

Now, in his soiled dressing gown, with down-at-the-heel slippers on his bare feet, with his sleepy air, unshaven, with down in his hair, he resembled but a little a son of Peter. After the effects of yesterday's spree, he had slept the whole day and had gotten up but recently, just before the very evening. Through the door opening into an adjacent room one could glimpse the unmade bed with its rumpled, enormous pillows of down, and its soiled linen.

His work table, at which he was seated, was cluttered with rusted and dust-covered mathematical instruments, an antique broken thurible with frankincense, a tobacco grater, meerschaum pipes, a small box that once contained powder for the hair but which now served as an ashtray; mounds of papers and heaps of books in the same disorder as everything else,—manuscript comments on *The Universal Chronicles of Baronius* were covered by a heap of tobacco in packets; a half-eaten salted cucumber reposed upon an open page of *The Book Entitled Geometry, or Land Surveying with the Radix and the Compass, for the Instruction of Seekers After Wisdom* (all dog-eared and with its backbone gone); upon a pewter plate lay a clean-gnawn bone and a small goblet sticky from orange liqueur in which a fly was struggling and buzzing. And over the walls with their tattered, smudged panels of dark-green flowered oil-cloth, and over the soot-covered ceiling, and over the turbid panes of the windows (which, despite the heat of June, still had double-frames),—everywhere the flies buzzed, thronged and crawled in thick black swarms.

The flies were buzzing over his head. . . . In his mind the sleepy thoughts, too, swarmed like flies. He recalled the set-to with which yesterday's drinking bout had terminated. Clodhopper had hit out at Sleepy-head,—Sleepy-head had let fly at Whip-hand, while Father Hades and Rook, together with Moloch, had fallen in a heap under the table,—these were the names bestowed by the Czarevich upon his bottle companions,—"for a bit of home fun." While he himself, Alexei the Sinful (also a nickname), had been pummeling somebody and yanking his hair,—but who precisely it was he could not remember. At the time it had been funny, but now it seemed vile and shameful.

His headache was getting worse. If he could but have a little more orange brandy to sober up.... But he was too lazy to get up, to summon the servants,—too lazy even to move. And right now he would have to dress, to draw on his narrow uniform *kaftan*, to put on his sword, and his heavy wig, from which the head ached still more, and then ride to the Summer Garden, for the masked Assembly, which everybody had been bidden to attend, under threat of "severe penalties."

The voices of children skipping rope and playing puss-in-a-corner reached him from the yard. The ailing, ruffled siskin in its cage over the window emitted a piteous chirp at rare intervals. The pendulum of a tall upright English clock, with chimes, an old present of his father's, was ticking away monotonously. From the apartment above one could hear dismal, interminable scales of a quavering German clavecin, ancient and diminute, played by the wife of Alexei, the Crown Princess Sophia Charlotta, daughter of the Duke of Wolfenbüttel. He suddenly recalled how, yesterday, when drunk, he had been cursing her before Clod-hopper, and Whip-hand:

"There, they've tied a she-devil round my neck for a wife: no matter when I come to see her, she's forever ruffled up and will not speak to me. What a German *frau!*"—"That's bad," he reflected. "When I'm drunk I say a lot of things I shouldn't, while afterwards I reproach myself very much. . . ." And wherein was she at fault because, when she was almost a child, she had been coerced into marrying him? And why call her a *frau*,—ailing, lonely, abandoned of all in a land of strangers,—she was just as unhappy as he was. And she loved him,—perhaps she was the only one who did love him. He recalled their recent quarrel. She had cried out: "The least cobbler in Germany treats his wife better than you do!"—He had shrugged his shoulders spitefully: "Then return to Germany, and God be with you! . . ."—"Why, if I were not . . ." and she could not finish, bursting into tears, as she pointed to her abdomen,—she was pregnant. He sees, as if they were actually before him, those swollen, pale-blue eyes, and the tears which, washing off the powder (the poor little thing had just now put the powder on for his particular benefit), were coursing down her face,—a face with traces of smallpox, haughtily supercilious, grown still homelier and thinner from pregnancy, and so pitiful, so childishly helpless. Why, he loves her in his turn,—or, at least, pities her at times, with a pity impulsive and hopeless, unbearable and so poignant that it hurts. Why, then, does he torture her? How is it he does not feel his conscience bothering him, or shame? He was bound to answer to God for her.

The flies were overcoming him. An oblique, warm, red beam of the setting sun, striking right through the window, was hurting his eyes. He finally shifted his armchair, turning his back to the window, and fixed his eyes on the stove. This was an enormous Dutch stove, with little carved pillars, intricately designed hollows and projections; made of Russian pictured tiles, fastened at the corners with small nails of brass. In rich reddish-green and dark-violet pigments, on a white field, were drawn sundry ingenious beasts, birds, people, vegetables,—and under every little figure there was an inscription in Slavic characters. In the dark-purple sunbeam the pigments flamed with a magic vividness. And for the thousandth time, with a dull curiosity, the Czarevich was scrutinizing these little figures and reading over the inscriptions. A *mouzhik* with a balalaika: *I make great music;* a man sitting in an armchair with a book: *I am improving myself;* a tulip in bloom: *The odor of it is sweet;* an old man kneeling before a beauty: *I do not want to be an old man's darling;* a couple sitting under some bushes: *Our counsel is good for thee also;* there were also a country wife of Berezina, and French mountebanks, and priests,—one Chinese, the other Japanese,—and Diana, and the fabulous bird Malkopheia.

But the flies were buzzing, buzzing, buzzing; and the pendulum was ticking, and the siskin dismally whimpering; and the scales of the clavecin were coming down from above, and the shouts of the children floating in from the yard. And the cutting red beam of the sun was growing duller, darker. And the little multicolored figures were stirring. The French mountebanks were playing leap-frog with the country wife of Berezina, the Japanese bonze was winking at the bird Malkopheia. And everything was mingling,—his eyes were closing. And.if.it were not for these enormous, sticky black flies, which were no longer buzzing in the goblet but in his head, and tickling it, everything would be well, peaceful, and there would be nothing except a quiet, dark, red murk.

Suddenly he shuddered all over and became wide awake.

"Have compassion, father, thou hope of all the Russias!" He heard the words within him, sounding with a staggering force. He cast his eye over the untidy room, and over himself—and even as the dark purple beam of the sun, which cut the eyes, had flooded his face, so did shame sear him. A fine "hope of all the Russias"! Vodka, sleep, indolence, lying, filth, and this eternal vile fear before Batiushka, his father.

Could it really be too late? Could it be all over? If he might but shake off all this, go off, fly! "To suffer for the word of Christ!" the words of Dokukin sounded within him again. "God has ordained man to be self-ruled." Oh, yes, to go to them as quickly as possible, while it was not yet too late! They were summoning him and awaiting him,—these "mystical martyrs."

He jumped up as though he was actually about to fly somewhere, to come to some decision, to take some irretrievable action,—and froze on the spot, tense with expectation, hearkening.

The brazen, slow, canorous rumble of the clock chimes boomed through the stillness. It struck nine, and when the last sound had died away the door opened very softly, and the head of his old *valet de chambre*, Ivan Aphanasich Bolshai, was thrust in.

" 'Tis time to be going. Will you order your clothes?" he grumbled,—as was his wont, with such malicious glumness as though he had sworn at the Czarevich.

"No need. I am not going," said Alexei.

"As ye will. Only everybody is ordered to come. Batiushka will again be wroth."

"There, go on, go on," the Czarevich was about to drive him away; but, having glanced at his rumpled head, with down in his hair, with the same sort of unshaven, rumpled, sleepy face as his own, he suddenly recalled that it was precisely this Aphanasich whom he had been dragging by the hair yesterday. The Czarevich contemplated the old man for a long while, in dull incomprehension, as though only now he had become fully awake.

The last red reflection died out in the window, and at once everything turned gray, just as if the cobwebs, coming down from all the sooty nooks, were filling the room, weaving it around with a gray net.

But the head in the doorway still stuck there, as though it were glued there, neither retreating nor advancing.

"Are you ordering your clothes, or what?" repeated Aphanasich, with still greater glumness.

Alexei made a hopeless gesture with his hand.

"Well, come what may,—let's have them!"

And, seeing that the head still did not vanish, as though expecting something else, he added:

"What about a little orange brandy, to sober up on? My head is splitting sorely, because of yesterday. . . ."

The old man made no answer, but looked at him as if he were fain to say:

"It's not *thy* head that ought to be splitting because of yesterday's affair!"

Left to himself the Czarevich slowly crackled his hands, so that all his finger joints snapped; he stretched himself and yawned. Shame, fear, sorrow, a thirst for repentance, a thirst after some great deed, some sudden exploit,—everything found an end in this slow, hopeless yawning, which was unrestrainable,—to the verge of pain, to convulsiveness of the jaws; a yawn more dreadful than any outcry and sobbing.

An hour later, washed and clean shaven, sobered up, in his tightly fitting, narrow uniform coat of green German broadcloth, with red lapels and gold braid,—the uniform of a sergeant in the Guard of the Transfiguration, he was on his six-oared wherry, floating down the Neva, toward the Summer Garden.

II

On that day, the 26th of June in the year of seventeen hundred and fifteen, there was going to take place a Festival of Venus in the Summer Garden, in honor of an antique statue, which had just been brought from Rome and was going to be placed in the gallery over the Neva.

"I shall have a better garden than the French King's Versailles," boasted Peter. Whenever he was on the sea or in foreign lands his royal consort sent him news about his favorite child: "Our pleasance has spread out rather well, and better than last year; the way leading from our chambers is almost shaded over with maples and oaks; and whenever I walk out I often regret, dearest little friend of my heart, that I am not strolling together with you."—"Our pleasance hath become most pleasantly green; there is already an odor of resin in the air"—*i.e.*, the resinous odor of buds.

And, actually, everything in the Summer Garden was arranged regularly, according to plan, as in the "splendid pleasance of Versailles." The trees were smoothly clipped, just as though they had come from a barber's; the flower-beds in geometrically regular figures; the canals running in straight lines; the ponds quadrangular, with swans, ates, and arbors; the fountains most ingenious; the walks interminable,— called *"perspectives"*; the hedges high and leafy; the espaliers resembled the walls of ceremonial reception halls,—"people were urged to stroll about, and if any did tire, he or she would at once find near a sufficiency of benches, theaters [pavilions], labyrinths, and plats of green grass, to which they may withdraw, as though it were into some most delectable solitude."

Nevertheless, the Czar's pleasance was still very far from equaling the Gardens of Versailles.

The wan sun of Peterburgh drew but very puny tulips out of the pinguid Rotterdam bulbs. Only the unassuming flowers of the North—the fragrant tansy, beloved of Peter, the dark-scarlet peonies, and the despondently vivid georginas,—grew freely here. Saplings, brought with unbelievable trouble and toil upon ships, upon rafts, from thousands of versts away,— from Poland, Prussia, Pomerania, Denmark, Holland,—also pined away. Their weak roots were but niggardly nurtured by a land strange to them. But then, "just as in Versailles," marble busts—"torso pieces"—and statues were placed along the main alleys. Roman emperors, Greek philosophers, Olympian gods and goddesses were, it seemed, exchanging glances of incomprehension as to how they had found themselves in this savage land of Hyperborean barbarians. These were, however, no antique originals, but merely new imitations by second-rate Italian and German artists. The gods, as though they had but now taken off their wigs and their embroidered *kaftans*, and the goddesses, as though just released from their lacy furbelows and bustles, and as if they were all somewhat at sea about their not altogether decorous nakedness, seemed more like demure cavaliers and dames, who had been taught "the degrees of French politeness" at the court of Louis XIV or the Duke of Orleans.

Czarevich Alexei was walking over one of the side paths of the Garden, which led from the large pond to the Neva. By his side hobbled a funny little figure of a man upon spindle shanks, in a worn German *kaftan*, an enormous wig, and with a flustered, overwhelmed expression on his face, like that of a man suddenly awakened. This was the head director of the Chancellory of Armaments and of the new Press, the first master printer in the town of Peterburgh,— one Mikhailo Petrovich Avramov.

The son of a deacon he had found himself, as a seventeen-year-old schoolboy, straight from his Book of Hours and his Psalter, upon a trading vessel, sent from Kronslot to Amsterdam with a freight of pitch, Russia leather, hides, and half a score of "Russian infants," chosen from among the "sharper lads," to learn overseas, by Peter's *ukase*. In Holland, having learned something of geometry (and still more of mythology), Avramov had been "by the denizens of those parts greatly praised and publicly cited in the current chronicles." Not at all silly by nature, being even a "sharp lad," he yet seemed to have been astounded for all time, knocked out of his senses by too sudden a transition from the Psalter and the Book of Hours to the fables of Ovid and Virgil,—and could nevermore come to himself. In his emotions and thoughts something had taken place which resembled that natal hysteria which occurs with little children who are scared in their dreams, and ever since there remained upon his face, unchanged, this eternal expression of one flustered, overwhelmed.

"Lord Czarevich, Your Highness, I shall confess to thee

as to God himself," Avramov was saying in a monotonous, lugubrious voice, just like the whimpering of a midge. "My conscience vexes me sorely for that, being Christians, we do extend worship unto pagan idols. . . ."

"What idols?" the Czarevich voiced his wonder.

Avramov pointed to the marble statues flanking both sides of the alley.

"Our sires and our grandsires did place holy ikons in their houses and upon the crossways, whereas we are ashamed so to do, and, instead, place shameless pagan images. The ikons of God have within them the power of God; similarly, in the idols, which are the ikons of the Fiend, there dwelleth the power of the Fiend. We did say a mass but the other day to a certain drunken god Bacchus, called in our tongue Ivashka the Tipsy, during an All-Fools' Conclave or Council, presided over by a mock Prince-Pope; whereas right now we are preparing to say mass for this most vile Venus, the whoring goddess. They do be calling these services 'masquerades' now, nor are they deemed a sin; for verily, say they, these very gods have no actual being in nature, while their soulless representations of wood and stone are placed in houses and pleasances with no other object than ornamentation. And in that they do err most grievously, unto the utter perishing of their souls, inasmuch as these ancient gods do have a natural and actual existence. . . ."

"Thou believest in the gods?" the Czarevich wondered still more.

"I believe, Your Highness, according to the witness of the Holy Fathers, that the gods be verily the fiends, which, driven out of their idol-temples in the name of Christ crucified, did flee into places desolate, dark, abysmal, and did make their nests there, and did pretend to be dead and as though they were not,—until their time is come. But when ancient Christianity did wax meager, and new ungodliness came thrusting up out of the ground into the light of the sun, the gods thereupon also became alive once more, and did crawl out of their lairs; and, just as every useless worm, and humming bug, and other venomous vermin, as soon as they come crawling out of their eggs, do start stinging man, thus the fiends, coming out of these ancient idols, their masks, do wound Christian souls and make them to perish. Dost thou remember, Czarevich, the vision mentioned in the holy writings of Father Isaac? Most comely maids and youths, whose faces were like unto the sun, having seized this most sainted man by his hands, did sault and dance with him to most delectable voices of music, and, after tiring him out, left him barely alive, and, having thus reviled him, did evanish. And thereupon the holy Abba fathomed that these were the ancient Hellenic-Roman gods,—Jove, Mercury, Apollo, Venus, and Bacchus. And now the fiends are appearing to us poor sinners also in similar guises. Yet we receive them graciously, and, wearing abominable masks and mingling with them, do sault and dance. Yea, and we shall all plunge together into nethermost Tartarus, even as the herd of swine did into the depths of the sea, without reflecting, ignorant that we are, how much more fearful than the most cloutish and black Ethiopian phizzes these new, comely, sun-like, candid devils verily are!"

It was almost dark in the Garden, despite the light June night. Low, black, stifling storm-clouds were drawing a pall over the sky. The illuminations had not yet been lit,—the festival had not begun. The air was as calm as an inclosed room. Heat lightnings,—or perhaps very distant lightnings, without any thunder,—flared up occasionally, and, at each flare-up, in its bluish sheen, the marble statues would suddenly stand out, with a whiteness which was almost blinding and which cut the eyes, against the black verdure of the espaliers along both sides of the alley,—just as though white phantoms were stepping forward and then vanishing. The Czarevich, after what he had heard from Avramov, regarded them now with a new emotion. "Why, in very sooth," he reflected, "they are just like white devils!"

Voices were heard. By the sound of one of them,—not at all loud, rather hoarse—as well as by the red dot of an ember, probably glowing in a Dutch clay pipe (the height of this dot indicated the Titanic stature of the smoker), the Czarevich recognized his father.

He quickly turned the corner of the alley into a little side-path of a labyrinth of lilac bushes and boxwood. "Just like a rabbit scurrying into the bushes!" he immediately reflected, with malice, upon this move of his, which was almost involuntary, yet nevertheless debasingly poltroonish.

"The devil knows what thou art saying, Abramka!" he continued with assumed vexation, in order to mask his shame. "One can see thy mind has strayed off from too much reading."

" 'Tis the very truth I speak, Your Highness," retorted Avramov, without becoming offended. "I have experienced this unclean power of the gods upon my own self. Satan did prompt me to ask Batiushka, our liege Lord, for leave to print certain books, tomes of Ovid and Virgil. I have already seen through the press one such book, with outline drawings of these vile gods and of their sundry hare-brained deeds. And ever since I have been as one mad, and have fallen into insatiable lechery, and the power of the Lord has been withdrawn from me, and there have begun to appear in my dreams visions of all sorts of gods, but especially of Bacchus and Venus. . . ."

"In what guise?" asked the Czarevich, not without curiosity.

"Bacchus appears in that guise in which the person of the heretic Martin Luther is drawn,—a German with a red phiz, his belly like your beer tun. But as for Venus,—in the beginning she pretended to be a certain wanton wench with whom, when I was living in Amsterdam, I did wallow in lechery; her body stark naked, candid, like sea foam; her lips scarlet, her eyes lascivious. And then, when I woke up in the first steam-room of the baths, where this abominable pass did befall me, this crafty witch turned into Akulka,—a wench who is a serf of the Father Archpresbyter. And, reviling me for that I did hinder her from taking a steam bath, she most brazenly did swipe me with a wet birch-besom right in my face, and, having jumped out into the yard, into a snowdrift —this took place in winter—did fall down and immediately scatter into snow drifting before the wind."

"Why, mayhap this was none other than Akulka!" The Czarevich burst into laughter.

Avramov was about to make some retort, but suddenly fell silent.

Voices were heard again; again, in the darkness, glowed

the red, seemingly bloody, dot. The narrow path of the dark labyrinth again brought father and son together in a spot too narrow to pass each other by. Even here a desperate thought flashed through the Czarevich's mind,—to hide, to slip by, or again to dart into the bushes like a rabbit; but it was too late. Peter caught sight of him from afar and called out:

"*Zoon!*"

In Dutch *zoon* signifies son. He styled him thus only during rare moments of graciousness. The Czarevich was all the more amazed, inasmuch as, of late, his father had entirely ceased speaking with him,—not only in Dutch, but even in Russian.

He walked up to his father, took off his hat, made a low bow, and first kissed the hem of his *kaftan*,—Peter had on a much-worn uniform, of a Colonel in the Guard of the Transfiguration, of dark green cloth with red lapels and brass buttons; after that the Czarevich kissed his rough, calloused hand.

"Thanks, Alësha," said Peter, and this "Alësha," which he had not heard for a long while, made Alexei's heart leap. "Thanks for the present. It came in the very nick of time. My oak-wood, now, which was rafted down from Kazan in floats was all smashed up on the Ladoga by a storm. So, were it not for thy gift, we would not have had the new frigate ready even by autumn, like as not. And then the timber itself,—of the very best, as strong as your iron,—I have not seen such fine oak-wood for many a day!"

The Czarevich knew that there was nothing which pleased his father more than goodly ship timber. On his hereditary estate in the Poretzkaya district of the Nizhegorodsky region he had long been guarding, and cherishing, a splendid oakgrove, against the day when he would have especial need of Batiushka's favor. Having learned that the admiralty would soon have need of oak-wood, he had felled the entire grove, had the logs rafted in floats down the Neva in the very nick of time, and had presented this timber to his father. This was one of those timid, occasionally clumsy, little services, which he had formerly shown more frequently to his father, but now more and more rarely. However, he did not deceive himself,—he knew that this service, as well as all the former ones, would be soon forgot, and that his father would subsequently avenge this casual, momentary caress by still greater severity. Nevertheless, Alexei's face flared up from a timorous joy; his heart began to flutter from an insane hope. He managed to mumble out something barely audible about his "being always glad to exert himself to the utmost for Batiushka," and once more attempted to kiss his hand,—but Peter took his son's head in both his hands. For one instant the Czarevich beheld the familiar, awesome and endearing face, with full, almost chubby cheeks, with turned-up and fluffy little mustaches,—like those of the fairy-tale tom-cat Kotabryss, the wags were wont to say,—with a splendidly beautiful smile upon his sinuous, almost femininely tender lips; he beheld the great, dark, radiant eyes,—also so awesome, so endearing, that on a time they had appeared to him in a dream, as the eyes of beautiful women may appear in a dream to a youth in love; he sensed an odor familiar to him since childhood,—a mixture of strong snuff, vodka, sweat, and some other, coarse, soldierly barrack odor, yet not disagreeable, which always prevailed in the workroom—the "office"—of his father; he also sensed the rough touch, familiar to him since childhood, of the not altogether smoothly shaven chin, with the little dimple in the middle of it,—so odd, almost amusing, upon this ominous face; it seemed to him (or perhaps he had merely dreamt it) that, when he was a child, when his father would take him on his knees, he used to kiss this funny little dimple and say with rapture: "It's just like grandma's!"

Peter, kissing his son on the forehead, said in his broken Dutch:

"Good beware ù! May God keep you!"

And this somewhat stilted Dutch "you" instead of "thou" appeared to Alexei bewitchingly amiable.

He saw all this, he sensed it all, as though in a flash of heat-lightning. The heat-lightning expired—and everything vanished. Peter was already walking away from him, as usual convulsively jerking one shoulder, throwing his head back, swinging his right arm powerfully, soldier fashion, as he walked at his accustomed pace, so rapid that his companions, in order to keep up with him, were forced practically to run.

Alexei went off in another direction, but still following the same narrow path of the dark labyrinth. Avramov kept pace with him. He again began talking, this time about the Archimandrite of the Alexandro-Nevskaya Abbey, the Czar's spiritual adviser,—one Theodosius Yanovsky, whom Peter, by having designated him the Administrator of Spiritual Affairs, had placed on a higher footing than that of the first dignitary of the Church, the most ancient occupant of the Patriarchal Throne,—Stepan Yavorsky. Many suspected Yanovsky of "Luthorstvo" (Lutheran leanings), of secret machinations, to do away with all worship of ikons and the bones of saints, all observance of feasts, the whole monastic structure, the Patriarchate, and all the other statutes of the Orthodox Church. Others supposed that Theodosius (or simply Fedosska) was cherishing dreams of becoming Patriarch himself.

"This Fedosska is a veritable atheist, and a brazen vile wretch to boot," Avramov was saying. "Having wormed his way into the greatly burdened, holy soul of the Monarch, and having seduced him, he is boldly demolishing the traditions and laws of Christianity; he is introducing the vainglorious and voluptuous Epicurean—or, rather, the swinish —mode of life. It was he, too, this frenzied Heresiarch, who did tear the wreath off the miracle-working ikon of the Mother of God at Kazan: 'Give us a knife, sacristan!' he kept on yelling, and slashed at the wires, and tore off the adornments of etched gold and put them in his own pocket, brazenly, right before the eyes of everybody. And, with great wailing, all the beholders were amazed at such obscene doings on his part. 'Twas also he, this evil vessel and most vile of vile wretches, who did turn away from God, and give the fiends a compact under his sign manual, wanting, mischievous goat that he is, to trample and spit upon the Life-Giving Cross and the holy image of Our Saviour. . . ."

The Czarevich was not listening to Avramov. He was thinking of his joy, and striving, through reason, to down this unreasoning,—as it now seemed to him,—puerile joy. What was he expecting? Whereon did he pin his hopes?

Upon reconciliation with his father? Was it possible,—and, besides, *did* he want reconciliation? Had not that taken place between them which it was impossible to forget, impossible to forgive? He recalled how, just now, he had been hiding with a base, rabbity poltroonery; he recalled Dokukin, his denunciatory supplication against Peter, as well as a host of other, still more dreadful, unanswerable denunciations. It was not for his sake alone that he had risen up against his father. And yet, it required but a few kindly words, a single smile,—and his heart had softened, had thawed anew, and he was all ready to fall at his father's feet, to forget and forgive all things, to be the first to implore him for forgiveness, as though he himself were at fault. He was ready for one more such caress, for a single smile, to give up his soul to him anew. "But can it be," reflected Alexei, almost with horror, "can it be that I love him so?"

Avramov was still talking, just like a wakeful midge humming in one's ear. His last words caught the Czarevich's attention:

"When the most devout Mitrophanii Voronezhsky beheld upon the roof of the Czar's palace Bacchus, Venus, and the idol-images of other gods, he spake, saying: 'Until such time when the Sovereign orders to be cast down the idols which tempt the people, I cannot set foot in his house.' And the Czar did respect the holy man, ordering the idols to be removed. Such was the way of things in the past. But who is there now to tell the truth to the Czar? Fedosska, perhaps, —the most impious one, who styles ikons idols and who creates idols into ikons? Woe, woe is us! Things have come to such a pass that on this very day, at this very hour, having cast down the image of the Mother of God he is rearing up in its place, for Venus, an ikon pleasing to the fiends and inciting lechery. And the Sovereign, thy Batiushka. . . ."

"Do get away from me, thou fool!" the Czarevich cried out suddenly and maliciously. "Do go away from me,—all of you! What are you sniveling about? Why do you all come creeping to me? Why, may you all go to . . ." He swore indecently.

"What have I to do with ye? I know naught,—nor do I

want to know aught. Betake yourselves to my father with your complaints! He shall judge between ye! . . ."

They were approaching the small Skipper Square, near the fountain of the Central alley. The place was crowded. People were already watching them and trying to catch their conversation. Avramov paled, seeming to lose height and shrink into himself, looking at the Czarevich with his distracted gaze,—the gaze of a child frightened in his dreams, who is likely at any moment to fall into a fit of eclampsia. Alexei felt pity for him.

"Well, have no fear, Petrovich," said he, with a kindly smile which resembled the smile not of his father but of his grandfather, the Most Pacific Alexei Mikhailovich. "Have no fear,—I shan't betray thee. I know that thou lovest me . . . and Batiushka as well. Only, in the future, do not chatter too much. . . ."

And, with a sudden shadow darting over his face, he added softly:

"Even if thou art in the right, what's the good of it? Who hath need of the truth now? Thou mayest as well knock thy head against a wall, or try to break a log with a straw. None will listen to thee. . . . Or me, for that matter."

Between the trees flashed out the first lights of the illuminations: small, multicolored lanterns, shallow bowls filled with tallow, pyramids of tallow candles in windows and between the turned little pillars of the open, roofed gallery over the Neva. There, as designated in the program of the festival, everything had been "decorated most formally, with a most great plenitude in all things."

The gallery consisted of three narrow and long arbors. In the main—the central—one, under a glass cupola, built especially for the purpose by the French architect Leblon, had been prepared a place of honor—the marble pediment for the Venus of Peterburgh.

III

"I have purchased a Venus," Beklemishev wrote to Peter from Italy. "She is held in very high esteem in Rome. In naught doth she differ from the glorious Florentine one

(Venus de' Medici),—but is even better. It was come upon
by some ignorant folk,—they found it as they were digging
the foundation stone for a new house. For 2,000 years has
she lain in the ground. She has stood for a long time in the
Vatican Gardens of the Pope. I am guarding it from those
who would fain get it. I much fear me it will not be allowed
to leave the country. Nevertheless, 'tis already Your Majesty's
property."

Peter, through his trusted agent Savva Yaguzhinsky, and
through the Cardinal Ottobani, had carried on negotiations
with Pope Clement XI, seeking permission to remove the
purchased statue to Russia. For a long while the Pope would
not agree,—the Czar was ready to ravish the Venus. Finally,
after many diplomatic circumventions and stratagems the
permission was received.

"Sir Captain," Peter wrote to Yaguzhinsky, "this most
excellent statue of Venus is to be dispatched from Livorno
[Leghorn] to Innsbruck by land, and thence, by water, over
the Dunai to Vienna, with a special escort,—and in Vienna
it should be addressed to you. But since this statue is, as
you yourself know, celebrated even there, let there be made
in Vienna a carriage body on springs, which would facilitate
its dispatch to Cracow, lest it be harmed in any way, and
from Cracow it can also be sent by water."

Over seas and rivers, across mountains and plains, through
cities and deserts, and, finally, through poverty-stricken Russian settlements, impassable forests, and swamps, everywhere
carefully guarded by the will of the Czar, swaying now upon
the waves, now upon the soft springs in its dark box, just
as in a cradle or in a coffin, did the goddess perform her
distant pilgrimage from the Eternal City to the new-born
town of Peterburgh. When she had finally arrived in safety,
the Czar, strong as was his desire to look upon the statue
which he had awaited so long and of which he had heard so
much, nevertheless managed to conquer his impatience, and
decided not to unpack the box until the first, triumphant
appearance of Venus at the festival in the Summer Garden.

Sloops, wherries, skiffs, flat-bottomed boats, and other
"new-fangled" vessels, were drawing up to the small wooden
steps which descended right into the water, and moored to

the iron rings of piles driven in near shore. The arrivals, on stepping out of their boats, went up the small steps into the central gallery, where, amid the lights of the illuminations, a well-dressed throng was already milling around, becoming ever greater and noisier. The gallants were in colorful *kaftans* of silk and velvet, in tricornered hats and with swords at their sides, stockinged and in buckled, high-heeled shoon, flaunting their showy, pyramidal wigs of unnaturally luxurious locks,—wigs black, flaxen-fair, and a few powdered ones; the ladies in most voluminous, hooped skirts upon frameworks of whale-bone,—*robes rondes*, "on the very latest Versailles manner,"—with long trains, or "draggle-tails," and lacy furbelows; and beauty spots graced their faces, and feathers and pearls their hair. But in this brilliant throng one also came upon simple military frocks of coarse soldier's broadcloth,—even sailors' and skippers' jackets, and greased boots smelling of pitch, and the three-cornered leather caps of Dutch shipmen.

The throng parted before a strange procession: the stalwart heydukes and grenadiers of the Czar carrying upon their shoulders, with great difficulty, and stooping down under its weight, a long, narrow, black box, resembling a coffin. Judging by the proportions of the coffin, the demised was not of human height. The box was stood up on the floor.

The Sovereign, single-handed, without allowing anybody to help him, began opening it. The carpenter's and joiner's tools simply flashed in the accustomed hands of Peter. He hurried so, and pulled the nails out with such impatience, that he scratched a hand so badly that blood came.

Everybody thronged closely, standing up on tiptoes, peeping with curiosity over shoulders and heads.

The Privy councilor, Peter Andreievich Tolstoi, who had long resided in Italy, a man of learning, and an author to boot,—he was the first in Russia to try his hand at translating *The Metamorphoses of Ovid*,—was telling the ladies and maids surrounding him about the ruins of an ancient temple of Venus:

"While on my way to the Castello-di-Baia, near Naples, I did see a temple reared in the name of this goddess Venus. The town was all in ruins, and the place where that city

had stood was grown over with a forest. The temple was built
out of plinths, of fine architecture, with gray pillars. Upon
the arches were graven depictions of a multiplicity of pagan
gods. I saw other temples as well,—to Diana, to Mercury,
to Bacchus, to all of whom, in the regions thereabouts, that
most accursed torturer Nero did bring sacrifices,—and for
this his love toward them he is now enduring with them in
everlasting flames. . . ."

Peter Andreievich snapped open his mother-of-pearl snuff-
box,—upon its lid were depicted three lambs and a shepherd
lad who was untying the girdle of a little sleeping shepherdess. He offered the snuffbox to the rather pretty little
Countess Cherkasskaya, took a pinch himself, and added with
a languorous sigh:

"During this same sojourn in Naples,—I can remember it
as if it were right now,—I was *inamorato* with a certain
cittadina Francesca, who was renowned for her comeliness.
She cost me more than two thousand gold pieces,—and even
to this day that *amore* cannot leave my heart. . . ."

He spoke Italian so well that he even interlarded his Russian speech with Italian words,—as *inamorato* instead of "in
love," *cittadina* instead of "a citizen's wife," and so forth.

Tolstoi was seventy years old but did not look more than
fifty,—so strong, vigorous and fresh was he. In his amiability
to the ladies he could have "tucked behind his belt even the
young devotees of Venus," to use an expression of the Czar's.
A velvety smoothness in his movements, his voice soft, velvety; a velvety, tender smile; his eyebrows velvety, amaz-
ingly thick, black (however, they were hardly innocent of
dye),—no wonder they said of him: "He's a velvety thing,
yet he hath his sting." And even Peter himself, who was
none too circumspect with his "fledglings," held that "when
you have to do with Tolstoi, keep your weather-eye peeled."
On the conscience of this "elegant and most excellent squire"
there was more than one dark, evil, and even sanguinary,
deed,—but he knew well how to cover up his tracks.

The last nails bent, the wood crackled, the lid went up,
and the case opened. At first they saw only something gray,
or yellow, resembling the dust of bones rotted in their grave.

These were the pine shavings, sawdust, felt, and woolen combings, used for the sake of softness.

Peter was pawing them aside, rummaging with both hands and, having finally felt the marble body, exclaimed joyously:

"There,—there she is!"

The lead for the welding of the iron tie-rods which were to join the pediment with the base of the statue was already being melted. The architect Leblon was bustling about, preparing something in the nature of a crane, with little ladders, ropes, and blocks. But at first it was necessary to take the statue out of the case by hand. His orderlies were helping Peter. But when one of them, by way of an immodest jest, attempted to grab the "naked wench" at a place where he should not have, the Czar bestowed such a slap on his cheek as immediately inspired universal respect for the goddess.

Balls of wool, like gray clods of earth, were falling from the smooth marble. And once more, just as she had done two hundred years ago, in Florence, the resurgent goddess was emerging from her sepulcher.

The ropes were tautening,—the blocks creaking. She was ascending, rising higher and higher. Peter, standing upon a little ladder and attaching the statue to the pediment, clasped her with both arms, just as though he had embraced her.

"Venus in the embraces of Mars!" The greatly touched Leblon, well versed in the humanities, could not restrain himself, despite his best efforts.

"The two of them are so handsome," exclaimed one young thing, who was maid-of-honor to the Crown Princess Charlotta, "that, were I in the place of the Czaritza, I would wax jealous!"

Peter was almost of the same superhuman height as the statue. And his face of a mortal remained noble alongside of the divine; the mortal was worthy of the goddess.

Once more—but now for the final time—she swayed, quivered,—suddenly stood immovable, erect, firmly rooted on the pediment.

This was a sculpture of Praxiteles',—Aphrodite, Anadyomene, the Foam-Engendered; and Urania the Heavenly, the ancient Phœnician Astarte,—the Babylonian Melitte,— the first mother of actuality, the First Mother of All Being,

—the Great Foster Mother: she who had filled the heavens
with stars as with seed, and who had shed the milk out of
her breasts to form the Milky Way. Even here she was the
same as she had been upon the knolls of Florence, where a
pupil of Leonardo da Vinci's had gazed upon her in superstitious horror, and as she had been before that, within the depths
of Cappadocia, near the ancient castle of Macallum, where,
in a desolated temple, there had prayed to her her last wor-
shiper,—a pale, puny, little lad in dark garments, the future
Emperor Julian the Apostate. Still as innocent and sensuous;
stark naked, and unashamed of her nakedness. From the
very day when she had come out of her grave, there, in
Florence, she had gone, ever on and on, from age to age,
from nation to nation, halting nowhere until, finally, in her
triumphant procession she had reached the last limits of the
earth,—Hyperborean Scythia, beyond which there is naught
save Night and Chaos. And, having become firmly rooted
upon her pediment, she for the first time looked, with orbs
that seemed astonished and curious, upon this new land, so
foreign to her, upon these flat, mossy quags, upon this strange
city, resembling the settlements of nomadic barbarians, upon
this sky which was neither of the day nor of the night, upon
these black, slumbrous, fearful waves, which were like to
the waves of subterranean Styx. This land did not resemble
the radiant, Olympian land of her birth; it was as devoid of
hope as the Land of Oblivion, as dark Hades. Yet notwithstanding, the goddess smiled her eternal smile, as the sun
might have smiled, were it ever to penetrate into dark Hades.

Peter Andreievich Tolstoi, at the entreaty of the ladies, declaimed some verses of his own composition, *On Cupid*,—
an ancient Anacreontic hymn to Eros:

> Once Eros, 'mid the roses,
> A sleeping bee awakened,
> Which on the finger stung him.
> His heart was filled with sorrow.
>
> Half-running and half-flying,
> He sought his goddess mother,
> The beautiful Kythera:
> "Alas, O mother," crying,

"Olola, I am dying.
A little winged serpent,
A bee, the shepherds name it,
Has stung me on my finger."

His mother said: "If bee-stings
Are found to be so painful,
Thou seest how mortals suffer
When wounded by thy arrows!" [1]

To the ladies, who up to then had known no Russian verses of any sort, save church chants and psalms, this little song seemed enchanting. Then, too, it came very much apropos, inasmuch as at that same instant Peter ignited, and released with his own hands, instead of the first rocket of the fireworks, a flying machine in the semblance of Cupid with a burning torch. Gliding along an invisible wire, Cupid flew from the gallery to a ferry-boat on the Neva, whereon screens had been placed for "fire·diversion, following a scheme of fuses," and with his torch ignited the first allegory,—a sacrificial altar of brilliant fires, with two flaming, ruby-tinted hearts. On one of them, in emerald fire, was traced a Latin *P*, and, on the other, a *C*.—*P*etrus, *C*aterina. The hearts blended into one, and an inscription appeared: *Out of Two I create One,* signified that the goddess Venus and Cupid were blessing the connubial union of Peter and Ekaterina.

Another figure appeared: an illuminated pictorial transparency, with two representations: to one side the god Neptune was contemplating the Fortress of Kronslot, which had only very recently been erected in the midst of the sea; this picture bore the inscription: *Videt et stupescit.* He beholds and is amazed. On the other side was Peterburgh, the new town in the midst of swamps and forests, with the inscription: *Urbs ubi sylva fuit.* A town where once all was forest.

Peter, who was exceedingly fond of fireworks, and always took charge of everything himself, was explaining the allegories to the spectators.

With a rumbling whizz in sheaves of fiery ears of grain, countless rockets snaked up to the very sky, and, from the dark heights, showered down in a rain of slowly falling and dissolving stars,—red, blue, green, violet. The Neva reflected and doubled them in its black mirror. Fiery wheels began to turn,—fiery fountains to play; serpents started hissing and jumping; water and air balloons, bursting like bombs, crashed forth with deafening crackling. A fiery mansion was revealed, with blazing pillars, vaults, and staircases,—and in its very depth, which was as blinding as the sun, the final picture flared up: A sculptor, who looked something like the Titan Prometheus, standing before an unfinished statue which he is hewing with a chisel and mallet out of a rough block of marble; above him was the All-Seeing Eye surrounded by rays, with the inscription: *Deo Adjuvante*. With God's Help. The block of stone bowlder represented ancient Russia. The statue, though unfinished, already had some semblance to the goddess Venus,—or the new Russia; the sculptor, of course, was Peter.

The picture did not quite come off: the statue burned down too soon, toppling at the feet of the sculptor and falling in pieces, while he seemed to be hitting the empty air. The mallet, too, crumbled, and his arm stumped. The All-Seeing Eye grew dim, as though narrowing suspiciously, with a sinister wink.

However, no one paid any attention to this, since all were taken up with a new spectacle. In swirls of smoke, illuminated by a rainbow of Bengal fires, an enormous monster appeared, —one could not make out whether it was a horse, or a serpent with scaly tail and prickly fins and wings. It was swimming along the Neva, from the Fortress toward the Summer Garden. A multitude of boats, filled with rowers, towed it upon a rope. In a gigantic sea-shell upon the back of the monster was seated Neptune, with long white beard and trident; at his feet were sirens and tritons, trumpeting their horns; "The Tritons of the Northern Neptune, as though marching upon the seas, are spreading the fame of the Russian Czar," explained one of the spectators, Gabriel Buzhinsky, the Chaplain of the fleet. The monster, in its turn, was drawing in tow six pairs of empty, tightly bunged kegs, upon which the Cardinals of this All Fools' Council were sitting astride, securely fastened, lest they tumble off into the water,—one Cardinal to each keg. Thus they navigated, in pairs,—one pair behind the other,—and resoundingly trumpeted through their cow-horns. These Cardinals were followed by nothing less than a raft of just such other kegs, bearing an enormous vat of beer, wherein, seated in a wooden dipper, as if it were a bottle, was the mock Prince-Pope, the prelate of the god Bacchus. Bacchus himself was also seated here, upon the flat rim of the vat.

Amid sounds of triumphant music this whole water contrivance slowly drew near the Summer Garden, and moored at the central gallery, where all the gods made their entrance.

Neptune proved to be Czar's jester, the old *boyarin* (noble) Semion Turgeniev; the sirens, with long fish tails which dragged behind them like trains, so that their feet were almost invisible,—turned out to be serf wenches; the tritons, —the hostlers of General-Admiral Apraxin; Satyr, or Pan, who accompanied Bacchus,—the French dancing master of Prince Menshikov. The nimble Frenchman executed such saults, one might really have thought that his legs truly were ægipedal, like those of a veritable faun. Bacchus, wearing the skin of a tiger, garlanded with glass grapes, bearing a sausage in one hand and a decanter in the other, was in everyday life the director of the court singers, one Konon Karpov, an extraordinarily fat fellow with a red phiz. For the sake of greatest verisimilitude he had been mercilessly drenched with liquor for three days running, so that, to use an expression of his bottle companions, Konon had swollen like a juicy huckleberry, and had become a living Ivashka the Tipsy.

The gods surrounded the statue of Venus. Bacchus, reverently supported under his arms by the Cardinals and the Prince-Pope, got down on his knees before the statue, bowed before her to the very ground, and proclaimed in a thunderous bass, which was fully worthy of an Archdeacon:

"Most honorable mother Venus, thy humble churl Ivashka-Bacchus, the extractor of that merriment which is imprisoned in grapes,—Bacchus, born of fire-consuméd Semele,—doth knock his forehead in the dust before thee, petitioning against thy little son Eremka [Eros]. Command him, this mischievous Eremka, not to inflict hurt upon us, thy serfs, nor to win our hearts, nor to cause our souls to perish. Yea, sovereign mistress, be gracious and have pity!"

The Cardinals, in a chorus, thundered: "Amen."

Karpov,—since his eyes were bleary from drink,—did

launch off into the beginning of the Psalm, "Blessed *are* the undefiled," [2] but was checked in the nick of time.

The Prince-Pope, the decrepit preceptor of the Czar, a *boyarin* who had also served as dapifer to Czar Alexei, one Nikita Moiseich Zotov, wearing a jester's mantle of scarlet velvet trimmed with ermines, in a triple-crowned tiara of tin, adorned with an unseemly representation of the naked Eremka-Eros, put down before the pediment of Venus, upon a three-legged altar made of kitchen turnspits, a round copper basin which was usually used for making hot punch; he poured vodka therein and ignited it. Upon long poles, bending from the weight, the Czar's grenadiers brought in an enormous tub of *pertzovka,*—peppered brandy. Not only persons of the spiritual calling, whose presence here was no exception, since they attended all such burlettas, but all guests, ladies as well as gentlemen,—even young girls,— were obliged to approach the tub in turn, accept a wooden ladleful of the peppered brandy from the Prince-Pope, and, having practically drained it, to throw the few remaining drops upon the burning sacrificial altar; the gallants then kissed Venus, each in accordance with his age: the younger men kissing her little hand, the elder her minim foot; whereas the ladies, making her a bow, curtsied, "in ceremonial compliment."

All this, planned beforehand, down to the least trifle, and designated by the Sovereign himself, was being carried out punctiliously, under pain of a "severe fine," or even beating with rods. The old Czaritza Praskoviya Fedorovna, Peter's sister-in-law, the widow of his brother, Czar Ioann Alexeievich, also drank the vodka out of the tub, and made a bow to Venus. As a general thing she strove to please Peter, submitting to all the innovations; 'twas no use, now, spitting against the wind, as far as Peter was concerned. But this time the venerable little crone, in her dark, countrified, widow's jerkin (Peter permitted her to dress according to the old fashion), as she curtsied "in the German manner" before the "shameless naked wench," nevertheless felt cats scratching at her heart. "I'd liefer be stretched out under ground, only that I might not see all this!" she was thinking. The Czarevich also submissively kissed the little hand of Venus. Mikhailo Petrovich Avramov did want to hide himself, but was sought out and dragged forth against his will; and, although he trembled, grew pale, squirmed, was bathed in sweat, and almost fell into a swoon when, in applying his lips to the fiendish ikon he actually felt the touch of the cold marble, he nevertheless carried out the rite punctiliously, under the stern gaze of the Czar, whom he dreaded even more than he dreaded these pagan white devils.

The goddess seemed to contemplate these sacrilegious masks of the gods, these pranks of the barbarians, without any wrath. They were serving her against her will, even in their very sacrilege. The burlesque three-legged altar was turned into a veritable sacrificial altar, whereon, in the bluish flame, darting and slender, like the tongue of a snake, was burning the soul of Dionysos, a god akin to her. And, illuminated by this flame, the goddess was smiling a sage smile.

The feast began. At the upper end of the table, under a canopy of hops and red bilberry plants,—the latter gathered from the tussocks of indigenous swamps, and supposed to serve in lieu of the classic myrtles,—was seated Bacchus, astride a keg, out of which the Prince-Pope was drawing glasses of wine. Tolstoi, addressing Bacchus, declaimed other verses of his own composition,—a translation of an Anacreontic madrigal:

> When the child of Zeus, Lyaios,
> The care-dispelling Bacchus,
> Into my spirits enters,
> He brings me tipsy pleasure,
> And how to dance instructs me,
> There are other joys to charm me
> Than mirth and tipsy frolic.
> In the midst of song and revel
> Then Aphrodite charms me
> And again to dance I hasten.[3]

"One must admit, judging by these verses," remarked Peter, "that this Anacreon was a most valiant drunkard, and a man of most easy life."

After the customary toasts,—for the well-being of the Russian fleet, for the Sovereign and Sovereign's spouse,—

the Archimandrite Theodosius Yanovsky arose, solemn of
mien and with a glass in his hands.

Despite an expression of Polish hauteur on his face (he
was by birth of the petty Polish nobility), despite the blue
ribbon of his order and a diamond panagia with the Sovereign's likeness on one side and with the Crucifix on the
other (the first not only had more diamonds than the other,
but they were also larger),—despite all this Theodosius, to
use an expression of Avramov, was in appearance "like your
marasmus,"—i.e., a puny child, or one of premature birth.
Exceedingly small, exceedingly thin, exceedingly sharp, in a
most lofty cowl with long folds of black crêpe, in a most
broad cassock of finest wool, with fluttering, wing-like, black
lappets, he reminded one of an enormous noctule. Yet when
he was in a jocose vein, and, especially, when he scoffed at
sacred things, which was always the case when he was in
his cups, his most crafty little eyes sparkled with such caustic
intellect, with such impertinent merriment, that his lugubrious little phiz of a bat, or of one of premature birth,
would become almost attractive.

"That which I am going to say is not soothing," Theodosius
turned to the Czar, "but, verily, I say it from my very heart:
through the deeds of Your Sovereign Majesty we have come
out of the darkness of ignorance upon the theater of glory,
out of non-existence into existence, and are already numbered among the community of politic nations. Thou, Sovereign, hast in all things made new,—or, rather, hast brought
to new birth,—thy subjects. What has Russia been hitherto,
—and what is she now? Shall we look upon her edifices? In
place of rude cabins there have appeared radiant palaces,
in place of dry brushwood,—blossoming vineyards. Shall we
look upon the fortresses of our towns? We have such things
in actuality as would formerly have been considered visionary
if beheld as merely charted figures. . . ."

For long did he speak of law codes, free learning, the arts,
the fleet—"these fully-bearing arks,"—and the reformation
and restoration of the Church.

"And thou," he exclaimed in conclusion, in his oratorical
ardor brandishing the broad sleeves of his cassock as if
they were black wings, and looking more than ever like a

noctule,—"and thou, the new, the newly regnant Town of
Peter,—verily, doth not the fame of thy founder soar on
high? There, where none had even thought of as a habitation
for man, was speedily builded a region worthy of a Czar's
throne. *Urbs ubi sylva fuit.* A town where once all was forest.
And who can refrain from praising the site of this city?
Not only doth this place surpass in beauty any in Russia,
but even in some European countries one cannot find its
like! 'Tis built upon a most pleasant spot. Verily, Your
Majesty, thou hast made out of Russia a very metamorphosis,
or transformation!"

Alexei listened and looked at Fedosska closely. When the
latter spoke about the "most pleasant site" of Peterburgh,
his eyes, apparently by chance, for one moment encountered
the eyes of the Czarevich, to whom it suddenly seemed (or
perhaps he merely thought so), that in the depth of the
other's eyes there flashed, flittingly, a certain sparkle of
mockery. And he recalled how frequently, in his presence,—
and, of course, in the absence of his father,—as Fedosska
reviled this pleasant spot, he would dub it "the devil's
swamp" and "the devil's own home-town." However, it had
long since seemed to the Czarevich that Fedosska was laughing at his father,—almost openly, to his face, but so dexterously and with such refinement that none noticed it save
Alexei himself, with whom on every such occasion Fedosska
exchanged a quick, sly look,—like that of a fellow conspirator.

Peter, as always in the case of ceremonial speeches, answered briefly:

" 'Tis my most earnest wish that all my people may learn
forthright what the Lord hath done for us. For the future,
it behooves us not to weaken, but to strive for the common
weal and wealth, which God doth place before our very
eyes."

And, dropping into his usual speech, he expounded, in
Dutch,—so that foreigners might also understand,—an idea
which he had recently heard from the philosopher Leibnitz,
which was very much to his liking,—concerning the "rota-
tion of the sciences"—all sciences and arts were born in the
East and in Greece; thence they had passed on to Italy, then

into France, Germany, and, finally, through Poland into Russia. Now it was the turn of the Russians. Through Russians they, the arts, would return anew to Greece and to the East, to the first land of their birth, having during their course fulfilled a complete circle.

"This Venus," concluded Peter,—but now in Russian,—with that odd, simple-hearted floweriness peculiar to him, and indicating the statue, "this Venus has come to us from thence,—from Greece. Already, by the plow of Mars, everything in our land is plowed and sown. And now we expect a goodly bringing forth,—wherein we crave thy help, O Lord! And may this fruit of ours not be delayed like unto dates, which they that plant the tree do not live to behold. For now even Venus, the goddess of all pleasant amity, of comity, of domestic and political peace, is joining in matrimony with Mars, to the glory of the name of Russia."

"*Vivat! Vivat! Vivat,* Peter the Great, the Father of the Fatherland, the Imperator of all the Russias!" the entire gathering shouted, raising aloft their glasses, filled with Hungary wine. The title of Imperator, not yet made public in Europe, or even in Russia, was already accepted here, in the circle of Peter's fledglings.

In the left,—or ladies',—wing of the gallery the tables had been pushed aside and dancing had begun. The sounds of the military tubas, hautboys, and kettle-drums of the Simeon Guards and the Guards of the Transfiguration, issuing from behind the trees of the Summer Garden, softened by the distance,—and, perhaps, also by the enchantment of the goddess,—sounded here, at her pediment, like the tender flutes and *violes d'amour* in the kingdom of Cupid, where lambs browsed upon soft meadows and shepherd lads untied the girdles of little shepherdesses. Peter Andreievich Tolstoi, who was treading the minuet with the Princess Cherkasskaya, was humming in her ear in his velvety voice, to the sounds of the music:

> Thy arrows, Cupido, forego—
> For not a heart here but doth know
> A most delectable, dear woe;
> Not one but that has, to its sorrow,
> Felt of thy barbéd, golden arrow;
> We in submission all bow low.

And, coyly curtsying to the gallants, as required by the ritual status of the minuet, the rather pretty little Princess responded with the languorous smile of the little shepherdess Chloe to this septuagenarian youth Daphnis.

While in the dark alleys, the arbors, and every modest nook of the Summer Garden, one could hear whisperings, rustlings, susurrations, kisses, and sighs of love. The goddess Venus was already regnant in Hyperborean Scythia.

The imperial orderlies and pages of the chamber,—seated in a knot of their own in a small oak-grove near the Summer Palace, away from everybody, so that none might hear them, —were discussing, like veritable Scythians and barbarians, the love pranks of their gossips, the ladies of honor, and the court demoiselles,—or, to put it very simply, the "wenches."

In the presence of women they were modest and shy, but among themselves they spoke about the "country wives" and "wenches" with the shamelessness of wild animals.

"This Hamentova wench, now, slept the night through with the Master," apathetically declared one of them.

"Hamentova" was Maria Williamovna Hamilton, maid of honor to the Sovereign's consort.

"The Master is a gallant,—he can't live without *metress-kas*," remarked another, corrupting the French *maîtresse*.

"He won't be the first she's done that with," retorted a page of the chamber, a mere urchin of some fifteen years, spitting with an important air and drawing a new lungful from his pipe, which was nauseating him. "Even before the Master, now, Mashka begot a big belly with Vassiukha."

"And wherever do they get rid of their brats, now?" the first fellow voiced his wonder.

"Well, now, no man knoweth where his wife goeth!" sniggered the urchin who was having such a time with his pipe. "Aye, brethren, I myself saw from behind some bushes how Villka Monsov was making up to the Mistress. . . ."

Wilhelm Mons was Gentleman of the Chamber to Her Imperial Highness,—"a German of most base origin," yet most adroit, and handsome to boot.

And, huddling closer as they sat, whispering in the very ear, they fell to imparting to one another still more curious rumors of how, recently, right here in the Czar's pleasance, when men were at work cleaning some stopped-up pipes in one of the fountains, the body of an infant had been found, wrapped up in a palace napkin. . . .

In the Summer Garden there was, in keeping with the plan for all French gardens, the inevitable grotto,—so called, —a small, quadrangular building on the bank of the small Fontannaya river; from the distance it seemed rather incongruous, being reminiscent of a Dutch kirk, but within really resembling an under-water cavern, adorned with great shells, mother-of-pearl, corals, porous stones, and having a multitude of fountains and slender water jets, all spurting into marble bowls, with that lavishness of water of which Peter was so fond, yet which was so excessive when one considered the dampness of Peterburgh.

Here venerable little ancients, senators and dignitaries, were conversing,—also about love and about women.

"In the olden times, now, one led a virtuous married life, but now adultery is held to be a form of gallantry,—and this by the husbands themselves, who, calm at heart, behold their wives amorous with others, and even call simpletons those who, like us, place honor on so weak a basis. We have given the women a free hand,—bide a while, they'll be sitting on all our necks yet!" grumbled the most ancient of these little ancients.

One little ancient, who was somewhat younger, remarked that " 'Twas a pleasant thing, for people young and not yet rooted in ancient customs, to be on a free footing with the feminine sex"; that "The passion of love, which, when manners are coarse, is almost unknown, has nowadays begun taking possession of sensitive hearts"; that "Marriage reaps in a single day all the flowers which love has been cultivating for many years"; and that "Jealousy is the fever of love."

"Fair women have ever been wanton," decided a little ancient of medium age. "For sure, the fiends themselves must have built their houses in the ribs of the gadabout women-folk of this, our age. And such is their state of mind, that they do not even want to hear of anything save amours. And, watching them, even the little lasses fall to considering how they may love a bit, but cannot understand, the poor little things, that the elder women have to make baby-faces to encompass their ends. Oh, what an influence the desire to please has over the emotions of women!"

At this point the Empress Ekaterina Alexeievna entered the grotto, accompanied by Mons, her Gentleman of the Chamber, and her maid of honor, Hamilton,—a proud Caledonian with the face of Diana.

The little ancient who was somewhat younger, seeing that the Empress was lending an ear to their conversation, amiably took the ladies under his wing.

"Truth itself proves to us the worthy nature of woman-kind, by the fact that God, as a fit climax to all things, on the last day, did create Adam's woman, as if to show that without her the universe itself would be incomplete. 'Tis asserted that in the unique structure of a woman's body is gathered everything that the whole universe holds of the best and the most splendidly beautiful. Add to such advantages the beauty of her mind,—and can we help but wonder at their virtues? And what excuses can a gentleman offer who does not evince that deference which is their due? But if, in truth, there be certain tender frailties on their part, then we must remember that tender also is the matter from which they are derived. . . ."

The ancient little ancient merely shook his head at intervals. One could see by his face that he held to his former opinion: "A lobster is no fish and a woman is not human; a fiend and a dame weigh much the same."

In a rent between tattered clouds, upon the fathomlessly radiant and melancholy, aureately green sky, the slender silver sickle of a new-born moon flashed out and cast a tender beam into the depth of the deserted alley, where, near a fountain, in a half-circle of lofty espaliers of clipped greenery, at the foot of a marble Pomona, upon a bench of turf was seated a lonesome girl of seventeen, in a hooped *robe ronde* of pink taffeta with yellowish Chinese flowerets, her waist so tightly drawn in that it looked like an hourglass; her coiffure was in the latest mode,—Blossoming Delight,—yet, withal, her face was so Russian, so simple, that one could easily see that she was but very recently come from a rustic peace, amid which she had grown up, surrounded by nurses and sundry servants, under the thatched roof of some olden estate. Looking about her timorously she unfastened two or three buttons of her dress and nimbly extracted, from its hiding place in her bosom, a bit of paper rolled up into a little tube and still warm from contact with her body. This was a *billet-doux* from a nineteen-year-old second cousin of hers, who, in accordance with the Czar's *ukase,* had been taken out of the same rustic peace straight to Peterburgh, into the Admiralty School of Navigation, and, only the other day, had been sent away on a war frigate, with some other midshipmen, either to Cadix [Cadiz] or to Lissabon [Lisbon],—or, as he himself expressed it, to hunt snipe with the devil.

By the glow of the white night and the moon the maid read over the *billet-doux,* scrawled along ruled lines in large and round childish characters:

"My heart's treasure and my Nastenka! I fain would know why thou hast not sent me a last kiss. Cupidon, the accursed thief, has pierced my heart with his arrow. Great is my yearning,—my heart is clotted with ruddy gore."

Here, between the lines, a heart was sketched in, in blood instead of ink, transpierced with two arrows: red dots designated drops of blood. Further on followed verses,—probably pilfered somewhere or other,—it might have been from Tolstoi, who, in his turn, may have done it into bleak Russian from the sunny Tuscan of Carico, ballad monger and mountebank, also known as The Satyr:

> O, my beloved, my dear!
> O, my adored, my sweet—
> Wish for the moon, and I
> Will lay it, a toy, at thy feet.
>
> O, my adored, my sweet!
> O, my beloved, my fair—
> I'll crush thee a handful of stars
> For diamond dust on thy hair.
>
> O, my beloved, my fair!
> Hearken, adored, to my lute—
> And I'll sing thee a silvern song
> To make all the heavens mute. . . .

Having read over the *billet-doux* Nastenka once more rolled it up painstakingly into a little tube, hid it in the

bosom of her dress, let her head sink and covered her eyes
with a little kerchief scented with Sighs of Amour. But when
she took it away and glanced up into the sky, a black cloud
that looked like a monster with gaping maw had already all
but devoured the silver crescent. Its last beam glittered on
a little tear drop that hung upon the girl's lashes. She gazed
at the vanishing moon and hummed, barely audibly, the only
love madrigal she knew,—God knows whence or how it had
come to her:

> Rosemary, rosemary,
> Rosemary and rue,—
> I took the heart from out of me
> And gave it all to you.
> I sighed my love to every wind,
> And every rose that grew;
> I made my songs of shining words—
> I sang them all for you;
> But O, you never heard my songs!
> And O, you never knew!
> Rosemary, rosemary,
> Rosemary and rue,—
> I took the heart from out of me
> And gave it all to you!

Everything around her and upon her was foreign, artificial,—"on the manner of Versailles":—the fountain, and the
espaliers, and Pomona, and the crinoline, and the *robe ronde*
of pink taffeta with yellowish Chinese flowerets, and the coiffure of Blossoming Delight, and the Sighs of Amour perfume.
Only she alone, with her quiet grief and her quiet song was
simple, Russian,—precisely as she had been under the
thatched shelter of the homestead of her grandsires.

Yet alongside, in the dark alleys and arbors, in all the
modest nooks of the Summer Garden, one heard, as before,
whisperings, rustlings, susurrations, kisses, and sighs of love.
And the sounds of the minuet were wafted to her like the
pastoral flutes and *violes d'amour* from the kingdom of Venus,
as a languorous refrain:

> Thy arrows, Cupido, forego—
> For not a heart here but doth know
> A most delectable, dear woe,
> Not one but that has, to its sorrow,
> Felt of thy barbéd, golden arrow;
> We in submission all bow low.

In the gallery, at the Czar's table, conversation was still in progress. Peter was discussing with certain monks the origin of Hellenic Polytheism, puzzled as to how the ancient Greeks, "having a rather sufficient conception of the laws of nature and the principles of mathematics, could call their soul-less idols gods, and believe in them."

Mikhailo Petrovich Avramov could not restrain himself; he mounted his hobby-horse and set out to prove that the gods existed, and that the supposed gods were in reality veritable fiends.

"Thou speakest of them," Peter voiced his wonder, "as thou hast seen them thyself!"

"Not I, but others, 'tis true, have beheld them, Your Majesty,—beheld them with their own eyes!" exclaimed Avramov.

He took out of his pocket a thick leather wallet, rummaged in it, took out of it two yellowed clippings from Dutch newspapers, and began reading them, translating them into Russian:

"Out of Hispania we are informed: 'A certain person has brought with him into the city of Barcelona a Satyr,—a country lout grown over with wool, as if with fir bark, having also the horns and hoofs of a goat. He subsisteth upon bread and milk and hath no speech, but merely bleateth like to a goat. Which monstrous figure doth attract many spectators.'"

The second clipping proclaimed:

"In Jutland certain fishermen did haul in a Siren or merwoman. The said sea monster doth resemble, in its upper half, a human being, but below that, a fish; the color of its body is a pale yellow; its eyes are closed; its head is covered with black hair, while its hands are webbed between the fingers with skin, like unto the feet of geese. The fishermen had drawn the net out on shore with great difficulty, tearing it entirely to boot. And the inhabitants of those parts have made a most huge barrel, and have filled it with brine, and have placed the merwoman therein,—by these means they hope to preserve it from corruption. This is noted for the reason that, although there has been a great number of fables about the marvels of the sea, this can be asserted as true, for that the said so-amazing sea monster hath been actually captured. *Dated Rotterdam,* 28th of April, A.D. 1714."

Anything in print was believed, but especially foreign news, —for, if they lied overseas, where in the world was one to seek truth? Many of those present believed in water pixies and trolls, forest demons, hobgoblins, changelings and war-locks,—and not merely believed in them, but had even seen them with their own eyes. And, if there be forest demons, then why not satyrs as well? If there be water pixies, why not merwomen with fish-tails? But in that case, now, perhaps other gods, and even this same Venus, might actually exist?

Everybody fell silent and quieted down,—and through this silence there flitted some eerie emotion, as though they had all suddenly sensed, dimly, that they were doing that which they should not.

Ever lower, ever darker, did the cloud-covered sky de-scend. Ever more brightly did the blue heat-lightnings flash, —or were they lightnings without thunder? And it seemed that in these flares against the dark sky were being reflected exactly similar flares of bluish flame upon the sacrificial altar, still burning before the pediment of the statue; or that in this same dark sky, as though within the inverted chalice of a titanic sacrificial altar, a blue flame was concealed behind the clouds, as if under blackened embers, and that this flame, occasionally escaping thence, was flaring up in lightnings. And the flame in the heavens, and the flame on the sacri-ficial altar, responding to each other, seemed to be holding converse about an ominous mystery, unknown to mortals, but already being consummated upon earth and in the sky.

The Czarevich, who was seated not far from the statue, now, after the reading of the newspaper excerpts, bestowed his first close look upon her. And the white naked body of the goddess appeared to him as familiar as though he had already seen it,—and even more than seen it: as though that virginal curve of her back and those dimples at the shoulders had appeared to him in his sleep, in dreams most sinful, passionate and secret, which he was ashamed of before his own self. Suddenly he recalled that just such a curve of the back, just such dimples at the shoulders he had seen upon the body of his mistress,—the serf wench Aphrosiniya. His head was turning,—probably from the wine, the heat, the stuffiness,—and from all this monstrous delirifacient festival. He glanced at the statue once more, and this white, naked body in its double light,—from the red, smoky platters of the illuminations, and from the blue flame upon the tripod, —appeared to him so imbued with life, so fearful and seductive, that he cast down his eyes. Was it possible that to him also, even as to Avramov, the goddess Venus would at some time appear as a horrifying and repulsive changeling, as the house wench Aphroska? Mentally he made the sign of the cross.

" 'Tis not to be wondered at that the Hellenes, knowing not the law of Christ, did bend their knees before soul-less idols," Fedosska restarted the conversation, which had been interrupted by the reading of the clippings. "What is to be wondered at, however, is that we, who are Christians, knowing not true reverence for ikons, do bow our knees to ikons just as to idols!"

There sprang up one of those conversations which Peter was so fond of,—concerning all sorts of false miracles and portents and the knavery of monks, hysterical women, the possessed, innocents, and also dealing with "old wives' tales and long beards wagging at the country louts,"—a dig at the superstitions of the Russian priests. Once more Alexei had to listen to all these stories, which he had long known and grown heartily sick of: about the shift of the Most Holy Mother of God, brought by monks from Jerusalem as a gift to the Czaritza, Ekaterina Alexeievna,—apparently it was indestructible, and even not to be consumed by flames, which shift upon investigation proved to be woven out of the fibers of a special non-inflammable woven stuff,—amianth; about the life-like sacred remains of the Maid of Livonia, Von Grot by name: the skin on these remains was "like to dressed and tautened pigskin, and when one pressed a finger thereon, it did regain its former state quite springly"; about other bogus sacred bones, made out of ivory, which Peter had ordered to be dispatched to the recently established Cabinet of Curiosities at Peterburgh, as a memento of "superstition, now already being extirpated through the zeal of the clergy."

"Aye, there's been a great, great deal of knavish work in

the Church of Russia as far as miracles are concerned!"
concluded Fedosska, apparently perturbed but in reality with
malicious joy, and recalled the last false miracle: in a certain poverty-stricken church in the Peterburgh region there
had been discovered an ikon of the Mother of God which
exuded tears, foretelling, it would seem, great misfortunes
and even the final destruction of the new city. Peter, getting
wind of this from Fedosska, had set out without any delay
for this church, looked this ikon over, and had exposed the
deception. This had happened recently: there had not yet
been time to send the ikon off to the Cabinet of Curiosities
and it was still kept in the Sovereign's quarters at the Summer Palace,—a small Dutch house in this very Garden, just
a step or so from the gallery, at the confluence of the Neva
and the Fontannaya. The Czar, wishing to show it to his
audience, ordered one of the orderlies to fetch the ikon.

When the fellow returned, Peter got up from the table,
stepped out on a small platform before the statue of Venus,
where there was more room, leaned back against the marble
pediment, and, with the holy image in his hands, began to
explain in detail and painstakingly the "knavish mechanics."
Everybody surrounded him, just as eagerly crowding, and
getting up on their toes, and looking over the heads and
shoulders of one another as they had done at the unpacking
of the case with the statue. Fedosska was holding up a
candle.

The ikon was an ancient one. Its visage was dark, almost
black; its large, sorrowful eyes alone, seeming to be a trifle
swollen from tears, looked as if they were alive. The Czarevich from his childhood had loved and revered this image,—
the image of the Mother of God, the Bringer of Joy to All
That Sorrow.

Peter took off the silver trimming, studded over with
precious stones,—it barely held together, since it had already been torn off during the first inspection. Next he un-
screwed the new copper screws by which a small panel of
linden (this, too, was new) was fastened to the underside of
the ikon; in the middle of this panel was set in another and
smaller board which moved freely upon a spring, yielding
and buckling in under the lightest pressure of the hand.

Having taken off both boards he showed two lunettes or little cavities, chiseled out in the wood, just against the eyes of the Mother of God. Two small Greek sponges, saturated with water, were placed in these lunettes, and the water oozed through two barely perceptible little holes bored through the eyes, forming drops that looked like tears.

For the sake of greater clarity Peter performed an experiment on the spot. He wet the sponges, placed them in the lunettes, pressed down the little board,—and the tears began to flow.

"There is your source of the miracle-working tears!" said Peter. "The mechanics are far from complicated!"

His face was calm, as if he were explaining a curious "freak of nature" or some other oddity in the Cabinet of Curiosities.

"Yea, there's been a great deal of knavish work," Fedosska repeated, with a soft smile.

Everybody was silent. Some one emitted a dull moan,— probably some one overcome by drink, in his sleep; some one giggled,—so strangely and unexpectedly that everybody looked around at him, almost in fright.

Alexei had been long making attempts to get away, but a catalepsy had fallen upon him, as in a delirium, when a man strives to run yet his legs will not stir,—when he wants to cry out and has no voice. In this catalepsy he stood and watched Fedosska holding the candle, Peter's deft hands nimbly busied with the wooden parts of the ikon, the tears coursing down the sorrowing Visage,—and, above all this, the white sheen of the naked, dreadful and seductive body of Venus. He watched,—and tedium, like unto a deathly nausea, was welling up towards his heart, was constricting his throat. And it seemed to him that this would never end, that all this had been, was now, and would be, through all eternity.

Suddenly there came a flash of blinding lightning,—as though over their very heads a fiery abyss were opening up. And through the glass cupola an unbearable, flaming, white light,—whiter than that of the sun, inundated the marvelous statue. Almost at the same instant a crash pealed,—short, but as deafeningly crackling as if the vault of heaven had fallen apart and were toppling.

Darkness descended,—impenetrably black after the glitter of the lightning,—like the darkness of a subterrain. And at once, amid this blackness, the storm broke,—whistling, rumbling, its whirlwind like that of a hurricane, with lashing rain and hail.

All was confusion in the gallery, punctuated by the piercing squeals of women. One of them, in a hysterical fit, was making the noises of the possessed, and her weeping sounded like laughter. Panic-stricken, the people dashed about, not knowing themselves where they were going. Colliding, they fell and crushed one another. Some one was wailing, with a most desperate wail:

"Nikola, thou Miracle Worker! . . . Most Holy Mother of God! . . . Have mercy upon us! . . ."

Peter, having let the ikon fall out of his hands, dashed off in search of the Czaritza. The flame of the overturned tripod, as it sputtered out, flickered up for the last time in an enormous blue tongue, double, like the feeler of a serpent, and lit up the face of the goddess. In the midst of the storm, the murk, and the horror, it alone was calm.

Some one stepped upon the ikon. Alexei, bending down in order to pick it up, heard the crunching of the wood. The ikon had split in two.

BOOK TWO

ANTICHRIST

I

A coffin of pine wood
For me has been hewed;
Therein I me lay
To bide Judgment Day.

THIS was the song of the Coffin-Sleepers,—schismatic sectarians whose coffins served them for beds as well. "Seven thousand years after the creation of the world," said they, "the Second Coming of Christ will arrive; but, should it not, then we will burn the Evangel itself; as for other books, 'tis no use in e'en believing them."

And they abandoned their houses, their lands, their cattle, their goods; going off each night into the fields and forests, they clad themselves in clean, white shifts which were also their shrouds, lay down in their wooden coffins, hewn all in one piece, and, chanting their own requiems, momently bided the voice of the Judgment trumpets,—they were "meeting Christ."

Opposite the promontory formed by the Neva and the Little Nevka, at the very widest reach of the river, near the Gagarinsky rope factory and landing stages, amid other rafts, barks, barges and row-boats, were moored the oak floats of the Czarevich Alexei, which had been rafted down from the Nizhegorodsky region to Peterburgh, consigned to the Admiralty's wharf. On the night of the Festival of Venus in the Summer Garden, an old *bourlak* (bargeman) was sitting at the rudder of one of these floats; he had on a ragged short coat of sheep's-wool (despite the sultry weather) and wore bast sandals. They called him Ivannushka the Little Fool, deeming him an innocent or madman. It was already thirty years,—from day to day, from month to month, from

48

year to year, every night through till "the call of chanticleer"
(or cock's crow),—that he had kept vigil, met Christ, and
always sung the selfsame song of the Coffin-Sleepers. Sitting
over the very water upon the slippery logs, hunched up, with
his arms clasping his raised knees, he expectantly contemplated the gaps of aureately-green sky, yawning between
black, rent clouds. The immobile gaze from under his tangled,
gray hair, his immobile face, were filled with terror and hope.
Slowly rocking from side to side, he sang in a long-drawn-out,
dismal voice.

> A coffin of pine wood
> For me has been hewed;
> Therein I me lay
> To bide Judgment Day.
> By angels' trumpets shaken
> From my coffin I shall waken,
> To God's Judgment I shall wend.
> Two roads to Him ascend:
> They are long and they are broad,
> Now if ye take the one road,
> It up to Heaven doth go;
> As for the other road,—
> It leads to the Dark, below.

"Ivannushka, come to supper!" they called out to him
from the other end of the float, where a fire laid upon
stones was burning,—a semblance of a hearth, with a cast-
iron caldron suspended over it upon three sticks, in which
caldron a fish chowder was coming to a boil. Ivannushka
heard them not and kept on with his song.

Seated in a circle about the fire and conversing there were,
besides *bourlaki* and boatmen, a saintly Raskolnik, Kornilii
by name, who preached self-immolation by fire, on a pilgrimage from Pomorië to the Kerzhenskiya forests beyond
the Volga; his disciple, Tikhon Zapolsky, a runaway scholar
from Moscow; Alexei Semisazhennyii ("Furlong"), a runaway cannoneer from Astrakhan; Ivan Ivannov, son of Budlov, a runaway sailor belonging to the Admiralty Bureau,
who had been a calker; Larion Dokukin, the erstwhile government pettifogger; the ancient woman Vitalia, belonging
to the sect of the runners, who, to use her own expression,
led the life of a bird, forever on some pilgrimage,—that,

now, was the very reason they called her Vitalia, inasmuch as she "privitala," or fluttered, here, there, and everywhere, without ever roosting anywhere; her inseparable fellow way-farer, Kilikeia the Barefooted, a hysteric, who was "possessed of devils in her womb," was also here, besides other "folks in hiding," of all sorts of ranks and callings, who had run away from unbearable taxes, the recruited soldier's lot, running gauntlets, penal servitude, having their nostrils torn out, or having their beards shaven off, or making the sign of the cross with only two fingers, and from others such "fears of the Antichrist."

"There's a great weariness come upon me!" Vitalia was saying,—a little crone, still vigorous and sprightly, her face all wrinkled yet rosy-cheeked, like a little autumn apple, with a dark kerchief loosely tied upon her head. "But the wherefore of this weariness I myself know not. The days be so somber, and it seems as if the sun doth not shine as it did of yore."

"These latter days be tearful days; the dread of Antichrist is wafted upon the universe,—hence, also, the sadness," explained Kornilii,—a thin little ancient, with an ordinary *mouzhik* face, freckled and apparently purblind, but, in reality, with piercingly sharp eyes, that seemed to bore through one like a gimlet; he was wearing the head covering of the Raskolniki,—something in the nature of a monk's cowl,—a black, rusty under-cassock, and a leather belt of interwoven straps; his every move was followed by the soft clinking of his harness, which had eaten into his flesh,—consisting of a ninety-pound chain formed of cast-iron crosses.

"I am also thinking, Father Kornilii," continued the pilgrim woman, "isn't it likely that these be the last times? 'Tis not long the world will last, they do be saying. Let but a half of the first half of the eighth millennium pass,—and then the end?"

"Nay," retorted the ancient with assurance. " 'Twill not take even that long. . . ."

"May the Lord have mercy upon us!" Some one sighed deeply. "God knoweth,—but all we know is: May the Lord have mercy upon us!"

And everybody fell silent. The clouds covered up a gap in

the sky, and the Neva turned darker. The heat-lightnings began to flare more vividly, and each time, by their pale-blue glow, the slender, pale-gold spire of the Fortress of SS. Peter and Paul glittered, reflected in the Neva. The stone bastions, and the shallow, seemingly depressed shore line, whose plastered buildings, consisting of warehouses, garrison depots, and hemp-barns, also seemed flat, all showed darkly against the sky. In the distance, upon the other bank, through the trees of the Summer Garden, twinkled the flames of the illuminations. From Birch Island, on Lake Keivusara, was wafted the last breath of late spring,—an odor of firs, of birches, and of aspens. The tiny handful of people, lit up by a red flame, upon the flat float, itself a barely perceptible black blotch, seemed lonely and lost between the black thunder-clouds and the black, smooth expanse of the river, as if suspended in the air between two heavens, between two abysses,

When all had fallen silent it grew so still that one could hear the slumbrous gurgling of the streams of water under the logs, and, from the other end of the float, floating clearly over the water, came the never-varying, dismal song of Ivannushka:

> A coffin of pine wood
> For me has been hewed;
> Therein I me lay
> To bide Judgment Day.

"But what say ye, my little falcons," began Kilikeia the Possessed,—a woman still young, with a tenderly translucent face, just as though it were made of wax, and with frost-bitten, black, frightful feet, that looked like the roots of an old tree,—she always walked about barefoot, even in the most ferocious cold,—"but what say ye,—is it true, as I heard the other day, right here in Peterburgh upon the Gluttons' Mart, that, now, there is no Sovereign in Russia; but such as there is, he is not the real thing, not of Russian breed, nor even of any kingly blood, but, on the contrary, either a German, or the son of a German, or a Swedish changeling?"

"Neither a Swede nor a German is he, but an accursed

Jew from the tribe of Dan," proclaimed Kornilii the ancient.

"Oh, Lordy, Lordy!" some one again sighed heavily. "D'you see, the generations of the Czars, now are running to madness."

A dispute sprang up as to whether Peter was a German, a Swede, or a Jew.

"Well, the Devil alone knows what he is! Whether a witch has hatched him out in a mortar, or whether he was spawned from the dampness of a bath-house,—one thing alone is sure: he's a warlock," decided the runaway sailor Budlov, a lad of some thirty years, with a sober and common-sense expression on his intelligent face,—at one time probably handsome, but now disfigured by a black prison brand upon the forehead and by his nostrils being torn out.

"I, little fathers of mine, know,—downright everything do I know about our Sovereign," Vitalia chimed in. "I heard about it at Kerzhenetz, from an ancient woman, a wandering beggar; the singing nuns at the convent of the Ascension, in Moscow, also spake of it, the same way: 'twould seem, now, that our Czar, the pious Peter Alexeievich, was beyond the seas, amongst the Germans; and did travel in the lands of the Germans, and did visit Stekolnoë [the Glass Kingdom, —a corruption of Stockholm]; and in this German land, now, a certain maid doth hold reign in a Glass Kingdom; and this maid, now, being wishful for to revile our Sovereign, did put him upon a heated frying-pan, and afterward, shutting him up in a barrel studded with nails, did cast him into the sea."

"Nay, 'twas no barrel," somebody corrected her, " 'twas into a pillar that they walled him in."

"Well, whether 'twas a pillar or a barrel, all we know is that he's vanished, leaving nary a word, and there's nor hide nor hair of him to be seen. And in his place there has bobbed up, from these very regions overseas, a certain accursed Ebrew from the tribe of Dan, born of this most foul maid. And at that time no one found him out. But, no sooner had he appeared in Moscow than he began to act in everything after the ways of the damned Jews: he would take no blessing from the Patriarch, nor visit the miracle-working sacred bones at Moscow,—inasmuch as he knew that the power of the Lord would not let him, the accursed one, draw near to the holy place; nor did he bow down before the sepulchers of the former, pious Czars,—for that he knew them to be no kin of his and hateful to him. He would see of the royal line,—neither the Czarina, nor the Czarevich, nor the Czarevni, fearing that they would show him up,—that they would say to him, the accursed one, 'Thou art none of us; thou art no Czar, but an accursed Jew.' Nor did he appear before the people on the day of the anniversary, fearing that he would be shown up, even as Grishka the Unfrocked [4] had been before all the people,—and in all things does he act after the manner of one unfrocked: he doth not keep the holy fasts; he doth not go to church, nor to the baths every Saturday; he lives dissolutely in the same house with damned Germans, and now in the kingdom of Muscovy a German hath become a great person: the measliest German is now held above a *boyarin* or the very Patriarch. Why, he himself, this accursed Ebrew, doth dance with German wantons before all the people; he drinketh wine not to the glory of God, but somehow uncouthly and unseemly, as abandoned sots in low-down inns do, wallowing and raising Cain in his drink; as for the drunkards about him, he dubs one of them the Most Holy Patriarch, while the others he dubs Metropolites and Prelates, and, as for himself,—a Protodeacon, no less; he mixes up all sorts of shameful things with sacred words, raising up his voice most lustily for the amusement of the German folk about him,—but mostly for the sake of desecrating all Christian sanctity. And this," concluded Kornilii the holy ancient, "is the abomination that maketh desolate, as prophesied by the prophet Daniel,[5] and now come to pass in the holy place!"

Sundry voices became audible in the gathering:

"And the Czaritza Avdothea Fedorovna, now, who is immured in the Suzdal Nunnery, doth say: Endure ye, now, keep to your Christian faith,—for this is not my Czar; he that is come is another."

"He is bringing e'en the Czarevich to his own state,—but the latter will not listen to him. And the Czar, now, is fain to do away with him, so that the Czarevich may not rule."

"Oh, Lordy, Lordy, look ye, what a trial God hath sent

us,—that the father is set against his son, and the son against the father."

"What father is he to him! The Czarevich himself says: 'This is no Batiushka of mine, nor my Czar.'"

"Our Sovereign loves the Germans, but the Czarevich loves them not; 'Give me time,' says he, 'I'll bring them up short.' There did come to him a certain German, and did say certain words to him,—but what they were, we know not; and the Czarevich did set his clothes on fire and scorch him. The German did complain to the Sovereign, and the latter said: 'Wherefore go ye to him? Whilst I am alive, ye also live.'"

"That's so! All of the people say: When our Sovereign Czarevich, Alexei Petrovich, will be ruling, then our Sovereign Czar, Peter Alexeievich, will have to betake himself off, and the others with him!"

"Verily, verily, that is so!" joyous voices confirmed. "He, the Czarevich, burneth at soul for the things of old."

"He is a man who seeketh after God!"

"The hope of Russia! . . ."

"There be also many old wives' tales floating about now among the people: one can't believe everything," Ivan Budlov began,—and all involuntarily lent ear to his calm, common-sense speech. "But I will again say,—whether he be a Swede, or a German, or a damned Jew,—the devil alone knows what he is,—only, sure enough, soon as God set him to reign over us, we have not beheld any radiant days,—there's a heaviness weighing down upon the world; nor is there any rest. Why, take even us of the brotherhood that have served Czar and country: 'tis fifteen years that we've been warring with the Swede; nowhere have we made a poor showing, and have shed our blood without stint, and yet to this day can see no peace ahead of us; in season and out, in summer and in fall, we sail the high seas; we winter upon cold stones; we perish of hunger and cold. Yet he hath ruined his own domain,—so that in some places you won't find e'en a sheep remaining to a *mouzhik*. They do be saying: A clever head, a clever head! If his were really a clever head he would be able to judge such poverty in man. Wherein do we see his wisdom? He has issued something about civil rights; he has set up the Senate. What profit is there in that? They do but take a great deal in pay, these Senators. But if he were only to ask of the humble plaintiffs,—did they adjudge the affair of any one of them without pettifoggery, straight off? Well, wherein is the use of talking! . . . Brazen-faced wrongs are upon all the people. He contrives so that in our souls there be not the least Christianity; he is exhausting our last life forces. How doth God tolerate such hard-heartedness? Well, this matter will not pass for naught,—there is bound to be a turn: sooner or later, their blood will flow back upon their heads!"

Suddenly one of the audience, Alena Ephimova, a country wife with a very simple kindly face, who up to now had not opened her mouth, interceded for the Czar.

"We do not even know how to say it," she uttered softly, as though to herself, "but we do but pray: Lord, turn our Czar to our Christian faith!"

But here indignant voices rang out:

"What Czar is he? He is but a Czarlet! He's all petered out. He walks about like he's lost his head."

"He has turned into a damned Jew, and he could not even live without drinking blood. On the day that he drinketh blood, on that day is he merry; but on the day that he does not drink his fill,—why, he can't down even bread!"

"He devours the world! He hath devoured all the world,— but there is no end to him,—the wastrel!"

"May he fall through the ground!"

"You fools, you offspring of dogs!" the cannoneer Alexei Semisazhennyi cried out in sudden fury,—he was a red-haired fellow of enormous stature, with a face that had in it something of the beast and something of the child. "You fools,—for that ye cannot stick up for your own heads! Why, ye have all perished, soul and body: ye shall all be chopped up, even like to cabbage worms. Why, I'd take him and mince him into little bits, and rend his body in pieces!"

Alena Ephimova merely emitted a feeble oh! and crossed herself; she confessed, later on, that these words threw her as if into a flame. And the others also turned around to look at Semisazhennyi with fear. But he, with his bloodshot eyes fixed at one point, clenched his fists hard and added quietly, as though pensively,—yet in this quietness of his there was something still more dreadful than fury:

"I do be wondering how it is he hasn't been put away up to now. He rides about of nights, early and late, with but few men about him. 'Twould take but five knives to cut him up."

Alena turned all pale, wanted to say something, but merely moved her lips without making a sound.

"Thrice did they want to slay the Czar," Kornilii the ancient shook his head, "but they'll ne'er kill him: fiends walk behind him and safeguard him."

The diminutive albinoid of a soldier, whose little face, ravished with drink and sickly, had in it something of the simpleton,—altogether a little lad as yet, a fugitive conscript by the name of Petka Zhizla, began speaking,—hurriedly, stammering, confused, and piteously sniveling like an urchin, his eternal refrain of: "Oh, little brothers of mine, little brothers of mine!" He informed them that there had been brought from overseas, upon three ships, branding irons for to brand men with; they were shown to nobody and were kept under a strong guard upon Kotlin Island, and there was a constant watch of soldiers about it. These were the special recruiting marks which were introduced through an *ukase* of Peter's, and of which the Czar, in the year seventeen hundred and twelve, wrote to the General-Plenipotentiary, Jacob Dolgorukyi:

"And as a mark for the recruits, let crosses be tattooed on the left hand with a needle, and let gunpowder be rubbed thereon."

"He that shall have the imprint upon him, to him shall bread be issued; but to him that hath no imprint upon him, to him no bread shall be issued,—go thou and die from hunger. Oh, little brothers of mine, little brothers of mine, 'tis a frightful thing! . . ."

"All, because of the pressure brought upon them by lack of food, shall come to the son of perdition, and shall bow down before him," Kornilii the ancient confirmed.

"And there's some has already been branded," continued Petka. "And me too, now, oh, little brothers of mine, little brothers of mine,—and me too, accursed that I am. . . ."

With difficulty he lifted up, with his right hand, his left, which hung down impotently, like a whip-lash, brought it up to the light, and pointed out the recruit mark upon the back of it, between the thumb and the index finger, pricked out with the iron needles of the government stamp.

"As soon as they did imprint it, the hand began to wither. And it withered up completely. At first the left hand, and then the right is going, too: I try to make the sign of the cross with it, but it will not lift. . . ."

Everybody, with fear, inspected the pale yellow skin of the withered, apparently dead hand, a small dark blotch, which seemed to consist of pock marks. This was a human brand,—the black cross of the government.

"That's it, sure enough!" decided Kornilii the ancient, " 'tis the seal of Antichrist. 'Tis said: he shall mark them with a sign upon the hand, and he that accepteth his brand shall have no power to make the sign of the cross over his limbs; but 'tis not by bonds that his hand will be bound, but by an oath,—and for such there is no repentance."

"Oh, little brothers of mine, little brothers of mine! What have they wrought with me! . . . Had I but known I'd never have given myself up alive into their hands. They have spoiled a human being, have branded me with a branding iron like cattle, putting their mark upon me!" Petka sobbed convulsively, and great tears coursed down his piteous little urchin's face.

"Fathers of mine." Kilikeia the Possessed wrung her hands, as though she had been struck by a sudden thought. "Why, everything leads up to one thing: this Czar Peter is verily the . . ." She did not finish,—the fearful word froze upon her lips.

"What else, didst thou think?" Kornilii the ancient looked at her with his keen, gimlet-like little eyes. "He, and none other. . . ."

"Nay, fear not. He himself has not yet come. Mayhap this is his forerunner . . ." Dokukin attempted to contradict.

But Kornilii rose up to his full height; the chain of cast-iron crosses which hung upon him clanked; he raised up his hand, folded it in the schismatical, two-fingered sign of the cross, and exclaimed solemnly:

"Pay heed, ye of the righteous faith, who it is that reigns, who lords it over us since the year of sixteen hundred and sixty-six,—the date of the Beast. Czar Alexei Mikhailovich, with the Patriarch Nikon, was the first to renounce the faith, and be the forerunner of the Beast; and, following their example, Czar Peter has torn up piety by its very roots,—has ordained that there be no Patriarch, and has seized all churchly and Godly power unto himself, and has raised himself up against Our Lord, Jesus Christ, has established himself the sole Head of the Church, with no other Head above him, and its absolute Pastor. And, being jealous of the primogeniture of Christ, of whom it is said: *I am the first and the last,*[6] he called himself *Peter the First.* And in the year of seventeen hundred, on the first day of Januarius, the anniversary of the ancient Roman god Janus, he proclaimed, on a shield, in a show of fires: *My time is at hand.*[7] And on the eve of the high church mass for his victory over the Swedes at Poltava he did call himself Christ. And whenever he was met, upon his visits to Moscow, he saw to it that little lads were dressed up in white under-surplices and placed at the triumphal arches and among the processions, and did glorify himself, and did command that they sing: *Blessed is he that cometh in the name of the Lord! Hosanna in the highest!*[8] *The Lord hath appeared to us!*—as, by the will of God, the Hebrew children did sing praise to Our Lord Jesus Christ, the Son of God, upon His entry into Jerusalem. And thus, by his titles, is he raising himself up above any name given to God. As has been prophesied of yore: *In the name of Simon Peter there shall be in Rome a proud Prince of this world, one Antichrist;* in Russia,—that is to say, the Third Rome,—he hath verily appeared: the said Peter, the son of perdition, a blasphemer and an adversary of God; he is the Antichrist. And as it is written: *In all things will this false one strive to make himself like to the Son of God,—this* said false one, praising himself, doth say: 'Unto the orphaned am I a father, unto the wayfarers a haven; I am a helper to those in trouble, I am the deliverer of the wronged; for the incapacitated and the aged I have established hospitals, and, for those under age,—schools; the people of Russia, who were not reckoned among the great powers, I have made to be reckoned among them, and in all branches of knowledge to be equal to the peoples of Europe; I have expanded my czardom, have gotten back that which hath been ravished; have raised up anew that which hath crumbled; have restored to its glory that which hath been debased, and renewed that which was decrepit; have awakened them that slumbered in ignorance, and created that which hath not been before. I am beneficent, I am meek, I am gracious. Come all ye and bow down before me, the living and powerful God, inasmuch as I am God,—nor is there any other God save me! Such are the dissembling benefits of this Beast, of whom it is said: *a beast dreadful and terrible, . . . and it was diverse from all the beasts;* [9] thus under the skin of a sheep is hid a ferocious wolf; yea, he shall capture all and devour them. Hearken then, ye of the righteous faith, to the word of the prophet: *Go ye forth out of Babylon, O my people, flee ye from the Chaldeans!* [10] Save yourselves, inasmuch as there is no salvation in the cities of the living; flee, ye pursued, ye faithful, who have no real city, who seek after that which is coming; flee ye into the forests and the deserts; hide your heads under the ground,—among the mountains and the caverns and the abysses of the earth,—inasmuch as ye yourselves see not, brethren, that we stand upon the most huge mountain-top of our evil: the real Antichrist hath come, and with him doth this our age end. Amen!"

He fell silent. A blinding heat-lightning,—or a flash of real lightning,—suddenly illuminated him from head to foot, and to those who were looking upon him this little ancient appeared as a giant in this glow; and the reverberations of the distant, seemingly subterranean thunder appeared a reverberation of his words, filling heaven and earth. He fell silent,—and they, too, all kept silent. Again it became so quiet that one could hear only the slumberous gurgling of the water streaming under the logs, and, from the other end of the float, the long-drawn-out and dismal song of Ivannushka:

> O ye coffins made out of oak-logs tall,
> Our Eternal Homes ye shall be for all.
> Day is over, and the night draws nigh,

The sun is sinking toward the West,
And the ax so sharp at the root doth lie,
And the end of time is about to fall. . . .

And still deeper and more sinister did the silence become
because of this song.

Suddenly, with a rumbling whizz, a rocket snaked up, and
in the dark height scattered in a rain of rainbow stars. The
Neva, reflecting them, also doubled them in her black mirror.
And now the fireworks flared up. Screens with transparencies
burst into flame; enormous wheels fell to turning; fiery
fountains began to play; and there were revealed mansions,
resembling a temple made of flame as white as the sun. From
the galleries over the Neva, where Venus was already in her
place, the shouts of the revelers reached them, plainly transmitted over the reverberant, smooth expanse of waters:
"*Vivat! Vivat! Vivat!* Peter the Great, the Father of our
Fatherland, the Imperator of all the Russias!" followed by a
thunder-burst of music.

"This, brethren, is the consummation of the last portent!"
exclaimed Kornilii the ancient, pointing with his extended
hand to the fireworks. "As St. Hippolytus witnesseth: They
shall praise him, this Antichrist, with songs untold, and with
many voices, and with lusty-lunged shouting. And a light,
greater than any light, will enfold him, this chieftain of darkness. He will change day into darkness, and night into day,
and the moon and the sun into blood, and will draw down fire
from heaven. . . ."

Within the flaming chambers appeared the visage of Peter,
the Sculptor of Russia, like to the Titan Prometheus.

"And all shall bow down before him," concluded the
ancient, "and shall cry out: *Vivat! Vivat! Vivat!* Who *is*
like unto the Beast? Who is able to make war with him? [11]
He maketh fire come down from heaven! . . ." [12]

They all stared at the fireworks in a catalepsy of horror.
But when, amid swirls of smoke, illuminated by the vari-
colored Bengal fires, there appeared a sea-monster with a
scaly tail, and prickly fins and wings, floating down the
Neva from the Fortress of SS. Peter and Paul toward the
Summer Garden,—they imagined they were beholding the very
Beast (prophesied in the Revelation) that ascendeth out of

the bottomless pit.[13] They expected, at any moment, to see the flying Antichrist coming toward them upon the water, with "feet dry-shod," or upon the air, amid thunders and lightnings, on fiery wings, with an incomputable host of friends.

"Oh, little brothers of mine, little brothers of mine!" Petka was sobbing, trembling like a leaf, and with his teeth chattering. " 'Tis a frightful thing. . . . We are speaking of him, —but what if he be here himself, right nearby? Ye can see what confusion there is even amongst us. . . ."

"I can't figure out why ye are overcome by such womanish fright. . . . Drive an aspen stake down his throat and there is the end on't. . . ."[14] Semisazhennyi made an attempt to put on a brave front; but he, too, turned pale and took to shivering when Kilikeia the Possessed, who was sitting alongside of him, suddenly emitted a piercing squeal, fell flat on her back, and, beating about in cramps, began "calling in voices."

The damage had been done to Kilikeia in her childhood. Once,—as she herself told the story,—her mother had poured out some stew into a dish, and had given it to her to eat, at the same time upbraiding her: "Stuff that down your gullet, now, the devil take thee!"—and, the third week after that, she, Kilikeia, had begun to ail, and plainly heard something growling in her belly, like a puppy; and the said growling had been heard of everybody; and truly, now, her belly was possessed of a devil, and this devil spoke loudly, both with the tongue of man and with the voices of beasts. She had been put in a guardhouse, according to the Czar's *ukase* dealing with possessed women; she had been tried, put to the question, beaten with rods and with birch switches. She had given promises, pledged and signed, that "henceforth she would refrain from calling with voices, under penalty of severe punishment with the *knout* and life banishment of hard labor at the rope works." But birchings could not expel the fiend, and she continued to call with voices.

Kilikeia kept on repeating: "Oh, 'tis qualmish I feel, 'tis qualmish I feel . . ." and she laughed, and she wept, and she barked like a dog, and bleated like a sheep, and croaked like a frog, and grunted like a pig, and called in sundry other voices.

The watch-dog, which stayed right on the float, crawled out of its kennel, awakened by all these unusual sounds,—a starved, gaunt bitch, with her sides falling in and her ribs sticking out. She halted near the very water's edge, alongside of Ivannushka,—who went on singing, as though seeing naught and hearing naught,—and, with her muzzle tilted upward and her tail tucked in between her legs, set up a piteous howling against the blaze of the fireworks. The howling of the bitch blended with the yelling of the possessed woman into a single dreadful sound.

Kilikeia was being brought to by buckets of water thrown over her. The ancient, bending over her, was reading spells of exorcism, blowing and spitting into her face, and also striking it with his leather strap. Finally she quieted down and fell into a dead sleep, resembling a swoon.

The fireworks died out. The embers of the fire on the float barely glimmered. All was again dark. Nothing had happened. Antichrist had not come. There was no more horror. But a tedium fell upon them, more horrible than all horrors. As hitherto, they were sitting upon the level raft, which faintly showed as a black blotch between the black sky and the black water,—a mere handful of human beings, lonely, lost, seemingly suspended in the air between two heavens. Everything was calm. The float did not move. Yet it seemed to them that they were flying headlong, falling into this darkness as into some black abyss,—into the very maw of the Beast, toward the ineluctable end of all things.

And in this black, sultry darkness, filled with the blue quivering of heat lightnings, there came floating to them from the Summer Garden the tender sounds of a minuet, like the languorous sighs of love from the realm of Venus, where the shepherd lad Daphnis was untying the girdle of the little shepherdess Chloe:

> Thy arrows, Cupido, forego—
> For not a heart here but doth know
> A most delectable, dear woe;
> Not one but that has, to its sorrow,
> Felt of thy barbéd, golden arrow;
> We in submission all bow low.

II

On the Neva, alongside of the floats of the Czarevich, was anchored a large barque, come from Archangelsk with a freight of pottery, baked out of Kholmorskaya clay. The master of this ship, one Pushnikov, a rich merchant who was one of the Raskolniki who lived along the sea-shore, usually concealed on his vessel those fugitives and people in hiding who adhered to the old pieties. Below-decks the poop was partitioned off into diminutive cells of boards, something in the nature of cubby-holes. The country wife Alena Ephimova had found a snug shelter in one of them.

Alena was a peasant woman, the wife of a Moscow mint master, one Maxim Eremeëv, a secret ikonoclast. When Fomka, the Barber, the chief proponent of the ikonoclasts, had been burned at the stake, Eremeëv had fled to cities lower down the river, abandoning his wife. She herself was something between and betwixt a schismatic and one professing Orthodoxy: she made the sign of the cross with two fingers, at the instigation of a certain ancient, who, whenever he came to her, would say: "Thou canst not placate God with the three-fingered sign"; yet she also frequented Orthodox churches, and confessed to Orthodox confessors. Despite the fearful rumors concerning Peter, she believed that he was the true Czar of Russia, and loved him. She prayed God that she might look into the eyes of His Imperial Majesty. And she had come to Peterburgh for no other purpose save beholding the Sovereign. She was pursued by one idea: to supplicate God for Czar Peter Alexeievich, so that he might repent, return to the faith of his fathers, and cease his persecution of the people of the old belief; and that the latter, in their turn, might become one with the Orthodox Church. Alena had made up a special prayer for the unification of the different faiths, and had wanted to make that prayer known to her father confessor, but had not ventured to do so, "for that 'twas poorly written." She made pilgrimages to monasteries; she had hired, both in the Cathedral of the Ascension, and in the Church of the Mother of God at Kazan, ancient women to say the acathistus for the Czar, for six consecutive weeks; she herself made, daily,

two or three thousand bows for him. Yet all this seemed in-
sufficient to her, and she conceived a last, desperate remedy:
she ordered her nephew Vassiya, a fourteen-year-old boy,
to write down for her the prayer she had composed about
Czar Peter Alexeievich and the unification of the faiths;
contrived a pall for a holy image, sewed up her prayer in
the lining thereof, and gave it in to a priest of the Cathedral
of the Assumption, without saying anything concerning the
secreted writing.

After the talk on the float, Alena returned to her cubicle
upon Pushnikov's barque, and, as she recalled everything
she had heard about the Sovereign that night, a doubt assailed her for the first time in her life: perhaps that which
had been said of the Czar was true? And was it possible to
placate God for such a Czar?

For long did she lie in the stuffy darkness of her cubby-
hole, her eyes staring into the darkness, inundated with a
chill sweat, without stirring. Finally she got up, lit a little
candle-end of wax, put it before an ikon of the Mother of
God of All That Sorrow, which hung in a corner of the tiny
cabin, upon the partition of boards,—the same sort of ikon
as that which Czar Peter had used in his demonstration at
the pediment of Venus,—sank to her knees, made three
hundred bows, and began to pray in tears, with deep sighs;
praying a despairing prayer,—the same one that was sewn
into the pall for the image in the Cathedral of the Assumption:

"Hearken unto me, thou Holy Cathedral Church, with all
thy thrones of cherubim and seraphim, with thy prophets
and thy patriarchs, thy worthy saints and thy martyrs, and
with thy Evangel; and as many holy words as there be in
that Evangel,—let them all be applied to our Czar, Peter
Alexeievich! Hearken unto me, thou Holy Cathedral, Apostolic Church, with all thy stationary ikons, and all other true,
small images; with all thy Apostolic books and thy holy
lamps, and thy censers and thy stationary candles, and thy
sacred palls, and thy fair chasubles; with thy walls of stone
and thy plates of iron; with all thy fruit-bearing trees and
blossoms! Oh, I pray to thee also, thou splendidly beautiful
sun: raise up thy prayer to the Czar in Heaven for Czar

Peter Alexeievich! Oh, thou young, bright moon, and ye stars! Oh, thou sky, and ye clouds! Oh, ye thunder-laden clouds, and ye tempestuous winds and whirlwinds! Oh, ye birds in the sky! Oh, thou blue sea, and ye great rivers, and ye shallow springs, and ye small lakes! Raise up your voices in prayer to the Czar in Heaven for Czar Peter Alexeievich! And ye fish in the sea, and ye cattle on the lea, and ye beasts in the forests deep; and ye fields, and ye forests, and ye mountains, and all ye that are born of the earth,—raise up your voices in prayer to the Czar in Heaven for Czar Peter Alexeievich!"

The cubby-hole of Alena the country wife was divided off by a board partition from the roomier cell occupied by Kornilii the ancient and his disciple Tikhon. Never a word had Tikhon uttered during the entire conversation on the float, yet he had listened with an excitement greater than anybody else's. When all had dispersed the ancient had gone ashore in a small boat to a meeting and conclave with other schismatics, about a forthcoming grand self-inflicted holocaust of thousands upon thousands of people, persecuted for their adherence to the old faith, which holocaust was to take place in the Kerzhenskiya forests, beyond the Volga. Tikhon returned to his floating cell alone and lay down, but could not fall asleep, even like the country wife Alena in the adjacent cubby-hole, and pondered over what he had heard that night. He felt that all his future depended upon these thoughts, that there was impending an instant which, like a knife, would divide his life in two. "I am now upon the sharp edge of a knife as it were," he was saying to himself. "Whichever direction I fall in, that one I shall follow."

Simultaneously with the future, the past also rose up before him.

Tikhon was an only son, the last scion of the line of the Princes Zapolsky,—a line at one time noble, but long since fallen into disfavor and upon evil days. His mother had died in childbirth. His father, a chief of the Streltzi, had participated in the uprising, taking his stand against Peter and for the Miloslavskys, for old Russia, and for the old faith. During the inquisition of sixteen hundred and ninety-eight [15] he had been condemned, tortured within the dungeons of the

Fortress of the Transfiguration, and executed at the Kremlin, upon the Red Square. All his kindred and friends were likewise executed or banished. The eight-year-old Tikhon was left a total orphan, in the care of an aged retainer, Emelian Pakhomich. The boy was weak, and puny; he suffered from fits which resembled the black death. He had loved his father with a passionate tenderness. Apprehensive of the boy's health, Emelian had concealed his father's death from him, telling Tikhon that his father, now, had gone to attend to certain matters in an estate of his in distant Saratov. But the child wept and yearned, wandering like a shade through the vast, empty house, and, at heart, sensing misfortune. Finally he could endure no more. One day, after long and vain questionings, he ran away from home, all by himself, in order to make his way to the Kremlin, where his uncle lived, to find out from him about his father. His uncle at that time was no longer among the living,—he had been executed together with Tikhon's father.

Near the Gates of Our Saviour the boy came upon huge wains, loaded up to the top with corpses of the executed Streltzi, half-naked and thrown in every which way. Just like slaughtered cattle being freighted from the shambles, they were being driven to a common grave, to the knackers' pit, where they were thrown in together with all sorts of filth and carrion: such was the *ukase* of the Czar. From the embrasures of the Kremlin's walls logs jutted out; innumerable corpses hung upon them "like *polti*,"—a salted Astrakhan fish which is hung out in bundles to dry in the sun.

The people, dumbfounded, milled for days at a time upon the Red Square, without venturing any nearer to the place of the execution, but looking at it from afar. Jostling his way through the crowd, Tikhon caught sight, near Forehead Place, amid pools of blood, of some long, thick logs, which did duty as executioners' blocks. The condemned, huddling to one another, at times thirty men at once, would put their heads down upon these logs, in a row. And, as the Czar feasted in his chambers, the windows of which looked out upon the Red Square, his intimates among the *boyars,* and his jesters and favorites, would try their hands at chopping off these heads. Once, dissatisfied with their work—the hands of the unskilled headsmen trembled—the Czar commanded twenty of the condemned to be brought to the table at which he was feasting, and, right on the spot, executed them with his own hands, to jubilant shouts, to the sounds of music: he would toss off a glass and chop off a head,—glass after glass, blow after blow; the wine and the blood were poured out simultaneously,—the wine was mixing with blood.

Tikhon likewise saw a gallows, built in the semblance of a cross, for the mutinous chaplains of the Streltzi, who had been strung up by the most jocose of the jesters, the mock Patriarch, Nikita Zotov; and a multiplicity of torture-wheels, behung with the shattered members of those broken thereon; and iron spikes and stakes, upon which half-rotted heads were stuck: they could not be taken off, by *ukase* of the Czar, until they had rotted completely. There was a stench in the air. Ravens soared in flocks over the square.

The boy looked more closely at one of the heads. It showed clearly and darkly against the limpid blue sky with its tenderly-aureate and rosy clouds; in the distance the cupolas of the Kremlin cathedrals burned like glowing embers. The evening angelus was ringing. Suddenly it seemed to Tikhon as though everything—the sky, and the cupolas, and the cathedrals, and the earth under them—were quaking; that he himself was falling through the ground. In this one head, stuck up on a spike, with black holes where the eyes had oozed out, he recognized the head of his father. The rataplan of a drum rolled forth. From around a corner stepped out a division of the Guard of the Transfiguration, convoying tumbrils with fresh victims. The condemned, calm of face, were sitting in their white shifts, with burning tapers in their hands. Ahead of them, upon a steed, rode a man of enormous stature. His face, too, was calm, but awesome. This was Peter. Tikhon had never before seen him, yet now he recognized him at once. And it appeared to the child that the death's head of his father was looking straight into the eyes of the Czar with its empty eye-sockets. At that very instant he lost all consciousness. The crowd, ebbing back in its horror, would have trampled the boy, had he not been noticed by an old man, an old crony of Pakhomich,—a certain Grigorii Talitzky. He lifted him up and brought him home. That night Tikhon had such an epileptic fit as he had never had before. He barely managed to survive.

Grigorii Talitzky, a man obscure and poor, who eked out an existence by transcribing ancient books and manuscripts, was one of the first to expound the idea that Czar Peter was the Antichrist,—to quote the charge read against him subsequently, during the inquisition: "From his so great zeal against the Antichrist, and his dubious apprehension, he began to utter among the people evil words of obloquy and slander concerning the Sovereign." Having composed sundry pamphlets, *Of the Coming of Antichrist into this Our Universe,* and *Of the End of the World,* he had conceived the idea of printing them and of "throwing the broadsides among the people without moneys," to arouse them against the Czar. Grigorii had frequently visited Pakhomich and conversed with him about the Czar-Antichrist and the approaching end of time. Kornilii the ancient, who at that time also lived in Moscow, had taken part in these conversations. The little Tikhon listened to these three old men, who, like three sinister ravens, gathered at twilight, in the desolated house, and cawed: "The end of time is drawing near; cruel times have befallen us, and the years of hardship; true faith is no more,—there is no longer a wall of stone, nor are there any longer any pillars of strength, —Christian faith hath perished for aye. And at the very end of time there shall be the coming of Antichrist: all earth shall burst into flame, and shall burn to the depth of sixty ells, for this our great iniquity."

They spake about the vision of "A certain abominable and most fearful black Serpent that, in the Nikonian churches, during the high mass, hangs, instead of the sacred omophorien, upon the shoulders of the prelates, crawling and rattling; or at nights, entwining around the walls of the Czar's palaces, having his head and trunk within the palace whispers in the ear of the Czar."

And these dismal conversations passed over into still more dismal songs:

> Christ did speak, Our Heavenly King:
> O my dearest ones, unto me most dear,
> Flee ye one and all into deserts drear,
> Into forests grim, into caverns dim;

Cover ye yourselves, my beloveds all,
With the sands that are like to yellow ore,
Sands, and ashes, too, over your heads pour.
Die the death, my beloveds all:
Death shall not touch you,—ye will live anew
In God's Kingdom true!

With special avidity did he listen to stories of secret cloisters in the midst of impassable forests and marish lands beyond the Volga, of the invisible and faëry City of Kitezh upon the Lake of the Radiant Crag. The site thereof has the appearance of a forest wilderness,—yet are there not only churches, but houses, and monasteries, and people in great number. Of summer nights one may hear upon the lake the pealing of bells, and in its clear waters are reflected the golden domes of churches, each dome like the dry seed-pod of the poppy. There, truly, is the Kingdom of this earth; peace dwelleth there, and quiet, and an eternal joyance: the holy fathers have come to flourish there, like to lilies,—like to cypresses and date-palms,—like to most precious beads and the stars in heaven; from their lips issues an unceasing prayer to God, like unto sweet smelling incense and a chosen thurible; and when night falls their prayer becomes visible, even like unto pillars of fire with sparks, and so great is the light thereof that one can read and write by it, without any candle. God hath come to love them, and doth guard them like the apple of His eye, sheltering them invisibly with His palm, to the end of time. And they shall know nor grief, nor sorrow from the Beast-Antichrist; 'tis only because of us sinners that they grieve day and night,—because of our apostasy and that of the whole Czardom of Russia, for that Antichrist doth reign therein. Into this invisible city there leads, through groves and thickly wooded dales, but a single narrow path, surrounded by all kinds of wonders and terrors,—the Path of the Father, which none may find save those whom God Himself shall direct into that haven of blessed serenity.

Listening to these stories, Tikhon yearned to go thither, into these impassable forests, and the deserts. With pensiveness and delectation inexpressible did he repeat after Pakhomich the ancient lay of the youthful desert-anchoret, Josiphiah the Czarevich:

Thou wilderness resplendent, dear mother of mine!
I shall wander through forests, and through marish lands,
I shall wander over hills and through caverns deep;
I shall build a small hut for to shelter me;
I shall revel then,—I, who am a youth,
E'en I, Josiphiah, who am son to a Czar,—
In the greenwood, in the forest green:
The cuckoo will sound her call as I pass by,
She will eye me with a kindly eye,
E'en her silly song doth a sermon hold.
O, thou wilderness, dear mother mine!
The old tree-stumps that on thy bosom rot
Shall afford to me manna heaven-sent,
And a food most sweet;
Thy chill waters shall
Be as a honeyed drink. . . .

Since early childhood Tikhon had been visited, occasionally, by a queer feeling,—especially preceding his seizures; a feeling like no other,—unbearable, eerie and, at the same time, delectable; ever new,—ever familiar. In this feeling were both fear and wonder,—and a remembrance, just as if of some other world; but, most of all, there was in it curiosity, and a longing that that which was fated to happen might happen as speedily as possible. He never spoke to any one of this,—and, besides, he would not have been able to put this feeling into any words. Subsequently, when he had already begun to ponder, and to be conscious of things, this inward feeling of his began to blend with the idea of the end of the world, of the Second Coming.

At times the most sinister croakings of the three old men would leave him indifferent, while something casual, momentary,—a color, a sound, an odor,—would awaken this feeling within him with sudden force.

His house stood in Moscow-beyond-the-River, upon the slope of the Sparrow Hills; the garden terminated in a precipice, from whence could be seen all of Moscow,—mounds of black huts, of log cabins, recalling a village; rising over these were the white stone walls of the Kremlin and the gold cupolas of innumerable churches. From this precipice the boy would gaze for long at those magnificent and awesome sunsets which are occasionally to be seen in late, stormy autumn. In the deathly-livid, lilac, black, or enflamed-red, seemingly-ensanguined clouds, he imagined he saw: now the gigantic Serpent, coiled about Moscow; now the seven-headed Beast upon which sat the Whore with her cup of abominations; now the hosts of angels, pursuing fiends and wounding them with fiery arrows, so that rivers of blood flowed over the sky; Sion the resplendent, the unseen City, descending from heaven to earth amid the glory of the coming Lord. It seemed as though there, in the sky, was already being consummated, in mystic portents, that which was fated to be consummated upon the earth also. And the familiar feeling of the end would envelop the boy. This same feeling was born in him also by certain everyday trifles of life: by the smell of tobacco; by the first Russian book which met his eye,—printed in Amsterdam by *ukase* of Peter, in newly-invented "civil letters"; by certain sign-boards over the new shops in the German colony; by a peculiar form of perukes with amusing ringlets,—long, like the ear-locks of the Jews, or dog-ears; by the peculiar expression upon aged Russian faces,—recently bearded and but newly clean-shaven. One day the octogenarian gaffer Eremeich, a bee-keeper who had his place in their garden, had been seized by the Czar's wardens at the city gates, had his beard shaved off by force, and the skirts of his *kaftan* cut down and abbreviated to knee-length, to conform to the designated measurements. The gaffer, upon his return home, had wept like a baby; soon after he fell ill, and died from grief. Tikhon loved and pitied the old man; yet, when he first saw the weeping, bob-tailed and clean-shaven gaffer he could not refrain from laughter,—so strange, so unnatural, that Pakhomich grew scared lest Tikhon have a seizure. And, in this laughter, there was the horror of the end.

One winter there appeared a comet,—a star with a tail, as Pakhomich styled it. The boy had long wanted to have a look at it, yet did not dare; he deliberately turned away and puckered up his eyes in order not to see it. But he beheld it accidentally when one evening his guardian was carrying him in his arms into the bathhouse, through a blind alley, swept over with snow drifts. At the end of the lane between the black huts, over the whiteness of the snow, below the very edge of the blue-black sky, glittered an enormous, limpid, tender star,—somewhat declined, as though it were fleeing into immeasurable distances. It was not fearful, but as if it were kin to one, and so desired, so endearing that he gazed upon it nor could not have his fill of gazing. The familiar feeling contracted his heart, more powerfully than ever before, with unbearable rapture and terror. He was drawn toward it with all his body, as though he were awakening, with a tender, sleepy smile. And, that same instant, Pakhomich felt a dreadful spasm pass through the lad's body. A cry escaped the boy's breast. He was overcome by his second fit of the falling sickness.

When he had passed his sixteenth year he, along with other children of the petty nobility, was taken into the "School of Mathematical and Nautical Sciences,—that is, the Arts and Crafts of Seamanship." The school was located in the Sukharev Tower, where General Jacob Bruce busied himself with astronomical observations,—he was deemed a wizard and deeply versed in books of black magic: the old woman with twisted ribs who hawked pickled apples upon the Second Street of the Burghers had, one winter night, seen Bruce take off in flight from his high tower straight toward the crescent moon, astride his spy-glass. Pakhomich would not, under any circumstances, have given up the child to have him go to such an accursed place, if the youngsters were not taken by force.

The legal "minors" of the nobility,—some of them married, were infants of thirty and even forty years, were brought under convoy from their estates, where they had been in hiding, and had to sit side by side with real children, sharing the same form and learning by rote out of the same book,—which had a woodcut showing a schoolmaster armed with an enormous bundle of birch-rods and flogging a scholar spread out across a bench, with the inscription: *Let every man learn in silence*. All the a-b-c books were copiously adorned with verses glorifying the birch-rod:

> Thy blessing, Lord, on yon birch-groves bestow,
> That through the future ages the punitive rods may grow.
> To Youth birch-rods afford instructive delectation,
> E'en as Age needs oak-staves for ambulation.

Even the Czar's *ukase* prescribed: "There shall be chosen certain men from among the worthy retired soldiers of the Guards, and one of these shall be stationed in every room during instruction, and he shall have a lash in his hands; and should any of the pupils misbehave, the same shall be beaten, no matter of what family the guilty one be."

But no matter how hard learning was knocked into the heads of the scholars (lash and birch being used on the youngsters, and whips and cudgels on the big fellows), all alike learned poorly. At times, during moments of despair, they would sing "the song of Babylon." The older pupils would lead off in bass voices hoarse from too much drinking:

> Life in school is far from gay,—
> We are birched five times a day.

The small fry caught up in squealing falsettos:

> We be in sad plight,—
> Birched both day and night!

And the falsettos and the basses would blend into a well-timed chorus:

> Birches beat the empty belly,
> Sticks beat our hands to jelly.
> If you murmur,—watch your chin!
> They will flay your very skin.
> Euclid's science you must know—
> On food that would kill a sow.
> We be in sad plight,—
> Birched both day and night!

> And our black ink,—may it rot!
> It has made our heart's blood clot.
> E'en our paper and our quills
> Are to us but grievous ills.
> It matters not how good the lad—
> In the end school makes him bad.
> We be in sad plight,—
> Birched both day and night!

Tikhon would have learned but little in school had it not been for his having attracted the attention of one of the teachers, Pastor Glück, a German from Königsberg. Having gotten only a fair-to-middlin' knowledge of the Russian

tongue from a fugitive Polish monk, Glück had come to
Russia to instruct "the youths of Muscovy, who were like
to clay, soft and fit to be molded into anything." He was
disillusioned soon enough,—not so much in the youths themselves, as in the Russian method of "training them on the
manner of gypsy horses," by driving learning into their heads
with lashes. Glück was a man intelligent and kindly, even
though a drunkard. As for his drinking,—it was due to the
fact that not only the Russians but even the Germans deemed
him mad. He was writing a brain-racking work,—commentaries on Newton's commentaries on the Apocalypse;
in Glück's opus all the Christian revelations about the end
of the world were proved by the most exact astronomical
calculations, upon the basis of the laws of gravity, as laid
down in the recently issued *Philosofiæ Naturalis Principia
Mathematica* of Newton.

In his pupil, Tikhon, he had discovered unusual aptitudes
for mathematics, and had come to love him as his own kin.
Old Glück himself was a child at soul. With Tikhon, especially when half-seas over, he spoke as if the lad were
grown-up, and his only friend. He told him about new
philosophical doctrines and hypotheses; about the *Magna
Instauratio* of Bacon; about the geometrical ethics of
Spinoza; about Descartes' theory of vortices; and about the
monads of Leibnitz. But most inspiredly of all did he discourse upon the great astronomical discoveries of Copernicus,
Keppler, and Newton. There was a great deal that the boy
did not understand, but he listened to these relations of the
wonders of science with the same curiosity as he had to
the conversations of the three old men about the invisible
City of Kitezh.

Pakhomich deemed all the sciences of the Germans in
general as godless, but particularly so "star-gazing," also
dubbing astronomy *ostroumeia,*—keenness, or pride, of intellect.

"This accursed Copernic," he would say, making the
name rhyme with *sopernik,* or rival, "sets himself up as a
rival to God: he has raised the ponderous earth from its
center up into the air. 'Tis he alone who has been visited by
the dream that the sun and moon, now, are standing still,

whilst the earth doth turn around, contrary to the Holy Scriptures. The theologians do be laughing at him!"

"True philosophy," Glück would say, "is not only useful to faith but actually necessary. Many holy fathers were most excellently learned in the philosophical sciences. A knowledge of nature is not opposed to Christian law; and he who strives to investigate nature doth know and revere God; physical considerations of the creature serve for the glorifying of the Creator, even as is said in the Scripture: *The heavens declare the glory of God.*" [16]

Yet Tikhon surmised, through a dim instinct, that in this concurrence of science with faith everything was not quite so simple and evident even to Glück himself as he thought it was, or as he tried to think. 'Twas not for naught that occasionally, at the conclusion of a learned dispute with himself concerning the multiplicity of worlds, or the incomprehensibility of cosmic distances, the old man, very much under the weather, forgetting the presence of his pupil, would let his bald head drop on the edge of the table, as though in exhaustion,—a head grown heavy not so much from wine as from his vertiginous metaphysical thoughts, with its wig sliding off to one side,—and would dully moan, repeating Newton's famous utterance:

"Oh, physics,—deliver me from metaphysics!"

On one occasion Tikhon (who by now was already nineteen, finishing school, and able to read Latin well) chanced to open a manuscript collection of Spinoza's letters, lying upon his teacher's work-table, and read the first lines his eyes fell upon: "Between the properties of man and God there is just as little in common as between the constellation of the Dog and the dog, a barking animal. If a triangle had the gift of the word, even it would say that God is nothing else save a perfect triangle, while a circle would say that the nature of God is in the highest degree circular." And in another letter,—dealing with the Eucharist: "Oh, mad youth! Who has so bewitched you that you have come to imagine that 'tis possible to swallow the sacred and the eternal,—as if the sacred and the eternal could ever find a place within your inwards? Dreadful are the mysteries of your church,—for they contradict common sense." Tikhon closed the book and read no further. For the first time in his life he was experiencing, through thought, that feeling which he had formerly experienced only through external impressions: the horror of the end.

General Jacob Williamovich Bruce had, in the Sukharev Turret, an extensive library and a "cabinet of mathematical, mechanical and other instruments; likewise a *naturalium*, with specimens of animals, insects, roots, sundry ores and minerals, as well as antiquities, ancient coins, medals, engraved stones, masks and curiosities in general, foreign as well as domestic." Bruce had entrusted Pastor Glück with compiling a manual or description of all the objects and books. Tikhon was assisting him, and passed whole days in the library.

One clear summer evening he was perched on the very top step of a folding library-ladder, which moved upon wheels before a wall lined with books from top to bottom, pasting numbers on their backs and comparing the new list with the old,—illiterate, with the titles of the foreign books transliterated into Russian characters. Through the tall windows, with their small, round leaded panes, like those in ancient Dutch houses, the sun's rays fell in oblique, dusty sheaves upon the sparkling copper apparatuses,—celestial spheres, astrolabes, compasses, squares, drafting instruments, levels, spy-glasses, *microscopiums;* they fell upon stuffed specimens of all sorts of wondrous beasts and birds, upon the enormous bones of a mammoth's head; upon monstrous idols of China and marble visages of the splendidly beautiful gods of Hellas; upon interminable shelves of books in monotonous bindings of leather or parchment. Tikhon liked this work. Here, in the realm of books, reigned the same sort of soothing calm as in a forest, or in some old cemetery, abandoned of men, beloved of the sun. The evening angelus alone floated in from the street, recalling the pealing of the bells of faëry Kitezh, and, through the doors opening into the adjacent room, one could hear the voices of Pastor Glück and Bruce. Having supped they were sitting at a table, smoking and drinking as they conversed.

Tikhon had just pasted new numbers on certain quartos and octavos, illiterately designed in the old list as: No. 473

—Philosophy of Francisco Bakon, in the Englishe tongue, in three tomes; No. 308—*Meditation de Prima Philozophia, of Decartes, in the Dutch tongue;* and No. 532—*Mathematicall Elemens of Natural Philozophy, of Isaac Nephton.* As he was putting the books on the shelf his hand came upon an exceedingly ancient, mouse-nibbled octavo which had fallen back of the other books. It bore No. 461—*Lionardo Davinci, Tractate on Painting, in the German Tongue.* This was the first German translation of *Trattato della Pittura,* issued in Amsterdam in 1582. On a separate leaf laid into the book was a woodcut portrait of Leonardo. Tikhon gazed intently at this face,—odd, unknown, yet, at the same time, seemingly familiar, as if seen in some immemorial dream,— and reflected that, probably, Simon the Magus, who had flown through the air, must have had exactly the same sort of face.

The voices in the adjacent room had a louder sound by now. Bruce was carrying on some controversy with Glück. They were speaking in German. Tikhon had learned this language from the Pastor. A few isolated words struck him, and, his curiosity aroused, he listened more closely, with Leonardo's book still in his hand.

"How is it you do not perceive, my most worthy sir, that Newton was not of sound mind when he wrote his *Commentaries on the Apocalypse?*" Bruce was saying. "However, he himself confesses this in his letter to Bentley, under date of the thirteenth of September, in the year sixteen hundred and ninety-three: 'I have lost all coherence of thought, and do not feel my former assurance of mind,'— to put it plainly, it means that he had bats in his belfry."

"Your Excellency, I had rather be mad with Newton than of sane mind with all the rest of the two-legged creatures!" exclaimed Glück, and drained his tumbler in one draught.

"*De gustibus non disputandum est,* my dear Pastor;" Jacob Williamovich went on, breaking into his dry, harsh, seemingly wooden laughter; "yet here is the most curious thing of all: that, at the same time when Sir Isaac Newton was composing his *Commentaries,*—precisely here, in our midst, in Muscovy, at the other end of the world, those savage fanatics, who are called Raskolniki, or Schismatics of the Old Faith, had also composed their own commentaries on the Apocalypse, and had come to well-nigh the same conclusions as Newton. Awaiting, from day to day, the end of the world and the second coming of Christ, some of them lie down in coffins and sing their own requiems; others immolate themselves through fire. For this reason they are hunted and persecuted; yet in speaking of these unfortunates I would use the words of the philosopher Leibnitz: 'I have no love for tragic events, and would fain have everybody on earth live happily; as concerning the delusion of those who calmly await the end of the world,—it seems to me to be entirely innocent.' This, then, say I, is the most curious thing of all: in these Apocalyptic ravings the extreme West meets with the extreme East, and the greatest enlightenment with the greatest ignorance, which might, really, inspire the thought that the end of the world is approaching, and that all of us shall shortly go to the Devil! . . ."

He again broke into his harsh, wooden laughter and added something which Tikhon could not catch,—probably something very unorthodox, inasmuch as Glück (whose wig, as was usual after supper, had sidled down), suddenly jumped up in fury, pushed his chair away, and wanted to run out of the room. But Jacob Williamovich held him back and calmed him down with a few kindly words. Bruce was the sole patron of Glück, whom he respected and liked for his disinterested love of learning. But, being a skeptic, and even —as many asserted—an absolute atheist, he could never look at the poor Pastor, this "Don Quixote of Astronomy," without teasing him and poking fun at his ill-fated commentaries on the Apocalypse, at his reconciliation of science with faith. Bruce's stand was that one must choose one of the two,— either faith without science, or science without faith.

Jacob Williamovich filled Glück's tumbler, and, in order to console him, began questioning him about the details of Newton's Apocalypse. At first the old man replied unwillingly, but soon became infatuated once more and imparted to Bruce Newton's conversation with his friends about the comet of sixteen-hundred-and-eighty. On one occasion, when asked about it, he, instead of an answer, opened his *Principia*, and pointed out the passage which reads: "*Stellæ fixæ refici possunt.* Fixed stars can be renewed through the fall of comets upon them."—"Why, then, have you not written as frankly about the sun as about the stars?" "Because the sun concerns us more nearly," Newton had answered, and then added, laughing, "however, I have said sufficient for those who wish to understand!"

"Like a moth flying toward a flame the comet shall fall upon the sun!" exclaimed Glück. "And from this fall the heat of the sun shall increase to such a degree that everything on earth shall be consumed by fire. It is said in the Scripture: *The heavens shall pass away with a great noise, and the elements shall melt with fervent heat, the earth also and the works that are therein shall be burned up.*[17] Then both prophecies shall be fulfilled,—of him who believed, and him who knew."

" '*Hypotheses non fingo!* I do not invent hypotheses,' " he concluded inspiredly, repeating Newton's great phrase.

Tikhon listened,—and the prophetic croaking of the three ancients, of the three ravens, was, to him, becoming one with the most exact deductions of knowledge. Shutting his eyes, he beheld a blind alley, swept over the snow drifts, and, at its end, below, over the whiteness of the snow, between the black huts, on the rim of the blue-black sky, an enormous, limpid, tender star. And, just as in childhood, the familiar feeling contracted his heart with unbearable rapture and horror. He dropped Leonardo's book, which, in falling, caught the tube of an astrolabe and sent it crashing to the floor. Glück came running,—he knew that Tikhon was afflicted with fits. Seeing him atop the ladder, pale, trembling, he darted toward him, took him around, supported him, and helped him to come down. This time the seizure did not occur. Bruce also came in. They both questioned Tikhon solicitously, but he kept silent: he felt that he must not speak with any one of *this.* . . .

"Poor lad!" Jacob Williamovich remarked to Glück, leading the latter aside. "Our conversation must have frightened him. They're all like that hereabouts,—the end of the world is all they ever think of. I have noticed of late that there's some sort of madness spreading among them, like a plague. God knows where this unfortunate nation will wind up!"

Upon leaving school Tikhon, like all the children of the petty nobility, would have had to enter military service. Pakhomich had died. Glück was getting ready to go to Sweden and England, upon a commission from Bruce to purchase new mathematical instruments. He was inviting Tikhon to come along,—Tikhon who, having forgot his childhood fears and the warning of Pakhomich, was giving himself up with ever greater love to the study of mathematics. His health had become better; there was no recurrence of his fits. Long-cherished curiosity was drawing him on to regions new, —into the Glass Kingdom [Stockholm], almost as mysterious to him as the unbelievable Kitezh Town. And so, through the negotiations of Jacob Williamovich, the student of navigation Tikhon Zapolsky, among a number of other "infants of Russia," was sent by the Czar's *ukase* to finish his schooling over-sea. They arrived with Glück in Peterburgh at the beginning of June, in the year of seventeen hundred and fifteen. Tikhon had passed his twenty-fifth birthday; he was of the same age as the Czarevich Alexei, yet still had the appearance of a boy. A merchant ship was to leave Kronslot in a few days, on which they were to sail to Stockholm— which was popularly corrupted into the Stekolnoë—or Glass Kingdom.

Everything underwent a sudden change. Peterburgh, whose appearance was so dissimilar to that of Moscow, amazed Tikhon. He roved the streets for days at a time, gaping and being amazed: the endless canals; the perspectives; the houses on piles, hammered into the quaggy silt of marshes, but built in ranks, "all in a line," in accordance with an *ukase,* "so that no structure whatsoever be built out of line or back of the line"; wretched hovels, daubed over with clay and thatched, after the Chukhon fashion, with sods and birch bark; palaces of ginger-bread architecture, "on the Prussian manner," and standing amid forests and waste places; dismal garrison magazines; arsenals; sheds; churches with Dutch spires and clockwork chimes,—everything was flat, vulgar, workaday,—yet, at the same time, it all resembled a dream. At times, of foggy mornings, in the haze of the dirty-yellow fog, he had the hallucination that this whole town would float upward, together with the fog, and disperse, like a dream. In Kitezh Town all that had being was invisible, while here in Peterburgh, on the contrary, that was visible which had no being; but both towns were alike phantasmal. And again there would be born within him that eldritch sensation which he had not experienced for a long time by now,—the sensation of the end. Yet it did not resolve itself, as formerly, into rapture and horror, but oppressed him dully, with infinite sadness.

One day, at the Coffee House of the Four Frigates, on the Square of the Trinity, he encountered a man of tall stature, in the leather jacket of a Dutch skipper. And, just as in Moscow, on the Red Square, near the Brow Place, where the death's-head of his father had gazed with its empty eye-sockets straight into the eyes of this very man,—Tikhon at once recognized him: this was Peter. The awesome face had somehow immediately explained this dread city to him,— the same impress was upon both.

On the same day he had met the ancient, Kornilii,—had been as glad to see him as if the old man were of his kin, and thereafter left him no more. He slept at night in the ancient's cell; he passed his days on the floats, on the barques, with the runaways, with the folk in hiding. He listened to stories from the lives of the patriarchs who dwelt in the wildernesses of the far North, in the forests of Pomorsk, Onezhsk, and Olonetzk, where Kornilii, after having left Moscow, had passed many years; he heard of the dreadful holocausts which had taken place there,—*autos-da-fé* of thousands. The old man was now making a pilgrimage from thence to Kerzhenetz, beyond the Volga, to preach the "Red Death."

Tikhon's learning had not been wasted. A great deal that these people believed in he no longer believed; his ways of thought were different, yet his emotions were the same as theirs. The chiefest thing of all—the sensation of the end— they had in common with him. That which he would never have discussed with anybody, that which none of the learned would have comprehended, they did comprehend,—it was the only thing they lived for. All that he, since his earliest childhood, had heard from Pakhomich now suddenly sprang to

life within his soul, with new force. He was again drawn
to the forests, to the deserts, to the jealously guarded cloisters,
to the "haven of benign peace." It was as though in the light
of the white nights, over the vast expanse of the Neva,
through the chimes of Dutch clocks, he once more heard the
peal of the bells of Kitezh. And again, with a languishing
sadness and sweetness, he repeated the lay of Josiphiah the
Czarevich:

> Thou wilderness resplendent, dear mother of mine!
> I shall wander through forests and through marish lands,
> I shall wander over hills and through caverns deep. . . .

He had to decide,—he had to choose one of two things:
either returning for all time into the world, in order to lead
the life that all men lead; to serve the man who had destroyed
his father, and, perhaps, would destroy Russia; or to withdraw for all time from the world,—become a pauper, a vagrant,
one of the folk in hiding, one of the fugitive folk, "having
no real city,—seekers after the times to come"; he would
either have to go West, with Pastor Glück, into the Town of
Glass,—or East, with Kornilii the ancient, into the never-seen
Kitezh Town. Which would he choose,—whither would he go?
He himself knew not as yet, wavering, putting off the final
decision, as though awaiting something. But on this night,
after the discussion on the raft concerning Peter-Antichrist,
he felt that he must not procrastinate. The ship for Stockholm
was setting out on the morrow; and, also on the morrow,
Kornilii the ancient, who was threatened by denouncement,
would have to flee Peterburgh. He was summoning Tikhon to
go with him.

"I am now as if upon the sharp edge of a knife," he again
reflected. "Whatever direction I fall in, that shall I follow.
There is but one life, and one death. Once I err, there is no
second time for reparation."

But at the same time he felt that he had not the strength
to decide, and that the two fates, like the two ends of a dead
noose, joining, drawing together, were squeezing and strangling him. He arose, took down from a shelf a book in manuscript, *The Utterances of St. Hippolytos anent the Second
Coming*, and, as a respite from his thoughts, fell to looking

through the rubricated pictures, by the light of a lampad burning before an image. On one of them, toward the left margin, was depicted Antichrist, seated on a throne, in the uniform of the Guards of the Transfiguration,—green, with red facings and brass buttons,—with cocked hat and sword; his face resembled that of Czar Peter Alexeievich, and one hand pointed straight ahead. Before him, to the right, a division made up of the Simeon and Transfiguration Guards was marching in the direction of a cloister in the midst of a dark forest. Above, upon some mountains with three caves, certain friars were at prayer. The soldiers, led by blue fiends, were clambering up the mountain slope. Beneath was the inscription: "Then shall he send into the mountains, and antres, and clefts of this earth his hosts of fiends, that they may seek out them that hide from his eyes, and bring them to worship him." Upon another picture the soldiers were firing away at certain trussed-up ancients; the legend read: "They shall fall by the weapons of the devil."

On the other side of the board partition, in an adjacent cubby-hole, the country wife Alena was still sighing and weeping, praying to the King in Heaven for Czar Peter Alexeievich. Tikhon laid down his book, and sank to his knees before the image. But pray he could not. Sadness had fallen upon him,—a sadness such as he had never yet experienced. The flame of the holy lamp, burning low, blazed up for the last time and expired. Darkness fell. And something was crawling up, stealing up in this darkness, seizing him by the throat with its dark, warm, soft, seemingly shaggy paw. He was stifling. A chill sweat was coming out on his body. And again it seemed to him that he was flying headlong, plunging into a black darkness that was like a yawning abyss, —the maw of the Beast Itself. "Nothing matters," he reflected, and suddenly, as an unbearable light, the thought flared up in his consciousness: It did not matter which of the two paths he would choose, or whither he would go,—to the East or the West; both here and there, on the ultimate bounds of East and West was but one thought, one emotion: the end would come soon. *For as the lightning cometh out of the east, and shineth even unto the west; so shall also the coming of the Son of man be.*[18] And it was as if within him also there flashed this last, conjoining lightning: "Yea, come Thou, Lord Jesus!" he exclaimed, and at the same instant, at the other end of the cell, there flared up a white, fearful light. A deafening crash resounded, as though the heavens had fallen asunder. This was that same flash of lightning which had so frightened Peter that he had let the ikon drop out of his hands at the pediment of Venus. The country wife Alena caught, through the howling, whistling, and rumbling of the storm, a horrible, inhuman cry,—a fit of the falling sickness had overcome Tikhon.

He came to at the stern of the barque, whither, while he was in his fit, he had been carried out of the stuffy cell. It was early morning. Above was the blue sky,—below, the white mist. A star was glittering in the East, through the mist,—the star of Venus. And, upon the Island of Keivoussar, on the Peterburgh side, the Great Street of the Nobles, above the cupola of the house where Bouturlin lived,—Bouturlin, the Metropolitan of the Most-Drunken Conclave,—a gilt statue of Bacchus flared up under the first ray of the sun as a fiery-red, bloody star through the mist,—as though the terrestrial star had exchanged a mysterious glance with the celestial. The mist took on a rosy glow, as though living blood had poured into the bodies of wan phantoms. And the marble body of the goddess Venus, in the middle gallery over the Neva, turned rosy and warm, just as though it were alive. She smiled her eternal smile to the sun, as though rejoicing that the sun was rising even here, in this Hyperborean midnight. The body of the goddess was ætherial and rosy hued, like a bank of mist; the mist was glowing and alive, like the body of the goddess. The mist was her body,—and everything was in her, and she was in everything.

Tikhon recalled his thoughts of the night, and felt in his soul a calm resolution,—not to go back to Pastor Glück, but to run away with Kornilii, the ancient.

The barque on which he was lying, having been shifted from its mooring by the storm, had its stern jammed up against that same float where the night conversation about Antichrist had taken place. Ivannushka, who had managed to have his full sleep, was sitting on the same spot as before, and singing the self-same little song. And the music—or merely the phantom of music, the sounds of the minuet, stifled by the mist—

> Thy arrows, Cupido, forego—
> For not a heart here but doth know
> A most delectable, dear woe . . .

blended with the dismal, drawn-out song of Ivannushka, who, looking toward the East, the beginning of day, was singing to the West, the end of all days:

> O ye coffins made out of oak-logs tall,
> Our Eternal Homes ye shall be for all.
> Day is over, and the night draws nigh,
> The sun is sinking toward the West,
> And the ax so sharp at the root doth lie,
> And the end of time is about to fall!

III

On the bank of the Neva, near the Church of the All that Sorrow, alongside of the house of the Czarevich Alexei, was situated the house of the Czaritza Martha Matveievna, the dowager of the half-brother of Peter, Czar Fedor Alexeievich. Fedor had died when Peter was ten. The eighteen-year-old Czaritza had lived in wedlock with Fedor only four weeks. After his death she had gone out of her mind from grief, and spent thirty-three years in seclusion. She went nowhere out of her chambers,—she recognized nobody. At foreign courts she was accounted as one already long dead. Peterburgh, which she caught fleeting glimpses of through the windows of her chamber,—a Peterburgh which was a collection of clay-daubed buildings, built "on the Dutch and Prussian *manière*," its spired churches, Neva with its wherries and barques, and the canals,—it all appeared to her as a fearful and absurd dream; whereas visions seen in dreams seemed to her actuality. She imagined that she was living in the Kremlin at Moscow, in chambers hallowed by antiquity, and that, were she to look out of the window, she would behold the Kremlin belfry, called Ivan the Great because of its height. Yet look out she never did,—she dreaded the light of day. Perpetual darkness reigned in her chambers; the windows were covered with hangings. She lived by candlelight. Age-old screens and jalousies hid from the gaze of men the last Czaritza of Muscovy. Regal ceremony, solemn and pompous, was observed in the "Upper Chambers." The servitors durst not enter farther than the anteroom without "an announcement." Here time had stopped, and everything stood still forever,—just as it had been in the times of the Most Pacific Czar, Alexei Mikhailovich. An insane fairy tale had taken form in her afflicted mind,—her husband, Czar Fedor Alexeievich, was apparently alive, and dwelling in Jerusalem, at the Sepulcher of Our Lord, praying for the land of Russia, which was about to be attacked by the Antichrist, who was advancing with incomputable hosts of Poles and Germans; there is no Czar in Russia,—whatever Czar there was, he was not the real one; he was an impostor, a warlock, a Grishka Otrepiev, a runaway cannoneer, a German from the Kukuevskaya Borough; but the Lord was not completely wroth with those of the orthodox faith; when the times and days appointed would be fulfilled, the sole Czar of the true faith, the Czar of all the Russias, Fedor, the beautiful little sun, will return to his land with his terrible army, in might and glory, and the hosts of the Paynim shall flee before him, even as night flees before the sun, and he will take his place on the throne of his grand-sires with his Czaritza, and will raise up anew justice and truth throughout his land; all his people shall come to him and bow down before him, and the Antichrist, with all his Germans, shall be cast down. Then, too, would be immanent the end of the world, and the second dread coming of Christ. All this was nigh,—standing on the very threshold.

Some two weeks after the Festival of Venus in the Summer Garden, Czarevna Maria invited Alexei to the house of the Czaritza Martha. This was far from the first time that they had held secret meetings there. His aunt transmitted to him news and letters from his mother, the disgraced Czaritza Eudoxia Fedorovna, who had fallen into disgrace and out of favor, whose name as a nun was Ellena,—the first wife of Peter, who had forced her to take the veil and had shut her in in the Suzdalsko-Pokrovsko nunnery.

Alexei, upon entering the house of the Czaritza Martha, for a long while had to grope his way through sundry dark, beamed passages, anterooms, pantries,—both above stairs and below,—and staircases. Everywhere was an odor of wood-oil, cluttery furnishings, of ancient, worn-out fripperies,—as if one were breathing the odor of the dust and rot of ages. Everywhere were tiny cells, closets, secret rooms, nooks formed by angles, tiny cubby-holes, tiny lumber rooms. All these afforded snug nests to the upper stratum of the noble dames and damsels—ancient, most ancient,—as well as chamber-maids, nurses, treasuresses, laundresses, women who took care of furs, others who took care of bed-linens, inno-cents, beggars, female palmers, canting pilgrims, fools,—male and female,—little orphaned girls, centenarian story-tellers or bards and players upon the *domra*,[19] who sang sagas to the sounds of their dismal instruments. Decrepit servitors in *kaftans* of faded fustian,—hoary, shaggy, seemingly grown over with moss,—clutched the Czarevich's coat-tails, kissing his hand, or his shoulder. The blind, the mute, the halt; gray-beards; beings leaden-hued from age; creatures without faces,—all, dogging him, slithered along the walls, like phantoms; they swarmed, they wriggled, they crawled through the darkness, like multipedes in damp cracks. He stumbled upon Shamyra, the fool, who was forever snigger-ing and exchanging pinches with Manka, the female fool. The most ancient of the ladies of honor, Sundulia Vakhrameëvna, —a favorite of the Czaritza, and, like her mistress, out of her mind through sheer senescence; stout, all bloated with yellow fat, and shaking like frozen jelly,—threw herself down at his feet and, for some reason or other, set up a howl, keen-ing over him as if he were one dead. The Czarevich was en-compassed by an eldritch feeling. He recalled what his father had said: "The said court of the Czarevna Martha is, because of its piety, naught save a hospital for monsters, for the feeble-minded, for bigots, and for mischief-makers."

Alexei sighed with relief upon stepping into a lighter and fresher corner-chamber, where his aunt, Czarevna Maria Alexeievna, was expecting him. The windows looked out upon the blue and sunny expanse of the Neva with its ships and barques. The walls, made of logs, like those of a hut, were bare, save where, in the wonted corner, there stood a niche with images, a lampad dully glowing before them. There were benches along the walls. The Czarevich's aunt, who was seated at a table, arose and kissed him with tenderness. Maria Ivannovna was dressed in the old fashion, in a peasant woman's head-dress and woolen jerkin of an "humble"—that is, a dark, widowy-color, with brown dots. Her face was far from handsome,—pale and puffy, like the faces of old nuns. But in her malicious, thin lips, in her clever, keen, seemingly pricking eyes, there was something imperious and resolute, reminiscent of the Czarevna Sophia,—"the evil seed of the Miloslavskys." Just as Sophia did, she hated her brother and all his deeds, "flaming at soul for the times of old." Peter spared her, but called her an old crow, inasmuch as she was forever croaking in his ears.

The Czarevna handed over to Alexei a letter from his mother in Suzdal. This was in answer to her son's recent little note, all too stiff and brief: "Mother, I greet thee! Forget me not in thy prayers." Alexei's heart began pounding as he fell to deciphering the illiterate lines of clumsily scrawled, child-like characters in the familiar handwriting:

"Czarevich Alexei Petrovich, I greet thee. For I, poor that I am, am scarce alive because of my sorrows, for that thou, my dear one, hast forsaken me, for that thou hast left me in the midst of such sorrows, for that thou hast forgotten her who has given thee birth. And yet I tended thee like to a slave. And yet thou hast forgot me so soon. And yet 'tis for thy sake that I am still alive to this day. And yet, were it not for thy sake, I could not bear to be in this world, amid such disasters, and misfortunes, and poverty. Bitter, most bitter is this my existence! 'Twould have been better had I never seen the light of day. I know not the wherefore of my sufferings. And yet, I have not forgot thee,—I ever pray for thy health to the Most Holy Mother of God, that she may preserve thee, and keep thee in all purity. There is an image here of the Most Holy Mother of God at Kazan,—the church has been built upon the site of her appearance. And I did make a vow for thy health, and had this image brought and hung in my house, and did bring it back myself, carrying it upon my shoulders. And I had a vision in the month of May, on the twenty-third day thereof. The Most Radiant and Most Pure Queen of Heaven did appear, and did promise to intercede

before the Lord God, her Son, and this my sorrow to trans-
mute into joy. And I did hear, unworthy that I am, from the
Most Radiant Woman,—she spake, saying: 'Thou didst
prefer my image, and didst follow it to my temple and therefore shall I make thee great, and preserve this thy son.' And
as for thee, my joy, the child of my womb, keep then the fear
of God in thy heart. Do write me, my friend Olëshenka, if it
be but one line; slake my tearful sobbing; do let me, if but
a little while, have surcease of grief; have mercy upon thy
mother and thy slave; do, please, write a little! I bow before
thee, like a slave."

When Alexei had finished reading the letter, the Czarevna
Maria handed to him certain presents from the nunnery,—a
little image; a small kerchief, broidered in silks, with her
own hand, by the humble nun Ellena; as well as two small
cups of linden wood, "the same to be used for drinking
vodka." These pitiful gifts touched him more than the letter.

"Thou hast forgotten her," Maria uttered, looking him
straight in the eyes. "Thou dost not write her, nor dost thou
send her aught."

"I am afraid," spoke the Czarevich.

"And of what?" she retorted with animation, and her keen
eyes seemed to prick him. "And even if thou wert to suffer?
'Tis naught! Why, 'tis for thy mother,—and for no other. . . ."

He kept silent. Thereupon she fell to telling him, whispering in his ear, what she had heard from one who had come
from the Suzdal cloister, a certain innocent by the name of
Mikhailo the Barefooted: the joy of that region had created
universal gladness; in that locality there was no end of
visions, of portents, of prophecies, of images speaking with
tongues; Job, the Prelate of Novgorod, was saying: "There
is evil preparing for the Czarevich in Peterburgh; God alone,
I wot, will deliver him; see what will take place there." While
Vissarion, the ancient who dwelt immured in the wall about
Yaroslav, had had a revelation, that a change was imminent:
"Either the Sovereign would die, or Peterburgh would fall to
wrack and ruin." And to Bishop Dositheus of Rostov there
had appeared St. Dimitri the Czarevich, and had foretold:
that there would be a certain uprising, and that there would
be *a consummation soon*.

"Soon! Soon!" concluded the Czarevna. "There are many raising an outcry: Lord, avenge us, and give us a *consummation,* and thus let matters end!"

Alexei knew that *consummation* meant the death of his father.

"Mark my words!" Maria exclaimed prophetically. "Peterburgh will not last long after us! May it be desolate!"

And, having glanced through the window at the Neva, at the little white houses amid the green, quaggy meadows, she repeated with an evil joy:

"May it be desolate! May it be desolate! May it sink to the Devil through the quagmire! Even as it has sprung up, so may it rot,—the vile toadstool! And may the spot whereon this accursed town once stood be never found!"

The old crow now fully launched upon her croaking.

"Old wives' tales!" Alexei made a hopeless gesture. "Have we not heard enough of prophesying? 'Tis all nonsense!"

She was about to offer some contradiction, but suddenly looked at him again with her keen, prickling eyes.

"Why hast thou such a look, Czarevich? Art ailing, or what? Or art thou drinking?"

"I am. Drink is forced upon me. Three days ago, at the launching of a ship, I was carried out as one dead. 'Twould be better were I condemned to hard labor, or lying in a fever, than be there!"

"Why, thou shouldst take medicines,—make believe thou art taken with illness, so as to avoid attending those launchings, since thou knowest thy father's way."

Alexei was silent a while; then sighed deeply.

"Oh, Mariushka, Mariushka, but mine is a bitter lot! . . . Why, I scarce know myself for bitterness. Were it not for the sustaining power of God, a man could scarce keep sane. . . . I would be glad to hide almost anywhere. . . . If one could but go away,—away from all this!"

"Whither art thou to go from thy father? His arm is long. He would find thee anywhere!"

"I feel sorry," Alexei went on, "that I did not do what Kikin urged me to do,—go off to France, or to the Kaiser. There I would live in greater peace than here, as long as God willed. For there have been many like me who have saved themselves by flight. But then, there is nothing to countenance my leaving. Why, I really know not, dear aunt of mine, my darling, what the end of me will be! . . . There is nothing I desire, —save to be given my freedom and be left in peace. Or else,—to be allowed to enter some monastery. Even my succession would I renounce,—I fain would live away from everything, in peace; I would withdraw into my hamlets, where I might end my days!"

"That will do, now,—that will do, Petrovich! For the Sovereign, now, is no immortal man: when it is God's will, he shall die. There, now, they do be saying that he hath the falling sickness,—and such folk are not long-lived. God will grant the *consummation*. . . . I feel it will not be delayed. . . . Bide a while, say I,—we, too, shall have our say. Thou art beloved by the people, and they drink thy health, naming thee the hope of Russia. The succession will not pass thee by!"

"What matters the succession, Mariushka! 'Tis fated that I take the tonsure, and it isn't only now, from my father, but even after him, that I must expect the same fate as Vasilii Shuisky's,—that, after shaving the crown of my head, I shall be thrown into captivity somewhere. Evil are my days. . . ."

"But what can we do, my little falcon? Be patient an hour, —and live for an age. Be patient a while, Aleshenka!"

"Long have I been patient,—I can no more!" he exclaimed, with an irresistible impulse, while his face blanched. "If but the end itself would come! Languishing is worse than death. . . ."

He wanted to add something else, but his voice broke. He moaned out dully: "Oh, Lord, Lord!" dropped his arms on the table, pressed his face against his palms, and then clutched his head,—and, while he did not burst into tears, he seemed to shrink into himself, as if from unbearable pain. Convulsive yet tearless sobbing made his whole body quiver.

Czarevna Maria bent over him, and laid upon his shoulder her firm and imperious little hand,—Czarevna Sophia had precisely such hands.

"Be not faint of heart, Czarevich," she spake slowly, with a quiet and kindly sternness. "Provoke not the wrath of God, —murmur not. Remember Job: 'tis good to place thy trust in God, 'in whose hand *is* the soul of every living thing, and the breath of all mankind.' [20] Mayhap He will even so contrive that those who are opposed to us will prove of benefit to us. 'But the Lord *is* with me as a mighty terrible one: therefore my persecutors shall stumble, and they shall not prevail. [21] Though an host should encamp against me, my heart shall not fear,' [22]—for the Lord shall avenge me! Place all thy trust in Christ, Alëshenka, dearest friend of my heart: He will not allow any temptation beyond thy strength."

She fell silent. And to the sound of these pious words, familiar and beloved even from his childhood, under this kindly, firm hand, he, too, grew quiet.

There was a knock at the door. It was Sunduleia Bakhrameëvna, come after them from Czaritza Martha. Alexei raised his head. His face was still pale, yet almost calm by now. He glanced at the image, with the dully glowing lampad before it, made the sign of the cross, and said:

" 'Tis the truth thou speakest, Mariushka! Let God's will be wrought in all things. He, through the prayers of the Mother of God and all the saints, shall consummate or resolve all those things concerning us. On which I had placed, and shall place, all my hopes."

"Amen!" pronounced the Czarevna.

They got up and set out for the sleeping quarters of the Czaritza Martha.

IV

Despite the sunlit day, it was as dark as night within the chamber, and the candles were burning. Never a ray penetrated through the windows, closely nailed over with lengths of felt, and hung with rugs. In the close air there was an odor of calamint, milfoil brandy, rose water, and incense, which was put in the fuel, to scent the place. The room was cluttered with benches near the stoves, and cupboards, wardrobes, chests from Little Russia, strong-boxes, hampers, caskets; coffers of wrought iron; treasure chests meant to be kept under one's pillow, bound with strips of tinned iron; cypress presses with all sorts of furs, garments, and "white treasure-trove,"—*i.e.*, linen. In the middle of the room reared up the Czaritza's couch, sheltered, as if by a tent, by a canopy of cloth of gold,—scarlet-hued, with a design of grasses in pale-green, and covered by a comforter of gold Kizilbash damask, lined with sables and fringed with ermines. Everything was magnificent,—yet ancient, threadbare, disintegrated, so that it seemed as if it would scatter, like grave-yard dust, from a breath of fresh air. Through an open door one could see an adjacent room,—the chapel, all flooded with the refulgence of lampads before ikons in gold and silver chasubles, thickly bossed with precious stones. All sorts of sacred things were preserved there: crosses, panagias, triptychs, scapularies, reliquaries, shrines with sacred bones; myrrh from Smyrna, olibanum, wonder-working metheglins, holy water kept in cere-cloths, cassia in saucers, chrism, consecrated by Patriarchs, stored in a leaden vessel; candles lit by fire from heaven; sand from the Jordan; slivers of the Ever-Burning Bush and of the oak of Mamre; some milk from the breasts of the Most Pure Mother of God; lapis lazuli,—"a bit of the heavens where Christ had stood on air"; a stone in a cloth pouch,—"giving forth a goodly odor, yet what manner of stone it be, none knoweth"; the footclouts of Pahnutius of Borov; a tooth of Antipas the Great,— a sovereign remedy against toothache,—appropriated for his own use by Ivan the Terrible from the treasury of his slain son.

Czaritza Martha Matveievna was seated by the bed, in a gilt armchair, resembling a "Czar's seat" or throne, with a double-headed eagle and a *"coruna"* or crown carved on its back. Although the green glazed stove, with its intricate festoons and scrolls, was at red-heat, the chilled, ailing old woman was muffling herself in a warm jacket lined with Arctic fox. A banded fringe of pearls hung down on her forehead from under her high headgear of gold. Her face was not aged, but rather dead, stony. Thickly whitened and rouged, according to the ancient usage of the Czaritzas of Muscovy, it seemed still more death-like. The eyes alone were alive,— limpidly light, yet with an unmoving, apparently unseeing gaze,—such a gaze as night-birds have in the day-time. A little old friar was sitting at her feet, in the midst of some narration.

When the Czarevich entered with his aunt, Martha Matveievna greeted them kindly and invited them to lend ear to the dear little pilgrim of God. This was a diminutive ancient, with a face altogether childish, yet exceedingly gay; his piping voice, too, was gay, sonorous and pleasant. He told of his travels, of the cloistered life in Athon and the Solovki. Comparing the two, he gave the preference to the Greek cloister over the Russian.

"The said Cloister at Athon is called *The Garden of the Most Holy Mother of God*,—for the Most Pure Mother doth ever gaze down upon it from above, providing for it and guarding it unscathed. And by her help it stands and flourishes, and bringeth forth fruits, both without and within,—the fruits without are to behold; those within are good for the salvation of the soul. And whoever doth penetrate into that garden, which is like to the fore-court of Paradise itself, and doth perceive its goodness and its beauty, will never want to retrace his steps. The air there is buoyant, and while the height of the knolls and the mountains, and the warmth, and the light of the sun, and the diversity of trees and fruits, and the nearness of that most desired region, Jerusalem,—all create a joy eternal.

"The Island of Solovetzk, on the other hand, is filled with despondency and dread, with despair and darkness, and a most bitter cold, like unto that of Tartarus. Also, there is to be found upon that island something that is e'en harmful to the soul: certain white birds—sea-gulls—make their homes there, in great numbers. All summer long they multiply, bringing forth their young, weaving their nests on the ground, along the ways which the monks use in going to church. And great is the mischief wrought by these birds upon the friars. Fi stly, they are deprived of their blessed peace. Secondly, when they behold these birds fluttering about, and playing and coupling, their minds are captivated, and they are made passionate. Thirdly, there is the fact that women, and maids, and nuns, come frequently to that cloister. But as for the Mount of Athos, it has no such temptations: the gulls come not a-flying; neither do women come a-visiting. One Woman only, soaring upon the twin pinions of a she-eagle—The Holy Mother Church—hovers over that delectable wilderness, until such time when the will of the Lord, and the days He has appointed, shall be fulfilled,—to Whom be glory, for ever and aye. Amen."

When he had finished his tale, the Czaritza requested that everybody,—even Maria,—leave the room, and was left alone with the Czarevich.

She practically did not know him, did not remember just who he was and how he was related to her,—she even kept on forgetting his name, and simply called him her little grandson; she did not love him, but rather pitied him with a certain strange, fatidical pity, as though she knew that about his destiny which he himself as yet knew not. She gazed at him for long in silence, with her bleak, unmoving eyes, seemingly veiled over with a pellicle, like the eyes of night-birds. Then she suddenly smiled, sadly, and her hand fell to stroking softly his cheek and hair:

"My poor little orphan, thou! Nor father nor mother hast thou. There is ne'er a soul e'en to intercede for thee. The fierce wolves shall rend the poor little lamb to pieces; the black ravens shall peck to death the little white pigeon. . . . Oh, but I am sorry for thee,—sorry for thee, my own dear little one! Thou art not long for this world. . . ."

From this insane delirium of the last of the Czaritzas, who here, in Peterburgh seemed a pitiful specter of old Muscovy, —from this dry-rot of pomp,—from this quiet, warm room, in which time seemed to be standing still,—there was wafted upon the Czarevich the chill of death, and the tenderness of his most remote childhood. A sad and sweet ache sprang up in his heart. He kissed the dead-white, emaciated hand, with its thin fingers, from which the ancient, ponderous, regal rings were slipping.

The Czaritza had let her head droop, as if she had fallen into deep thought, as she told her round coral beads: from these *kralki* (corals) the Foul One flees, "for that the *Kralek* doth grow in the form of a cross."

"All is confusion,—all is confusion; evil deeds are being wrought!" she began anew, as though in delirium, with increasing disquiet. "Hast read in the Scriptures, little grandson,—*Little children, it is the last time: and as ye have heard that antichrist shall come, even now are there many antichrists; whereby we know that it is the last time?* [23] 'Tis said of him, of the Son of Perdition. He hath already come to the gates of the court. Soon, soon, he will be here. For I e'en know not whether I shall live to see the day, whether I shall behold the dearest friend of my heart, my little fair sun, the righteous in faith, Czar Fedor Alexeievich? If I might but peek at him out of the corner of one eye, when he shall come in his might and glory, and give battle to the infidels, and conquer, and take his seat on the throne of majesty; and all the nations shall bow down, and cry out: "Hosanna; Blessed *is* he that cometh in the name of the Lord!" [24]

Her eyes blazed up for an instant, but immediately were drawn over anew, like embers by ashes, with their former turbid film.

"Oh, nay, I shall not live to see that day,—I shall not behold him! I have provoked the Lord's wrath, sinner that I am! . . . My heart senses misfortune,—oh, but it senses it! Heavy am I at heart, little grandson,—most heavy. . . . And the dreams I dream now are all so evil, so ominous. . . ."

She turned around to look apprehensively, drew her lips to his very ear, and whispered:

"Dost know, little nephew, what a dream I had the other day? *He* himself—whether in a dream or a vision, I know not,—only *he* himself came to me; 'twas none other than *he!*"

"Who, Czaritza?"

"Dost thou not understand? Listen, then, how I came to dream this dream,—mayhap thou wilt then understand. I was lying, 'twould seem, on this very bed, and I seemed to be waiting for something. Suddenly the door flies open, and *he* enters. I recognized him at once. Such a tall fellow, and a stout, yet his wretched *kaftan* was skimpy, of a German cut; he hath a pipe in his mouth, and is pulling away at it,—and most vile tobacco it held; his phiz is clean-shaven, and his mustachios are like a tom-cat's. He walked up to me, looks at me, and keeps silent. And I, too, keep silent,—what is going to be the upshot of this?—thinks I. And I felt ill, and sad,—so sad that I thought my death were come. . . . I fain would make the sign of the cross,—but my hand won't rise; I fain would say a prayer,—but my tongue won't stir. I lie there as one dead. But he takes me by the hand, and feels my pulse. Fire and frost run down my spine. I glance at a holy image,—but even the image appears to me in different guises: as though it were not the Most Pure Visage of Our Saviour, but of some vile German,—his phiz all puffed up, blue, like that of a drowned man. . . . But *he* keeps on hammering away at me all the time: 'Thou art ill, Martha Matveievna,' says he,—'thou art seriously ill. Say the word, and I'll send my doctor to see thee. But why dost thou gaze at me so? Or hast thou not recognized me?'—'How can one help but recognize thee,' said I. 'I know thee, right enough. We have seen enough of the likes of thee!'—'Who, then, am I?' says he. 'Tell me, if thou knowest.'—'Any one,' says I, 'knows who thou art. Thou art a German, and the son of a German; thou art a drummer in the army.' Whereupon he bared all his teeth, and spat at me, like a tom-cat gone crazy. 'Thou art out of thy mind, crone,—thou art altogether out of thy mind! No German am I, and no drummer, but the God-crowned Czar of all Russia, as well as own half-brother to thy late husband, Czar Fedor.'—Right there and then I gave way to anger entirely. Fain would I have spat right in his phiz, and fain would I have cried out: Thou hound, thou son of a dog, thou false pretender, thou Grishka Otrepiev, thou anathema,—that's who thou art! Ah, well, thinks I, the Foul One take him! Wherefore should I bandy curses with him? 'Tis not even worth the while to out and spit on him. For this is but a dream of mine; a foul vision that I am imagining through a visitation of God. I have but to puff, and 'twill perish, will scatter into dust. 'Well, if thou be the Czar,' said I, 'what name dost thou go by?'—'Peter,' says he, 'is my name.' No sooner had he said 'Peter' than it was just as though a light dawned upon me. 'Eh,' thinks I to myself, 'so that's who thou art! Well, bide thee a while, then.' Being no fool, though I could not move my tongue, I e'en begin reciting a holy incantation in my mind: 'Thou our adversary, Satan! Take thyself off into the waste places, into forests impenetrable, into the clefts of the earth, into the bottomless seas, into the mountainous wildernesses, where there is nor house nor mankind,—for the light of the face of the Lord ceaseth never! Thou accursed maw! Get thee hence from me into Tartararus,[25] into the uttermost pit of hell, into the fires infernal! Amen! Amen! Amen! Scatter into dust! I blow upon

thee, and spit out!' No sooner had I finished the spell, than
he simply up and vanished, just as though he had fallen
through the ground; there was ne'er a trace of him,—save for
the stench of his vile tobacco. I woke up, and cried out;
Vakhrameëvna came on the run, sprinkled me with holy
water, and burned incense over me. I arose, went off into the
oratory, fell down on my knees before the image of the
Most Pure Queen, the Mother of God at Vlakherna; and it
was only when I had recalled and thought over everything
that I at last comprehended who it was."

The Czarevich had long since gathered that his father had
visited her, not in a dream but in reality. Yet, at the same
time, he felt that the delirium of this madwoman was being
transmitted to him, was infecting him.

"Who was it, then, Czaritza?" he echoed her last words,
with an avid and eerie curiosity.

"Dost thou not comprehend? Or hast forgotten that in the
book of Ephraim, now, 'tis said of the Second Coming: 'The
proud prince of this world, Antichrist, shall come in the name
of Simon *Peter*?' Dost hear? His name is Peter. 'Tis he,
himself!"

She fixed him with her eyes, dilated with horror, and, in a
gasping whisper, repeated:

" 'Tis he, himself. Peter is Antichrist . . . Antichrist!"

BOOK THREE

DIARIES OF THE CZAREVICH ALEXEI
AND FRAULEIN ARNHEIM

I

THE DIARY OF FRÄULEIN ARNHEIM

1st of May, 1714.

An accursed land,—an accursed people! vodka, blood, and dirt,—'tis hard to decide which predominates. Dirt, apparently. The King of Denmark put it well: "If the envoys of Muscovy ever pay me another visit, I shall build a pigbyre for them, inasmuch as any place they may stay at is uninhabitable for half a year thereafter, because of the stench." According to the definition of a certain Frenchman the Muscovite "is the man of Plato,—an animal without feathers, who has all the attributes of the human save cleanliness and reason." [26]

And these stenchful savages, these baptized bears, who are changing from something fearful into something pitiful, transforming themselves into European apes, nevertheless deem themselves the only human beings, and all the others beasts. But especially against us, against Germans, do they harbor hatred,—innate, inconquerable. They consider themselves defiled by our mere touch. Lutherans are, for them, but little better than the Devil himself.

Not for a moment would I stay in Russia, were it not a matter of dutiful love and loyalty to Her Highness, my gracious mistress and heartmost friend, the Crown Princess Sophia Charlotta. No matter what befall, I shall not forsake her!

I will write this diary in the same language that I speak,—in German; also, partly in French. However, certain jests, by-words, songs, citations from *ukases*, and snatches of conversation, I will retain in the original Russian, but with their translations next to them.

My father is a thoroughbred German, of an ancient line of Saxon knights; my mother was a Pole. With her first husband, a Polish nobleman, she had lived for a long while in Russia, not far from Smolensk, and had thoroughly mastered the Russian tongue. I was educated in the town of Torgau, at the court of the Queen of Poland, where there were also many Muscovites. I heard Russian speech from my childhood on. I speak it poorly; I do not like this language; but I understand it well.

In order to have something to lighten my heart at least, when things become too sad, I have decided to keep notes, imitating the babbler in the ancient fable who, not daring to entrust his secrets to men, did whisper them to swampreeds. I would not want these lines ever to come to light; yet it affords me joy to think that they may come to the eyes of the only human being whose opinion is to me the dearest thing in the world,—my great teacher, Gottfried Leibnitz.

*　　*　　*

Just when I was thinking of him, I received a letter from him. He requests me to make inquiries as to what salary is due him, as one filling in the Russia service the position of Privy Councilor of Justice in the Russian Service. I much fear me he will never see this salary.

I almost wept, for sadness and joy, as I was reading his letter. I recalled our quiet strolls and our conversations in the galleries of the Salzdallen Castle, in the alleys of lindens at Herrenhausen, where the caressing zephyrs among the leaves, and the swish of the fountains, seem to be eternally humming our favorite little song from *Mercure Galant:*

> *Chantons, dançons, tout est tranquille*
> *Dans cet agréable séjour.*
> *Ah, le charmant azile!*
> *N'y parlons que de jeux, de plaisirs et d'amours.*

I was recalling the words of my teacher, which at one time I almost believed: "I am a Slav, even as you are. You and I ought to rejoice because Slavonic blood flows in our veins. There is a great future appertaining to this race. Russia shall unite Europe with Asia, shall reconcile the West with the East. This country is like a new pot, that has not yet taken on any foreign flavor; it is like a sheet of blank paper, whereon one may write whatever one wills; like a new land, which shall be plowed up for a new sowing. Later Russia may be in a position to enlighten even Europe itself, thanks to the fact that she may have avoided those errors which are much too deeply rooted within us." And he concluded with an inspired smile: " 'Twould seem I am called by destiny to be the Russian Solon, the law-giver of a new world. To gain sway over the mind of one such man as the Czar is of greater significance than winning a hundred pitched battles!'"

Alas, my poor, great dreamer, if you did but know and see that which I have come to know and see in Russia!

Even right now, as I write, sad reality reminds me that I am not within the delectable shelter of Herrenhausen, that German Versailles, but within the depths of Muscovite Tartary!

Shouts, screams, curses resound under my window: these are the servants at the court of our neighbor, the Czarevna Nathalia Alexeievna, fighting with ours. The Russians are beating the Germans. Alas,—I am seeing the actual working out of the union of Asia with Europe, of the West with the East!

Our secretary has come running,—pale, trembling, his clothes all torn, his face all in blood. Upon seeing him, the Crown Princess almost fell into a swoon. The Czarevich was sent for. But he is suffering from his usual ailment,—he is drunk.

2nd of May.

We live in the palace of Crown Prince Alexei,—a clay-daubed little house of two stories, roofed with tiles, on the very bank of the Neva. These quarters are so cramped that almost all of the court suite of Her Highness has disposed itself in three adjacent houses, which the Senate has hired. One of these has neither doors, nor windows, nor stoves, nor any furniture. Her Highness had to finish it at her own expense, and to build an adjoining stable.

Yesterday the owner of this house, a certain Gideonov, in the service of the Czarevna Nathalia, returned, and ordered our people to be driven out and their things to be thrown

out into the yard. Then he began to lead Her Highness' horses
out of the stable, and installing his own. The Crown Princess
ordered the stable to be dismantled, in order to rebuild it on
another site. But when our head hostler brought workmen,
Gideonov sent his own people there, who drove ours off, after
cruelly beating them. The head hostler threatened to complain
to the Czar. Gideonov answered: "Complain to your heart's
content,—but I shall lodge my complaint ahead of yours!"

Worst of all, he affirms that everything he does is by order
of the Czarevna. This Czarevna is an old maid, the most
malignant creature in the universe. She is amiableness itself
to Her Highness' face, but, behind her back, the Czarevna
spits every time she utters her name, adding: *What a German! A friya!* [She can't even pronounce *frau* right!] Who
does she think she is? She'll have to run off with her tail
betwixt her legs, yet!"

And so our poor hostlers have to live under the open sky.
It was impossible to find a place for them in the whole town,
not even for a hundred gold pieces,—such is the lack of
quarters. When this is mentioned to the Czar he answers that
in a year's time there will be houses a-plenty. But by that
time they will no longer be needed,—at least not for our
people, for, most probably, the greater number of them will
have passed on into the other world.

* * *

The people in Europe would not believe if they were to
hear what poverty we live in. The moneys appropriated for
the maintenance of the Crown Princess are issued so irregu-
larly and niggardly that they never suffice. Yet, at the same
time, things are frightfully expensive here. That which one
pays a *groschen* for in Germany, one pays four for here. We
have run up debts with all the merchants, and they will soon
cease to extend credit to us. To say nothing of our servants,
we ourselves are occasionally pinched for candles, fuel, edibles. One can get nothing from the Czar, because he is
eternally busy. And the Czarevich is forever drunk.

"The world is filled with bitterness," Her Highness remarked to me to-day. "Beginning with my very childhood,—
that is, from the age of six,—I know not what joy is, and I

doubt not that fate is preparing still greater misfortunes for me in the future. . . ."

Gazing into the distance, as though already beholding this fateful future, she kept on repeating: "I am not fated to escape misfortune!"—with such a hopeless calm, that I could not find words of consolation, merely kissing her hands in silence.

A cannon shot boomed, and we had to hurry to prepare for a pleasure excursion on the Neva,—an Aquatic Assembly.

Things are so arranged here that, when given the signal by cannon-fire, and by flags hung out in different quarters of the city, all the barques, wherries, yachts, shallops, and sloops have to gather near the fortress. Absence means a fine.

We immediately set out on our sloop manned with ten rowers, and for a long while rowed up and down the Neva with the other boats, steadfastly in the wake of the Admiral, daring neither to fall behind nor to get ahead,—also under penalty of a fine: there are fines for everything.

We had music,—tubas and other wind instruments. The echo in the fortress bastions repeated the sounds of the music.

We were sad enough even without all this. Yet the chill, pale-blue river, with its low, shallow banks; the pale-blue, ice-like, limpid sky; the sparkling of the golden spire on the church of SS. Peter and Paul,—built of wood, but painted yellow and marble-grained; the dismal chiming of clocks,—everything brought on still greater sadness,—a peculiar sadness, such as I have never experienced anywhere save in this town.

Nevertheless, its view is rather good. Along the low wharf, paved with black, tarred piles, are houses of pale-pink brick, of pretentious architecture, resembling Dutch kirks,—with pointed spires, dormer windows and peaked roofs, and enormous stoeps with lattice-work. One might think it was really a city. But, right alongside, are miserable hovels, thatched with turf and birch-bark; farther on lie marshland and forest, where deer and wolves are still to be found. On the very sea-marge are windmills, just as if one were in Holland. Everything is bleakly-bleak, and wan, and sad,—just as if it were limned, or artificially made. One thinks one's self asleep, and beholding an impossible city in one's dream.

The Czar—with all his family—was standing at the rudder of a special sloop, steering. The Czaritzas and the Princesses, in little blouses of dimity and in red skirts, wearing round oil-skin caps (everything is on the Dutch manner), look like downright sailors' wives of Saardam. "I am accustoming my family to water," says the Czar; "whoever would live with me must be often at sea." He takes them along on practically every occasion,—especially when a fresh wind is coming on to blow; locks them up in the cabin, and keeps on steering against the wind, until he has rocked them a-plenty, and, *salve honore,* has made them throw up,—only then is he satisfied!

We were afraid that it might be decided to sail for Kronslot. The participants of one such excursion last year cannot recall it without horror: being overtaken by a storm they barely escaped drowning, ran up on a shoal, sat several hours through up to their waists in water; finally, they managed to make their way to some island or other, made a fire, and, absolutely naked,—they had had to take off their wet clothes,—covered themselves with coarse sleigh-robes they managed to get from some peasants, and passed the whole night thus, warming themselves by the bonfire, without drink, without food,— like new Robinson Crusoes.

This time fate was gracious to us: a red flag was let down on the Admiral's sloop, which signaled the end of the excursion. We returned by way of the canals, and looked the town over.

Of canals there is a vast number. "If God prolong my life and health, Peterburgh shall be another Amsterdam!" boasts the Czar. "Arrange everything as it is done in Holland," are words frequently recurring in the *ukases* dealing with the building of the town.

The Czar has a passion for straight lines. Everything that is straight, regular, seems splendid to him. Were it possible, he would build the whole town according to rule and compasses. The inhabitants are bidden to "build in line, so that no structure be built out of line or back from it, but that the streets and lanes be even and aligned." The houses which project beyond the line are ruthlessly torn down.

The Czar's pride is the interminable, straight "Nevskaya Pershpectivá" [Nevsky Prospect] which bisects the whole town. It is altogether a wasteland in the midst of the swampy wastes, yet it is already planted with puny little lindens— there are three and four rows of them,—and resembles an avenue. It is very well kept. It is swept by Swedish prisoners every Saturday.

Many of these geometrically regular lines, or imaginary streets, are almost devoid of houses,—with nothing but a stake sticking up here and there. Upon other sites, already built up, one can still see the traces of plows, and furrows of recent plantings.

Although the houses are constructed of brick baked "according to the specifications of Vitrivius," they are built so hurriedly and precariously that they threaten to collapse. If a vehicle passes through the streets, they shake; the marish soil is too quaggy. The Czar's enemies prophesy that the whole town will fall through the ground one of these days.

One of our companions, the old Baron Lewenwald, Commissioner General of Livonia, a man both amiable and clever, told us much that was curious about the founding of this city.

For erection of the first earth-works of the Fortress of SS. Peter and Paul dry earth was needed, yet there was none to be found nearby,—there being nothing save quagmire and moss. Thereupon the idea was conceived of hauling earth to the bastions from distant places, in old mats, sackings, or simply in coat-skirts. At this labor of Sisyphos two-thirds of the miserable wretches perished, especially as a consequence of the thievery and cheating of those to whom their maintenance was entrusted. For whole months at a time they never as much as saw bread,—which, however, is at times not to be gotten for any money in this desolate region; they kept themselves alive on cabbages and grapes; they suffered from dysentery and scurvy; they became bloated from hunger; they shivered in their earth-huts, which resembled animal lairs; they died off like flies. The erection of but a single fortress upon the Merry Island—Lust-Eiland—(what a fine name!) cost the lives of a hundred thousand settlers who had been driven thither by force, like cattle, from all parts of Rus-

sia. Verily, this unnatural city, this dreadful Paradise as the
Czar styles it, is builded upon human bones!

There is no standing upon ceremony here, either with the
living or with the dead. It has happened to me to see, with my
own eyes, upon the Provender Market (or it may have been
in the Hostel Yard) the corpse of a working-man, wrapped up
in matting, tied with ropes to a pole, borne by two men; also
many who were being carted off upon lumber-sleighs, mother-
naked, to the cemetery, where they are earthed thus, without
any rites whatsoever. There are so many poor folk dying every
day that there is no time to bury them in a Christian manner.

On one occasion, one hot summer day, as we were boating
on the Neva, we noticed gray spots on the blue water: these
were mounds of the dead bodies of mosquitoes, they abound
in the swamps hereabouts. They were floating down from the
Lake of Ladoga. One of our rowers scooped up a whole hatful
of them.

As I listened to Lewenwald's stories of how Peterburgh had
been built, I repeatedly shut my eyes, and it seemed to me
that dead human bodies, gray as gray as can be, and of the
tiniest, innumerable, like these mounds of dead mosquito
bodies, were floating down the Neva with never an end,—and
none knows them, none remembers them. . . .

Upon returning home, I sat down to write my diary in my
diminutive closet,—a vertible coop,—in the mezzanine, under
the very roof. It was stuffy,—I opened the window. An odor
of vernal waters, of pitch, and of pine shavings floated in.
On the very bank of the Neva two carpenters, one young
and one old, were repairing a boat. One could hear their
hammering, and a drawn-out, mournful song, which the
younger man was singing with exceeding slowness, forever
reiterating the same refrain. Here are some of the words of the
song, as far as I could make them out:

> Oh, 'twas in the great town, in Sanctpeter,
> Oh, 'twas on the river, on the River Neva,
> That upon the grand Island of Vassiliev,
> A young sailor lad was a-riggin' ships . . .

Looking at the evening sky of this Paradise,—a sky pale-
green, like ice, pellucid and chill, I listened to this sad song,
which was like to a lament, and I felt like weeping myself.

3rd of May.

To-day Her Highness paid a visit to the Czaritza, and complained against Gideonov,—she also made a request for a more regular issuance of monies. I was present at this inter·view.

The Czaritza was amiable,—as usual.

"Czaarische Majestaät Euch sehr lieb," she, in her broken German, protested her love to the Crown Princess, among other things.

"Aye, aye,—His Majesty the Czar is exceedingly fond of you. 'Truly, Katerina,' says he, 'thy daughter-in-law is most pleasing, both in form and in manners.' 'Your Majesty,'' says I, 'you love your daughter-in-law more than you do me.' 'Nay,' says he, and laughs to himself, 'not more,—but I shall love her just as much, soon. My son,' says he, 'to tell the truth, does not really deserve such a good wife.' "

From these words we could gather that the Czar was none too fond of the Czarevich.

When Her Highness, almost with tears in her eyes, fell to interceding for her husband, the Czaritza promised to be his advocate, asserting, with still the same amiability, that she 'loved her like her own child, and that she could not love her more even if she had carried her under her own heart.'

I find this Russian mawkishness not to my liking; I much fear me lest in this case it merely prove to be honey upon the sharp edge of a knife. However, it would seem that Her Highness is not deceiving herself either. On one occasion, in my presence, she voiced her opinion that the Czaritza is 'the worst of all—*pire que tout le rest.*' To-day, on our way home from the interview, she remarked:

"She would never forgive me were I to give birth to a boy."

One old woman, of the common people, when the talk veered to the Czaritza, whispered in my ear: " 'Tis not fit for her to be a Czaritza,—why, she's neither of the gentry nor a Russian; and we know full well how she was captured: she was brought under our flag in naught but her shift, and placed under guard; and it was our officer of the guard, who put a *kaftan* upon her. God knows what station of life she comes from. They say she used to wash shirts with other Finnish washerwomen."

I recalled this to-day when Her Highness, in greeting the

Czaritza, was about to kiss the latter's garments. True, Her Majesty would not permit this,—she herself embraced Her Highness and kissed her. But still, what a mockery of fate it is that the Princess of Wolfenbüttel,—a descendant of the great Guelphs, who contested with the German Emperors for their crown, even in those days when the Hohenzollerns and the Hapsburgs were not so much as heard of,—has to kiss the garments of this woman, who had at one time washed clothes with other Finnish washerwomen!

4th of May.

After some warm days, which made one think it was summer, winter is here again. Cold,—wind,—snow turning to rain. Ice from the Lake of Ladoga floats down the Neva. They do say, however, that snow falls here even in June.

Our "palace" has fallen into such a state of neglect that the roof was found to be full of holes, and this night, during a hard rain, there was a leak in the ceiling of Her Highness' sleeping chamber,—it was a good thing that it missed her bed, at least. But a pool formed on the floor.

The ceiling is adorned with an allegorical painting: a flaming sacrificial altar, entwined with roses; on each side are cupidons bearing two coats of arms,—the eagle of Russia and the steed of Brunswick: between them are two joined hands with the inscription: *"Nun unquam junxit nobiliora fides. Fidelity never joined any two more noble."* It was precisely on the sacrificial altar that a black blotch appeared because of the dampness, and it was from the flame of Hymen that the dirty, cold water dripped.

I recalled the epithalamium of the archæologist Eckhardt, which set forth that both bride and groom were sprung from the Byzantine Emperor, Constantine Porphyrogenitus. A fine land this, where there are leaks almost right over the nuptial couch of a female descendant of "him who had been born to the purple"!

5th of May.

The Crown Prince has finally put in an appearance from the other half of the house, where he lives apart from us, so that at times we do not see him for weeks at a stretch. An explanation took place. I heard everything from an adjoining room, where I had to remain at the desire of Her Highness. To all her requests and complaints about the Gideonov matter, and the failure to issue money, he replied, shrugging his shoulders:

"*Mich nichts angehn. Bekümmere mich nicht an Sie.* That does not concern me. I have nothing to do with you!"

Then he burst into reproaches because she, apparently, spoke against him to his father.

"Aren't you ashamed?" Her Highness burst into tears. "Spare your own honor at least! There is never a cobbler or a tailor in Germany who would permit himself to treat his own wife so. . . ."

"You are in Russia, and not in Germany."

"I feel that only too well. Yet if everything that has been promised had been fulfilled. . . ."

"Who made the promises?"

"Was it not you yourself, with your father, who signed the marriage compact?"

"*Halten Maul! Ich Sie nichts versprochen.* Hold your tongue! I promised you nothing. You know very well that you were saddled upon me!"

He jumped up and overturned the chair he had been sitting on. I was ready to rush to the help of Her Highness. It seemed to me that he was about to strike her. I hated him so at that moment that I probably was ready to kill him.

"*Das danke Ihnen der Henker!* May the hangman pay you out for this!" the Crown Princess cried out, beside herself from wrath and grief. He walked out with an obscene oath, slamming the door.

It seems as if all that is savage and vile in this savage and vile land has been embodied in this man. There is only one thing I cannot resolve,—which trait is more predominant in him: that of the fool or the scoundrel?

Poor Charlotta! Her Highness, who with every day evinces an ever greater friendship for me, out of all proportion to my deserts, has herself begged me that I call her thus,—poor Charlotta! When I approached her, she threw herself into my arms and for a long while could not utter a word, but merely kept on trembling. Finally she said, through her sobs:

"Were I not pregnant, and able to return to Germany without difficulty, I would joyfully agree to subsist there upon

stale bread and water! I am almost going out of my mind
from grief; I know not what I am saying or doing. I pray to
God that He strengthen me, lest grief lead me to do something horrible!"

Then she added, but now with tears already subdued, and
with her wonted submissiveness, which trait of hers at times
frightens me more than any despair:

"I am the unhappy sacrifice of my family, to whom I have
not brought the least benefit, while I myself am dying a slow
death because of grief. . . ."

* * *

Both of us were still crying, when messengers came to tell
us that it was time to go to the masquerade. Gulping down
our tears, we began dressing ourselves in our disguises. Such
is the custom hereabouts: willy, nilly, yet you must make
merry when you are told.

The masquerade took place on the Square of the Trinity,
near a coffee house or "hostelry," under the open sky. Since
this spot is low, swampy, with mud that never has a chance
to dry, part of the square was laid with logs, with boards on
top of them; a flooring was thus formed, and it was upon
this that the masks thronged. Fortunately, the weather had
unexpectedly changed once more,—the evening was calm and
warm. But toward night a fog rose up from the river,—thick
as thick could be, and white as milk,—and enveloped the
whole square. Many,—the ladies especially,—in costumes that
were too light, caught cold from the dampness, and were
sneezing and coughing. Instead of medicine, they were made
to drink vodka. Grenadiers carried it about in tubs,—quite the
usual thing. In the white cloud of the fog, lit up by the
glaucous light of the prolonged evening glow (later on, in
July, the glow lasts the whole night here), all these masks,—
harlequins, scaramouches, pagliacci, Dresden shepherdesses,
nymphs, Chinamen, Arabs, bears, cranes, dragons,—seemed
ludicrous and frightful phantoms.

And right here, alongside of the flooring on which we were
dancing, one could see the black stakes with iron spikes, upon
which were stuck the death's-heads of the executed, almost
rotted away. In the resinous fragrance of the vernal pine-
needles, and of the birch buds, with which odors the whole

town now seems permeated, I imagined I caught the stench of these heads. And again it seemed—as everything always seems here—that all this was but a dream.

6th of May.

There has been an unexpected reconciliation. Having approached the half-open door of Her Highness' chamber, I inadvertently caught sight of her in a mirror, as she sat in an armchair, and of the Crown Prince, bending over her and holding her head in his hands, kissing her with deferential tenderness. I was about to hide myself, but she, noticing me in the mirror made a sign to me with her hand. I understood it as ordering me to remain in the adjoining room. The poor little thing probably wanted to flaunt her happiness.

"*Der mensch, der sagen, ich Sie nicht liebe habe, lügt wie Teuffel!* He who says that I love you not, lies like the very devil!" The Czarevich was speaking, as I surmised, about one of those contemptible slanders at the expense of Her Highness, of which there are a great many current here (she is even accused of infidelity to her husband). "I believe you; I know that you are kind, while those who speak evil of you are not worth your little finger. . . ."

He questioned her about her affairs and the unpleasantnesses she has to endure, about her health and her pregnancy; he evinced such concern, and his words, and the features of his face, were full of such intellect and goodness that it seemed as if an entirely different man were before me. I could not believe my eyes and ears, recalling what had taken place in this very room no further back than yesterday. When he was gone and we were left alone, Charlotta said to me:

"What an amazing man! He is not at all what he seems. No one understands him. How he loves me! Ah, my darling Juliana,—if only there be love, everything is well, and one can bear anything. . . . When my child shall be born—I pray that it be a son—I shall be perfectly happy!"

I did not contradict; I would not have had the heart to shake her faith,—she was so happy, even now. But,—would it be for long? The poor little thing,—the poor little thing!

*   *   *

Perhaps I am unjust to the Czarevich? Perhaps he really is "not at all what he seems"?

He is the most secretive of men. When he is not drunk he sits locked up with his old books and manuscripts; he is studying—so they say—universal history, and theology,—not only Russian, but the Catholic and Protestant as well,—he is reputed to have read the German Bible through eight times; or else he holds converse with monks, pilgrims, saintly ancients, and people of the lowliest station in life.

One of his retainers, Fedor Evarlakov, a young man not at all foolish and also a great lover of reading,—he takes all sorts of books from me, even in Latin,—once told me something about the Crown Prince which I noted down in Russian right there and then, in a memo book, presented to me by Leibnitz, and which I always carry about with me: "The Czarevich hath a very ardent feeling toward priests, and so do the priests have toward him, and he reveres them as much as he does God,—while they style him a saint, and always beatify him among the people."

I remember Leibnitz once telling me that when he had been presented to the Czarevich at the Ducal Castle of Wolfenbüttel, in the summer of the year seventeen hundred and eleven, the Czarevich had conversed with him long about his, the Czarevich's, favorite subject,—the union of the East with the West, of China and Russia with Europe,—and had subsequently sent him, through his tutor, the Baron Huissen, an abstract of certain writings dealing with Chinese affairs. Leibnitz affirms that, contrary to everything which is said about the Czarevich, he is very intelligent; his mind, however, is of an altogether different order from that of his father's. "Probably he takes after his grandfather," Leibnitz had remarked.

Her Highness showed me the copy of a letter from the Berlin Academy of Sciences to Duke Ludwig Rudolph of Wolfenbüttel (the father of Charlotta). In this letter the imminent possibility of spreading true Christian enlightenment in Russia is spoken of, "thanks to the special and extraordinary inclination of the Heir Apparent toward the sciences and books."

I have likewise seen an account of a session of this same Berlin Academy in the year of seventeen hundred and eleven, wherein one of its members, the Associate Rector Frisch, announced: *"The Czar's heir has a love for the sciences still greater than the Czar's, and in his turn, will be no lesser a Mæcenas to them."*

Strange! To-day, when I was looking at both of them in the mirror,—just as in a magic "mirror of divinations,"—I thought I perceived in these two faces, so different, one trait of similarity,—a shadow of some premonitory sadness, as though they were both victims, and some great suffering lay before them both. Or was it that I had merely imagined all this in the dark mirror?

8th of May.

We were present at the Admiralty, at the launching of a great ship of seventy guns. The Czar, dressed as a common carpenter, in a red knitted jersey that was soiled with pitch, and with an ax in his hands, was crawling between the stays, under the very keel, to see if everything were in order, and paying no heed to the danger,—recently, during a launching, two men had been crushed to death. "I toil over the ark of Russia, like to another Noah," I recalled the words of the Czar. Doffing his hat before the Grand Admiral, like any subordinate before his superior, he asked if it were time to begin, and, having received the order, struck the first blow with his ax. Hundreds of other axes began to chop away the props; at the same time the under-beams, which supported the ship on both sides on the stocks, were jerked away. It slid down the greased runways, at first slowly, then flying like an arrow, so that the runways were smashed to smithereens, it floated out on the water, pitching and cleaving the waves for the first time, amid the thunder of music, and cannon peals, and the huzzas of the people.

We took our seats in sloops and went off to the new ship. The Czar was already there. Having changed his dress for the uniform of a Flag Officer, the naval rank he now has attained, and with a star and a blue order ribbon over his shoulder, he was holding a reception for his guests. As they stood on deck, the new-born ship was christened with the first goblet of wine. The Czar made a speech. Here are some isolated words which come to my memory:

"Our people are like unto children, which do not take to their a b c's till they be compelled, and to whom this at first seems a vexing matter; yet when they have learned, they are thankful,—which is made clear by all our present works: have they not all been consummated against their will? And even now one can hear thanksgiving for much which has already brought forth fruit. . . . Without having taken the bitter, one will never attain the sweet. . . ."

"Feed me not with sweet white bread, and break no bricks upon my head . . ." one of the court fools, an old *boyar* or noble, probably already in his cups, put in, whispering in the ear of one of his neighbors, right behind my back.

"We have," the Czar went on, "as examples, the other enlightened peoples in Europe, who have also had small beginnings. 'Tis time for us as well to take up our tasks,—at first the small ones, while at a later day there shall be men who shall not shun even great deeds. I know that I shall not consummate this, nor behold it myself, inasmuch as the length of our days is not certain,—however, I shall make a beginning, so that it may be easier for others to work after me. But as for us, even this glory doth suffice us now,—that we are making the beginning. . . ."

I admired the Czar. He was splendid.

We went down into the cabins. The ladies seated themselves apart from the gentlemen, in the saloon adjoining, which none dared enter during the feast, save the Czar. In the partition dividing the two saloons was a small round window, something in the nature of a port-hole, drawn over with red taffeta. I took my seat alongside of it; by lifting the hanging a little I could see and partly hear that which was taking place in the men's division. Some of the things I jotted down in my memo book on the spot, as is my wont.

The long, narrow tables, disposed in the shape of a horseshoe, were laden with cold delicacies, and all sorts of fish, either smoked or pungently salted, and all thirst-provoking. The food cheap,—the wines expensive. For such festal occasions the Czar issues to the Admiralty, out of his own treasury, a thousand rubles,—an enormous sum, according to the standards prevailing here. The guests seated themselves wherever they happened to be, without any discrimination as to rank,—ordinary shipmen alongside of the foremost dignitaries. At one end of the table was enthroned the scaramouche

Prince-Pope, surrounded by his Cardinals. He proclaimed solemnly:

"Peace and blessing on all this honest company! In the name of Father Bacchus and his Son, Ivashka the Drunken, and the Spirit of wine, take ye communion! May the drunkenness of Bacchus be with ye!"

"Amen!" responded the Czar, who filled the post of proto-deacon to this Pope.

Every one in turn drew near to His Holiness, bowing down to his very feet, kissing his hands, accepting and draining a large spoon of *pertzovka*,—this consists of pure spirits, infused with red Indian pepper. 'Twould seem that, in order to extract a confession from a malefactor, it would suffice merely to threaten him with this horrible *pertzovka*,—yet here everybody has to drink it,—even the ladies.

The healths of all the members of the Czar's family were drunk,—with the exception of the Czarevich and his spouse, although they were present. Every toast was accompanied by a salvo of cannons. There were so many volleys that the panes of one window were shivered.

Guests grew drunk all the sooner, because vodka was poured into the wine on the sly. It became stuffy in the low-ceiled cabins, packed with humanity. The men threw off their waistcoats; they tore the wigs off one another by force. Some were embracing and kissing one another, others were quarreling,—especially the prime ministers and the senators, who were accusing each other of taking bribes, of knaveries and chicaneries.

"Thou hast a *maitresska* that is *coshting* thee twice thy salary!" one of them was shouting, mangling the foreign words horribly, as is the way of these barbarians.

"But hast thou forgot the little orange agaric mushrooms in the little flat-bottle?" retorted the other.

The orange agaric mushrooms were the red gold pieces, offered by a deft seeker after favors in a little keg (and not a bottle), in the guise of pickled mushrooms.

"Yes? And how much didst thou grab out of supplying the Admiralty with hemp?"

"Eh, brethren,—what is the use of reproaching one another? Every living soul longeth after sweets. A sinner may

be honest, a sinner may be a knave,—for we all in sin our
being have!"

"Bribes are really nothing but one's perquisites."

"Not to take anything from petitioners would be a preter-
natural thing."

"However, according to law . . ."

"What is law? It's a whiffle-tree,—where'er you want to
go, that's how you swing it. . . ."

The Czar was listening attentively. It is a way he has:
when everybody is already three sheets to the wind,—and
the fourth fluttering,—a double guard is placed at the doors,
with orders to let no one out; at the same time the Czar, who
never gets drunk, no matter how much he drinks, purposely
makes those about him quarrel and sicks them on; from these
drunken squabbles he frequently learns that which he would
never have learned otherwise. Just as in the proverb,—when
thieves fall out, honest men get their own back. The feast
becomes an investigation.

The most illustrious Prince Menshikov had a falling-out
with the Vice-Chancellor Shaphirov. The Prince had called
him a Jew.

"I may be a Jew, but thou art a pastry-cook,—'sourdough
pies, hot from the oven!'" retorted Shaphirov. "Thy father
used to sup his stew with a bast shoe. Thou wast brought
into the world under a wine-barrel. Thou art not much of a
prince,—thou wast mud not long since, then they made thee
a prince! . . ."

"Ah, thou mangy Jew! If I were to crack thee betwixt my
two thumbs, there'd be nought but a wet spot left of
thee. . . ."

They bandied curses for a long while. Russians are, as a
rule, great hands at cursing. It seems to me one can never
hear such foul language anywhere else. The air is pestilent
with it. In one of their oaths, and that the most ignominious,
—although everybody, both small and great, uses it,—the
word "mother" is joined with the most vile words. They call
it just that,—the maternal word. Yet this people deems itself
the most Christian!

Having exhausted oaths, the grandees fell to spitting in
the faces of one another. Everybody stood around, looking

and laughing. Such encounters are an everyday matter here, and wind up without any consequences.

Prince Jacob Dolgorukyi came to blows with the meek Prince-Cæsar Romodanovsky. These two venerable hoary ancients, also cursing with maternal oaths, sank their talons into each other's hair and fell to fisticuffs and strangling one another. When an attempt was made to separate them, they snatched out their swords.

"Ei, dat ist nit parmittet!" the Czar shouted in Dutch, walking up and taking his stand between them. This royal Protodeacon, Peter Mikhailov, has instructions from the buffoon Pope: "During a disturbance abate the contenders, both by word and action."

"I demand satisfaction!" Prince Jacob kept on vociferating. "A great affront has been put upon me. . . ."

"Kamrat," retorted the Czar, "who, save God, can afford thee redress against a Prince-Pope? For I, too, am subjected to him, and am placed under His Majesty's commands. And, besides, wherein is the affront? Now the whole company has not been scorned by Bacchus. *Sauffen—rauffen:* drink a barrel, and then quarrel; sleep, and wake,—and your peace make."

The enemies were fined,—they had to drink *pertzovka,* and soon both of them tumbled together under the table.

The merry-andrews were exceedingly noisy; they gabbled, and spat, and spewed,—not only in the faces of one another, but even in those of decent folk. A separate choir, a so-called *Spring,* rendered the songs of birds in a forest, from the nightingale to the warbler, by different whistles, so loud that the sound was thrown back from the wall in a deafening echo. A savage dancing song rang out,—its words almost meaningless, recalling the outcries at a Witches' Sabbath:

> Ho, burn,—ho, burn!
> Mince, stump, ye low knaves!
> Thump out jigs and reels,—
> Till you wear out all your heels!

In our ladies' compartment the drunken old female buffoon, the Princess-Abbess Rzhevskaya, a downright witch, also set or went off into a dance, with her skirt turned up and singing in a voice hoarse from too much drinking:

Oh my club, start in to swirl,
Oh my bag-pipes, start to skirl!
My man's father fell with a thump
Right behind a big tree-stump;
I'd have been only too glad,
Higher to have made his bed,—
Higher to have made his bed,—
So that he might break his head.

Looking at her the Czaritza, with her head-dress tumbled all to one side, all sweating, red, drunken, kept on clapping her palms and beating time with her feet: "Ho, burn,—ho, burn!"—and laughed like one insane. At the beginning of the drinking bout she importuned Her Highness, persuading her to drink with rather strange proverbs,—the Russians have a multitude of them, dealing with this subject: "When cup 'gainst cup clicks, 'tis not like two sticks.—Even cabbage withers if one water it not.—Even a hen drinks." But, seeing that the Crown Princess was almost swooning, she took pity upon her, left her in peace, and even, on the sly, herself added water to her wine,—and, at the same time, to the drink of us, the maids-of-honor,—this, during such celebrations, is deemed a great crime.

When the night was on the ebb,—we had sat at table from six o'clock in the evening until four in the morning,— the Czaritza walked up to the door several times, calling out the Czar, and asking him:

"Is it not time to start for home, father dear?"

"No matter, Katenka! To-morrow is a day for idling," the Czar would answer.

Lifting up the hanging and peeping into the men's division, I would see something new every time.

Some one, striding right across the table, had set his boot right in a platter of fish-jelly. The Czar had just been shoving this very jelly by force into the mouth of his Chancellor, Golovkin, who could not stand fish; orderlies held him by his arms and legs; he beat about, gasped for breath, and had turned all purple. Dropping Golovkin, the Czar applied himself to Weber, the Hanoverian Resident; he caressed and kissed him; he embraced his head with one hand, holding a tumbler near Weber's mouth with the other, imploring him to drink. Then, having taken off Weber's wig, the Czar kissed now the nape of his neck, now the crown of his head; he raised up Weber's lips and kissed his gums. They say the reason of all these tendernesses was the Czar's desire to extract some diplomatic secret or other out of the Resident. Mussin-Pushkin, whose neck they were tickling,—he is very much afraid of tickling, yet the Czar is teaching him to overcome this fear,—was squealing like a suckling pig under a knife. Grand Admiral Apraxin was weeping with great sobs. Tolstoi, the Privy Councilor, was crawling about on all fours, —however, as it turned out afterwards, he was not at all very drunk, and was merely dissembling, in order not to drink any more. The head of Vice-Admiral Kruiss had been split open. Prince Menshikov had fallen down as one dead,—his face had turned a frightful blue; they were massaging him and trying to bring him to, lest he die,—men frequently die during these sprees. The Archimandrite Theodosius, the Czar's spiritual adviser, was nauseated. "Oh, 'tis the death o' me! Most Pure Mother of God!" he kept on moaning piteously. The Prince-Pope was snoring, sprawling with all his body on the table, his face in a puddle of wine.

The whistling, the roaring, the clatter of dishes breaking, the maternal cursing, the buffets on ears, to which none any longer paid any attention,—all these sounds soared in the air. The stench was like that of the filthiest of pot-houses. Were some one to be brought in here out of the fresh air, he would be nauseated at once, I think.

Everything was turning dark before my eyes; at times I almost lost consciousness. Human faces seemed like some sort of bestial maws; and the most fearful of all was the face of the Czar; broad, round, with a somewhat oblique slit for the eyes,—great, convex, just as though they were popping out; his small mustaches are sharply pointed, and stick upward; it is the face of some enormous feral cat, or of a tiger. His face was calm and mocking; his gaze clear and penetrating. He alone was sober, and, with curiosity, peered into the most abominable secrets, the exposed inwards of human souls, which were turned inside out before him in this torture chamber, where the implement of torture was wine.

The Prince-Pope was awakened and lifted up from the

table. The Prince-Cæsar had also managed to have his full
sleep under the table. The two of them were forced to dance
facing one another, being supported under the arms, inasmuch as both of them could hardly stand on their feet. The
Pope, in a buffoon's tiara, wherewith he had been crowned
by the naked Bacchus, held in his hand a cross made out of
pipe-stems. The Cæsar had on a buffoon's crown and scepter
in his hand. The Czarevich was sprawled out on the floor,
absolutely drunk, like one dead, between these two merry-
andrews, these two phantoms of ancient grandeur,—the phantoms of a Russian Czar and a Russian patriarch.

What took place later on I do not remember, nor do I
even want to recall it,—it is all too vile.

The reveille was sounded on the ships lying next to us.
And the sound of a drum was heard on our ship also: the
Czar himself—an excellent drummer,—was beating a retreat.
This signified: "There has been a great battle with Ivashka
the Tipsy [the Russian Bacchus] and he has overwhelmed
all." Grenadiers were carrying out the drunken grandees in
their arms, like the bodies of the slain from a field of battle.

When we caught sight of the sky, it seemed to us—to put
it in the grand style—that we were emerging out of Hades;
or, to put it vulgarly,—out of a cess pool.

9th of May.

To-day the Czar set out from Peterburgh with a great
fleet, for war operations against the Swedes.

20th of May.

I have not written in my diary for a long time. Her Highness was unwell after the drinking bout. I did not leave her
side. And what is there to write? Everything is so sad that
one does not want to speak or think. What will be, will be.

25th of May.

I was not mistaken. The peace proved short-lived. A black
cat has again dashed between the Czarevich and Her Highness; again they do not see one another for weeks at a time.
He, too, is ailing. The doctors say it is *chakhotka* [consump-
tion]. I think it is simply vodka.

4th of June.

The Czarevich arrived, dressed for a journey, in a gray German traveling cloak; he spoke of something irrelevant, and suddenly announced:

"Adieu. Ich gehe nach Karlsbad."

The Crown Princess was so flustered that she could not find what to say,—she did not even ask if he would be gone long. I thought he was jesting. But, as it turned out, almost immediately upon leaving us the Czarevich took his seat in a mail coach,—and that was the last we saw of him. They are saying that he is really going to take a trip to the waters for the cure. And so we are alone, with neither the Czar nor the Czarevich.

The parents of Her Highness, having probably come to believe the silly slanders current here, have become angry with her and have likewise ceased writing her. We are abandoned of all.

7th of July.

Here is the Czar's letter to Her Highness:

"I would not want to inconvenience you, nor to hold any opinions contrary to my conscience; but the absence of my son, your spouse, compels me so to do, in order to guard against the yapping of tongues uncurbed, which have become accustomed to pervert truth into falsehood. And inasmuch as the rumor has already gone the rounds everywhere for over a year, concerning your pregnancy,—therefore, when it pleaseth God, and you shall near your time, there should be a certain form observed, which will be imparted to you by the Chancellor, Prince Golovkin, which form you will observe undeviatingly, that thereby the lips of all those who love lying may be stopped up."

The form was observed: three women, almost total strangers, were attached to her person,—the wife of the Chancellor Golovkin, the wife of General Bruce, and that old country-wife, the mock Princess-Abbess Rzhevskaya,— the same who had danced during the orgy. These three vixens never let their eyes off her, "guarding," or simply spying, upon—her.

What is the meaning of all this? What do they fear? What deception? Can it be a substitution of another infant, a boy for a girl, at the machination of those who desire to secure the succession in the Czarevich's line? Or is this the excessive amiability of the Czaritza?

It is only now that we have grasped what objects of suspicion and hatred we are. All the fault of Charlotta lies in this: that she is the wife—of her husband. Father against son,—and we are between them, as between two fires.

"I shall submissively carry out the behest of Your Majesty anent the appointment of three women to act as my guard," Charlotta wrote in reply to the Czar, "all the more so since there has never even entered my mind any intention of deceiving Your Majesty or the Crown Prince; for this reason such a strange and so undeserved an order grieves me very much. It would seem that the oft-promised favor and love of Your Majesty ought to serve as a guarantee that no one will offend against me by slander, and that the offenders will meet the punishment due to criminals. It is most sad that those who envy and persecute me should enjoy sufficient power for such an intrigue. God is my hope in this land which is not my own. And, since I am forsaken of all, He will hear my heartmost sighs, and shall abridge my sufferings!"

12th of July.

At seven o'clock in the morning Her Highness was safely delivered of a daughter.

There is never a word or sign from the Czarevich.

1st of August.

We have received news of the Russian victory over the Swedes, on the 27th of July, at Gangout; a whole squadron under the command of Ernschild has been captured, 'twould seem. The bells peal and the cannons fire all day long. However, they are not at all chary of gunpowder here, and, on account of the paltriest victories, whenever they seize three or four water-logged galleys, they blaze away as if they had conquered the universe.

9th of September.

The Czar has returned to Peterburgh. Again cannons volley, as in a besieged town. We have become almost deaf. There are endless triumphal processions, and fireworks with boastful allegories: the Czar is glorified as a conqueror of the universe, as a Cæsar and an Alexander. There was a debauch at which, glory be to God, we were not present. They all, so 'tis said, again got as drunk as swine.

13th of September.

Rain, mire. A low-hanging, dark, apparently stony sky meets the eye when one looks out of the windows. Drenched crows caw upon the bare boughs.

Ennui,—ennui!

19th of September.

I came upon the Crown Princess weeping over some old letters of the Czarevich, written to her when he was courting her. Crooked, disjointed characters, upon lines drawn in pencil. Vapid compliments,—diplomatic amenities. And she weeps over them, the poor little thing!

We found out, in a roundabout way, that the Czarevich is living in Karlsbad *incognito;* he is not returning hither before winter.

20th of September.

In order to forget myself, not to think upon our affairs, I have resolved to write down all that I see and hear concerning the Czar.

Leibnitz is right: *"Quanto magis hujus Principis indolem prospicio tanto eam magis admiror.* The more I observe the ways of this Prince, the more wonder-struck I am."

1st of October.

I have seen how the Czar forged iron at the Admiralty smithy. The courtiers served him,—making the fire, blowing the bellows, carrying coals,—soiling the silk and velvet of their gold-embroidered *kaftans*.

"There's a Czar for you that is a Czar! He doesn't eat his bread in idleness. He works better nor any bargeman!" said one of the common laborers standing near-by.

The Czar had on a leathern apron; his hair was caught up with a whipcord; his sleeves were rolled back from his bare arms, with their bulging muscles; his face was smudged with soot. This smith of gigantic stature, lit up by the red glow of the smelting furnace, resembled a subterranean Titan. He struck the white-hot iron with his sledge-hammer so that the sparks sprayed like rain,—the anvil quivered and rumbled, as though ready to fly into smithereens.

"Thou art fain, Sire, to forge a new Russia out of Martian iron,—but 'tis a painful matter to the hammer, and a painful matter for the anvil as well!" I recalled the saying of a a certain aged *boyarin*.

* * *

"Time is like to hot iron,—which, if it cools, is not malleable," is one of the Czar's sayings. And this smith of Russia forges it while the iron is hot. He knows not rest, just as though he were rushing somewhere all his life. It seems as if he could not rest, or halt, even if he wanted to. He kills himself with feverish activity, an unbelievable straining of his powers, resembling an eternal spasm. The physicians say that his strength is undermined, and that he will not live long. He is forever treating himself with the ferruginous waters of Olonetz, but, at the same time, drinks vodka, so that the treatment merely results in harm.

The first impression upon looking at him is that of impetuousness. He is all motion. He never walks, but runs. The Kaiser's envoy, Count Kinsky, who is rather stout, asserts that he would liefer sustain several pitched battles than go through two hours of an audience with the Czar, inasmuch as he, Kinsky, must, for all his corpulency, run after the Czar all the time, so that he is all inundated with sweat, even during a Russian frost. "Time is like Death," reiterates the Czar. "Letting time slip by is like to irrevocable death."

* * *

His elements are fire and water. He loves them like one born in them,—water, like a fish; fire, like a salamander. He has a passion for cannon fire, for all sorts of experiments with fire, for fireworks. He always lights them himself, and crawls into every fire,—once, when I was present, he had his hair singed off. He says that he is making his subjects accustomed to the fire of battles. But this is merely a pretext, —he is simply in love with fire.

He has the same passion for water. This descendant of the Czars of Muscovy, who had never seen the sea, had conceived a yearning for it even when he was yet a babe in the stuffy chambers of the Kremlin Palace, even like some wild gosling in a hennery. He navigated toy boats in the pleasure ponds which were parts of the aqueducts. But as soon as, after much straining, he got to the sea, he never parted from it. He passes the greater part of his life on the water. He has his after-dinner siesta every day on a frigate. When he is ill, he shifts his quarters there altogether, and the sea air almost always cures him. He finds the summer sultry in the enormous gardens at Peterhof. He has arranged a sleeping chamber for himself at Monplaisir,—a little house one side of which is washed by the Bay of Finland; the windows of this sleeping chamber look directly on the sea. In Peterburgh the Observatory Palace is built entirely on water, upon the sandy shoal at the mouth of the Neva. The palace in the Summer Garden is also bounded by water on two sides: the front steps descend into the water, as in Amsterdam and Venice. On one occasion, during winter, when the Neva was already frozen over and the only remaining hole in the ice was before the Palace,—not more than a hundred paces in circumference, —he navigated back and forth even on that, in a diminutive outrigger, like a duck in its pond. But when the entire river was covered over with thick ice, he ordered a space to be cleared along the wharf, some hundred paces long and thirty wide, ordering the snow to be swept off it every day, and I myself have seen him coursing along on this plaza, upon small, beautiful sloops or boyers placed upon skates and runners of steel. "We navigate on ice," he says, "so that e'en in winter we may not neglect maritime exercises." Even in Moscow, during Yuletide, he once rode through the streets upon an enormous sleigh,—an effigy of a real ship, with sails. He loves to release wild ducklings and goslings upon water,— which young fowl are presented to him by the Czaritza. And how he rejoices over their joy! Just as though he himself were a water fowl.

*   *   *

He says that he first began thinking of the sea when he read the narrative of the chronographer Nestor about the naval expedition of Oleg, Prince of Kiev, against Czargrad. If that be so, he is resurrecting the ancient in the new, that which is kin to him in that which is foreign. From one sea, across dry land, to another sea,—such is the path of Russia.

*   *   *

At times it seems that the contradictions of fire and water, the two elements native to him, have been blended within him into a single being, strange and foreign,—I know not if it be good or evil, divine or fiendish,—but it is surely inhuman.

*   *   *

His is a savage shyness. I have seen myself how, at a magnificent reception of ambassadors, sitting on his throne, he grew confused, blushing and perspiring, frequently taking snuff to bolster up his courage, not knowing what to do with his eyes, avoiding even the glances of the Czaritza; but when the ceremony was at an end, and he could descend from the throne, he was as glad as any school-boy. The Margravine of Brandenburg was telling me (at least that is her version of it) that at his first interview with her the Czar,—true, he was altogether a lad then,—had turned away, covered his face with his hands, like a green girl, and merely kept on repeating one and the same thing: *"Je ne sais pas m'exprimer. I am not a good conversationalist. . . ."* However, he gained confidence soon enough, and became even too free and easy, —he desired to have first hand confirmation of the fact that the firmness of the waists of the German women, which amazed the Russians so, was not due to their native boniness, but to the whale-bone in their corsages. *"Il pourrait être un peu plus poli!* He might have been a bit politer about it!"* the Margravine remarked. Baron Manteufel imparted the following to me about the interview of the Czar with the Queen of Prussia: "He was polite to such a degree that he even extended his hand to her,—having first put on a rather soiled glove. At supper he surpassed himself,—he did not pick his teeth, nor eruct, nor produce any other unseemly sounds (*il n'a ni roté, ni pété*)."

When he was traveling through Europe, he demanded that nobody look at him, that the highways and streets, when he rode through them, be deserted. He entered and left houses through secret passages. The museums he visited by night. On one occasion, in Holland, when he had to pass through a hall where the members of the States-General were in session, he requested that the President order them to turn their backs; but when they, out of respect for the Czar, declined to do so, he pulled his wig down over his nose, crossed the hall and the foyer rapidly, and ran down the staircase. Riding on a canal in Amsterdam, and seeing that a boatful of the curious was maneuvering to approach, he fell into such a frenzy that he threw two bottles at the head of the helmsman and almost split his skull. A veritable cannibal—savage. A Russian demon of the wild places within an enlightened European,—there you have the Czar.

He is a savage and a child. However, all Russians in general are children. In their midst the Czar merely pretends to be grown up. Never shall I forget how, at a country fair near Wolfenbüttel, the hero of Poltava rode astride the wooden hobby-horses of a wretched little carrousel, catching brass rings on a small stick, and amusing himself like a little boy.

Children are cruel. The Czar's favorite amusement is to compel people to do whatever is against their natures,—whoever cannot abide wine, oil, cheese, oysters or vinegar, has his mouth filled forcefully therewith by the Czar, on every opportune occasion. He tickles those who dread tickling. Many, in order to get into his good graces, pretend on purpose that they cannot endure whatever he likes to tease them with.

At times these jokes are horrible, especially during the Yuletide drinking bouts,—the so-called celebrations. "This Yuletide diversion," a certain aged *boyarin* told me, "turns out to be so arduous that many prepare for those days as if for death." Men are dragged on a rope from one hole in the ice to another. They are made to sit with bare posteriors on the ice. Many are plied with liquor till they die therefrom.

Thus, playing with mortals, a being of another nature—a faun or a centaur—maims and slays them, by chance.

In Leyden, in the Anatomical Theater, observing the denuded muscles of a cadaver being saturated with turpentine, and noticing utmost aversion in one of the Russians accompanying him, the Czar seized him by the nape of his neck, bent him toward the table, and compelled him to tear a muscle off the cadaver with his teeth.

At times it is almost impossible to decide wherein, in these little pranks, childish exuberance ends and bestial ferocity begins.

* * *

Hand in hand with this savage shyness goes a savage shamelessness,—especially with women.

"*Il faut que Sa Majesté ait dans le corps une légion de démons de luxure*. It seems to me that there is, in the body of His Majesty, a whole legion of the demons of lechery," says the Royal Physician, Blumentrost. It is his supposition that the "scorbutus" of the Czar originated from another disease of old, which he contracted in early youth.

To use the expression of one of the modern Russians, the Czar "has a politic condescension toward sins of the flesh." The more sins, the more recruits,—for he has need of them. As for himself, love to him is "merely an incitement of nature." Once, in England, on the occasion of a certain courtesan's complaint about her dissatisfaction over a present of five hundred guineas, he said to Menshikov: "Dost think I am the same sort of wastrel as thou? Old men serve me with zeal and intelligence for five hundred guineas; whereas this creature has served me but illy—thou knowest with what!"

The Czaritza is not at all jealous. He tells her of all his adventures, but always ends with amiability: "Still, thou art the best of all, Katenka!"

Strange rumors are current about the orderlies of the Czar. One of them, General Yaguzhinsky, pleased the Czar through such means as it is not expedient to talk about. The Adonis, Lefort, if one is to take the word of a certain amiable little ancient here, was on a footing with the Czar of "such extreme confidence as to amorous intrigues" that they had a mistress in common. They say that even the Czaritza, before she became intimate with the Czar, had been the mistress of Menshikov, who supplanted Lefort. Menshikov, "this man of vile origin," who, to use an utterance of the Czar's, "has been conceived in iniquity, born full of sins by his mother, and who shall end his life in knavishness," has an almost incomprehensible sway over him. There were occasions when the Czar beat him like a dog, knocking him down and trampling him underfoot,—everything was at an end, 'twould seem; and yet, when one looked again, they had made their peace and were kissing one another. I have heard with my own ears the Czar calling him his own "darling little Alexasha," "the dear little child of his heart (*sein Herzenskind*)," while the other responded in kind. This quondam street huckster of pies has attained such brazenness that once— true, it was in his cups,—he said to the Czarevich: "Thou art no more fated to see the crown than thy ears. 'Tis mine!"

8th of October.

To-day was held the funeral of a certain Dutch merchant's wife, who had been afflicted with dropsy. The Czar performed an operation upon her with his own hands, to let out the water. They say she died not so much from the disease as from the operation. The Czar attended both the funeral and the wake. He drank and waxed merry. He deems himself a great chirurgeon. He always carries about him a lancet in a case. All who have any abscesses or swellings conceal them, lest the Czar fall to cutting them up. He has some sort of an unwholesome curiosity about anatomy. He cannot look at a corpse without performing an autopsy. He anatomizes his nearest of kin when they die.

He is also fond of extracting teeth. He learned the art in Holland, from the tooth-jerkers who work the public squares. In the Cabinet of Curiosities here there is a whole bag of carious teeth he has pulled.

He has both a cynical curiosity toward sufferings, and a cynical compassion. He pulled a tape-worm with his own hands out of his blackamoor page.[27]

* * *

His whole being is a combination of strength and weakness. This can be seen in his face as well: awesome eyes, from whose mere look men fall into a swoon,—the eyes are too truthful; whereas his lips are thin, tender, with a sly smile,— almost feminine. His chin is soft, plump, rounded, with a dimple.

The incident of the hat shot through at Poltava has been dinned into our ears. I doubt not that he is capable of being brave,—especially in victory. However, all conquerors are brave. But has he always been as brave as it seems?

Hallart, the Saxon engineer who took part in the Narva campaign in the year seventeen hundred, told me that the Czar, having learned of the approach of Carl XII, transferred the entire direction of the troops to Duke De Croy, by a letter of instruction, hastily written, undated, unsealed, —altogether, it would seem, incongruous (*nicht gehauen, nicht gestochen*), while he himself withdrew, "in great perturbation."

I have seen a medal struck off by the Swedes, owned by the Swedish prisoner, Count Pipper: on one side is the Czar, warming himself at the fire of his cannons, out of which bombs are flying in the direction of besieged Narva; the inscription reads: *And Peter warmed himself at the fire*,[28]—a hint at Peter the Apostle in the courtyard of Caiaphas; on the reverse are the Russians, in flight from Narva, and Peter is at their very head; his regal crown is tumbling off his head,—his sword has been cast away,—he is wiping his eyes with his handkerchief; the inscription proclaims,—*And Peter went out, and wept bitterly*.[29]

Admitting that all this is false,—but how is it that none would even have dared to cavil Alexander or Cæsar thus?

In the Prutsky campaign as well something queer happened: at the most hazardous moment the Czar was ready to abandon his army,—so that he might return with fresh forces. And if he did not abandon them, it was merely because all retreat was cut off. "Never," he wrote to the Senate, "since I began in the service, have we been in such desperation." This, too, practically means that "he went out, and wept bitterly."

Blumentrost says—and physicians know things about

heroes that posterity knows nothing of—that the Czar apparently cannot bear any bodily pain. During one serious illness, which was considered mortal, he did not at all resemble a hero.

"And it is impossible to conceive," a certain Russian, who had been glorifying the Czar, had exclaimed in my presence, "that this great and intrepid hero should be afraid of such small vermin as cockroaches!" When the Czar travels through Russia, new huts are built for him to lodge in, inasmuch as it is hard to seek out in Russian villages any dwelling free from cockroaches. He is also afraid of spiders and all sorts of insects. I myself once observed how, upon catching sight of a cockroach, he shook and grew all pale, his face becoming distorted,—just as though he had seen a wraith or some supernatural monster; a little more, it seemed, and he would have swooned or fallen in a fit, just like a timorous woman. If the same sort of prank that he plays upon others were to be played upon him, and half a dozen or so of spiders or cockroaches were to be liberated upon his bare body,—he, like as not, would die on the spot; and, of course, the historians would never believe that the conqueror of Carl XII died from the touch of cockroach legs.

There is something amazing about this fear before this tiny, harmless creature of the gigantic Czar, in whose presence all tremble. The teaching of Leibnitz concerning monads came to my mind: it would seem that it is not the physical, but the metaphysical, protoplastic nature of insects which is inimical to the nature of the Czar. To me his fear was not only amusing, but also frightening: as though I had suddenly peered into some ancient, most ancient mystery.

*　　*　　*

On one occasion, in the Cabinet of Curiosities here, when a certain German savant was demonstrating to the Czaritza some experiments with a pneumatic pump, and a swallow had been placed under a crystal bell, the Czar said, upon seeing that the suffocating little bird was staggering and beating its wings:

"That will do,—take not the life of an innocent creature; it is not a brigand."

"Methinks its little ones are weeping for it in its nest," added the Czaritza; then, having picked up the little bird, she carried it over to the window and set it free.

Sensitive Peter! How odd that sounds. . . . And yet, in those thin, tender, almost feminine lips of his, in the plump chin with its little dimple, something resembling sensitiveness persisted in coming to my mind's eye at the moment when the Czaritza was saying in her sweetish little voice, with her mawkishly demure little smile: "Its little ones are weeping for it in its nest!"

Was it not on this very day that the frightful *ukase* was issued?—

"His Majesty the Czar has taken cognizance of the fact that the nostrils of those convicts who have been sentenced for life to hard labor have been slit hardly noticeably; therefore, His Majesty the Czar has issued an order that the nostrils be torn off to the very bone, so that, if these convicts happen to escape, they might not be able to hide themselves anywhere, and shall be known, so as to make their capture easier."

Or take another *ukase*, from the Admiralty Regulations:

"If any shall kill himself, he, even though dead, shall be hanged by his feet."

*　　*　　*

Is he cruel? That is a question.

"He who is not cruel is no hero,"—such is one of the utterances of the Czar, in which I do not place great trust: they have too much about them of being intended for posterity. And yet,—posterity shall learn that, while pitying swallows, he has tortured his sister to death, is torturing his wife, and, apparently, will torture his son to death as well.

*　　*　　*

Is he really as full of homespun virtues as one might think? That is another question. I am fully aware of the number of anecdotes now current about the Czar-carpenter at Saardam. I could never, I confess, listen to them without boredom,—for they are all far too moralizing, resembling the woodcuts that illustrate copy book maxims.

"*Verstellte Einfalt,*—sham simplicity," one clever German

has said of him. There is also a Russian proverb: Simplicity is worse than thieving.

In ages to come all pedants and schoolboys shall learn, of course, that Czar Peter darned his own socks, that he thriftily cobbled his own shoes. But, as likely as not, they shall not learn what a certain Russian merchant told me the other day,—he supplies building lumber:

"There are many great oak beams lying near Ladoga,—all drifted over with sand and rotting. Yet men are flogged and hung for cutting down oaks. Human flesh and blood are cheaper than oak wood!"

I might have added: cheaper than socks full of holes.

"*C'est un grand poseur!* What a great actor!" some one has said of him. It is a sight to behold when, being at fault in having infringed some rule of his merry-andrew gatherings, he kisses the hand of the mock Prince-Cæsar:

"Pardon, sire, of thy graciousness. Our brotherhood of shipmen are not skilled in ceremonies."

One looks on, and cannot believe one's eyes,—one cannot distinguish the demarcation between Czar and buffoon.

He has surrounded himself with masks. And this "Czar-carpenter"—is it not also "a masquerade on the Dutch manner"? And isn't this new Czar, with his supposed simplicity, in his carpenter's costume, farther from the common folk than were the ancient Czars of Muscovy, in their raiment woven of gold?

"Times now be far more cruelly hard than of yore," the same merchant complained to me. "No one durst make any complaint,—the truth is never brought to the Czar's attention. Things were simpler in the old days!"

The Czar's spiritual adviser, the Archimandrite Theodosius, once praised the Czar to his face, in my presence, for his "dissimulation," which, it seems, "political preceptors account among the first principles of government."

*   *   *

I do not judge him. I merely repeat that which I see and hear. Many see the hero,—few the man. And, even if I do gossip a little, 'twill be forgiven me,—for I am a woman. "This is a man who is both very good and very bad," some one has said of him. But I repeat once more: Whether he be better or worse than other people, I know not; but to me it seems that he is not quite a human being.

* * *

The Czar is pious. He himself reads the Epistles from the choir, and sings with just as much assurance as the priests, inasmuch as he knows all the lauds and services by heart. He himself composes prayers for his soldiers.

Sometimes, during conversations dealing with matters military and governmental, he will suddenly roll his eyes up to heaven, make the sign of the cross over himself, and devoutly utter, from the depths of his heart, a brief prayer: "God, take thou not away, in times to come, thy Graciousness from us!" Or: "O Lord, let thy graciousness be over us, for that we place our trust in Thee!"

This is not hypocrisy. He, of course, believes in God,—as he puts it himself, he "places his trust in Him Who is strong in battles,—the Lord." But at times it seems that his God is not at all the God of the Christians, but the ancient, pagan Mars,—or Fate itself: Nemesis. If ever there has been a man who least of all resembled a Christian, that man is Peter. What concern has he with Christ? What connection is there between the iron of Mars and the lilies of the Evangel?

Side by side with devoutness there is a scoffing at sacred things.

The Prince-Pope, the mock Patriarch, replaces the panagia by clay flasks with little bells; the Bible,—by a cellarette in the shape of a book, filled with vials of vodka; his cross is made of pipestems.

During a mock marriage of dwarfs, arranged by the Czar some five years ago, the espousal took place in church amid general laughter; the priest himself could hardly pronounce the words because of the laughter choking him. The mystic rite recalled a comedy in a show-booth at some fair.

This sacrilege, however, is unconscious, child-like, and savage, even as all the rest of his madcap pranks are.

* * *

I have just read through a rather curious new book, issued in Germany under the title of: *Curieuse Nachricht von der itzigen Religion I. K. M. in Russland Petri Alekzieviz und seines grossen Reiches, dass dieselbe itzo fast nach Evangelische-Lutherischen Grundsätzen eingetrichtet sei.—A Curious Relation concerning the Religion of Czar Peter Alexeievich, and of the said Religion in Russia Being now Conducted almost in Accordance with the Evangelistic-Lutheran Ritual."*

Here are a few extracts:

"We would not err in saying that His Majesty pictures true religion to himself in the form of Lutheranism.

"The Czar has set aside the Patriarchality, and, following the example of Protestant Princes, has proclaimed himself Supreme Bishop,—*i.e.*, Patriarch of the Russian Church. Returning from his travels in foreign lands, he immediately entered into disputes with his priests, became convinced that they understood nothing in matters of faith, and founded schools for them, that they might study the more diligently, since before that they could barely read.

"And now, when the Russians are intelligently taught and educated in schools, all their superstitious notions and customs must vanish of themselves, inasmuch as no one can believe in such things save simple and unenlightened folk. The system of instruction in these schools is absolutely Lutheran, and the youth of the land is brought up in accordance with the principles of true Evangelical religion. The monasteries have been greatly circumscribed, so that they cannot, as of yore, serve as a den for a multitude of idle people, who represent for the government a heavy burthen and the danger of sedition. All the monks are now obligated to master some useful calling, and everything is arranged in a praiseworthy manner. Also, miracles and the holy bones of saints no longer enjoy their former esteem,—in Russia, even as in Germany, people have already come to believe *that there has been a great deal of hocus pocus* about such matters."

I know that the Czarevich has read this book. What must his emotion have been when he was reading it?

* * *

Once, while I was present, and they were sitting at their wine in the small oak-grove near the Palace, in the Summer

Garden, where the Czar is fond of holding converse with the clergy, the Archimandrite Theodosius, who is the Administrator of Spiritual Affairs, was discoursing on "through what causes, and in what sense, the Roman Emperors—Christian as well as Pagan—served and were designated as Pontifexes, the Archpriests of a polytheistic faith." His deduction was that the Czar is the Supreme Archprelate, the High Priest and the Patriarch. Most artfully and dexterously did this Russian monk prove, according to *The Leviathan* of the English atheist "Hobbezia" (Hobbes), that *civitatem et ecclesiam eandem rem esse,*—the government and the church are one and the same—is not to be understood to mean that the government should be changed into the church, but, on the contrary, the church should be transformed into the government. The monstrous beast-machine, Leviathan, was swallowing the Church of God, so that not even a trace of it was left. These ratiocinations might serve as a curious memorial of monastic flattery and toadyism to the will of the Sovereign.

* * *

They say that, even at the close of last year (seventeen hundred and fourteen), the Czar, having convened his dignitaries of the clergy and the laity, solemnly announced to them that "he desired to be the sole Head of the Russian Church, and left it to them to designate an ecclesiastical Council, under the name of the Most Holy Synod."

* * *

The Czar is considering an expedition against India, following the footsteps of Alexander the Great. Imitating Alexander and Cæsar,—the union of the East and the West,—the founding of a new world-wide monarchy,—these constitute the deepest and most secretly cherished thought of the Russian Czar.

* * *

Theodosius tells the Czar to his face: "Thou art a god of this earth." That is precisely what *Divus Cæsar* means,— Cæsar the Divine, Cæsar the God.

* * *

At the Poltava triumph the Czar of Russia was represented in a certain allegorical picture in the guise of the ancient god of the Sun, Apollo.

* * *

I have found that the death's-heads, which are stuck up on stakes near the Church of the Trinity, opposite the Senate, are the heads of Raskolniki executed for calling the Czar the Antichrist.

20th of October.

A certain little ancient, an invalided master-at-arms, is wont to drop in at our kitchen,—a pitiful creature, seemingly moth-eaten, with a trembling head, a red nose, and a wooden leg. He himself styles himself "a magazine rat." I regale him with tobacco and vodka. We discuss military affairs in Russia.

He is forever laughing, and speaks in waggish quips: "A hundred years a soldier man, but hasn't a hundred drops in his can; a crumb is a feast, and with water he's pleased; he shaves with a spoke, and warms himself over smoke; three doctors he hath,—Vodka, Garlic, and Death."

Having been apprenticed, when almost an infant, "for to learn the drummer's trade," he took part in all the campaigns from Azov to Poltava; yet all he received in reward from the Czar was a handful of nuts and a kiss on his head.

When he speaks of the Czar, the man seems to become entirely transfigured. To-day he told of the battle at Red Farm:

"We stood up bravely for the House of the Most Holy Mother of God, for His, our Sovereign's, Most Illustrious Majesty, and for the Christian Faith, dying for one another. We did all cry out, in a great voice: 'Help us, Lord God!' And, through the prayers of the miracle-working saints of Moscow, we did massacre the Swedish troops, both horse and foot."

He tried to repeat for my benefit the Czar's address to his troops:

"Little lads of mine, I have brought ye into this world through the sweat of my toilings. No government can exist without ye,—no more than a body without a soul. Ye have cherished love for God, for me, for your fatherland,—ye did not spare your lives. . . ."

Suddenly he leapt up, leaning on his wooden leg,—his nose turned a still deeper red; a little tear-drop hung suspended at its very tip, like a dew-drop on a ripe plum; and, brandishing his miserable little hat, he exclaimed:

"*Vivat! Vivat!* Peter the Great, Emperor of All the Russias!"

No one has yet called the Czar Emperor in my presence. But I was not amazed. In the turbid little eyes of this magazine rat such a fire began to glow that an odd chill ran through my body,—as though a vision of ancient Rome had swept by before my eyes: there was the swish of victorious banners, the trampling of brazen-armored cohorts, and the clamor of the soldiers, in greeting to "Cæsar the Divine, the Imperial,"—*Divus Cæsar Imperator!*

23rd of October.

We made a trip to the Hostel Court, on Trinity Square,— a long, clay daubed courtyard, built by the Italian architect Trezina; it is roofed with terra-cotta tiles, and has a covered way with arches, as if it were somewhere in Verona or Padua. We dropped in at a bookshop,—the first and only one in Peterburgh, started by the Czar's *ukase*. It is conducted by Vasilii Eudoximov, the printer. Here, besides books in Slavic and translations, are sold calendars, *ukases*, reports, alphabets, battle-maps, "the Czars' persons,"—*i.e.*, portraits and prints showing triumphal entries. The books go but poorly. Certain editions do not sell a single copy in two, and even three, years. Calendars, and *ukases* having to do with bribery, enjoy the best sale of all.

The head director of the first typographical establishment in Peterburgh, who happened to be in the shop,—a certain Avramov, a very queer fellow, but not at all a stupid one,— tells us what difficulties are to be met with in translating foreign books into the Russian tongue. The Czar is forever rushing the translators, and demands, under threats of a great penalty,—*i.e.*, the bastinado,—that the "book be not translated in a slip-shod fashion, but understandably and in a good style." Whereas the translators complain: "Because of the exceedingly involved German style speed is impossible; the thing is most incomprehensible, obdurate, and bitter hard; there have been times when one could not translate intelligently ten lines a day." Boris Volkov, a translator in the Foreign College, falling into despair over the translation of *Le Jardinage de Quintiny* (a book on gardening), and dreading the Czar's wrath, cut his own veins.[30]

Learning does not come easy to the Russians.

The greater part of these translations, which cost such immeasurable efforts, sweat, and—one may say—blood, is of no need to anybody, and is read by none. Recently a huge quantity of books, which had not sold and for which there was no room in the shop, were placed in a barn in the yard of the Arsenal. During an inundation they were flooded. One part was water-stained, another damaged by flax-seed oil, which, it was found, had been stored together with the books, while a third part were nibbled away by the mice.

14th of November.

We visited the theater. A large, wooden structure, or "Comedy Booth," not far from the Foundry Court. The performance began at six in the evening. The "labels" or tickets of admission, printed upon thick paper, are for sale in a separate cubby-hole. Forty kopecks is charged for the worst seat. There are few spectators. If it were not for the court, the players would starve to death. The hall, although its walls are covered with lengths of felt, is cold, damp, and draughty on all sides. The tallow candles smoke. The execrable music is always off-key. Those in the stalls are forever nibbling nuts, cracking them resoundingly, and swearing. The play was *The Comedy of Don Pedro and Don Jan*, —a Russian translation of a German adaptation of the French *Don Juan*. After every scene the "panel" or curtain was lowered—leaving us in darkness—to denote a change of locale. This caused exceeding vexation to my companion, the chamberlain Brandenstein. He kept on remarking in my ear: "What the devil kind of a comedy is this! *Welch ein Hund von Komödie ist das!*" I could hardly keep from laughing. Don Juan, in a garden, was saying to a woman he had seduced:

"Come, my love! Recall that time, filled with pleasure, when we were able to enjoy the gayety of spring, without hindrance,—and, without qualms, the *vegetable* of love could use. Let us, through gazing at the flowers, fill our eyes, —and, through the strong odor of the same, our emotions."

I rather liked the little song:

> He who is to love a thrall
>   Hugs a shadow, kisses wind:
> Wormwood wine and serpents' gall
> He who is to love a thrall
> Deems the sweetest fare of all!
>   Deaf, and mad, and mute, and blind,
> He who is to love a thrall
>   Hugs a shadow, kisses wind!

After every act there was an intermede ending in a fracas. Bibernstein, who had contrived to fall asleep, had his pocket picked of a silken handkerchief, while young Lewenwald was relieved of a silver snuff-box.

There was also another piece: *Daphnis, turned into a Myrtle Tree, through being Pursued by Apollo.* Apollo threatens the nymph:

> By force my hands thee shall secure
> For I shall not such torture endure.

The latter replies:

> Since thou dost act with such effrontery
> Abandon hope of e'er possessing me.

Just at this moment some hostlers, much the worse for drink, started a fight at the entrance to the theater. Men ran out to stop them,—and flogged them right on the spot. The words of the god and the nymph were drowned by screams and indecent curses.

In the *Epilogue* certain "engines and aerial effects" were introduced.

Finally, Phosphorus, the Morning Star (played by an actress), announced:

> Let us, then, bring this act to a close;
> We thank ye humbly,—and 'tis time for repose.

A hand-written play-bill was distributed to us, about a spectacle which was to take place in another show-booth: "Price of Admission Half-A-Ruble per Person. Italian Marionettes or Dolls, A Yard and a Half in Height, shall walk through the Theater, with the Utmost Ease, And shall represent, as Artfully as though They were Living, *The Comedy of Doctor Faustus*. Also, the Learned Horse will Perform, as Hitherto."

I must confess, I did not expect to come upon Faustus in Peterburgh,—and side by side with a Learned Horse, at that!

Recently, in this very theater, they had given *The Dear Bemocked,* or *A Most Precious Sport,*—I forget exactly how they butchered the title in Russian of Molière's *Précieuses ridicules*. I obtained a copy and made a point of reading it through. The translation was made, by order of the Czar, by one of his fools,—"The Samoyed [Cannibal] King,"—probably when the latter was blind-drunk, inasmuch as one cannot understand a word of it. Poor Molière! The monstrous cannibal "gallantries" have all the grace of a dancing white bear.

23rd of November.

Cruel frost and a piercing wind,—a real ice storm. Pedestrians have their noses and ears frost-bitten before they have time to perceive it. There is a rumor that 700 working men froze to death in a single night, between Peterburgh and Kronslot.

Wolves have appeared on the streets,—even in the heart of the town. Recently, at night, near the Foundry Court,—which means that it was at no great distance from the theater where *Daphnis and Apollo* was staged only the other day—the wolves fell upon a sentry and knocked him off his feet; another soldier came running to his aid, but was immediately torn into pieces and devoured. Also, on Basil Island, near the palace of Prince Menshikov, in broad daylight, the wolves chewed up a mother and her child.

Not less to be dreaded are the brigands. Sentry-boxes, turnpikes, chevaux-de-frise, sentries with "great angulous clubs," and night patrols, such as they have in Hamburg, do not, evidently, deter the black-legs in the least. Every

night there is either burglary with forcible entry, or robbery
with murder.

30th of November.

A humid wind set in,—and everything thawed. The mire
is impassable. There is a stench of swamps, of liquefied
manure, of spoilt fish. There are epidemics,—throat abscesses and exanthematous and peritoneal fevers.

4th of December.

Again a frost. Exposed ice everywhere. It is so slippery
that one cannot make a step without fear of breaking one's
leg. And such sharp changes go on all winter. The Nature
here is not merely ferocious, but also, apparently, mad. An
unnatural city. What chance have the arts and sciences to
flourish here! As a local proverb puts it,—there's no time
to thrive,—be glad you're alive.

10th of December.

There was an assembly at Tolstoi's. Mirrors, crystal, powder, beauty spots, crinolines and furbelows, curtsies and
scrapings,—altogether as if in Europe,—somewhere in Paris
or London.

The host himself is a man of amiability and learning. He
is translating *The Metamorphosis, or Transformation, of
Ovid* and *The Political Counsels of Nicòlo Machiavelli, A
Noble Citizen of Florence*. He danced the minuet with me.
He paid me "compliments" out of Ovid,—comparing me with
Galatea because of the whiteness of my skin, "which is like
to marmor," and because of my black hair, "which is like to
the flower the hyacinth." An amusing old chap. A clever fellow,—but a rogue of the highest degree. Here are some of
the utterances of this new Machiavelli:

"One should, when luck is going one's way, seize at it not
only with both hands, but with the mouth also, and gulp it
down."

"To live at the height of good fortune is like walking on
a glass floor."

"A citron, squeezed to excess, yields bitterness in lieu of
a goodly flavor."

"To know the intellect and manners of mankind is a great philosophy; and to know men is harder than to remember many books by heart."

Listening to the intelligent discourses of Tolstoi,—he spoke with me now in Russian, now in Italian,—to the tender music of a French minuet, and contemplating the elegant gathering of gallants and fair ladies, where everything was almost the same as in Paris or London, I yet could not forget that which I had just witnessed on my way here: before the Senate, upon Trinity Square, were still the same stakes, with still the same heads of the executed, which had been sticking there even in May, at the time of the masquerade. They were drying up, soaking, freezing, thawing, and freezing again, and yet, notwithstanding all this, they had not rotted away entirely. An enormous moon was rising from behind the Church of the Trinity, and against its red glow the heads showed blackly, with the utmost distinctness. A raven, perched upon one of them, was pecking tatters of skin from it, and cawing. This vision floated before my eyes all through the ball. Asia was screening Europe from sight.

The Czar arrived. He was out of sorts. His head shook and his shoulder jerked so that all were inspired with terror. Entering the hall where the dancing was going on, he found that it was too warm in there, and wanted to open a window, —but the windows were nailed down from the outside. The Czar ordered an ax to be brought, and, assisted by two orderlies, fell to work. He would run outside every so often to see how, and wherewith, the window was battened down. At last he had his way, by taking out the window-frame. The window did not remain long open,—furthermore, another thaw was coming on out of doors, and the wind was blowing directly from the west,—never the less, such draughts sprang up throughout the house that the lightly-clad ladies and the easily-chilled little ancients did not know where to hide themselves. The Czar tired himself out, getting up a sweat from his labor, but was content,—he even grew merry.

"Your Majesty," said Pleier, the Austrian Resident (and a great master of the compliment), "you have chopped a window through into Europe."

*   *   *

Upon the wax seal used in closing up the Czar's letters to Russia, during his first journey through Europe, there is a representation of a young carpenter, surrounded by naval instruments and military engines, with the inscription: "Since I am enrolled among apprentices, instructors are what I demand."

*   *   *

Another emblem of the Czar's: Prometheus, returning to mortals from the gods, bearing a lit torch.

*   *   *

The Czar says: "I shall create a new race of men."

*   *   *

From the stories of the "magazine rat": The Czar, desiring that the oak be grown everywhere, was himself planting acorns one day in the vicinity of Peterburgh, on the road to Peterhof. Noticing that one of the dignitaries standing near had a sneering smile for his efforts, the Czar spake wrathfully:

"I can read thee. Thou art thinking that I shall not live to see the oaks full-grown. True enough. Yet art thou a fool. I am leaving an example unto others, so that, if they do the same, our descendants will in due time be building ships out of them. 'Tis not for myself I moil,—weal of the state comes first."

*   *   *

More of the same:

"In accordance with an *ukase* of His Majesty it was ordered that the children of the nobility be registered in Moscow and enrolled in the Sukharev Tower, to study navigation. And the said nobility did enroll their children in the Monastery of Our Saviour, which is in back of the Ikonnaya Row, in Moscow, for to learn Latin. And, hearing of this, the Sovereign was sorely wroth, ordering Romodanovsky, who was the head of Moscow, to take the children of the nobility out of the Monastery of Our Saviour and to take them to Peterburgh, for to drive down piles on the Moika River, which piles would form the foundation for certain hemp storehouses being built. And the Head-Admiral, Count Fedor

Matveievich Apraxin, and the most Illustrious Prince Menshikov, and Prince Jacob Dolgorukyi, as well as other Senators, not daring to vex His Majesty, did implore His Most Gracious helpmate, Our Sovereign Empress Ekaterina Alexeievna, getting down on their knees and shedding tears,—only 'twas impossible to pacify His Majesty's wrath. And the said Head-Admiral, Count Apraxin, did take measures to set himself up as an example: he ordered a lookout to be kept, to spy out when His Majesty would be on his way to the hemp storehouses, past the toiling children of the nobility; and, upon being told that the Sovereign had set out for those storehouses, Apraxin went to those toiling minors, threw off his Order of a Cavalier and his *kaftan*, and hung them up on a post, whilst he himself took to driving the piles with the youngsters. And when the Czar was on his way back, and did catch sight of the Admiral, that he was at the same work as the minors, using his powers in the driving of piles, he halted and spoke to the Count:

" 'Fedor Matveich,—thou art the Head-Admiral and a Cavalier,—wherefore art thou driving piles?'

"And, in answer to this, the Admiral replied to the Sovereign:

" 'My nephews and my little grandchildren are driving piles. Yet who am I? What privilege of lineage have I got? As for the Order of a Cavalier, which Your Majesty was gracious enough to grant me, 'tis hung up on a wooden post,—I have brought no dishonor upon it.'

"And, upon hearing this, the Czar rode off to his palace, and, four and twenty hours later, having issued an *ukase* relieving the minors, specified that they be sent into foreign lands, for to learn sundry arts and crafts,—his wrath had been so aroused that, even after driving piles, they did not escape being employed in sundry arts and crafts."

*   *   *

One of the few Russians who sympathize with the new order of things told me of the Czar:

"No matter what you look at in Russia, it hath him for a beginning, and, no matter what Russians may achieve in the future, they shall be but dipping out of this spring. This man has in all things renewed Russia,—or, rather, hath given it a new birth."

28th of December.

The Czarevich has returned,—just as suddenly as he departed.

6th of January, 1715.

We had visitors: Baron Lewenwald; Pleier, the Austrian Resident; Weber, Secretary of Hanover; and the Czar's physician, Blumentrost. After supper, at their Rhenish wine, the conversation touched upon the new ways which are being introduced by the Czar. Since no outsiders were present, and no Russians, they expressed themselves freely.

"The Muscovites," said Pleier, "do everything through coercion, and, were the Czar to die,—farewell to learning! Russia is a land where all sorts of things are begun—and none finished. The Czar acts upon it as *aqua forte* acts upon iron. He knocks learning into his subject with cudgels and sticks, acting in keeping with the Russian proverb: A stick cannot speak, but 'twill make thy wit quick; none faster goes than he that gets blows. Puffendorf spake truth of this people: 'This slavish people slavishly submits and, through the severity of those in power, is constrained in submission to love those in power.' One may also apply to them that which Aristotle said of barbarians in general: '*quod in libertate mali, in servitute boni sunt*. Evil in freedom, they are good in servitude.' True enlightenment inspires hatred for servitude,—whereas the Russian Czar, through the very nature of his power, is a despot, and has need of slaves. That is why he is so zealously introducing ciphering, navigation, fortification, and other lower applied sciences among the people, yet never permits his subjects to draw near to true enlightenment, which demands liberty. Besides, he himself does not comprehend, or love, real enlightenment. Utility is all that he seeks for in science. He prefers *perpetuum mobile*— this ludicrous conception of that charlatan Orphireus,—to all the philosophy of Leibnitz. He deems Æsop the greatest of philosophers. He has forbidden the translation of Juvenal. He has proclaimed that 'for composing a satire its creator shall be put to the greatest tortures.' Enlightenment is to the might of the Czars of Russia the same as the sun is to snow: when the sun is not strong, the snow shines, and is iridescent; when the sun is strong, the snow melts."

"Who knows," remarked Weber, with a subtle smile, "perhaps the Russians have done Europe greater honor than it deserves, by taking it as an example? Imitation is always dangerous; virtues do not lend themselves to it as readily as vices. A certain Russian has put it rather well: 'The infectious putrescence of foreign lands is gnawing away the soundness of Russian souls and bodies; coarseness of manners has grown less, but the place made vacant thereby has been filled by flattery and vulgarity; we have outlived our old sense, yet have not gained any new,—we shall die fools!' "

"The Czar," Baron Lewenwald retorted, "is not at all as passive a pupil of Europe as he is thought to be. Once, when enraptured praises of French manners and customs were being sung in his presence, he remarked: ' 'Tis a good thing to take over their arts and sciences from the French; but, in other respects, Paris stinks.' And he added, with a prophetic mien: 'I am sorry that this town will die out because of its stench.' Although I have not heard them at first hand, other words of his have also been transmitted to me,—it might not be out of place for all the friends of Russia in Europe to bear them in mind: *L'Europe nous est nécessaire pour quelques dizaines d'années; après cela nous lui tournerons le dos*. We have need of Europe for but a few decades more; after that we shall turn our backs upon her.' "

Count Pipper cited excerpts from a recently published book: *La crise du Nord—The Crisis of the North,* dealing with the Russo-Swedish War, wherein it is set forth that "the victories of the Russians prognosticate the end of the world," and that "Russia's insignificance represents a necessary condition for the welfare of Europe." The Count also recalled the words of Leibnitz, uttered prior to Poltava, when Leibnitz was still friendly to Sweden: "Muscovy shall be a Second Turkey, and shall open the way for a new barbarity, which shall destroy all European enlightenment."

Blumentrost reassured us by saying that vodka and the venereal pox (*Venerische Seuche*), which of late years has

spread with amazing rapidity from the boundaries of
Poland to the White Sea, would make Russia a wilderness in
less than a century. Vodka and Syphilis,—these, it would
seem, are the two scourges sent by the very Providence of
God for deliverance of Europe from a new invasion of the
barbarians.

"Russia," Pleier concluded, "is an iron Colossus upon feet
of clay. It will topple, shiver into pieces,—and naught shall
be left of it!"

I bear no very great love for the Russians; but still, I had
no idea that my compatriots hated Russia so. At times it
seems that a secret fear lurks in this hatred, as though we
Germans had a premonition that some one would gobble up
somebody,—either we them, or they us.

17th of January.

"Well, which do you think I am, Fräulein Juliana,—a fool
or a scoundrel?" the Czarevich asked me, meeting me this
morning on the stairs.

At first I did not understand, thinking that he was drunk,
and wanted to pass him in silence. But he blocked my way,
and he continued, looking me straight in the eyes:

"It would also be a curious thing to know who will gobble
up whom,—we you, or you us?"

It was only then that I surmised that he had read my
diary. Her Highness had borrowed it from me for a little
while,—she, too, had wanted to read it; the Czarevich had
probably dropped into her room, when she was not there,
had seen the diary, and read it through.

I was so abashed that I was ready to fall through the
ground. I blushed and I blushed, to the very roots of my
hair; I almost wept, like a schoolgirl caught red-handed.
But he kept on looking at me in silence, as though enjoying
my discomfiture. Finally, making a desperate effort, I made
a new attempt at flight. But he seized my hand. I simply
froze from fright.

"There, now, you have put your foot in it!" He burst into
jolly, kindly laughter. "Be more careful in the future. 'Tis
a good thing, now, that 'twas I and not some other who
was the reader. My, but Your Grace has a sharp little tongue,

—like a razor! Everybody got his share. And yet, 'tis no use deluding one's self, there is much truth in that which you say of us,—aye, aye, much truth! And, though you rub our fur the wrong way,—thanks for the truth!''

He ceased laughing, and, with a radiant smile, squeezed my hand hard, as one comrade might another's, as if he really were thanking me for the truth. A strange fellow. All these Russians, in general, are strange folk. One can never foresee what they will say or do. The more I think of it, the more it seems to me that there is something about them which we Europeans do not understand, and which we never shall understand,—to us they are like the dwellers of another planet.

2nd of February.

When I was passing through the lower gallery this evening, the Czarevich, having probably heard my steps, called after me and asked me to step into the dining room, where he was seated before a small fire-grate,—alone, in the dusk; he made me sit down in an armchair facing him, and began to talk,—at first in German, and then in Russian, as kindly as if we were old friends. I heard much that was curious from him. But I shall not write down everything,—it is not without danger, both for me and for him, while I am in Russia. Here are but a few unrelated thoughts:

I had been struck most of all by the fact that he is not at all as great a defender of the old things and a foe of the new as he is held to be.

"The good old days did ever their bald pate praise," he quoted a Russian proverb to me. "And it must be said that with us, in Russia, iniquity has grown most hoary, so that, without tearing down the whole time-worn structure, and carefully inspecting each and every beam, one cannot clear away the ancient decay. . . ."

The Czar's mistake, it seems, consists of his hurrying too much.

"Batiushka is fain to do everything in a hurry: slap, dash, and you have your ship. And yet he cannot understand that haste makes waste. A tap and a clout,—and your wheels are turned out; away you go,—what a goodly show; then you turn with a start,—and your spokes fall apart."

18th of February.

The Czarevich keeps a note-book into which he copies excerpts from *The Civil and Ecclesiastical Chronicles* of Baronius; excerpts which, as he himself puts it, "are applicable to myself, to my father, and to others,—showing in a manner, that formerly things were different from what they are now." He gave me this note-book to scan through. In the notations one can perceive an inquisitive and free mind. Referring to certain legends which are too miraculous, —true, Catholic ones,—one finds such parenthetical addenda as: [compare with the Greek]; [rather dubious]; [this is not entirely the truth].

But most curious of all appeared to me the notes in which he makes analogies between the past of other lands, and the present time of Russia:

A.D. 395.—"The Cæsar Arcadius commanded that all those be styled heretics who are to be distinguished even in the least particular from Orthodoxy." *A hint at the unorthodoxy of the Russian Czar.*

A.D. 455.—"The Cæsar Valentinian was slain for infringing the laws of the Church and for adultery." *A hint at the abolition in Russia of the Patriarchate, at the Czar's marriage to Ekaterina during the lifetime of his first wife, Avdothea Lopukhina.*

A.D. 514.—"Long garments were being worn in France, for Carlus the Great did forbid the short; there was praise for long garments, and condemnation for the short." *A hint at the change in Russian dress.*

A.D. 814.—"Cæsar Leo was seduced by a certain monk into ikonomachy. The same state of affairs prevails with us." *A hint at the Czar's spiritual adviser, the monk Theodosius, who, they say, is counseling the Czar to do away with the worship of ikons.*

A.D. 854.—"Cæsar Michael did use the Sacraments of the Church as a game." *A hint at the establishment of the Most Drunken Conclave, the wedding of the Mock Patriarch, and many other pastimes of the Czar.*

Here are several other thoughts:

Concerning the power of the Pope: "Christ did make all prelates equal. But as to what they say about salvation being impossible without the absolution of the Church,—that, too, is an evident falsehood, inasmuch as Christ Himself said: Whosoever liveth and believeth in me shall never die,[31]— 'in me,'—and not in the Church of Rome, which at that time had no being, and, until the Gospel of the Apostles reached Rome, many souls must have thus sneaked into salvation."

"The impieties of Mohammed have spread through women-folk. Women-folk are much inclined toward false prophets."

Whole learned researches on Mohammed have less to say than is said in these few words, worthy of the great skeptic Beyle!

* * *

Recently Tolstoi, in speaking of the Czarevich, told me with his vulpine smile:

"To make one's self loved, the best expedient is this: when the occasions arise one must know how to cover one's self with the skin of the simplest of beasts."

I did not understand him at the time; it is only now that I am beginning to understand him. Among the works of a certain old English writer,—I have forgot his name,—which work bears the title of *The Tragedy of Hamlet, Prince of Denmark*, its unhappy prince, persecuted by his enemies, pretends to be either a simpleton or a madman. Is not the Russian Prince emulating the example of Hamlet? Is he not covering himself 'with the skin of the simplest of the beasts'?

* * *

They say that the Czarevich dared on one occasion to be frank, informing the Czar about the miseries of the people. It is since then that he has fallen out of favor.

23rd of February.

He loves his daughter Natasha most tenderly. To-day, the whole morning through, sitting on the floor with her, he built turrets and little houses for her out of wooden blocks; crawling about on all fours he acted out for her a dog, a horse, and a wolf. He tossed a ball to her, and, whenever it rolled behind a bed or wardrobe, would crawl in after it, covering himself with dust and cobwebs. He carried her off to his room, dandling her in his arms, showing her to everybody and asking:

"A fine little lassie, eh? Where will you find such another?"

He, himself, looks like a little boy.

Natasha is intelligent beyond her age. If she stretches her hands out for something, and some one threatens to tell her mamma, she quiets down immediately; but, if she be simply told to stop, she begins to laugh and becomes more mischievous than ever. When she sees that the Czarevich is out of sorts she quiets down, merely contemplating him closely; but, when he turns around to look at her, she starts laughing loudly and waving her tiny arms. She caresses him altogether like a grown-up.

I experience a peculiar emotion when I see these caresses, —it seems that the tot not only loves the Czarevich, but pities him as well, as though she sees, as though she knows, something concerning him that no one has yet known. It is a strange, eerie sensation,—as at the time when I was looking at my father and mother through a dark—most dark—clairvoyant's mirror.

* * *

"That she loves me, I know full well,—why, she left everybody behind for me," he once told me, speaking of his wife.

Now, when I have come to understand the Czarevich better, I cannot place the entire blame upon him because they find it so hard to get along together. Both are blameless,—both are at fault. They differ too much, and are too unhappy,—each in his or her own way. A small, or moderate, grief draws people together; too great a grief draws them apart.

They are like two people seriously ill or wounded, sharing one bed. They cannot help one another,—yet each move of the one inflicts pain upon the other.

There are people who have become so accustomed to suffering that it seems as if their very soul was as habituated to tears as a fish is to water,—without tears, they are like a fish on dry land. Their thoughts and emotions, having once drooped to the earth, will never rise up more like the branches of the weeping willow. Her Highness is one of these.

The Czarevich has enough woe of his own, besides hers; yet every time when he comes to her he sees another's woe as well,—a woe which cannot be alleviated. He pities her. But love and pity are not the same thing. If you would be loved, shun pity. Ah, I know,—I know through my own experience,—what a torture it is to pity when one cannot be of help! One finally begins to shun that person whom one has pitied too much.

Yes,—both are blameless, both are unhappy, and none can help them,—none save God. Poor, poor things! One dreads to think how this will end; one dreads,—and yet it would be better if the end were to come as soon as possible.

7th of March.

Her Highness is again pregnant.

12th of May.

We are in Rozhdestvenno, a farmstead belonging to the Czarevich, in the Koporsky district, some seventy *versti* from Peterburgh.

I have been ill for a long time. They thought I would die. Still more fearful than the thought of dying was the thought of dying in Russia. Her Highness brought me along with her here, into Rozhdestvenno, in order to afford me an opportunity of resting and recuperating in the pure air.

All around is the forest. All is quiet. There is naught save the murmur of the trees, and the twitter of birds. The rapid little river of Oredezh, for all the world as if it were a mountain stream, burbles below under the steep banks of red clay, upon which the first greenery of the birches shimmers wispily, like smoke, and the greenery of the firs shows darkly, like blackened embers.

The log-cabins on this estate look like common huts. The main building, in two stories, with a lofty attic, like those of the old Muscovite palaces, is not yet completely built. Alongside of it is a tiny chapel, with a belfry and two small bells, which the Czarevich likes to ring himself. At the gates is an old Swedish cannon and a small round of cast-iron cannon-balls, rusted, with green grass and spring flowers springing up between them. Taken all in all, it is a veritable forest monastery.

Within the buildings, the walls are yet bare, with the logs showing. There is a smell of resin; everywhere the amber drops ooze, like tears. There are holy images, with tiny lampads burning before them. Everything is radiant, fresh, clean, and has the innocence of youth. The Czarevich is fond of this place. He says he would live here forever, and would ask for nothing more than to be left in peace.

He reads and writes in his library; he prays in the chapel; he works in the garden and the vegetable plat; he angles, and roams the forest. I can see him right now out of the window of my room. He has been delving among the flower-beds, planting some Haarlem tulip buds. He is resting, as he stands leaning on his spade, seemingly rooted to the spot, trying to catch some sound. The silence is infinite. Only the ax of some wood-chopper is hammering somewhere far, far away, in the forest, and a cuckoo is sounding its silly call. And his face is calm, joyous. He is whispering, humming something,—probably one of the prayers he likes so well: an akathistus to his patron saint, Alexei the Man of God; or the Psalm beginning:

"I will extol thee, my God, O king; and I will bless thy name for ever and ever." [32]

Never have I beheld such even-glows as here. To-day's sunset was especially peculiar. The whole sky was in blood. The incarnadined clouds were scattered about, like tatters of bloodied garments, just as though a murder had been consummated in heaven, or some sort of fearful sacrifice. And blood was dripping from heaven upon the earth. Among the sharp bristles, as black as embers, of the fir-forest, the blotches of red clay seemed like blotches of blood.

While I was contemplating this and marveling, somewhere from above, as though it were from the dreadful sky, there came a voice:

"Fräulein Juliana! Fräulein Juliana!"

It was the Czarevich calling me, as he stood in the dove-cote, with a long pole in his hands, such as pigeon fanciers here use to make the pigeons circle. He is very fond of them.

I went up the shaky little ladder and, when I set foot on the small platform, the white pigeons soared up, like snow-flakes grown roseate in the even-glow, the wind and swish of their wings beating down upon us.

We seated ourselves on a bench, and, one word leading to another, began disputing, as is often the case of late, about faith.

"Your Martin Luther did issue all his laws in accordance with worldly reasoning and his own whim, and not in accord-ance with spiritual integrity. But you, you poor dears, did wax glad over an easy life; ye did believe what that se-ducer had said so light-heartedly, and did forsake the strait and hard path which Christ himself did ordain. And he, this Martin, turned out to be this whole world's fool, and in his teaching is secreted the great venom of the Asp of Hell. . . ."

I have grown accustomed to Russian pleasantries, and al-ways let them enter at one ear and out the other. To use the arguments of reason in disputing with them is the same as entering a fight with a sword against a cudgel. But this time, for some cause, I became angry, and suddenly gave full and free utterance to all the things that had long been seething in my heart.

I demonstrated that the Russians, while deeming them-selves better than all the Christian nations, in reality led a worse mode of life than pagans; they profess the law of love, —and work such cruelties as are to be seen nowhere else in the whole world; they fast—and, during the fast, drink bestially; they go to church—and, in church, swear maternal oaths. They are so ignorant that, among us Germans, a five-year-old infant knows more about faith than, among them, grown ups, and even priests, do. Out of half a dozen Rus-sians scarcely one can be found who can read a Paternoster. To my question as to who the third person of the Holy Trin-ity was, one pious little crone named Nikola the Miracle Worker. And, truly, this Nikola is veritably the Russian God, since one might think that they have no other. It was not for nothing that in sixteen hundred and twenty the Swedish theologian Johannes Botwid, had defended, at the Academy of Upsala, his dissertation on *Are the Muscovites Really Christians?*

I know not how far I might have gone, had I not been stopped by the Czarevich, who had been listening to me all the while calmly,—it was this very calmness which maddened me so.

"Well, now, *fräulein,*—here is something I have been wanting to ask you for a long while,—do you, yourself, believe in Christ?"

"What,—do I believe in Christ? Why, doesn't Your Highness know that we are all Lutherans? . . ."

"I do not speak of all,—but merely of Your Grace. I once spoke with your very teacher, Leibnitz; well, that fellow shillied and he shallied, and led me about by the nose, and I got the idea right then that he did not believe in Christ the right way. Well, and where do you stand?"

He was regarding me intently. I let my eyes drop, and for some reason at once recalled all my doubts, my disputes with Leibnitz, the unsolvable contradictions of metaphysics and theology.

"I think," I, in my turn, began to shilly-shally, "that Christ is the justest and wisest of men. . . ."

"But not the Son of God?"

"We are all children of God. . . ."

"And he, even as all?"

I did not feel like lying,—I kept silent.

"Well, there it is!" he let drop, with such an expression on his face as I had never yet seen. "Ye are wise, powerful, honest, splendid. Ye have everything. Yet Christ ye have not. Besides, what need have ye of Him? Ye are your own salvation. Whereas we be foolish, beggared, naked, drunken, stenchful,—worse than barbarians, worse than the beasts, and are always perishing. Yet Christos Batiushka is with us, and shall be, world without end. 'Tis through Him, the Light, that we seek salvation!"

He spoke of Christ as, I have noticed, the simplest folk—the *mouzhiks*—speak of him here: as though He were their own, their very own, a member of their households,—just such a *mouzhik* as any of them. I know not what this is,—the greatest pride and sacrilege, or the greatest humility and piety.

We were both silent. The pigeons were again flocking, and, between us, joining us, their white wings fluttered.

Somebody from Her Highness came to fetch me. Getting down from the turret, I turned around for the last time to look at the Czarevich. He was feeding the pigeons. They had surrounded him. They settled upon his arms, upon his shoulders, upon his head. He stood on the height, over the black, seemingly charred forest, in the red, seeming ensanguined sky,—all covered, as though he were clad in them, with white wings.

> 31st of October, 1715.

Now, when everything is at end, I end this diary.

In the middle of August (we had returned to Peterburgh from Rozhdestvenno toward the end of May), some ten weeks before her confinement, Her Highness fell on a staircase and struck her left side against the top step. They say that she stumbled because the heel of her slipper had broken. In reality she lost consciousness when she caught sight of the Czarevich below, drunk, kissing and hugging the serf wench Aphrosiniya, his mistress.

He has long been living with her, almost before everybody's eyes. Upon his return from Karlsbad he took her into his house,—into his quarters. I did not write about this in my diary, fearing lest Her Highness read of it.

Did she know? Even if she did know, she did not want to know it, did not believe it until she saw. A base wench, the rival of the Duchess of Wolfenbüttel, the daughter-in-law of the Emperor! "Even the impossible is possible in Russia," as a certain Russian said to me. The father gallivants with a laundress,—the son with a base wench.

Some say that she is a Finn, taken prisoner by the soldiers, —even as the Czaritza had been; others, that she is a serf wench of the Czar's preceptor, Nikiphor Viyazemsky. The latter is probably nearer the truth.

She is rather handsome,—but one can at once see her "base breeding," as they say here. Tall, red-haired, white-skinned; her nose somewhat snub; the eyes big, light, with oblique and almond-shaped openings, like a Kalmuck's, with some sort of a wild, goatish gaze,—and, in general, there is something of a she-goat about her, like that of the Satyr's female in the *Bacchanal* of Rubens. One of those faces which make us women indignant, yet in almost every case is pleasing to the men.

The Czarevich, they say, has gone mad over her. When she first met him she was—apparently—a virgin, and for a long while resisted him. He was not at all to her liking. Neither promises nor threats availed. But once, after a drinking bout, intoxicated, he threw himself at her in one of those fits of insane fury,—which he, as well as his father, is subject to,—and beat her up, almost killing her, threatening her with a knife, and thus possessed her by force. Russian bestiality,—Russian filth!

And this is that very man who had resembled a saint so much, when, in the forests of Rozhdestvenno, he had been singing an akathistus to Alexei, the man of God, and, encircled by pigeons, spoke of Christ-Batiushka! However, to combine such extremes is a talent especially Russian,—which, Glory be to God, it is not given to us silly Germans to understand.

"We Russians," the Czarevich himself once told me, "do not know how to keep to moderation in anything, but are forever straying about brinks and precipices."

Her Highness, after her fall on the staircase, felt a pain in her left side. "It is just as if I were being pricked with pins all over my body," she kept saying. But, in general, she was calm, just as though she had come to some decision and as though she knew that nothing would change her decision. She never again spoke with me about the Czarevich, or complained against her fate. Only once did she say:

"I hold my ruin to be inevitable. I hope that my sufferings will be terminated soon. I do not long for anything in the world as much as for death. That would be my sole salvation."

On the 12th of October she was safely delivered of a boy, the future heir to the throne, Peter Alexeievich. The first few days after her confinement she felt well. But whenever she was tendered felicitations and wishes for her good health, she would become angry and requested everybody to pray that God might send her death.

"I want to die, and I shall die," she kept on saying, with the same unvarying, awful, calm resolution, which never left her to the very end. She paid no attention to the physicians and the midwife, seeming to do purposely everything she was forbidden to. On the fourth day she seated herself in an armchair, ordering herself to be carried to another room,— she was nursing the child herself. That same night she grew worse; she ran a fever, had fits of vomiting, convulsions, and such pains in her abdomen that she cried out louder than she had while in labor.

Learning of this the Czar, who was ill himself, sent Prince Menshikov with four royal physicians,—Areskin, Polikola, and the two Blumentrosts,—to hold a consultation. They found her at death's door,—*in mortis limine.*

Whenever they urged her to take some medicine, she would throw the glass on the floor, saying:

"Torture me not. Let me die in peace. I do not want to live."

The day before her death she summoned Baron Lewenwald to her and imparted to him her last behest: That none of those about her person, neither here nor in Germany, should dare speak evil of the Czarevich; she was dying before her time,—before she had thought she would,—but was satisfied with her fate, and made no accusations of any sort against any one.

Then she said good-by to all. She gave me her blessing, as a mother might have.

On the last day the Czarevich did not leave her bedside. His face was such that it frightened one to look at it. Three times did he fall into a swoon. Only before the very end, when he had his lips to her hand, did she bestow a long look upon him, and said something, in a very low voice. All I caught was:

"We shall see each other again. . . . Soon. . . . Soon.
. . ."

She passed away just as though she had fallen asleep. Her

face, when living, had never been as happy as it was when she was lying there, dead.

By order of the Czar the body was anatomized. He himself was present when this was done.

The funeral took place on the 27th of October. For a long while there were long disputes as to whether, according to court etiquette, cannon were supposed to be fired at the interment of Crown Princesses, and, if they were supposed to be fired, how many times? Inquiries were made of all the foreign ambassadors. The Czar was more concerned about these salvos than he had ever been about the entire destiny of Her Highness. It was decided not to have any salvos.

The coffin was carried out over a board-walk built especially for the purpose, directly from the doors of the house to the Neva. The Czar and the Czarevich walked behind the coffin. The Czaritza was not present. She expected, from hour to hour, to be delivered of a child. A funereal frigate was anchored on the Neva,—all draped in black, with black flags.

Slowly, to the sounds of funereal music, we floated down to the Cathedral of SS. Peter and Paul, still not completely built, where the tomb of the Crown Princess will have to remain under the open sky until the vaulted roof is completed. Her whole life had been inclement,—the elements will be inclement to her even when she is dead.

Th evening was drab, calm. The sky was like a sepulchral vault; the Neva like a dark—most dark—mirror; the whole city, enveloped in fog, was for all the world like a phantom, or a vision seen in a dream. And everything that I had experienced, seen, and heard in this fearful city, now, more than ever, seemed to me a dream.

From the Cathedral we returned at night to the house of the Czarevich, for the funeral feast. Here the Czar handed to his son a letter which, as I subsequently learned, threatened the Czarevich, in the event of his not mending his ways, with deprivation of his succession to the throne, and with a father's curse.

On the following day the Czaritza was delivered of a son.

Between these two children—the son and the grandson of the Czar—waver the destinies of Russia.

1st of November.

Yesterday, just before evening, I dropped in on the Czarevich, to talk over with him my departure for Germany. He was seated before a brightly blazing stove, burning papers, letters, and manuscripts therein. Probably he apprehends a raid.

He had in his hand a small, scuffed, leather-bound book, and was just about to cast it in the fire, when, with a sudden indiscretion at which I myself am now amazed, I asked him what it was. He handed the book to me. I peeped into it and saw that it consisted of the Czarevich's notes, or his diary. The ruling passion of women in general, and mine in particular—curiosity—instigated me to the still greater indiscretion of asking him to lend me this diary to read.

He considered for a minute or so, gave me an intent look, and suddenly smiled that endearing, child-like smile of his, which I love so:

"One good turn deserves another. I read your diary,— you may read mine."

But he demanded my word of honor that I would not speak to a soul about these notes, and would return them to him to-morrow morning, to be burned.

I pored over them the whole night long. They are, correctly speaking, an ancient Russian calendar,—or Church calendar,—done into a book at Kiev. It was presented to the Czarevich in seventeen hundred and eight by the late Metropolitan, Dimitri Rostovsky, who, among the common folk, is held as a saint. Partly on the margins and blank spaces of the book's pages, partly upon separate small sheets, inserted or pasted in, the Czarevich had been jotting down his thoughts and the incidents of his life.

I decided to transcribe this diary.

I shall not break my word: as long as I live, and the Czarevich lives, none shall learn of these, his notes. But they must not be lost without a trace.

God shall judge between father and son. But by men the Czarevich is slandered. Let, then, this diary, if it be fated to reach posterity, convict or exculpate him,—but, at any rate, reveal the truth.

II

THE DIARY OF THE CZAREVICH ALEXEI

Blessed be the crown of the years of thy goodness, O Lord.

*   *   *

While sojourning in Pomerania for the purpose of buying up provender, in accordance with the instructions of the author of my being [*Note by Fräulein Arnheim:* This is how the Czarevich always styles his father], I heard that in Moscow, in the Usspensky Cathedral, Stepan, Metropolitan of Riyazan, denouncing the *ukase* concerning *fiscals,*—that is to say, informers in matters of state and church,—and other laws detestable to the church, did cry unto the people:

"Let it be no matter of wonder to ye that this so greatly troubled Russia is up to this very day tossed about amid bloody tempests. O, how far removed from the Law of God are the laws of man!"

And the dignitaries of the Senate, having called upon the Metropolitan did upbraid and admonish him for that he was inciting the people to rioting and insurrection, and for touching upon the dignity of the Czar. And they did make a report of all this to the Czar.

And I, too, did speak with Riyazansky, urging him to make his peace with Batiushka the best way he could; what profit, now, was there in any disagreement being between them? And that he should seek this peace earnestly, inasmuch as, were he to be deprived of his office, there would never be found another like him.

Before this predicament he used to write to me, and I to him, although, with the exception of important matters, not frequently. But, since hearing of that predicament, I have cut the said correspondence short, and do not call upon him, neither am I at home to him, inasmuch as he is held in great hatred by the author of my being, and, because of that, 'tis dangerous for me to correspond with him. And 'tis said he is to be deprived of the office he now occupies.

And the said exhortation Riyazansky did conclude with a prayer to Alexei, the Man of God, for me, sinful servant of God:

"Oh thou accepted of God! Forget not also thy namesake, the zealous guardian of the behests of God, and thy most righteous follower, the Czarevich Alexei Petrovich. Thou didst forsake thy home,—he, too, is a wanderer in the houses of others; thou hast been deprived of slaves and subjects, friends and kinsmen,—he has been, likewise; thou art a man of God,—he, too, is a faithful servant of Christ. Yea, we pray thee, saint of God, protect thy namesake, our sole hope; hide him within the shelter of thy wings, like a beloved chick; like to the apple of thy eye, guard him unharmed from every evil!"

*   *   *

While sojourning in foreign regions, also by order of the author of my being, for the study of navigation, fortification, geometry and other sciences, I was overcome by great fear of dying without absolution. I wrote of this to Moscow, to my confessor, Father Jacob, as follows:

"We have no priest with us, nor can we obtain one anywhere. I pray Your Holiness,—seek out some priest in Moscow, to come out here to me secretly, putting off his marks of priesthood,—that is, shaving off his mustache and beard, and also letting his tonsure grow over, or shaving his head entirely, and putting on false hair; also, let him wear German clothes. And let him say he is an orderly of mine. Please,—please, Father! Show compassion for my soul,—let me not die impenitent! Not for aught else do I need him, save in case of death,—also, when well, for holy confession. And 'twould be a good thing if he were a man without house or wife, so that, hiding away in such guise from those that know him in Moscow, he might seem to have disappeared without news. As for the shaving of the beard,—let him not hesitate, inasmuch as necessity knows no law: 'tis better to offend in small things than to let a soul go to perdition through dying without absolution. Work this diligently, but if thou art not inclined so to do, God will call thee to account for my soul."

When I did return from foreign lands to the author of my being in Sanct Peterburgh, he did receive me graciously, and did question me: Whether I had forgot that which I had been studying? To which I answered that I thought I had not, and he did order me to bring him some plans of my draughtsmanship. But, fearing lest he compel me to draw in his presence—inasmuch as I could not do so—I conceived the idea of maiming my right hand, so that I might not be able to use it for anything, and, having primed my pistol, taking it in my left hand, I shot it off at the palm of my right, in order to shoot a bullet through it; and, although the bullet did miss the hand, it nevertheless was scorched painfully by the gunpowder; as for the bullet, it made a hole in the wall of my room, which hole can be seen to this day. And the author of my being saw my burnt hand at the time, and asked me for the cause of the accident. And I did tell him somewhat at the time, but not the truth.

* * *

From the Military Code, Chapter VII, Article 63:
"He that malingers, or breaks his joints and maketh himself unfit for service, the same shall have his nostrils slit, and afterwards be sentenced to Penal Servitude."

* * *

A statute from the Code of Czar Alexei Mikhailovich, Chapter XXII, Clause 6:
"In the event of a son petitioning against his father, no judgment shall be granted him against his father; and, after a lashing with the *knout*, he·shall be, for such a petition, given over to his father."

And that, on the whole, is but just; although, even if children are subject to the parental will, they are not so on the manner of dumb brutes. It is not the sole qualification of having brought a child into the world, but virtue, which makes men fathers.

* * *

I have heard that it displeases the author of my being to have any one build houses in Moscow,—inasmuch as it is his will to live in Peterburgh.

* * *

We cannot, merely by ourselves, change any general national custom.

Whatever land shifts its customs,—that land shall not long stand.

The people of Russia have forgot the water of their own vessels, and have greedily and wantonly begun drinking out of the stirred-up waters of strangers.

*   *   *

Job, the Archprelate of Novgorod, did say to me:

"There is evil brewing for thee in Peterburgh,—only God, I feel, can deliver thee. Thou shalt see what events will take place in our land."

*   *   *

God hath so worked his will upon us that the aliens all but have us saddled and bridled.

We are afflicted with an invasion of foreign fiends. This death-bearing malady, this furious love of foreign things and peoples, has infected all our nation. Truly doth the prophet Baruch speak: *Let an alien come near thee, and he shall bring thee to ruin.*[33]

The Germans boast, and have actually made that boast a by-word: Let him that would eat his bread in idleness go to Russia. They style us barbarians and number us among the brutes rather than among humankind. They try to make us appear as worse than dead dogs before all the nations.

Certain of their petty German machinations could very well be put a stop to. Otherwise, by hook or by crook, we will try to ape them and their ways. To be by Germans ruled is but a step from being befooled. We do but degrade our own selves, our tongue, and our nation, making ourselves a laughing-stock for all.

*   *   *

The purity of the Slavic tongue has, because of the foreign ones, crumbled into ashes. Why we have to use foreign words I do not know. Is it in boast? If so, there is but little glory therein. At times we speak so that neither we nor others can understand.

Sit not nigh the hedge of strangers, but near your own, even though among nettles. A stranger's wit won't bring thee far. We ought to stick to our own common-sense. Music far over the hills hath a fine sound,—but, when it comes near, it turns out to be naught but the thundering of an empty barrel.

*   *   *

The Germans are a great deal cleverer than we in the matter of sciences; whereas our folk, through the beneficence of God, are no whit inferior to them in sharpness of penetration, and 'tis in vain that they belittle us. I feel that, as a people, God has created us not inferior to them.

*   *   *

I doubt whether the whole well-being of man lies verily in science alone. For have not men, in ancient times, studied less than now, yet experienced more well-being than now, with many sciences? With great enlightenment there can also be great misery. Science, when the heart is corrupt, is a cruel weapon to wreak evil with.

In our country men are not treasured. Taxes of blood and tears are tyrannically gathered from the subjects. Tributes have been devised on land, on serfs, on yokes, on beards, on bridges, on bees, on baths, on hides, and on other things,—there is no numbering them. One ox has two or three hides flayed off it, yet they can flay nary a one that is whole, and, no matter how they toil, all they flay off are tatters. That is why none of tributes come in readily, while the people still waste away from day to day. Don't let the *mouzhik* grow all woolly, say they, but clip him to the very skin. And, working on this principle, they devastate the whole land. Impoverishment of the peasant is impoverishment of the ruler. Our administrators will lay down their lives over a crumb,—but, where thousands of rubles go for naught, they deem it a matter of no import whatsoever.

At this feast of Herod they eat men, and for drink have their blood and tears. The lords have everything a-plenty, unto satiation, whereas the poor peasants cannot get at even a heel of a loaf of poor bread. The first are over-eating,—the others are enhungered.

The Russian people have arrived at the last stage of penury. And no one reveals the truth to the Czar. Our country is perished.

*   *   *

We Russians have no need of bread. We eat one another, and are filled thereby.

* * *

The *boyari* are a fallen, frost-riven tree. The Czar cannot see the forest [the people] for the thick trees [the *boyari*].

See what a clever fellow Batiushka is,—yet Menshikov aye hoodwinks him.

* * *

All the statesmen, from the little to the great, have become crawling, creeping creatures. The ancient statutes have become decrepit, while the new ones are held at naught. How many of them have been issued! Yet how much effect have they? And, because of that, things go on in the same old way. And, e'en in the future, I cannot foresee much good.

When, by order of the author of my being, I was cutting down timber for scout-boats in the Novgorod district, I had a talk with a peasant from the Pokrovsky hamlet, one Ivashka Pososhkovii, about a territorial assembly and a council of the people,—men should be chosen out of every calling, and from among the people, of good intelligence, that they might compile a new code of laws, witnessed by a free vote of all the people. Inasmuch as God did divide intelligence among all men in moieties, giving to each according to his ability. And through those of but humble mind doth He frequently make known His will and truth. To degrade such men doth harm to the soul. Therefore, a Czar cannot do without many counsels and a free voice of the people.

* * *

Concerning the duty of a Czar:

Not to put his trust in his own haughty intellect, but to be concerned for the land and the people, and for all the regions and hamlets of that land; and to bear love, and use all care, and discretion, and protection, for the lesser brethren of Christ, inasmuch as there shall be a Dread Judgment day for the great and the powerful of this earth. The lesser man shall be forgiven; as for the mighty, there shall be a mighty trial for them.

This is to be borne in mind, unfailingly, if God grant that I be Czar.

*   *   *

On the day of the Protomartyr Eustace we had a merry gathering and did drink greatly. Our faces were bashed in with tympani. Clod-hopper had his eye blackened, and Whip-hand a tooth knocked out. But I remember naught of it,—I barely managed to make my way home. I was most abundantly pleasured by the gifts of Bacchus.

*   *   *

I stayed alone at home at Rozhdestvenno. The days have passed like waters flowing by. There was naught save utmost peacefulness.

*   *   *

Time passeth, and bringeth us closer to death,—the end of our days is nearer than ever.

The full corruption of this our age I now do learn;
No desires have I, and no fear; I for death but yearn.

*   *   *

I am somewhat under the weather,—after drinking.

*   *   *

My helpmeet [*Note by Fräulein Arnheim:* The Czarevich thus styles his spouse, the Crown Princess Charlotta] hath conceived in her womb.

Eremka, Eremka, thou pagan god! Since my very youth the passions beset me greatly. I do accuse others of ungodliness, yet am myself the most ungodly of all.

Aphrosiniya. . . . I have known my iniquity, and have not atoned for my sin. May Thy hand lie heavy upon me, O Lord! When shall I come and appear before the face of God? For tears are my bread and meat, day and night; my soul longeth and fainteth to appear in the mansions of the Lord.

We did swill away until late at night with the Proto-presbyter of the Cathedral of the Annunciation, Jacob, our spiritual father. We drank not in the German manner, but in the true Russian. We were done rather to a turn.[34]

Aphroska! Aphroska! [*Note by Fräulein Arnheim:* Here follows an indecent oath.]

* * *

A verse from *An Enemy of the Cross of the Lord,*—from a requiem which had been sung during the sacred services after Poltava,—was sung during a drinking bout, openly, in the presence of all, to the very face of Theodosius, Archimandrite of Neva.

* * *

I wonder greatly at Batiushka,—wherefore does he love this Fedosska so? Can it be because Fedosska is introducing Lutheran ways, and allows all sorts of things to pass? He is a downright atheist,—truly, an Enemy of the Cross of the Lord!

* * *

Such a subtile knave I have rarely beheld! He is a politician,—he will work no evil openly; only one must be on a wary footing with him, and not dwell in open enmity with him, but rather hypocritically, when things so fall out that one is under his orders.

* * *

Pity for Thy House doth consume me, O God! Fear hath come upon me, and a trembling, lest Christianity perish utterly in Russia!

* * *

Fedosska the heresiarch, and others like him, have openly begun to beset the whole Church; to do away with fasts; to preach that repentance and mortifying of the flesh should be taken as some sort of a fable; to put celibacy and self-imposed poverty to laughter, and to change the other arduous and strait ways of a strict Christian life into smooth and broad ways. They preach boldly that one should lead every debauched and indulgent mode of life; they acknowledge no sin in anything,—everything is sacred with them, and by this baying of theirs they bring the lovers of this world into such a state of fearlessness and sensuousness that many of them have fallen into Epicurean ways of thinking: eat, drink, and be merry,—for there is no rendering of accounts after death.[35]

The holy ikons are called idols; church singing,—the lowing of bulls. Chapels are demolished,—but, where the walls have been standing, men have been licensed to trade in tobacco, and to shave beards. Miracle-working ikons are brazenly carted off on rotting wains, under filthy matting, to make a mock of them before all the people. They have set their feet upon all piety and the Orthodox faith,—but in such a manner and under such a pretext as to convey the idea that it is not the faith that they are extirpating, but an obnoxious and quite harmful superstition. Oh, what a great number of the clergy have been done away with, unfrocked, and tortured to death through this subterfuge! But, shouldst thou ask wherefore, thou shalt get no other answer save this: Thou superstitious one, thou zealot, thou useless Pharisee!— He that keepeth fasts is a zealot; he that prayeth,—a Pharisee; he that worships ikons,—a hypocrite.

And all this is done with such craft and premeditation in order to do away entirely in Russia with the Orthodox clergy, and to initiate their newly-conceived Lutheran and Calvinistic priestless ways.

Yea, he hath no sense of smell who scents not in this the odor of atheism!

* * *

When this slight attack of Lutheranism shall spread, and increase because of the great number of its victims, and corrupt the entire body,—ponder thou on what will be then!

If there be but a little leaven, we shall have mead in good time. . . .

* * *

The very pealing of church bells has been changed. The peals are now all jangled, as if summoning to a fire, or beating a tocsin. And there is a change in all other things as well. The ikons are not limned upon panels of wood, but upon canvases,—insane portraitures of German faces. Look upon the image of Emmanuel the Saviour,—He is all like some

damned German, pot-bellied and fat, of the flesh fleshly.
People have fallen in love with fleshly girth, they have cast
down that of the heavenly heights. Nor are the churches
built as they were of yore,—but with spires, on the style
of kirks, and orders have been given to chime the bells, after
the manner of Lutheran organs.

Woe, woe is thee, poor Russia! What has made thee get
a hankering after German doings and ways?

* * *

They want to extirpate monasticism. An *ukase* is being
prepared,—to the effect that none shall take the tonsure
henceforth, and that superannuated soldiers fill the places
that fall vacant in the monasteries.

And yet the Evangel saith: *Him that cometh to me I will
in no wise cast out.*[36]

But—the Holy Scripture is by them held as naught.

* * *

Faith has become a Spiritual Code, even like unto the
Military Code.

But—what will that prayer be like, which is prayed because of an *ukase,* under fear of punishment?

* * *

"Beggars shall be taken under guard, mercilessly beaten
with cudgels, and sent into penal servitude, that they may
not eat their bread in idleness."

Such is the Czar's *ukase.* But Christ's, on Dread Judgment
Day, shall be: *For I was an hungred, and ye gave me no
meat: I was thirsty, and ye gave me no drink: I was a
stranger, and ye took me not in: naked, and ye clothed me
not. Verily I say unto you, Inasmuch as ye did it not to one
of the least of these, ye did it not to me.*[37]

Thus, under the best police regulation, are men taught
to revile Christ, the Czar of Heaven,—in the guise of beggars they beat Him with a cudgel and send Him into penal
servitude.

The whole Russian nation is wasting away through spiritual
hunger.

The sower soweth not, and the earth receiveth not; the
pastors watch not, and the people go astray. Rural priests

are in naught to be distinguished from the *mouzhiks* who till the soil: the *mouzhik* taketh to the plow,—and so doth the priest. And in the meantime Christians are dying like cattle. Drunken priests use obscene language at the altar, cursing with maternal oaths. The chasubles upon their shoulders are woven in gold,—but their feet are clad in dirty bast sandals. The Holy Wafers are baked of rye flour; the awesome Sacrament of the Lord is kept in most vile little vessels, infested with bed-bugs, crickets and cockroaches.

The black-robed monks have become a pack of sots and thieves.

All of monasticism and priesthood requires great correction, inasmuch as there is scarce a trace to be found of true monasticism and priesthood.

We are branded with the disgrace of understanding naught of our faith, such as it is, nor of spiritual decency, for we live almost on the manner of dumb brutes. I think that there is hardly to be found in Moscow one man in a hundred who knoweth what the true Orthodox Christian faith is, or who God is,—and how to pray to Him, and how to work His will.

There is not to be found in us a single mark of Christianity, save that, in name, we pass for Christians.

*   *   *

We have all become a nation of innocents. In devotion we waver like to a leaf on a tree. We have deviated to strange and diverse teachings,—some, to Romanism; others,—to Lutheranism; we go knock-kneed,—we are baptized idolators. We have forsaken the paps of our Mother the Church; we seek after other paps,—Egyptian, outlandish, heretical. Like fallen blind puppies, each one of us goeth his own way,—but whither, none knows.

*   *   *

In the Monastery of the Miracles Fomka the barber, an ikonoclast, did chop up with an iron hedge-bill the image of the Metropolitan Alexei, the Miracle Worker, for that he, Fomka, doth not worship holy ikons, nor the Life-Giving Cross, nor the holy remains of the Martyrs of God; the holy ikons, now, and the Life-Giving Cross, are the works of human hands; as for the holy remains, they do not remit any of his, this Fomka's, sins; nor will he accept the dogmas and traditions of the Church; nor doth he believe that the Eucharist is the true Body and Blood of Christ,—but that it is simply a wafer and some church wine.

And Stepan, the Metropolitan of Riyazan, did give this Fomka up to the anathema of the Church, and to secular punishment,—burning him at the stake in Red Square.

Whereupon the dignitaries of the Senate did summon the Metropolite to Peterburgh, to answer charges therefor, and did extend encouragement to the heretics: they did acquit the ikonoclast Mitka Tveretinov, a leech, who had been Fomka's teacher in this, whereas the priestly one was expelled from the Senate chambers in ignominy; and he went, weeping, and spake:

"Christ our God, our Saviour! Thou Thyself didst say: *If they have driven me out, they will also cast you out.*[38] Lo, they are driving me out but 'tis not me, but Thee Thyself, whom they are driving out. Thou Thyself, All-Seeing, seest that their judgment is unrighteous,—judge Thou them, Thyself, then!"

And when the Metropolitan did walk out of the Senate into the square, all the people did feel pity for him, and did weep.

Yet the author of my days is most sorely wroth at Riyazansky.

*   *   *

The Church is greater than the kingdom of the earth. But now this kingdom hath taken supremacy over the church.

In times of antiquity the Czars did bow down to the ground before Patriarchs. But now the occupant of the Patriarchal Throne signs his missives to the Czar as "Your Majesty's slave and footstool, the humble Stepan, the little poor shepherd of Riyazan."

The head of the Church hath become a footstool for the Czar to conculcate; and the entire Church consists of serfs.

Take Dmitri, the Metropolitan of Rostov,—as saintly a man as you would want to find,—yet when the author of my days did make him drunk with Hungary wine, and did fall to questioning him about matters of spiritual policy, the saintly ancient did make no answer to him, but merely kept on making the sign of the cross over the Czar, in silence. And thus escaped through the sign of the cross!

* * *

One cannot swim against a river's current, say the holy Fathers; and one can't break a log with a straw.

But how is it that the sainted martyrs did not spare their blood for the Church?

* * *

The Prelates sit at the Czar's table,—well, "He that feeds my belly, owns my body."

* * *

Former churchmen were the petitioners for all of the Russian land; but the Prelates of this our day not only do not petition the Czar, but are, rather, yea-sayers, and do corrupt the pious dignity of the Czar.

* * *

If the people go astray, the Czar can pray for them; if the Czar go astray, the people cannot pray for him. God punishes the whole land if the Czar transgresses.

* * *

The other day, at a drinking bout, the "shepherd lad of Riyazan" was saying to the author of my being: "Ye Czars, the gods of this earth, are like unto the Czar of Heaven Himself."

But the mock Prince-Pope, a drunken jester, did revile the son of the Church:

"I," says he, "even though I be a jester-patriarch, would never have said anything like that to the Czar! The Godly is greater than the Czar-like."

And the Czar praised his jester.

* * *

During the same drinking bout, when the Prelates began speaking of the widowhood of the Church, and of the necessity of a Patriarchate, the author of my being did in great wrath snatch out of its scabbard his naval dirk so that all fell to trembling, thinking he would start laying about him, struck its blade flat on the table, and began yelling:

"There's your Patriarch! Two in one,—Patriarch and Czar!"

* * *

Fedosska is talking the author of my days into adapting the Imperial title for the Russian Czars,—that is, the title of the ancient Roman Cæsars.

* * *

In Moscow, on the Red Square, in the year of seventeen hundred and nine, during the triumph over the Poltava victory, there was erected, by persons of the spiritual calling, a certain semblance of an ancient Roman temple, with a sacrificial altar dedicated to the virtues of the Russian god Apollo-Mars,—to wit, the author of my being. And upon this ancient Hellenic idol-temple was inscribed:

"*Basis et fundamentum reipublicæ religio*. Faith is the basis and foundation of a state."

What sort of faith? In what God—or what gods?

During the same triumph was given *A Political Apotheosis of the Hercules of All the Russias*,—to wit, the author of my being,—slaying many beasts and men, and, upon the completion of these feats, soaring up to heaven upon the chariot of the god Iovish [Jove], drawn by eagles over the Milky Way —with the inscription: "*Viamque effectat Olympo*—Seeking a road to Olympus."

While in a certain little book, the work of the Archmonk Joseph, the Prefect of the Academy, there is said of this Apotheosis: "It should be noted, that this is not in truth any Temple or Church, erected in the name of some saint, but a political—that is to say, a civic—tribute of praise."

* * *

Fedosska is urging the author of my days that the following words be made known to all the people, in the *ukase* concerning the proposed Spiritual College—the Holy Synod,— and even in the Russian oath of allegiance:

"Hold ye the name of Your August Sovereign in honor as

your Head, and the Father of the Fatherland, and as high
as that of Our Lord Christ."

* * *

Men are fain to usurp the glory of God, and the honor of
Christ, the Eternal and Sole Czar of Czars. It is precisely
in the Codex of the Laws of Rome that one reads the impious
and blasphemous words: The Sovereign of Rome is Lord to
all the world.

* * *

We profess and believe that Christ alone is the Czar of
Czars and the Lord of Lords, and that there is no man who
is Lord to all the world.

* * *

Jesus Christ, the rock unhewn of hands from an unhewn
hill, did smite and destroy the Roman Empire, and did shat-
ter to dust its feet of clay. Whereas we be erecting and building that which God hath destroyed. Is this not contending
with God?

* * *

Consider the history of Rome. Cæsar Caligula said:
"Everything is permissible to the Emperor. *Omnia licent.*"
Well, everything is permissible not only to the Cæsars of
Rome, but to all sorts of knaves and louts,—and four-legged
brutes.

* * *

Nebuchadnezzar, Czar of Babylon, spake, saying: *I am
God.* But it was not a God he became, but a beast.[39]

* * *

Upon the Vassilievsky Island, in the house of the Czaritza
Praskoviya Matveievna, there dwells a certain holy ancient,
by the name of Timothei Arkhipich,—a haven for the
despairing, the hope of the hopeless, a madman to the world,
but not to himself. He knoweth the innermost hearts of men.

One night recently I went to see him, and did converse
with him. Arkhipich doth say that the Antichrist, now, is a

false Czar, a veritable lout. And this Lout, this Ham of the Bible, will come.

*   *   *

I have read *The Portents of the Coming of Antichrist*, by the Metropolitan of Riyazan, and have been thrown into trepidation over this Coming Beast.

Grigorii Talitzky had been burnt in Moscow for that he had lifted up his voice among the people anent the coming of Antichrist. Talitzky was a man of great intellect. And Vasilii Levin, captain in a regiment of dragoons, who had traveled with me from Lvov to Kiev in the year of seventeen hundred and eleven, and the priest Lebedka, the spiritual Father of the Most Illustrious Prince Menshikov, and the clerk Dokukin, and many others, hold like opinions concerning Antichrist.

In forests and in wildernesses men leap into great fires, immolating themselves, for fear of the Antichrist.

*   *   *

Outside the body there are contentions; within the body,—fears. I can see that we are perishing, yet we know of no help or salvation anywhere. We pray and fear. How many iniquities, how many wrongs, cry out to heaven and arouse the wrath and vengeance of God!

*   *   *

The mystery of iniquity is being consummated. The time has drawn near. Upon the very summit of evil do we all stand, yet there is no faith in us.

*   *   *

A certain Raskolnik spilt the sacrament of Christ underfoot, to the last drop, and did trample thereon.

*   *   *

Near Liubech there was a flight of locusts, lasting from noon till midnight, and upon their wings was writ: *The Wrath of God*.

*   *   *

The days are short and overcast. Old people say even the sun doth not shine as it used to.

*   *   *

Drinking, we did down a mighty deal of vodka. God sees, we drink out of fear, to forget ourselves.

*   *   *

The fear of death hath fallen upon me.

The end is at the threshold; the ax most sharp at the root is laid; the scythe of Death is swishing overhead.

*   *   *

Save, O Lord, the land of Russia! Intercede for us, and have compassion, Most Pure Mother of God!

*   *   *

The goodly and most saintly Simeon, who was a madman in Christ, as his end was drawing nigh, did say unto his friend, Deacon Ioannes: "Among the common folk and the tillers of the soil, who live in loving-kindness and with simple hearts, wronging none, but eating their bread in the sweat of their brows,—among such there are many truly great saints, inasmuch as I have seen them, arriving in town and taking communion, and they were like to unalloyed gold."

*   *   *

O, ye men, the martyrs of these our latter days, Christ dwelleth in ye now as if in His own body! The Lord loveth them that are sorrow-laden,—and ye are ever in tears. The Lord loveth them that are an hungred and athirst,—and there is but little ye have of meat and drink: some of ye have not even sufficient to make a loaf half-mixed with bran. He loveth them that suffer unjustly,—and among ye unjust suffering is not to be computed: some among ye can scarce keep your body and soul together. Languish not as ye endure, but render thanks to your Christ,—and he, upon His Resurrection, shall come as a guest to ye,—and not as a mere guest only, but to abide with ye inseparably. Christ is in ye, and shall be, and therefore ye should say: Amen!

III

THE DIARY OF FRÄULEIN ARNHEIM

With these words the diary of the Czarevich Alexei came to an end. He threw it into the fire in my presence.

31st of December, 1715.

To-day died the last Russian Czaritza, Martha Matvei-èvna, widow of Peter's half-brother, Fedor Alexeievich. At foreign courts she had long since been accounted dead,—ever since the death of her husband, for the duration of thirty-two years she was out of her mind, living like a recluse in her chambers, and never showed herself to any-body.

She was buried at even-dusk, with great pomp and cere-mony. The funerary procession proceeded between two rows of torches, placed along the whole way, from the home of the departed—she lived in the next house to us, near the Church of the All-Sorrowing—to the Cathedral of SS. Peter and Paul, across the Neva, over the ice. This is that very same route over which, a little over two months ago, Her Highness' body had been borne to the funereal frigate. Then they had been burying the first Czarevna of foreign birth; now they were burying the last Russian Czaritza.

The priests headed the procession in their magnificent vestments, with candles and censers, and with funebrial chant-ing. The coffin was borne upon a sleigh. The Privy Councilor, Tolstoi, walked behind it, bearing the crown, all studded with precious stones.

During this funeral the Czar had for the first time abro-gated the ancient Russian custom of keenings and lamenta-tions at the grave,—a strict order had been issued that none should weep loudly. Everybody walked along in silence. The night was calm. All one could hear was the crackling of burning resin, the crunch of feet on snow, and the funebrial chanting. A muffled horror was wafted upon one from this speechless procession. It seemed as if we were gliding along the ice after the dead woman,—ourselves as if we were dead, —into black, eternal darkness. It also seemed that, in bury-ing the last Russian Czaritza, the new Russia was burying the old,—that Peterburgh was burying Moscow.

The Czarevich, who had loved the departed as if she had been his own mother, is much shaken by this death. He deems it a bad portent for himself, for all his destiny. Several times during the funeral he said, in my ear:

"This is the end of everything!"

1st of January, 1716.

To-morrow morning, together with Baron Lewenwald, we are leaving Peterburgh, going directly to Riga, and through Danzig into Germany. I am forsaking Russia forever. This is my last night in the house of the Czarevich. In the evening I dropped in upon him to say good-by. By the way we parted I felt that I had come to love him, and that I would never forget him.

"Who knows?" said he. "Perhaps we may see each other again. I fain would pay you Europeans a visit. I have grown to iike the regions thereabouts. Things are well with you,—and free and jolly."

"Well, wherein is the hitch, Your Highness?"

He sighed deeply:

"I fain would get into paradise,—but my sins will not let me."

And he added, with his kindly smile:

"Well, the Lord be with you, Fräulein Juliana! Remember no evil of me, and give my best regards to the lands of Europe, and to your Leibnitz, that dear old man. Mayhap he is right: if God grant it, we may yet be of service to one another, instead of gobbling one another up!"

He embraced and kissed me with a brotherly tenderness. I burst into tears. Departing, I turned around to him once more and bestowed one final look in farewell. And again my heart contracted from premonition, as on that day when, in the dark, most dark, prophetic mirror, I had caught sight of the joined faces of Charlotta and Alexei, and it had appeared to me that they were both victims destined for some great suffering. She has perished. The turn is now his.

And I also recalled how, on the last evening in Rozhdestvenno, he had been standing in the dove-cote, on high, over the black, seemingly charred forest, against the red, seemingly ensanguined sky, all covered, as though he were clad therewith, with the white wings of the doves. Thus will he ever remain in my memory.

I have heard that prisoners, given their freedom, occasionally sigh for their prison. I now feel something of the sort toward Russia.

I commenced this diary with execrations. But I shall end it with benedictions. I shall say only what many others in Europe might probably say, were they to know Russia better: A mysterious land; a mysterious people.

BOOK FOUR

THE INUNDATION

I

THE Czar had been warned, when he was founding Peterburgh, that the site was uninhabitable because of inundations; that, twelve years before, the whole countryside, up to Nienshantz, had been flooded, and that such calamities were repeated almost every five years; the aborigines at the mouth of the Neva never built permanent houses, but merely small hovels; and when, by certain signs, an inundation was anticipated, they dismantled these dwellings, tied the logs and boards into rafts, and made them fast to trees; as for themselves, they sought escape on the Duderov Mountain. But to Peter the new town seemed a "Paradise,"—precisely because of the plenitude of waters. He himself loved bodies of water like some water fowl, and hoped that here, with greater expediency than elsewhere, he would be able to accustom his subjects to water.

Toward the end of October, in the year seventeen hundred and fifteen, ice started floating down the river and snow fell,—men took to sleighs, and expected an early and friendly winter. But there came a thaw. In a single night everything melted away. A wind from the sea drove up a fog,—a putrid and stifling yellow murk, from which men sickened.

"I pray to God to lead me out of this abysmal place," a certain old *boyarin* wrote to Moscow. "Verily, I apprehend falling sick; as soon as the thaw began, there came such a balsamic odor and such a murk, that one cannot go out of one's hut, and many die in this same Paradise because of the air."

The Sou'wester blew for a duration of nine days. Water in the Neva rose. The inundation began several times.

Peter issued *ukases*, which commanded the inhabitants to bring their belongings out of their cellars, to hold their boats

182

in readiness, and to drive their cattle to high places. But each time the water abated. The Czar, noticing that his *ukases* were alarming the people, and having concluded, through certain signs known to him alone, that the inundation would not be a great one, decided to pay no attention to the rises of the water.

On the sixth of November the first Assembly of the winter was to take place, at the house of the President of the College of the Admiralty, Fedor Matveievich Apraxin, on Wharf Street, alongside of the Winter Palace.

The evening preceding the water had again risen. People who knew foretold that this time there was no escaping calamity. They imparted the signs: the cockroaches in the palace were creeping from the cellar to the garret; the mice were scurrying away from the flour barns; Her Royal Majesty had dreamt of Peterburgh all in flames,—and as every one knows, to dream of a conflagration really means a flood. Not having recuperated entirely after her confinement, she was unable to accompany her spouse to the assembly, and implored him not to go.

Peter read in all eyes that ancient dread of water with which he had vainly contended all his life: "Expect woe where deep seas flow; misfortune mutters in deep waters; where water rides misfortune, too, abides; even the Czar cannot make the waters abate." . . .

On all sides they warned him, importuned him; and, finally, this had palled upon him so that he forbade them even to mention the inundation. He almost beat up with a cudgel the Head of Police, Devier. A certain little *mouzhik* had frightened the whole town with his prognostications,—that the water, now, would cover the tall alder-tree that stood on the Neva's bank, near the Church of the Trinity. Peter commanded the tree to be chopped down, and the little *mouzhik* to be punished by whipping, on this very place, to the sound of drums, and "a persuasive reassurance" to be delivered to the people.

Before the Assembly Apraxin came to the Czar and craved permission to hold it in the house proper, and not in the wing (where it was usually held), standing in the courtyard and connected with the main building by a narrow, glass-roofed gallery, which would not be without danger in the event of a sudden rise of water,—the guests might be cut off from the staircase leading to the upper chambers. Peter pondered a while, but decided to have things his own way, and ordered that the rout be held in the little house generally used for assemblies.

"An Assembly," the *ukase* explained, "is a free gathering or meeting, not only for amusement, but for business also."

The host was not obligated to meet the guests, or speed them, or regale them. "During the Assembly all are free to sit, walk about and play; and none shall hinder any other from doing the same, or make him or her abate; nor let any one even durst to be ceremonious, by arising, seeing people off, and the like, under penalty of the Great Eagle."

Both rooms,—in one they ate and drank, in the other they danced,—were spacious, but with exceedingly low ceilings. In the first the walls were faced with pictorial Delft tiles, as Dutch kitchens are; pewter utensils were placed about on shelves; the brick floor was strewn with sand; the enormous tiled stove was stoked till it was red-hot. Upon one of three long tables were the cold delicacies,—Flensburgh oysters, of which Peter was so fond, pickled lemons, sprats; upon a second were sets of draughts and chess; upon a third, packets of tobacco, baskets of clay churchwardens and short pipes, and mounds of fuses to light up with. The tallow candles glimmered dully among the swirls of smoke. The low-ceiled room, packed with people, reminded one of a skipper-frequented wine cellar somewhere in Plymouth or Rotterdam. The resemblance was completed by the great number of the English and Dutch ship-masters present. Their wives—rosy-cheeked, stout, as smooth of skin as though they had been glazed, with their feet stuck into warming-pans,—knitted away at socks, chatting and obviously feeling themselves right at home.

Peter, puffing away at the cannister tobacco in his clay pipe, of a species so abbreviated that they were styled nose-warmers, sipping away at his glass of *phlin,*—a kind of shandygaff, made of beer, mulled with cognac, rock-candy and lemon juice,—was deep in a game of draughts with the Archimandrite Theodosius.

Timorously shrinking, and slinking just like a beaten dog, Anton Manuilovich Devier approached the Czar,—this Head of Police was either a Portuguese or a Yid, with a muliebrile face and that expression of sweetness and weakness which is sometimes so peculiar to Southern countenances.

"The water is rising, Your Majesty."

"How much?"

"Two feet, eight and three-quarters inches."

"And the wind?"

"West-sou'west."

"Thou liest! I tested it myself but recently,—'twas sou'-west-south."

"It has changed," Devier protested, with an air as though he were personally to blame for the direction of the wind.

"No matter," decided Peter. "The water will soon begin to decrease. The burometer points to a let-up in the atmosphere. Never fear,—'twill not deceive!"

He believed in the infallibility of the barometer, even as in all mechanics.

"Your Majesty! Isn't there going to be some *ukase?*" Devier implored him piteously. "For, as it is, I know not what to do. People are greatly alarmed. Men who know say . . ."

The Czar looked at him intently.

"One of the said knowing ones I have already had soundly whipped near the Church of the Trinity,—and thou wilt get the like, if thou dost not pipe down. Get thee gone, thou fool!"

Devier, shrinking still more, like the wheedling little bitch Lisetta under a stick, instantly vanished.

"What, then, is thy opinion, Father, concerning this unusual pealing?" Peter turned to Theodosius, beginning anew the conversation about the information recently lodged, that, apparently, in the churches of Novgorod, the bells were rumbling of night through some miracle; rumor proclaimed that this tunding foreboded great misfortunes.

Fedosska stroked his scandent little beard, toyed a little with his double panagia bearing the Crucifixion and the portrait of the Czar, looked out of the corner of his eye at the Czarevich Alexei, who was sitting right alongside of them, puckered up one eye, as though he were taking aim,—and suddenly his whole diminutive face, the phiz of a flitter-mouse, was illuminated by the subtlest shyness:

"That which the said wordless rumbling teacheth men, any that hath a mind can discern: 'tis, plainly, from the Arch Adversary; the fiend is sobbing for that his seductive-ness is being cast out from the peoples of Russia,—from hysterically possessed women, from the Raskolniki, and from bigoted ancients, with whose correction Your Majesty is concerned."

And Fedosska led his speech around to his favorite subject, —upon a discourse on the harmfulness of monasticism.

"The monks are, truly, drones. They do flee from taxes, that they may eat their bread without paying therefor. But what profit is there in that to society? They transform their civic status into nothingness, ascribing it to the vanity of this world,—the which is even attested by the proverb: He who hath taken the tonsure, say they, had been working for the Czar of this world, but now has gone to work for the Czar of Heaven. They do lead a brutish life in their 'deserts.' But what they cannot discern is that in Russia, because of its cold climate, there can be no real deserts. . . ."

Alexei comprehended that this speech about bigots was a stone shied over his fence. He got up. Peter looked at him and said:

"Keep thy seat."

The Czarevich sat down submissively, casting down his eyes,—with, as he himself felt, a "hypocritical" mien.

Fedosska was in fine mettle; encouraged by the attentive-ness of the Czar,—who had taken out a note-book and was making in it notes for future *ukases*,—he kept on proposing ever new measures, apparently for reformation, but in reality, as it seemed to the Czarevich, for a definite extirpation of monasticism in Russia.

"Establish well-regulated hospitals for retired dragoons in the monasteries,—also schools of ciphering and geometry; in the nunneries,—reformatories for wayward children; the nuns shall earn their keep by weaving for manufac-tories. . . ."

The Czarevich strove not to listen; but detached words reached him, like imperious shouts:

"The sale of honey and oil in churches should most decidedly be put a stop to. The burning of candles before ikons placed outside the churches is most decidedly to be forbidden. Chapels are to be demolished. Holy relics are not to be brought out. Prohibit the trumping-up of miracles. Beggars shall be taken under arrest, and mercilessly beaten with cudgels. . . ."

The shutters on the window began to tremble under an onslaught of the wind. A breath of air went through the room, making the flames of the candles sway. It was as though an incomputable adverse force was advancing to attack and was battering at the house. And to Alexei there seemed to be, in the words of Fedosska, the same evil force, the same attack of a storm from the West.

In the second room, set aside for the dances, panels woven of worsted graced the walls; there were mirrors in the spaces between doors and windows; there were wax candles in candelabra. Musicians, with deafening wind instruments, were seated on a small dais. The ceiling, with an allegorical picture, *A Journey to the Island of Love*, was so low that the naked loves, plump of buttocks and thighs, almost touched the wigs.

The ladies, when there was no dancing going on, sat around like so many deaf mutes, bored and wasting away; when dancing, they hopped about like clock-work dolls tightly wound up; they answered questions with "ay" and "nay"; if compliments were tendered them, they eyed one askance, like wild creatures. The daughters seemed, for all the world, to be stitched to their mammas' skirts, while on the faces of their mammas one could plainly read: " 'Twould be better were we to put our maidens into the midst of deep waters, rather than bring them to these here assemblies!"

Wilhelm Ivannovich Mons was delivering a compliment (translated and stolen from a German book) to that same Nastenka who was in love with a midshipman, and who, during the Festival of Venus, had been so tenderly weeping over her *billet-doux* in the Summer Garden:

"Through oft-repeated contemplation of your fair self, which is verily like that of an angel, I have come to experi-

ence such a desire to know you that I can no longer conceal
the same, but am compelled to acquaint you with the facts,
with all due deference. I fain would with all my heart, that
you, as my sovereign mistress, might have found in me a
person so well versed that I, with my ways and pleasant discourses, might prove entirely pleasing to you, my sovereign
mistress; but inasmuch as Nature has favored me but little in
this regard, deign to receive all I can offer,—my devoted
faithfulness and service. . . ."

Nastenka was not listening to him—the sound of the monotonously humming words was inclining her to sleep. Subsequently she complained to her aunt against her gallant: "He
seems to be saying something and apparently even in Russian,
yet I cannot make out a word of it, for the life of me."

Ushka Proscurov, son of a petty government clerk in Moscow, and now a secretary of the Ambassador of France,—a
young man who had long sojourned in Europe, and had there
been metamorphosed into a *Monsieur George,* a perfect *petit
maître* and *galant'uomo* was singing for the ladies the fashionable *chansonette* about the peruke-maker Frison, and the
street trollop, Dodun:

> *La Dodun dit à Frison:*
> *Coiffez-moi avec adresse.*
> *Je prétends avec raison*
> *Inspirer de la tendresse.*
> *Tignonnez, tignonnez, bichonnez moi.*

He recited, as well, certain Russian verses concerning the
charms of life in Paris:

> Beautiful site, thou Seine's shore so dear!
> Where manners bucolic dare not even appear,
> Inasmuch as all hold there to a most noble code—
> Verily, of gods and goddesses art thou the native abode;
> My heart can forget not, nor my mind's eye help seeing
> Thee, as long as on this earth I have my being!

Aged Moscow *boyarin,* foes of the new customs, were sitting apart, warming themselves at the stove, and carrying on
conversation in half-hints, half-riddles.

"And how, my dear sir, doth thee like life in Peterbur*kh?*"
"May the ashes of the grave overcome ye, and this life of

yours! Your new-fangled cheats and your German news-sheets! From the so-great compliments hereabouts, and tail-waggings, and cates from overseas, things are growing black before my eyes!"

"Well, what wouldst thou have one do, brother? One can't leap into the sky, nor bury one's self underground."

"Thy burthen lug, till thy pit be dug."

"Whether one crack or no,—yet bend one must."

"Oh, oh, and oh again,—but my poor sides do me pain; my sides they do ache, yet no rest must I take!"

Mons was whispering in the ear of Nastenka a madrigal he had just composed:

> Sans love, sans passion's fire,
> All our days are but cold;
> We must sigh, and aspire
> That love's sweets be our gold.
> Life doth sad prove
> If we do not love.

Suddenly she imagined that the ceiling was swaying as during an earthquake, and that the naked loves were falling right on her head. She cried out. Wilhelm Ivannovich calmed her: 'Twas but the wind; 'twas only the canvas of the picture, nailed to the ceiling and bellying in the wind, that was swaying. Again the shutters shook,—but this time so that everybody turned around to look, in fear.

But a *Polonaise* struck up, the couples began to whirl,—and the music drowned out the storm. The chilled little ancients alone, warming near their stove, heard the wind howling in the chimney, and they whispered, and sighed, and shook their heads; in the sounds of the storm, still more ominous through the sounds of the music, they could hear: "Expect woe where deep seas flow; misfortune mutters in deep waters."

Peter, continuing his conversation with Fedosska, questioned him concerning the heresy of the ikonoclasts of Moscow, Fomka the barber and Mitka the leech. Both heresiarchs, in propagating their teaching, referred to the recent *ukases* of the Czar: "Nowadays, here in Moscow, every one is free,—for which glory be to God!" said they. "Whatever faith one chooses, that's the one he believes in."

"According to their—this Fomka's and Mitka's—teaching," Theodosius was saying, with a smile so ambiguous that one could not tell whether he were condemning or condoning the heresy, "the true faith is to be learned only through holy writings and good works, but by no means through miracles and human traditions. One can find salvation through all faiths, in the words of the Apostle: 'In every nation he that feareth Him, and worketh righteousness, is accepted with him.'" [40]

"Quite reasonable," remarked Peter, and the smile of the monk was reflected in a precisely similar smile of the Czar,— they understood one another without any need of words.

"As for the ikons—teach they—they be the works of man's hands,—therefore plain idols," Theodosius went on. "How can painted panels ever work miracles? Throw such a one in the fire,—it will burn, even as any other wood. 'Tis not before ikons that we should bow down to the ground, but to God up in heaven. And whoever hath bestowed such long ears upon the accepted saints of God, now that they can hear, in heaven, the supplications of those on earth? 'And if,' say they, 'some man's son be slain with a knife or a stone, how could the father of the slain love the said stick or knife? Even so,—how can God love the tree upon which His Son hath been crucified? And as for the Mother of God,' they query, 'wherefore do ye revere her so? She, now, is like unto a common sack, filled with precious stones and seed pearls; but when the said stones of great price have been emptied out of the sack, what value and reverence doth it deserve?' And concerning the Mystery of the Eucharist they reason: 'How can Christ be divided and distributed everywhere, and consumed during all the masses, when there is such a huge number of them being held all over the world, all at the same time hour? And, too, how can bread be transmuted into the Body of the Lord through the prayers of the priests? As for the priests, there be all sorts of them,— sots and lechers, and downright evil-doers. Therefore, this thing cannot be,—and we do have strong doubts thereof: sniff at it,—and it hath the odor of bread; likewise the Blood, through the witness of the senses given us, turns out to be simply red wine. . . .'"

" 'Tis shameful for us of the Orthodox faith e'en to listen to such heretical indecencies!" the Czar stopped Fedosska. The latter fell silent, but kept on smiling,—ever more brazenly, ever more maliciously.

The Czarevich lifted up his eyes and stealthily glanced at his father. It seemed to him that Peter was abashed: he was no longer smiling; his face was stern, almost wrathful, but, with all this, helpless, distraught. Had he not himself just accepted as reasonable the basis of the heresy? Having accepted the premise, how could one not accept the conclusions as well? It was easy enough to interdict,—but how to contradict? Clever was the Czar, but was not the monk cleverer, and was he not leading the Czar—as an evil leader of the blind might—to a pit?

Thus thought Alexei, and the crafty smile of Fedosska was reflected in a precisely similar smile,—this time, however, not the father's, but the son's: the Czarevich and Fedosska also understood one another now, without the need of words.

"There's no need to wonder at Fomka and Mitka," Mikhailo Petrovich Avramov suddenly blurted out, amid the general awkward silence. "As the piper pipes, so the dancers dance; whither the shepherd goeth, the sheep go also. . . ." And he looked point-blank at Fedosska. The latter understood the hint, and, in his malevolence, resembled a hissing, coiled-up snake, about to strike.

At this moment something struck the shutters,—as though thousands of hands had begun to beat upon it; then this something began to squeal, to howl, to keen,—and then, somewhere far off, died away. The force of the adversary was ever more ominously coming to the onslaught and breaking into the house.

Devier ran out of doors every quarter of an hour to learn about the rise of the water. There was but ill news. The small rivers Miya and Fontannaya were coming out of their banks. The whole town was in terror.

Anton Manuilovich lost his head. Several times he drew near the Czar, trying to catch his eye, to draw his attention; but Peter, engrossed in conversation, paid no heed to him. Finally, unable to restrain himself, Devier with desperate resolve bent to the Czar's very ear and babbled out:

"Your Majesty! The water . . ."

Peter turned around to him in silence and with a quick, seemingly involuntary movement, slapped his cheek. Devier experienced nothing save strong pain,—an everyday affair. " 'Tis flattering," Peter's fledglings were wont to say, "to be beaten by such a Sovereign, who, during the same minute, will beat one and then extend favors to one."

And Peter, with a calm face, as though nothing untoward had happened, turning to Avramov asked why, up to the present, the work of the astronomer Huyghens; entitled *The Contemplation of the Universe, or a Consideration of the Celestial and Terrestrial Globes,* had not been printed. Mikhailo Petrovich was abashed at first, but, immediately recovering himself and looking the Czar straight in the eyes, answered firmly:

"The said tome is most ungodly; 'twas not written with ink, but with charcoal out of hell, and is fit only for a speedy burning at the stake. . . ."

"What ungodliness does it contain, then?"

"The earth's revolution around the sun is presupposed, and a multiplicity of worlds, and all these worlds, 'twould seem, are but other earths, even like to this one,—and there be men upon them, and fields, and meadows, and forests, and beasts, and all other things, even as on our earth. And thus, having insinuated himself, he strives everywhere, craftily, to glorify and confirm nature,—that is, self-existent life. As for the Creator and God, he reduces Him to non-existence. . . ."

A dispute sprang up. The Czar was proving that "Copernicus' Chart of the Universe explains easily and conveniently all the phenomena of the planets." Under the protection of the Czar and of Copernicus ever more daring thoughts were expressed.

"Nowadays all philosophy has become mechanical!" Alexander Vassilievich Kikin, a Councilor of the Admiralty, suddenly declared. "Nowadays 'tis believed that the whole universe is in its greatness as a watch is in its smallness, and that everything within it works through a certain established motion, which depends upon an orderly disposition of atoms. The mechanics are one and the same everywhere. . . ."

"Insane, atheistical reasoning! A corrupt and infirm basis

of thought!" Avramov waxed horrified, but none heeded him. Each one tried to outdo the other in flaunting his freedom of thought.

"A most ancient philosopher, one Dicæarchos, wrote that man has his being in the body, while the soul is a mere incidental and an empty name, signifying nothing," the Vice-Chancellor Shaphirov informed the gathering.

"Through the microscopium there have been detected, in the male seed, certain animals, on the manner of frogs or tadpoles," Ushka Proscurov smiled scoffingly,—with such evil joy that the deduction was clear: There was no soul whatsoever. Following the example of all Parisian dandies, he had his own "bit of a philosophy,— *une petite philosophie*," and he gave expression to it with the same elegancy with which he hummed the little song about the peruke-maker, with "*Tignonnez, tignonnez, bichonnez moi*" for its burden.

"According to the opinion of Leibnitz, we are but hydraulic thinking machines. An oyster is inferior to us in intelligence. . . ."

"Thou liest,—'tis not inferior to thee!" some one remarked, but Ushka continued, unperturbed:

"An oyster is inferior to us in intelligence, having its soul stuck to a shell, and for this reason it hath no need of five senses. But perhaps there are, in other worlds, beings endowed with ten or more senses, to such a degree superior to us that they wonder at Newton and Leibnitz as much as we wonder at the actions of the apes and spiders. . . ."

The Czarevich listened, and it seemed to him that in this conversation there was taking place, with ideas, the same thing that took place with snow during a Peterburgh thaw: everything was crawling apart, melting, becoming corrupt, turning into mire and mud, under the breath of a rotten wind from the West. A doubt of everything, a negation of all, without retrospection, without restraint, was on the increase, like the waters of the Neva, held back by the wind and threatening with an inundation.

"There, that'll be enough of lying!" concluded Peter, rising. "He that believeth not in God is a madman, or a fool from birth. He that hath eyes must recognize the Creator from His works. As for the godless ones, they bring shame upon a state, and must under no circumstances be tolerated therein, inasmuch as they undermine the foundation of the laws whereon oaths, and the oath of allegiance to the authorities, are based."

"The reason for impieties," Fedosska could not restrain himself, in spite of everything, from putting in, "does it not lie in hypocritical zealotry, rather than in godlessness? For the atheists themselves proclaim that God should be preached among the people; otherwise, say they, the people will mistrust those in authority. . . . "

Now the whole house was trembling with a ceaseless tremor from the onslaught of the storm. But all had so grown used to these sounds that none noticed them. The Czar's face was calm, and, by his air, he reassured all.

Some one had set the rumor afloat that the direction of the wind had veered, and that there was hope for a decrease of water soon.

"You see?" said Peter, growing merry. "There was e'en no need of being chicken-hearted. Never fear,—the burometer will not deceive!"

He passed into the adjoining hall and took part in the dancing.

When the Czar was merry, he infatuated and infected all with his merriment. When dancing, he would hop, stamp his feet, and perform certain intricate figures—*caprioli*—with such animation that the most laggard were overcome with a desire to join the dance.

In the English contra-dance the lady of the first couple would invent a new figure. The Princess Cherkasskaya kissed her partner, Peter Andreievich Tolstoi, and pulled his wig down over his nose, all the ladies having to repeat this after her, while during this each gallant stood as motionless as a pillar. Bustle, laughter and pranks sprang up. They were all as mischievously spry as schoolboys,—and the gayest of all was Peter.

Only the little ancients sat, as before, in their corner, hearkening to the deep howling of the wind, and whispered, and sighed, and shook their heads.

"The giddy dancing of women," one of them recalled a fulmination against dancing in the ancient books of the Holy

Fathers, "doth alienate men from God, and doth draw them toward the very bottom of hell. The laugh-makers shall change to unconsolable weeping; the dancers shall be hung up by their navels. . . ."

The Czar approached the little ancients and invited them to take part in the dancing. In vain did they decline, pleading their ignorance of the art and all sorts of ailments,—rheumatism, asthma, podagra,—the Czar insisted upon having his way, and would listen to no excuses. The musicians struck up a pompous, quaint Grandfather's Dance,—the *Grossvater*. The little ancients—they had purposely been assigned the liveliest of the young women—at first barely stirred, stumbling, becoming confused and confusing others; but, when the Czar threatened them with the penalizing glass of the awful *pertzovka*, they began to leap as sprightly as the youngsters. But then, when the dance was over, they keeled over into their chairs, half-dead from fatigue, grunting, moaning and oh'ing.

They had scarcely had a chance to rest, when the Czar ordered a new dance, still more difficult,—a chain-dance. Thirty couples, tied by handkerchiefs, followed the musician, —a little hunchback, who went hopping ahead with his fiddle.

At first they made a circuit of both halls of the wing. Then, through the gallery, they stepped into the main building, and thus, through the whole house, from room to room, from staircase to staircase, from floor to floor did the dance whirl, with shouting, hallooing, whistling and laughter. The hunchback, scraping away on his fiddle and leaping madly, twisted his face into such funny phizzes as though the fiend had taken possession of him. After him, in the first couple, followed the Czar; after the Czar, the others, so that it seemed that he was leading them, as bound captives, while he himself, the Czar-Titan, was led and twirled along by an imp.

Returning to the wing, they beheld in the gallery some people running to meet them, waving their arms and shouting in terror:

"The water! The water! The water!"

The leading couples halted,—those behind flew against them and crushed them. Everything was thrown into confusion. They collided, fell, tugged and tore at the handkerchiefs with which they were tied. The men swore,—the ladies squealed. The human chain was torn. The greater number, together with the Czar, dashed back, toward the exit from the gallery into the main building. The others, who were fewer, and were ahead, and nearer the opposite entrance into the wing, impetuously started to go where every one else was going; but they had scarcely managed to reach, by running, the middle of the gallery when the shutter on one of the windows began to crack and give way; it fell down with a crash and a shower of fragments of glass, and the water, in a turbulent torrent, lashed through the window. At the same time, the pressure of air from below, from the cellar, began to raise the floor, breaking it up and making it buckle, with reverberations and crashes which were like to volleys of cannon-fire.

Peter, from the other end of the gallery, was shouting to those who had fallen behind:

"Back,—back into the wing! Be not afraid,—I'll send boats after you!"

They could not hear his words but understood his signs, and stopped.

Two people alone continued their flight over the flooded floor. One of them was Fedosska. He had almost run up to the exit where Peter was waiting for him when suddenly a broken floor-board yielded,—Fedosska fell through and began to drown. A stout woman, the wife of a Dutch skipper, picking up her skirts, jumped over the monk's head; over his black cowl flashed her fat calves in red stockings. The Czar rushed to his aid, grabbed him by his shoulders, dragged him out, lifted him up and carried him off in his arms, like a little child,—shivering, and flapping the black wings of his cassock, from which the water ran in streams, he resembled an enormous, dripping bat.

The hunchback with the fiddle, having run up to the middle of the gallery, had also fallen through, vanishing in the water; then he bobbed up and started swimming. But at that very moment the middle section of the ceiling crashed down and crushed him under the ruins.

Thereupon the handful remaining,—there were some ten of

them,—seeing that they were definitely cut off from the main building, rushed back to the wing, as to a last haven.

But even here the water was catching up with them. One could hear the waves plashing under the very windows. The shutters creaked and cracked, ready to tear loose from their hinges. Through the broken panes the water penetrated through the cracks, woozing in, spurting, gurgling, running down the walls, flooding the floor.

Almost all were bewildered. Only Peter Andreievich Tolstoi and Wilhelm Ivannovich Mons had retained their presence of mind. They had found a small door, hidden behind some hangings. It revealed a small step-ladder, leading to the garret. Everybody ran thither. The gallants, even the most amiable, now that death was staring them in the face, were not concerned for the ladies; they cursed and shoved them,—each one thinking only of himself.

It was dark in the garret. Groping their way among beams, boards, empty kegs, and boxes, they huddled in the farthest corner of all, somewhat protected from the wind by the projection of the stove chimney, which was still warm; they snuggled up against it and for some time sat thus in the darkness,—overwhelmed, stupefied by fear. The ladies, in their light ball dresses, felt their teeth chattering from the cold. Finally Mons decided to go below, to see if he could not find help.

Below the hostlers, wading in water up to their knees, were bringing into the hall their master's horses, which had almost drowned in their stalls. The Assembly hall was transformed into a stable. The muzzles of the horses were reflected in the mirrors. Tatters of the torn canvas of *A Journey to the Island of Love* dangled and fluttered from the ceiling. The naked loves fluttered about as if in mortal terror. Mons gave some money to the hostlers. They obtained for him a lantern, a demijohn of exceedingly vile vodka, and several rough, short coats, lined with wool. He learned from them that there was no exit from the wing: the gallery was demolished, the yard covered over with water; they, the hostlers themselves, would have to escape to the garret; they were waiting for boats, but, evidently, would have to wait a mighty long while. Subsequently it turned out that the boats which had been sent off by the Czar could not draw up at the wing,—the courtyard was surrounded by a high fence, while its only gates were blocked up with the débris of a fallen building.

Mons returned to the people sitting in the garret. The light of the lantern put a little heart into them. The men drank off some of the vodka. The women muffled themselves up in the sheep-lined coats.

The night dragged on without end. Under them the whole house would quiver occasionally from the onslaught of the waters, like a frail vessel on the verge of wrecking. Above them the hurricane was flying by,—now with frenzied roaring and thudding, like a herd of beasts, now with piercing whistling and whizzing, like a flight of titanic birds,—and tearing tiles off the roof. And at times it seemed that, at any moment, it would tear off the roof itself, and carry everything away. In the voices of the storm they thought they heard the voices of the drowning. From moment to moment they expected the whole town to topple.

From fright one of the ladies, the wife of the Danish resident, got such pains in her abdomen—she was pregnant—that the poor little thing cried as if she were under the knife. She feared a miscarriage.

Ushka Proscurov was praying to the Holy Father, Nikola, the miracle-worker, and the most Saintly Sergei, imploring their aid and mercy. And one could not believe that this was that same free-thinker who had, only a short while ago, been striving to prove that there was no such thing as a soul.

Mikhailo Petrovich Avramov was also quaking,—but, at the same time, he was deriving a malicious joy from it all.

"One can't dispute with God! Righteous is His wrath. This town shall be wiped off the face of the earth, even as Sodom and Gomorrah were. 'And God looked upon the earth, and, behold, it was corrupt; for all flesh had corrupted his way upon the earth. And God said . . . The end of all flesh is come before me; . . . And, behold, I, even I, do bring a flood of waters upon the earth, to destroy all flesh, wherein *is* the breath of life, from under the heaven; *and* every thing that *is* in the earth shall die.'" [41]

And, listening to these prophecies, his hearers experienced

a new, unknown horror, as though the end of the world, the Dread Judgment Day, were imminent.

Through the little dormer window the glow of a conflagration sprang up against the black sky. Through the noise of the hurricane they heard a bell,—the sounding of a tocsin. The hostlers, who had arrived from below, said that the huts of the laborers and the rope warehouses in the Admiralty borough nearby were burning. Despite water being so near a fire was especially to be dreaded with the wind blowing so hard,— the flaming fire-brands were carried all over the city, which might, at any minute, blaze up on all sides. It was perishing between two elements,—burning and drowning at the same time. The prophecy of "Peterburgh shall be desolate" was being fulfilled.

Toward dawn the storm abated. In the transparent gray of a dull day the gallants in wigs covered with dust and cobwebs, the ladies in *robes rondes* and crinolines on "the Versailles manner," under sheep-skin jerkins, their faces turned blue from the cold, appeared as apparitions to each other.

Mons looked out of the garret window, and saw, where once the town had stood, a shoreless lake. It was agitated,— as though not only on its surface, but down to its very bottom, it were seething, burbling, and coming to a boil, like water in a caldron over a strong fire. This lake was the Neva, —as mottled as the skin of a snake's belly,—yellow, tawny, black, with whitecaps; tired, but still riotous, fearful, under the dreadful and low-hanging sky, which was as gray as earth.

Broken barques, overturned boats, beams, boards, roofs, the skeletons of whole houses, trees torn up by the roots, the bodies of animals,—were all whirling along upon the waves.

And pitiful, in the midst of this exulting element, were the traces of human life,—the towers, spires, cupolas and roofs of the inundated houses, sticking up out of the water here and there.

Mons saw on the Neva, in the distance, opposite the Fortress of SS. Peter and Paul, several oar-driven galleys and boyers. He picked up from the floor a long pole—such as are used to make pigeons take to wing—tied to it Nastenka's neckerchief of red silk, thrust the pole out the window, and fell to waving it,—signaling to summon help. One of the boats drew away from the others, and, cutting across the Neva, began approaching the little house once used for Assemblies.

These boats were accompanying the Czar's sloop.

All night had Peter toiled, without rest, rescuing people from water and fire. Like a common fireman he clambered up burning buildings; fire had scorched off his hair; he had barely escaped being crushed by the fall of a huge beam. In helping to drag the humble belongings of the poor out of their cellar dwellings, he had stood in water up to his waist, and had been chilled to the bone. He suffered with all,—and put heart into all. Everywhere the Czar appeared the work was tackled with such speed and team-work that water and fire gave way before it.

The Czarevich was in the same boat with his father,—but every time he made an attempt to be helpful in some way Peter declined this help, as if with squeamishness.

When the fire had been put out, and the water had begun to go down, the Czar recalled that it was time to go home to his wife, who had passed the whole night in mortal apprehension for her spouse. On his way home he felt a desire to approach the Summer Garden, to see what devastations the water had wrought.

The gallery over the Neva was half-ruined,—but Venus was unscathed. The pediment of the statue was submerged, so that the goddess seemed to be standing on the water; the Foam-Engendered was emerging from the waves,—but not blue and caressing ones, as of yore, but ominous, dark, heavy, seemingly of iron—the waves of the Styx.

At her very feet, upon the marble, something showed darkly. Peter looked through his spy-glass and saw that this was a human being. By an *ukase* of the Czar's, some soldier was on sentry-duty day and night near the precious statue. Caught by the water, yet not daring to flee, he had clambered up on the pediment of Venus, had huddled close to her legs, embracing them, and must have perched thus the whole night through,—benumbed by the cold, half-dead from fatigue.

The Czar hurried to his aid. Standing at the helm, he

steered the sloop against the waves and the wind. Suddenly an enormous billow swept up, lashed over the board, spattering all with its spume, and careened the vessel so that it seemed as if it would keel over. But Peter was a helmsman of experience. Gaining purchase against the poop, putting all the weight of his body against the rudder, he was conquering the fury of the waves, and with a firm hand steered straight toward his goal.

The Czarevich looked up at his father, and suddenly, for some reason, recalled that which he had once heard his tutor Viyazemsky say—they had both been half-seas over when the conversation took place:

"Theodosius used to sing, with his choristers, in the presence of Batiushka: *Where it is the will of God, the course of nature is overcome,*[42] and other such verses; and they sing thus for to flatter thy father,—'tis to his liking to be likened to God; but what he cannot understand is that the course of nature can be changed not only by God, but by the fiends also,—there are also fiend-miracles!"

In a plain skipper's jacket, in high leather boots, with his hair fluttering,—his hat had just been torn off by the wind,— the titanic Helmsman was gazing upon the flooded city,—and there was no consternation, nor fear, nor pity upon his face, which was calm, firm, just as though it were carven out of stone,—as though, in reality, there was in this man something not human, which held sway over men and the elements, which was as powerful as fate. Men would settle down, reconciled, the winds would quiet down, the waves would surge back,—and there would be a city where he had commanded a city to be, inasmuch as *the course of nature is overcome,— where it is the will of—*

"The will of whom?" the Czarevich asked himself, without daring to finish,—"of God or of the Fiend?"

A few days later, when the usual appearance of Peterburgh had almost concealed the traces of the inundation, Peter wrote in a jocose epistle to one of his fledglings:

"Last week a West-Sou'west wind drove up such a mass of water as, so they say, has never been seen before. At one time the floor of my chambers was more than 21 inches under water; while in the pleasance and in the street opposite men rowed about freely in boats. And it was most droll to see people perching in the trees and upon the roofs of houses,—not only men, but women as well,—as if it had been the Flood. The water, although it was most high, did not work any great harm."

The letter was dated: *From Paradise*.

II

Peter fell ill. He had contracted a cold during the inundation, when, in salvaging the goods of the poor from the cellars, he had had to stand up to his waist in water. At first he paid no attention to his illness, trying to down it on his feet; but on the fifteenth of November he took to his bed, and his physician, Blumentrost, announced that the life of the Czar was in danger.

During these days the fate of Alexei was being decided. On the very day of the funeral of the Crown Princess, the twenty-eighth of October, having returned from the Cathedral of SS. Peter and Paul to the house of his son for the funeral repast, Peter had given him a letter, "A Declaration to My Son," in which he demanded the latter's immediate reformation, under threat of bitter displeasure and deprivation of his succession to the throne.

"I know not what to do," the Czarevich said to his intimates, "whether to embrace poverty, and hide with beggars for a while, or to withdraw into some monastery and dwell there with the petty clergy, or to depart for some kingdom where refugees are sheltered and not given up . . . to none?"

"Join the monks," urged Alexander Kikin, the Councilor of the Admiralty,—long an accomplice and confidant of Alexei. "The cowl is not nailed on to the head,—it can e'en be taken off. Thou wilt find peace when thou shalt have left all this behind thee. . . ."

"I rescued thee from thy father and the headsman's block, one might say," Prince Vassilii Dolgorukyi told him. "Now thou canst rejoice,—thou wilt not have aught to do with anything. Submit e'en a thousand letters as to giving up the throne. One can never tell what will turn up; there is an old proverb: The snail is on its way,—but when will it get here? This is no contract with a demurrer."

" 'Tis a good thing that thou dost not want the succession," Prince Uriah Troubetzkoy consoled him. "Just think,—does gold prevent tears from flowing? . . ."

The Czarevich held many discussions with Kikin concerning a flight into foreign lands: "To the end that he might remain there somewhere, for no other purpose save to live there in peace, withdrawn from everything."

"Should there be an opportunity," Kikin advised him, "go thou off to Vienna, to the Kaiser. There they will not give thee up. The Kaiser has said that he will receive thee like his own son. Or else,—go to the Pope, or, if it pleases thee, to the French court. There even kings are given protection, and 'twould be no great matter for them to keep thee. . . ."

The Czarevich listened to their councils, but could not come to any decision, and lived on from day to day, biding "the will of God."

Suddenly everything changed. Peter's death threatened an overturn not only in the destinies of Russia alone, but of the whole world. He who had but yesterday wanted to hide himself among beggars might to-morrow ascend to the throne.

Fair-weather friends suddenly surrounded the Czarevich; they came together, whispering, talking in hushed tones.

"Bide and wait,—something is bound to turn up."

"All things come to them that wait; they will come, as sure as fate."

"We shall say our say yet!"

"E'en mice can drag a dead cat to its burial."

On the night between the first and the second of December the Czar felt so bad that he commanded his spiritual father, Theodosius, to be summoned; he confessed, and took the Viaticum. Ekaterina and Menshikov did not leave the room of the sick man. The Residents of foreign courts, Russian ministers, and Senators, passed whole nights in the chambers of the Winter Palace. When, in the morning, the Czarevich arrived to learn the state of the sovereign, the latter would not receive him; but, by the sudden speechlessness of the throng that made way for him, by the slavish bows, by their searching glances, by their pale faces,—especially those

of his stepmother and the Most Illustrious Prince Menshikov, the Czarevich gathered how near was that which had
always seemed to him so distant,—well-nigh impossible.
His heart sank, and his breath was cut short,—he himself
knew not why: whether from joy or from terror.

That same day, in the evening, he paid a visit to Kikin
and for a long while conversed with him privily. Kikin lived
on the very outskirts of the town, directly opposite the
Okhten Boroughs, not far from the Smolnii Court. From
there he rode home.

The sleigh raced through the deserted pine forest and
through the broad streets, just as deserted, resembling forest
trails, with a barely noticeable row of dark log-cabins,
snowed under drifts. The moon was not visible, but the air
was saturated with vivid lunar sparks and needles. The snow
was not falling, but swirling up in pillars in the wind, and
smoldered like smoke. And the radiant, lunar snow-storm
sparkled, like foam, in the bluishly turbid sky, as if it were
wine in a chalice.

He breathed in the frosty air with enjoyment. He felt gay,
as though in his soul, too, a radiant snow-storm were playing,
—riotous, tipsy, and making one tipsy. And even as there was
a moon behind the snow-storm, so, behind his gayety was a
thought which he himself did not perceive as yet, which he
was afraid to perceive; yet he sensed that it was because of
this thought that he was so tipsy, afraid, and gay.

In the rime-covered windows of the huts, under the icicles
hanging down from the roofs, like tipsy eyes under hoary
eyebrows, little lights glowed dimly through the bluish lunar
murk. "In there, perhaps," the thought came to him, "they
are drinking to me,—*to the Hope of Russia!*" And he grew
still merrier.

Upon returning home he sat down at the grate with its
smoldering embers, and ordered his valet Aphanasiich to prepare some hot punch. It was dark,—no candles had been
brought in, since Alexei was rather fond of meditations at
dusk. In the rosy reflection of the embers there suddenly
began to quiver the blue heart of the spirits-flame. The lunar
snow-storm peeped in at the windows with its blue eyes
through the transparent flowers of the frost, and it seemed

that, behind them, there was also pulsating a living, enormous, blue, tipsy flame.

Alexei was telling Aphanasiich of his conversation with Kikin,—it had consisted of a whole plan for a conspiracy, in the event of his having to flee; and then, in the event of the death of his father, which he sensed would take place soon (the Czar, now, was afflicted with epilepsy and such people are not long-lived), he would return to Russia from foreign parts. The ministers and senators,—Tolstoi, Golovkin, Shaphirov, Apraxin, Streshnev, the Dolgorukyis,—were all friends of his, would all adhere to him,—Bour in Poland, too, and the Archimandrite Pechersky in the Ukraine, and Sheremetev, with the main army:

"Everything from the frontier of Europe would be mine!"

Aphanasiich listened with his usual obdurate and glum aspect, as if to say: Sweet is thy song, but where wilt thou perch?

"And Menshikov?" he asked, when Alexei had finished.

"Why, spit Menshikov through on a stake!"

The old man shook his head:

"Wherefore, my master Czarevich, dost thou speak so provokingly? Well, now, suppose some one were to eavesdrop, and convey the news where it belongs? 'Curse not the king, no not in thy thought; and curse not the rich in thy bedchamber; for a bird of the air shall carry the voice. . . .' " [43]

"There, that will be enough of thy grousing!" The Czarevich waved him away with a gesture of vexation,—yet, at the same time, with unrestrainable gayety. Aphanasiich lost his temper:

" 'Tis not grousing I am, but talking sense! Praise the dream when it comes true. Thou art pleased, Highness, to build castles in Hispania. Thou wilt not listen to humble folk such as I. Thou dost put thy trust in others, but they are deceiving thee. Judas Tolstoi, and Kikin the atheist,—they are betrayers! Beware, master: thou wilt not be the first they have gobbled up. . . ."

"I would spit upon them all,—if only the rabble be with me!" exclaimed the Czarevich. "When the time comes and my father will no longer be, I shall whisper to the Archpresbyters; the Archpresbyters will whisper to the parish priests;

while the rural priests will whisper to their parishioners. Then they shall make me Czar, even though they may not want to!"

The old man kept silent, still with the same obdurate and glum air: Sweet is thy song, but where wilt thou perch?

"Why art thou silent?" asked the Czarevich.

"What am I to say, Czarevich? Thou art thy own master; yet I am not the one that would counsel thee to fly from thy Batiushka."

"For what reason?"

"Why, for this: if it comes off well, well and good; but if it does not, thou wilt be the first to be wroth with me. I have taken all sorts of things from thee, as it is. Humble, unenlightened we,—yet our skins, too, tender be. . . ."

"Well, come what may, see to it, Aphanasiich, that thou tell no one of all this. Thou art the only one who knows this about me,—save Kikin. Shouldst thou tell, thou wilt not be believed; I shall deny everything stoutly, but thee they'll put to the torture. . . ."

The Czarevich had dragged the torture in in order to tease the old man.

"But I say, master, when thou shalt be Czar, since thou choosest to speak and act so,—wilt thou be frightening thy faithful servants with the torture then?"

"Fear not, Aphanasiich! If I be Czar, I shall treat all of you with honor. . . . Only, I am not fated to be Czar. . . ." he added softly.

"Thou shalt be,—thou shalt!" retorted the old man, with such assurance that once more, as shortly before, Alexei's breath was cut short for joy.

The sounds of sleigh-bells, the scraping of a sleigh over the snow, the snorting of horses, and voices reached them from beyond the windows. Alexei exchanged glances with Aphanasiich,—who could this be, at such a late hour? Could it possibly be some one sent from the palace, from Batiushka?

Ivan ran to the entry. The visitor was the Archimandrite Theodosius. The Czarevich, upon beholding him, thought that his father was dead,—and turned so pale that the monk observed this despite the darkness as he blessed him, and smiled the faintest of smiles.

When they were left *tête-à-tête*, Fedosska took his seat near the fire-grate, opposite the Czarevich, and, occasionally glancing at him with still the same scarcely perceptible sneer, fell to warming his chilled hands over the embers, now unclenching, now clenching his crooked fingers, resembling the talons of a bird.

"Well, and how is Batiushka," Alexei finally let drop, getting himself in hand.

"Badly," the monk sighed deeply, "so badly that we do not expect him to live. . . ."

The Czarevich crossed himself:

"God's will be done."

"Man is like the cedars of Lebanon to look upon," Theodosius began, chantingly, as if he were in church, " 'his breath goeth forth, he returneth to his earth; in that very day his thoughts perish. . . .' " [44]

But suddenly he broke off, drew his diminutive wrinkled phiz up to Alexei's very face, and fell to whispering in a stealthy whisper,—rapidly, more rapidly:

"God's patience is long, but his chastisement strong. The Sovereign hath been visited by a mortal sickness because of his unbounded drinking, his venery, and through God's vengeance, because of his attempt at the spiritual and monastic orders, which he was fain to do away with. As long as there will be tyranny over the Church, so long may one expect no good. What Christianity have we? Our faith seems striving to become that of the Turks, perhaps,—but even among Turks such things do not take place. Perished is our state! . . ."

The Czarevich listened, and could not believe his ears. He expected anything from Fedosska's brazenness,—but not this.

"But what of yourselves,— ye Archpresbyters, the administrators of the Russian Church,—where are your eyes? Who else should stand up for the Church if not you?" he managed to say, looking at Fedosska point-blank.

"Come, now, Czarevich! What administrators are we? Our Archpresbyters are so bridled that one can lead them where one lists. They are appointed the same way as are the besotted rural guards. Whomever they fear, him they revere. They are ready to turn this way or that, all in the space of an hour. They are no Archpresbyters, but scare-crows. . . ."

And, hanging his head, he added softly, as though to himself— Alexei thought he caught the voice of the ages in this soft utterance of the monk:

"We once were eagles,—we have now become bats of the night!"

In his black cowl, with the black wings of his cassock, with his hideous, keen little face, lit up from below by the red reflection of the expiring embers, he did, in very sooth, resemble an enormous noctule. Only in the intelligent eyes was there the dull glow of a fire worthy of an eagle's gaze.

" 'Tis not thou who shouldst say such things, nor I who should listen, Your Reverence!" exclaimed the Czarevich at last, unable to contain himself. "Who has subdued the Church to the State? Who was it that urged the Czar to bring the ways of Luther among the people, to demolish chapels, to revile ikons, to bring down monasticism? Who gives him dispensation to do all these things? . . ."

Suddenly he stopped. The monk was regarding the Czarevich with such an intense, piercing gaze that the latter felt eerie. Was not all this guile, now, or a trap? Had not Theodosius been sent to him as a spy from Menshikov, or from Batiushka himself?

"But does Your Highness know,"—Fedosska began, puckering up one eye with an infinitely cunning smile, "does Your Highness know that figure in logic which is called *reductio ad absurdum?* Well, that is the very thing I am doing. The Czar is set against the Church, yet dares not fight it openly, —he makes it fall into ruins, makes it rot, and oppresses it all on the sly. But to my way of thinking, if you are going to demolish anything,—then go ahead and demolish! Whatever you do, do it expeditiously. Better straightforward Lutheranism than a devious Orthodoxy; better straightforward atheism than devious Lutheranism. The worse,—the better! That is what I am leading up to. What the Czar begins, I conclude; that which he whispers in my ear, that I cry out before all the people. Through him, himself, I expose him,— letting all know how the Church of God is dishonored. If this should pleasant be, we will bear it patiently; but if it should not,—we shall bide till our time befall, and then out of our holes crawl. The cat shall be repaid for the tears mice have shed! . . ."

"Downright clever!" The Czarevich began to laugh, almost admiring Fedosska—and not believing a single word of his. "Well, but thou art crafty, father,—crafty as the fiend. . . ."

"But do not, my master, despise e'en the fiends. The Devil serves God despite himself. . . ."

"Art comparing thyself with the Devil, Your Reverence?"

"I am a politician," retorted the monk modestly. "When one lives with wolves, one must howl like a wolf. Dissimulation is placed in the first rank of the rules of governing not only by teachers of statecraft, but even God Himself instructs us in politics,—like to a fisher that hideth his hook with a worm, thus hath the Lord hidden His Holy Ghost with the Flesh of His Son, and hath let His angle into the troubled depths of the universe, and has outwitted and caught the Enemy, the Devil. The craftiness of the Supreme Wisdom of God! Celestial politics!"

"But, Holy Father,—dost thou believe in God, now?" The Czarevich again looked at him point-blank.

"What politics, my master, can there be without the Church,—and what a Church can there be without God? *For there is no power but of God.*" [45]

And, with a queer snigger,—one could not tell if it were timid or brazen,—he added:

"Aye, but thou too art clever, Alexei Petrovich! More clever than Batiushka. Batiushka, e'en though he be clever, yet he knoweth not men,—we used to lead him by the nose quite a bit, now. But thou wilt know clever men better. Dearest little one! . . ."

And, stooping suddenly, he kissed the Czarevich's hand so quickly and dexterously that the latter had not time to jerk it away,—merely shuddering all over. But, even though he felt that the flattery of the monk was honey upon the sharp edge of a knife,—the honey was sweet, withal. He turned red, and, in order to hide his confusion, began with assumed severity:

"Look, Brother Theodosius, do not miss thy step! The

pitcher that goeth to the well too oft is bound to get broken thereat. Thou art provoking Czar Batiushka like a puss with her paw, but, were that bear to turn around and squeeze thee,—there would not be as much as a sniff of thee left! . . ."

Fedosska's little phiz contracted painfully, his eyes widened, and, looking around, just as though some one were standing behind his back, he began in the same whisper as before,—a whisper rapid, disjointed, like that of delirium:

"Oh, my dearest little one,—oh, that too is frightful! I have ever thought that my death would befall me at *his* hands. When, even in my early years, I did come to Moscow with others of the petty Polish nobility, and we were brought to the palace, and graciously permitted to kiss the royal hand, I did make obeisance to thy uncle, Czar Ioann Alexeievich; but when it came to kissing the hand of Czar Peter Alexeievich, such a fright fell upon me,—such a fright that my knees began to shake; and I could hardly stand, and ever since that time I have always reasoned that my death would come from the same hand! . . ."

He was all a-tremble from terror even now. But hatred was stronger than fear. He began to speak of Peter in such a way that the Czarevich imagined that Fedosska was not lying,—or practically not lying. In the ecclesiastic's thoughts he was recognizing his own most secret, evil thoughts against his father:

"A great ruler, say they,—a great ruler! But whereof does his greatness consist? In a tyrannous manner doth he reign. With ax and *knout* doth he enlighten. One can't ride far on a *knout*. And the ax is but an instrument of iron,—and of no great rarity: 'twill fetch but half a ruble! He is forever seeking out conspiracies and seditions, now. And yet he cannot see that all this sedition is because of him. He himself is the chiefest insurrectionist. He breaks up, he knocks down, he swings his ax straight from the shoulder,—yet all this without rhyme or reason. How many men have been executed, —how much blood has been spilt! And yet thievery doth not abate. The conscience of men is not curbed. And blood is not water,—it cries out for vengeance. Soon, soon, shall the wrath of God descend upon Russia, and when internecine strife comes, then, then shall all see, from the first to the least; there will be such an upheaval, such a chopping-off of heads, that one will hear naught save *swish—swish— swish.* . . ."

He was passing his hand across his throat and *swishing,* imitating the sound of an ax.

"And thereupon, out of those great floods of blood, shall the Church of God emerge, washed clean, made whiter than the snow, like to the 'woman clothed with the sun,' [46] reigning it over all kings. . . ."

Alexei was looking at his face, distorted with rage; at his eyes, blazing with a savage fire, and it seemed to him that a madman was before him. He recalled the story of one of the abbey cubicularies: "There doth occasionally fall upon him, this Father Theodosius, a melancholy; and, tortured of the fiend, he doth fall to the ground, and remembereth not himself what he doeth."

"That is what I foresaw, that is what I was leading up to," concluded the monk. "Aye, 'tis evident that God hath taken pity upon Russia: hath punished the Czar, and spared the people. He hath sent us thee,—thee, our deliverer, our joyance, our little radiant child, thou churchly, pious Sovereign, Alexei Petrovich, Autocrat of All the Russias,—Your Majesty! . . ."

The Czarevich sprang up in horror. Fedosska also arose, threw himself at his feet, embraced them, and lifted up his voice in a frenzied and inexorable, seemingly threatening supplication:

"Protect and forgive thy slave! All, all, all shall I give up to thee! To thy father I would not give it up, wanting it for myself, thinking to be Patriarch myself; but now I want it not, I have no heed of it,—I have need of naught! . . . All for thee, my dear little one, my joyance, friend of my heart, Aleshenka darling! I have come to love thee! . . . Thou shalt be Czar and Patriarch both! Thou shalt unite the earthly and the heavenly, the Crown of Constantine— the White Cowl—with the Crown of the Monomachi! [47] Thou shalt be greater than all the Czars of this earth! Thou— the first; thou—the only one! Thou,—and God! . . . But I—I am thy slave, thy hound, a worm crawling at thy feet,

—Fedosska, the miserable one! Yea, Your Majesty,—I swear it, embracing thy little feet as though they were those of Christ Himself!"

He bowed down to the earth before him, and the black wings of his cassock spread out, like the gigantean wings of some noctule, and the diamond panagia, with the portrait of the Czar and with the Crucifix, emitted a tinkle as it struck against the floor. Revulsion filled the soul of the Czarevich; a chill ran through his body, as if from the touch of a reptile. He wanted to thrust him away, to strike him, to spit in his face; but he could not stir, as though he were in the catalepsy of a fearful dream. And it seemed to him that it was no longer "miserable Fedosska" the knave who was sprawling at his feet, but some one powerful, ominous, regal, he who had been an eagle, and had become a bat of the night; was it not the Church itself, subdued to the State, dishonored? And through his revulsion, through his horror an insane rapture and an intoxication with power were making his head swim. It was just as though some one were raising him up on gigantean black wings to the heights, showing him all the kingdoms of the earth and all their glory, and saying: *All these things will I give thee, if thou wilt fall down and worship me.*[48]

The embers in the grate were barely glowing under the ashes. The blue heart of the spirit flame was barely beating. And the blue flame of the lunar snow-storm had grown dim beyond the windows. Some one wan, with wan eyes, was peering in through the windows. And the flowers of frost upon the panes showed whitely, like the wraiths of dead flowers.

When the Czarevich recovered himself, there was no one else in the room. Fedosska had vanished, just as though he had fallen through the ground, or had melted into thin air.

"What lies was he telling here? What was he raving about?" Alexei reflected, as though coming out of a sleep. "The White Cowl . . . The Crown of the Monomachi. . . . Madness,—melancholy! . . . And how,—how does he know that my father will die? What makes him think so? How many times was he not expected to remain alive,—yet God had mercy upon him."

Suddenly he recalled Kikin's words during their recent conversation:

"Thy father is not seriously ill. He confesseth and taketh the Viaticum with premeditation, to show people that he is seriously ill, yet 'tis all pretense; he is putting thee and others to the test,—to see, now, how ye will act when he will be no more. Thou knowest the fable,—the mice had foregathered to bury the cat; they leap and they dance, but the cat giveth one spring and a pounce,—and the dance is at an end. . . . As for his taking the Viaticum,—he construes the law in his own way, and not in that of the mice. . . ."

On that occasion something shameful and vile had pricked the Czarevich's heart at these words. But he had deliberately let them pass,—for he had been all too gay, and did not want to think of anything.

"Kikin is right!" he decided now, and it was just as though somebody's dead hand had squeezed his heart. "Yes, everything is pretense, deception, dissimulation,—the Devil's politics,—the playing of a cat with a mouse. 'But the cat giveth one spring and a pounce. . . .' There is nothing,—there was nothing. All hopes, raptures, dreams of freedom, of power,—all these are but dreaming,—delirium,—madness. . . ."

The blue flame flared up for the last time and went out. Only a single ember, glowing under the ashes, was peeping out, as though it were winking, laughingly, like an eye slyly puckered up. The Czarevich grew frightened; it seemed to him that Fedosska had not gone, that he was still here, lurking in some corner,—that he was keeping quiet, with his fangs all set, and that, at any moment now, he would begin circling, rustling, swishing over him with his black wings, like a noctule, and whispering in his ear: *All this power will I give thee, and the glory of the kingdoms of the world: for that is delivered unto me; and to whomsoever I will I give it.*[49]

"Aphanasiich!" the Czarevich cried out. "Lights! Bring lights as fast as thou canst!"

The old man launched into angry coughing and grumbling, as he crawled off his warm couch—a ledge projecting from the stove.

"Come,—what have I gotten so joyous over?" the Czarevich asked himself,—with full consciousness for the first time in all these days. "Can all this really be true?"

Aphanasiich, his bare feet pattering, brought in a tallow candle with a thief on its wick. The light struck Alexei straight in the eyes,—it was blinding, cutting after the darkness.

And it was as if a light had flashed within his soul: he suddenly perceived that which he did not want, did not dare to perceive,—that which had made him so high-spirited: the hope that his father would die.

III

"Dost remember, my master, how in the hamlet of Preobrazhensky [Transfiguration], in thy bed-chamber, before the Holy Evangel, I did ask thee: Wilt thou revere me, thy spiritual Father, as an angel of God, and an apostle, and as a judge of thy deeds, and dost thou believe that I, sinful that I am, have the same priestly power to bind and to loose which Christ bestowed upon His apostles? And thou didst answer: I believe."

Thus to the Czarevich spoke his spiritual adviser, Archpresbyter of the Kremlin Cathedral of Our Saviour On High, —Father Jacob Ignatiev, who had come to Peterburgh from Moscow, three weeks after the Czarevich's interview with Theodosius.

Ten years ago Father Jacob had been to the Czarevich precisely what the Patriarch Nikon had been to his grandfather, Alexei Mikhailovich, the Most Pacific Czar. The grandson had fulfilled the behest of his grandfather: "Hold ye the priesthood dearer than your head, with every submission, without any contradiction; the Priesthood is above the State." Amid the general desecration and enslavement of the Church, the Czarevich found delectation in bowing at the feet of the humble priest Jacob. In the face of the pastor he beheld the face of the Lord Himself, and believed that the Lord was the Head over all heads, the Czar over all czars. The more autocratic Father Jacob was, the more humble the Czarevich, and the more sweet this humility was to him. He gave to his spiritual father all that love which he could not give to his father in the flesh. This was a friendship jealous, tender, passionate,—seemingly enamored. "I call the Most True God to witness that I have not in the whole Empire of Russia such another friend as Your Holiness," he wrote to Father Jacob from foreign parts. "I fain would not say this, but, come what may, say it I shall: may God grant you a long life; but, if your translation from this world to the next occur, a return to the Russian Empire would become altogether undesirable to me."

Suddenly everything changed.

Father Jacob had a son-in-law, a pettifogger, by the name of Peter Anphimov. Through the request of his spiritual adviser, the Czarevich had taken Anphimov into his service, and had entrusted him with the management of his estate at Poretzkaya, in the Alatorskaya district of the Nizhegorodsky region. The pettifogger had ruined the *mouzhiks* with his high-handedness, and all but brought them to uprising. Many a time did they petition the Czarevich, complaining against Petka the Thief. But the latter always came off scot-free, inasmuch as Father Jacob shielded and extricated his son-in-law. Finally the *mouzhiks* hit upon the idea of sending a walking delegate to their fellow-villager and old friend, the Czarevich's *valet de chambre,* Ivan Aphanasiich. Ivan had himself made a trip to the Poretzkaya estate, had investigated the affair, and, upon returning, had put in his complaint in such a manner that there could be no doubt of Petka's knaveries, and even malefactions,—but, mainly, that Father Jacob was fully aware of them. This was a cruel blow to Alexei. It was not for himself, nor for his peasants, but for the Church of God which, to him, seemed dishonored in the person of an unworthy pastor, that the Czarevich rose up in arms. For a long while he refused to see Father Jacob, hiding his hurt and keeping silent,—but at last he could restrain himself no longer.

Under the nickname of Father Hades, together with Clodhopper, Sleepy-Head, Whip-Hand, and other bottle companions, the Archpriest participated in the "band" or "Most-Drunken Council" of the Czarevich,—a likeness, in little, of his Batiushka's Great Council of a similar nature. In one of these drinking bouts Alexei fell to exposing the Russian Archpriests, calling them "Judases-betrayers," "Sellers of Christ."

"When will a new prophet Elijah arise, that he may bow down your backs, ye priests of Baal!" he exclaimed, looking Father Jacob straight in the eyes.

"Thou art pleased to utter unseemly things, Czarevich," the other began with severity. " 'Tis not fitting for thee thus to reproach and anger us, thy insignificant pious ones, who pray for thee to God. . . ."

"We know all about your prayers," Alexei cut him short. " 'Lord, thy mercy is untold,—but let us get into the fold, help us grab all we can hold, and then get off, scot-free and bold.' Batiushka, Czar Peter Alexeievich, did right well in plucking off some of your down, ye long-beards! And that is naught to what really ought to be done to you, ye Pharisees, ye hypocrites, ye generation of vipers, ye whited sepulchers! . . ."

Father Jacob got up from the table, approached the Czarevich, and asked him in solemn tones:

"Whom meanest thou, master? Our humble self perhaps?"

At this moment the "Most Benignant Father, the Proto-Presbyter of Verkhosspask," resembled the Patriarch Nikon, —the son of Peter, however, no longer resembled the Most Pacific Czar, Alexei Mikhailovich.

"Thou too,—" answered the Czarevich, also arising and, as before, looking point-blank at Father Jacob, "thou, too, father, art not to be told from the others! Thou, too, hast sold thy soul to the Devil,—thou hast sought the Christ-head, not for Christ but for thy bread! . . . Wherefore art thou puffed up with pride? Art fain, no doubt, to be numbered among the Patriarchs? Well, these be not the times for that, brother. There's many a slip 'twixt the cup and the lip! Bide a while,—the Lord shall surely cast thee down from the Golden Altar-Rail, which is in the Cathedral of Our Saviour On High, with thy heels up in the air, and thy damned maw down,—right into the mire,—into the mire, into the mire. . . ."

He added an obscene oath,—everybody burst into laughter.

Everything grew dark before Father Jacob's eyes; he, too, was drunk, but not so much from wine as from wrath.

"Keep still, Aleshka!" he shouted. "Keep still, thou puppy! . . ."

"If I be a puppy, then, father, thou art a hound!"

Father Jacob turned purple; he began to quiver, raised both his arms over the head of the Czarevich, and cried out in the same voice in which, when he had been Protodeacon of the Cathedral of the Annunciation, he had thundered anathemas from the ambo against all heretics and apostates:

"I shall curse thee! I shall curse thee! Through the power given us from the Lord Himself, through Peter the Apostle. . . ."

"What art thou yelling thy lungs off for, shave-pate?" the Czarevich retorted with a malevolent sneer. "Not Peter the Apostle, but Peter Anphimov, the pettifogger, the thief, thy own dear little son-in-law,—that's the fellow thou shouldst invoke! 'Tis he that hath thee in his hold, and he it is that makes thee talk so bold,—Petka the varlet, Petka the fiend! . . ."

Father Jacob let his arm fall and struck Alexei in the face, —"barring the impious one's lips."

The Czarevich threw himself upon him; with one hand he seized him by the beard, with the other he groped on the table for a knife. Distorted by a convulsion, with eyes blazing, Alexei's face suddenly took on a momentary, fearful, and seemingly unearthly, phantasmal resemblance to the face of Peter. This was one of those attacks of rage which occasionally possessed the Czarevich, and during which he was capable of committing any evil deed.

Their bottle-companions jumped up, threw themselves upon the brawlers, seized their arms and legs, and, after great efforts, pried them apart and dragged them off.

This quarrel, like all such quarrels, ended in naught: whoever is drunk isn't his own man, now; 'tis an everyday matter: drink a barrel and then quarrel; sleep, and wake,—and your peace make. And they made their peace. But there was no more of their former love. This Nikon fell out of favor with the grandson, even as his predecessor had done with the grandsire.

Father Jacob was the intermediary between the Czarevich and a whole secret league—almost a conspiracy—of the foes of Peter and Peterburgh, who surrounded the "desert-dweller," the disgraced Czaritza Avdothea, immured in the Suzdal. When the news came of the—apparently—mortal illness of the Czar, Father Jacob hastened to Peterburgh, by instruction from the Suzdal, where great events were expected upon Alexei's accession to the throne.

But, by the time the Archprelate had arrived, everything had changed. The Czar was getting well, and so rapidly that his recovery seemed miraculous—or his illness merely assumed. Kikin's prophecy had been fulfilled: the tomcat Kotabriss had jumped up,—and the dance of the mice began; they all rushed off helter-skelter, and again hid themselves under the floor boards. Peter attained his end; he learned what the power of the Czarevich would be, if he, the Sovereign, were really to die.

Rumors reached Alexei that his father was most cruelly wroth with him. Some one of the spies—was it not Theodosius himself?—had, it would seem, whispered to his father that the Czarevich had been pleased to wax merry over the death of Batiushka; he had been joyous and radiant of mien, now, just as though it were his birthday.

Again he was suddenly abandoned of all,—swerved aside from, as if he were plague-stricken. Again,—from the throne to the executioner's block. And he knew that now there would be no more pardon for him. From day to day he waited for the fearful interview with his father. But fear was stifled by hatred and indignation. Base and vile did all this deception, this "dissimulation," this feline craftiness, this blasphemous playing with death seem to him. There also came to his memory another "dissimulation" of Batiushka's: the letter with the threat of depriving him of the succession, *A Declaration to My Son*, given him on the very day of the death of the Crown Princess Charlotta, on the 22nd of October, seventeen hundred and fifteen; it had been signed on the eleventh of that same October,—that is, right on the very eve of the birth of the Czarevich's son, little Peter Alexeievich. At that time he had paid no attention to this substitution of dates. But now he understood what craftiness lay herein: the Batiushka would not have been able to avoid mentioning the Czarevich's son in the *Declaration;* he would not have been able to threaten the Czarevich with an unconditional deprivation of his succession, when a new heir-apparent had appeared. Through substituting different dates, a lawful appearance had been given to a lawless action.

The Czarevich smiled as he recalled how fond Batiushka was of appearing a just man.

He would have forgiven everything to his father,—all his great falsehoods and malefactions,—everything, but not this petty craftiness.

It was precisely in the midst of these thoughts that Father Jacob found the Czarevich. Alexei, in his loneliness, was overjoyed to see him, even as he would have been to see any other living soul, but the spirit of Nikon was strong in the Archpresbyter,—sensing that Czarevich now needed his help more than ever, he decided to remind him of the old grievance.

"Now, my master Czarevich," Father Jacob continued, "thou hast made as naught that promise of thine, given to us in the Cathedral of the Transfiguration upon the Holy Evangel, transforming the said promise into a sport or a mockery. Thou dost hold me no more as an angel of God, nor as an Apostle of Christ and a judge of thy actions; but dost thyself judge us, wounding us with words of opprobrium; and as for the affair of my son-in-law, Peter Anphimov, with the *mouzhiks* of Poretzkaya,—thou hast caused much weeping in our humble little household, and didst drag me, thy spiritual father, by the beard, which Thy Grace shouldst not have done, out of fear for the living God. Even though I be a sinful man and a vile,—nevertheless am I a servitor to the Most Pure Body and Blood of the Lord. We shall be judged therein, my child, before the Czar of czars, on the day of the Second Coming, where there is no favor shown. When earthly power shall be at an end, then even a czar shall stand under judgment, even like to one of the humble. . . ."

The Czarevich raised his eyes in silence, but with such an expression—neither of sorrow, nor of despair, but of an apathetic, apparently dead vacuity—that Father Jacob sud-

denly fell silent. He comprehended that this was not the
time to settle old scores. He was a kindly man, and he loved
Alexei as if the latter was of his own kin.

"Well, God will forgive," he concluded. "And now, my
little friend, do forgive me, sinner that I am. . . ." Then he
added, looking into his face with tender solicitude:

"But why art thou so down-hearted, Alëshenka? . . ."

The Czarevich cast down his head and made no answer.

"Come,—I have brought thee a present," Father Jacob
smiled with a merry and mysterious air. "A little letter from
thy mother. I did journey recently to the *desert-dwellers*.
The joy I saw there has greatly cheered me; there were also
visions, voices,—there will be a consummation soon, now.
. . ."

He reached for his pocket to get the letter.

"No need," the Czarevich stopped him. "No need, Ignatiich!
'Twere better if thou wert not to show it. What would be
the good of it? 'Tis oppressive enough without that. Like as
not the word will go forth,—my father will learn of it. There
be many who keep watching us. Go thou not to the desert-
dwellers, and, in the future, do not bring me any letters.
There is no need. . . ."

Father Jacob bestowed another long and intense look
upon him. "So that is what they have brought him to," he
reflected. "The son denies his mother,—blood denies blood!"

"Are things as bad as all that with Batiushka?" he asked
in a whisper.

Alexei made a hopeless gesture and let his head sink still
lower. Father Jacob understood all. Tears welled up in the
eyes of the old man. He stooped toward the Czarevich and
placed his hand upon one of the latter's; with the other he
fell to stroking Alexei's hair, with a soft caress, as if the
Czarevich were a sick child, and spoke soothingly:

"Why grieve so, my little chick? Why grieve so, my own
little one? The Lord be with thee! If thou hast aught upon
thy heart, tell me, conceal it not,—'twill be easier then; we
can reason together. For I am thy father. Even though I be
sinful, yet the Lord may send me wisdom. . . ."

The Czarevich still kept silent, turning away. But suddenly

his face puckered up,—his lips began to quiver. With stifled, tearless sobbing he toppled at the feet of Father Jacob:

"I am most heavy-hearted, batiushka,—most heavy-hearted! . . . I know not what to do. . . . There's no more strength in me. . . . For I did wish, now, that my father might . . ." And he did not end his speech, as though he himself had become frightened of what he had wanted to say.

"Let us go to the chapel! Let us go, speedily; I'll tell thee all there. I fain would confess. Father, judge between me and Batiushka, before the Lord! . . ."

In the chapel, a tiny room adjoining the bed-chamber, the walls were literally lined with ikons in vestments of gold and silver, studded with precious stones,—heirlooms of Czar Alexei Mikhailovich. Not a single ray of daylight penetrated here; never-extinguished lampads glimmered in the eternal dusk.

The Czarevich got down on his knees before a *prie-dieu* on which an Evangel was lying. Father Jacob, clad in his sacerdotal vestments, solemnly triumphant, as though he had been entirely transfigured,—his face, near at hand, was of the commonest *mouzhik* type, somewhat heavy and puffy from age, but, at a distance, it was still benign, recalling the face of Christ upon ancient ikons,—was holding a cross and saying:

"Lo, my child, Christ is standing invisibly near, receiving thy confession,—be not ashamed, nor afraid, nor keep aught from me, but without hesitation tell me all, so that thou mayst receive manumission from Our Lord, Jesus Christ."

And, even as Alexei enumerated his sins one after another, in accordance with the rite of confession, as his spiritual father put the questions and the penitent replied, he felt lighter and lighter, as though some powerful being were lifting off one burden after another,—as though some ætherial being were touching with ætherial fingers the wounds of his conscience, and they were being healed. He felt a delectation of fear; his heart was a-flame, as though it were not Father Jacob who stood before him, but Christ Himself.

"Tell me, my child, hast thou not, perchance, slain a man,—either willingly or unwillingly?" This was that question which the Czarevich awaited and dreaded.

"I have sinned, father," he managed to babble, barely

audibly. "Not in deed, not in word, but in thought. I wished that my father might . . ."

And again, as recently, he halted, as though becoming frightened himself at that which he wanted to say, but the all-seeing gaze was penetrating to the most secret depths of his heart. One could conceal naught from this gaze. With an effort, trembling, blanching, bathed in a cold sweat, he concluded:

"When Batiushka was ill, I did wish his death."

And he shrank into himself, contracting like a hedgehog, letting his head sink and closing his eyes in order not to see Him Who was standing before him; he was rooted to the spot from horror, as though he expected that a word like unto heavenly thunder would peal forth,—a final condemnation or vindication, as on Dread Judgment Day.

And suddenly the familiar, ordinary, human voice of Father Jacob pronounced:

"God will forgive thee, child,—for e'en all of us wish him death."

The Czarevich raised his head, opened his eyes and beheld a face that was also familiar, ordinary, human, not at all awesome,—with fine little wrinkles around the kindly and somewhat crafty brown eyes, a mole with three hairs upon the round, chubby cheek, and a grizzled red beard—that very same beard by which he had, some time ago, been dragging the father around, during the fight, when he was drunk. A priest like any priest,—there was nothing and nobody beyond him. But, had a thunder peal really burst over the Czarevich's head, he would have been, apparently, less overwhelmed than by these simple words: "God will forgive thee,—for e'en all of us wish him death."

But, as though nothing had happened, the priest went on with his questions, in accordance with the missal:

"Tell me, my child, hast thou tasted of any carrion, or of blood, or of aught that hath been strangled, or aught slain of wolves, or aught killed by birds of prey? Hast thou been defiled by any other thing, such as is forbidden in the rules of holy living? Or hast thou during Lent, or on Holy Wednesday or Friday, tasted of butter or cheese?"

"Father!" exclaimed the Czarevich. "Great is my sin,— God sees it is great. . . ."

"Hast thou failed to keep thy fast?" Father Jacob asked with alarm.

" 'Tis not of that I speak, father! I speak of the Sovereign, my Batiushka. How can such things be? For I am his own son,—his own son, the blood of his blood. The son hath wished death to his father. And whoever hath wished death to another, that man is the murderer of the man he wished death unto. I am a parricide in thought. 'Tis a fearful thing, Ignatiich,—a fearful thing. Aye, father, I confess to thee like unto Christ Himself! Judge, help, have mercy upon me, O Lord! . . ."

Father Jacob regarded him at first with wonder, and then with wrath.

"That thou hast risen up against thy father in the flesh,— thou dost repent of; but that thou hast done so against thy father in the spirit,—that thou dost not even recall? Even as the spirit is greater than the flesh, thus is the spiritual father greater than the father in the flesh. . . ."

And he again began speaking lengthily, bookishly, vapidly, on the same unvarying subject: "Hold the spiritual dearer than your own head."

"Thou, my child, hast had thy own way too long. Like to a raging or to a butting ram, thou hast raised thy voice against me. May the Lord not hold it against thee, inasmuch as it did not come from thee; but 'tis the devil within thee that is working spite against me, through thee,—he hath bridled thee as if thou wert bony nag, and doth ride thee, making himself grand, as if upon a swine, according to the visions of the Holy Fathers, riding thee wherever he lists, until he shall cast thee into eternal perdition. . . ."

And, one word leading to another, he managed, in the end, to bring his discourse around to the affair of the Poretzkaya *mouzhiks* and his son-in-law, Peter Anphimov.

Something gray, most gray, slumbrous, viscid, like a cobweb, was veiling the eyes of the Czarevich; and the face of him who stood before him was dissolving, doubling, as if in a fog,—as if behind this face another face were coming out also familiar, with a red, sharp little nose, perpetually sniffing

the air; with purblind, rheumy, crafty, feral little eyes,—the
face of Petka the clerk; as if on the face of "His Reverence,"
the Most Beatific Father, Archpresbyter of the Cathedral of
Our Saviour on High,—a face most benign, recalling the face
of Christ in the ancient ikons, the face of the Lord were
being united and blended, in a fearful and sacrilegious blending, with the vile little phiz of Petka the thief, Petka the lout.

"Our Lord and God, Jesus Christ, through the benevolence
and largesses of His loving-kindness, will forgive thee all thy
sins, my child Alexei," pronounced Father Jacob, covering
the head of the Czarevich with his stole, "and I, His most
unworthy priest, through His power, bestowed upon me, do
forgive and absolve thee in the name of the Father, the Son,
and the Holy Ghost, Amen!"

There was a void in the heart of Alexei, and these words, to
him, had an empty sound, without any power, without any
mystery, without any awe. He felt that he was forgiven *here*,
but that he would not be forgiven *there;* that absolution had
been granted upon earth, but that there had been no absolution in heaven.

On that same day, just before evening, Father Jacob went
to the steam-baths; upon his return he sat down near the fire-
grate opposite the Czarevich, to partake of a sort of tea, made
of spiced honey and hot water, steaming, in a kettle of bright
red copper, that reflected the face of the Archprelate, which
was also as red as copper. He drank one mug after another,
leisurely, and wiped the sweat off his face with a huge checkered handkerchief. He steamed himself at the bath, and even
drank the spiced honey, as if he were performing a rite. In the
way he sipped the drink, and smacked his lips, and bit off
small pieces of crunching, sweet cracknel, there was the same
benign decorum and pomp as in a church service; one could
perceive the guardian of ancestral customs,—one could hear
the behest of all orthodox antiquity: Be thou steadfast like
unto a pillar of marble,—deviate neither to the right nor to
the left.

The Czarevich listened to disquisitions on which besoms
were best for a steam-bath, what herbs, mint or tansy gave off
the sweetest odor in the bath; he also heard the saga of how
the Archprelate's spouse had upon the Day of St. Nicholas

almost steamed herself to death. There were also appropriate precepts and edifying maxims out of the Holy Fathers: "The worm is exceedingly meek, and scant of flesh, whereas thou art vainglorious and proud; but if thou art wise thou wilt thyself destroy thy pride, contemplating on how thy stubbornness and strength shall be food for worms. Beware of prideful thoughts; shun wrathfulness. . . ."

And again, and again,—the affair of the Poretzkaya *mouzhiks*, and the ineluctable Petka Anphimov.

The Czarevich felt sleepy, and at times it seemed to him that this was no man speaking before him, but an ox ruminating, and regurgitating, and ruminating anew its endless, sleep-inducing cud.

The dismal twilight was advancing. There was a thaw out of doors, with a yellow, filthy fog. The pale flowers of the frost were melting and weeping in the windows. And the sky, too, was peeping in at the windows,—a filthy, purblind sky, and rheumy, like the crafty, vile little eyes of Petka the clerk.

Father Jacob was sitting opposite the Czarevich on the same place which had been occupied three weeks ago by the Archimandrite Theodosius; and Alexei was involuntarily comparing both pastors,—of the old Church and the new.

"No priests, we, but riff-raff! We were eagles, but have become bats of the night," the priest Theodosius had said. "We were eagles, but we have become yoke-oxen," the priest Jacob might have said.

Behind Fedosska was the Eternal Politician, the ancient Prince of This World; and behind Father Jacob was the same Politician, the new prince of this world—Petka the lout. One was worthy of the other,—the ancient was worthy of the new. And could it be possible that behind these two faces, the past and the future, there was but a third face: the face of the Church as an entity?

He contemplated, by turns, the filthy sky and the red face of the priest. Both in the one and in the other there was something flat, most flat, and vulgar,—the eternally vulgar, that which always exists, and yet is still more phantasmal than the wildest delirium. And there was a void in the heart of the Czarevich, and a tedium as fearful as death.

And again, as on the other occasion, there came the jingle of a sleigh-bell,—at first indistinct, in the distance, then ever louder, ever nearer. The Czarevich hearkened and suddenly became all alert.

"Some one is driving up," said Father Jacob. "Coming here, perchance?"

They heard the splashing of horses' hoofs in puddles of thawing snow, the whine of runners upon the bare cobbles, voices at the front entrance, and then steps in the entry. The door opened and a giant entered, with a handsome, stupid face,—a strange blend of a Roman Legionary with a Russian Ivannushka the Simpleton. This was the Czar's orderly, Alexandre Ivanovich Rumyantzev, a Captain in the Guards of the Transfiguration. He handed a letter to the Czarevich. The latter broke the seal and read:

"Son.—Come to us on the morrow, at the Winter Palace. —Peter."

Alexei was neither frightened nor surprised, as though he had known beforehand of this interview,—and it did not at all matter to him.

That night the Czarevich dreamt a dream,—a dream which came to him frequently, and was always the same. This dream was connected with a story which he had heard in his childhood.

During the trial of the Streltzi, Czar Peter had ordered to be disinterred, from where it was buried in the refectory of the Church of Nikola Stylites, and where it had lain for seventeen years, the body of his enemy, and Sophia's friend, —the arch-rebel, the *boyarin* Miloslavsky; he had ordered the opened coffin to be drawn by swine into the Cathedral of the Transfiguration, and there, in the torture-chamber, he had it placed underneath the headsman's block where the heads of the traitors were being lopped off,—so that their blood would pour into the coffin upon the dead man; then the corpse was to be chopped up into parts and buried right on the spot, in the torture vault, under the strappado and the headsmen's blocks,—"In order that," proclaimed the *ukase*, "the said vile parts of the thief Miloslavsky might be watered by the multiplied blood of thieves forever, according to the words of the Psalmist: *'The Lord will abhor the bloody and deceitful man.'* [50]

In this dream of his, Alexei at first did not seem to see anything; he merely heard a soft, exceedingly soft, dreadful little song from the fairy-tale about Alënushka, the little sister, and Ivannushka, her little brother, which had been frequently told to him by his grandmother, the old Czaritza, Nathalia Kyrillovna Narishkina, the mother of Peter. The little Ivannushka, turned by witchcraft into a kid, is calling to his little sister, Alënushka, but in the dream, instead of 'Alënushka,' it sounded like 'Alëshenka'—and sinister and ominous did this coincidence in the sounds of the names seem.

> Alëshenka, Alëshenka!
> Fires are lit most hot;
> Water seethes in many a pot,
> Knives sharpened are of steel,—
> 'Tis thee they fain would kill!

He next beheld a deserted cul-de-sac of a street, porous, thawing snow, a row of black, rude log-cabins, and the leaden cupolas of the decrepit little church of Nikola Stylites. It was early morn, and dark,—as though it were evening; at the edge of the sky was "an enormous star with a tail,"— or a comet,—as red as blood. Monstrous swine,—fat, black, their hairless skins maculated with pink, are dragging along a buffoonesque sleigh. An open coffin rests on the sleigh. Within the coffin there is something black, something slimy, like musty leaves in a rotted, hollow tree-trunk. In the ray of the comet, the wan cupolas give off a bloody reflection. Under the sleigh, the thin ice of the vernal puddles crunches, and the black mire spurts forth like blood. There is a stillness,—like that preceding the end of the world, just before the trumpet of the Archangel. The swine alone grunt. And then somebody's voice (it resembles the voice of St. Dmitri of Rostov, a hoary little ancient in a wretched cassock of faded green, whom Alesha had seen in his childhood) was whispering in his ear: *"The Lord will abhor the bloody and deceitful man."* And the Czarevich realizes that the bloody man is Peter himself.

He awoke from this dream in horror, as always. Early

morning, and dark,—as though it were evening,—was peering in at the windows. There was a stillness,—like that preceding the end of the world.

Suddenly he heard a tapping on the door, and the sleepy, angry voice of Aphanasiich:

"Get up, get up, Czarevich! 'Tis time to go to thy father!"

Alexei wanted to cry out, to jump up,—and could not,—just as though he had been deprived of the use of all his limbs. He was lying as one dead, and it seemed to him that this was a continuation of his dream,—that his awakening was only part of his dream; and, at the same time, he heard a tapping on the door and the voice of Aphanasiich:

" 'Tis time,—'tis time to go to thy father!"

And the voice of his grandmother,—senile, quavering, like the bleating of a kid, was singing a song over him,—a song soft, exceedingly soft, and a terrible little song:

> Alëshenka, Alëshenka!
> Fires are lit most hot;
> Water seethes in many a pot,
> Knives sharpened are of steel,—
> 'Tis thee they fain would kill!

IV

Peter was saying to Alexei:

"When the war with the Swede began,—oh, what great routs we suffered because of our lack of skill; with what bitterness and patience did we have to go through our schooling, until we deservedly beheld that the same enemy, before whom we once trembled, now trembling still more before us! All of which has been attained through the poor efforts of myself and other true sons of Russia. And to this day we eat bread in the sweat of our brow, in accordance with God's commands to our first father, Adam. As much as in our power lay did we toil, like unto Noah, over the ark of Russia, having always but one thing in mind,—that Russia might be glorious before all the world. But when, after contemplating this joy bestowed by God upon our Fatherland, I do look upon my line of succession, I am consumed by a bitter grief almost equal to my joy, seeing thee altogether unfitted for the conduct of matters of state. . . ."

Going up the staircase of the Winter Palace, and passing the grenadier standing sentry-duty near the doors leading to the little office, or work-room of the Czar, Alexei experienced, as he always did preceding his interviews with his father, an unreasoning animal fear. Everything grew dark before his eyes, his teeth chattered, his legs gave way under him,—he was afraid he would fall.

But in proportion as his father went on, in a calm, even tone, with his lengthy, evidently premeditated speech,—which he seemed to have gotten down by heart,—Alexei was growing calmer. Everything was congealing, petrifying within him,—and again it was all one to him, as though his father were not speaking with him, nor about him.

The Czarevich stood like a soldier, eyes-front, his arms along the seams of his trousers; he was listening, and at the same time was not, stealthily scrutinizing the room with a distracted and apathetic curiosity. Turning-lathes, carpenter's tools, astrolabes, water-levels, compasses, globes and other mathematical, artillery and fortification appliances cluttered the cramped little office, giving it the air of a ship's cabin. Along the walls, paneled in dark oak, hung the seascapes of the Dutch master beloved of Peter, Adam Silo,—"useful for acquiring a knowledge of the art of seamanship." These were all objects familiar to the Czarevich since childhood, engendering in him a whole series of recollections: upon a newspaper sheet,—a Dutch *News Current*—lay great, round, metal-rimmed spectacles, twined round with a blue silk thread in order not the rub the bridge of the nose; alongside was a night cap of white ribbed dimity, with a green tassel, which Alësha had once happened to tear off when he had been playing with it,—but at that time his father had not become angered; he had merely put aside the *ukase* he had been writing and had immediately sewed the tassel on with his own hands.

Peter was seated at a table piled up with papers, in an old, high-backed, leather armchair, near an exceedingly heated stove. He had on a blue dressing-gown, faded and much worn, which the Czarevich remembered seeing even

before the battle of Poltava, with the same patch of a
brighter color upon a spot burned through by a pipe; he also
wore a jersey of red wool, with white bone-buttons,—one
of these was broken off, only half remaining; the Czarevich
recognized it, and counted it,—a thing he always did, for
some reason or other, during the lengthy admonitions of his
father,—this button was the sixth, counting from below; his
small clothes were of coarse blue woolen stuff; he had on
gray darned stockings of worsted, and old slippers trodden
down at the heels. The Czarevich scrutinized all of these
trifles,—so familiar, so homely,—and so remote. The face
of Batiushka was the only thing he could not see. Through
the window, beyond which the snowy, smooth expanse of
the Neva gleamed whitely, an oblique ray of the yellow
wintry sun fell between them,—slender, short, sharp, like
a sword. It divided them and screened them from one another. In the quadrangle of sunlight which the window-pane
cast on the floor, at the very feet of the Czar, slept his
favorite little bitch, the red-haired Lizetta, curled up in a
ball. And the Czar spoke on in an even, monotonous voice,
somewhat hoarse because of his cough,—just as though he
were reading a written *ukase:*

"God is not to blame for thy incapacity, inasmuch as He
hath not deprived thee of reason, nor hath He taken away
thy bodily strength; even though thou art not of a strong
nature, still thou art no weakling; but, worst of all, thou
wilt not even hear of matters military, through which we
have come from darkness to light, and because of which we
are now respected in the world, where before we were not
even known. I am not teaching thee to be eager for war,
without any lawful cause, but to love matters military, and
in every way possible further and learn them; inasmuch as
the military science is one of the two things indispensable
for governing,—to wit, order and defense. From a contempt
of war general ruin is bound to follow, of which we have a
clear example in the fall of the Greek Empire,—have they
not perished because they abandoned their arms and, overcome by love of peace alone, being desirous of living in
tranquillity, ever yielded to their adversary; has not this
tranquillity of theirs given them over into the never-ending

bondage of tyrants? But if thou hast at the back of thy mind the idea that generals can direct military affairs according to thy will, that is not true reasoning, inasmuch as everybody looks to the leader, so as to fall in with his likes: whatever the man at the head likes, the others like as well; but that which he turns away from, the others also care naught for. Besides, having no heart therefor, thou studiest naught and thus art ignorant of matters military. And, without knowing how to command others, how canst thou render their deserts to the deserving and punish the laggards without understanding all the factors of their calling? Thou wilt be forced merely to gape at them, like a fledgling to gape at them. Dost thou put forth thy weak health as an excuse for being unable to bear the toils of a military life? But even that is no reason, inasmuch as it is not so much hard work that I desire as willingness, which no illness could deprive thee of. Art thou harboring the thought that there are many who do not go to the war themselves, yet whose affairs are well run? True, although they do not go themselves, yet they have the will to do so; take the late French king, Louis, who did not often go to the wars himself, yet had such a great zeal therefor, and evinced such fine strategies, that his warring was called a theater and school of the world; and it was not only for war that he showed a zeal, but even for other matters, and for various industries, through all of which he made his realm celebrated above all others! Putting all of these factors before thee, I shall revert to what I said first, in speaking of thee. Inasmuch as I am but a man, and subject to death . . .”

The sunbeam which separated them faded away, and Alexei glanced into the face of Peter. It had changed greatly, —as if years, and not merely a month, had gone by since he had seen his father last; at that time Peter was in the full bloom of his powers and manhood; now he was almost an old man. And the Czarevich realized that his father’s illness had not been assumed; that probably he had actually been nearer death than the Czarevich, or all of them, had thought. In his denuded skull (his front hair had fallen out), in the pouches under his eyes, in the jutting lower jaw, in the whole pale-yellow puffy face, seemingly swollen and bloated, there was something ponderous, crushing, frozen, as in a death mask. Only in the exceedingly bright glitter—like the glitter of inflammation—of the enormous eyes, widened like those of a captured bird of prey, eyes so prominent that they seemed to bulge out—was there an expression of former youthfulness,—yet that very expression now infinitely weary, weak, almost pitiable.

And Alexei also realized that even though he had thought a great deal about the death of his father, and had awaited and desired his death, he had never really grasped its significance, as though not believing that his father could actually die. Only now, for the first time, did he suddenly come to believe. And there was incomprehension in this emotion, and a new, never heretofore experienced fear, no longer for himself, but for his father: What must death be like to such a man? How would he meet death?

"Inasmuch as I am but a man, and subject to death," Peter went on, "to whom should I bequeath this which I have planted with the help of the All-Highest, and which has already grown to some extent? To him who hath made himself like unto the wicked and slothful servant in the Gospels, who hid his talent in the earth,—that is to say, who cast from him all that God gave him? And I must also dilate upon the evil and stubborn nature which is thine. For how greatly have I not upbraided thee for this,—and not only upbraided, but even chastised? And, too, have I not e'en refused to speak with thee,—actually for years at a time? Yet naught of this availed,—naught proved of any good; everything was in vain, everything went by the board, and thou dost not want to do anything save to take thy ease at home, make merry forever,—as if thou wert not of our house, and contrary in everything! For while, on the one hand, thou hast the kingly blood of a high lineage, on the other hand thou hast vile opinions, like the lowest of low varlets, ever communing with shiftless folk from whom thou canst learn naught save evil and abominable ways. And wherewithal dost thou repay thy father for having brought thee into the world? Dost thou help me in these my griefs and trials, so unbearable, now that thou hast attained years of maturity? Nay, not so,—which is known to all men!

Rather, thou hatest my works, which I do for the people of my nation, without sparing my health; and, verily, thou shalt be a destroyer of these works after me! Pondering upon all of this with bitterness, and perceiving that I cannot incline thee toward good, I have thought it best to make known to thee my last testament, and to bide a while longer, hoping that thou wilt reform,—yet not hypocritically, but truly. But if not, let it be known . . ."

At these words he was taken by a coughing fit,—prolonged, excruciating,—a residue of his illness. His face turned scarlet, his eyes were popping out,—the sweat stood out on his forehead, and his veins were swollen. He was suffocating, and, from his frantic and vain efforts to clear his throat, he strangled still more, as little children do, who do not know how to cough. In this blending of the childish and the senile there was something both laughable and awful.

Lizetta awoke and fixed an intelligent and seemingly pitying gaze upon her master. The Czarevich also glanced at his father,—and suddenly something poignant,—most poignant, —pierced his heart, just as if it had been stung:

"Even a dog has pity, whereas I . . ."

Peter finally managed to clear his throat, spat, cursed roundly in his usual indecent oath and, wiping the sweat and tears from his face with his handkerchief, at once went on from the very place where he had stopped; and, although his voice was now still hoarser, it was as dispassionate and even as before, as though he were reading a written *ukase*.

"I therefore affirm,—let it be known unto thee . . ."

The handkerchief chanced to fall out of his hands,—he was about to bend down in order to pick it up, but Alexei forestalled him. He darted over, picked it up, and handed it over to his father; and this little service suddenly recalled to him that timid, tender, almost enamored emotion which he had at one time felt for his father.

"Batiushka!" he exclaimed, with such expressiveness of voice and face that Peter looked at him intently, and immediately dropped his eyes. "God sees, I have nothing crafty against thee on my conscience; but as for depriving me of the succession,—I crave it myself, because of my weakness; for what would it profit me to take upon my shoulders that which I cannot bear? For how could I ever do it! And then, too, Batiushka . . . How could I ever wish that thou . . . That thou shouldst . . . Oh, Lord!"

His voice broke; he lifted up his hands despairingly, convulsively, as though he wanted to clutch his head,—and froze so, all pale and trembling, with a strange, distracted smile on his lips. He himself knew not what this was,—he merely sensed, growing, welling up within him, a something that was striving, with a shattering force, to escape from his bosom. One word, one glance, one sign from his father,—and the son would have fallen down at his feet, would have embraced them, would have begun to sob with such tears that the fearful wall between them would have crumbled, would have melted away like ice under the sun. He would have explained everything, finding such words that his father would have forgiven him, would have understood how Alexei had loved him all his life,—him alone; and that he still loves him, more than ever; and that he does not ask for anything, save being allowed to love his father, to die for him, if only the latter would just once take pity upon him, and say, as he used to say during Czarevich's childhood, pressing him to his heart: "Alësha, my darling little boy!"

"Drop this childishness!" resounded the voice of Peter; it was rough, but somehow the roughness seemed assumed, for, in reality, it was uncertain, and strove to cover up that uncertainty. "Do not make excuses—of any sort. Show us faithfulness by thy works,—as for words, they are not worthy of belief. For even the Scripture sayeth: Neither *can* a corrupt tree bring forth good fruit. . . ." [51]

Avoiding Alexei's eyes, Peter was looking to one side; yet at the same time something was flitting, trembling on his face,—as though, through a death-mask, a living face could be glimpsed,—all too dear, all too familiar to the Czarevich; but Peter had already managed to overcome his emotion. As he talked, his face was becoming ever more deathlike, his voice ever firmer and more merciless.

"Nowadays drones are not held very highly. He that eateth bread, yet profiteth not God, the Czar, and the Fatherland, is like to a worm, which turneth everything to corruption and worketh only abomination, being not of the least good to men. Even the Apostle proclaimeth: If any would not work, neither should he eat; and the sluggard shall be accursed.[52] Whereas thou hast shown thyself to be a ne'er-do-weel. . . ."

Alexei practically did not hear his words. But every sound wounded his soul and cut into it with unbearable pain, as a knife cuts into the living flesh. This was akin to murder. He wanted to cry out, to stop his father,—but he felt that the latter would not understand anything, would not hear him. Again a wall was rising, an abyss was yawning, between them. And his father was receding from him, ever farther and farther, with every word, ever more irretrievably, even as the dead leave the living.

Finally even his pain abated. Everything again turned to stone within him. Again nothing mattered to him. He was merely languishing from a sleepy tedium, induced by this dead voice, which no longer even wounded, but merely rasped on, like a dull sword.

In order to end matters, to get away as soon as possible, he chose a moment of silence to make a long-considered answer, delivering it with the same dead expression of countenance, and the same dead voice, that Batiushka had used:

"Most Gracious Sovereign,—Batiushka! I have naught to say save this: if thou art pleased to deprive me, because of my unfitness, of the succession to the crown of Russia,— let thy will be done. I implore you most humbly, Sire, to do so,—since I perceive myself to be unfit and incapable for this station, inasmuch as I am of quite poor memory, without which naught can be accomplished, for all my powers, mental and bodily, have become debilitated through sundry ailments, and have made me unfit to rule such a people, which hath need of a man less spent than I. Therefore, I have no pretensions to succeed to the rule of Russia after you,— even though I had no brother; but all the more so since there is one now, for which God be thanked, and to whom God grant health; nor shall I have any pretensions in the future, in which I call God to witness to my soul; and, as a true acknowledgment, I am ready to write this oath in my own hand. I entrust my children to you; as for myself, I crave naught save subsistence until my death."

A silence fell. In the stillness of the wintry noonday, one could hear only the measured, brassy ticking of the wall-clock's pendulum.

"Thy renunciation is but procrastination, and not real!" Peter finally uttered. "For, since thou art unafraid now, and dost not regard highly the admonitions of thy father, how wilt thou keep my behests after me? As for thy taking an oath,—'tis not worthy of belief, because of the hardness of thy heart. One may also cite the words of David: All men *are* liars.[53] Also, even though thou shouldst want to follow my behests, certain long-beards, priests, and holy ancients, who, because of their idle life are none too well off now, will be able to sway and compel thee,—for thou art very partial to them. As for remaining, as thou fain wouldst, neither fish, flesh, nor good red herring,—that is impossible. Therefore, thou must either mend thy ways, and, without any hypocrisy, make thyself worthy to be my successor,—inasmuch as my spirit cannot be at rest without one, all the more so now, since my health hath grown poor,—or else become a monk. . . ."

Alexei, his eyes cast down, kept silent. His face now seemed the same death-mask as the face of Peter. Mask against mask, —and in both there was an unexpected, strange, seemingly spectral resemblance: a similarity of contrasts. It was as though the broad, round, puffy face of Peter, reflected in the long and gaunt face of Alexei, as in a concave mirror, had become monstrously narrowed, elongated.

Peter, too, kept silent, but on his right cheek, at the corner of his mouth and of his eye,—over the entire right side of his face,—a rapid tremor or twitching began: gradually increasing, it changed into a convulsion, which made his face, neck, shoulder, arm and leg writhe. Many considered him subject to the "falling sickness," or even demoniacally possessed, because of these convulsive cramps, which were forerunners of attacks of frenzied rage. Alexei could not look at his father without horror during such moments. But now he was calm, just as though girt about by an invisible, impenetrable armor. What else could Batiushka do to him? Kill him? Let him. Why, was not that which he had just done to him worse than murder?

"Why art thou silent?" Peter suddenly cried out, striking his fist on the table in one of the convulsive spasms which shook all his body. "Beware, Alëshka! Dost think I do not know thee? I know thee, brother,—I can see thee through and through! Hast thou risen up against thy own blood, thou whelp,—dost wish thy father's death? . . . Ugh, thou snake-in-the-grass, thou accursed bigot! 'Tis from the priests and the holy ancients, never fear, that thou hast learned such politics! 'Tis not in vain that the Saviour enjoined His apostles to fear no one, yet enjoined them most particularly concerning this: Beware ye, said He, of the leaven of the Pharisees,— [54] which is the hypocrisy of the monks,—their dissimulation. . . ."

A sinuous, evil sneer sparkled in the downcast eyes of the Czarevich. He barely restrained himself from asking his father as to the meaning of the substitution of dates in the *Declaration to My Son,*—that of October 11th instead of the 22nd. From whom, now, had Batiushka learned this dissimulation, this knavery, worthy of Petka the clerk, Petka the lout, or of Fedosska, "the prince of this world," with his "most divinely wise craftiness," his "celestial politics"?

"One more admonition,—the last," Peter began again in his former voice,—even, almost dispassionate,—restraining his convulsion by an unbelievable effort. "Consider everything thoroughly, and, having come to a resolution, give me thy answer without any delay. But if not, then let it be known unto thee that I shall positively deprive thee of the succession. For, if gangrene were to set in my finger, must I not lop it off, even though it be part of my body? Thus will I lop off even thee, like to a gangrenous member! And think not that I am saying this merely to frighten thee: verily, before God, I will fulfill what I say. For I have not spared my life, nor do I spare it now, for my people and for my fatherland,—how, then, can I spare thee, thou worthless one? Better a worthy stranger than one of the blood who is worthless. Therefore we reiterate: one of two things must be definitely done: either mend thy ways, or else take the tonsure. But shouldst thou do neither . . ."

Peter drew himself up to his full gigantic height. Convulsions were again overcoming him,—his head trembled, his arms and legs jerked. The death-mask of his face, with its unblinking, inflamed gaze, yet grimacing as if it were indulging in merry-andrew antics, was horrible. One heard the muffled growling of a beast in his voice.

"But shouldst thou do neither, I shall treat thee as a malefactor! . . ."

"I desire monkhood, and beg your gracious consent," uttered the Czarevich, in a quiet, firm voice.

He was lying. Peter knew he was lying. And Alexei knew that his father knew this. The malevolent joy of revenge filled the soul of the Czarevich. In his infinite submission there was infinite contumacy. Now the son was stronger than the father,—the weak was stronger than the strong. Of what benefit to the Czar would be his son's taking the tonsure? "The cowl is not nailed on to the head,—it can e'en be taken off." Yesterday a monk,—to-morrow a Czar. Batiushka's bones would turn in the grave when his son would make mock of him,—would squander, ruin everything, leaving not a single stone standing upon another, sending Russia to perdition. He should not be tonsured but slain, extirpated, wiped off the face of the earth.

"Get thee gone!" Peter moaned out in impotent frenzy.

The Czarevich raised his eyes and looked at his father point-blank, from under his brows: thus a wolf-cub regards an old wolf, its young fangs bared, its back bristling. Their glances crossed, like swords in a duel, and the father's gaze fell, just as if it had broken, like a knife striking granite.

And he again launched his low roar, like a wounded beast, and with a maternal oath suddenly raised his fist above the head of his son,—ready to throw himself upon him, ready to maul him, to kill him.

Suddenly a tiny, tender and strong hand descended upon Peter's shoulder.

The Empress Ekaterina Alexeievna had long been eavesdropping at the door of the room, and had made attempts to spy through the keyhole. Katenka was inquisitive. As always, she came to the rescue of her spouse at the moment of greatest danger. She had opened the door noiselessly and stolen up to him from behind, on tiptoe.

"Petenka! Batiushka!" she began, with a humble air,

which was yet somewhat jocose and humoring, such as kindly wet-nurses use in speaking to stubborn children, or nurses use with the sick. "Do not fash thyself, Petenka; break not thy heart, my dearest, or else thou wilt tire thyself out beyond thy strength and then take to thy bed again, and fall sick. . . . As for thee, Czarevich, do go,—do go, my own, and God be with thee! Thou canst see our Sovereign is not feeling well. . . ."

Peter turned around, caught sight of the calm, almost jolly face of Katenka, and at once came to his senses. The uplifted arms fell and hung down as if of wood, and the whole huge, corpulent body sank into an armchair, just as if an age-old tree had crashed down, cut at its very roots.

Alexei regarded his father point-blank, as before, from under his brows,—stooping, shrunken, just as if he had his back up, like one beast against another, he was slowly backing toward the exit, and, only on the very threshold, did he suddenly make a quick turn, opening the door and going out.

As for Katenka, she perched sideways on the arm of the chair, embraced Peter's head, and pressed it to her bosom,— full, as soft as a pillow: the bosom of a real foster-mother. Side by side with his yellow, ailing, almost aged face, the rosy-cheeked face of Katenka seemed altogether young,— all in little downy birthmarks, resembling beauty-spots, with its charming little prominences and dimples, and arched sable eye-brows, and painstakingly curled ringlets of dyed black hair upon her low brow, and large, rather bulgy eyes, with the unchanging smile of the portraits of royalty. However, on the whole she resembled not so much a Czaritza as a German tavern-maid or a Russian soldier-woman,—a laundress, as the Czar himself styled her, who accompanied her "old man" on all his campaigns, "washing and sewing" for him with her own hands; and, when he had "the colic fits," she warmed hot compresses for him, rubbed down his abdomen with the unguents prescribed by Blumentrost, and "physicked him."

No one save Katenka could tame those fits of insane, regal wrath, which those about him dreaded so much.

Clasping his head with one hand, she stroked his hair with

the other, to the unvarying, soothing refrain of: "Petenka,
Batiushka,—my dearling,—dearest little friend of my
heart! . . ." She was like a mother lulling a sick child,—
and like a lion-tamer fondling one of her beasts. Under this
measured, soft caress, the Czar was growing calmer, as if he
were falling asleep. His bodily convulsions were abating. It
was only the death mask of his face, now altogether turned
to stone, with the eyes shut, which still twitched occasionally, as though it were grimacing like a merry-andrew's.

Katenka had been followed into the room by a little
monkey,—brought as a present to Lizanka, the youngest
Czarevna, by a certain Dutch skipper. This madcap jacka-
napes, following the Czaritza like some page, strove to catch
the train of her dress, as though it wanted to lift it up with
bold shamelessness. But, catching sight of Lizetta, it grew
frightened and leapt on the table, and from the table on to
a sphere which represented the course of celestial luminaries,
according to the system of Copernicus,—the slender brass
arcs bent under the beastie, the globe of the universe emitted
a soft tinkle,—and then the monkey leapt still higher, to the
very top of the upright English clock, in its cabinet of tulip-
wood and glass. The last beam of the sun fell upon the clock,
and the pendulum, as it swayed, flashed like lightning. It
was a long time since Jocko had seen the sun. As if trying to
recall something, it looked with melancholy wonder at the
alien, wan, wintry sun, and puckered up its eyes and made
funny little faces, as though mimicking the convulsions on
the face of Peter. And dreadful was the resemblance of the
merry-andrew grimaces on these two faces,—that of the tiny
beastie and of the great Czar.

Alexei was on his way home.

He was in that state in which people who have had a leg
or arm amputated find themselves: coming to, they try to feel
the place where the member had been, and perceive that it
is no longer there. Thus did the Czarevich feel about that
spot in his soul where his love for his father had been,—and
perceived that it no longer existed. "I'll lop thee off like to a
gangrenous member," he recalled Batiushka's utterance. It
was as though, together with his love, everything had been
extracted from the Czarevich. There was a void,—no hope,

no fear, no sorrow, no joy,—everything was a void, buoyant and frightful.

And he was astonished how quickly, how simply his desire had been fulfilled: his father had died.

BOOK FIVE

THE ABOMINATION THAT MAKETH DESOLATE

I

"WHEN the Czar had journeyed to Voronezh to build ships, in the year seventeen hundred and one, a great fire occurred in Moscow, through the will of God. The Czar's residence in the Kremlin burned down,—the mansions of wood, and the interiors of those that were built of stone, and the holy churches, and their crosses, and their roofs,—and, within, even the ikonostases and the holy images burned. And, on the John the Great Tower, a great bell weighing near a hundred and thirty ton was weakened by the fire, and fell, and cracked; that of the Cathedral of the Annunciation, as well, was shattered, and sundry other bells fell. And so great was the fire that the very earth did burn. . . ."

This was told to the Czarevich Alexei by the sacristan of the Cathedral of the Annunciation, Father Ivan, a septuagenarian.

Peter had gone off to foreign parts immediately after his illness, on the twenty-seventh of January, seventeen hundred and sixteen. The Czarevich remained alone in Peterburgh. Receiving no communications from his father, he had "put off" the Czar's ultimatum,—either to mend his ways in order to succeed to the throne, or to take the tonsure, and lived on as before, taking no care beyond the day, resigning himself to the will of God. He passed the winter in Peterburgh,—the spring and summer in Rozhdestvenno. In the autumn he made a trip to Moscow to see some of his kindred.

On the tenth of September, in the evening, just before his departure, he paid a visit to an old friend, the sacristan of the Cathedral of the Annunciation, the husband of his wet nurse, and in his company had gone to inspect the old palace at the Kremlin, made desolate by the conflagration.

Long did they wander from one suite to another, from chamber to chamber, through the endless ruins. That which the flames had spared was being destroyed by time. Many of the suites were left without doors, without windows, without floors, so that it was impossible to enter them. Crevices yawned in the walls. Vaults and roofs had fallen down. Alexei could not find, or did not recognize, the rooms in which he had passed his childhood.

Even though it was not put in words, he surmised the thought of Father Ivan,—that the conflagration, which had occurred the very year when the Czar had begun to break down the times of old, was a portent of the wrath of the Lord.

They entered the small, crumbling oratory,—so old that even the Terrible Czar had prayed there for the son whom he had slain.

The sky peeped in through a crevice,—a sky as deep, as blue as it can be only among ruins. The cobwebs clinging to the edges of the crevice gave off all the colors of the rainbow, and a cross, wrenched off by some storm, on the very verge of falling, barely hung upon torn chains. The small window-panes of mica had been broken by the wind. Jackdaws, flying in through the holes, wove their nests under the vaults and defiled the ikonestasion. Their droppings, in white streams, furrowed the visages of the saints. One wing of the bema gates was torn off its hinges. In the altar, before the communion-table, was a stagnant, dirty puddle.

Father Ivan told the Czarevich how the chaplain, an old man, almost a centenarian, had long petitioned all the departments, bureaus, and even the Sovereign himself, pleading for the temple to be repaired, inasmuch as, "because of the dilapidation of the vaults, the leaks have multiplied so that there is danger of the Most Holy Eucharist being spoilt." But no one paid any attention to him. He had died from grief and the chapel had fallen into ruins.

The alarmed jackdaws soared upward with ominous cries. A draughty wind, rushing in through a window, began to moan and wail. A spider started scurrying up and down his web. Something fluttered out of the altar,—probably a bat, —and began to circle over the very head of the Czarevich.

An eerie feeling fell upon him. One felt pity for the dese-
crated church. He recalled the words of the prophet anent
the abomination that maketh desolate set up in the sanctuary.[55]

Passing by the Golden Altar Rails, through the front corridors of the Grand Entry, they descended to the Granite
Suite, which had fared better than the others. But, instead
of the former receptions of ambassadors and Imperial receptions, new comedies,—*dialogues* were presented here now;
the place was also used for the weddings of jesters. And, in
order that the old might not conflict with the new, the pictorial chronicles upon the walls had been whitewashed, and
daubed over with ochre, in a gay little design, in the new
"German manner."

In one of the cubby-holes of a ground-floor lumber-room,
Father Ivan showed the Czarevich two lion effigies. He immediately recognized them, since he had frequently seen
them in his childhood. Placed, during the times of Czar
Alexei Mikhailovich, near the Imperial throne in the Kolo-
mensky Palace, they used to growl, move their eyes, and
open their maws. Their brass bodies were glued over with
the skins of rams, to simulate lion skins. The mechanism
which emitted the "leonine roaring," and which gave motion
to their maws and eyes, was placed alongside, in a separate
cubby-hole, where a work-bench fitted out with bellows and
springs had been built. Probably they had been transferred
to the Kremlin palace for repairs, and here in the store-
room, amid the other lumber, they had been forgotten. The
springs had broken; the bellows had become full of holes;
the skins had become moth-eaten; rotted soaked-bast pro-
truded from their bellies,—and pitiful now seemed the one-
time awesome lions of the Russian autocrats. Their maws
were full of sheepish stupidity.

Those suites which had been neglected, but had remained
undamaged, were now used to house new departments. Thus,
the two fronting the quay, formerly the Chamber of Reports
and the Requiem Hall, were now the Court Chambers; under
the roof were the Departments of the Senate; in the Com-
missary and Granary building were the Salt Office, the Military Bureau, the Chancellories of Equipment and Expedi-

tions; the hostlers' quarters were now the stores of cloth and ammunition. Every department had moved in not only with its archives, its clerks, its watchmen and petitioners, but even with its prisoners, who lived for years in the ground-floor quarters of the palaces. All these newcomers swarmed and milled about in the old palace, like maggots in a corpse, and created much filthiness.

"All this noisome waste and manure from the privies, and from the horse-stalls, and from the prisoners," Father Ivan told the Czarevich, "greatly endanger the Czar's treasures and the precious utensils which are kept in the palace from the years of old, inasmuch as an evil odor is engendered by this foulness. One may expect serious harm to the gold and silver plate, and all the treasures of the Czar, from the said odor,—for it may make all these things turn black. The refuse ought to be cleared away, and the prisoners removed to other places. Much have we petitioned and complained concerning this, but none heeds us . . ." the old man concluded despondently.

It was Sunday; the chancellories were empty; but there was an oppressive odor in the air. Everywhere one could see the greasy traces where the backs of the petitioners had rubbed against the walls, and ink spots, and obscene drawings and inscriptions. But the austere visages of the prophets, patriarchs and Russian saints still looked down from the dimmed gilding of the ancient murals.

In the Kremlin, near the palaces and cathedrals, close to the Secret Gates, was a public house for the clerks and petti-foggers, called The Slope, because of the steepness of the descent from the Kremlin hill. It had sprung up like a foul toadstool, and flourished these many years on the sly, despite *ukases* that: "the said tavern is to be immediately removed from the Kremlin; but, in order not to lose such a sum from the revenue on liquor, several other taverns, instead of this one tavern, may be added at discretion, in some convenient and fitting place."

In one of the chancellory suites the stuffiness and the stench were so great that the Czarevich made all haste to open a window. Floating up from below, out of The Slope, packed to overflowing, came a savage roaring, just like that

of some beast, the thump of dancing, the tinkling of a
balalaika, and a drunken song:

> Oh, my mother was a-dancing when she gave me birth;
> I was christened midst the tavern's mirth;
> I was baptized in a wine green and strong . . .

a familiar song,—the same that was sung by the mock Princess-Abbess Rzhevskaya at Batiushka's feasts.

And it seemed to the Czarevich that out of The Slope, as
out of a dark, yawning maw, together with the song and the
maternal curses, and the effluvia of wretched spirits, there
was rising up to the Imperial chambers, and filling them, a
stifling stench, which made one nauseous, made everything
grow dark before one's eyes, and made one's heart contract
with a deathly ennui. He lifted up his eyes to the vault of
the suite, whereon were depicted the "celestial courses," the
lunar and solar orbits, the angels who served the stars, and
divers other "works of God"; there, too, was Christ Emmanuel, seated upon heavenly rainbows with many-spoked
wheels; in His left hand was a chalice of gold, in His right
a staff; on His head,—a seven-beamed nimbus; on a field of
gold, underlaid with green, was the inscription: *Eternal Word
of the Father, Thou Who art in the image of God, and Who
makest and createst every creature from Non-Being into
Being,—grant peace to Thy Churches, and victory to Thy
faithful Czar.*

Yet in the meanwhile, below, the song was rollicking on
and on:

> Oh, my mother was a-dancing when she gave me birth;
> I was christened midst the tavern's mirth. . . .

The Czarevich read the inscription in the solar orbit:
The sun knoweth his going down, and it is night.[56]

And these words echoed within his soul as a prophecy:
the ancient sun of the Czardom of Muscovy had come to
know its westering, its going down on this dark Finnish bog,
in this putrid, autumnal mire; *and it was night,*—not a black
night, but the white, fearful, Peterburgh night. The ancient
sun had grown dim. The ancient gold, the crown and the
coronation mantle of Monomachos had turned black from the

new mephitic air. And the abomination that maketh desolate had been set up in the holy place.

As though escaping from an invisible pursuit, he fled from the palace, without looking back, through corridors and passages and up and down staircases, so that Father Ivan, with his old limbs, could hardly keep up with him. Only out on the square, under the open sky, did the Czarevich halt and breathe more freely. Here the autumnal air was clean and chill. And the ancient white stones of the cathedrals seemed clean, and new.

On the corner, by the very wall of the Cathedral of the Annunciation, near the chantry dedicated to the Protomartyr Georgii, beneath the cells in one of which Father Ivan lived, was a low bench daubed with clay, something on the manner of those found near stoves. The old man frequently sat there warming his old bones in the sun. The Czarevich sank down in exhaustion on this bench. The old man toddled on homewards, in order to see about the night's lodging. The Czarevich was left alone.

He felt fatigued, as though he had traversed a thousand versts. He wanted to weep, yet had no tears, his heart was afire, and the tears dried up within it, like water upon a heated stone.

The soft light of evening glowed, was reflected warmly upon the white walls, like the light of some holy lamp. The gold cupolas of the cathedrals glowed like living embers. The sky was darkening, turning lilac,—its color was like to the color of a wilted violet. And the white towers seemed gigantic blossoms with fiery corollas.

Bells began to chime the time,—at first on the Saviour's Secret and Investiture Gates, then upon various other towers, near and far. The slow waves of prolonged booming and pealing quivered in the vibrant air, as though the clocks were calling to one another, talking over the mysteries of the past and the future. The old fellows "struck the hours" by means of a multitude of small bells, that chimed in "in half-tones" with the huge military bell, which, although hoarse, nevertheless produced triumphant churchly music; but the new Dutch bells answered them with babbling chimes and fashionable dance tunes, "somewhat on the manner of those in Amsterdam." And all these sounds, ancient and new, were recalling to the Czarevich his distant—most distant—childhood.

He narrowed his eyes, and his soul was plunged into a half-oblivion, into that dark region between sleep and reality where the shades of the past dwell. As motley shadows flit across a white wall when a sunbeam penetrates within a dark room through some crack, so recollections, visions were flitting before him. And over all of them one horrifying image was dominant,—his father. And as a wayfarer, looking down at night from a height, suddenly beholds the entire distance he has traversed by the light of a lightning gleam, so did he, in the fearful gleam of this image, behold his whole life.

II

He is six. He is being held in the arms of his grandmother, in an antique, regal carriage, "built for the hardships of the road," all begilt, but as clumsy and jouncing as a common cart, its interior upholstered in velvet with clove designs, with shutters of mica and curtains of taffeta, amid down-pillows, and linen-women and nurses who are as puffy as pillows. His mother, the Czaritza Avdothea, is also here. Under a frontlet, fringed with pearls, her face is round, perpetually astonished,—altogether like that of a little girl.

From behind a hanging, through the open little window of the carriage, he is peeping at the triumphal review of the troops, on the occasion of the Azov expedition. He likes the unvarying formation regularity of the regiments, the brass cannons flashing in the sun, and the rudely daubed allegories on the shields: two shackled Turks with the inscription:

> Ah, Azov, we did let go
> And thereby begot much woe!

And, in a sea as blue as blueing, a naked, ruddy man, "the famed sea-god, Neptunus," was astride the scaly, green beast, Cytovrass, with a harpoon in his hands: *Verily, I do felicitate you on the capture of Azov, and do submit to you.* Magnificent does the German savant Vinius seem to him, clad as a Roman warrior and declaiming Russian verses from the heights of the triumphal arch, through a trumpet over three yards long.

In the ranks, side by side with the common soldiers, marches a bombadier of the Guard of the Transfiguration, in a dark green frock with red facings, and wearing a tri-cornered hat. He is so much taller than all the rest that he can be seen towering from afar. Alësha knows that this is his father, but his face is so youthful,—almost like a child's, that to Alësha he appears not his father but an elder brother, a dear playmate,—just as much of a little lad as he, Alësha, is. It is stuffy in the old carriage, amid the down-pillows, and the nurses, and the wet-nurses, who are as puffy as pillows. Alësha longs for freedom and the sun, and for this jolly, curly-haired lad with his sprightly eyes.

The father has caught sight of the son. They smile to each other; and Alësha's heart is pounding for joy. The Czar approaches the carriage-doors, opens them, takes his son from his grandmother's arms almost by force,—the nurses simply 'Oh'd!'; tenderly, much more tenderly than his mother,—the Czar kisses and embraces him; then, raising his son high on his hands, he shows him to the troops, to the people, and, setting him on his shoulder, carries him over the heads of the troops. At first near at hand, and then ever farther and farther, over the sea of heads, there resounds a thousand-throated shout, like to a joyous thunder.

"*Vivat! Vivat! Vivat!* Hail to the Czar and the Czarevich!"

Alësha feels that all are looking at him, and that all love him. He is both frightened and gay. He holds fast to his father's neck, nuzzling against him trustingly, and the latter carries him carefully,—most carefully; never fear, he won't let Alësha drop. And it seems to him that all his father's movements are his own movements; that all of his father's strength is his own strength; that he and his father are one. He wants both to laugh and to cry,—so joyous are the shouts of the people, and the thundering of the cannons, and the pealing of bells, and the golden cupolas of the cathedrals, and the blue skies, and the free wind, and the sun. His head is swimming; he cannot catch his breath,—and he is flying, flying straight up into the sky, toward the sun.

In the meanwhile the head of his grandmother pops out of the window of the carriage. Her ancient, kindly, wrinkled little face is both funny and dear to Alësha. She waves her hand and shouts, and implores, almost weeping:

"Petenka, Petenka, Batiushka! Don't tire out Olëshenka!"

And again the nurses and the wet-nurses tuck him up in his downy bassinet, under a soft coverlet of damask cloth-of-gold, made in Kizilbash, lined with sable bellies, and sing lullabies to him, and pamper him, tickling the soles of his tiny feet to make his sleep sweeter, and bundle him up, and muffle him up, lest a breeze breathe on him,—safe-guarding the kingly babe like the apple of their eyes. They hide him as if he were a beauteous maiden, behind age-old screens and curtains. Whenever he goes to church, lengths of woolen cloth screen him from all sides, that none might see the Czarevich till that he be "proclaimed," in accordance with ancient custom; but when they shall have proclaimed him, people will come from the most distant places, with the sole purpose of beholding him, as if he were some "great marvel."

It is stuffy in the rather low-ceiled, small chambers of the old palace. The doors, the shutters, the windows,—all openings,—are painstakingly covered over with felt, lest a draft penetrate from anywhere. The floor is also covered with felts, "for warmth and to make walking soft." The tiled ovens are red-hot; there is an odor of garrow brandy, and cala-mite, which is put into the oven fires "for the sake of the smell." The light of day, when it penetrates in here through the mica of the distorting small window openings, becomes amber-yellow. The little flames of lampads are warmly glowing everywhere. Alësha feels languid, but, at the same time, tranquil and comfortable. Seemingly, he is forever dozing and cannot awaken. He is dozing, and listens to the monotonous conversations of how "one's house should be arranged in accordance with God's dictates; everything ought to be tidy, and most clean, and swept up, and kept from every sort of filth,—lest there be spoilage from mildew or rot,—and always locked up, and not exposed to theft or wanton waste; honor should be rendered to the worthy, while the wicked should go in fear"; how "left-overs should be care-fully saved"; how split and dried fish should be rolled up in matting. How to preserve pickled mushrooms, red and brown, in tubs,—and a warm faith in the Trinity, one and indivisible, in one's soul. He dozes to the dismal sounds of Tartar balalaikas played by blind men who chant the ancient sagas; he dozes, too, to the sounds of fairy tales told by centenarian bards,—ancients who had amused even his grandfather, the Most Pacific Czar Alexei Mikhailovich. He dozes and daydreams as he listens to the stories of pious palmers, coming from up-river, and of little mendicant pilgrims,—stories concerning the Mount of Athos,—mountain as pointed as pointed can be, like to a pine-cone; on its very summit, away above the clouds, stands Our Mother, the Most Holy Mother of God, and shelters the mountain under the cover of her vestments; stories concerning Simeon Stylites, who, letting his own body rot, was all a-swarm with maggots; stories concerning the site of the earthly paradise, which Moïslav of Novgorod had caught a glimpse of from his ship; and stories concerning all sorts of Divine miracles and Satanic visitations. But should Alëshenka become bored, all sorts of fools and female zanies, and innocents, and little orphan girls, and Mongolian idiots, and blackamoors, would, at the command of his grandmother, fall to dancing before him, and fighting, and tumbling about the floor, and pulling each other's hair, and scratching one another until blood came. Or else his little old grandmother would sit him on her knees and would begin telling his fingers, one after the other, from the thumb to the little finger itself, chanting the nursery rhyme of the magpie crow that cooked some porridge; "she hopped without stop, bidding friends come to sup; this fellow ate, and this fellow ate,—but this fellow got naught, save a thwack on his pate!" And his grandmother tickles him, while he laughs and swings his arms. She stuffs him with greasy baked puddings, and pancakes, and onion-patties, and puffed-up dumplings, with the stuffing all at one end, and little sour-sweet pancakes fried in nut-oil, and buckwheat prepared in milk of poppies, and gruel made of white flour, after a Mozhaisk recipe, and obovate pears in treacle.

"Eat, Olëshenka,—eat hearty, my dearest little dear!"

But when Alësha's little tummy begins to ache, there appears a knowing old country-wife, who treats little children by whispering spells, and medicates them with herbs against internal and hysterical ailments, says charms by putting pots on their little bellies, and makes incantations over a thunder-arrow, as well as a bear's claw; and all this lightens the ills of man. No sooner does he sneeze or cough, than he is drenched with strawberry-infusions, rubbed down with spirits of wine mixed with camphor, or made to sweat in a trough, over steaming malope.

Only on the very hottest day is he led out to stroll in the Upper Garden, also called the Beautiful, built up on timber work on the slope of the Kremlian Mountain, which is near the river-bank. This garden, a simulacrum of the Hanging Gardens, is a continuation of the old palace. Here every-thing is artificial: hot-house flowers in boxes, diminutive ponds in tubs, trained birds in cages. The boy gazes down upon Moscow, spreading out at his feet; upon streets which he has never trod; upon roofs, towers, belfries; upon distant Moscow-Beyond-the-River, upon the Sparrow Hills, show-ing blue in the distance; upon ætherial aureate clouds. And he feels bored. He longs to escape from the old palace, and from this toy forest, into a real forest, into the unknown dis-tance; he longs to run away, to fly off,—he envies the swal-lows. It is sultry, and a haze is rising up. The hot-house flowers and the medicinal herbs,—marjoram, thyme, savory, costmary, hyssop,—emit a spicy and oppressive aroma. A blue cloud, as blue as blue can be, is creeping up. Sudden shadows begin to scurry along, there is a breath of fresh-ness,—and rain spatters down. He puts his face and hands under it, avidly catching the cold drops, but the nurses and wet-nurses are already seeking him, calling him:

"Olëshenka! Olëshenka! Come on home, dear little baby! Thou wilt get thy little feet wet."

But Alësha does not heed them, and hides amid some bushes. There is a new odor of mint, of fennel, of damp black loam, and the moist verdure has become a vivid dark; the dark red peonies have burst into scarlet flame. The last sunbeam has pierced a cloud, and the sun has mingled with the rain into a single golden, tremulous net. His feet and his dress have already become soaked through and through. But, as he admires the great drops breaking up into radiant dust in the puddles, he hops and prances, clapping his palms and singing a gay little snatch to the noise of the rain, echoed by the reverberating vault of the aqueduct tower:

> Rain, rain, go away
> Come again some other day.
> To Jordan we will go,
> And to Christ and God bow low.

Suddenly, over his very head, just as though a cloud had split, came a blinding lightning-flash,—there was a peal of thunder, and a whirlwind sprang up. He froze on the spot from horror and joy,—as at the time when he had been perched on the shoulders of his father, during the triumphal procession on the occasion of the Azov victory. He recalled the gay, curly-headed, quick-eyed lad,—and he felt that he loved him as much as he loved this frightful lightning. His breath was cut short. He fell on his knees and stretched out his arms toward the black sky, dreading, yet longing, that the lightning might flash out once more,—still more ominous, still more blinding.

But trembling, senile hands are already snatching him up, carrying him off, undressing him, tucking him up in his crib, rubbing him down with spirits of wine mixed with camphor, giving him internal doses of special vodka used against apoplexy, and drenching him with linden blossoms until he sweats seven times, and wrapping him up, and bundling him. And he is again dozing. And there comes to him in his dream the Aspic-Beast, which dwelleth on mountains of stone, having the face of a maid, the proboscis of a serpent, and the limbs of a basilisk, wherewith it can split iron; it is killed by the sound of trumpets: being unable to bear this, it pierces its ears and expires, inundating the stones with its blue blood. There also comes to him in his dream the Sirin [Siren], the bird of paradise, which sings kingly songs, and in the gardens of Aiden in the East, dwelleth, and to the righteous that joy foretelleth which is promised to them of God; no man that draws the breath of life, can bear to hear its voice,—for, should he hear it, he is taken captive with thoughts of it, and following after it and listening to its song, he dieth. And it seems to Alësha that he is following the singing of the Sirin, and, hearing its delectable song, is dying, falling into an eternal sleep.

Suddenly it seems as if a storm had burst into the room and, throwing open the doors, screens, and hangings, and snatching the blanket from Alësha, had enveloped him in cold. He opened his eyes and beheld Batiushka's face. But he did not become frightened, nor even wonder-struck, as though he knew that his father would come, and had awaited his coming. The paradisaical song of the Sirin still ringing in his ears, with a tender, sleepy smile, he stretched out his hands, cried out, "Batyia, Batyia! My dearest!" Sprang up and threw himself at his father's neck. The latter clasped him hard to his breast, until it hurt, and squeezed him, kissing his face, and his neck, and his bare little legs, and his whole body,—warm, sleep-laden, under his tiny night-shift. His father had brought him from over-seas a new, cunning toy: in a wooden box, under glass, were three little waxen figures of German women, and a tiny babe, and behind them a small mirror; below this was a handle of bone,—if one turned it, the German women and the child would start turning round and round, dancing to music. The toy is very much to Alësha's liking. But he barely glanced at it,—and is again gazing, and cannot gaze enough at Batiushka. The latter's face has grown thinner and sunken; he has matured, and appears to have grown still taller. But to Alësha it seems that even though his father is big—exceedingly big,—yet he is still little, just the same as he had been before: a gay, curly-headed, quick-eyed lad. There is an odor of wine and fresh air about him.

"Why, Batyia has grown mustaches! And how tiny they are! One can barely see them! . . ."

And, curious, he passes a tiny finger over the upper lip of his father, over the soft dark down.

"And there is a tiny dimple on your chin,—every little bit like grandma's!" He kisses his father's dimple.

"But why has Batyia callouses on his hands?"

"From an ax, Alëshenka. I was building ships over-seas. Wait till thou art grown up, I'll take thee along with me too. Wouldst go over-seas?"

"I would. Where Batyia goes, I go too. I always want to be with Batyia. . . ."

"But art thou not sorry to leave grandma?"

Alësha suddenly noticed in the half-open door the thoroughly scared face of the little old woman, and the pale,—most pale,—seemingly dead face of his mother. Both were looking at him from afar, without daring to approach, and were making the sign of the cross over him, and also crossing themselves.

"I do feel sorry for grandma! . . ." Alësha spoke up, and wondered why his father did not ask him about his mother as well.

"But whom dost thou love more,—me or grandma?"

Alësha keeps silent. It is hard for him to decide, but suddenly he hugs his father still closer and all atremble, almost swooning from bashful tenderness, whispers in his ear: "I love Batyia,—I love him more than everybody else! . . ."

. . . And at once everything vanished,—the palace chambers, and the downy little bed, and his mother, and his grandmother, and the nurses. It was just as though he had fallen into some black pit,—had fallen, like a fledgling out of its nest, upon the frozen, hard earth.

He is in a large, cold room, with bare gray walls, with iron bars on the windows. He no longer sleeps now, but merely always wanting to sleep, and cannot get his fill of sleeping,—they wake him up much too early. Through a fog which is making his eyes smart he sees long barracks, yellow military buildings, striped sentry-booths, earth ramparts with yawning cannon and pyramids of cannon-balls, and the Falcon Field, covered with thawing gray snow under a gray sky, dotted with dripping crows and jackdaws. He hears the tattoo of drums, the commands of military drill: "Eyes front! Shoulder arms! Present arms! Right-about face!"—and the crisp rattle of musketry,—and once more the tattoo of the drums.

His aunt is with him,—the Czarevna Nathalia Alexeievna, an old maid, yellow of face, with bony fingers that pinch most painfully, and malicious, prickly eyes, that look upon him as if they would gobble him up: "Ugh, thou mangy whelp of Avdothea! . . ."

Only a long time afterward did he learn what happened.

The Czar, having returned from Holland, had packed off the Czaritza Avdothea, his wife, into the Suzdalsky Nunnery, where she had been forced to take the veil under the name of Ellena, while he had taken his son out of the old palace at Kremlin to the hamlet of the Transfiguration, into the new Pleasure Palace. Adjoining this palace, were the torture-chambers of the Privy Chancellory, where the investigation of the Streletsky Mutiny was being conducted. There, every day, blazed more than thirty bonfires, upon which the mutineers were being put to the question.

Whether that which he afterward recalled had been real, or had come to him in a dream, he himself did not know. It seemed to him that, at night, he was stealing along the palisade of sharpened logs which surrounded the prison-yard. One could hear moans issuing thence. A gleam of light came through a crack between the logs. He put his eye to it and saw a similitude of Hell.

> Fires are lit most hot;
> Water seethes in many a pot,
> Knives sharpened are, of steel:
> 'Tis thee they fain would kill.

Men were being broiled over a fire; men were being lifted up and stretched on a strappado, so that their joints crackled; their ribs were being broken with iron-pincers made red-hot; their nails were being "trimmed," by driving heated needles under them. Amid the executioners stood the Czar. His face was so frightful that Alësha does not recognize his father: it was he, and yet it was not he,—seemingly it was his double, or some warlock. He is torturing one of the ringleaders with his own hands. The latter endures everything and keeps silent. His body is already like a bleeding carcass that has been flayed by butchers. But he still keeps silent, merely looking straight into the eyes of the Czar, as though he were mocking him.

The dying man suddenly raised up his head and spat in the eyes of the Czar:

"Take that, thou son of a dog, thou Antichrist! . . ."

The Czar snatched his dirk out of its scabbard and plunged it into the man's throat. The blood spurted into the Czar's face.

Alësha fell down unconscious. In the morning some soldiers found him by the palisade, at the edge of a ditch. He lay for a long time ill, without regaining his senses.

When barely recovered, he was present, at the will of his father, at the solemn dedication of Le Fort's Palace to the god Bacchus. Alësha was in a brand-new German frock-coat, with stiff lapels on wires, with an enormous peruke pressing down on his head. His aunt was in a magnificent *robe-ronde*. They were in a room apart, adjoining the one wherein the guests were feasting. Hangings of taffeta,—a last vestige of the seclusion of old palaces,—hid them from the guests, yet Alësha could see everything: the participants of the Most Drunken Conclave,—bearing, instead of sacred utensils, goblets of wine and flagons of mead and beer; instead of the Evangel,—a cellarette, opening on the manner of a book, and holding bottles of sundry vodkas; tobacco burning in brazier was sending up its fumes, in lieu of frankincense. The high priest, the Prince-Pope, in a motley simulacrum of a patriarchal chasuble, with dice and playing-cards sewn thereto, in a miter of tin crowned wih a naked Bacchus, and with a crozier adorned with a naked Venus, was blessing the guests with two pipe-stems laid crosswise one upon the other. The drinking bout was under way. The jesters were reviling the old *boyars*, beating them, spitting in their faces, pouring wine over them, dragging them by the hair, clipping off their beards by force,—or plucking them out, together with flesh and blood. The feast was becoming an inquisition. It seems to Alësha that he is beholding all this in a delirium. And, again, he cannot recognize his father: this is his double, or a warlock.

"His porphyrogene and serene Highness, the Grand Czarevich Alexei Petrovich, having made beginning of the Alpha That Hath No Beginning, and in a short while having mastered letters and syllabification, by way of the alphabet, is now learning the Breviary," Nikishka Viyazemsky, "The least of the Czar's slaves," and the Czarevich's preceptor, reported to the Czar. He taught Alësha in accordance with the *Domostroi*,— [57] "concerning contact with all sacred things: miracle-working images and all-healing holy relics

should always be kissed with the utmost caution, nor should
the lips be smacked, and one's breath ought to be held, inasmuch as our stench and smell is abominable to the Lord; the
holy wafer should be consumed with the utmost care, dropping no crumbs to the ground, it should not be bitten off with
the teeth, as other forms of bread are,—but, breaking it off in
little bits, it should be put in the mouth and eaten with faith
and fear." Listening to these admonitions, Alësha recalled
how in Le Fort's Palace, before the shameless German wench
Monsikha, the intoxicated Nikishka, together with the Prince-
Pope and other merry-andrews, had been executing the squatting figure of the Russian dance to the whistling of the *Spring
Song* and the words of a tavern snatch:

> On the priest's meadow green,—*ikh, vokh!*
> I did lose my tambourine,—*ikh, vokh.*

The German savant, Baron Huyssen, presented to the
Czar his *Methodus Instructionis*,—"Instructions, to be fol-
lowed by whosoever shall be entrusted with the education of
His Royal Highness the Czarevich:

"Love for virtues should ever be inculcated and affirmed,
both in sentiment and in the heart; also, efforts should be
made to instill within him aversion and dislike to everything
which may be called evil-doing before God; and the serious
consequences flowing therefrom should be thoroughly represented, and be illustrated by applications from the Divine
Scriptures and temporal history. The French tongue should
be taught,—there is no better way of mastering it than
through daily use. Colored geographical maps should be ex-
hibited to him; he should be accustomed, little by little, to
the use of the compasses; the regularity and usefulness of
geometry should be represented to him. The rudiments of
military exercises, attacking, dancing, and equitation should
be taught him. He should be led to use a good Russian
style,—*i.e.*, diction. On mail days he should read diligently
the French gazettes, as well as *The Historical Mercury*, and,
in conjunction therewith, observations of political and moral
significance should be presented to him. *Telemachus* should
be used for the guidance of His Highness, like to a life-long
mirror and rule for his future reign. But, lest through cease-

less studies and efforts his capacities be wearied, the game of Backgammon should be moderately resorted to as an amusement. All these projects could be conveniently consummated within two years, and thereafter His Highness might be led to perfect himself in certain studies, without any loss of time, in order that he might arrive at a fundamental knowledge of: All universal political matters; the true weal of this realm; and all the necessary arts,—such as fortification, artillery, civic architecture, navigation, and so on, and so on,—to the great pleasure of His Majesty and to the immortal glory of His Highness himself."

For the execution of these *Instructions,* they chose the first German who came to hand,—Martin Martinovich Neubauer. He taught Alësha the code of "European compliments and courtesies," in accordance with a certain book entitled *The True Mirror of Youth.*

"Children should above all, hold their father in great honor. And when anything is told them by their parents, children ought to hold their hats in hand, and never stand alongside of them, but somewhat behind them, withdrawn to one side, like to a page or a servant. Also, upon meeting, halting three paces before reaching them, they should greet their parents, doffing their hats in a pleasant manner; inasmuch as it is better to have it said of one: He is polite, a diffident gallant, and a goodly youth, than to have it said: He is a vain blockhead. Lean not against tables, nor benches, nor aught else, and be not like unto some country bumpkin, who spendeth his time lolling in the sun. Youths of tender years ought not to snort through their noses, nor blink their eyes. Nor is it the least of vilenesses when some one blows his nose frequently, as if he were blowing a trumpet, or sneezeth loudly, and thereby frighteneth other people, or, when he is in church, frighteneth little children. Trim thy nails, lest they appear to be edged with velvet. At table sit decorously erect; do not clean thy teeth with a knife, but with a tooth-pick, and cover thy mouth with one hand when thou dost clean thy teeth. Do not smack thy lips over thy food, like to a swine, and scratch not thy head, inasmuch as that is the way of clodhoppers. Youths of tender years should ever converse among themselves in foreign tongues, that they

may grow adept therein, and so that they may be distinguished
from other ignorant blockheads. . . ."

Thus did the German sing into one ear of the Czarevich,
whereas the Russian sang into his other ear: "Do not spit,
Olëshenka, to the right,—for your guardian angel is there;
spit to the left,—that is where the fiend is. Do not put the
shoe on thy left foot first, my dear little one,—'tis a sin.
Gather into a bit of paper and preserve thy nail-parings,—
that thou mayst have wherewithal to climb up Mount Zion,
into the Kingdom of Heaven. . . ." The German jeered at
the Russian, the Russian jeered at the German,—and Alësha
knew not which one to believe. This "haughty student, the
son of a burgher of Danzig," hated Russia. "Is this a language?" he was wont to say. "There can be no rhetoric or
grammar in this language. The Russian priests themselves
are unable to explain that which they read in churches. The
Russian language breeds only unenlightenment and ignorance!" He was forever drunk, and, when in his cups, was
even more bitterly reviling:

"You know nothing at all, now; ye are all barbarians! Ye
dogs,—dogs! *Hundsfötte! . . .*"

The Russians teased the German by nicknaming him
"Martinushka-Martishka"—Martinushka-Jackanapes, and
informed on him to the Czar, to the effect that, "instead of
instructing the Prince Czarevich, he, this Martin, was giving
him evil counsels, forming in him an aversion for studies and
having anything to do with foreigners." To Alësha it seemed
that both his preceptors,—the Russian as well as the German,—were equally louts.

Martin Martinovich used to bore him so during the day-
time that even at night he would come to him in his dreams,
in the form of a little monkey that, in accordance with all
the rules of European compliments and courtesies, was
grimacing before the true mirror of youth. The ancient Czars
of Muscovy, the patriarchs and holy men, were standing all
around, just as they did upon the walls of the Golden Suite,
with its mural ikons, while Martishka was mocking and
reviling them: "Ye dogs,—dogs! *Hundsfötte!* All of you
know nothing,—ye are barbarians!" And Alësha thinks he
sees a resemblance between this simian muzzle and a certain

convulsion-distorted face,—not of the Czar, the Batiushka, but of that other, that fearful double of his,—the warlock. And the shaggy paw is stretching toward Alësha, and seizing his hand, and dragging him off.

And again he is falling, falling,—but now it is to the very edge of the world, to a flat sea-marge, with mossy tussocks of swamps whose stagnant waters seem rusty; the wan sun seems dead, the low-hanging sky seems to be the sky of some subterrain. Everything here is misty, phantomlike. And he himself seems a specter, as though he had died long, long ago, and descended into the terrain of shadows.

At the age of thirteen the Czarevich has been enrolled as a soldier in a company of bombardiers and taken along in the expedition against Noteburgh. From Noteburgh to Ladoga; from Ladoga,—to Jamburgh, to Koporië, to Narva, —he is dragged everywhere behind the troops in a wagon-train, in order to inure him to military exercises. Almost a child, he endures privations, dangers, cold, hunger, endless fatigue, on a footing with adults. He sees blood and mire, and all the horrors and abominations of war. He sees his father, but only in glimpses, from a distance. And each time he sees him his heart swoons from a mad hope: lo, he will approach, call Alësha near him, and caress him. Had there been but a single word, a single glance,—Alësha would then have taken on new life, would have understood what was wanted from him. But his father never has the time: now it is a sword that he has in his hand,—and next it is a quill, or the compasses, or an ax. He is warring with the Swede, and is driving down the first piles, building the first small houses of Sanct Peterburgh.

"My Most Gracious Lord and Batiushka:

"I beg of thee, My Lord, as a favor, to see that I be informed by a letter concerning thy health, which would cause me joy,—since I ever long zealously to hear about this matter.

"Thy little son Alësha,
    imploring thy blessing and offering his homage."
Writ in Peterburgh, the 25th Day of August, A.D. 1703.

Even in his letters, which he writes to the dictation of his teacher, he dares not add a single heartfelt word, either of endearment or caress or complaint. Alone, wild, thoroughly cowed, he is growing up like the quitch grass under the palisades of the military buildings and in the ditches.

Narva has been taken by assault. The Czar, celebrating the victory, reviews his troops to the sound of cannon fire and music. The Czarevich stands in front of the troops and sees from afar a youthful giant, with a gay and awesome face, approaching him. This is he, he himself,—neither his double nor the warlock, but his own Batiushka, as of yore,—the real one. The boy's heart beats violently, swooning once more with an insane hope; their eyes meet,—and it is as if a lightning flash had blinded Alësha. If he could but run up to his father, throw himself on his neck, embrace and kiss him, and weep for joy . . .

But, instead, words which are like to the wording of *ukases* and military articles rattle forth distinctly and abruptly, like the tattoo of a drum:

"Son! I have taken thee along in this campaign so that thou mightest see that I fear neither exertions nor danger; inasmuch as I, being but a mortal man, may die to-day or on the morrow, thou shouldst remember that thou wilt have but little joyance if thou dost not follow my ensample. Spare no efforts for the common weal. But should my counsels be merely dispersed by the wind, and thou shalt choose not to do as I desire, then I shall not recognize thee as my son, and shall pray to God that He may punish thee, both in this and in the future life. . . ."

His father lifts Alësha's chin with two fingers and looks intently into his eyes. A shadow flits across Peter's face. It is as though he beheld his son for the first time,—this puny little lad, narrow-shouldered, with sunken chest and a gaze obdurate and dismal, is his only son, the heir to his throne, the one who is to crown all his toils and great deeds with success. Come,—is this really so? Whence had come this pitiful marasmus, this jackdaw fledgling in an eagle's eyrie? How could *he* have fathered such a son?

Alësha has become all shrunken, all huddled up like a hedgehog, as though he were surmising all his father's thoughts and were at fault before him,—a fault unknown yet infinite. He feels such shame and fear that he is ready to start bawling like a little boy, before the eyes of all the troops. But, making an effort, he babbles the greeting he has memorized in a quavering little voice:

"Most gracious Sire,—Batiushka! I am yet too young, and do what I can, but I assure Your Majesty, as an obedient son, that I shall exert all my powers to emulate all your deeds, and follow your ensample. May God preserve you for many a long year in steadfast health, that I may long continue to take joy in having such an illustrious parent. . . ."

After doffing his hat in "a pleasant manner, like an obedient squire," as instructed by Martin Martinovich, he extends a German "compliment":

"*Meines gnadigsten Papas gehorsamster Diener und Sohn.*

And he feels himself a little monster, a silly little ape before this Titan, who is as splendidly beautiful as a youthful god.

His father thrust out his hand toward him. Alësha kissed it. Tears spurted out of his eyes, and it seemed to him as if his father, having felt the warmth of those tears, had jerked his hand away in revulsion.

During the triumphal entry of the troops into Moscow, on the seventeenth of December, in the year seventeen-hundred-and-four, on the occasion of the victory of Narva, the Czarevich marched along in the full-dress uniform of the Guards of the Transfiguration, carrying a musket, like any common soldier. It was zero weather. He was chilled,—almost freezing to death. In the Palace, during the customary drinking bout, he drank a tumbler of vodka for the first time in his life, in order to warm himself, and immediately became tipsy. His head began to swim,—everything grew dark before his eyes. Through this darkness, with its rapidly revolving and intertwining circles of turbid green and red, he saw clearly only the face of Batiushka, who was regarding him with a smile of contempt. Alësha experienced the pain of an unbearable affront. Staggering, the Czarevich arose, walked up to his father, looked at him from under his brows like a cornered wolf-cub, was about to say or do something, but suddenly paled, emitted a feeble cry, swayed, and dropped at his father's feet as one dead.

III

"The days of my life are drawing toward old age, and loss of voice, and deafness, and blindness; therefore I implore you to retire me from my office of sacristan and to let me end my days in peace in some cloister. . . ."

Plunged in his recollections, the Czarevich did not listen to the monotonously murmuring words of Father Ivan, who, having come out of his cell, had once more sat down beside him on the bench.

"Likewise my small house, and the humble furnishings thereof, and whatever superfluous poor chattels I may have, ought to be sold; and the two little orphans who live with me, my two nieces, that have nor sib nor kin, ought to be put in some nunnery. As for whatever dowry might accrue, it ought to be put into the treasury of some cloister, so that I, sinner that I am, may not eat the bread of the monastery without paying therefor, and may it be found acceptable from me, like the two mites of the widow in the Evangel. And may it be granted to me to live a little while more under a vow of silence, and in repentance, until such time as, through the decree of God, I shall be taken from this into the future life. As for my years, I think them drawing nigh to death, inasmuch as e'en my father did when he had attained my years,—cease this life."

Coming to, as if from a deep sleep, the Czarevich saw that night had fallen long since. The white towers of the cathedrals had become ætherially blue and they resembled, more than ever, gigantic flowers, or lilies of paradise. The gold cupolas now showed in dull silver against the black-blue of the star-strewn sky. The Milky Way glimmered feebly. And, in the wafting of the celestial freshness,—as even as the breathing of a sleeper,—there was descending upon the earth a premonition of an eternal sleep,—an infinite calm.

And the slowly-murmurous words of Father Ivan blended with the calm:

"If they would but let me go to my rest in some holy cloister, to live there under a vow of silence until such time as I shall be taken from this into the future life. . . ."

He spoke on for a long while yet, alternately falling silent and speaking again. He went away; he returned; he called the Czarevich to supper. But the latter saw nothing and heard nothing. He again narrowed his eyes and was plunged into forgetfulness, into that dark region between reality and dreaming wherein dwell the shadows of the past. Again, recollections,—visions passed before him,—image threading upon image, like a long chain, link upon link; and over all of them reigned one terrifying image,—his father. And, even as a wayfarer who looks back at night from a summit may suddenly perceive by a lightning gleam all of the way he has traversed, so did he, in the fearful gleam of this image, perceive all his life. . . .

He is seventeen years old; when former Czareviches of Moscow attained this age, and were first "proclaimed," the people came from far and near to gaze upon them, as upon some "great wonder." But a task beyond his strength is already shouldered upon Alësha: he travels from town to town, buying up provender for the troops; felling timber for the fleet and floating it down; building forts; printing books; casting cannon; writing *ukases;* levying troops; searching out minors in hiding, under penalty of capital punishment,—he, almost an infant, "performing executions without any pardons" over other lads like himself; he most vigilantly watches in person over everything, "lest any falsehood be wrought," and dispatches the most detailed of reports to Batiushka.

He passes from German declensions to building bulwarks, from bulwarks to drinking bouts, from drinking bouts to searching for fugitives,—his head is going round and round. The more he tries, the greater the demands made upon him. There is neither leisure nor rest. It seems as though he would pass out from fatigue, like a foundered horse, yet he knows that all this is in vain,—"no one can, in any way, please Batiushka."

At the same time he is studying like any schoolboy. "For a fortnight we shall keep on repeating naught save the German language, to become firm in the declension; and after that we shall study French and Arithmetic. As for studying, it takes place every day."

Finally his strength snapped. In the January of seventeen-hundred-and-nine, during a spell of great frosts, when he was marching the five regiments he had himself recruited from Moscow to the city of Summi (which regiments were to take part in the Battle of Poltava), he caught cold, and lay unconscious for several weeks,—"his life was despaired of."

He regained consciousness on a sunny day in early spring. The whole room was flooded with oblique beams of yellow light. There were still snowdrifts outside the windows, but the icicles were already dripping. One could hear the murmur of vernal waters, and the song of the lark was tinkling in the heavens like a little bell. Alësha sees Batiushka's face bending over him,—familiar, endearing, filled with tenderness.

"My dearest little dear, art better? . . ." Having no strength to answer, Alësha merely smiles.

"Well, glory be to God, glory be to God!" His father piously makes the sign of the cross. "The Lord has been gracious,—He hath heard my prayers. Now thou wilt get better, never fear!"

The Czarevich subsequently learned that Batiushka had not left his side during his entire illness; he had neglected all his affairs, and had not slept nights. When Alësha worsened, he commanded masses to be said, and made a vow to build a church in the name of St. Alexei, the Man of God.

Slow, joyous days of convalescence followed. It seemed to Alësha that the caresses of his father were making him whole, like the light and heat of the sun. In a blessed exhaustion, a delectable weakness suffusing all his body, he lay for whole days without moving, looking upon the simple yet majestic face of Batiushka,—his radiant, awesome, endearing orbs,—the splendidly-beautiful smile, that seemed somewhat sly, of his femininely exquisite, sensuous lips; and the Czarevich could not get his fill of gazing. His father did not know how to caress Alësha enough, or how to please him. On one occasion he presented him with a snuff-box of his own workmanship, turned out of ivory, with the inscription: *A small gift, but given in all goodness of heart*. The Czarevich treasured it for many years, and every time he looked at it, something poignant, searing, akin to immeasurable pity for his father, would pierce his heart.

On another occasion, as he was stroking his son's hair, in utmost gentleness, Peter let drop in confusion, and very timidly, as though apologetically: "If I have ever told thee, or have done, anything to cause thee grief, then for God's sake be not grieved thereat. Forgive me, Alësha. In an arduous life even petty opposition can make one vexed at heart. For, truly, my life is an arduous one,—there's never a soul to think things over with. Not a single helper have I! . . ."

Alësha, entwined his father's neck with his arms, as he used to do in his childhood, all atremble, swooning with bashful tenderness,—and said in his ear:

"Batyia dear, my own, I love thee,—I love thee!"

But, in proportion as he returned to life, his father receded from him. It was as though an implacable vow of abstinence had been placed upon them: To be forever akin yet strangers to each other; to love each other in secret, and to hate each other openly.

And again everything resumed its old course: the collection of provender; the search for fugitives; the cast of cannon; the felling of lumber; the construction of bulwarks; the wandering from town to town. Alexei is again working like a galley-slave. Yet Batiushka is forever dissatisfied,—it forever seems to him that his son is idling,—that "having abandoned work, he walketh in the ways of idleness." At times Alësha would like to remind him of that which had taken place in Summi,—yet his tongue refuses to speak.

"*Zoom!* We instruct you to journey to Dresden. At the same time, we command that, while sojourning there, you lead an upright life, and be more diligent in your studies,— to wit: Languages, Geometry, and Fortification; and partly to political matters as well. And when you have finished Geometry and Fortification, write us thereof."

In foreign lands he lived as an exile, abandoned of all. His father had again forgotten about him. He recalled him only to marry him off. His bride, Charlotta, the daughter of the Duke of Wolfenbüttel, was not to the Czarevich's liking. He did not want to marry an alien. "What a she-devil they have saddled my neck with!" he would curse in his cups.

Before his wedding he had to go through degrading haggling about the dowry. The Czar tried to pull every possible *groschen* out of the Germans.

After having lived with his wife for half a year, Alexei forsook her for new "vagabondage": from Stettin to Mecklenburg, from Mecklenburg to Abo, from Abo to Novgorod, from Novgorod to Ladoga. Again endless fatigue, endless dread. This dread in anticipation of each audience with his father was growing into an insane horror. Approaching the doors of Batiushka's rooms, the Czarevich would whisper, crossing himself: "Remember, O Lord, King David and all his meekness"; he would senselessly repeat his lesson in Navigation,—such barbarous words as *Krupp-Kamera, balc-vegers, geigen-bloken* and *unchor-stops*, being beyond his power to remember,—and finger upon his breast a scapulary presented to him by one of his nurses, consisting of a bit of herb over which a spell had been uttered, and which had been kneaded into wax, and a bit of paper upon which was written an ancient incantation for the softening of parental hearts: "On a high holiday did my birth befall; of iron I built about me a hedge most tall, and I set out to see Batiushka, who had brought me into the world. And my own dear one, that had brought me into the world, did break my bones, did pinch my flesh, did trample me underfoot, and did drink my blood. Thou radiant sun, ye bright stars, thou calm sea, and ye yellow fields,—ye all abide in peace and quiet; may my own Batiushka be as quiet and peaceful, enduring all days, enduring all hours,—at nights and at midnights."

"Well, brother, I must say this is a great fortification!" his father would shrug his shoulders, as he scrutinized the plan which his son had handed to him. " 'Tis easy to see thou hast learned a great deal in foreign lands." Alësha would lose his head completely, becoming as confused as a guilty schoolboy before a birching.

In order to escape this torture, he would take medicines, "feigning that he was ill."

Horror was being transformed into hatred.

Shortly before the Prutsky campaign the Czar became

seriously ill,—"knowing not whether he were alive." It was
when the Czarevich learned of this that the thought of the
possible death of his father, together with a certain joy, first
flashed through his mind. He became affrighted at this joy,
and drove it away, yet extirpate it he could not. It found a
secret hiding-place in the very depth of his soul, like some
beast lying in wait.

Once, during a drinking-bout, when the Czar, after his
wont, was egging the tipsy men against one another, in order
to learn through their squabbling the secret thoughts of those
around him, the Czarevich, who was intoxicated, began to
speak of matters of state, and about the oppression of the
people.

Everybody quieted down. Even the jesters stopped their
hullabaloo. The Czar was listening attentively. Alësha's heart
was swooning from the hope: What if his father would comprehend, would heed?

"There, enough of thy lies," the Czar suddenly stopped
him, with that sneer which was so familiar and hateful to
Alësha. "I can see, brother, that thou art as well versed in
matters political and civil as a bear is in playing the
organ. . . ." And, turning away, he made a sign to his fools.
They once more started up their din. Prince Menshikov, intoxicated, whirled off in a dance with some other grandees.
The Czarevich still kept on saying something, shouting in a
breaking voice, but his father, paying no attention to him,
stamped and clapped his hands and whistled in time with the
dancers:

> *Tari-bari, rastobari,—*
> Where the fields in white snow lie
> Rabbits gray go loping by,—
> Ho, burn! Ho, burn!

Even his face was that of a soldier,—coarse, the face of
him who wrote: "The foe had good treatment from us,—
inasmuch as there were but few left of even the babes."

Prince Menshikov, puffing from the dance, suddenly halted
before the Czarevich, his arms akimbo, with a brazen sneer
which was a reflection of the Czar's.

"Ho, Czarevich!" cried out His Illustriousness, pronounc-

ing "Czarevich" in his usual manner, so that it sounded like
psaverich (keeper of the hounds).

"Oh, Czarevich Theodul, why sulk like a fool? Come now,
dance with us a bit!"

Alësha turned pale and seized his sword, but immediately
recalled himself, and, without looking at him, said through
his teeth:

"Louse! . . ."

"What? What didst thou say, thou puppy? . . ."

"I say it: louse! The glance of a louse is worse than a
curse. . . ."

At that very instant Batiushka's face, distorted by a convulsion, flashed before Alësha. He struck his son's face so that
blood ran from his mouth and nose; then he seized him by
the throat, felled him to the floor, and began to strangle him.
The aged dignitaries Romodanovsky, Scheremetev and
Dolgorukyi, whom the Czar had instructed to restrain him
during his attacks of fury, threw themselves upon him and
dragged him away from his son. They were afraid he might
kill him.

In order to "give satisfaction" to His Illustriousness, the
Czarevich was driven out of the house and placed on sentry
duty at the door, as schoolboys are put in a corner. It was
a wintry night, frosty and with a snowstorm. He was merely
in his frock coat, without any fur coat. Tears and blood were
freezing on his face. The snowstorm howled and whirled,
just as if, drunken, it were singing and dancing; and, behind
the illuminated windows of the house, the drunken old she-
fool, the Princess-Abbess Rzhevskaya, was also dancing and
singing. Her savage song blended with the savage howling
of the snowstorm:

> Oh, my mother was a-dancing when she gave me birth;
> I was christened midst the tavern's mirth;
> I was baptized in a wine green and strong. . . .

Such anguish fell upon Alësha that he was ready to dash
his brains out again the wall.

Suddenly, in the darkness, some one stole up to him from
behind, threw a fur coat over his shoulders, then sank on his
knees before him and fell to kissing his hands,—just as if an

affectionate hound were licking them. This was an old soldier of the Guard of the Transfiguration, Alësha's chance companion in sentry duty,—he was a secret Raskolnik.

The old man gazed into his eyes with such love that it was evident he was ready to render up his soul for him, and wept, and whispered as though he were praying to him.

"Master Czarevich, our darling, our Batiushka, our red little sun! Thou poor little orphan,—neither father nor mother hast thou. May the Father in Heaven and the Most Pure Mother save and preserve thee! . . ."

His father had beaten Alësha more than once,—unceremoniously, with his fists, and ceremoniously, with a cudgel. The Czar did everything in some new-fangled way, yet he beat his son in the good old way, according to the *Domostroi* of Father Sylvester, the counselor of the Terrible Czar, the filicide:

"Give not power to thy son in his youth, but break his spirit while he is growing. If thou beatest him with a rod he shall not die, but be all the better for it."

Alësha felt a brute fear of beatings ("he may slay or maim me"), but he had grown used to psychic pain and shame. At times a malicious joy would blaze up within him. "Very well, go ahead and beat me! 'Tis not me thou shamest but thyself," he seemed to be saying to his father, regarding him with an infinitely-submissive and infinitely-provoking gaze.

But his father had probably surmised this: he ceased his beatings, and conceived something more evil: he ceased speaking with his son entirely. When Alësha himself would begin, Peter kept silent, as though he did not hear, and looked at the spot where his son stood, as if it were empty. Such a silence would last for weeks,—for months,—for years; the Czarevich felt it always, everywhere, and becoming more and more unbearable with every day. It was more humiliating than any upbraiding, more vicious than any beating. It seemed to him slow murder,—cruelty such as would not be forgiven, either by man or by God.

This silence was the end of everything. Further there was nothing save darkness, and in the darkness was the dead, immobile face of Batiushka, just like a mask of stone, as he had seen him the last time. And dead words issued from the

dead lips: "I'll lop thee off like to a gangrenous member;
I'll treat thee as if thou wert a malefactor. . . ."

The thread of his recollections broke off. He came to, and
opened his eyes. The night was as calm as ever; as ever, the
white towers of the cathedrals showed bluely; the golden
cupolas were dull silver against the black, starry sky; the
Milky Way glimmered feebly. And, in the breath of the
celestial freshness, as even as the breathing of a sleeper,
there was descending upon the earth a premonition of eternal
peace,—an infinite calm.

The Czarevich seemed to be experiencing at this moment
the fatigue of his whole lifetime,—his back, his arms, his legs,
all his members were aching; his bones throbbed dully from
fatigue. He wanted to get up, but had not the strength to do
so; he merely raised his arms to the sky and emitted a moan,
as though he had invoked Him Who could answer:

"My God! My God! . . ."

But no one answered. Silence was upon the earth and upon
the sky, as though the Heavenly Father as well had abandoned him, even as the earthly father had done.

He covered his face with his hands, bowed his head upon
the stone bench, and fell to weeping,—at first softly, piteously,
as forsaken children do; then ever louder and louder, ever
more insanely. He wept and beat his head against the stone,
and shouted because of the wrong done him, because of his
indignation and horror. He wept for that he had no father,—
and in this weeping was the outcry of Golgotha, the eternal
outcry of the Son to the Father:

My God, my God, why hast thou forsaken me? [58]

Suddenly he realized, as on that time during the wintry
night when he stood sentry duty, that some one had approached him in the darkness, had bent over him and embraced him. This was Father Ivan, the old sacristan of the
Cathedral of Good Tidings.

"What is it, my own? The Lord be with thee! Who has
wronged thee, my own little dear one?"

"My father! . . . My father! . . ." Alësha could but
moan.

The old man comprehended everything. Sighing deeply,
he was silent for a while, and then began whispering, with

such hopeless submission that it seemed as if the wisdom of the ages itself, ancient and decrepit, were speaking with his lips:

"What can one do, Alëshenka? Reconcile thyself,—do, my little one. There's no use in dashing one's head against a stone wall. Who can cope with the Czar? God is in his heaven,—and the Czar is on the earth. The will of the Czar is beyond judgment. A sovereign is responsible to God alone. And to thee he is not only the Czar, but also thy God-given father. . . ."

"He is no father, but an evil-doer, a torturer, a murderer!" cried out Alësha. "May he be accursed,—may he be accursed, this monster of cruelty! . . ."

"Master Czarevich, Your Highness, provoke not the wrath of God,—utter not words of violence! Great is a father's power. Even in the Scriptures 'tis said: *Honor thy father.* . . ."

The Czarevich, suddenly ceasing to weep, turned around quickly and bestowed a long and searching look upon the old man:

"But, Father, there is something else said in the Scriptures, now: *Think not that I am come to send peace on earth: I came not to send peace, but a sword. For I am come to set a man at variance against his father.*[59] Dost thou hear, old man? The Lord hath set me at variance against my father! From the Lord am I sent, as a sword and an adverse host, into the heart of the author of my days; I am his judgment and his punishment, sent by the Lord. Not for myself have I risen up, but for the Church, for the state, for all the Christian people! Being zealous, I have become zealous for the Lord! And I shall not abate, I shall not submit to him, even unto death! The world is too small to hold us both! It has to be either he or I! . . ."

His face distorted by a spasm, his lower jaw quivering, his eyes blazing with a sinister fire, he took on a sudden, seemingly spectral resemblance to his father. The old man regarded him with horror, as if the Czarevich were possessed, and crossed himself, and shook his head, and mumbled with his time-eaten lips words of time-eaten wisdom:

"Reconcile thyself,—reconcile thyself, little one! Submit to thy father! . . ."

And it seemed that the ancient walls of Kremlin, and the palaces, and the cathedrals, and the very earth itself, with its graves of the holy fathers,—it seemed that everything here was repeating: "Reconcile thyself, reconcile thyself! ..."

When the Czarevich entered the house of the sacristan of the Cathedral of Good Tidings, the latter's sister, Martha Aphanasievna, a little crone who had been wet-nurse to Alësha, thought he was ill when she caught sight of his face. She grew still more uneasy when he refused supper, passing straight into the bedroom. The little crone made an attempt to drench him with linden blossoms and rub him down with camphorated spirits of wine. In order to calm her, he was forced to take some vodka, especially prepared against apoplexy. With her own hands she tucked him into bed,—a soft, most soft bed, with a whole mound of feather bolsters and pillows, such as he had not slept in for a long time. So peaceful was the glowing of the lampad before an image, —so familiar was the odor wafted upon him of dried medicinal herbs, of cypress and olibanum, so sleep-inducing was the whisper of the little crone, who on a time had told him old nursery tales of Ivan the Czarevich and the gray wolf, of the Cockerel-with-the-Golden-Comb, of the bast sandal, the bladder and the wisp of straw, who had all wanted to cross the river together: the wisp of straw had broken, the sandal had sunk, while the bladder had puffed and puffed, until he burst,—so peaceful were all these things that it seemed to Alësha, through his dozing, that he was once more a little boy, lying in his little bed in the chambers of his grandmother, and that everything which had taken place no longer was; and that it was not Martha Aphanasievna, but his grandmother who was bending over him, covering him up, tucking him in and crooning:

"Sleep, Olëshenka, my darling; sleep, and God be with thee, little one."

And everything is quiet,—so quiet. And Sirin, the bird of paradise, is singing kingly songs. And, as he listened to its delectable singing, he seemed to be dying, to be falling into an eternal sleep, devoid of any dreams.

Yet, before morning, a dream came to him: he seemed to be walking about in the Kremlin, on the Red Square, among a throng of people, on Palm Sunday, taking part in the Procession of the She-Ass, Palm Week. Arrayed in gala regal dress, in a purple mantle of gold, in the golden crown and coronation mantle of Monomachos, he is leading by its bridle the ass, upon which is mounted the Patriarch,—an ancient, most ancient little man, as hoary as hoary can be, all white, radiant because of his hoary hair. But, as he looks more closely, Alësha sees that this is no old man, but a youth in raiment as white as snow, with a countenance like to the sun: 'tis Christ himself. The people either do not see or do not recognize Him. All have fearful, gray, earthy faces, like those of dead men, and they all keep silent; the stillness is such that Alësha can hear the beating of his own heart; and the sky, too, is frightful, filled with a cadaverous grayness, as before an eclipse of the sun; while under Alësha's feet a hunchback is darting about,—he has on a tri-cornered hat, a clay pipe is stuck in his teeth, and he puffs the stinking smoke of Dutch canister tobacco right into the Czarevich's nostrils, and he is gibbering about something, and brazenly sneering, and indicating with his finger the place whence there is coming a growing, approaching rumble, like to the rumble of a hurricane. And Alësha sees that this is a procession coming to meet them: Czar Peter Alexeievich, the Proto-deacon of the Most Drunken Conclave, who is leading by the bridle, instead of the She-Ass, an unbelievable beast; upon the beast is mounted some one with a dark visage; Alësha cannot see him clearly, but it seems to him that he resembles both the knavish priest Fedosska, and Petka the thief, Petka the lout,—save that this some one is more frightful, more vile than both of the others; marching ahead of them is a shameless, naked wench,—either Aphrosiniya or the Venus of Peterburgh. In greeting to this procession all the bells are being rung,—including the biggest of them all, upon the belfry of John the Great, which bell is nicknamed the Roarer; and the people are shouting, as at the time of the wedding of the Prince-Pope Nikita Zotov:

"The Patriarch is married! The Patriarch is married! All hail to the Patriarch and to the Patriarch's wife! . . ."

And, falling on their faces, they bowed down before the Beast, the Whore, and the Coming Lout:

"Hosanna! Hosanna! Blessed be he that cometh!"

Abandoned of all, Alësha is alone with Christ in the midst of the maddened rabble. And the wild procession is moving directly upon them, with shouting and yelling, with darkness and stench, which tarnish the gold of the regal vestments and the very sun of Christ's Visage. Lo, they will rush upon him, crush him, trample him, sweeping everything along,— and there will spring up in the holy place the abomination that maketh desolate.

Suddenly everything vanished. He is standing upon the shore of a broad, desolate river,—apparently on the high road from Poland to Ukraine. It is late evening in late autumn. Wet snow,—black mire. The wind is tearing off the last leaves from the trembling aspens. A beggar in tatters, chilled and grown blue from the cold, is piteously begging alms: "Give, if but a kopeck, for Christ's sake!"—"See, he is a branded man," reflects Alësha, looking upon the beggar's arms and legs, with their bloody sores, "probably a runaway recruit." And he feels so sorry for the "frozen lad" that he wants to give him not merely a kopeck but seven *gulden*. He recalls in his dream the entry he had made in his travel diary, among other expenses: "22nd of November, for ferrying across river, three *gulden:* for lodgings in a Jew's inn, five *gulden;—for the frozen lad,* seven *gulden.*" He is just about to extend his hand to the beggar, when suddenly somebody's rough hand is placed upon Alësha's shoulder, and a rough voice,—probably that of the soldier on sentry duty near the barrier,—says to him:

"For giving alms, there's a fine of five rubles; while beggars, after being beaten with cudgels and having their nostrils torn out, shall be exiled to Rogerwick."

"Have pity," implores Alësha. "Foxes have holes and birds of the air have nests, but the Son of man hath not where to lay his head. . . ." [60]

And, looking more closely at the frozen lad, he sees that His face is like to the sun,—that this is Christ Himself.

IV

"My Son!

"Some time ago, when I parted with thee, I did ask thee about thy decision regarding a certain matter, to which thou didst make the same answer thou didst ever make: that thou couldst not succeed to the throne, because of thy debility, and that thou wouldst liefer enter a monastery; but I told thee at that time that thou shouldst consider this matter seriously, and write me as to what resolution thou didst come to.—for which resolution, I have waited seven months, yet up to this time thou dost write naught thereof. Therefore (inasmuch as thou hast had sufficient time for deliberation), upon receipt of this letter, thou must now come to a resolution without delay,—either one way or the other. And shouldst thou resolve upon the first course, do not delay for more than a week, and come here, inasmuch as then thou wilt still have time to take part in the maneuvers. But, shouldst thou resolve upon the other course, then write me what monastery thou wilt enter, and the time, and the very day (so that my conscience may know peace, in knowing what to expect from thee). And thou canst send thy definite answer by this messenger: if it be the first course,—the date of thy departure from Peterburgh; if the other, when thou wilt carry it out. And this we do reiterate gravely, so that this matter may be definitely concluded, inasmuch as I can see that thou art merely frittering away thy time in thy usual fruitless indolence."

Saphonov, the courier, had brought the letter from Copenhagen to the promontory of Rozhdestvenno, whither the Czarevich had returned from Moscow.

He immediately sent a reply to his father that he was setting out at once to see him. Yet he had not come to any resolution. It seemed to him that here it was not a matter of choosing one of two things,—either of becoming a monk or of mending his ways to become worthy of the succession,—but merely a double trap: to take the tonsure with the mental reservation that the cowl, now, is not nailed to the head meant giving a false oath to God,—thus destroying his soul; as for mending his ways to become worthy of the succession, as Batiushka demanded,—he would have to reënter his mother's womb, and be born anew.

The letter caused neither grief nor fright to the Czarevich. There had fallen upon him that unfeeling and senseless coma which of late fell upon him more and more frequently. In such a condition he would say and do everything as if in a dream, without himself knowing what he would say and do the next minute. There was a frightful buoyancy and emptiness in his heart,—either a desperate cowardice or a desperate daring. He set out for Peterburgh and stopped at his house near the Church of All that Sorrow, and ordered his *valet de chambre*, Ivan Aphanasiich Bolshoi, "to get everything together necessary for a trip, as he had done before, when they had gone to Germany."

"Art going to Batiushka?"

"I am going, but God knows if it be to him or elsewhere," Alexei dropped listlessly.

"Lord Czarevich, where else? . . ." Ivan Aphanasiich grew frightened,—or pretended to do so.

"I would like to have a look at Venice. . . ." The Czarevich was about to smile, but immediately added in a despondent and low tone, as though he were speaking to himself: "I am doing this for no other reason but to save myself. . . . However, keep thou thy counsel. Thou art the only one who knowest this about me,—thou, and Kikin. . . ."

"I am ready to keep thy secret," answered the old man, with his usual gloominess, under which, however, there now glowed in his eyes an infinite loyalty. "Only, 'twill be an ill-hap for us when thou dost depart. Bethink thee of what thou art doing. . . ."

"I never thought I would get a message from Batiushka," the Czarevich went on, just as sleepily and listlessly. "It never even entered my mind. But now I can see that God is guiding me on my way. Also, I have seen a dream pertaining thereto, that I was building churches,—and that means that I will complete a journey. . . ."

And he yawned.

"Many a man in thy fix," remarked Aphanasiich, "has

sought salvation in flight. However, such a thing has never occurred in Russia,—not that any one could recall. . . ."

Directly from his house the Czarevich rode to Menshikov, and informed him that he was going to his father. The Prince spoke with him kindly. Toward the end he asked him:

"But where wilt thou leave Aphrosiniya?"

"I shall take her as far as Riga, and then let her return to Peterburgh," the Czarevich answered at haphazard, almost without thinking of what he was saying. Afterwards he was himself astonished at this unaccountable guile.

"Why let her go?" spake the Prince, looking him straight in the eyes. "Why let her go,—better take her with thee. . . ."

If the Czarevich had been more attentive, he would have wondered: Menshikov could not but know that the son who wanted "to mend his ways to be worthy of the succession," could not appear at Batiushka's camp "for the study of military maneuvers" accompanied by the loose wench Aphroska. What, then, did these words mean? When subsequently Kikin learned of them, he urged the Czarevich to thank the Prince by letter for this counsel; "Mayhap, now, thy father may find thy letter in the possession of the Prince, and will suspect him of complicity in thy flight."

When they were saying farewell to each other, Menshikov bade him drop in at the Senate, in order to get his passport and money for the journey.

In the Senate all strove to out-vie one another in serving the Czarevich,—as though they desired to express secretly their sympathy, which must not be avowed. Menshikov gave him, for the journey, one thousand pieces of red gold. The gentlemen of the Senate voted as their share another thousand and, right on the spot, arranged a loan of five thousand in gold and two thousand in smaller coins, from the Head Commissioner at Riga. No one questioned him,—as if all had conspired to keep silent as to what reason he had for needing such a lot of money.

After the session, Prince Vassilii Dolgorukyi led him aside:

"Art going to Batiushka?"

"How else, Prince?"

Dolgorukyi looked around cautiously, drew his thick, soft

lips, like those of an old woman, to Alexei's very ear, and said in a whisper:

"How? Why, here's how: Pick up the hoe, and away we go; seek high and seek low,—yet where none will know! . . ."

And, after a silence, he added, still whispering in the Czarevich's ear:

"Were it not for our Sovereign's cruel nature, and for the Czaritza, I would have been the first to betray them at Stettin, and show a clean pair of heels!"

He squeezed the Czarevich's hands, and tears welled up in the crafty and kindly eyes of the old man.

"If I can serve thee in any way in the future, I would be glad e'en to lay down my very life for thee. . . ."

"I pray thee, forsake me not, my dearest Prince!" spake Alexei,—without any emotion or thought, merely through old habit.

In the evening he learned that the most faithful of the Czar's servants, Prince Jacob Dolgorukyi, had sent him a message, in a roundabout way, advising him not go to his father: "There is an ill brew brewing for thee there, now."

And the following morning, the twenty-sixth of September, in the year seventeen hundred and sixteen, the Czarevich took his departure from Peterburgh in a postchaise, with Aphrosiniya and her brother, Ivan Fedorov, a one-time serf.

In the final upshot he had not come to any decision as to his destination. From Riga, however, he took Aphrosiniya farther with him, saying that he "was bidden to go secretly to Vienna, for the formation of an alliance against the Turk, and to live there secretly, lest the Turk learn thereof."

In Libau he was met by Kikin, who was returning from Vienna.

"Hast thou found any refuge for me?" the Czarevich asked him.

"I have; go thou to the Kaiser,—thou wilt not be given up there. The Kaiser himself has said to the Vice-Chancellor, Schönborn, that he will receive thee like a son."

The Czarevich asked:

"When Batiushka's emissaries come to me at Danzig, what am I to do?"

"Steal away in the night," answered Kikin, "or, if there be

but one, take him with thee, and leave thy servants, as well as the baggage, behind. Or, if two be sent for thee, pretend to be sick,—send one ahead and escape from the other."

Noticing his indecision, Kikin said:

"Remember this, Czarevich: thy father will not make thee a monk now, even though thou shouldst want to be one. Thy friends, the Senators, have persuaded him to hold thee constantly by his side, and to take thee about with him everywhere, to the end that this knocking about from pillar to post might prove the death of thee, inasmuch as thou wilt not be able to bear such hardship. And thy father has said 'tis a goodly plan. And Prince Menshikov did reason with him that in thy black monk's raiment thou wouldst have peace, and that thou mayst live long. And, considering this, I do wonder that thou hast not been taken long ago. Then, again, they may do this: When thou wilt be in the land of Denmark, thy father, having placed thee upon some manof-war, under pretext of training thee, will issue orders to the captain to give battle to a near-by Swedish ship, so as to bring thy death,—concerning which matter we have information from Copenhagen. That is why they are summoning thee now, and, save in flight, there is no salvation for thee. As for putting thy head in the noose thyself,—that would be sheer brute stupidity," concluded Kikin, and glanced at the Czarevich searchingly.

"But why art thou so sleepy, Your Highness, as if thou wert not thyself? Or art thou out of sorts?"

"I have tired very much," the Czarevich answered simply.

After they had already bidden each other farewell, and separated, Kikin suddenly turned back, caught up with the Czarevich by running, stopped him, and, looking into his eyes, uttered slowly, stressing each word and there was such assurance in his words, that the Czarevich, despite all his apathy, felt a chill run through his body:

"Should thy father send any one to persuade thee to return, and promising thee forgiveness, do not go,—he will cut thy head off before all the people."

Upon his departure from Libau Alexei had not come to any decision, just as before, at his departure from Peterburgh. However, he hoped that there would be no necessity for a decision, because envoys from his father would be waiting for him at Danzig. From Danzig the road branched into two: one led to Copenhagen; the other, through Breslau to Vienna. As it turned out, there had been no envoys. It was impossible to delay decision. When the master of the post-inn where Alexei had put up for the night came in the evening to ask what destination the Czarevich wanted to order horses for on the morrow, he gazed at the inn-keeper for a moment absent-mindedly, as though he were thinking of something else, then said, almost without realizing his words:

"To Breslau."

And immediately he himself was frightened by this utterance, which was deciding his fate; but then he reflected that he could change his mind in the morning.

In the morning, the horses were driven up,—all that was left was to take his place and ride off. He put off his decision until the next stop; at the next stop, he put it off until they should arrive at Frankfort-on-the-Oder; in Frankfort,—until Tübingen; in Tübingen—until Grossen; and so on without end. He rode ever farther and farther, and could no longer stop, just as though he had lost his footing and were rolling down a slippery steep. The same fear-engendered force which hitherto had restrained him was now driving him onward. And, keeping pace with the distance he traversed, his fear increased. He comprehended that there was naught to fear,—his father could not yet know of his flight. But his fear was blind, senseless.

Kikin had supplied him with false passes. The Czarevich posed now as a Polish cavalier, one Kremenetzky, now as Kohkansky, a lieutenant-colonel, or Balk, a corporal, or else as a merchant connected with the Russian army. Yet it seemed to him that the hosts of the inns, and the postillions, and the guards, and the post-masters, all knew that he was the Russian Czarevich and that he was fleeing from his father. During the night stops he would awaken and jump up in horror at the least sound, the scrape of footsteps, or the creak of a floor-board. On one occasion, when a man in a long gray coat, resembling the traveling dress of his father, and almost of the same stature as Batiushka, entered the half-dark dining-room where the Czarevich was supping, the latter almost fainted. He imagined he saw spies everywhere. The generosity with which he scattered his money did really inspire the thrifty Germans with suspicion that they actually had to do with a personage of royal blood. At the main posts he was given the best horses, and the drivers drove them at full speed. Once, at twilight, when he saw a carriage riding behind them, he imagined there was pursuit. He promised ten *gulden* for *trink-gelt* to the driver. The latter set off on a gallop, at a break-neck pace. At a turn the axle caught on a stone and the wheel snapped off. They were forced to stop and crawl out. Those riding behind were catching up with them. The Czarevich became so frightened that he wanted to drop everything and go off on foot with Aphrosiniya into the woods, where they might hide. He was already dragging her off by the hand,—she could barely restrain him.

Having left Breslau behind, he made practically no other stops. He galloped day and night, without rest. He neither slept nor ate. His throat would spasmodically contract whenever he attempted to swallow anything. He had but to doze off to awaken immediately, with a shudder that shook his whole body, and bathed in cold sweat. He felt like dying, or being captured at once,—anything to be rid of this torture.

Finally, after five sleepless nights, he fell into a dead sleep. He awoke in his carriage very early in the morning, while it was still dark. His sleep had refreshed him. He felt almost lively. Aphrosiniya was sleeping by his side. It was cold. He wrapped her up more warmly and kissed her as she slept. They were passing through an unknown small town, with tall, narrow houses and cramped streets, in which the rumble of the wheels reverberated sharply. All shutters were closed; probably the whole town was asleep. In the middle of the market-square, before the *rathaus,* murmured the jets of a fountain, dripping from the edges of a mossy-green stone shelf, propped up by the shoulders of powerful tritons. A holy lampad, in the depression of a wall, glowed warmly before a Madonna.

Having traversed the town, they went up a knoll. From the knoll, the road descended to a broad, somewhat sloping plain. The chaise, harnessed with six horses abreast, flew like an arrow. The wheels rustled softly through the dew-covered dust. The night mist still lay down below; but above light was already breaking, and the mist was rising like a curtain, leaving clinging threads of cobweb upon the last year's stalks of grass, which were threaded with dewdrops as if with beads. A blue sky was revealed, in which an autumnal flock of cranes, lit up by the first ray of the sun which had not yet risen over the earth, was flying along with summoning cries. At the edge of the plain, some mountains showed bluely,—these were the mountains of Bohemia. Suddenly a blinding ray flashed out from behind them, straight into the eyes of Czarevich. The sun was rising, and joy was rising in his soul,—a joy as blinding as the sun. God had saved him,—and none other than God.

He laughed and wept for joy, as though he were beholding for the first time the earth, and the sky, and the sun, and the mountains. He looked at the cranes—and it seemed to him that he, too, had wings, and that he was flying.

Freedom! Freedom!

V

Saphonov, the courier, sent ahead from Peterburgh, reported to the Sovereign that the Czarevich was following him. Yet two months passed, and the latter did not appear. The Czar, for a long while, could not believe that his son had fled, — "He's not the sort,—he has not the pluck!"—but finally he believed, dispatched sleuths over all the highways and byways and issued a personal *ukase* to the Resident in Vienna, Avram Veselovsky: "Thou art to make inquiries in Vienna, in Rome, in Naples, in Milan, in Sardinia, as well as in Switzerland. When thou learnest the whereabouts of our son, having made sure thereof, thou shalt go and follow him to those regions, and immediately write us thereof through special staffettas and couriers; at the same time, thou shalt be most circumspect."

Veselovsky, after lengthy searching, fell upon a scent. "The scent leads to this place," he wrote to the Czar from Vienna. "A certain lieutenant-colonel, by the name of Kokhansky, stopped at the hostelry of *The Black Eagle,* on the outskirts of the city. A drawer says that he recognized him to be some man of distinction, inasmuch as he paid out his money with great generosity, and seemed to bear a resemblance to the Czar of Muscovy,—possibly his son,—for this fellow had seen the Czar here, in Vienna."

Peter was amazed. There was something strange, seemingly eldritch, for him in these words,—"he seemed to bear a resemblance to the Czar." The thought that Alexei resembled him in countenance had never occurred to him.

"After staying but four and twenty hours in the said place," Veselovsky's report went on, "he put his belongings upon a hired vehicle, while he himself, on the next day, after paying the reckoning, went off on foot, so that none knows whether he has left for other parts or not. And, while sojourning in the said hostelry, he did buy a ready-made man's costume, of a coffee color, for his wife, and she did put on masculine garb. All further traces have vanished. In all the local hostelries and post-offices, as well as in private dining-rooms and ordinaries, have I made inquiries, but so far all of them have everywhere proven fruitless. I have also instituted searches through spies; I have made trips over both the post-roads leading to Italy,—the Tyrolean and the Carinthian. None could give me any news."

The Czar, surmising that the Kaiser had received the Czarevich and given him sanctuary in his domains, sent him a letter from Amsterdam:

"Most Illustrious and Most Sovereign Kaiser!

"I am forced to inform Your Cæsaric Majesty, in fraternally friendly confidence, and with heart-felt sorrow, of a certain untoward occurrence that hath befallen me,—to wit, concerning my son Alexei; we have good reason to believe it is not unknown to Your Majesty that our son did, to our utmost displeasure, ever act in a manner opposed to our parental will, and has also led a dissolute life when married to your kinswoman. Some time ago, having received our order to come to us, that he might thereby be drawn away from his dissolute mode of life and from commerce with dissolute men, he, without taking with him any of the servants whom we had appointed for him, but taking along several other young people, did leave the road leading hither, and secreted himself we know not where, so that up to this time we have not been able to learn his whereabouts. And inasmuch as we apprehend that he has been induced to take the said contumacious course through following the misguided counsel of certain persons, and inasmuch as we bear paternal pity for him (lest through his unrighteous action he bring upon himself irretrievable ruin, and, most of all, lest he by some chance fall into the hands of our adversaries),—we have therefore commissioned Veselovsky, our Resident at the court of Your Majesty, to seek out this our son and bring him to us. To that end we request Your Majesty, if he be residing secretly or openly in your domains, to command that he be sent back to us, with this our Resident, giving them, for safety, a few men from among your officers, so that we may paternally chastise him for his own weal; by your compliance you will bind us forever to your services and friendship. We remain,

"Your Cæsaric Majesty's Faithful Brother,
"Peter."

At the same time, the Kaiser was made cognizant, in a roundabout way, that, if he did not release the Czarevich of his own free will, the Czar would seek the latter out as a traitor, "with an armed hand."

Every fresh bit of news concerning his son was an affront to the Czar. The secret, malicious joy of Europe peeped out from under its hypocritical commiseration.

"A certain major-general returned hither from Hanover," Veselovsky reported, "when in attendance at court, told me plainly in the presence of the Ambassador from Mecklenburg, that he grieved over the illness which hath come upon Your Majesty through sundry sorrows, of which the most widely known is that your Crown-Prince has, apparently, 'made himself invisible,'—he used the French term: *Il est éclipsé.* I inquired from whom he had such false information. He replied that the information was true and authentic, and that he had received it from the Hanoverian Ministers. I retorted that this was a slander, instigated by the malice of the Court of Hanover."

"The Kaiser has a far from inconsiderable reason to second

the Crown-Prince," Veselovsky transmitted an opinion openly expressed at the foreign courts, "inasmuch as the said Crown-Prince is in the right before his father, and had good reasons for escaping out of his father's domains. It is held that it all began when Your Majesty had, soon after birth of the Czarevich Peter Petrovich, apparently compelled the Czarevich Alexei, by force to a reversion, whereby he renounced the crown and promised to retire for the rest of his life into some desert hermitage. And, when Your Majesty departed for Pomerania, and perceived that he did not become an anchorite, as by the terms of his reversion he had undertaken to do, you did then,—so they say,—devise another means,—to wit: to summon him to you, to the land of Denmark, and there, having placed him upon a certain warship of yours, under the pretext of training him, you would command the captain to give battle to a Swedish ship, which was to be near by, and thus kill the Czarevich. Wherefore he was forced to flee from such a mishap."

Reports were also made to the Czar concerning the secret negotiations of the Kaiser with the King of England, George I: "The Kaiser, who had given shelter and protection to the son of the Czar, through kinship, sympathy for the sufferings of the Czarevich, and the magnanimity of the Imperial House toward all those innocently persecuted," was asking the King of England whether the latter "as an Elector and one related to the House of Braunschweig," did not intend "to protect the Prince"; in addition, the "miserable state—*miseranda conditio*—of the good Czarevich" was pointed out, as well as the "patent and unceasing tyranny of the father,—*clara et continua paterna tyrannidis,*—not devoid of a suspicion of poison, and other such Russian *galanterien*."

The son was becoming his father's judge.

What else did the future hold? The Czarevich could become a weapon in the hands of the enemy; he might kindle an uprising within Russia, might make all Europe to rise up in war,—and God alone knew wherewith all this would end.

"Even to kill him,—to kill him!—would not be enough!" thought the Czar in his fury.

But the fury was drowned out by another, hitherto unknown, emotion: the son was an object of fear to the father.

BOOK SIX

THE FUGITIVE CZAREVICH

I

THE Czarevich and Aphrosiniya were boating on the Bay of Naples; it was a moonlit night.

He was experiencing an emotion resembling that which is engendered by music: there was music in the lunar gold, which lay stretching into the distance, like a fiery path on the water, from Posilipo to the rim of the heavens; there was music in the plaint of the sea, and in the barely audible breath of wind, which, together with the briny freshness of the sea, brought the sweet fragrance of orange- and lemon-groves on the shores of Sorrento; there was music, too, in the silvery-azure outlines of Vesuvius, which, through the murk of the crescent moon, was emitting a white smoke, and occasionally glared with a red fire, like some sacrificial altar of the gods who had died, had been re-born, and had died anew.

"Little mother, dearest friend of my heart,—how splendid al this is!" the Czarevich uttered in a whisper.

Aphrosiniya contemplated the whole scene with the same apathetic air with which she used to regard the Neva and the Fortress of SS. Peter and Paul.

"Aye, 'tis warm; we are on the water, yet the air is not raw," she answered, suppressing a yawn.

He closed his eyes,—and before them appeared a chamber in the house of the Viyazemskys, on the Lesser Okhta,—the oblique rays of the sun on an evening in spring,—the serf-wench Aphroska, with her skirt caught up high and with her legs bare, bending low and mopping the floor . . . most ordinary of country wenches, the kind of whom the yokels say: Look ye,—she's all juicy, and as round and white as a washed turnip. Yet there were times when, as he looked at her, he would recall an old Dutch picture he had seen in his Batiushka's room at Peterhof,—*The Temptation of Anthony:* a naked, rufous she-devil is standing before the anchorite; her legs are covered with wool, and terminate in cloven goat-hoofs,—like the legs of a female faun. About Aphrosiniya's face,—in her lips, much too full, in her somewhat upturned nose, in her great, light eyes, languishing, and with slightly oblique, elongated slits,—there was something caprine, wild, innocently shameless. The Czarevich also recalled the adumbrations of the old bookmen anent the fiendish beauty of women: Sin had its beginning with woman, and she is the death of us all; whether one falls in love with her, or falls into a fire,—'tis all one.

Even he himself did not know how it had come about, but he had come to love her almost at first sight, with a coarse, tender love that was strong as death.

Even here, on the Bay of Naples, she was still the same Aphroska that she had been in the little house on the Lesser Okhta; and even here, she was nibbling the small nuts of the cedar (for lack of sun-flower seeds), just as she had been wont to do, of holidays, while sitting on a bench with the other servants, spitting out the shells into the waves of lunar gold. Saving this: that, arrayed in the French fashion, with beauty spots and in farthingale and *robe-ronde*, she seemed still more indecorously enticing, innocently shameless. No wonder both of the Kaiser's bodyguards who were with them made eyes at her, and even the elegant and rather young Count Esterhazy himself, who accompanied the Czarevich on all his excursions from the Fortress of St. Elmo. Alexei abominated these masculine oglings, which seemed forever drawn to her, as flies are drawn to honey.

"Well now, Æsopka, hast thou wearied of the life here? Thou art fain go home, never fear?" she uttered in her lazy, canorous voice, addressing the chap sitting next to her in the boat,—a diminutive, homunculus of miserable appearance,—one Alëshka Urov, an apprenticed seaman,—he was called Æsopka because of his merry-andrew antics.

"Yea, Aphrosiniya Fedorovna, little mother of mine,— we have fallen upon most evil days here. That which we have been set to learn is so exceedingly complicated that, were we to spend all our lives studying, yet would we not absorb it, inasmuch as we do not know which to learn first,—the language or the sciences. Yet, in Venice, our lads are actually perishing from hunger,—they give them three kopecks a day all-in-all to live on, and they have verily come to such a pass that they have naught to drink or eat, nor a stitch of clothing,—'tis a shame the way they walk about, showing their nakedness. They abandon us poor fellows to die like cattle. And the worst of all hardships to me is the fact that I cannot stand the sea,—inasmuch as I am a very sick man. No seaman I! I am sure to die, unless a godly mercy be shown me. Gladly and readily would I start out on foot for Peterburgh,—anything at all to avoid sea-travel. I would rather beg alms along the road, than go by sea,—let His Majesty do what he will!"

"Well, brother, watch lest thou fall out of the frying-pan into the fire: in Peterburgh thou wilt be whipped for having run away from thy apprenticeship," remarked the Czarevich.

"Thou art in bad straits, Æsopka! Whatever will become of thee, thou poor orphan? Where canst thou go?" asked Aphrosiniya.

"Aye,—where am I to go, little mother? I shall either hang myself, or go off to Mount Athos and turn monk. . . ."

Alexei looked at him in pity and involuntarily compared the fate of this fugitive navigator with the fate of a fugitive Czarevich.

"Never mind, brother,—it may yet be God's will for us to return happily to our Fatherland!" he uttered with a kindly smile.

Their boat had emerged from the lunar gold, and they were turning back toward the dark shore. Here, near the foot of the mountain, was a neglected villa, built during the Renaissance upon the ruins of an ancient temple of Venus.

Gigantic cypresses, treading closely upon each other's heels, like torch-bearers at a funeral procession, flanked both sides of the half-ruined stairs leading to the sea; their tattered, pointed summits, forever bending before the wind from the sea, had in the end remained inclined, just like heads bowed in sorrow. Gods in white marble gleamed whitely, like specters, amid black shadows. And the jet of a fountain, too, seemed a pallid specter. Glow-worms glimmed like funerary candles within the laurel thicket. The oppressive odor of magnolias recalled some aromatic used for anointing the dead. One of the peacocks kept about the villa, awakened by the voices and the noise of the oars, strutted forth on to the stairs and spread out his tail, which began to play in a dim rainbow in the lunar effulgence, like a flabellum of precious stones. And the plaintive calls of the peahens resembled the piercing wails of keening women. The waters of the fountain, running down from an overhanging crag, along grasses as long and fine as hair, fell into the sea, drop by drop, like subdued tears,—just as though, there in the cavern, some nymph were weeping for her perished sisters. And this melancholy villa recalled in its entirety some somber Elysium, a subterranean grove of shades,—a cemetery of gods who had died, had been re-born, and had died anew.

" 'Tis scarcely to be believed, my gracious mistress,—but 'tis already the third year that I have not had a good Russian steam bath!" Æsopka went on with his complaints.

"Oh, for bath-besoms of fresh birch twigs,—and then just a sip of cherry-mead after such a fine bath!" sighed Aphrosiniya.

"When one drinks the sour, wretched slops of this region, and recalls vodka, how can one help bursting into tears?" Æsopka moaned.

"Oh, for a bit of pressed caviar!" Euphrosinia chimed in.

"Or a bit of salted sturgeon steak!"

"Or some White Lake smelts!"

Thus did they vie with one another, irritating their heart-wounds.

The Czarevich was listening to them as he contemplated the villa, and he involuntarily smiled: the contradiction between these everyday longings and the spectral reality was decidedly odd.

Another boat was also moving over the fiery pathway of the sea, leaving a black trail on its quivering gold. They heard the sound of a mandolin, and a song chanted by a young feminine voice:

Quant 'è bella giovenezza,
Si fugge tuttavia;
Chi vuol esser lieto, sia;
Di doman non c'è certezza!

This song of love had been composed by Lorenzo de'
Medici, the Magnificent, for a triumphant procession of
Bacchus and Ariadne, during some Florentine festival. It
held the brief joyousness of the Renaissance, and an eternal
yearning for it.

The Czarevich listened without understanding the words;
but the music filled his soul with a delectable sadness:

> Youth is wondrous, but how fleeting!
> Sing, and laugh, and banish sorrow;
> Give to happiness good greeting,—
> Place thy hopes not on the morrow.

"Come, little mother,—let's have a Russian song!" implored Æsopka,—he even made an effort to get down on his
knees, but swayed and almost fell into the water: he was
unsteady on his pins, inasmuch as he had been pulling all
the time on the "sour, wretched slops" out of a straw-bound
flask, which he bashfully concealed under his coat-skirt. One
of the rowers, a half-naked Adonis, catching Æsopka's meaning, smiled to Aphrosiniya, winked at the manikin, and
handed him a guitar. Æsopka fell to tinkling upon it, as
though it were a three-stringed *balalaika*. Aphrosiniya
smiled, glanced at the Czarevich, and suddenly began singing in the loud, somewhat strident voice of a country wife,—
just as she had been wont to sing in the round dances at
even-glow, in spring, near a birch-grove overhanging a river.
And the shores of Naples, of ancient Parthenope,[61] reëchoed
sounds they had never heard before:

Ah, the entry to my house, built of maple-wood, and new;
Entry with the latticed windows, where each thing is fair to view!

There was infinite longing for the past in the alien song:

> *Chi vuol esser lieto, sia:*
> *Di doman non c'è certezza!*

There was infinite longing for the future in their native
song:

Fly away, my Falcon,—fly thou far and fly thou high,—
Fly thou high, and fly thou far, to my own native land!
In my native land, in my own land, my dread father dwells:
He is dread, fair master,—he is dread and merciless.

Both songs,—their own and the alien one,—blended into one.

The Czarevich could barely restrain his tears. Never yet, it seemed to him, had he loved Russia as much as he loved her now. But he loved her with a new love, that embraced the whole universe; he loved her together with Europe,—he loved this alien land as if it were his own. And his love for his native land, and his love for this alien land blended, like these songs, into one.

II

The Kaiser, having received the Czarevich under his protection, had lodged him, in order to conceal him the more surely from his father, under the name of a certain Hungarian Count (or, as the Czarevich himself expressed it, on the manner of a captive), in the isolated, inaccessible castle of Ehrenberg,—a veritable eagle's eyrie, upon the summit of a towering crag in the mountains of Upper Tyrol, on the road from Fussen to Innsbruck.

"Immediately upon receipt of this," ran the Kaiser's instructions to the commander of the fortress, "order two rooms, with stout doors and iron-barred windows, to be prepared for the chief personage; the soldiers, as well as their wives, are not to be permitted to leave the fortress, under penalty of severe punishment, or even death. Should the chief prisoner desire to speak with thee, thou mayst grant his wish in this instance, as well as in others,—if, for example, he should demand books, or any other thing for his diversion; or even if he invite thee to dinner, or to participate in some game. Over and above this, permit him to walk through the rooms, or in the yard of the fortress, for the sake of the air,—but always taking precautions lest he leave."

Alexei had lived in Ehrenberg for five months,—from December to April.

Despite all precautions, the Czar's spies (a Captain of the Guards, by the name of Rumyantzev, and three other officers), who had secret orders to seize "a certain person" at any cost, and to carry him off to Mecklenburg, learned of the Czarevich's stay in Ehrenberg, arrived in Upper Tyrol, and settled secretly in the little village of Reite, near the very foot of the Ehrenberg crag.

Veselovsky, the Resident, declared that his Sovereign would be "exceedingly perturbed to hear the answer of the ministers, given in the name of the Kaiser, purporting that a certain person is not to be found within the domains of the Kaiser, while, at the same time, the courier dispatched has seen this person's attendants in Ehrenberg, where he is maintained at the cost of the Kaiser. Not only Captain Rumyantzev, but even all of Europe, probably, knows that the Czarevich is in the Kaiser's realm. If the Archduke, leaving his father, were to seek an asylum in the lands of the Russian Sovereign, and such asylum were to be proffered him secretly,—how grievous this would be to the Kaiser!"

"Your Majesty," Peter wrote to the Emperor, "can judge yourself how painful it is to us, as a father, that our first-born son, evincing such disobedience toward us, and going off without our will, is kept under the protection of others, or, rather, under arrest; which matter we can hardly credit, and desire an explanation thereof from Your Majesty."

It was announced to the Czarevich, that the Emperor left it to him either to return to Russia or to remain under his protection; but, in the latter instance, he deemed it necessary to transfer him to another remote place,—to wit, Naples. At the same time, he was made to feel that the Kaiser's desire was for him to leave behind in Ehrenberg, or altogether dismiss from him, his companions, of whom his father had spoken with displeasure in his letter; in order that by such action the Czar might be deprived of every pretext for reproaching the Emperor with taking dissolute people under his protection. This was a hint at Aphrosiniya. It really did seem unbecoming for the Czarevich, while imploring the Kaiser for protection, in the name of the late Charlotta, the sister of the Empress, was keeping near his person "a wanton wench" with whom he had formed a liaison even while his wife was alive.

He announced that he was ready to go wherever the Kaiser might order him to, and to live as he commanded, if only he be not given up to his father. On the fifteenth of April, at three o'clock in the morning, the Czarevich, paying no heed to the spies, departed from Ehrenberg, under the name of an imperial officer. He had only one servant with him—Aphrosiniya, disguised as a page.

"Our Neapolitan pilgrims have arrived safely," reported Count Schönborn. "At the first opportunity I shall send my secretary with a full report of their journey,—the most amusing imaginable. Among other things, our little page is finally acknowledged to be a woman, but, evidently, neither wife nor maid, since she is admitted to be a mistress, and necessary for the prisoner's health."—"I am exerting all possible means to restrain our company from frequent and immoderate drinking, but vainly," reported Schönborn's secretary, who accompanied the Czarevich.

He journeyed through Innsbruck, Mantua, Florence, and Rome. On the midnight of the sixth of May, sixteen-hundred-and-seven, he arrived at Naples, and stopped at the hostel of *The Three Kings*. On the evening of the next day, he was borne off in a hired carriage out of the city to the sea; then, though a secret passage, brought into the king's palace, and thence, two days later, as soon as special chambers were ready for him, into the Fortress of St. Elmo, located on a high hill overlooking Naples.

Although he lived even here "on the manner of a captive," he was not low in spirits nor felt himself in prison; the higher the walls and the deeper the moats in the fortress, the more securely did they guard him from his father.

In these chambers the windows, with a covered way before them, looked out directly on the sea. Here he passed whole days; he fed, just as he used to do in Rozhdestvenno, the pigeons which flocked to him from everywhere and which he quickly tamed; he read books of history and philosophy, and sang songs and acathists; he gazed upon Naples, Vesuvius, and upon Ischia, Procida and Capri, ablaze with a blue fire, as though they were formed of sapphires; but, most of all, he gazed upon the sea,—he gazed upon it, and could not have his fill of gazing. It seemed to him that he was beholding it for the first time. The northern sea, gray, given up to commerce and war,—the sea belonging to the Department of Ships and the Peterburgh Admiralty,—that sea which his father loved,—did not at all resemble this southern sea, blue and free.

Aphrosiniya was with him. Whenever he managed to forget about his father, he was almost happy.

He succeeded, although with the greatest difficulty, in gaining entry for Alexei Urov into St. Elmo, despite the strictest watch. Æsopka managed to make himself indispensable: he amused Aphrosiniya whenever the latter was in low spirits, playing cards and draughts with her, and diverting her with jests, fairy-tales and fables, as if he were really Æsop. But it was of his travels through Italy that he discoursed most willingly. The Czarevich listened to him with curiosity, as though he were reliving his own impressions. No matter how much Æsopka longed to be in Russia, no matter how he yearned after Russian baths and vodka, one could see that he, too, like the Czarevich, had come to love this alien land as his own, that he had come to love Russia together with Europe, with a new, universal love.

"The road over the Alpine Mountains is most grievous and arduous," he described the crossing of the Alps. "The road is of the narrowest. On one side are the mountains, as high as the very clouds; while on the other are precipices, most deep, and, because of rapid running waters, filled with ceaseless noise, like that of a mill. And a great horror comes upon a man, when he beholds the said depths. And there are great snows lying upon the mountains, inasmuch as the sun never casts its beams among them. . . .

"And when we would come down from those mountains, winter was still upon them, yet, below, there was summer in all its beauty. On both sides of the road were vineyards and fruit trees,—lemons, oranges, and others,—in great number; and there were wattled enclosures, most comely, guarding the trees. Come to think of it, all Italy is a garden, a similitude of God's Paradise! On the seventh day of March did we see fruits,—lemons and oranges,—ripe, and almost ripe, and some quite green or yet germinating, and there were also blossoms,—all this on the same tree. . . .

"And, near the very mountains, on a most comely site, was built a certain house, called a villa,—most seigniorial, of beautiful architecture. And around the said house were most marvelous gardens and pleasaunces,—people stroll there for the sake of coolness. And in those gardens the trees are kept to a certain regularity, and even their leaves are clipped with that end in view. And flowers and grasses are planted and placed about in accordance with the laws of architecture. The perspective is most exquisite! In the same gardens a multitude of most glorious fountains has been built, spouting most pure water which then flows into all sorts of cunning devices. And, in lieu of posts, lads and wenches of marble there are placed along the paths: Jove, Bacchus, Venus, and divers other pagan gods; the workmanship is splendid,—they seem alive. And these be images belonging to the ages of antiquity, dug up out of the earth. . . ."

Of Venice he told such marvels that Aphrosiniya for a long while would not believe him, and confused Venice with Rock-Candy Town, which is spoken of in Russian fairy-tales.

"How thou canst lie, Æsopka!" she would laugh, yet she listened with avidity.

"All of Venice is situate upon the sea, and sea-water runs through all of the streets and by-ways, and people ride about in boats. As for horses or any sort of cattle, there is none; also, there are no chaises, carriages, or carts of any sort,—nor do they even know about sleighs. The air in the summertime is very oppressive, and there is a very bad odor from the putrid water, even as is the case with us in Peter-burgh, from the Fontannaya water-way, which is clogged up. And, throughout the whole town, there are many boats for hire, which are called *goondallas*, built on a style all their own: they are long and narrow, something like dugouts; the bow and the stern are pointed; there is an iron comb on the bow while in the middle is a structure somewhat like an attic, with small windows of crystal and with damask curtains; and these *goondallas* are all black, they are covered over with black cloths, and look like coffins; as for the rowers,—one man stands at the bow and the other at the stern; each rows and steers with his single oar; of rudder there is none,—however, they make out very well even without it. . . .

"In Venice they give most marvelous operas and comedies, which none can describe to perfection, and nowhere else in all the world are such marvelous operas and comedies to be found, or even possible. And those structures wherein these operas are acted are grand and circular, and the Italians style such a place a theatrum. In those structures are many small chambers, running five tiers high, done in most cunning gold work. And these operas consist of plays on the manner of ancient histories, and deal with illustrious men and the gods of Hellas and Rome; whoever hath a favorite story, will find it presented in some theatrum. And these operas are attended by a multitude of people in maskherats,—or as we say, funny false-faces,—so that none may recognize them. Also during the entire duration of the carnival,—that is to say, during Shrovetide,—they go in maskherats and curious garb; all of them roam about without any let or hindrance, each wherever he lists, and they ride in their *goondallas*, with music aboard; they dance, eat sweets, and drink all sorts of fine lemonades and chocolates. And so they are always making merry in Venice, and their desire is never to be without merriment; and in these their merry-makings they do oft fall from grace, inasmuch as when they do come together in their maskherats many women and maids will take foreigners by the arm, and stroll with them, and amuse themselves, without any shame. . . .

"As for the womenfolk of Venice, they are exceedingly comely, tall and graceful, and polite, and most neatly dressed; but as for handicrafts, they are not very prone thereto,—they would liefer live in idleness, being fond of gallivanting and participating in all diversions, and rather prone to carnal sin, and that for no other reason save to enrich themselves, inasmuch as they get great riches thereby, nor have they any other calling. And many wenches live in special houses, nor deem it a sin nor shame unto themselves, considering it to be their way of trading; while others, who have no houses of their own, live in streets set aside, in small one-story houses; each house has a door leading into the street, and when they see a man coming to them, each with great diligence doth call him to her; and that day when any one of them has the most visitors is considered by her to be the most fortunate; and because of all this, they are not only afflicted by the Frankish malaises themselves, but do also bestow that sort of largesse upon their visitors, plentifully and with all dispatch. As for the clergy, they oppose them only through admonitions, but not through force. And they are most skilled in Venice at curing the Frankish malaises. . . ."

With the same deep feeling that he described Venetian amusements did he also describe all sorts of churchly sanctities, miracles and holy relics.

"I was found worthy of seeing a certain cross; in the said cross, under glass, were arranged and placed a particle of the Navel of Christ, and a particle of His Circumcised Foreskin. And in another cross there was a tiny particle of the sainted Baptist's nose. In the town of Bara I saw the myrrh-exuding remains of St. Nikola the Miracle Worker,—one can see his thigh-bone, and this bone is covered over with sacred myrrh, something like the purest oil to look at, and never does it diminish. A great quantity of this sacred myrrh is taken away by the worshipers, who come day in and day out, and yet it never decreaseth, flowing like water out of a well-spring, and the whole world is copiously supplied and is sanctified by the said sacred myrrh. I have also beheld the boiling blood of St. Januarius, and a bone of the martyr-saint, Laurentius; and the said bone is placed in crystal, and when one kisseth it, a warmth is transmitted through the crystal, which is a matter for no small astonishment. . . ."

With no lesser wonder did he describe the marvels of science as well.

"In Padua, at the Academy of Medicine, embalmed in balsam, are to be found certain infants,—usually abortions; while others, cut out from their dead mothers, swim about in spirits, in jars of glass, and they can stay so for even a thousand years without ever putrefying. There also, in the libraries, I did see exceedingly great globes, terrestrial and celestial, fashioned with a most beautiful mastery of mathematics. . . ."

Æsopka was a lover of the humanities. The medieval seemed to him barbaric. He was thrown into raptures by the emulation of ancient architecture, by all regularity, or rectilinearity, or "proportion,"—that which his eyes had already become accustomed to even in young Peterburgh.

Florence did not prove to his liking.

"Of very beautiful houses, such as might be called well-proportioned, there are but few; all the houses in Florence are of ancient construction; and, even though there are high edifices of three or four stories, yet they are simply built, without much heed to architecture. . . ."

Most of all was he struck with Rome. He spoke of it with that reverent, almost superstitious emotion, which the Eternal City always inspired in barbarians.

"Rome is a most vast place. Even now the boundaries of ancient Rome are perceptible, and one knows that the grandeur of Rome was beyond telling; those places which, in times of antiquity, were in the very heart of the town, are now great fields and farms, where wheat is sown and many vineyards are planted, and herds of buffaloes and oxen and all other kinds of cattle graze; and upon those fields are many structures of stone, immeasurably vast, which because of their great age have fallen into ruins, even though builded with most splendid skill, and most beautiful proportioned,—builded as none can build now. And from the mountains, up to Rome proper, one beholds stone pillars of ancient construction, with sluices, and on top of those pillars are troughs of stone, through which spring-water, of the purest, used to flow from the mountains. And those pillars are known as aqueducts, while the fields are the "Campagna di Roma."

The Czarevich had had merely a glimpse of Rome, but now, as he listened and remembered, it seemed to him as if some ominous shadow of a "grandeur beyond telling" were passing over his head.

"And amid those fields, in the midst of a ruined Roman edifice, is an entrance to certain caverns; in those caverns the Christians sought refuge during their persecutions, and were there martyred, and to this day many bones of those holy martyrs are to be found there. The said caverns, styled catacombs, are so vast that there is said to be a passage underground to the very sea; and there are also other passages, not yet explored. And near those catacombs, in a certain small chapel, stands the Sepulcher of Bacchus hewn out of porphyry stone,—a most huge sarcophagus, yet there is no one therein,—it stands empty. Yet, in times of antiquity, they say, it did hold a body,—incorruptible, of a comeliness indescribable; which body, through the influence of Satan, did resemble that unclean god Bacchus. And sainted men did cast out the said vileness, and did sanctify the place, and builded the church. . . .

"Then I visited a certain place called the Colosseum, wherein sainted martyrs used to be thrown to be devoured of wild beasts, in the presence of the Roman Cæsars of antiquity, who persecuted those of Christian Faith and tortured those who cherished the name of Christ. This place is built in a circle, and is of a huge size; it is at least one hundred and five feet in height; the walls, along which these torturers of old used to stroll and gaze upon the beasts rending the holy martyrs, are of stone. And near those walls, underground, certain pits had been made, also, of stone, in which the wild beasts were kept. And in this same Colosseum St. Ignatius Theophorus was devoured of beasts; and the soil of that place is all encrimsoned with the blood of the martyrs. . . ."

The Czarevich recalled how, since his very childhood, it had been dinned into him that in the whole world Russia alone was a holy land, while the people of all other lands were pagans. He also remembered that which he had said on one occasion to Fräulein Arnheim, in the dove-cote at Rozhdestvenno: "Christ is with us—and us only." "Come, is that really so?" he now reflected. "What if these people, too, have Christ; and what if not only Russia, but even all of Europe, be a holy land? The soil of the place was all encrimsoned with the blood of the martyrs. Could such a land be pagan?"

That the third Rome, as the graybeards styled Muscovy, was very far from the first, authentic Rome, even as Peterburgh's attempt at being European was far from being really Europe,—of that he became convinced with his own eyes.

"Before one even heard of the beginnings of Moscow," Æsopka asserted, "there were many other kingdoms in the West, of greater age and held in greater esteem than Moscow. . . ."

He concluded his description of a Venetian carnival in words which remained in the Czarevich's memory:

"There they are forever making merry, and do not interfere with one another in any way, or fear aught from anybody: each, according to his will, does whatever he feels like doing. And such freedom is always to be found in Venice, and the Venetians always live in absolute peace, without fear, and without hurt, and without crushing taxes. . . ."

The unfinished thought was clear: not at all the sort of thing, now, which prevails with us in Russia, where none durst even peep about any kind of freedom.

"One custom of all European nations that is particularly praiseworthy," Æsopka remarked on one occasion, "is that their children do not meet with indifference or cruelty either from their parents or from their teachers, but are brought up in undeviating freedom and courage through kindly and sharp rebuke, rather than through beatings. And, knowing this, the people of Muscovy in the days of old did not send their children at all to learn abroad, fearing lest, having learned the beliefs and customs of those lands, and their blessed freedom, they might change their own faith and take to others, and neither care nor think about returning to their homes. But now, even though they are sent, there is still little use therein, inasmuch as, even as a bird cannot be without air, so sciences cannot be without freedom; whereas with us, even new things are taught in the old manner: Mute is a stick, yet it maketh the mind quick; to make a man spry, let thy fists fly. . . ."

Thus both of them, the fugitive navigator as well as the fugitive Czarevich, dimly sensed that that Europeanization which Peter was introducing into Russia,—ciphering, navigation, fortification,—was still not the whole of Europe, and not even the chiefest thing in it; that the true Europe had a higher truth, which the Czar did not know. Whereas, without this truth, with all the sciences, there would merely be a new Peterburgh loutishness, instead of the old barbarism of Muscovy. Was not the Czarevich himself turning to it, to this blessed freedom, calling upon Europe to judge between him and his father?

On one occasion Æsopka told them *The history of the Russian Sailor, Vasilii Koriotsky, and of the Beauteous Heraklea, the King's Daughter, of the Land of Florence.*

Perhaps to his hearers, even as to the narrator himself, the meaning of this fairy-tale was not clear and yet mysteriously-understandable: the espousal of the Russian sailor with the daughter of the King of Florence, the vernal land of the Renaissance (the most splendidly-beautiful blossom of European freedom), was like an imaging-forth of a yet unknown, impending union of Russia with Europe.

The Czarevich, having heard the *History* to the end, recalled a certain picture which his father had brought from Holland: the Czar, in a sailor's costume, embracing a most robust Dutch wench. Alexei involuntarily smiled, reflecting that this raddle-faced wench was just as far from the Florentine king's daughter, "as radiant as the sun in its nakedness," as all of Russian Europe was from the real.

"Well, I dare say thy sailor never returned to Russia?" he asked Æsopka.

"What would he miss there?" the latter grumbled, with sudden apathy for that very Russia which he had been yearning for so, only a little while ago. "In Peterburgh, through the *ukase* dealing with fugitives, he would have been, like as not, flogged with a cat-o'-nine-tails, and sent off to Rogerwick; while the Florentine king's daughter would have been packed off to a weaving factory, like some loose wench! . . ."

But Aphrosiniya unexpectedly voiced her conclusions:

"There, Æsopka, thou canst see to what high honors thy sailor attained through learning; but, had he been fleeing from learning, like thee, he would have seen as little of the Florentine king's daughter as of his own ears. As for thy praise of the liberty here, 'tis not meant for the likes of thee.

How is one to teach such fools as all of you are otherwise than with a stick, when you will not learn of your own will? Czar-Batiushka ought to be thanked. Serve you fellows right!"

III

My own father Don,
Flowing gentle on,—
Cleanse me in thy wave.
Thou dank mother earth,
That didst give me birth,—
Cover me, and save.

Aphrosiniya was singing, sitting at a table near a window in the chambers of the Czarevich, within the Fortress of St. Elmo; and, as she ripped off the lining of red taffeta from the sand-colored waistcoat of her masculine garb, she announced that she refused to dress up any longer like a merryandrew at a fair.

She had on a dressing-gown of silk,—soiled and with the buttons torn off,—and upon her bare feet, silver slippers trodden down at the heel. In a tin receptacle placed before her,— her workbox,—was a confusion of bright bits of cloth and ribbon, a woman's fan, "mittens," or gloves of kidskin, loveletters from the Czarevich, and little paper packets with incense, as well as some frankincense given her by a certain sainted ancient, and Maréchal face powder from the famous wig-maker Frizon, of Rue Saint Honoré; there were also prayer-beads from Mount Athos, and beauty-patches and little jars with "pomatum" from Paris. She passed whole hours in massaging and touching-up her face,—which was altogether unnecessary, since she had a splendid complexion. The Czarevich, seated at the same table, was writing letters, which were meant to be "scattered throughout Peterburgh," as well as submitted to the heads of the clergy and the senators.

"To the Most Excellent Gentlemen of the Senate:
"I feel that my absence from the land of Russia, as well as my unknown existence since, must be a matter of wonder not only to Your Graces, but to all of the people as well;

I have been forced to adopt the course I have through naught else save the perpetual malice causelessly held against me, and constant strife; but most of all, because of that which had taken place at the beginning of last year, when I was almost forced to put on the black raiment of a monk, without, as you know, any fault of mine. But through the prayers of the Consolatrice of all that sorrow, the Most Holy Mother of God, as well as through the prayers of all the saints, the All-Gracious Lord did deliver me therefrom, and did grant me an opportunity of saving myself by absenting myself from my beloved Fatherland, which, had it not been for this opportunity, I would never have forsaken; and now I dwell in peace and health under the safeguard of a certain great sovereign, until such time as the Lord, who hath preserved me, shall command me to appear again in Russia,—in which case, I beg of you, not to consign me to neglect. But, should there be any news, tending to erase memory of me among the people be bruited about, to the effect that I am not among the living, or announcing some other ill-haps, pray put no credence therein, and assure the people, so that they, too, might not credit such news. Since God preserves me, I am still alive, and remain a well-wisher, always, not only to Your Graces, but also all of my Fatherland, till that I be in my grave.

"ALEXEI."

He glanced through the open door of the gallery at the sea; under the fresh northern wind it was blue, shadowed over as though it were smoking,—tempestuous, with white-caps, and with white sails, as arch-bosomed as swans, billowing in the wind. It seemed to the Czarevich that this was that very same blue sea which was sung of in Russian songs, and over which prophetic Oleg had journeyed with his band against Czargrad.

He got out several sheets folded together, written in German by his own hand,—in a large, seemingly childish handwriting. The margin bore a notation: *"Nehmen sie nicht Übel, das ich so schlecht geschrieben, weil ich kann nicht besser.* Please overlook my having written this so poorly, inasmuch as I cannot do better." This was a lengthy letter to the Kaiser,—a whole speech of accusation against his father. He had begun it a long time ago, constantly correcting and blotting out, writing anew, and never able to finish it; that which seemed true in his thoughts, proved untrue in words,—between words and thought was an insuperable obstacle,—and the main thing could not be told in any words whatsoever.

"The Emperor must save me," he read over detached passages. "I am not at fault before my father; I was ever obedient to him, loving and respecting him in accordance with the commandment of God. I know that I am but a frail man,—but I was thus brought up by Menshikov. He taught me nothing, ever estranging me from my father, treating me as if I were a serf or a dog. I was purposely made to drink a great deal. I grew faint in spirit from deathly drunkenness and from persecutions. However, in former days, my father was kind toward me. He entrusted me with the administration of affairs of state, and everything went well,—he was satisfied with me. But, since the time when my wife began bearing children,—the new Czaritza having also borne a son,—they began treating the Crown-Princess poorly, forcing her to work like a serving-wench, and she did die from grief. The Czaritza and Menshikov have set my father up in arms against me. Both of them are filled with malice,—they know neither God nor conscience. The heart of the Czar, if he be left to himself, is kind and just; but he is surrounded by evil folk; in addition to that, he is unbelievably fiery-tempered, and is cruel in his wrath. He thinks that he, like God, hath the right of life and death over men. Much innocent blood has he shed, and has tortured and executed condemned men,—aye, with his own hands. Should the Emperor surrender me to my father, it would be the same as if he were to kill me. Even were my father to spare me, my stepmother and Menshikov would not abate until they had made me drink myself to death, or had poisoned me. My abdication from the throne was extracted from me by force; I do not .vant to retire to a monastery; I have sufficient intellect to rule. But I call God to witness that I never contemplated making the people mutiny, even though this would not have been difficult to do, inasmuch as the people love me, while they hate my father because of his unworthy Czaritza, his evil and debauched favorites, his desecration of the church and contempt for the good old customs, and also because he is a tyrant and an enemy to his people, 'sparing neither money nor blood. . . .'

" 'An enemy to his people?' " repeated the Czarevich, and, after reflection, crossed out these words,—they seemed false to him, for he knew his father loved his people, even though his love was at times more merciless than any enmity: Him whom I love I do chastise. It would be better, it seemed, to love a little less! And he loved him, his son, as well. If he did not love him he would not torture him so; and now, as always, when he re-read this letter, he dimly sensed that he was in the right before his father, but not altogether in the right; a single line, a single hair, divided this "not altogether in the right" from "altogether not in the right," and in his accusations he was constantly, even though involuntarily, stepping over this line. It was as though each one of them had a truth of his own, and these two truths were forever irreconcilable. And one truth had to annihilate the other. But, no matter who conquered, the conqueror would be at fault,—the conquered would be in the right.

He would not have been able to put this into words, even to himself to say nothing of others; and, besides, who would have understood him, who would have believed him? Who, save God, could serve as judge between father and son?

He put aside the letter with an oppressive feeling, with a secret desire to destroy it, and began listening closely to the song of Aphrosiniya, who, having done with ripping out the lining, was trying on the new French beauty-patches before a mirror. This eternal quiet singing in the midst of prison tedium was, in her case, involuntary, like the singing of a bird in its cage. She sang, even as she breathed, almost without realizing it. Yet the contrast between the to-do with the French beauty-patches and her native, dismal song seemed strange to the Czarevich:

> Thou dank mother earth,
> That didst give me birth,—
> Cover me, and save.
> Woodland nightingale,

Little brother dear,—
Sing thy song for me.
Thou greenwood cuckoo small,
Fairest sister mine,—
Sound thy call for me.
Thou birch, slim and white,
Like a youthful wife,—
Whisper thou o'er me.

Steps, sentry-calls, the ringing of opening locks and
bolts came echoing down the reverberating passages. The
officer on sentry-duty knocked at the door and announced
Weingart, the high and many-titled secretary to the Kaiser's
Viceroy in Naples,—or, as the Russians phrased it, the
Vice-King.

A roly-poly asthmatic entered the room, with a low bow,—
his face was as red as raw meat, his lower lip hung down,
and his little porcine eyes were sunk in blubber. Like many
knaves, he had a most ingenuous air. "This most stout German is a most exquisite rogue," Æsopka was wont to say
of him.

Weingart brought a case of old Falernian and Moselle as
a gift to the Czarevich, whom, observing his incognito in
the presence of strangers, he styled a nobly-born Count;
while for Aphrosiniya, whose hand he kissed (he was a great
ladies'-man), he had brought a basket of fruit and flowers. He
also transmitted certain letters from Russia, and verbal instructions from Vienna.

"The news that the highly-born Count is in good health
and well-being was pleasurably received in Vienna. Much
patience is needed,—now more than ever. I beg to report,
as the latest news, that it is already beginning to be said
in the world that the Czarevich has disappeared. Some suppose that he has gone because of the great ire of his father;
according to the opinion of others, he has been deprived of
his life through the Czar's will; others think that he has
been done away with by assassins, while traveling. But none
knows truly his whereabouts. Here is a copy of the report
of Pleier, Kaiser's Resident in Peterburgh, in case the highly
born Count be curious to learn what is written concerning
him. Here are the authentic words of His Majesty, the
Kaiser: 'Our beloved Czarevich is advised, for his own well-

being, to keep as hidden as possible, inasmuch as upon the return of the Sovereign, his father, to Peterburgh, a great investigation will be instituted.'"

And, stooping to the Czarevich's very ear, he added in a whisper:

"Rest assured, Your Highness! I have the most exact information: The Emperor will not surrender you for any cause; but, should the occasion arise, after the death of your father, he is even willing to help you, with an armed hand, to attain the throne. . . ."

"Ah, no, whatever are you saying,—whatever are you saying! You must not . . ." the Czarevich stopped him, with the same oppressive feeling with which he had just recently put aside his letter to the Kaiser. "May God grant that affairs never reach such a state,—that there be no war because of me. That is not what I am supplicating you for,— I would have naught save that you keep me under your protection. As for this other thing, I do not wish it. . . . However, I am grateful. May the Lord reward the Kaiser for all his graciousness to me!"

He ordered a bottle of Moselle wine from the case presented to him to be opened, in order to drink the Kaiser's health.

Having stepped out for a minute into an adjoining room for certain necessary letters, he found Weingart upon his return, explaining to *mademoiselle Eufrosyne,* with gallant amiability (not so much in words, however, as by signs), that it was a pity she no longer wore her masculine garb,— it became her so greatly.

"L'Amour même ne saurait se presenter avec plus de grâces!" he concluded in French, looking point-blank at her with his little porcine eyes, with that peculiarly masculine gaze which the Czarevich abominated so.

Aphrosiniya, upon the arrival of Weingart, had managed to throw a new festal robe of two-faced taffeta over her soiled dressing-gown and a cap of precious Brabant lace over her unkempt hair, had powdered herself, and even contrived to stick a beauty-patch over her left eyebrow, just as she had seen a certain Parisian jade wear hers on the Corso, in Rome. The expression of ennui vanished from her face; she grew more animated and, although she did not understand a word of either German or French, she contrived to understand even without words that which the German was saying about her masculine garb, and was laughing slyly, and artfully blushing, and covering her face with her sleeve, like any country lass.

"What a carcass of pork! Faugh, the Lord forgive us,— thou surely hast found some one to flirt with!" the Czarevich looked at them in vexation. "Well, it makes but little difference to her who it is, as long as it be some one new. Oh, ye daughters of Eve, ye daughters of Eve! A fiend and a dame, they both weigh the same. . . ."

When Weingart had taken his departure, the Czarevich began to read the letters. Pleier's report was the most important of all.

"The regiments of the Guards, consisting for the most part of nobles, together with the rest of the army, have formed a conspiracy in Mecklenburg, to assassinate the Czar, to bring the Czaritza hither, and, together with the younger Czarevich and both the Czarevnas, to immure her in that same monastery where the old Czaritza now abides; and, having freed the last, to entrust the government to her son, the legitimate successor."

The Czarevich drained off two tumblers of Moselle, got up, and began pacing the room rapidly, muttering something and waving his arms. Aphrosiniya followed him with her eyes,—silently and closely, yet apathetically. Her face, upon Weingart's departure, had assumed its wonted expression of ennui.

Finally, halting before her, he exclaimed:

"Well, little mother, thou wilt be eating White Lake smelts soon. These be good tidings. Never fear,—God will grant us an opportunity to return in joy. . . ."

And in full detail, he imparted to her the whole report of Pleier,—he read its concluding words in German, evidently unable to get his fill of joyance from them:

"*Alles zum Aufstand allhier sehr geneiget ist.* Everybody in Peterburgh, now, has strong leanings toward revolt. Everybody complains that the well-born and low-born are considered equal, that all alike are enrolled as sailors and soldiers, while whole villages have fallen into wrack and ruin because of the building of cities and ships."

Aphrosiniya listened to him in silence, still with the same apathetic ennui on her face, and, only when he ended, did she ask in her drawling voice:

"But, now, Alexei Petrovich,—should they slay the Czar and send for thee, wilt thou throw thy lot in with the rebels?"

And she looked at him out of the corner of her eyes in such a manner that, had he been less taken up with his thoughts, he might have been struck by this question,—might even have sensed a secret sting in it. But he did not notice anything.

"I know not," he answered, after brief thought. "Should they send for me after the death of Batiushka, then I might even throw in my lot with them. . . . But what avails trying to foretell the future! The Lord's will be done!" he seemed to recollect himself. "All I say is this: thou canst see, Aphrosiushka, what God is doing,—Batiushka doth as he pleases, and God doth as He pleases!"

And, tired out by joy, he sank down in a chair and again began, without looking at Aphrosiniya, as though he were talking to himself:

"There is a printed report that the Swedish fleet has set out for the shore of the Bay of Livonia to transport people there. Great will be the harm thereof, if this be true: there will be disagreement in Peterburgh between Prince Menshikov and the Senators. And our main army is far away. The Prince and the Senators will sulk at one another, and will not help,—the Swedes are likely to work great havoc. Peterburgh, now, is right nearby! If our troops have gone far off, to Copenhagen, we may lose Peterburgh thereby, even as we lost Azov. Peterburgh is not fated to be ours long: either the Swedes will capture it, or it will fall into ruins. May it be desolate,—may it be desolate!" he kept on repeating, like an incantation, the prophecy of the Czarevna Martha Alexeievna, his aunt.

"But as for its being quiet now,—even that quiet bodes no good. Here is what Avram Lopukhin, my uncle, writes me: People of all ranks are discussing me,—asking about me and commiserating with me, always, and are ready to stand up for me; while all around Moscow, now, things are already beginning to stir up, and, down south on the Volga, there cannot help but be unrest among the people. And is there any cause for wonder? How is it that they are enduring everything even up to now? For all this will not go unavenged. Methinks that, losing their patience, they are bound to do something or other. And, on top of it all, there is the uprising in Mecklenburg, and there are the Swedes, and the Kaiser, and myself! Misfortune on all sides! Everything is in a turmoil,—in a turmoil and tottering. Then will come a shattering sound, and a crash,—and then all one will see will be dust rising in a pillar. The very earth will quake so that men shall cry out! Nor will even Batiushka himself get off scot-free! ..."

For the first time in his life he felt himself powerful and an object of dread to his father. He could not catch his breath for joy, as on that memorable night, during Peter's illness, when, outside the frost-covered window, the moonshot blizzard had been giving off a blue sheen, as though it were burning with a blue flame, as though it were intoxicated. Joy intoxicated him more potently than the wine which he kept on drinking, almost without noticing it himself, tumblerful after tumblerful, as he contemplated the sea,—also blue, as though it were burning with a blue flame, likewise intoxicated and intoxicating.

"In German gazettes they write that my younger little brother, Petenka, was almost killed by lightning in Peterhof this summer; a wet-nurse was holding him in her arms,—and she was barely left among the living; while the soldier on duty was struck dead. Ever since that time the infant has been ailing and failing,—evidently he is not long for this world. And yet, see how they guarded him, how they cherished him! I feel sorry for Petenka. His baby soul is innocent before God. He is suffering for the sins of others, for those of his parents, the poor little fellow. May the Lord save him and spare him! And yet I see it is all the will of God,—this was a miracle, a portent! And how is it that Batiushka will not pause to think? 'Tis a dreadful thing,—a dreadful thing!—to fall into the hands of the living God! ..."

"But who among the Senators will stand up for thee?"
Aphrosiniya suddenly asked, and again the same strange
spark flickered in her eyes, and at once expired,—as though
a candle had been borne past behind an opaque hanging.

"But what dost thou want to know that for?" the
Czarevich looked at her in wonder, as though he had forgotten about her entirely and only now recollected that she
was listening to him.

Aphrosiniya did not put any other questions. But some
barely perceptible shadow—the shadow of some third person—seemed to pass between them.

"Even though not all are my enemies, yet they all work
evil to please Batiushka, inasmuch as they are all poltroons,"
continued the Czarevich. "But then, I have no need of anybody. I can spit upon them all,—if but the rabble be whole-
hearted!" (He was repeating his favorite saying.) "When
I shall be Czar, I shall oust all of the old men and choose
new ones for myself, according to my will. I shall lighten
the burdens of the people,—let them rest a while. I shall
take some of the flesh off the bodies of the *boyars*. They
have been waxing fat long enough; I shall take heed of the
peasantry, of the sick and the orphaned, of the lesser
brethren of Christ. And I shall inaugurate an ecclesiastical
and an agrarian council, chosen of all the people,—let them
all bring the truth to the Czar, without fear, with the fullest
freedom of speech, so that state and church may be set right
through the general counsel of the many, and through the
coming of the Holy Ghost, forever and ever! . . ."

He was dreaming aloud, and his dreams were becoming
ever more misty, ever more fairylike.

Suddenly an evil, poignant thought stung his heart like
a gadfly: Nothing would come of it; the whole thing was
his mere vaporing; much bruit, little fruit.

And he saw vividly that, side by side with his father, the
giant forging a new Russia of iron, he himself, with his
dreams, was a little boy blowing soap-bubbles. Come,—who
was he to contend with Batiushka?

But he immediately drove this thought from him, waving
it away like some annoying fly: God's will would be done
in all things; let Batiushka forge his iron to his heart's

content; he was doing as he willed, while God was doing as He willed; God had but to will it, and the iron would burst, even like a soap-bubble.

And he gave himself up to reveries even more delectable. Feeling no longer powerful but weak (however, this was a pleasant weakness) with a smile which was becoming ever more meek and intoxicated he listened to the surge of the sea, and he thought he caught in this surge something familiar, something old,—most old: was it his grandmother singing a lullaby, or was it Sirin, the bird of paradise, singing kingly songs?

"And, later on, when I shall have put the whole land in order, and have made things easier for the people, I shall set out against Czargrad with a great army and fleet. I shall kill off all the Turks, free the Slavs from under yoke of the infidels, and raise up the cross once more a-top the St. Sophia. And I shall convene a universal council for the unification of all of the churches. And I shall bestow peace upon all the world, and all the nations shall come flocking from the four ends of the earth, to the shadow of Sophia, the All-Highest Wisdom of God, into the sacred, the eternal kingdom, to meet the Coming Christ! . . ."

Aphrosiniya had ceased listening long ago; she was constantly yawning and making the sign of the cross over her mouth. Finally she got up, stretching and scratching herself.

"I am all broken up somehow. I guess it's because I have not had my full sleep, having waited for this German ever since dinner. I think I had better go and lie down, Petrovich,—eh?"

"Do so, little mother; sleep, and may God watch thee. I may go myself after a while,—only I must feed the little pigeons first."

She went into the next room,—the bed-chamber, while the Czarevich went out into the gallery. The pigeons were already flocking in anticipation of their usual feeding.

He scattered crumbs and grain for them, with a soft, caressing call:

"Ghul, ghul, ghul!"

And, just as they used to do in Rozhdestvenno, the pigeons, cooing, crowded at his feet, fluttered over his head, perched on his shoulders and arms, covering him with their wings as if they were clothing him. He looked down at the sea from the height, and, amid the fluttering beating of the wings, it seemed to him that he himself was flying upon wings thither, into the infinite vista, over the blue sea, toward Sophia, the Highest Wisdom of God, as radiant as the sun.

The sensation of flight was so strong that his heart swooned and his head swam. A feeling of fear came upon him. He puckered up his eyes and convulsively seized a projection of the railing. He was no longer flying, it seemed, but falling.

With uncertain steps he returned to his room. Aphrosiniya, now altogether disrobed, barefooted, in nothing but her shift, bustlingly entered the same room from the bed-chamber, clambered up in a chair, and began fixing the lampad before an image. This was an antique ikon,—that of the Mother of All the Sorrowing,—beloved of the Czarevich; he carried it about with him everywhere and never parted with it.

"What a sin! To-morrow is the Assumption of the Queen of Heaven, and yet I had forgot about it. The Dear Mother might have been left just so, without any lamp. Art thou going to read the hours, Petrovich? Shall I get the reading desk ready?"

Before every high holiday, since they had no priest, he himself performed the services, read the hours, and sang the canticles.

"Nay, little mother,—although I may do so toward night. I have become tired out, somehow; my head aches."

"Thou shouldst drink less wine, batiushka."

" 'Tis not because of the wine; 'tis because of my thoughts, rather,—the news has been so exceedingly joyous! . . ."

Having lighted the lampad, on her way back to the bed-chamber, she paused near the table to pick out the ripest peach from the basket of fruit presented to her by the German. She had a fondness for eating something sweet in bed, before falling asleep. The Czarevich walked up to her and embraced her.

"Aphrosiushka, dearest little friend of my heart, art thou not glad? For thou shalt be a Czaritza, whereas the Silver One. . . ."

The Silver One—or, as he more tenderly put it, imitating the pronunciation of children, the Silvel One, was his pet-name for the child which Aphrosiniya was going to bear,—it was bound to be a son, he thought; she was in the third month of pregnancy. "Thou art my golden one, while my little son shall be of silver," he was wont to say to her in moments of tenderness.

"Thou shalt be a Czaritza, while the Silvel One shall be heir to the throne!" continued the Czarevich. "We shall call him Vannichka,—the Most Pious and Autocratic Czar of All the Russias, Ioann Alexeievich! . . ."

Most gently she freed herself from his embraces, looked over her shoulder to see if the little holy lamp were burning right, bit into the peach, and only then answered him calmly:

"Thou art pleased to jest, batiushka. How am I, a serf wench, ever to become a Czaritza?"

"Why, when I marry thee thou wilt become one,—for even Batiushka himself managed things that very way. My stepmother, Ekaterina Alexeievna, also did not spring from any too well-known a line,—she used to wash shirts with the Finnish women, and was taken captive in naught but her shift; and yet, look ye, there she is, reigning. And thou, too, Aphrosiniya Fedorovna, shalt be a Czaritza,—and, never fear, thou wilt be no worse than the others! . . ."

He longed to, yet could not, tell her everything that he felt: that perhaps the very reason he had come to love her was because she was a simple serf wench; for he, too, even though he was of the blood of Czars, was also simple, disliking the high pride of the *boyars* yet liking the rabble; it would be e'en through the rabble, now, that he would come to rule; one good turn deserved another,—the rabble would make him Czar, while he would make her, Aphrosiniya, a serf wench sprung from the rabble, a Czaritza.

She kept silent, with her eyes cast down, and all that one could tell by her face was that she wanted to sleep. But he was embracing her ever harder and harder, feeling through the thin stuff of her shift the resiliency and freshness of her naked body. She resisted, pushing away his arms. Suddenly, through a chance movement, he pulled down her half-buttoned shift, which had been barely hanging on one shoulder. The shift unbuttoned entirely, slipped down, and fell at her feet. All naked, with the dull gold of her rufous hair, as if in a nimbus, she stood before him, and strange and seductive did the black beauty-patch over her left eyebrow seem. And there was something caprine, unashamed, and wild in the oblique, elongated slits of her eyes.

"Let me go, let me go, now, Alëshenka! 'Tis ashamed! . . ." But, if she were ashamed, she was not so to any great extent, —she merely turned away slightly, with her habitual, indolent, somewhat contemptuous smile, remaining under his caresses, as always, cold, innocent, almost virginal, despite a barely perceptible roundness of her abdomen, foreshadowing the fullness of her pregnancy. At such moments it seemed to him that her body was slipping out of his hands and melting, as ætherial as a specter.

"Aphrosiya! Aphrosiya!" he was whispering, striving to catch, to retain this specter, and suddenly sank on his knees before her.

" 'Tis a shame," she was repeating. "We are on the eve of a holiday. Look,—there is even the holy lamp burning. . . . 'Tis a sin,—'tis a sin!"

Yet the next instant, just as apathetically, insouciantly, she brought the bitten peach up to her half open mouth, which itself was as scarlet and fresh as some fruit.

"Aye, 'tis a sin," flashed through his mind, "all sin has sprung from woman, and because of her do we all die. . . ."

And he, too, involuntarily turned around to look at the holy image, and suddenly recalled how just such another image, on that night in the Summer Garden, during the tempest, had fallen out of the hands of Batiushka and had broken to pieces at the pediment of the Venus of Peterburgh, —the white She-Devil.

Against the quadrangle of the doorway, opening on the blue sea, her body stood out, as though, aureately white, like the foam of the waves, it were emerging out of the flaming blueness of the sea. One hand held the fruit; the other she had let fall in a chaste gesture, covering her nakedness, like the Foam-Engendered One. And, behind her, the blue sea flashed and seethed, like a chalice of ambrosia, and its surge was like to the eternal laughter of the gods.

This was that same serving wench Aphroska who, on a certain evening in spring, in the little house of the Viyazemskys on the Lesser Okhta, had been mopping the floor, bending low and with her skirt tucked up. This was both the wench Aphroska and the goddess Aphrodite in one.

"Venus, Venus,—the White She-Devil!" reflected the Czarevich, in superstitious awe, and was ready to jump up, to flee. But from the sinful and yet innocent body, as from an opened flower, there was wafted upon him a familiar, heady and sinister odor, and, without himself understanding what he was doing, he bowed still lower before her and kissed her feet, and glanced up into her eyes, and whispered like a suppliant:

"Czaritza! My Czaritza! . . ."

And the dim little flame of the lampad flickered before the holy and sorrowful Visage.

IV

The Kaiser's Viceroy in Naples, Count Daun, invited the Czarevich to an audience with him at the Royal Palace, designating the evening of the 26th of September.

During the last few days one felt in the air the approach of the sirocco, a wind out of Africa, bringing with it clouds of incandescent sand out of the depths of the Sahara. Probably the hurricane had already burst and was raging in the higher strata of the air, but below there was breathless calm. The fronds of the palms and the branches of the mimosas hung motionless. The sea alone was turbulent with enormous, foamless rollers, breaking against the shore in a dead swell with shattering reverberations. The distance was veiled over with a turbid murk, and, upon the cloudless sky, the sun seemed dim, as if viewed through a smoky opal. The air was shot through with the finest dust,—it penetrated everywhere, even into closely shut chambers, and a sheet of white paper or the pages of books would become covered with it in a gray layer; it crunched in one's teeth; it inflamed one's eyes and throat. The air was sultry, becoming sultrier with every hour. One felt in nature the same sensation one feels in one's body when an abscess is ripening. Men and beasts, knowing not where to find refuge, were in restless agony. The people were expecting calamities,—war, or the plague, or an eruption of Vesuvius.

And, actually, during the night from the twenty-third to the twenty-fourth of September, the inhabitants of Torre del Greco, Resina and Portici felt the first subterranean tremors. Lava appeared. The fiery torrent was already approaching the very highest vineyards, disposed on the slope of the mountain. To placate the wrath of the Lord, penitential processions were formed, with lit candles, soft chanting, and the loud wails of self-flagellants.

But the wrath of God would not abate. By day black smoke poured out of Vesuvius, as if out of a smelting furnace, spreading out in a long cloud from Castellamare to Posilipo; while at night a red flame reared upward, like the glow of some subterranean conflagration. The peaceful sacrificial altar of the gods was becoming transformed into the awesome torch of the Eumenides. Finally came the first reverberations of the earthquake, like to subterranean thunders, as if the ancient Titans were awaking anew. The city was in terror. The days of Sodom and Gomorrah were being recalled. And, of nights, in the midst of the dead quiet, a high-pitched—exceedingly high-pitched whimper, as of some creature caught fast (like the buzzing of a captured mosquito), would spring up somewhere in the cracks of a window, or under a door, or in the hearth chimney: this was the sirocco striking up its song. The sound would grow in volume and intensity, and it seemed as if it would break out into frenzied howling at any second; but suddenly it would die out, would break off, and again quiet would fall, deader than ever. It was as though evil spirits, from both below and above, were calling to one another, communing about the Lord's dread Judgment Day wherewith the world would end.

All these days the Czarevich felt unwell. But the physician reassured him, having told him that this was because he was unused to the sirocco, and prescribing a sour mixture,—which really did make him feel better. At the designated day and hour he drove to the palace, for his audience with the Viceroy.

The officer on duty, who met him at the entry, transmitted to him Count Daun's most respectful apologies, because His Highness would have to wait a few minutes in the reception hall, since the Viceroy had had to absent himself on a very important and undeferable matter.

The Czarevich entered the enormous and deserted reception hall, furnished with a somber, almost sinister, Spanish pomp: walls hung with blood-red silk; an abundance of heavy gilt; cupboards of carved ebony, resembling sepulchers; mirrors, so dim that it seemed they reflected the faces of phantoms only. Upon the walls were huge dark canvases, the devout paintings of old masters: Roman soldiers, who looked like butchers, were burning, chopping, cutting up, sawing, and torturing the Christian martyrs in all sorts of other ways. This recalled a shambles, or the torture-chambers of the Most Holy Inquisition. And above, on the ceiling, among gilded scrolls and shells, was a representation of the Triumph of the Olympian Gods: in this pitiful mongrel art aping Titian and Rubens one could perceive the end of the Renaissance,—in its precious effeminateness one could perceive barbaric savagery and coarsening of art,—mounds of naked flesh,—naked meat,—fat backs, plump bellies, all in creases; misshapen legs, monstrous, pendulous feminine breasts. All these gods and goddesses, as fatted as pork carcasses, and these little loves who resembled rosy, suckling pigs,—this entire bestial Olympus,—seemed predestined for the Christian shambles, for the implements of torture of the Most Holy Inquisition.

The Czarevich, for a long time, paced the hall; finally he grew tired and sat down. The twilight was crawling in at the windows, and gray shadows, like spiders, were weaving their webs in the corners. Only here and there catching the light, some gilt lion-paw stood out, or some arch-breasted griffin, supporting the jasper or malachite top of a round table, and the crystal pendants of the lusters, covered with cheese-cloth, emitted an occasional dim gleam, like gigantic cocoons besprinkled with dew-drops. It seemed to the Czarevich that from this copiousness of naked flesh, of naked meat,—well-fed, pagan above, and martyred, Christian below,—the oppressiveness of the sirocco was increasing. His distrait glance, roving over the walls, paused upon one picture which did not resemble the others, emerging from their midst like a bright spot: it represented a maiden, with rufous hair, naked almost to the waist, with a bosom almost like that of a child and innocent, with limpidly yellow eyes and an unmeaning smile. In the upturned corners of her lips and the elongated slits of her eyes there was something caprine, wild and strange, almost uncanny, reminiscent of the wench Aphroska. Suddenly, dimly, he sensed some connection between this smile and the oppressiveness of the sirocco, like that of a gathering abscess. The picture was a poor one, a copy of an antique creation of the school of Lombardy, by some pupil of the pupils of Leonardo. In this vacuous yet enigmatical smile had been reflected the last shadow of the nobly-born citizen of Naples, Monna Lisa Gioconda.

The Czarevich wondered why the Viceroy, who was always so meticulously polite, was making him wait so long; and what had happened to Weingart; and why there was such silence. . . . Had everybody in the castle died out?

He wanted to get up, to summon somebody, to order that candles be brought. But a strange lethargy had fallen upon him as though he, too, were enmeshed within and plastered over with those gray cobwebs which the shadows, like spiders, were weaving in the corners. He felt too lazy even to move. His eyes were closing. He opened them with an effort, repeatedly, to avoid falling asleep. Yet, despite everything, he did fall asleep for a few moments. But, when he awoke, it seemed to him that a great deal of time had passed. He had seen something dreadful in his sleep, but could not recall just what. Still, there was left in his soul a sensation of unutterable heaviness, and he again imagined he perceived a connection between this fearful dream, the vacuous smile of the rufous maiden, and the oppressiveness of the sirocco like that of a ripening abscess.

When he opened his eyes he beheld a face right before him, —pale, most pale, like that of a specter. For a long space he could not understand what this was. Finally he understood that this was his own face, reflected in the dim pier-glass between two windows, before which he had fallen asleep as he sat in his armchair. In the same mirror he could see a closed door directly in back of him. And it seemed to him that his dream was still going on,—that the door would open at any moment, and that that horror which he had just now seen in his dream, and which he could not recall, would enter.

The door opened noiselessly. Faces, and the light of wax candles appeared in it. Gazing into the mirror as before he recognized one face, then a second and a third. He leapt up and turned around, thrusting his hands out with the desperate hope that this was but a hallucination seen in the mirror, —but he beheld in reality the same thing as in the mirror, and a cry of boundless horror escaped from his breast:

" 'Tis he! 'Tis he! 'Tis he!"

The Czarevich would have fallen flat on his back, but for the support of the secretary, Weingart, who was behind him.

"Water! Water! The Czarevich is unwell!"

Weingart solicitously seated him in an armchair, and Alexei saw the kind face of the aged Count Daun bending over him. He was stroking Alexei's shoulder and giving him some spirits of ammonia to sniff.

"Calm yourself, Your Highness! For God's sake calm yourself! Nothing untoward has happened. The news is of the best. . . ."

The Czarevich was sipping some water, his teeth chattering against the rim of the glass. He was trembling with all his body, with a ceaseless, frequent tremor, as if in a powerful ague-fit, without taking his eyes off the door.

"How many of them are there?" he asked Count Daun in a whisper.

"Two, Your Highness,—only two."

"But what of the third? I saw a third. . . ."

"It is probably your imagination."

"Nay, I saw him! Where is he, then?'

"What he?"

"My father! . . ."

The old man gave him a wondering look.

"This is caused by the sirocco," explained Weingart. "A

trifling rush of blood to the head. It is a frequent occurrence. Why, even I, since the very morning, have some sort of blue specks dancing before my eyes. Just let some blood, and the complaint will vanish as if by magic."

"I did see him!" the Czarevich kept on reiterating. "I swear by God that this was no dream. I saw him, Count, even as clearly as I see you now. . . ."

"Oh, my God, my God!" exclaimed the old man, with sincere consternation. "Had I but known that Your Highness was not feeling entirely well, I would never have permitted this, under any consideration. . . . However, perhaps it is possible to put off the audience even now? . . ."

"Nay, no need,—it matters but little. I fain would know all," uttered the Czarevich. "Let only the old man approach me; as for the other, do not let him near me. . . ."

He convulsively seized the Count's hand:

"For God's sake, Count, do not let that other one near me. . . . He is an assassin! You can see how he eyes me. . . . I know that he is sent by the Czar to slit my throat! . . ."

There was such terror in his eyes that the Viceroy reflected: "Who can tell about these barbarians,—perhaps this is really so? . . ."—And he recalled how the Emperor had worded his real instructions to him:

"The audience must be arranged so that none of the Muscovites (a desperate folk, and capable of anything!) might fall upon the Czarevich and lay violent hands upon him,— although I do not expect that."

"Rest assured, Your Highness,—I stake my life and honor that they will work you no harm."

And, to Weingart, the Viceroy whispered to increase the number of guards.

Yet, at the same time, Peter Andreievich Tolstoi was already approaching the Czarevich, with inaudible, gliding steps, his back bowed with the most respectful air, and making the lowest of obeisances.

His companion (a captain of the Guards and an orderly of the Czar's, of gigantic stature, and with the handsome and ingenuous face of a Roman legionary,—or of a Russian simple Simon), whose name was Alexandre Ivannovich

Rumyantzev, stopped at a distance near the door, at a sign from the Viceroy.

"Most Gracious Lord Czarevich, Your Highness! Here is a letter from Batiushka," said Tolstoi, and bowing still lower, so that his left hand almost touched the floor, he tendered him the letter with his right.

Simply by looking at the three words: *To my Son*, inscribed on the envelope, the Czarevich recognized his father's handwriting; he broke the seal on the letter with trembling hands and read:

"My Son!

"By now all men must know what disobedience and contempt of my will thou hast been guilty of; and that neither through verbal admonitions nor through punishment couldst thou be made to follow my instructions. But, in the end, having beguiled me, and swearing before God when thou didst bid me farewell, what didst thou do afterward? Thou hast gone off and submitted thyself, like to a traitor, to the protection of another! Which is a thing unheard of not only among royal scions but even among our lowest subjects. Whereby what affront and vexation to thy father, and disgrace to thy Fatherland, thou didst commit! Therefore, I now send thee this my last communication, that thou mayst act in accordance with my will, as Tolstoi and Rumyantzev will explain and propose to thee. Shouldst thou be afeared of me, I hereby reassure thee, and promise before God and His Judgment, that there shall be no punishment meted out to thee, but that I shall evince greater love for thee if thou wilt obey my will and return. But shouldst thou not do so, then, as a father, through the power given me of God, I do curse thee for all eternity; and, since I am thy sovereign, I shall proclaim thee a traitor, nor leave any means untried to punish thee as a traitor, and as a flouter of thy father,—wherein God will help me, for mine is the right. In addition to that, recall that I have not sought to use coercion upon thee in any matter; but should I have wanted to do so, would I have put any trust in thy good will? Whatever I might have wanted to do, that I would have done.

"PETER."

After reading the letter through the Czarevich once more glanced up at Rumyantzev. The latter made a bow, and was about to approach, but the Czarevich blenched, began trembling, rose up in his armchair and said:

"Peter Andreievich . . . Peter Andreievich . . . order him not to approach! . . . Or else I shall go away . . . go away immediately. . . . There, even the Count says that he should not dare to approach. . . ."

At a sign from Tolstoi, Rumyantzev again halted, astonishment written large upon his handsome and far from intelligent face.

Weingart brought up a chair. Tolstoi moved it nearer the Czarevich, perched himself respectfully upon its very edge, bent over, glanced right into his eyes with a simple-hearted, trusting glance, and began speaking as if nothing out of the way had happened and they had merely come together for a pleasant chat.

Now he was still that same exquisite and most excellent gentleman, Peter Andreievich Tolstoi, privy-councilor and gallant,—black, velvety eyebrows; a soft, velvety glance; a kindly, velvety smile, and an ingratiating, velvety voice: all a velvety thing, yet he hath his sting.

And although the Czarevich remembered Batiushka's saying: "Tolstoi is a clever man, but when thou hast dealings with him, keep thy weather-eye peeled,"—he nevertheless did listen to him with pleasure. Tolstoi's clever, sensible speech, was calming him, was awakening him from dreadful visions, was bringing him back to reality. In this speech everything was softened down, was smoothed out. It seemed that one could both run with the hare and hunt with the hounds. He spoke like an experienced old surgeon, who strives to convince a patient that a most difficult operation is so easy that it is almost a pleasure.

"Thou shalt use both gentleness and threats,—bringing to bear, however, appropriate reasons and arguments," ran the Czar's instructions; and, were the Czar to hear Tolstoi now, he would have been satisfied with him.

Tolstoi confirmed verbally the contents of the letter: complete restoration to favor and full pardon in the event of the Czarevich's returning. Then he cited the exact words in the instructions given to him by the Czar for negotiations with the Kaiser,—at which a ring of firmness appeared in his voice, through his former persuasive kindness.

"Should the Kaiser say that, our son having placed himself under his protection, he is unable to give him up against his will, and should he put forth other excuses and far-fetched apprehensions, make him see clearly that it can not be otherwise than painful to us that he should desire to judge between my son and myself, inasmuch as, through natural laws, especially in our land, no one can judge between father and son, even in the case of private subjects,— the son must submit to the will of the father. All the more so since we, an autocratic sovereign, are not in any way subject to the Kaiser, and it is not for him to interfere; it behooves him, rather, to send our son back to us; for our part, both as father and sovereign, we, through our parental duty, shall receive him most graciously, and shall forgive him his misdeed, and shall instruct him, so that, abandoning his former dissolute ways, he might enter upon the path of virtue and pursue our intentions; in this manner he can turn our paternal heart toward him, of a surety; by assisting him in this His Royal Majesty will be both evincing graciousness toward him and meriting a reward from God for himself, as well as gratitude from us; furthermore, our son shall be eternally grateful to him for this, more than he will be for being now kept like some prisoner or malefactor, under strong guard, hiding behind the name of a certain rebellious Hungarian count, to the prejudice of our honor and name. But should the Kaiser, contrary to my hopes, positively refuse this request, thou shalt declare to him that we will consider this an open rupture, and shall lodge our complaints before all the world against the Kaiser, and shall seek to avenge ourselves for this unheard of and unbearable affront to us and to our honor."

"Nonsense!" the Czarevich cut him short. "Batiushka would never start a war with the Kaiser over me."

"I think there will be no war," concurred Tolstoi. "But then, the Kaiser will give thee up e'en without a war. There is no advantage for him, but hardship, rather, because of thy sojourning in his domains. Moreover, he has fulfilled his promise to thee,—he has protected thee until such time as thy father would be willing to forgive thee; and now, since thy father has been pleased to forgive thee, there is no obligation on the part of the Kaiser to keep thee against all rights and bring on a war with the Czar, when, as it is, he is beset by war on two sides,—from the Turks, and from the Spaniards: it must be known even to thee, I think, that the Spanish armada is now anchored between Naples and Sardinia, and has intentions of attacking Naples, inasmuch as the petty nobility hereabouts have formed a plot, and would rather be under Spanish rule than that of the Kaiser. If thou believest me not, ask the Viceroy,—he has received a letter from the Kaiser written by His Majesty himself, instructing him to resort to all measures to influence thee to go to Batiushka,—and as a last measure, to persuade thee to go anywhere at all, so long as thou dost leave his domains. And should they not give thee up of their own free will, our Sovereign intends to get thee through armed force: of course, that is the very thing he is keeping his troops in Poland for, so as to place them soon in winter quarters in Silesia,—and from there it is no great distance to the possessions of the Kaiser. . . ."

Tolstoi peered into his eyes still most kindly, and most gently touched his arm:

"My Lord Czarevich, batiushka, do heed a parent's persuasion,—return to thy father! 'For,' says the Czar,—these are his very words,—'we shall forgive him, and receive him into our favor once more; and we promise to keep him like a father, in all freedom and plenty, without any ill-will or constraint.'"

The Czarevich kept silence.

"'But,' says he, 'if he prove intractable,'" Tolstoi went on, with a deep sigh, "'make it known to him, in our name, that for such disobedience, after giving him up to a father's curse and the anathema of the church, we shall proclaim him a traitor throughout all our realm; let him judge, then what his life will be like. Let him not think that he will be out of danger,—unless he be in perpetual confinement, and under a strong guard. And thus he will earn not only torment for his soul in the hereafter, but for his body even in the present.

As for us, we shall not cease seeking all means of punishing his disobedience. We shall even, with an armed hand, force the Kaiser to give him up. Let him judge of the consequences thereof.' "

Tolstoi fell silent, awaiting a reply; but the Czarevich was likewise silent. Finally he lifted his eyes and looked at Tolstoi intently.

"How old are you, Peter Andreievich?"

"I would hate to say it in front of ladies,—but I have passed my seventieth year," answered the old man, with an amiable smile.

"Yet it would seem, according to the Scriptures, that three score and ten is the limit of human life. How is it then, Peter Andreievich, that, with one foot in the grave, thou hast undertaken such a mission? And yet I thought right along that thou didst bear me love. . . ."

"And I do bear thee love, my own,—God sees that I bear thee love! Yea, unto my last breath, I rejoice to serve thee. I have but one thing in my thoughts,—to reconcile thee with Batiushka. 'Tis a sacred deed: Blessed, 'tis said, are the peacemakers. . . ."

"Come, enough of lying, old man! Or dost thou think I know not why thou hast been sent here with Rumyantzev? One need not wonder at *him*, murdering brigand that he is. But thou,—thou, Andreievich! . . . Thou hast raised up thy hand against thy future Czar and Sovereign. Ye are murderers,—murderers both! Ye have been sent by Batiushka to slit my throat! . . ."

Tolstoi wrung his hands in horror:

"God will be thy judge, Czarevich! . . ." There was such sincerity in his face and voice that, well as the Czarevich knew him, he nevertheless reflected: had he erred, perhaps, —had he done the old man an injustice? But immediately he burst into laughter,—even his malice passed: there was something ingenuous, something innocent, almost captivating in this lie, as in the guile of women, or the playing of great actors.

"Well, thou art surely crafty, Peter Andreievich! Only, brother, there is no artifice that can entice a sheep into the maw of a wolf. . . ."

"Is it thy father thou meanest when thou sayest 'wolf'?"

"Wolf or no wolf; but should I fall into his claws, there would be not e'en as much as my bones left of me! But wherein is the sense of trying to fool one another? Methinks thou thyself knowest. . . ."

"Alexei Petrovich,—oh, Alexei Petrovich, batiushka! If thou dost not believe my words, see it for thyself, written in the letter in His Majesty's own hand: *I promise before God and His Judgment*. Dost thou hear,—he takes God to witness! Will the Czar, then, go back on his oath before all of Europe? . . ."

"What are oaths to him!" the Czarevich cut him short. "If he himself cannot dispense with it, then Fedosska will do it for him. The matter won't fail because of the Higher Clergy. They will grant him dispensation in conclave. That is what he is the Autocrat of Russia for! There be two men on earth who are like unto gods,—the Czar of Muscovy and the Pope of Rome: whatever they will, that they do. . . . Nay, Andreievich,—thou dost waste thy breath. I shall never yield myself alive!"

Tolstoi took out of his pocket a gold snuff-box, upon the lid of which was a shepherd lad unbinding the girdle of a sleeping shepherd girl; leisurely, with an accustomed movement of his fingers, rubbed a pinch of snuff, let his head drop on his breast, and spoke in deep thought, as if he were speaking to himself:

"Well, evidently it will have to be so. Do as thou wilt. Thou hast not heeded me, an old man,—perhaps thou wilt heed thy father. He will be here himself soon, methinks. . . ."

"How,—here? . . . What art thou lying for, old man?" uttered the Czarevich, blenching and looking around at the fearful door.

Tolstoi, as leisurely as before, thrust a pinch of snuff first in one nostril, then in the other, drew in a deep breath, brushed the tobacco dust off the lace on his bosom with a handkerchief, and uttered:

"I have no permission to say anything; however, I see I have let the cat out of the bag. I have recently received from His Majesty, the Czar, a letter in his own hand, that he is pleased to journey to Italy without any delay; and, when he does come himself, who can forbid thy father to see thee? Think not that this cannot be, since there is not the least difficulty,—it is all a matter of His Majesty's pleasure. And besides, thou knowest well thyself that it has long been our Sovereign's intention to journey to Italy,—and now, because of this occasion, he is all the more set upon doing so."

He let his head drop still lower, and his whole face suddenly puckered up, becoming aged,—most aged; it seemed as though he was just about to burst into tears,—he even brushed away something that looked suspiciously like a little tear-drop. And once more the Czarevich heard the words which he had heard so frequently:

"Where canst thou hide thyself from thy father?—Where, save under the earth,—for otherwise he will find thee. The Czar's arm is a long arm. I feel sorry for thee, Alexei Petrovich,—I feel sorry for thee, my own. . . ."

The Czarevich got up,—again, as during the first moments of the interview, he was trembling with all his body.

"Wait a while, Peter Andreievich. I must say a word or two to the Count."

He approached the Viceroy and took him by the arm. They went into an adjacent room. Having ascertained that the doors were closed, the Czarevich told him everything Tolstoi had said, and, in conclusion, clutching the old man's hand with both of his own, which had turned cold, asked:

"Should my father demand me with an armed band, can I rely upon the protection of the Kaiser?"

"Be at rest, Your Highness! The Emperor is sufficiently powerful to defend those he takes under his protection, no matter what contingency may arise. . . ."

"I know, Count, but I speak to you now, not as to the Emperor's Viceroy, but as to a noble chevalier, as to a kind-hearted man. You have ever been kind toward me. Do tell me all the truth, then,—conceal nothing from me, for God's sake, Count! Away with politics! Tell me the truth! . . . Oh, Lord! . . . You can see how heavy my heart is! . . ."

He broke into tears and the look he turned upon the Viceroy was the look of a cornered beast. The old man involuntarily let his eyes drop.

Tall, rather spare, with a pale, thin face, resembling some-what the face of Don Quixote, a man kindly but weak and wavering, with double-minded thoughts,—both a knight and a politician,—Count Daun was forever vacillating between the old knighthood, devoid of politics, and the new politics, devoid of knighthood. He felt pity for the Czarevich, but, at the same time, also a fear lest he implicate himself in an affair of responsibility: the fear of a swimmer who is clutched at by a drowning man.

The Czarevich sank on his knees before him.

"I implore the Emperor, in the name of God and all the saints, not to forsake me! 'Tis frightful even to think of what would happen to me were I to fall into my father's hands. No one knows what sort of a man he is. . . . But I know . . . 'Tis frightful,—dreadful! . . ."

The old man bent over him, with tears in his eyes.

"Get up,—do get up, Your Highness! I swear by God that I am telling you the whole truth, without any politics: the Kaiser, as I know him, will not give you up to your father under any circumstances; this would be degrading to His Majesty's honor and opposed to universal rights,—it would be a mark of barbarism!"

He embraced the Czarevich, and kissed him on the forehead with a fatherly tenderness.

When they returned to the reception room the Czarevich's face was pale, but calm and resolute. He approached Tolstoi and said, without sitting down himself or inviting him to sit down, evidently giving him to understand that the in-terview was over:

"To return to my father is dangerous, nor am I unafraid to face him in his wrath: as for my reasons in not daring to return,—they shall be submitted in writing to His Cæsaric Majesty, my protector. I may write to my father in reply to his letter, and, in that event, I shall give a definite an-swer. But at this time I cannot say anything, inasmuch as this matter requires considerable reflection."

"If," Tolstoi again began ingratiatingly, "Your Highness has any conditions to propose, they can be made known even to me. Methinks Batiushka will agree to everything. He may even allow thee to marry Aphrosiniya. Think it over, think

it over, my son. Sleep upon the matter. Aye, thou and I will
have time to talk it over further. 'Tis not the last time we are
seeing one another. . . ."

"There is nothing more for us to talk over, Peter
Andreievich, nor is there any necessity for seeing one another. But art thou going to stay here long?"

"I have my orders," retorted Tolstoi quietly, and looked
at the Czarevich in such a way that it seemed to him that
Batiushka's eyes had looked at him out of the eyes of the
old man, "I have my orders not to depart from here until
I have taken thee along, and, wert thou to be transferred to
some other place, I would follow thee even there."

Then he added, still more quietly:

"Thy father will not let thee be until he gets thee, alive
or dead."

Claws had emerged from under the little velvet paw,
but were immediately sheathed again. He bowed, as he had
done upon his entrance, with a most profound obeisance,
and was even about to kiss the Czarevich's hand, but the
latter snatched it away.

"Your Gracious Highness' most obedient servant!"

And, accompanied by Rumyantzev, he went out of the
same door through which he had entered. The Czarevich
followed him with his eyes, and for a long while contemplated
this door with an unmoving gaze, as though a vision of
horror had again flitted before him.

Finally he sank into an armchair, covered his face with
his hands, and slumped down, huddled up like a hedgehog,
as though under a fearful burthen.

Count Daun placed his hand on the Czarevich's shoulder
and was about to tell him something in consolation, but
sensed that there was nothing to say and in silence walked
away to join Weingart.

"The Emperor insists," he whispered to him, "that the
Czarevich put away from him the woman with whom he is
living. I had not the heart to tell him of this to-day. When
the occasion arises, you tell him."

V

"My affairs are in an exceedingly difficult situation," Tolstoi wrote to the Resident Veselovsky, in Vienna. "Unless our child despairs of the protection under which he lives he will never think of leaving. Therefore it behooves Your Grace to exert yourself in all directions to the end that it might be clearly shown to him that he will not be defended by arms; for he doth place all his hopes therein. We must be grateful for the zealous efforts in our favor of the Viceroy here; but then, he cannot break down such hardened obstinacy. At this time I cannot write more, inasmuch as I am going to our quarry, and the post is going out."

Tolstoi had more than once found himself facing most difficult situations,—and always got off scot-free. In his youth he had taken part in the mutiny of the Streltzi; all had perished,—but he had saved himself. When he was filling the post of military commander in Ustiuzh, at the age of fifty, with a wife and children, he volunteered to go to foreign lands together with other "Russian infants" to learn navigation,—and had learned it. As an ambassador in Constantinople, he had thrice found himself in the underground dungeons of the Seven-Towered Castle,—and thrice did he issue thence, after earning the special favor of the Czar. On one occasion his own secretary indited a complaint against him, accusing him of embezzling treasury funds,—but died suddenly before he had a chance to send the complaint off; as for Tolstoi, he gave the following explanation: "That pettifogger, Timoshka, got the idea into his head to turn Mussulman, having struck up an acquaintance with some Turks; through God's help I learned of this; I summoned him secretly and had a talk with him; then I locked him up in my bedchamber, until nightfall; but that night he drank a goblet of wine and died soon after,—thus did God keep him out of mischief."

It was not in vain that he was studying and translating into the Russian tongue *The Political Discourses of Nicòlo Macchiavelli, a Nobly-Born Citizen of Florence*. Tolstoi himself was famed as the Macchiavelli-of Russia. "Thy head, thy head,—were another as clever to be had, I would long since have ordered it lopped off!" the Czar was wont to say.

And now Tolstoi was apprehensive, lest this head turn out to be but a simpleton's, and the Macchiavelli of Russia be numbered among the fools, in this affair of the Czarevich. And yet he had done everything possible; he had enmeshed the Czarevich in a strong and fine net; he had imbued each individual with the personal belief that all the others were secretly desirous of giving Alexei up, but that each, being ashamed of breaking his own word, was entrusting this task to others: the Kaiser's consort,—to the Kaiser; the Kaiser,—to his Chancellor; the Chancellor,—to the Viceroy; the Viceroy,—to the Secretary. To the last Tolstoi had given a bribe of one hundred and sixty pieces of red gold, and had promised to add thereto if he would convince the Czarevich that the Kaiser would not extend any further protection to him. But all efforts crumbled before Alexei's "hardened obstinacy."

Worst of all was the fact that Tolstoi had begged himself to go on this mission. "A man must know what planet he is born under," he was wont to say,—and it seemed to him that his lucky star would rise when he succeeded in capturing the Czarevich, and that thereby he would crown his entire career of statesmanship, receiving the Ribbon of St. Andrew, and a countship, becoming the founder of a new house, the Count Tolstoi,—a thing he had dreamt of all his life.

What would the Czar say when he would return empty-handed?

But now it was not of the losses of the Czar's favor, the Ribbon of St. Andrew, and the title of Count, that he was thinking; like a true Nimrod, having forgotten everything else in the world, he was thinking of one thing alone: the *quarry* would escape.

A few days after his first interview with the Czarevich, Tolstoi was sipping his morning cup of chocolate on the balcony of his luxurious quarters in the hostelry of the *Three Kings,* situated on the liveliest street of Naples,—the Via Toledo. In his dressing-gown, without a wig, his skull all bald, save for vestiges of gray hair only on the very nape of his neck, he seemed very ill,—almost decrepit. His youth, his own metamorphosis, consisting of small jars, tiny brushes, and a magnificent undress wig, with youthful locks, as black as pitch, was lying on a little dressing table before a mirror, together with *The Metamorphoses, or Transformations, of Ovid*, in which he was translating into the Russian tongue.

The cats of care were scraping at his heart; but, as always during his moments of deep meditations on matters political, he had an insouciant, almost frivolous air; he was exchanging glances with a rather pretty little neighbor of his, who was also sitting on her balcony, across the street,— a swarthy-faced, black-eyed Spanish woman, from the number of those, who, to quote Æsopka, being averse to any handicraft, "would liefer live in idleness"; he smiled to her with gallant amiability, although his smile recalled that of a death's-head, and hummed a love madrigal of his own composition,—*To a Maid*, an imitation of Anacreon:

> Fly not thus my brow of snow,
> Lovely wanton! fly not so.
> Though the wane of age is mine,
> Though the brilliant flush is thine,
> Still I'm doomed to sigh for thee,
> Blest, if thou couldst sigh for me!

> See, in yonder flowery braid,
> Culled for thee, my blushing maid,
> How the rose, of orient glow,
> Mingles with the lily's snow;
> Mark how sweet their tints agree,
> Just, my girl, like thee and me!

Captain Rumyantzev was narrating to him his amatory adventures in Naples. According to Tolstoi's opinion, Rumyantzev was "a man with a cheerful make-up,— evincing amiability in his social relations, and exceedingly fond of company; but rather lucky than fit in affairs of importance; having naught but the bravery of a good soldier," meaning, to put it simply, that the good Captain was a fool. Yet he did not despise him on that account,—on the contrary, he listened to him, and occasionally heeded him: "The universe is propped up by fools," Peter Andreievich was wont to remark. "Cato, the Roman senator, used to say that wise men have greater need of fools than fools have of wise men."

Rumyantzev was castigating some wench or other, by the name of Kamillka, who had in a single week bled him for more than a hundred gold pieces.

"The wenches hereabouts are an awful lot of robbers, as far as our kind are concerned!"

Peter Andreievich recalled how he himself had been in love, many years ago, right here in Naples. Concerning this love, he always spoke in never-varying words:

"I was *inamorato* with a certain Signora Francesca, and had her for my *maîtresse* during my whole sojourn, and I was *inamorato* to such an extent that I could not live for an hour without her, who did cost me, during two months, one thousand pieces of red gold. And I did part from her with such great sorrow that, even to this day, that *amor* doth not leave my heart. . . ."

He sighed languishingly, and smiled to his rather pretty little neighbor.

"But what about our *quarry?*" he suddenly asked with his casual air, as though this were a matter of the least import to him.

Rumyantzev told him of his conversation yesterday, with the navigator, Aleshka Urov,—the same who was called Æsopka. Frightened by Tolstoi's threat to seize him and send him off to Peterburgh as a runaway, Urov, despite his loyalty to the Czarevich, had agreed to act as a spy, keeping Tolstoi informed of everything he saw and heard in the Czarevich's place. Rumyantzev had learned from Æsopka a great deal that was curious and important for Tolstoi's consideration, concerning the Czarevich's excessive love for Aphrosiniya.

"The said wench finds her love quite profitable, and, through the great confidence engendered by the pleasures of the night, has attained such power over him that he durst not even peep before her. She has him under her thumb. Whatever she says, that he does. He would fain marry her, save that he cannot find a priest,—otherwise they would have been espoused a long time ago."

He also told of his interview with Aphrosiniya, arranged

without the Czarevich's knowledge during his absence, through the good offices of Æsopka and Weingart.

"A person comely in all ways, save that she is red-haired. To look at her, she is a quiet body, butter would not melt in her mouth,—yet she must be the devil and all: still waters run deep."

"But how did things look to you?" asked Tolstoi, a sudden idea flashing through his mind, "has she any inclination for a love affair?"

"That is,—to plant horns in our quarry?" smiled Rumyantzev. "Like all women, I suppose she would be glad to. But then there isn't anybody. . . ."

"And why not with thee, Alexander Ivannovich? Never fear, any woman would be flattered to have a likely lad like thee for a partner!" Tolstoi winked craftily.

The Captain guffawed, and with a self-satisfied air stroked his slender, turned-up mustache, like a tom-cat's,—precisely the same sort of mustaches as the Czar had.

"Kamillka is enough for me! What would I be doing with two?"

"But dost thou know, Sir Captain, the little song that goes:

> " 'Gainst love's ardent flame cease thy war to maintain,
>   Two maids without quarreling thy heart can contain;
>   Fear not that thy love surfeit may smother,
>   For with ease thou mayst serve now the one, now the other.
>   Then get rid of the first, and get rid of the second,—
>   For in love even tens can be easily reckoned. . . .' "

"Look ye, what a gay dog Your Excellency is!" Rumyantzev burst out laughing, like a downright orderly, showing all his white, even teeth. " 'The beard may be gray, yet the heart is gay!' "

Tolstoi countered with another madrigal:

> "The women tell me every day,
> That all my bloom has passed away,
> 'Behold,' the pretty wantons cry,
> Behold this mirror with a sigh;
> The locks upon thy brow are few,
> And like the rest, they're withering too!
> Whether decline has thinned my hair,
> I'm sure I neither know nor care;

But this I know and this I feel,
As onward toward the tomb I steal,
That still as death approaches nearer,
The joys of life are sweeter, dearer;
And had I but an hour to live,
That little hour to bliss I'd give!

"Listen to me, Alexandre Ivannovich," he went on, but
now no longer in jest, "instead of thy senseless carryings-on
with Kamillka 'twould be better if thou wert to strike up a
love affair with this distinguished person. Our affair would
benefit greatly thereby. We would so enmesh our child with
jealousy that he would not seek any other refuge, but give
himself up into our hands, of his own will. For there is no
better bait than one of the frail sex for gallants like us!"

"Whatever art thou saying,—whatever art thou saying,
Peter Andreievich? Come, now! I thought thou wert pleased
to jest, but thou seemest to be in earnest about it. This is a
ticklish matter. Suppose he comes to learn of this *amor*
when he is Czar,—why, there won't be room enough on my
neck for all the axes. . . ."

"Eh, nonsense! Whether Alexei Petrovich will ever be
Czar,—that, brother, is writ upon water, with a pitchfork;
but that Peter Alexeievich will reward thee,—that is certain. And then, how he will reward thee! Alexandre Ivannovich, batiushka, please render me this service as a matter
of friendship; I shall never forget it as long as I live, my
dearest fellow! . . ."

"But really, Your Excellency, I do not know even how to
go about this affair. . . ."

"We will go about it together. 'Tis not a complicated
matter. I will instruct thee,—do thou but heed me. . . ."

Rumyantzev still hemmed and hawed for a long time,
but finally concurred, and Tolstoi imparted to him his plan
of action. When he had gone, Peter Andreievich plunged
into deep thought, worthy of the Macchiavelli of Russia.

He had already dimly felt, for a long time, that
Euphrosinia alone could, were she so minded, convince the
Czarevich to return: a night cuckoo, now, can always drown
out with its call that of a day cuckoo; and he also felt that,
in any event, she was his last hope. He even wrote to the

Czar: " 'Tis impossible to describe how the Czarevich loves the said wench, and what solicitude he shows for her." He also recalled the words of Weingart: "His greatest apprehension in refusing to go to his father is lest the latter part him from this wench. I intend to threaten him soon, hinting that she will be taken from him without any delay, unless he goes to his father; even though I cannot carry out this threat without instructions, we shall nevertheless see what the upshot will be."

Tolstoi decided to go at once to the Viceroy and demand that he order the Czarevich to put away Aphrosiniya from him, in compliance with the wish of the Kaiser. "And then, besides, there's Rumyantzev and his love affair," he reflected, with such hope that his heart began to pound. "Help me, little mother Venus! Come, now,—that which wise men have failed to accomplish with politics, a fool may accomplish through an *amor*."

He grew downright merry, and, occasionally glancing at his fair neighbor, hummed with a liveliness which was no longer assumed:

> How the rose, of orient glow;
> Mingles with the lily's snow;
> Mark how sweet their tints agree,
> Just, my girl, like thee and me!

But the fair knave, screening herself with a fan, putting forth from under the black lace of her skirt a dainty little foot, in a tiny silver slipper and a rose-colored stocking embroidered with little golden arrows, was making eyes at him and smiling artfully: as though, in the guise of this girl, Goddess Fortune herself was once more smiling to him, as she had done so many times in his life,—promising him success, the Ribbon of St. Andrew, and the title of Count.

Getting up from his seat, in order to dress, he blew a kiss across the street to her, with his most gallant smile: a death's-head seemed to be smiling a shameless smile at Fortune, the strumpet.

The Czarevich suspected Æsopka of spying, of being in secret communication with Tolstoi and Rumyantzev. He had driven him out and forbidden him to come back, but on one occasion, returning home unexpectedly, he ran across him on a staircase. Æsopka, catching sight of him, paled and began to quake like a caught thief. The Czarevich surmised that he had been making his way to Aphrosiniya on some sort of secret errand, seized him by his coat-collar and threw him down the stairs.

As Alexei was shaking him, a small, round box of tin, which he had been painstakingly hiding, tumbled out of Æsopka's pocket. The Czarevich picked it up. It was a box of "French chocolate wafers," and inserted in its lid was a note, which began:

"My Gracious Mistress, Aphrosiniya Petrovna!

"Inasmuch as my heart is not fashioned with an ax out of wood, but has been imbued with the tenderest emotions,— since my very birth . . ." and ended with versicles:

> "My strength naught avails love's flame to subdue;
> 'Tis my heart that is ailing,—what can I do?
> Ever apart, sad is my heart,—
> Better never love know than suffer so.
> If thou my love spurn, in Vesuvius I'll burn!"

Instead of a signature, there were two initials,—A.R. "Alexandre Rumyantzev," surmised the Czarevich.

He had spirit enough to say nothing to Aphrosiniya about this find.

That same day Weingart informed him of an order, purporting to have come from the Kaiser: In the event of the Czarevich's wishing further protection he must immediately put away Aphrosiniya from him.

In reality there was no such order; Weingart had merely fulfilled his promise to Tolstoi: "I intend to threaten him soon; even though I cannot carry out this threat without instructions, we shall nevertheless see what the upshot will be."

VI

That night, between the first and second of October, the sirocco finally broke.

With particular vehemency did the storm howl upon the

heights of St. Elmo. Within the castle, even in the closely-shut chambers, the noise of the wind was as strong as in the cabin of a ship during a most terrific storm. Through the voice of the hurricane (now it was the howling of wolves, now the weeping of children, now the frenzied trampling of a stampeded herd, now the screeching and whistling of gigantean iron-winged birds), the surge of the surf resembled distant peals of cannon-fire. It seemed as if there, beyond the walls, everything was tumbling down, as if the end of the world had come and limitless chaos was raging.

It was dank and cold in the quarters of the Czarevich, but it was impossible to make a fire in the hearth, inasmuch as the wind beat back the smoke in the chimney. The wind penetrated the walls, so that draughts traversed the room; the candle-flames of the candles wavered, and the wax-drippings cooled into long, pendent needles.

The Czarevich was quickly pacing the room back and forth. His angular, black shadow flitted over the white walls, now contracting, now elongating and, as it leaned against the ceiling, breaking in two.

Aphrosiniya was seated in an armchair, with her feet tucked up under her, and, muffling herself in a fur jacket, followed him with her eyes, in silence. Her face seemed apathetic,—save that in the corners of her mouth something was quivering, with a scarcely perceptible quiver, and her fingers with a mechanical movement, now unwound, now wound a bit of gold cord, unraveled from a loophole of her coat.

Everything was the same as it had been a month and a half ago, the day he had received the joyous news. The Czarevich finally halted before her and uttered dully:

"There is no help for it, little mother! Get thee ready for traveling. To-morrow we are off to Rome, to the Pope. A certain Cardinal here was telling me that the Pope would receive me under his protection. . . ."

Aphrosiniya shrugged her shoulders.

"Nonsense, Czarevich! Since even the Kaiser won't keep a wanton wench,—how would the Pope do it? Certainly he could not do so, if only because of his spiritual rank. And he has no army to defend thee with, should Batiushka demand thee with armed force."

"What's to be done,—what's to be done, then, Aphrosiushka? . . ." He wrung his hands in despair. "An order has come from the Kaiser, that I put thee away from me without any delay. They barely agreed to wait till to-morrow morning. The first thing one knows they will take thee away by force. We must fly,—fly as fast as we can! . . ."

"But whither are we to fly? They will catch us anywhere. 'Twill all be the same in the end. Go thou to thy father."

"Thou too,—thou too, Aphrosya! Evidently Tolstoi and Rumyantzev have been at thee with their siren songs, while thou didst lend them a most willing ear."

"Peter Andreievich desires only thy good. . . ."

"My good! . . . What canst thou understand? Keep still, woman,—thy hair is long but thy wit is short! Or dost thou think they will not torture thee to death, as well as myself? Think it not! They will not take e'en thy big belly into consideration,—'tis no rare sight in our land to have wenches give birth on the strappado. . . ."

"But then, Batiushka promised forgiveness. . . ."

"I know,—I know my Batiushka's forgivenesses. Here's where they give me a pain!" He indicated the nape of his neck. "Should the Pope not receive me, then I am off to France, or England,—or to the Swede, or the Turk, or the devil's own horns,—only not to Batiushka! Durst not even speak to me of this, ever, Aphrosiniya,—dost thou hear?—durst not! . . ."

"As thou wilt, Czarevich; only, I shall not go with thee to the Pope," she uttered quietly.

"How dost thou mean, thou wilt not go? What hast thou gotten into thy head now?"

"I shan't go," she uttered, just as calmly as before, looking fixedly into his eyes. "I have even told that to Peter Andreievich already: I shan't go with the Czarevich anywhere, save to Batiushka; let him go alone wherever else he lists, but I shan't."

"What art thou up to,—what art thou up to, Aphrosiushka?" he began in a suddenly changed voice, and blenching. "Christ be with thee, little mother! For how can I . . . Oh Lord! . . . How can I be without thee? . . ."

"Do as thou knowest best, Czarevich; only I shan't go, and do not ask me any more." She finally tore off the bit of gold cord dangling from the loop and tossed it to the floor.

"Hast thou lost thy sense, wench, or what is it?" he cried out, clenching his fists, with sudden malice. "If I take thee, thou wilt go! Thou takest great liberties! Or hast thou forgotten what thou wert?"

"That which I have been, that I have remained: the faithful slave of His Imperial Majesty, Peter Alexeievich, my Liege Lord. Whither the Czar orders me to go, there shall I go. I shan't go against his will. I shan't go with thee against thy father."

"Oh, so that's thy talk now, is it! . . . Thou hast been sniffing about Tolstoi and Rumyantzev,—those who would work me ill, those who would assassinate me! . . . This in return for everything,—for the good I have done thee, for my love! . . . Thou sneaky viper! Thou lout, begotten of louts! . . ."

"Dost thou feel like quarreling, Czarevich? But wherein is the use? As I have said, so shall I do."

Fear fell upon him. Even his anger passed; he grew all weak, exhausted, sank into the armchair beside her, took her hand, and tried to peer into her eyes:

"Aphrosiushka, little mother, dearest friend of my heart,— what is this, what is this, now? Lord! Is this a time to quarrel? Why dost thou speak so? I know that thou wilt not do it,—wilt not leave me alone in such a strait; if thou wilt not take pity on me, thou wilt on the Silvel One methinks? . . ."

She made no answer, nor looked at him, nor stirred,— as though she were dead.

"Well, dost thou not love me?" he went on, with an infinitely supplicating tenderness, with the pitiful craftiness of those in love. "Well, then,—go, if thou wilt have it so. God be with thee. I shan't keep thee by force. Only tell me,—thou dost not love me? . . ."

She suddenly arose and looked at him so that the heart within him stood still from horror.

"And thou didst think that I loved thee? When thou didst revile a silly wench, raping her, threatening her with a knife,—that was the time thou shouldst have asked whether I loved thee or not! . . ."

"Aphrosiya, Aphrosiya, what art thou about? Or dost thou place no trust in my word? For I shall marry thee, shall atone for that sin before the altar. And, even right now, thou art to me e'en as a wife! . . ."

"I strike my forehead on the ground before thee, My Lord, for thy favors! For who shall say that 'tis not a favor! The Czarevich is pleased to marry a serf wench! And yet, look ye, what a fool she is,—she is not overjoyed at such an honor! I have endured, and endured, until there is no more strength in me! Whether I shall put my head in a noose, or whether I shall drown myself in a hole in the ice,—'twill be because of thee, whom I have grown sick of! 'Twould have been better if thou hadst killed me right off then,—if thou hadst slit my throat! 'Thou shalt be a Czaritza,'—look ye, what bait he has thought of. . . . But, mayhap, my virgin chastity and freedom were dearer to me than thy Czardom? I have seen enough of your kingly lines,—ye are all shameless and vile wretches! Your court's glare is the same as a wolf's lair,—each one watches his fellow, biding a chance to leap at his throat. Batiushka is a beast full-grown, while thou art a small one; and the beast shall surely eat up the beastie. What chance hast thou in contending with him? The Sovereign did well to deprive thee of the succession. How is a fellow like you to rule? Go join the petty clergy and pray forgiveness for thy sins, thou would-be saint! Thou hast done thy wife to death,—hast forsaken thy children,—hast taken up with a wanton wench and art unable to drop her! Thou hast grown weak,—altogether weak; thou hast squandered and bemired thyself! Aye, even now, 'tis but a woman upbraiding thee to thy eyes, and yet thou art silent, thou durst not e'en peep. Ugh! Thou shameless fellow! Were I to beat thee like a dog and then merely to beckon to thee, to whistle, thou wouldst run after me again, with thy tongue lolling out, like a hound after a bitch! But dost thou hanker after love to boot? Aye, do women love such fellows as thee? . . ."

He was looking at her, and could not recognize her. Amid the glow of her rufous hair her face, pale, as though it were illuminated by an unbearable radiance, was frightful, yet as splendidly beautiful as it had never been before. "A witch!" the thought came to him, and it suddenly seemed to him that all this storm was raging beyond the walls through her spells, and that the wild wails of the hurricane were repeating her frenzied words:

"Bide a while,—thou shalt see how I love thee! I shall repay thee for all,—for all! I shall mount the scaffold myself, yet I shan't screen thee! I shall tell Batiushka all: how thou didst beg the Kaiser for arms, so as to go warring against thy father; how thou didst rejoice over the mutiny in his troops, wanting to join the mutineers; how thou didst desire thy father's death,—thou villain! I shall inform him of everything,—everything! Thou wilt not get out of it! the Czar will torture thee to death,—will flog thee to death with a cat-o'-nine-tails, the while I'll stand there looking at thee and questioning thee: Well, now, Alëshenka darling, dearest friend of my heart, wilt thou remember how Aphrosiya did love thee? . . . As for thy puppy, this Silvel One, I shall, as soon as he's born, take him with my own two hands and . . ."

He closed his eyes and stopped up his ears, in order not to see and not to hear. It seemed to him that everything was tumbling down about him, and that he himself was falling through. As clearly as never before he suddenly comprehended that there was no salvation, and that, no matter how he struggled, no matter what he did, he was lost in any case.

When the Czarevich opened his eyes Aphrosiniya was no longer in the room. But he could see the light through the crack of the incompletely closed door leading to the bed-chamber. He surmised that she was there, approached the door, and peeped in.

She was hurriedly packing, tying her things in a bundle, as though she were preparing to leave him immediately. Her bundle was rather small,—a little linen, two or three simple dresses which she herself had made, and her girlhood casket, rather old and small, its lock broken, and with a moulting bird painted on its lid, picking at a cluster of grapes,—a casket he remembered only too well: the same in which, when she had still been a serving-wench in the house of the Viyazemskys, she had been hoarding her dowry. The expensive dresses, and other things which he had presented to her, she painstakingly put aside,—probably she did not want to take his gifts. This was a greater affront to him than all her evil words.

Having finished her packing, she sat down near the night-table, sharpened a quill and began writing slowly, with difficulty, outlining character after character as if she were drawing it. He approached her on tiptoe, from behind, looked over her shoulder, and read the opening lines:

"Alexandre Ivannovich.

"Seeing as how the Czarevich is wanting for to go to the Pope, and although I did try to talk him out of going he will not listen to mee,—but gets all wrought up, will your graice pleese send after mee as soon as may bee, and it would bee still better were you to come yourself, lest he take mee away with him by main force; for, like as not, he will go nowhere without mee."

A floor-board creaked, Aphrosiniya, quickly turning around, cried out and jumped up. They stood in silence, without moving, face to face, and looked into each other's eyes with a protracted gaze, precisely as at that time when he had thrown himself upon her, threatening her with a knife.

"So, thou art really going to him?" he managed to say, in a hoarse whisper. Her lips, which had paled the least trifle, were distorted by a quiet smile.

"If I want to, I'll go to him; if I want to, I'll go to another. I shan't ask thee." His face was distorted by a convulsion. Seizing her throat with one hand and her hair with the other, he knocked her down and began to beat her, dragging her about and kicking her.

"Creature! Creature! Creature!"

The slender blade of a dirk she had worn as part of her disguise as a page, and which she had just now used as a knife to cut off a quarter of a larger sheet of paper, lay gleaming on the table. The Czarevich seized it and swung it over her. He was experiencing an insane rapture, as at the time when he had been possessing her by force; he suddenly understood that she had always been deceiving him, that she had never belonged to him, even during the most passionate caresses, and that only now, having killed her, would he possess her to the end, would slake his unbelievable desire.

She did not cry out, nor did she call for help, but merely struggled in silence,—as nimble, as sinuous as a cat. During the struggle he pushed a table with a candle upon it,—the table overturned, the candle fell and was extinguished. All was dark. Fiery circles, like quickly-revolving wheels, began whirling before his eyes. The voices of the hurricane set up a howl, somewhere altogether near him, and burst into frenzied laughter.

He shuddered, as though he had come to out of a profound slumber, and, in the same instant, felt that she hung limp on his arm, without moving, like one dead. He unclenched the hand which still clutched her hair. The body slumped to the floor with a dull thud.

The horror that gripped him now was such that his hair stood up on end. He flung the dirk far from him, ran into the adjoining room, seized a candelabrum, the candles of which were in winding sheets, ran to the bed-chamber, and saw that she was lying on the floor, her arms flung out, with blood on her forehead, and with her eyes shut. He wanted to run off anew, to shout, to summon help, but it seemed to him that she was still breathing. He went down on his knees, bent over her, embraced her, carefully picked her up and placed her on the bed.

Then he began dashing about the room, without knowing what he was doing: now he gave her some spirits to smell, now he sought a quill, having recalled that burnt feathers are used to revive swooning people, now he dabbed her head with water. Then he would bend over her once more and, sobbing, kiss her hands, her feet, her dress, and call to her, and dash his head against a corner of the bed and tear his hair.

"I have killed her,—I have killed her,—I have killed her,—accursed that I am! . . ."

Or else he would pray:

"Lord Jesus! Most Pure Mother! Take my soul for hers! . . ." And his heart would contract with such pain that it seemed to him he would die that moment.

Suddenly he noticed that she had opened her eyes and was gazing upon him with a strange smile.

"Aphrosiya, Aphrosiya . . . What is the matter with thee, little mother? . . . The doctor ought to be sent for. . . ."

She still gazed at him in silence, with the same incomprehensible smile. She made an effort to sit up. He helped her, and suddenly felt that she had entwined his neck with her arms, and nuzzled her cheek against his, with a caress as gentle, as childishly-trusting as never before.

"Come,—thou wert scared, never fear? Didst think thou hadst done me to death? Nonsense! 'Tis not so easy to kill a woman. We are as hard to kill as cats. A lover's blow maketh one grow!"

"Forgive me, forgive me, little mother, my own little one! . . ."

She was gazing into his eyes and, smiling, was stroking his hair with a maternal tenderness.

"Ah, my little lad, my silly little lad! I look at thee,— and thou seemest altogether a little child. Thou canst not understand, thou knowest naught, of our women's ways. Ah, my little silly one,—didst thou really believe that I love thee not? Come hither, I would fain say one little word in thy ear."

She put her lips to his very ear and whispered in a passionate whisper:

"I love thee like my very soul,—thou, my soul, my joy! How could I live in this world without thee,—how could I be among the living? It would be better for my soul and body to part. Or dost thou not believe me?"

"I do believe,—I do believe! . . ." he wept and laughed for happiness.

She was snuggling to him, ever more closely.

"Oh, my lamb, my batiushka, Alëshenka,—and why art thou so dear to me? . . . Where thy mind is, there mine is also; whatever thy speech is,—that is mine also; and, at thy word, I would lay down my heart! In all things, at all times,

I am at thy will! . . . But then, here is my misfortune: all of us women are foolish, evil,—and I am the worst of all. Yet what am I to do if through the will of God, I have been born so unhappy? He hath given me a heart insatiable, greedy. For I can see thou lovest me, and yet 'tis all too little for me,—all too little; I myself know not what I want. Here I am thinking to myself: 'Can this lad of mine be so soft, so peaceful, that he will never say a contrary word to me, will never become angry, will never teach a lesson to silly me? . . . I do not feel his hand over me, I do not feel any fear of him. 'Tis not for naught they say: Whom I love, I chastise. Or doth he not love me? Well now, I shall anger him, shall try him to see what he will do. . . .' So that's the kind of man thou art! Thou hast nearly killed me. Thou dost take altogether after Batiushka. Why, my very breath left me just now, from fear. Well, now, 'twill be a lesson for the future; I shall remember and I shall love thee,—thusly! . . ."

It seemed as if he were for the first time beholding these eyes, smoldering with a sinister, dim fire,—kissing these half-open searing lips,—feeling this quivering body, as slippery as that of a serpent. "So that's how she really is!" he was thinking in beatific wonder.

"But didst think I knew naught of caresses?" she broke into soft laughter that set all his blood on fire, as though she had surmised his thought. "Bide awhile,—this is nothing to the way I shall caress thee! . . . Do but satisfy my foolish heart,—satisfy it, do what I shall ask of thee, so that I may know thou lovest me, even as I love thee,—unto death! Oh, my life, my love, my dearling! . . . Wilt thou not do so? . . ."

"I shall do everything! God sees there is nothing in the world which I would not do. I would go to my death,—say but the word. . . ."

She seemed to sigh,—a barely audible sigh,—rather than to whisper:

"Return to thy father! . . ."

And again, as shortly before, his heart stopped still from terror. It seemed as if under her tender hand the iron hand of Batiushka was stretching forth and seizing him. "She is

lying!" flashed through his head like lightning. "Let her lie,
—if she will but love me!" he added recklessly.

"I am sick,—most sick," she went on, "yea, even unto my
death, of having to live with thee in sin and outside the law!
I do not want to be a dissolute wench,—I want to be thy
honest wife before all men and before God! Thou sayest
that even now I am the same as a wife to thee. Come, now,—
what sort of wife am I? We were married near a pine tree
haunted, while the devils chaunted. And our boy, now, the
Silvel One, will be born in sin. But, as soon as thou returnest
to thy father, thou canst marry. Even Tolstoi says: Let the
Czarevich offer to return to Batiushka, if but the latter allow
him to marry; as for Batiushka, he says, he'll be only too
glad, if only the Czarevich will renounce the succession and
live in retirement in his villages. Whether he marries a
bondswoman or puts on a cowl, 'tis all,—he will nevermore
be a Czar. . . . But as for me, my little lamb, Alëshenka,—
that is all I need. For I fear this being a Czar most of all,
my own little one,—oh, how I fear it! Shouldst thou become a
Czar, thou wilt have no time for me. There will be other
things a-plenty on thy mind. Czars have no time for love. I
would not be a hateful Czaritza to thee,—I want to be thy
little leman forever! My love is my Czardom! Let us go to
the country,—either to the village of Poretzkoë, or to that
of Rozhdestvenno. We shall live in quiet and in peace,—I,
and thou, and the Silvel One,—and no cares shall touch us.
. . . Oh, thou, my heart, my life, my joy! . . . Or dost thou
not want it? Thou wilt not do so? . . . Or art thou sorry to
forego ruling? . . .

"Why dost thou ask, little mother? Thou knowest thyself
I will do it. . . ."

"Thou wilt return to thy father?"

"I will."

It seemed to him that now was being consummated the
opposite of that which had taken place between them at one
time. It was no longer he who was overcoming her by force,
but she who was overcoming him; her kisses were like to
wounds,—her caresses like to murder.

Suddenly she froze, put him from her softly by pushing
him, and again sighed a barely audible sigh:

"Swear it!"

He wavered, like a suicide at the ultimate moment, with a knife already raised over his head. Nevertheless he said: "I swear it before God!"

She extinguished the candle, and enveloped all of him in infinite tenderness, as deep and fearful as death.

It seemed to him that he was flying with her,—with this witch, this White She-Demon,—into a bottomless darkness, upon the wings of the hurricane.

He knew that this was annihilation, the end of everything, —and he rejoiced over this end.

BOOK SEVEN

THE RETURN OF THE CZAREVICH

On the following day, the third of October, Tolstoi wrote to the Czar, in Peterburgh:

"Most Gracious Liege Lord!

"We most humbly beg to report that your Majesty's son, His Highness the Lord Czarevich, Alexei Petrovich, has been pleased to declare his intention to us this day: Abandoning all his former resistance, he is submitting to Your Majesty's *ukase*, and is, without any further objections, going to St. Peterburgh with us, concerning which he has been pleased to write to His Majesty, in his own hand and has been pleased to give the said letter to us, unsealed, that we may send it to Your Majesty under our cover; a copy of which letter is subjoined herewith, while the original we have kept by us, being afraid to let it out of our possession under the circumstances. He is pleased to put forth but two conditions; the first, that he be permitted to live on his country estates, which are located near St. Peterburgh; while the other condition is that he be allowed to marry the wench who is now with him. And when we were first trying to pursuade him to go to Your Majesty, he would not even think of it if the abovementioned conditions were not granted him. He would very much like, Liege Lord, that we petition Your Majesty in his behalf for permission to marry this wench, before he reaches St. Peterburgh, and although these conditions of His Highness are immoderate, I have nevertheless taken the liberty, even without instructions, of granting them, verbally. Concerning this, I submit. my humble opinion to Your Majesty: If there be no objection thereto, he should be allowed to do so, to the end that he may thereby show clearly before all the world his true status,—since he did not fly because of any wrong done him, but only for

352

the sake of this wench; another reason is that this will vex the Kaiser considerably, and he will never again believe him in anything; and, in the third place, the damage of his contracting a suitable marriage among the quality will be done away with,—a danger which we are not free from even here. And should you grant your permission thereto, my Liege Lord, may it please you to write me concerning that in your letter, among other matters, so that I might but show it to him, without giving him the letter. But should Your Majesty deem it unseemly for such things to be, will you be kind enough merely to assure him graciously that this cannot be consummated abroad, but only in our own land,—to the end that, being reassured thereby, he may, without any further consideration, go to you in all confidence. And may it please you, Liege Lord, to keep secret for some time your son's return to you; should this become bruited about, we are not without danger of some one opposed thereto writing him of some tempting plan,—which (God forbid!) may frighten him and make him change his intention. Also, my Liege Lord, please send me an *ukase* to the commanders of your troops, if any be located along the line of our travel, that they are to give us convoy, should it be needed.

"We hope to leave Naples on the sixth of October, or, definitely, on the seventh. However, the Czarevich is pleased to go to Bari first, to see the remains of St. Nikola,[62] where we too, shall go with him. In addition thereto, the roads in these mountains be most vile, and even though one were to set out without any delay, haste would be impossible. As for the wench in question, she has been big-bellied for the fourth or fifth month, and by reason of this our travel may be protracted, inasmuch as he will not travel fast, for her sake,—for it is impossible to describe how much he loves her, or what solicitude he hath for her.

"And so, with the utmost submission and highest respect, we remain,

"Most humbly yours,
"PETER TOLSTOI.

"P. S. But when, my Liege Lord, I shall be in St. Petersburgh, through the grace of God, I may praise Italy without any danger, or having to pay the fine of drinking pepper-brandy, inasmuch as not only the actual expedition, but also our Majesty's mere intention to visit Italy, have had a good effect for Your Majesty and the whole land of Russia."

He also wrote to Veselovsky, the Resident in Vienna.

"Keep everything in the utmost secrecy, for fear some devil write to the Czarevich and frighten him from going. What difficulties this affair entailed, God alone knows! Truly, I cannot describe all the miracles we have wrought."

Peter Andreievich was sitting up at night, alone in his chambers in the hostelry of the Three Kings, at a writing-table, before a candle.

Having finished his letter to the Czar, and made a copy of the Czarevich's letter, he took some wax to seal both of them in the same envelope. But he put the wax aside, once more re-read the original letter of the Czarevich, sighing deeply and contentedly, opened his gold snuff-box, took out a pinch and, rubbing the snuff between his fingers, with a gentle smile fell into deep thought.

He could hardly believe his good fortune. Why, even this very morning he had been in such despair that, having received a note from the Czarevich: "I have the utmost need of speaking with thee, which will not be without benefit"—he did not want to go there: "He will merely waste my time with idle talk."

And lo, suddenly, this "accursed obstinacy" seemed never to have existed,—the Czarevich agreed to everything. "Miracles,—verily, miracles! It must be due to none save God and St. Nikola! . . ." It was not in vain that Peter Andreievich always paid particular honor to Nikola, and placed his hopes on "the holy protection" of the Miracle-Worker. And so he was glad to go with the Czarevich to Bari on this occasion. "Surely, the Saint deserves a candle now!" But, of course, besides St. Nikola, the goddess Venus had helped too,—Venus, whom he also zealously revered: after all, the little mother had not disgraced him, had pulled him out of a scrape! To-day, in making his adieux, he had kissed the little hand of the wench, Aphroska. But kissing her little hand was nothing,—he would have been willing to bow down to her very feet, as if to the goddess Venus herself. There was a likely lass! How she had got around the Czarevich! For, after all, he was not such a fool as not to see what awaited him at the end of his journey. That was just the trouble,—he was too clever. "As a general rule," Tolstoi recalled one of his utterances, " 'tis easy to deceive the wise, inasmuch as, even though they do know an exceedingly great deal, they do not, however, know anything of the ordinary things in life, which is a far greater need; to know the mind and character of mankind is a great philosophy, and it is a harder thing to know men than to remember many books by heart."

With what insouciant buoyancy, with what a gay face had the Czarevich announced to-day that he was going to his father! Just as though he were sleepy, or intoxicated; he had been laughing all the time, with an eldritch, pitiful laughter.

"Ah, the poor little fellow, the poor little fellow!" Peter Andreievich regretfully shook his head, and, having drawn a pinch of snuff up his nose, brushed away the little tear which welled up in his eyes,—either from snuff or from pity. "Like a voiceless lamb is he led to the slaughter. Help him, O Lord!"

Peter Andreievich had a heart that was kind,—and even sentimental.

"Aye, 'tis a pity,—yet there's naught to be done," he immediately consoled himself. "That's what the pike is placed in the sea for,—so that the perch may keep their eyes open! Friendship is friendship,—and statesmanship is statesmanship." For, after all, he, Tolstoi, had served his Czar and his Fatherland, had not fallen down, had proved a worthy disciple of Nikola Macchiavelli, had crowned his career,—now his lucky star would of itself come down to his breast in the guise of the Star of St. Andrew. Aye, the Tolstois would be Counts, and if, in ages to come, they should become celebrated, and attain the highest offices, they are bound to recall Peter Andreievich as well! Now Thou dost liberate thy slave, O Lord!"

These thoughts filled his heart with an almost puckish liveliness. He suddenly felt himself younger, as though some two-score years had dropped off his shoulders. He felt like launching into a dance at any second, as though his arms and legs had sprouted little wings, like those of the god Mercury.

He held the sealing wax over the flame of the candle. The flame wavered, and the enormous shadow of his bare skull— he had taken off his wig for the night—leapt on the wall, as though it were dancing and grimacing like a merry-andrew, and laughing, like a death's head. The thick drops of wax, as red as blood, bubbled and then trickled down. And, most softly, he hummed his favorite madrigal:

> Thy arrows, Cupido, forego—
> For not a heart there but doth know
> A most delectable, dear woe;
> Not one but that has, to its sorrow,
> Felt of thy barbéd, golden arrow;
> We in submission all bow low.

In the letter which Tolstoi was dispatching to the Czar, the Czarevich had written:

"MOST GRACIOUS LIEGE LORD, BATIUSHKA!

"Thy most gracious letter, my Liege Lord, I have received through Tolstoi and Rumyantzev; from which letter, as well as from what they have communicated to me by word of mouth, I gather that thou, Sire, hast extended thy forgiveness to me in the event of my return, even though I am undeserving of any grace, because of this my self-willed departure; for which I thank you, with tears, and prostrating myself at the feet of thy mercy, I, who am deserving of all punishments, do tearfully implore for the remission of my transgressions. And placing my trust in thy gracious promise, I place myself under thy will, and shall, within a few days leave Naples for St. Peterburgh, to see thee, with the envoys thou, my Sire, hast sent.

"Thy most humble and worthless slave, undeserving of being called thy son,

ALEXEI."

BOOK EIGHT

PETER THE GREAT

I

PETER had gotten up early. "What a devil of an early bird!" grumbled his sleepy orderly, lighting the stoves. A black November morning was peeping in at the windows. By the light of a tallow candle-lamp, in his night-cap, his dressing-gown, and his leather apron, the Czar was seated at a turner's lathe, and was turning a thurible of bone for the Cathedral of SS. Peter and Paul, as a token of gratitude for relief from his sickness, which relief he had obtained by drinking Martial [ferric] waters; then, out of bird's-eye maple, he turned a little Bacchus, bearing a cluster of grapes, for a goblet-lid. He worked with as much zeal as if he were earning his daily bread thereby.

At half-past four, his private secretary, Alexei Vassilievich Makarov, arrived. The Czar took his stand at a reading-desk of walnut wood, a very high desk, which would reach up to the neck of a man of medium height,—and began dictating *ukases* concerning Colleges [or Governmental Departments], which were being founded in Russia by advice of Leibnitz, "after the example and manner of other well-governed states."

"Even as in a watch one wheel is brought in motion by another," the philosopher used to say to the Czar, "thus, in a great governmental machine, one college must bring another into motion, and if everything be arranged in exact proportion and harmony, then the time-hand of life must inevitably indicate happy hours for the country."

Peter was fond of mechanics and he was captivated by the thought of turning his state into a machine. But that which seemed easy in conception proved difficult in reality.

The people of Russia neither understood nor loved the Colleges, contemptuously mispronouncing the very word, or

actually perverting it into *Kalleki* [cripples]. The Czar had
invited foreign savants and "men skilled in laws." These
managed their affairs through interpreters, which was incon-
venient. Thereupon young Russian clerks were dispatched to
Königsberg, "for to learn the German tongue, so that they
might be better fitted for each Collegium, and supervisors are
to be sent along with them, lest they spend their time in
idleness." But the supervisors spent their time in idleness together with those supervised.

The Czar issued an *ukase:* "All the Collegia are to formu-
late regulations for their work and procedure, point by point,
using the Swedish code as a basis; but as for such points in
the Swedish regulations which are not practical, or out of
keeping with the situation of this state, such shall be used according to their own discretion." But they had no discretion
of their own, and the Czar had a premonition that in the new
Colleges affairs would go on in the same way as in the old
departments. "Everything is in vain," he reflected, "until our
people come to realize the direct benefit of the Crown, which
is not to be hoped for even in the next hundred years."

The orderly announced a translator of the Foreign College,
Vassilii Koslovsky. A pale and consumptive young man entered. Peter sought out among his papers and handed over
to him a manuscript, greatly blotted and with many notations in pencil on the margins,—a treatise on mechanics.

"This has been badly translated,—correct it."

"Your Majesty!" Koslovsky began to babble, growing
timid and stammering. "The very creator of this book has
indulged in a style such as is most difficult to understand,
inasmuch as he wrote concisely and cryptically, without so
much regard for the benefit of mankind as for the subtlety
of his philosophical diction. Whereas I, because of the paucity
of my mind, find it impossible to understand him. . . ."

The Czar instructed him patiently:

"One should not keep closely to a word-by-word rendi-
tion, but, having gotten at meaning itself, write it over in
one's own language, as plainly as possible, merely guarding
against the matter in hand being lost track of, and by no
means running after style. Let not thy aim be any idle
elegancy, but utility, without any extraneous fables, which

are a waste of time, and take away the reader's desire to learn. And write not in a lofty Slavic style, but in plain Russian; there is no necessity of putting in big words,—use such words as are in use in the diplomatic department. Even as thou speakest, so shalt thou write,—simply. Hast understood?"

"Precisely so, Your Majesty," answered the translator, as a soldier might a command, and letting his head drop with a dismal air, as though he had recalled his predecessor, also a translator of the Foreign College, one Boris Volkov, who, despairing over a French book on gardening, *"Le Jardinage de Quintiny,"* and fearing the Czar's wrath, had cut his veins.

"There, go thy way with God, and do put forth thy best efforts. Also, tell Avramov that the type in the new books, as compared with that formerly used, is thick and not clean-cut. The letters *b* and *p* are to be re-cut,—they are much too thick. And the binding is bad, for the most part because he binds them much too tight in the backbone,—the books gape. The leaves should be sewn loosely and more space allowed in the back."

When Koslovsky had gone, Peter recalled the dreams of Leibnitz about a Universal Russian Encyclopedia,—"the quintessence of the sciences, such as has not yet been made," —and about an Academy of Peterburgh, a high college of learned administrators, with the Czar at its head,—and about a future Russia which, having outdistanced Europe in the sciences, would lead the latter after it.

" 'There's many a slip 'twixt the cup and the lip,' " the Czar smiled a bitter smile. "Before enlightening Europe we ourselves must learn the Russian speech, and writing, printing, binding and paper-making."

He dictated an *ukase:*

"In the cities and main districts, all sweepings of discarded cloth and all rags are to be gathered and sent to the Chancellory in St. Peterburgh; and those who gather and deliver the same shall be paid eight *denghi* per *poud* [eight half-kopecks for each thirty pounds avoirdupois]."

These rags were intended for paper mills.

Then followed *ukases* concerning tallow-refining; concerning better weaving of bast sandals, concerning the finishing of rough leather for footgear: "inasmuch as the leather used for footgear is quite unfit for wear, since it is tanned with pitch, and, upon coming in contact with water, falls apart and lets the water through; therefore the said leather should be tanned with blubber."

He glanced at a graphite slate which, together with a slate pencil, he hung overnight near the head of his bed, in order to write down upon awakening whatever ideas occurred to him concerning future *ukases*. During the night he had written down:

"Where should manure be dumped?—Mem.:

"A dump for manure, about Persia.—About mattings."

He ordered Makarov to read aloud the letter from Volinsky, the Ambassador to Persia:

"The man at the head here is such that I feel another Simple-Simon like him could hardly be found even among common folk, to say naught of crowned heads. God is leading this crown to a downfall. Even though our present war with Sweden were to hold us back, still, since I can see its weakness, we could annex a great part of Persia with but a small army, or even a small force, without any difficulty; no more convenient time than the present could be found."

In his answer to Volinsky Peter ordered a trading party to be sent down the Amu-Dariya River, in order to find a water-route to India, and, describing everything, to make a chart; he also ordered that an epistle to the Mogul,—the Dalai Lama of Tibet,—be prepared.

A road to India, the joining of Europe with Asia, was a long-cherished dream of Peter's.

As long as twenty years ago, an Orthodox Church in the name of St. Sophia of the Highest Wisdom of God had been founded in Pekin.

"Le Czar peut unir la Chine avec l'Europe. The Czar is able to join China with Europe," Leibnitz had prophesied. "Through the conquests of the Czar in Persia will be founded an empire more powerful than that of Rome," the foreign diplomats warned their sovereigns. "The Czar, like another Alexander, is striving to get the entire world into his possession," the Sultan used to say.

Peter got up and unrolled a map of the terrestrial globe, which he himself had once drawn, planning the future destinies of Russia; *EUROPE* was inscribed toward the West, *ASIA* toward the South, while in the space from the Chukotski Cape to the Niemen, and from Archangelsk to Ararat, was inscribed *RUSSIA* in letters just as large as those of *EUROPE* and *ASIA*. "Everybody makes a mistake," he used to say, "in calling Russia a state,—*it is one part of the world*."

But at once, through an habitual effort of his will, he turned from revery to reality,—from the grandiose to the petty. He began dictating *ukases:* "Concerning a suitable site for manure dumps"; concerning the replacement of bags of matting with those made out of hair for ship-biscuits, while those for grain- and salt-bags were to be replaced by kegs or canvas-bags,—"for matting must by no means be used henceforth"; concerning the conservation of lead bullets in instructing soldiers to shoot; concerning the preservation of forests; concerning the discontinuance of making coffins out of whole logs,—"they are to be made solely out of boards knocked together"; concerning the importation of a sample coffin from England into Russia.

He turned the pages of his notebook, checking up whether he had not forgotten some necessary matter. On the first page was the inscription: *In Gottes Namen—In the name of the Lord.* Further followed divers notations; sometimes a long train of thought was jotted down in two or three words.

"Concerning a certain conception, through which divers mysteries of nature may be discovered."

"An experimental device. How to extinguish naphtha with vitriol. How to boil hemp cooked in saltpeter water. *Mem:* purchase the secret of manufacturing sausage-casings."

"The *mouzhiks* are to have some instruction in theology, even if of the briefest, which is to be read aloud in churches, for their better understanding."

"Concerning the education of foundlings."

"Concerning the founding of a whaling industry."

"The fall of the Greek monarchy was due to contempt for war."

"Order French Gazettes to be sent."

"Find mummers in the land of Germany, for great pay."

"Concerning Russian proverbs. Concerning a Russian Lexicon."

"Concerning secrets of chemistry,—as applied to testing ore."

"If we accept the laws of nature as being rational, why do animals devour one another, and wherefore do we cause them such misery?"

"Concerning present and ancient dealings against atheists."

"Compose, personally, a prayer for soldiers: *O God,— Great, Eternal, and Holy, etc. . . . .*"

Peter's diary recalled the diaries of Leonardo da Vinci.

At six o'clock in the morning he began dressing. As he was pulling on his stockings he noticed a hole. He sat down, got out a needle and a ball of wool, and fell to darning it. Meditating on a route to India in the footsteps of Alexander of Macedonia, he darned his stockings.

After that he had a sup of anise brandy with a cracknel, lit his pipe, walked out of the palace, took his seat down in a carriole with a lantern,—inasmuch as it was still dark,— and set out for the Admiralty.

II

The spire of the Admirality, through the fog, smoldered dimly from the fires of fifteen forges. An unfinished ship showed its bare ribs, blackly, like the osseous frame of some monster. Anchor ropes dragged their length along like gigantean snakes; one heard the screech of blocks, the boom of sledge-hammers, the rumbling of iron, the bubbling of pitch. The Admiralty resembled a smithy in hell.

Peter visited every nook and inspected everything. In the Department of Ammunition he checked up the record of the caliber of the cannon-balls and grenades, which were piled up in pyramids, under sheds, "Lest rust get at them"; whether the barrels of the flint-locks and muskets were filled with grease; and whether his *ukase* concerning cannon had been carried out: "the bore should be inspected with a mirror, to see if it be smooth and if there be any fissures or obstacles, from the breach to the muzzle; should any fissures be found, they are to be probed, to ascertain their depth."

He could distinguish, by its odor, the quality of walrus blubber; his sense of touch told him of lightness of sail-cloths, and whether it were due to fine threads or to loose weaving. When he spoke with master workmen, it was as one master to another.

"Boards should be joined closely to one another. Select those seasoned for at least two years,—and if longer, so much the better, inasmuch as unless they be dried when they are calked, they will not only crack but will swell up from the water and make the calking bulge out. . . ."

"The shrouds are to be fastened with pins over the boards. Attach deadeyes at the ends, fasten to the wales, and splice on the inside. . . ."

"Only the very best green oak is suitable,—the wood should be bluish, rather than red. Made of such oak, the ship will become as iron, inasmuch as even a musket bullet will not go entirely through it,—not more than seven-eighths of an inch. . . ."

In the barns where hemp was stored he would take handfuls from the bundles, place it between his knees, painstakingly inspect it, shake it out and pick it in a masterly fashion.

"A ship's mooring cables are a great and awesome matter: they should be made out of the very best and stoutest hemp. If the rope be trustworthy, it means the ship's salvation; but if it be bad, it means perdition to ship and crew."

Everywhere one could hear the Czar yelling wrathfully at the chandlers and contractors:

"I can see that during my absence everything has been turned arsi-versy!"

"I'll have to make you sweat like slaves and go in fear of your lives until everything is brought into order!"

"Just bide a while,—I'll give you something to remember me by, so that you won't forget for quite a spell!"

He could not bear any long conversations. He spat into the face of a certain important foreigner who spoke of trifles, cursed him out with a maternal oath, and walked away.

To a rascally clerk, he remarked:

"That which thou failest to mark down upon paper, I shall not fail to mark up on thy back."

By way of answer to a petition for an increase in the yearly remuneration of the Councilors of the Admiralty he issued the resolution: "This is out of the question, inasmuch as it tends to fat living and lining the pocket rather than to true service."

Upon learning that on several vessels of the galley-fleet "the salt pork proved rotten, the marines having to subsist upon spoilt smelts and water, from which one thousand men did fall ill and were incapacitated for work," he became angry in downright earnest. He almost struck the face of an old, venerable captain, who had distinguished himself in the Battle of Gangut:

"If thou wilt act as stupidly as this in the future, do not blame me if, in the fullness of thy years, thou shalt be disgraced! Why is this most important work, which is a thousandfold more precious than thy head, carried on with such negligence? Methinks thou dost not read the Military Statutes often enough! The officers of the said galleys are to be hanged, and thou mayst also go the same way, because of thy loose command!. . ."

However, he let his hand drop and restrained his wrath.

"I never expected this from thee," he added, but quietly by now, yet with such reproach that it would have been much easier for the guilty man had the Czar struck him.

"See to it now," said Peter, "that such heartlessness does not take place in the future, inasmuch as this is the most onerous of all sins in the eyes of God. I have heard recently that here in Peterburgh on the works undertaken for the harbor, the people, during last summer, were so neglected,—especially those unwell,—that they fell down dead on the streets,—which is revolting to the conscience and seemliness not only of Christians but even of barbarians. How is it ye have no pity? For these be no cattle, but Christian souls. God will demand a reckoning for them!"

III

Peter was riding in his carriole along the quay toward the Summer Palace where, that year, he had stayed over until late fall, because alterations were going on in the Winter Palace.

He was pondering why formerly it had been a joy for him to be returning home to sup and to see his Katenka, yet now it was almost depressing. He recalled anonymous letters, containing innuendoes concerning his wife and a rather youthful, comely German lad,—Mons, the Chamberlain.

Katenka had ever been a faithful wife and a good help to her husband. She shared all his toils and dangers; she followed him on all his campaigns like any simple soldier-lass. During the Prutsky campaign, "acting rather like a man than like a woman," she had saved the whole army. Peter styled her his "mother." Left without her, he felt himself helpless and complained like a child: "Mother, there is no one to mend or wash for me!"

They were jealous of one another, in jest. "Having read thy letter, I fell into deep thought. Thou dost write that I ought not to come so soon; apparently 'tis for the sake of my cure, yet one can easily see how the matter really stands: Thou hast sought out some one younger than I. Please write me,—is it one of our own people, or one of the Germans? So that is what ye daughters of Eve do with us old men!"— "I do not consider thee an old man," she objected. "And it is a pity thou hast gotten this idea of being an old man into thy head,—such another darling old man is to be eagerly sought for. So that is how thou dost feel about me! But I, too, have a report,—that the Queen of Sweden is inclined to be in love with thee,—and I have my own doubts."

During the separations, they would exchange presents, like bride and groom. Katenka would send him, though he were thousands of leagues away, Hungarian wine, *vodka* (the "strong" kind), freshly pickled cucumbers, "citrons" and oranges,—"Inasmuch as our own fruit will be more pleasing to you. God grant you good appetite."

But the most precious presents she made him were children. With the exception of two elder ones, Lizanka and

Annushka, they were born puny and soon died. Most of all
did he love his last-born, Petenka,—Little Bud, the Master
of Peterburgh, who had been proclaimed successor to the
throne in lieu of Alexei. Petenka, too, had been born frail,
was forever ailing, and lived on nothing but medicines. The
Czar was in fear and trembling lest the Little Bud die. Katenka consoled the Czar. "I wot that if our good old man
were here there would be e'en another little bud burgeon-
ing next year."

In this marital tenderness there was a certain mawkishness,—a gallant sensitiveness, surprising in the sinister Czar.
"I have had my hair clipped here, and, although it may be
no pleasant gift, I am nevertheless sending the shaggy
clippings to thee." "I have received safely your darling locks,
and it gave me pleasure to have tidings of your good health."
—"I am sending thee, dearest friend of my heart, a flower
and a sprig of mint,—'tis the same thou didst plant thyself.
Glory be to God, all is joyous here,—save that when I enter
the garden in the back of the house, and thou not there, I
feel a great longing," he wrote to her from Reval,—from her
beloved garden, called Katerinenthal. Enclosed in the letter was a dried, bluish flower, a sprig of mint, and a clipping
from an English newspaper: "Last year, on the 11th day of
October, there arrived in England from the County of Mon-
mouth, a couple who have lived in Wedlock an hundred and
ten Years, the man being an hundred and twenty-six Years
of Age, and the woman an hundred and twenty-five." This
signified: God grant that thou and I live just as long in
happy matrimony.

And so now, in his declining years, on this dismal,
autumnal morning, recalling their past life, and thinking that
Katenka might prove untrue to him, might change her "old
man" for the first-come good-looking lad, a low-born German,
he experienced not so much jealousy, or malice, or indignation, as the defenselessness of a babe, forsaken by its
"mother."

He handed the reins over to an orderly and slumped in his
seat, with hunched-up shoulders and head drooping; and
from the jolts of the carriole over the uneven cobbles, his

head bobbed as though from senile feebleness, and he seemed altogether very senile, very feeble.

The chimes beyond the Neva struck eleven. But the light of morning resembled the glance of a dying man. It seemed as though day would not come at all. Snow and rain were falling. The horses' hoofs splashed through puddles,—the wheels spattered mud. Gray clouds crawled slowly along, as bloated as spiders' bellies, and so low that they shut off the view of the spire of the Fortress of SS. Peter and Paul; the gray waters, the gray houses, the trees, the people,—all, melting away in the fog, looked like specters.

When they rode up on the small wooden drawbridge over the Swan Canal, Peter was assailed by an odor of turned earth from the Summer Garden,—like the odor of the grave; an odor of dampness and of moldered leaves,—throughout the alleys the gardeners were sweeping them into mounds with their besoms.

Ravens were cawing upon the naked lindens. One heard the sound of hammers, the marble statues were being put into long narrow boxes for the winter, to safeguard them against the snow and the cold. It seemed as if the resurgent gods were being buried anew, were being nailed up into coffins.

Between the lilac-black sodden tree-trunks came the gleam of the light yellow walls of a small Dutch house, with a checkered roof of iron, a weather-vane in the shape of St. George the Conqueror, and white sculptured bas-reliefs on its walls, depicting the fabled wonders of the sea, its tritons and nereids; it was many-windowed, and its glass doors led directly into the garden. This was the Summer Palace.

IV

The palace reeked of sour-cabbage soup, cooking for dinner. Peter was fond of this dish, even as of other simple soldier-dishes.

The courses came and went in quick succession,—the Czar did not like to wait long at table,—being served right into the dining-room through a window communicating directly with the exceedingly neat kitchen, tiled throughout and with glistening copper utensils hanging on the walls, as in old

Dutch houses. In addition to the sour-cabbage soup, served with buckwheat porridge, there were oysters from Flensburg, fish-jelly, sprats, fried beef, served with cucumbers and pickles, lemons, and duck's feet with a sour sauce. As a general thing, he was fond of sour and salted things,—anything sweet he could not bear. After dinner there were nuts, apples, and Limburg cheese. For drink there was bread-cider and a French red wine,—Hermitage. There was only one waiter,—an orderly.

Guests had been invited for dinner, as always: Jacob Bruce; the royal physician, Blumentrost; some English skipper or other; the Chamberlain Mons; and a maid-of-honor, Miss Hamilton. Peter had invited Mons because Katenka did not expect him; but, when she had learned of this invitation, she had in her turn invited the maid-of-honor, Miss Hamilton,—perhaps for the purpose of giving her husband to understand that she, too, knew a thing or two about his "little mistresses." This was that same Hamilton, "the Hamilton wench," a Caledonian, in appearance proud, pure, and chill, like some marble Diana, whose name had been bruited about in whispers when the corpse of an infant, wrapped up in a napkin belonging to the palace, had been found in the water-pipe of a Summer Garden fountain.

At table she sat in silence during the whole dinner, all pale, without a drop of blood in her face.

The conversation did not get on very well, despite Katenka's efforts. She told about her latest dream,—that of an angry beast with white wool, with a crown on its head, and with three little candles on the crown, which beast kept shouting at frequent intervals: *Saldoreth! Saldoreth!*

Peter liked dreams, and not infrequently noted them down himself on his slate at night. He, too, told his dream: it all had to do with water, and naval maneuvers, and galleys; in his dream he had noticed that "the sails, as well as the masts, were out of proportion."

"Ah, Batiushka!" Katenka was touched. "Even in thy sleep thou hast no rest,—thou art forever fashing thyself over matters of ship-building!"

And when he again fell into a sullen silence she brought the conversation around to the new ships.

"*The Neptune* is a most beautiful ship, and so fleet that, like as not, 'tis the best in the fleet. *The Gangut* is likewise a good sailor, and obeys the helm,—but, because of its height, 'tis not very steady; it careens more than the others even under the slightest breeze,—now what will it be like in bad weather? As for the large sloop-boat built by the *Gaas* Van Renne,—I would not launch it before your arrival, and, lest it warp, have ordered it to be boarded up ashore."

She spoke of the ships as though they were her own children:

"*The Gangut* and *The Forest-Dweller* are like twin brothers,—they sicken when apart from each other; but now, when they are docked side by side, they are truly a joy to behold. As for those ships we have bought, when you compare them with our own,—truly, you can only call them foster-children, inasmuch as they are as far behind ours as in a father's eyes a foster-son is compared with his own! . . ."

Peter answered grudgingly, as though he were thinking of something else. He glanced stealthily now at her and now at Mons with his face as firm and smooth as though it were carved out of rose-quartz, and his eyes as blue as though they were of turquoise, the elegant chamberlain reminded one of a porcelain doll.

Katenka felt that the "old man" was observing them. But she had perfect self-control. Even if she knew about the anonymous letters, she did not reveal her uneasiness in any way,—unless it were that whenever she looked at her husband there was in her eyes a tenderness more ingratiating than ever, and, perhaps, she spoke a little too much, rapidly passing from one subject to another, as though she were seeking for something wherewith to divert her husband's mind,—"weaving her spells," he might have reflected.

She had barely done speaking of ships when she began talking about the children, Lizanka and Annushka, who, during the summer, "had almost had their darling faces marred by smallpox," and about the Little Bud, who "had become weak of health through cutting his last toothies."

"However, with the help of God, he is getting back to his right state now. The fifth toothie has already come out safely,

—God grant the same for all of them! But now his dear little
right eye is paining him."

Peter regained his animation for a minute and fell to questioning the royal physician about the health of the Little Bud.

"His Highness's little eye is much better," imparted Blumentrost; "also, it turned out that he has a little tooth on the
left lower jaw. He deigns to feel his gums with his little fingers, now. That means that even the molars are about to
come out."

"He'll be a brave general!" Katenka cut in. "He can't get
his fill of playing with his tin soldiers,—he's forever making
merry over mustering recruits and firing off the cannon. And
all he says is, 'papa, mama, soldier!' And also, Batiushka, I
ask for protection, inasmuch as he and I have no mean quarrel over you whenever you depart. Should I happen to mention that papa's gone away, he likes that speech not; he
likes it more and rejoices when one says papa's here," she
drawled out, in her sing-song little voice, and peeped into
her husband's eyes with a mawkish little smile.

Peter made no reply but suddenly looked at her and Mons,
so that an eldritch feeling crept over all those present.
Katenka let her eyes drop and paled the least bit. Hamilton
raised her eyes and smiled a quiet smile. There was a silence.
They all became frightened.

But Peter, as though nothing whatever had happened,
turned to Jacob Bruce and began speaking of astronomy,—
of Newton's system,—of the sun-spots which can be seen
through a telescope if the lens next to the eye be smoked
over; he also spoke of the forthcoming solar eclipse. He became so absorbed in this conversation that he paid no attention to anything until the end of the dinner. Without even
leaving the table he took a memorandum book out of his
pocket and jotted down: "Proclamations are to be made
among the people about the solar eclipses, that they may not
hold them to be miracles, inasmuch as when people know
thereof ahead of time, an eclipse is no longer a miracle. Also,
let no one dare trump up false miracles, or spread knowledge
of them, for the purpose of misleading the people."

There was a general sigh of relief when Peter arose from
the table and went into the adjoining room.

He sank into an armchair near the blazing fireplace, put on round, iron-rimmed glasses, lit his pipe and fell to looking through the latest Dutch newspapers, marking off in pencil, on the margins, whatever he deemed necessary to be translated for the Russian news. Once more he took out his book and jotted down:

"Everything should be printed, dealing with good fortune or bad, whichever befalls; nor should anything be held back."

A pale sunbeam flashed out from behind the clouds,—a sunbeam timid, feeble, like the smile of one mortally ill. A quadrangle of light, thrown by the window-frame, extended across the floor to the very fireplace, and the red flame lost body, grew more transparent. Beyond the window, against a sky that was like molten silver, slender twigs were silhouetted, like little veins. A young orange tree, frail and sensitive to the cold, in a tub which the gardeners were forever transferring from one hothouse to another, became overjoyed at the sun and its fruit, like little spheres of gold, began to glow amidst its dark clipped foliage. Between black tree-trunks showed whitely the marble gods and goddesses,—the last, not yet nailed up in their coffins; they, too, were sensitive to the cold, naked, apparently eager to warm themselves in the sun.

Two little girls ran into the room. The elder, the nine-year-old Annushka, had dark eyes, an exceedingly white face, and vividly glowing cheeks; she was staid, dignified, corpulent, and somewhat slow of gait, a "roly-poly," as Peter used to call her. The younger, the seven-year-old Lizanka, had golden curls and blue eyes, was as buoyant as a little bird; she was a lively madcap, a lazy-bones as far as learning was concerned, and liking nothing save games, dances and little songs, —a very pretty little thing, and already a coquette.

"Ah, you brigands!" Peter turned around to them, and putting aside his newspapers, stretched his arms out to them with a tender smile. He embraced them, kissed them, and seated one on each knee.

Lizanka pulled off his spectacles,—she disliked them, inasmuch as they aged him; when he wore them he looked like a grandfather. Then she fell to whispering in his ear, confiding to him her long-cherished dream:

"The Dutch skipper, Isaiah Koenig, was telling me that

in Amsterdam there's a little bit of a monkey, all of a green color; it is so teensy-weensy that it can be placed in an India nut. There, if thou wouldst get that little monkey for me, papa,—dearest little papa!"

Peter voiced his doubts as to the possibility of little monkeys being of a green color, but promised solemnly (he had to repeat "I swear it by God!" no less than three times) that he would write to Amsterdam about it by the next post. Whereupon Lizanka in her rapture launched into a game: trying to thrust her little hand into the blue rings of tobacco smoke issuing from Peter's pipe, making believe they were necklaces.

Annushka told him the marvels of the intelligence and good-nature of her favorite, Mishka,—a tame seal in the central fountain of the Summer Garden.

"Papa, dear, why not make a saddle for Mishka, and then ride him on the water, like a horse?"

"Well, now, suppose he were to dive,—wouldst thou not drown?" Peter objected.

He chattered and laughed with the children as though he himself were a child.

Suddenly he caught sight in a pier-glass of Mons and Katenka. They were standing by the fire in the next room, before a spoiled darling of the Czaritza's, a green parrot from Guiana, and were feeding it sugar.

"Your Majesty . . . is a fool! . . ." the parrot was saying, piercingly and hoarsely. He had been taught to shout: "Long life to Your Majesty!" and "Polly is a fool!" But he combined the two phrases into one.

Mons was bending toward the Czaritza and was saying something almost in her ear. Katenka had let her eyes drop, flushing just the least bit, and was listening to him with the demure, sweetish simper of the shepherdess in the mural of *A Journey to the Island of Love.*

Peter's face suddenly became overcast. Nevertheless he kissed the children and dismissed them kindly.

"There, go on, go on,—and God be with ye, ye brigands! Give my regards to Mishka, Annushka."

The sunbeam dimmed; the room became gloomy, damp and chill. The caw of a raven came from above the very window;

somewhere a hammer began to tap. This marked the coffining, the entombment of the resurgent gods.

Peter sat down to a game of chess with Bruce. He always played well, but to-day he was absent-minded. He lost his queen on the fourth move.

"Check to your queen!" said Bruce.[63]

"Your Majesty is a fool!" screamed the parrot.

Peter, happening to look up, again saw Mons and Katenka in the same mirror. They had become so engrossed in their conversation that they had not noticed how a little monkey, who resembled an imp, had stolen up on them from behind, and, stretching out its little paw and making a knavish little grimace, had raised up the hem of Katenka's dress.

Peter leapt up and overturned the chess-board with his leg,—all the pieces flew to the floor. A spasm distorted his face. The pipe fell out of his mouth, shattered, and spilled the burning ashes. Bruce, too, leapt up in terror. The Czaritza and Mons turned around upon hearing the noise.

At the same instant Miss Hamilton entered the room. She moved like a somnambulist, as though she neither saw nor heard aught. But, as she passed the Czar, she bowed her head the least trifle and looked at him intently. There was such chilliness wafted from her splendidly-beautiful face, as pale as in death, that she seemed one of the marble goddesses who were being nailed into their coffins.

The Czar's eyes followed her to the door. Then he turned around to look at Bruce and the overturned chess-board, with a guilty smile:

"Forgive me, Jacob Williamovich . . . 'Twas accidental!"

He left the palace, seated himself in a small sloop, and went off for a siesta on his yacht.

V

Peter's sleep was unwholesomely light. All traffic past the palace at night was prohibited,—even walking. In the daytime, since it is impossible to avoid noise in a dwelling, he slept on the yacht.

As soon as he lay down he felt great weariness,—probably he had gotten up too early and had tired himself out in the

Admiralty. Delectably yawning and stretching he closed his eyes, and was just dozing off, when he shuddered as if from a sudden pang. This pang was caused by the thought of his son, the Czarevich Alexei,—it was a constant, dull, nagging pain. But at times, amid silence or solitude, it would begin to ache with fresh force, like a real wound.

He strove to fall asleep, but sleep was no more. Thoughts forced their way into his head of themselves.

Within the last few days he had received the letter in which Tolstoi informed him that Alexei would not return under any circumstances. Would he really have to go to Italy and begin a war with the Kaiser and England, perhaps with all of Europe,—now, when he ought to think of naught save terminating his war with the Swedes, and concluding a peace? Wherefore had God sent him such a son as a punishment?

"Thou heart of Absalom, thou heart of Absalom,—hating thy father's works and wishing death to thy very father! ..." He moaned dully, squeezing his head between his hands.

He recalled how his son had called him a malefactor, a tyrant, a godless man before the Kaiser, before all the world; he recalled how the friends of Alexei,—the long-beards, the holy ancients and the monks,—had reviled him, Peter, as an "Antichrist."

"Simpletons!" he reflected with a calm contempt. Why, could he have accomplished what he did, if he had not had the aid of God? And how could he do otherwise than believe in God, when God,—lo, there He was!—was ever with him from the years of his infancy, up to this very hour? And, probing his conscience, as though he were his own confessor, he reviewed all his life.

Was it not God Himself Who had instilled in his heart the desire to learn? When he was sixteen years of age, he had barely known how to write; he knew addition and multiplication but so-so. But even then he had dimly sensed that which later on he came to understand clearly: "The salvation of Russia lies in education; all the other nations hold to the policy of keeping Russia in ignorance, and of restraining her from the light of reason in all matters, but especially in matters military, so that she might not realize her own strength."

He decided to go himself into foreign lands, to seek learning. When this became known in Moscow the patriarchs and *boyars*, the Czaritzas and the Czarevnas, came to him, placing his son Alëshenka at his feet, and wept, and knocked their foreheads on the ground before him, imploring him not to go off to the Germans,—such a thing had never happened since the beginning of Russia. And the people saw him off with weeping, as though he were going to his death,—yet go off he did, notwithstanding, and that which was unheard of was consummated. The Czar, in lieu of a scepter, had taken an ax into his hands,—had become a common workman.

"I am numbered among the learners, and demand those who can teach me. That which one does one's self, cannot be purchased at any price." And God had blessed his works: out of his boyhood retinue, supposed to amuse him, which retinue Sophia, in contempt, described as consisting of "madcaps and hostlers," there had formed an awe-inspiring army; out of the tiny toy dugouts, in which he had sailed the pools of the aqueduct in the Red Garden, there had formed a victorious fleet.

His first battle with the Swedes,—the defeat at Narva . . . "That whole affair was like to child's play, and not even to be regarded as a matter of military skill. And now, when I think thereon, I deem it to be God's Grace, inasmuch as when the said misfortune did befall us necessity drove away indolence and forced us to be industrious and skillful, day and night." The defeat had seemed hopeless. "We," boasted Carl, "could drive out the Russian *canaille* without even using a sword,—just with a common whip; and we could drive them out of this world entirely, to say nothing of their own land!" Had the Lord not helped Peter then, he would have perished.

There was no brass for his cannon,—he ordered the church-bells to be melted down into cannon. The holy ancients had threatened him,—"God will punish thee, now,"—yet he knew that God was with him. There were no horses; men, harnessing themselves, hauled the ordnance of this new artillery, "baptized with tears."

All the affairs were "fermenting like new mash." Without there was war; within,—sedition. There was an uprising at Astrakhan, under the leadership of Bulavin.[64] Carl crossed the Vistula and the Niemen; he entered Grodno two hours

after Peter had evacuated it. From day to day he expected
the Swedes to advance upon Peterburgh or Moscow. He
fortified both cities, preparing for a siege. Yet at the same
time he was ill,—so ill that his life "was quite despaired of,"
even by himself. But again God's miracle was manifested.
Carl, contrary to all expectations and suppositions, halted,
turned about, and marched towards the southeast, into Little
Russia. The uprising expired of itself. "In a miraculous manner, the Lord was pleased to put out the fire with fire, so as to
make it evident that all things depend truly not upon human,
but upon His, will."

The first victories over the Swedes . . . at the battle of
Lessonoë, putting Cossacks and Kalmucks, armed with pikes,
right back of his front line, he issued orders to stab, without any mercy, any deserters,—not excepting even himself,
the Czar. All day long they faced the fire without breaking
ranks, nor yielding even a foot's pace; four times did their
guns become red-hot from the firing; four times did they fill
their wallets and pockets with cartridges. "Why, ever since I
entered the army, I had never seen such a performance; however, we danced this dance rather well, with the ardent
Carolus looking right on!" Henceforth "the neck of the Swede
bends more flexibly."

Poltava . . . Never in all his life had he felt the hand of
the Lord to be as helpful as on this day. Again good fortune,
resembling a miracle. Carl, the night before, had been
wounded by a stray Cossack bullet. At the very beginning
of the battle a shot had struck the litter of the king; the
Swedes had thought he was killed,—their ranks were thrown
into confusion. Peter contemplated the fleeing Swedes, and it
seemed to him that he was borne upon invisible wings; he
knew that the day of Poltava, was "the day of the Resurrection of Russia," and that the refulgent sun of this day
was the sun of all the new Russia.

"Now the corner stone of Sanct Peterburgh has been
definitely laid. Henceforth, one may sleep in peace in Peterburgh." This city, created in despite of the elements, in the
midst of marish lands and forests,—"is like to a child growing
in its beauty; a holy land, a Paradise, God's Eden,"—is it
not also a great miracle of the Lord, a sign of God's gracious-

ness to him,—which now will not cease, and is evident before the face of all the coming ages?

And lo, now, when everything is almost consummated,—everything is tumbling down. God has withdrawn Himself, has forsaken him. Having granted him victories over external enemies, He has stricken him within his heart, through his own flesh and blood,—through his son.

His son's most dreaded allies were not the foreign troops, but the hordes of knaves, parasites, bribe-takers, and all sorts of other pernicious homunculi swarming within the realm. By the way things had gone during his last departure from Russia Peter saw how they would go when he would no longer be; during these few months everything had begun to creak, had become as shaky as some old, rotted hulk, stuck on a shoal during a storm.

"The greatest thievery has sprung up." *Ukase* followed *ukase,* each more severe than the preceding, in the fight against bribe-takers. Almost every one began with the words: "Should any disregard this, or last *ukase,*"—but this last one was followed by others, with the same threats and additional admonition as before.

At times his hands would drop in despair. He felt a dreadful impotence. One against many. Like some huge beast bitten to death by mosquitoes and midges.

Seeing that naught could be done through force, he resorted to craftiness. He encouraged secret information. He designated a special post,—that of the *fiscals* or informers. Whereupon chicanery and pettifoggery sprang up throughout the land. "The *fiscals* are utterly heedless; they contrive to live like real parasites, and screen one another, inasmuch as they are banded in common." Knaves were informing on knaves, —informers on informers—*fiscals on fiscals;* and the arch-fiscal was, apparently, the arch-knave.

An abominable abyss,—an abominable cess-pool,—Augean stables, which no Hercules could clean. Everything is seeping with mire, disintegrating like thawing snow. "Ancient rottenness" is coming to the surface. The stench that is spreading throughout all Russia is like to that after the battle of Poltava, from whence the army had had to retreat because the men stifled from the stench of the innumerable corpses.

Hearts are in darkness because minds are in darkness. None desires the good because none knows what good is. The minor nobility and the common people were like Erema and Phoma in the by-word: Erema does not teach, and Phoma can do naught. Here, too, no *ukases* of any sort will aught avail.

"Our minds are dull and our hands incapable; the people of our land are truly of sluggish minds," the oldsters were wont to say to him.

On one occasion he heard an ancient legend from a Dutch skipper: some mariners sighted an unknown island in the midst of the ocean; they moored their ship, disembarked, and lit a fire to cook their food; suddenly the ground began to sink, and they all but drowned,—that which had seemed to them an island was the back of a sleeping whale. Was not all the new enlightenment of Russia like to this fire, lit on the back of the Leviathan,—upon the sluggish mass of a sleeping people?

Accursed Sisyphean labor, like to the labor of the convicts at Rogerwick, where a jetty was being built; a storm would hardly spring up, when it would demolish in an hour all that it had taken years to raise up; they would build again, and again their work would be demolished, and so on without end.

"We all see," an intelligent *mouzhik* had once told him, "how hard thou, our great ruler, dost work thyself; yet thou wilt not succeed in aught, inasmuch as thy helpers are few,—suppose thou wert to pull uphill, thou thyself doing the work of ten men, while millions were to be dragging downhill,—who, then, would succeed fastest?"

" 'Tis a burthen,—a burthen unbearable! . . ." moaned Peter, as he lay in his berth, wide awake, in such as if the entire weight of Russia were verily crushing him down.

"Wherefore hast Thou afflicted Thy servant?" he repeated the words that Moses had addressed to God. "And wherefore have I not found favour in Thy sight, that Thou layest the burden of all this people upon me? Have I conceived all this people? Have I begotten them, that Thou shouldst say unto me, Carry them in thy bosom, as a nursing father beareth the sucking child, unto the land which Thou swarest unto their fathers? I am not able to bear all this people alone, because *it is* too heavy for *me*. And if Thou deal thus with me, kill me,

I pray Thee, out of hand, if I have found favour in Thy sight; and let me not see my wretchedness." [65]

Suddenly he again thought of his son, and felt that all this fearful weight, this dead sluggishness of Russia, was embodied in his son,—in him alone.

Finally, through an unbelievable effort of his will, he got himself in hand, summoned his orderly, dressed, embarked in his small sloop, and returned to the Palace, where he was awaited by the senators whom he had summoned for an investigation of their knavery and bribe-taking.

VI

Prince Menshikov, the Princes Jacob and Vassilii Dolgorukyi, Sheremetev, Shaphirov, Yaguzhinsky, Golovkin, Apraxin and others, were crowded in a little reception room, next to the royal turner's shop.

They were all in fear. They remembered how, two years ago, a pair of bribe-takers,—the Princes Volkonsky and Opukhtin,—were publicly knouted and had their tongues seared with heated irons. Strange rumors were transmitted in whispers,—that, apparently, officers of the guard and other persons of military rank had been designated as judges over the senators.

But, behind their fear, was the hope that the storm would blow over, and that everything would go on in the good old way. They reassured one another with utterances of ancient wisdom: "Who has not sinned before God? Who is not guilty before the Czar? Come, now, are they going to string up everybody? Every man does the best he can. There's not a living soul but longs for tidbits. Sinners honest, sinners mean, —not a soul but lives to sin."

Peter entered. His face was stern and hard-set, save for the gleaming of his eyes and a slight convulsive twitch in the left corner of his mouth. Without greeting anybody, without extending any invitation for them to sit down, he turned to the senators with a speech evidently premeditated:

"Gentlemen of the Senate! Whereas I have written and spoken to you so many times about your negligence and greediness, and contempt of civic laws; yet words are of no avail, and all *ukases* are nullified; therefore, I now, and for the last time, affirm: 'Tis vain to write laws if they be not observed, or to play with them as if they were cards in a game of solitaire,—which disregard of law is nowhere in the world as prevalent as with us. What, then, are the consequences of this? Seeing thievery going unpunished, it would be a rare man who would not be tempted; and so, little by little, all would come to despise the law, the people would be ruined, and the wrath of God provoked, and this, more than any private betrayal, can bring not only misfortune to the entire state but even its ultimate downfall. Therefore, it behooves us to punish bribe-takers, even as we ought to punish any man who violates his duty in time of battle, or a downright traitor to the state. . . ."

He spoke without looking into their eyes. Again he felt his impotence. All his words were about as effective as bombarding a wall with peas. In these submissive, frightened eyes, these humbly downcast eyes, was still the same thought: "Sinners honest, sinners mean,—not a soul but lives in sin."

"Henceforth let no one place hopes in his services, no matter what they might have been!" concluded Peter, and his voice began to quiver with wrath. "I hereby proclaim that no matter what the rank of the thief may be,—even if he be a senator,—he will be subject to court-martial. . . ."

"Such a thing cannot be!" began Prince Jacob Dolgorukyi, a corpulent old man, with long white mustaches on his bloated, purply-livid face,—his eyes, as clear as those of a child, were looking straight into the eyes of the Czar. "Such a thing cannot be, liege Lord,—soldiers cannot sit in judgment over senators. Thou wilt inflict an unheard of affront not only to our honor, but to the entire state of Russia!"

"Prince Jacob is right!" put in Boris Sheremetev, a Knight of the Order of Malta. "At the present day all Europe deems the men of Russia to be good knights. Wherefore, then, dost thou dishonor us, Sire, depriving us of our knightly rank? For we are not all thieves. . . ."

"Who among ye is no thief,—thou traitor?" shouted Peter, his face distorted with fury. "Or dost thou think I do not know ye? I know thee, brother,—I can see thee through and through! Were I to die this minute, thou wouldst be the first to stand up for that evil-doer, my son! Ye are all in cahoots with him!"

But again, through an unbelievable effort of his will, he downed his wrath. He sought out in the crowd Prince Menshikov, and uttered in a stifled, choked, but already calm voice:

"Alexandre, come with me!"

They went out together, into the turner's shop.

The Prince, a somewhat spare fellow, apparently fragile but in reality as strong as iron, and as mobile as quicksilver, with a thin, pleasant face and unusually lively, quick, intelligent eyes,—recalling that gamin vendor who, on a time, had shouted "Red-hot pies!"—darted through the door after the Czar, slinking just like a little dog which is about to be beaten.

The rather squat, stout Shaphirov was puffing and mopping the sweat off his face. The gaunt Golovkin, as long as a rail, was shaking all over, crossing himself, and whispering a prayer. Yaguzhinsky had slumped into a chair and was groaning; his stomach was queasy from fright.

But in proportion as the wrathful voice of the Czar, and the monotonously plaintive voice of Menshikov, issued from behind the door,—it was impossible to distinguish the words, —they were calming down. Some of them were even maliciously joyous: it wasn't the first time the Most Illustrious One had gotten his; his bones were rather sturdy; he had become used to the Czar's cudgel since his early years. It was nothing to him! He would manage to wriggle out of it somehow.

Suddenly noise, shouts and screams were heard on the other side of the door. Both halves of the door were flung wide open and Menshikov came flying out. His gold-embroidered frock was all in tatters; his blue Ribbon of St. Andrew was in shreds; the orders and stars on his breast were dangling, half-torn away; the wig made out of the Czar's own hair (Peter, at one time, as a mark of his friendship, had given him his hair every time he had it clipped) was knocked to one side; his face was all in blood. The Czar was pursuing him with a bared dirk and shouting frenziedly:

"I'll show thee, thou son of a bitch!"

"Petenka! Petenka!" the voice of the Czaritza rang out. She, as always, seemed to spring up from the very earth at the most necessary moment. She restrained him on the threshold, locked the door of the turner's shop, and, left alone with him, snuggled up against him with all her body and clung to him, hanging about his neck.

"Let me go, let me go! I'll kill him! . . . ." he was shouting in his fury.

But she embraced him, harder and harder, repeating:

"Petenka! Petenka! The Lord be with thee, dearest friend of my heart! Drop the little knife,—do drop it, now, before thou dost some harm. . . ."

Finally the dirk dropped out of his hand. He himself slumped into a chair. Fearful convulsions were contracting his members.

Just as at the time of the last meeting of father and son, Katenka perched on the arm of the chair, embraced Peter's head, clasped it to her bosom, and fell to stroking his hair softly, caressing and lulling him, as a mother might a babe; and little by little, under this quiet caress, he was calming down, his convulsions lessening. Occasionally a shudder would still shake his whole body, but it came at ever greater intervals. He no longer shouted, but merely moaned, as though he were sobbing,—weeping without tears:

" 'Tis hard,—oh, 'tis hard, Katenka! There is no more strength in me! . . . There is no one to think things over with,—never a helper, have I. I am always alone,—ever alone! . . . Can a man do everything, alone? Not even an angel, let alone a man! . . . Mine is an unbearable burthen! . . ."

His moans were becoming more and more subdued; finally they died out altogether,—he had fallen asleep. She listened to his breathing. Always, after such attacks, he slept very soundly, so that nothing could awaken him, as long as Katenka did not leave his side.

Still embracing his head with one hand, she explored and felt his bosom and within his frock with the other hand as though it, too, were caressing him, her fingers as nimble as those of a thief. Having felt a packet of letters in a side pocket she dragged it out, looked through its contents, saw a letter that was large and soiled,—most probably the anonymous one,—in a blue envelope, the red wax seal of which was unbroken. She surmised that this was the very one she sought, —a second report about Mons and herself, more dreadful than the first. Mons had warned her about this blue letter,—he himself had learned of it from the talk of some intoxicated orderlies.

Katenka was wonderstruck because her husband had not opened this letter. Or was he afraid of learning the truth?

Paling the least trifle, clenching her teeth hard, but without losing her presence of mind, she glanced into his face. His sleep was sweet,—like that of a little child after it has had its fill of weeping. Most gently she let his head rest against the back of the chair, unbuttoned a few buttons on her breast, crumpled up the letter, thrust it within the sweet valley of her breasts, bent down, lifted up the dirk, ripped the pocket in which the letters were lying as well as the skirt of the frock along the seam, in such a manner that these rips might be taken for chance holes, and restored the packet with the rest of the letters to their former place in his pocket. Should he notice the disappearance of the blue letter he was likely to think that it had fallen within the lining, and thence out through the hole below, thus getting lost. Holes were not unusual things in the much-worn clothing of the Czar.

Katenka finished all this in the twinkling of an eye. Then she again took Petenka's head, placed it on her bosom, and resumed stroking it most gently, caressing and lulling him, looking at the sleeping Titan even as a mother might at her sleeping child, or a lion-tamer at some ferocious beast she had subdued.

An hour later he awoke, lively and refreshed, as though nothing whatsoever had happened.

A dwarf, belonging to the Czar had died recently. His funeral was set for that very day,—one of those mock masquerade processions of which Peter was so fond. Katenka urged him to postpone the funeral until the morrow, and not to go anywhere else to-day, but to rest. But Peter would not heed her, ordered drums to be beaten, and flags to be put out as a general gathering signal; hurrying, as though it were a matter of the utmost importance, he got ready, dressed himself in a costume that was half mourning and half masquerade and went off.

VII

"Concerning monsters or freaks:

"Whereas monstrous births,—that is to say, freaks,—are known to occur among the different species of beasts and birds, even as among humankind, which freaks are collected in all countries as a matter of curiosity,—Therefore an *ukase* was issued several years ago, that such monsters be brought to us; but the ignorant keep such freaks secret, thinking that such freaks are born through the ministrations of the devil, or witchcraft and spells, which is impossible, since the sole Creator of every living thing is God and not the devil, to whom no dominion has been given over any creature; such births are due, rather, to internal injury, also to fear and the mother's thoughts during pregnancy, of which there are many examples: whatever causes fright in the mother also leaves its marks on the offspring. In view of all the foregoing, this *ukase* is again renewed, to the definite end that such human freaks, as well as those of cattle, and birds and beasts, shall be brought to the governor of each city or town; and they that bring such things shall be given pay therefor, to wit: for a human monster, ten rubles; for one among cattle or beasts, five; while a freak bird shall fetch three; this applies to dead monsters,—as for living monsters, one hundred rubles shall be paid for a human, while a freak among cattle or beasts shall fetch fifteen rubles; and a bird, seven rubles. But if it should be extraordinarily wondrous, even more shall be given. But should any, in violation of this *ukase,* conceal such freaks, they ought to be informed upon; and he that is found guilty shall be fined one-tenth of whatever he would have been paid for the freak or freaks, and such money shall be given to the informers. The aforementioned freaks, human as well as animal, should, when they die, be placed in spirits; but if there be no spirits, use wine of double strength, or, if need be, simply wine, and let the specimen be tightly sealed up, so that it spoil not; such wine shall be paid for separately, by our pharmacy."

Peter had loved his dwarf,—"a deliberate monster,"—and had arranged a magnificent funeral for him.

At the head walked thirty choristers, two by two,—all little boys. Behind them, in full vestments, with a censer in his hands, stalked a diminutive priest, who had been chosen out of all the priests in Peterburgh because of his small stature. Six small ponies, in black trappings reaching to the ground, drew the little coffin, almost like that of a child, upon a little catafalque, for all the world like a toy. Then, following solemnly, hand in hand, under the leadership of a diminutive marshal with an enormous baton, came twenty pairs of dwarfs, in long mourning mantles, trimmed with white crêpe, and the same number of female dwarfs,—all ranged according to their height, the smallest in front, the biggest in the back, on the manner of organ pipes,—hunch-backed, pot-bellied, pigeon-toed, wry-faced, bandy-legged, like the dogs bred for badger-baiting, and a multitude of other freaks,—not so much funny as frightful. On both sides of the procession, alongside of the dwarfs, walked giant grenadiers and the Czar's haiduks, with flaming torches and funereal tapers in their hands. One of these giants, dressed up in a child's pinafore, was guided along on leading-strings by two dwarfs who were the most diminutive of all and were also endowed with long gray beards; another giant, swaddled up like an infant at breast, was borne along on a small cart by six trained bears.

The procession was brought up by the Czar, with all his generals and senators. In the full-dress of a Dutch ship's drummer, he walked the whole way on foot, and, with the air of one engaged in a most necessary matter, kept on beating his drum.

The procession, followed by a mob, moved along the Nevsky Prospect, from the wooden bridge over the Fontannya River to the Yama Borough, where the cemetery was. People were gaping out of the windows and running out-doors; and, in a superstitious awe, the true Christian souls did not know whether to cross themselves or to spit over their left shoulders. As for the Germans, they were saying: "Such a procession one would hardly see anywhere save in Russia! . . ."

It was five o'clock in the evening. It was darkling fast. Snow was falling in large, wet flakes. Along both sides of the *perspective* two rows of denuded, small lindens and the low roofs of little houses gleamed whitely, because of the snow. The fog was thickening. And in the turbid, yellow fog, and the turbid, red light of the torches, this procession seemed delirium, a diabolical visitation. But the mob, even though it was afraid, ran along with it or followed behind, splashing through the mire and imparting to one another frightful rumors, also resembling delirium, and having to do with the unclean powers that, it would seem, had sprung up in Peterburgh.

Only the other night a sentry near the Trinity had heard a thumping, which was like to the sound of running feet, coming from the church refectory; and some one had run up and down the wooden ladder in the belfry, so that its rungs had quivered; while in the morning, when the sacristan went up to toll the bells, he saw that the step-ladder had been torn away, and that the bell-rope had been furdled into four lengths.

" 'Twas none other than the devil that did it all," some surmised.

"Not the devil, but a goblin," contradicted others.

A crone, who sold herrings on the Okhta, had seen this goblin, with her own eyes, sitting and spinning wool:

" 'Twas all naked, as thin as thin can be, and as black as black; while its little head was just *so* tiny, no bigger than a thimble, and you couldn't tell its upper body from a blade of straw."

"Is it not a hobgoblin, perhaps?" some one else asked.

"Hobgoblins don't live in churches," he was answered.

"But mayhap 'twas a strayed one? They're visited by a plague, now, the same as cows and dogs; that's why they are so mischievous."

"It means spring is coming on: in spring the hobgoblins shed their skins; when their old skin is peeling off, that's when they get frenzied."

"Whether it be a hobgoblin, or a devil, or just a plain goblin, there's just one thing sure,—'tis the unclean power!" they all decided.

In the turbidly yellow fog, and the turbidly red light of the torches, which made the monstrous shadows of the giants and the dwarfs dart about, this procession itself seemed sprung of the powers of evil, in a Peterburgh not of this world.

Still more fearful tidings were going around. On the Finland side of the river some priest or other, "in order to commit a certain madness," had togged himself out in a goatskin with horns, which skin had immediately grown to his skin, and, in this guise, he would be carried that night on a cart to his execution. Svarykin, the son of a dragoon, did sell his soul to the devil, who had turned up near the Foundry Court, in the guise of a German, and the compact had been signed with blood. In the Apothecary Garden, in the cemetery, resurrection men had opened a grave, breaking the coffin open with pick-axes, and had started dragging the dead man out by his feet; but, before they had succeeded, grew frightened and took to their heels; in the morning some one caught sight of the legs sticking up out of the grave,—and a rumor of the resurrection of the dead swept the town. In the Tartar Borough, beyond the fortified Crown Works, an infant had been born with a cow's horn where its nose should have been; while at the Custom House the monstrous birth had been that of a piglet with a human face.

"It bodes no good for the towns where such births happen!"

Somewhere a rooster with five legs had popped up. A rain of blood had fallen on the Ladoga; the earth had quaked and had roared like an ox; there had been three suns in the sky.

"Ill times are coming,—ill times are coming!" everybody repeated.

"Peterburgh is bound to be desolated!"

"And not Peterburgh alone,—the end of the whole world is coming! 'Tis the Judgment Day! Antichrist!"

Having had his fill of listening to these stories, a little boy, whom his mother was dragging by the hand through the crowd, suddenly began to weep, screaming from fright. A certain woman in tatters, with the face of a half-wit,—probably an hysterical case,—began calling in an inhuman voice. She was taken with all speed to a nearby court-yard. The Czar was in no mood for jesting with such hysterical women, —he exorcised their fiends with a *knout*. "The tail of a *knout* is longer than the fiend's tail!" he would say when reports were made to him concerning "superstitious pranks."

Among the grandees and senators there were also many frightened faces. Just before the setting out of the procession Shaphirov had handed to the Czar the letters from Tolstoi and the Czarevich, just come by courier from Naples. The sovereign had put them in his pocket, without breaking the seals. Probably he did not want to read them before witnesses. Shaphirov, however, already knew the frightful news, through a brief note he had received from Tolstoi. As if on wings the tidings sped from one to another:

"The Czarevich is coming back!"—"That Judas, Peter Tolstoi, has lured him back,—the Czarevich won't be the first he has gobbled up."—"Batiushka, I hear, has promised him that he can marry Euphrosyne."—"Marry her? A likely thing! Thou hast another guess coming! He is fated for a quick hanging and not for a wedding."—"But what if through God's grace there be a marriage!"—"That marriage will be solemnized on Goat's Swamp; while for ring and for frock he'll have the ax and the block!"—"What a fool, what a fool! He'll come to his end, and all in vain!"—"He's a bullock that will have but a short halter!"—"He won't have his head on his shoulders long!"—"He's headed straight for the butcher's mallet!"—"But, mayhap, they may e'en spare him, for he is no stranger, after all, but of the Czar's own blood: even the viper doth not eat her young. Mayhap, he'll be but taught a lesson, and forgiven?"—" 'Tis too late to teach him,—his baby-clothes don't fit him any more."—"They taught him not while he could be laid across a bench,—and now, when he's as long as a bench, they'll never teach him!" "Come into my mortar and nestle, and I'll caress thee with my pestle,—there's the whole gist of his learning!"— "They'll nurse this poor child along, so's there won't be a peep out of him,—and then knock him over the head!"— "Well, I guess we'll all be in such hot water, too, that we won't be able to see God's daylight."—" 'Tis an ill hap, brethren,—'tis an ill hap; even if one had two heads, he would lose them both!"

And in the throng of the grandees, they were all repeating, even as in the throng of the commonalty:

"Ill times are coming! Ill times are coming!"

But the Czar kept on and on, tramping through the mire and beating his drum, drowning the dismal chanting: "Rest thou with the saints. Eternal memory be thine!"

The fog was thickening. Everything was melting in it, dissolving, becoming phantasmal,—and it seemed that, at any second, the entire city, with all its people, and houses, and streets, would float upward, together with the fog, and scatter like a dream.

VIII

Upon returning to the Summer Palace from the funeral, Peter embarked in a small wherry, ferried across the dark, nocturnal Neva,—alone, without any rowers, working the oars himself,—and moored near a small wooden wharf, on the opposite shore. Here, near the very river, not far from the Cathedral of the Trinity, stood a small squat house, one of the first houses built by Dutch carpenters, at the very founding of Peterburgh,—Peter's first palace, resembling the poor hovels of the shipwrights of Saardarn. It was built of pine logs, chopped down right here, in the wild Keivussari swamp on the Island of Birches; it was painted in oil paint to resemble brick, and was roofed with shingles that resembled tiles.

The rooms were low-ceiled, cramped, and only three in all; to the right of the entry was a small office; to the left was the dining-room, and, next to it, the bedroom,—the tiniest of the three, approximately twelve feet in length and nine in width, —barely room enough to turn around in. The furnishings, although exceedingly simple, were nevertheless homy and neat, after the Dutch manner. The ceiling and walls were lined with whitened canvas; the windows were broad and low, glazed with small leaded panes and having oak shutters upon iron bolts. The doors did not conform to Peter's stature,—he had to bend his head to avoid striking the lintel.

After the erection of the Summer and Winter Palaces this house had stood vacant. Only on rare occasions did the Czar pass a night in it,—whenever he wanted to be left absolutely alone, without even Katenka.

Upon coming into the entry he prodded awake the orderly, who lay snoring on some felt, ordered him to bring a light, passed into the little office, and, turning the key in the door and placing the candle on the table, sat down in an armchair and took out of his pocket the letters of Tolstoi, Rumyantzev and the Czarevich. But, before breaking open the seal, he paused, as though in indecision, listening to the measured, reverberating chiming of the clock in the belfry of the Cathedral of the Trinity. It struck nine. The last sound died away, and then a silence fell,—such a silence as in the days when Peterburgh was not, and this poor house had been surrounded only by unending forests and impassable morasses.

Finally he broke open the seals. As he read, his face paled the least trifle, and his hands began to shake; but when he had read the last words in the letter of the Czarevich: "I shall leave Naples within a few days, to go to thee in Sanct Peterburgh, my liege Lord,"—his breath was cut short for very joy. He could read no further. He crossed himself.

Was not this, then, a miracle of God? Only a little while ago he had been in the last extremity, had despaired, had thought that God had forsaken him, had withdrawn from him forever,—and lo, the hand of the Lord was sustaining him again. He felt himself strong and vigorous once more, as though he had regained his youth and were ready for any toil or exploit. Then he let his head drop, and, looking into the flame of the candle, fell into deep thought. When his son would return, what was to be done with him? "Kill him!" he had formerly thought in his rage, when he had no hopes of his returning; but now, when he knew that his son would return, his rage had become extinguished, and for the first time he asked himself,—calmly, reasoningly: What is to be done?

Suddenly he recalled the words of the first letter he had dispatched to Tolstoi and Rumyantzev in Naples: "I promise, before God and His Judgment, that there shall be no punishment, but that I shall evince better love for thee, if thou wilt return." Now, when his son had come to believe this oath, it attained frightful force.

But in what manner should he fulfill it?

To forgive his son,—did it mean to forgive all the others as well, who were just as much as he traitors and evil-doers against the Czar, and the Fatherland? All these useless manikins,—bribe-takers, thieves, parasites, bigots, hypocrites, long-beards,—would join forces with him, and reach such a state of fearlessness that there would be no threat strong enough for them. They would bring about the utter downfall of the whole state. And, if the son mocked his living father so, what would happen after the father's death? He would ruin and dissipate everything,—would not leave one stone standing upon another,—would bring Russia to perdition!

Nay, even though he were to break his oath, yet forgive him he could not.

That meant an investigation again,—and again torture, burnings at the stake, executioners' axes, headsmen's blocks, and blood.

He recalled an occasion, during the executions of the Streltzi, when, as he was riding on horseback to the Red Square where three hundred heads were to fall that day, he had been met by the patriarch with a wonder-working ikon of the Mother of God,—the man of God implored him to spare the mutineers. The Czar had bowed to the ikon but had thrust the patriarch aside with a wrathful hand, saying: "Wherefore hast thou come here? I revere the Mother of God no less than thou dost, but my duty commands me to spare the good while punishing the evil. So get thee gone, old man! I know what I do."

He had known how to answer the patriarch,—but what answer would he make to God?

And there appeared before him, as in a vision, an endless row of heads, lying near the Brow Place, upon a long log instead of a block, with their heads down and the napes of their necks up: heads flaxen-fair, rufous, black, gray, bald, curly. . . . In a gay mood, having just come from a drinking bout, he, together with Danilich and other guests, is walking about with an ax in his hands, with sleeves rolled up, like a headsman, and is lopping these heads off, one after the other. And when he grows tired the guests take the ax from him, each one in his turn, and also do a little lopping. All have become blood-tipsy. Their garments are bespattered with blood; there are pools of blood on the ground; one's feet slip in the blood. Suddenly, one of these heads, when he has already swung his ax over it, very gently lifts itself up, turns about, and looks straight into his eyes. 'Tis he,—Alësha!

"Alëshenka, my own little boy!"—Another image came before him: how, on returning from abroad, he had secretly made his way by night into the bedchamber of the Czarevich, and bending over his little bed, had taken the sleepy little boy in his arms, and had embraced him, and kissed him, feeling through the boy's shirt the warmth of his little body.

"Kill his son!"—only now did he understand what this meant. A feeling came over him that this was the most fearful, the most important thing in all his life,— of greater importance than Sophia, the Streltzi, Europe, learning, the army, the fleet, Peterburgh, Poltava; that here a matter eternal was being decided: upon one scale of the balances would be placed all he had done that was great, that was good; on the other, —the blood of his son; and who knew which would outweigh the other? Would not all his glory grow dim from this bloody stain? What would Europe say,—what would posterity say of the perjurer, of the filicide? For any one who did not know all the circumstances it would be difficult to determine the Czar's innocence. And who did know all the circumstances?

And can man, before God, take upon his soul such a sin as the shedding of kindred blood,—even though it be for the good of his fatherland?

But then, what, what was to be done? To forgive his son meant to bring about the ruin of Russia; to put him to death, —bringing about his own. He felt that he would never resolve this problem.

Aye,—and it was impossible to resolve it alone. But who could help him? The Church? *Whatever ye shall bind on earth shall be bound in heaven: and whatsoever ye shall loose on earth, shall be loosed in heaven.*[66] Thus had it been formerly. But now,—where was the Church? And the Patriarch? He no longer was. He, the Czar, had himself abrogated the Patriarchate. Or was he to resort to the Metropolitan, to "Stepka, the Serf," who, falling down to the ground, himself proffers a petition to the sovereign? Or the Administrator of Affairs Spiritual, the knave Fedosska, with the other archpriests, who are "so bridled that one may lead them where one wills"? Whatever he would tell them, that would they do. He himself was the Patriarch,—himself the Church. He stood alone before God.

And, madman that he was, what had he rejoiced over, just now? Aye,—the hand of the Lord had been stretched out towards him, and had weighed down upon him with a frightful weight. 'Tis a fearsome, fearsome thing to fall into the hands of the living God!

It was as though an abyss had unrolled at his feet, and a horror were wafted therefrom,—a horror from which every hair on his head stirred. He covered his face with his hands.

"Withdraw from me, O Lord! Deliver me from blood guiltiness, O God, thou God of my salvation!" [67]

Then he arose and went into his bedchamber, where, in a corner, over the head of his bed, a never-extinguished lampad glowed warmly before the miracle-working ikon of Our Saviour of the Miracles,—it had been wrought for presentation to Czar Alexei Mikhailovich by his favorite ikonographer, Simon Ushakov, and at one time had been jealously guarded in the upper entry of the Kremlin Palace. This was a Russian adaptation from an immemorial, ancient Byzantine image: according to tradition, when the Lord was ascending Golgotha, He, languishing under His crucificial load, had wiped the sweat from His face with a frontlet, and His Visage had been imprinted thereon.

Since the day that Peter's mother, the Czaritza Nathalia Kyrillovna, had blessed her son with this Image, he nevermore parted with it. In all his expeditions and travels, on ships and in tents, at the founding of Peterburgh and on the battlefields of Poltava,—everywhere the Image had been with him.

On entering the bedchamber he added oil to the lamp and mended its wick. The flame took on a brighter glow, and, amid the gold that framed the dark Visage in its wreath of thorns, the diamonds began to gleam like tears, the rubies,—like blood.

He got down on his knees and began to pray.

He was so accustomed to this ikon that by now he was almost unconscious of it, and, without himself realizing it, always addressed his prayer to the Father and not to the Son; not to the God, dying, pouring forth His blood on Golgotha, but to the Living God, stalwart, and strong in battle,—the awesome Warrior, the righteous Bestower of Victories,—to Him Who says of Himself, through the lips of the prophet: *I have trodden the wine-press alone; and of the people there was none with me: for I will tread them in mine anger, and trample them in my fury; and their blood shall be sprinkled upon my garments, and I will stain all my raiment.*[68]

But now, when he raised up his gaze to the ikon, and was about to address his prayer, as always, past the Son to the Father, he could not. It was as though he beheld, for the first time the sorrowful Visage in the wreath of thorns, and this Visage had come to life and had looked into his soul with its meek gaze, it was as though he had come to understand, for the first time, that which he had heard about since childhood and which he had never understood: the significance of Son and Father.

And suddenly he recalled an awful ancient story, also about a father and a son:

"And it came to pass . . . that God did tempt Abraham, and said unto him . . . Take now thy son, thine only *son* Isaac, whom thou lovest . . . and offer him . . . for a burnt offering. . . . And Abraham built an altar. . . . And Abraham stretched forth his hand, and took the knife to slay his son." [69]

This was merely an earthly prototype of a still more awful heavenly sacrifice. For God had so loved the world, that He spared not His only begotten Son; [70] and through the ever-flowing Blood of the Lamb, through the Blood of His Son, the wrath of the Father is being appeased.

The Czar sensed about all this a mystery, near and most urgent, but so awful that he durst not think of it. His thought was exhausted, as if in madness.

Did God desire, or did He not, that he punish his son? Would this blood be forgiven him, or would he be called to account for it? And what if not he alone be called to account, but all his children, and his grandchildren,—and all of Russia?

"May this blood be upon my head, upon my head, alone! Punish me, God,—but spare Russia!"

BOOK NINE

THE WARLOCK

I

THE Czarevich was watching the door through which Peter was to enter.

The tiny reception room in the Palace of the Transfiguration (a palace, almost as humble as the Czar's little house in Peterburgh) was flooded with the yellow sunlight of February. The view through the windows was familiar to the Czarevich since childhood,—a snowy field with black jackdaws, gray barrack-walls, a prison building, a rampart of earth with pyramids of cannon-balls, a sentry-booth and a motionless sentry therein, silhouetted against the limpidly-green sky. The sparrows on the window-sills were chirruping as if it were already spring. Clear drops dripped from the icicles, like tears. It was the hour before dinner. One could smell the cabbage-dumplings. The pendulum of the wall-clock ticked monotonously in the silence.

During the voyage from Italy to Russia the Czarevich had been calm, even gay, but seemingly in a half-doze, or coma. He did not altogether understand what was going on,—where he was being taken and for what purpose.

But now,—sitting with Tolstoi in the reception room, and staring at the sinister door, just as on that night in the royal palace in Naples, during his delirium,—he seemed to be awakening, coming to a realization of things, and, just as at that time, he was trembling all over, with an incessant, slight tremor, just as though he were in a severe chill. Now he would make the sign of the cross and whisper prayers; now he would seize Tolstoi's arm:

"Peter Andreievich,—oh, Peter Andreievich,—what is going to happen, my own? I feel frightened, frightened! . . ."

Tolstoi was reassuring him in his velvety voice:

"Be of good cheer, Your Highness! The sword will not fall upon a repentant head. By God's grace everything will come right,—smoothly and gently, in peace and quiet. . . ."

The Czarevich was listening to him, and, not to forget, was mentally repeating the speech he had prepared:

"Batiushka, I cannot justify myself in anything, but, in tears, implore thy gracious forgiveness and paternal consideration, inasmuch as, save in God and in thy graciousness towards me, I have no other hopes, and give myself up in all things to thy will."

Familiar steps were heard beyond the door. The door was opened. Peter entered.

Alexei jumped up, swayed, and would have fallen flat on his face, had Tolstoi not supported him.

Before the Czarevich flashed two faces, as if at the instant of a warlock's transformation: an unfamiliar, fearful one, like a death-mask, and a kindred, endearing one,—that of his father, but as he remembered him from his earliest childhood.

The Czarevich approached him and was about to fall down at his feet, but Peter stretched out his arms towards him, embraced him, and clasped him to his breast.

"Greetings, Alësha! Well, glory be to God,—glory be to God! At last we have managed to see each other."

Alexei felt the familiar touch of his father's plump, shaven cheeks, and his familiar odor,—a mixture of strong tobacco and of perspiration; he saw the big, dark, clear eyes,—so awesome, so endearing; the splendidly-beautiful, somewhat shy smile upon the sinuous, almost femininely-exquisite lips. And, forgetting his long speech, he merely babbled:

"Forgive me, Batiushka. . . ."

And suddenly he burst into irrestrainable sobs, as he kept on repeating:

"Forgive me! Forgive me! . . ."

His heart had melted instantly, like ice cast upon fire.

"Come, come, Alëshenka! . . ."

His father was stroking his hair, kissing his forehead, his lips, his eyes, with the tenderness of a mother. But Tolstoi, as he regarded these caresses, was reflecting:

"The falcon will kiss the chick till there will not be as much as a feather left of it!"

At a sign from the Czar he vanished. Peter led his son into the dining-room. The little bitch, Lizetta, began to growl at first; but, after recognizing the Czarevich, fell to wagging her tail in embarrassment and licking his hand. The table was set for two. The orderly brought all the courses at once and walked out. They were left alone. Peter poured out two small glasses of anisette.

"To thy health, Alësha!"

They clinked glasses. The Czarevich's hands shook so that he spilt half his glass.

Peter prepared for him his own favorite snack,—a slice of black bread with butter, sprinkled with chopped onion and garlic. He cut the bread into halves, one for himself, one for his son.

"See how thin thou hast grown upon foreign fare," he said, scrutinizing his son. "Bide awhile,—we shall fatten thee speedily,—thou wilt fill out! Russian bread, now, is more nourishing than the German."

He helped him to the various dishes, adding rhymed adages:

"When glasses click, 'tis not like a stick against a stick. All good things go in threes. Make it four,—your guests will roar."

The Czarevich ate little, but drank a great deal, and was fast becoming tipsy,—not so much from the wine, however, as from joy.

His timidity still recurred; he could not recover his full senses,—could not believe his eyes and his ears. Yet his father was speaking with him so simply and gayly that it was impossible not to believe. Peter questioned him about everything he had seen and heard in Italy,—about the army and navy,—about the Pope and the Kaiser. He jested as one bosom crony with another.

"I must say thy taste is not at all bad," he winked at the Czarevich, laughing. "Aphrosiya is one fine lass! If only some ten years were to fall off my shoulders, the son, like as not, would have to watch out for his daddy, so's not to get horns. Evidently an apple doesn't fall far from its apple tree. The daddy took up with a washerwoman, and the son with a charwoman—they do be saying that Aphrosiya used to wash floors in the house of the Viyazemskys. But then, Katenka, too, used to wash clothes. . . . But art thou hankering to marry her?"

"If thou wouldst permit it, Batiushka."

"Well, what am I to do with thee? I promised, never fear, —that means I must permit it."

Peter poured out some red wine into crystal goblets. They raised and brought them together. The crystal tinkled. The wine, in the light of a sunbeam, took on the red glow of blood.

"To peace,—to eternal friendship!" said Peter.

Each drained his glass quickly to the very bottom, at a single draught.

The Czarevich's head was spinning. It was just as though he were flying. The heart within him now swooned, now pounded,—it would burst apart any second, it seemed, and he would instantly die from joy. The past, the present, the future,—everything vanished. He remembered,—saw,—felt one thing alone: his father loved him. What if it were but for an instant? Were it necessary to accept anew the torture of his whole life for one such instant, he would accept it.

And the Czarevich felt a desire to tell all, to confess everything.

Peter, as though surmising his thought, placed his hand upon his son's, with a gentle caress.

"Do tell me, Alësha, about thy flight."

The Czarevich felt that his destiny was being decided. And suddenly he comprehended clearly that which he had been striving not to think of all this time, ever since that moment when he had decided to return to his father. He had to do one of two things: tell all, give up his accomplices, and become a traitor; or seal his lips concerning everything, and let a bottomless pit again yawn between him and his father,— let a dead wall again rise up between them.

He kept silent, with his eyes downcast, fearing lest he see once more, instead of the kindred face he knew, that other unfamiliar, awesome face, which was like a death-mask.

Finally he arose, and, walking up to his father, fell on his knees before him. Lizetta, who had been dozing on a cushion at Peter's feet, got up and walked away, yielding her place to the Czarevich. He sank to the cushion. If he could but lie like this forever, at the feet of his father, like a dog, looking into his eyes and awaiting a kind pat.

"I'll tell thee everything, Batiushka,—only do thou forgive everybody, even as thou hast forgiven me!"—he lifted up his eyes with infinite supplication.

His father bent toward him and placed his hands on his son's shoulders, with still the same gentle caress.

"Harken, Alësha. How am I to forgive, when I know not the offense, nor the offenders? I can forgive for myself,—but not for the Fatherland. God will demand a reckoning thereof. He who winks at evil doth himself work evil. One thing I do promise: those whom thou shalt name I shall pardon; but to those whose guilt thou shalt conceal the severest punishment shall be meted out. And therefore thou wilt be no informer, but rather an intercessor for thy friends. Tell everything, then,—be not afraid. I shan't wrong anybody. We shall reason it out together. . . ."

Alexei kept silent. Peter embraced him, clasped his head to him, and with a profound sigh, added:

"Ah, Alësha, Alësha, if thou couldst but see my heart, couldst know my sorrow! Heavy is my heart,—most heavy, my little one! . . . None have I to help me. I am ever alone,—ever alone. All are enemies, all are evil-doers. Do thou, at least, take pity upon thy father. Be my friend. Or dost thou not want to,—dost thou not love me? . . ."

"I do, I do love thee, dear father, my own!" whispered the Czarevich, still with the same bashful tenderness as in his childhood, when his father would come to him in the night, secretly, and pick him up, a sleepy little boy, in his arms. "I shall tell everything,—everything; ask me! . . ."

But when his son had finished, Peter still waited for some revelation of greater importance. He was seeking for a plot, yet of plot there was none. There were merely word, rumors, gossip,—elusive phantasms that one could never seize upon as a pretext for a real investigation.

The Czarevich was assuming all the guilt himself and exculpating all the others.

"I, in my cups, would always utter all sorts of lying words, and could not keep my tongue behind my teeth in the company of others; I could not refrain from seditious talk, and, since I trust people, I gave a free rein to my idle hopes and fancies."

"Outside of words, was there not a plan of action, of inciting the people to rise up in revolt, or of making thee heir to the throne, through armed force?"

"There was nothing of the sort, Batiushka,—God sees there was naught! 'Twas all idle talk."

"Did thy mother know of thy flight?"

"I think not. . . ." And, after a little thought, he added: "I do not really know about that."

Suddenly he fell silent, letting his eyes drop. He recalled the visions, the prophecies of Dositheus, Bishop of Rostov, and of other holy ancients,—prophecies and visions his mother believed in and rejoiced over: concerning the downfall of Peterburgh, the death of Peter, her son's ascension to the throne. Should he speak thereof? Should he betray his mother? His heart contracted with a deathly sorrow. He came to feel that it was impossible to speak of this. And, too, Batiushka was not even asking him about that. What concern was that of his? Was such a fellow as his father to be afraid of old wives' ravings?

"Is this all? Or art thou keeping something back?" asked Peter.

"There is one other thing, but I know not how to tell it. I am afraid. . . ."

He clung closely to his father, hiding his face on his breast.

"Speak on. 'Twill be easier for thee. Utter thy thoughts and purge thy heart, as if thou wert at sacred confessional."

"When thou wast ill," the Czarevich whispered in his ear, "I thought thou wouldst die, and did rejoice thereat, I did wish thy death. . . ."

Peter, thrusting him away with the utmost gentleness, looked straight into his eyes, and saw in them that which he had never before beheld in human eyes.

"Didst thou plan my death with anybody?"

"Nay, nay, nay!" exclaimed the Czarevich, with such horror in his face and voice that his father believed him.

They gazed into each other's eyes in silence,—and their gazes were alike. And in their faces, although they were so different, there was yet a resemblance. They reflected and intensified each other to infinity, like two facing mirrors.

Suddenly the Czarevich smiled a feeble smile, and said, simply, but with such a strange, unfamiliar voice that it semed as though it were not he himself who was speaking, but some other being, at a distance, who was talking through him:

"Why, I know, Batiushka,—perhaps thou canst not forgive me, after all. Then do not. Punish me, slay me. I myself would die for thee. Do but thou love me,—love me always! and let no one know thereof. Thou and I alone. Thou and I. . . ."

His father, making no reply, covered his face with his hands.

The Czarevich was looking at him as though he were expecting something.

At last Peter took his hands away from his face, again bent toward his son, and, clasping his head with both his hands, kissed it without a word,—and the Czarevich thought he saw tears in the eyes of his father, for the first time in his life. Alexei wanted to say something else, but Peter quickly arose and went out.

On that same evening Father Balaam, his new father-confessor, came to the Czarevich.

Upon his arrival in Moscow Alexei had requested that his former father-confessor, Father Jacob Ignatiev, be allowed to see him; but his request had been refused, and Father Balaam had been appointed instead. He was a little old man, "of the simplest,—for all the world like a chick," to quote Tolstoi's jocose description of him. But the Czarevich was glad to get even him,—so that he might but confess himself as speedily as he could.

In his confession he repeated everything he had just told his father; but he also added that which he had concealed from him: concerning his mother, the Czaritza Avdothea, his aunt, the Czarevna Maria, and his uncle, Abraham Lopukhin, and about their common desire for "a speedy consummation," the death of Batiushka.

"Thou shouldst tell thy father the truth," remarked Father Balaam, and began to hurry and bustle, in an odd manner.

Something flashed between them,—queer, eerie, but so fleetingly that the Czarevich could not know, even himself, whether this had been something actual, or whether he had merely imagined it.

II

The second day after the first meeting between Peter and Alexei, on the morning of Monday, the third of February, in the year 1718, the ministers, senators, generals, arch-priests and others holding either secular or clerical posts, were ordered to convene in the Administrative Department, —the Audience Hall of the old Kremlin Palace,—to hear the manifesto of the Czarevich's abdication of the throne, and to take the oath of allegiance to the new heir, Peter Petrovich.

Battalions of the Transfiguration life-guards were stationed within the Kremlin,—throughout the squares, palace galleries and staircases,—there were apprehensions of an uprising.

All that remained of the old Palace in the Audience Hall was the fresco on the ceiling,—"the stars in their courses, the twelve months, and other heavenly motions." Everything else was new: panels of Dutch tapestry; crystal chandeliers; straight-backed chairs; narrow pier-glasses. In the middle of the hall, under a canopy of red silk, on a dais led up to by three steps, stood the Czar's Seat,—a gilded armchair, with the keys of St. Peter and the two-headed eagle embroidered in gold upon its dark-scarlet velvet.

The oblique rays of the sun fell through the windows upon the white wigs of the senators and the black cowls of the arch-priests. All faces betrayed that fear and that feral curiosity which can be seen in any mob witnessing an execution.

A drum began to beat. The crowd swayed and parted. The Czar entered, and took his seat upon the throne.

Two stalwart guards of the Transfiguration, with their swords bared, led in the Czarevich, as if he were a convict. Without a wig and without a sword, in a simple black suit, pale and yet calm and seemingly in deep thought, he walked without hurrying, his head downcast. Upon approaching the throne and beholding his father, he smiled a gentle smile, reminiscent of his grandfather, Alexei, the Most Pacific Czar.

Lanky, narrow-shouldered, his narrow face framed in the scandent locks of his straight, smooth hair, looking something like a village pettifogger, or like an ikon of Alexei, the Man of God, in the midst of these new Peterburgh faces, he seemed aloof, a stranger to everything, as if he were a visitant from some other world, or a specter of old Muscovy. And, through the curiosity, through the fear, pity for this specter flickered on many faces.

He halted near the throne, without knowing what to do.

"On your knees, on your knees, and say what thou hast memorized," Tolstoi ran up behind him and whispered in his ear.

The Czarevich sank to his knees and uttered in a loud, calm voice:

"Most Gracious Liege Lord, Batiushka! Inasmuch as I have come to realize my offense before you, both as my parent and my liege Lord, I did write a letter, acknowledging my guilt, and did send it from Naples; and so, even now, I repeat the same acknowledgment,—that I, having forgotten the duty of a son and a subject, sought flight, and submitted myself to the protection of the Kaiser, and did ask him to protect me,—in which matter I implore your gracious forgiveness and pardon."

And, not in accordance with court ceremony, but merely from the depths of his heart, he bowed to his father's very feet.

At a sign from the Czar, Vice-Chancellor Shaphirov began reading the manifesto, which on that very same day would be read to the people in the Red Square.

"We trust that the greater part of our faithful subjects know with what zeal and care we strove to educate our firstborn, Alexei. But all this effort proved of no avail, and the seeds of learning fell upon stony ground, inasmuch as he not only did not pursue learning, but actually hated it, nor did he evince any inclination whatsoever, either towards military or civic affairs, preferring always the society of dissolute and base people, whose ways of life were coarse and unregenerate."

Alexei was hardly listening. His eyes sought the eyes of his father. But the latter was looking past him with an unmoving, unfathomable gaze.

" 'Tis but acting, dissimulation!" the Czarevich was reassuring himself. "Now, though thou wert to revile me, though thou wert to beat me, I yet know that thou lovest me!"

"And upon Our seeing his stubbornness in keeping to such evil courses," Shaphirov went on reading, "we did make it known to him, that, should he not follow Our wishes in the future, We would deprive him of the succession. And We did grant him time to amend his ways. But he, having forgot fear and the commandments of God, which command obedience to all parents, to say nothing of potentates, did repay Us for these many said cares and good wishes towards him with unheard-of ingratitude; for when, upon Our departure to the land of Denmark, on certain military matters, We left him in Sanct Peterburgh, and thereafter wrote him to come to Us in Copenhagen, to participate in Our military forces and for the better training in the arts of war, Our son, instead of going to Us, did go off and give himself up to the protection of the Kaiser, taking along with him money and a certain woman, bedding and tumbling the same, without the bonds of wedlock; and, uttering many unjust slanders against Us, both as his parent and his Liege Lord, did implore the Kaiser that he not only conceal him from Us, but even lend his armed force against Us, as if We were an enemy and persecutor of his, from whom he feared meeting his death. And what ignominy and dishonor before the whole world he did bring upon Us and all Our state by his action, any one can judge, inasmuch as it would be difficult to find a similar example even in history! And although he, Our son, is deserving of death for his crimes, We, however, taking commiseration upon him within Our paternal heart, do forgive him, and exempt him from any punishment. However—"

Breaking in on the reading, the hoarse and awesome voice of Peter rang out, filled with such wrath and sorrow that all ceremony seemed to vanish, and all suddenly understood the horror of that which was taking place:

"I cannot leave such an heir, who would dissipate all that

which his father had won with the aid of God, and who would cast down the glory and honor of the Russian people; besides that, I would dread God's judgment were I to entrust the rule to one whom I know to be unworthy! As for thee . . ."

He gave the Czarevich such a look that the latter's heart sank: it seemed to him that this was no longer acting.

"As for thee,—remember this: even though I forgive thee, still, shouldst thou not declare everything and conceal aught, and should the same become known subsequently,—do not blame me: the pardon will not be a pardon then. Thy punishment will be death!"

Alexei had just lifted his hands and was all drawn to his father, wanting to say something, to cry out,—but the Czar was again looking past him with his immovable, unfathomable gaze. At a sign from the Czar, Shaphirov went on with his reading:

"And therefore, having regard for Our government, and Our faithful subjects, We, through our paternal authority, and as absolute monarch, do deprive him, Our son Alexei, for the said offenses and crimes, of the succession after us to the throne of all the Russias, even though there be not a single person of Our family left after Us. And We designate and proclaim as Our heir to the said throne Our other son, Peter, even though he be not of age, inasmuch as We have no other heir who is of age, and adjure Our son, by Our parental vow, that he seek not the said succession. We also desire all Our faithful subjects, and all the people of Russia, to hold Our son, Peter, appointed by Us as Our successor, as the lawful heir, in accordance with this Our express wish and determination; and that they affirm this promise before the holy altar, upon the Holy Evangel, and by kissing the Cross. As for those who at any time oppose this Our wish, and shall henceforth hold Our son Alexei as the heir, and shall render him aid with that end in view,—We do pronounce them traitors to Us and to Our Fatherland."

The Czar got up, and, stepping down from his throne, ordered all those present to go to the Cathedral of the Assumption, to kiss the Cross, without waiting for him.

When all, with the exception of Tolstoi, Shaphirov, and several other dignitaries nearest the Czar, had moved toward

the exit, and the hall began to empty, Peter said to Alexei:
"Come on!"

They passed together through the foyer of the Administrative Chambers and into the Secret Closet of the Judicial Chamber,—in which closet, in the days of old, the Czars of Muscovy, hidden behind hangings of taffeta, used to eavesdrop upon ambassadorial deliberations. This was a tiny room, somewhat in the nature of a cell, with bare walls and small windows of mica, admitting an amber-yellow light,— the light of an eternal evening, as it were. In a corner a never-extinguished lampad glowed before a dark-visaged image of the Saviour, in a wreath of thorns and with a meek, sorrowful gaze.

Peter closed the door and walked up to his son. Again, as at the time in Naples, during his delirium, and only the other day, in the Cathedral of the Transfiguration, the Czarevich was all a-tremble with an incessant, quick tremor, as though he had a severe chill. Yet he still had hopes,—lo! at any moment his father would embrace him, caress him, tell him that he loved him,—and all these fears would be ended forever.

"I know that thou lovest me! I know that thou lovest me!" he kept on repeating to himself, as though it were an incantation. Yet, notwithstanding, his heart was pounding in terror. He let his eyes drop and durst not lift them up, feeling upon himself the heavy, intent gaze of his father. Both were silent. It was very quiet.

"Hast thou heard," Peter at last uttered, "what has just been proclaimed before all the people,—that if thou dost conceal aught, 'twill mean thy death?"

"I have heard, Batiushka."

"And thou hast naught to add to that which thou didst make known three days ago?"

The Czarevich remembered about his mother, and again felt that he would not betray her, even though his instant death impended.

"There is naught," he managed to say, barely audibly, as though it were not he himself who had spoken but some one else for him.

"So,—there is naught?" repeated Peter.

Alexei kept silent.

"Speak! . . ."

Everything was growing dark before the eyes of the Czarevich; his legs were giving way under him. But again he answered, as though it were not he himself speaking but some one else speaking for him.

"There is naught."

"Thou liest!" cried out Peter, clutching him by the shoulder and squeezing it so that it seemed as if the bones would turn to putty. "Thou liest! Thou hast kept back everything concerning thy mother, thy aunt, thy uncle, Dositheus of Rostov,—about their whole accursed nest, the root from which all this evil-working sedition has sprung! . . ."

"Who has told thee, Batiushka?" the Czarevich babbled, and looked up at him for the first time.

"Aye, is it not the truth?" his father looked his son straight in the eyes. The hand on Alexei's shoulder was becoming heavier,—ever heavier. Suddenly the Czarevich swayed like a reed under this weight and fell at his father's feet.

"Forgive! Forgive! For 'tis my mother! My own mother! . . ."

Peter bent toward him and raised his fists above Alexei's head, swearing with maternal oaths. Alexei stretched out his hands, as though to fend off a mortal blow. He lifted up his eyes and saw a warlock-transformation taking place over his head,—even as he had seen it the other day, and just as quick: instead of the face he had known since birth, he beheld that other, unfamiliar, fearful visage of the beast,—like to a death-mask.

He cried out faintly and covered his eyes with his hands.

Peter turned to go. But the Czarevich, hearing his father move toward the exit, threw himself on his knees before him, crawling like a dog that is being beaten, but nevertheless implores forgiveness; he kissed Peter's feet, embracing his legs and holding them tight.

"Do not go! Do not go! Better kill me! . . ."

Peter wanted to thrust him away, to free himself, but Alexei held him, inextricably, clinging more and more tenaciously, and from these convulsive, clutching, tenacious hands an icy tremor of that revulsion which he felt all his life toward spiders, cockroaches, and all sorts of other crawling vermin, darted through Peter's body.

"Out, out, out! I'll kill thee!" he shouted in a fury, mixed with horror.

Finally, with a desperate effort, he shook him off, threw him aside, and kicked him in the face. The Czarevich, with a dull moan, fell to the floor, flat on his face, as if he were dead. Peter ran out of the room, just as though he were escaping from some horror.

As he was passing the dignitaries who were awaiting him in the Administrative Chambers they gathered from his face that something untoward had happened. He merely cried out: "To the Cathedral!"—and left the room.

Some ran after him; others,—Tolstoi and Shaphirov among the number,—ran to the Secret Closet of the Judicial Chamber to the Czarevich.

He was lying, as before, prone on the floor, as if he were dead. They started lifting him up and bringing him to. His members, cramped by convulsions, would not unbend, as though in *rigor mortis*. Yet this was no swoon. He breathed hard; his eyes were open. At last they raised him up and put him on his feet. They wanted to bring him into the adjoining room, in order to place him on a bench. He was looking about him with dimmed, apparently unseeing eyes, and was muttering, as though trying to recall something:

"What has happened? . . . What has happened? . . ."

"Fear not, fear not, my own!" Tolstoi was reassuring him. "Thou didst lose consciousness. Thou didst fall,—probably hurting thyself. 'Twill heal before thy wedding. Take a sip of water. The mediciner will be here any minute."

"What has happened? . . . What has happened? . . ." the Czarevich kept on repeating, mechanically.

"Ought we not to tell the Czar?" Tolstoi whispered to Shaphirov.

The Czarevich heard him, wheeled around, and suddenly his pale face turned scarlet. He was seized with a shaking fit and began tearing the collar of his shirt, as though he were stifling.

"What Czar?" he broke out weeping and laughing at the

same time, with such savage sobs and laughter that all felt eerie.

"What Czar? You fools,—you fools! Why, can ye not see? This is not he! This is no Czar and no Batiushka of mine, but a drummer-boy,—an accursed Jew,—Grishka Otrepiev,—a false pretender,—a warlock! Drive an aspen stake through his throat, and put an end to the vampire! . . ."

The royal physician, Areskin, came on the run.

Tolstoi, who was behind the Czarevich, first pointed to Alexei and then at his own forehead: "The Czarevich is going out of his mind, now."

Areskin made the sick man sit down in an armchair, felt his pulse, gave him some spirits to sniff, forced him to drink some sedative drops, and was just about to let his blood, when a messenger arrived and announced that the Czar was waiting in the Cathedral, and demanded the Czarevich's immediate presence.

"Tell him that His Highness has fallen ill—" Tolstoi began.

"No need of that," the Czarevich stopped him, as though coming out of a deep sleep. "There is no need of that. I am going right away. Let me but rest a little,—and I would like a bit of wine. . . ."

Some Hungarian wine was brought him. He drank it avidly. Areskin placed a towel wetted with cold water and vinegar on Alexei's head.

He was left in peace. They all went off to one side, to confer as to what was to be done.

After a few minutes, he said:

"Well, it isn't so bad now. The fit has passed. Let us go."

They helped him to rise and led him off, supporting him under his arms. In the fresh air, as he passed from the Palace to the Cathedral, he became almost his old self. Nevertheless, as he passed through the throng, every one remarked his pallor.

On the ambo, before the open altar grille, he was awaited by the newly appointed Bishop of Pskov, Theophan Procopovich, in full vestments, bearing the Cross and the Evangel. The Czar was standing by his side.

Alexei mounted the ambo, took the sheet of paper which Shaphirov handed him, and began reading in a weak, barely audible voice,—yet the throng was so hushed that every word could be heard:

"I, the undersigned, promise upon the Holy Evangel, inasmuch as I have been deprived of the succession to the throne of Russia, because of my offense against my parent and my Sovereign, that I do admit this deprivation to be just, and do swear by the Almighty God, glorified in the Trinity, and before His Judgment, to submit in all things to the said parental will, and never to seek or aspire to the said succession, or to accept it, under any pretext, and I acknowledge as the true heir my brother, the Czarevich Peter Petrovich. And I kiss the Holy Cross thereon, and sign this with mine own hand."

He kissed the Cross and affixed his signature to the abdication. And, while all this was going on, the Manifesto was being read to the people.

III

Through Tolstoi, Peter transmitted to his son certain "interrogatory points." The Czarevich was supposed to answer them in writing. Tolstoi advised him not to conceal anything, since the Czar apparently knew everything already, and was merely demanding confirmation from him.

"Whom did Batiushka learn it from?" asked the Czarevich.

For a long while Tolstoi would not tell him anything. But finally he read to him an *ukase*, as yet secret, but subsequently published at the establishment of the Spiritual College, the Most Holy Synod:

"Should any one, in confessing to his spiritual father, admit any evil and unrepentant plan against the honor and weal of the Sovereign, or, even worse, treason or sedition, the father-confessor is bound to lodge information thereof immediately, in the proper quarter,—in the Preobrazhensky [Transfiguration] precinct, or in the Privy-Chancellory. Nor does such a declaration violate the confessional, neither does the priest transgress against any of the Evangelical canons; he is, rather, fulfilling the teaching of Christ: 'If thy brother shall trespass against thee, go and tell him his fault: and if he shall neglect to hear, tell it unto the church.'" [71] If this be the Lord's decree in the case of brother sinning against brother, how much more applicable is it in the case of any maleficent or any evil-working machination against the Sovereign?"

Having heard the *ukase* to the end the Czarevich got up from the table,—he and Tolstoi were speaking alone, at supper,—and, just as on the other day, during his attack in the secret chamber, his pale face suddenly turned scarlet. He bestowed such a look upon Tolstoi that the latter became scared and thought that the Czarevich was getting another attack. But this time matters ended harmlessly. The Czarevich calmed down, and seemed to fall into deep thought.

For several days he did not emerge from this thoughtful mood. When any one attempted to speak to him he would look up distractedly, as though he did not altogether understand what the speech was about; then, too, he seemed all shrunken,—he did not seem a living man, somehow, as Tolstoi put it. However, he wrote an exact answer to the "interrogatory points" and confirmed everything he had said at confessional, although he had a premonition that this was useless, and that his father would not believe anything.

Alexei comprehended that Father Balaam had violated the secrecy of confessional, and he recalled the words of St. Dmitri of Rostov:

"Should any sovereign or secular court come and, by force, seek to compel a priest to divulge the sin of his spiritual son, and should the priest be threatened even with torture and death, he must rather die and be crowned with the crown of martyrdom than break the seal of confessional."

He also recalled the words of a certain Raskolnik, a schismatic holy ancient, with whom he had once talked in the depths of Novgorod forests, where, by Batiushka's orders, he had been felling pines for scampavias:

"God's blessing is not to be found nowadays either in the Church, or the priests, or the chanting, or the ikons,—or in anything whatsoever: everything has been withdrawn to Heaven. He who holds God in awe doth not go to church. Dost thou know to what the lamb of our communion is like? Ponder well on what I say: 'tis like to a dead hound, thrown outside the city walls. No sooner hath a man taken the communion he is done with life,—he hath died, the poor fellow! Your communion is as devastating as arsenic or corrosive sublimate,—'twill penetrate right speedily into all thy bones and very marrow; the Evil One darts to thy very soul,—rest thou then in flaming Gehenna, and moan in a burning furnace, like to Cain, the irredeemable sinner!"

These words, which had seemed vapid to the Czarevich at the time, now suddenly assumed a fearful force. What if the abomination that maketh desolate had really come to reign in the holy place,—what if the Church had withdrawn from Christ, and Antichrist were now ruler over it?

But who was Antichrist?—At that point delirium began. The image of his father was doubling: as if in the instantaneous transformation of a warlock the Czarevich was beholding two faces—one dear, lovable, the face of Batiushka, the author of his being; the other unfamiliar, dreadful, like a death-mask,—the face of a beast. And most fearful of all was the fact that he did not know which of these two faces was the real one,—that of his father, or that of the beast? Was his father becoming a beast, or was the beast becoming his father? And such horror took possession of him that it seemed to him he was going out of his mind.

Meanwhile, in the torture-chamber of the Chancellory of the Transfiguration, an investigation was going on.

On the day following the proclamation of the Manifesto,— the fourth of February,—couriers galloped off into Peterburgh and Suzdal, bearing orders that all those whom the Czarevich had mentioned in his confession be brought to Moscow.

Alexandre Kikin, Ivan Aphanasiich, the Czarevich's *valet de chambre*, Nikiphor Viyazemsky, his preceptor, and many others were seized in Peterburgh. Kikin, *en route* to Moscow, attempted to strangle himself with his fetters, but was prevented from doing so.

When questioned during the torture, he named Vassilii Dolgorukyi as the chief adviser of Alexei.

"I was taken from St. Peterburgh without knowing what it was all about," Prince Vassilii subsequently told the story himself, "and was dragged off to Moscow, in fetters,—all of which threw me into great desperation and perturbation,— and was brought to the Preobrazhensky precinct and placed under close arrest, and afterward brought into the General Court, before His Majesty, the Czar, at which I was still in the same fright, seeing that the words which the Czarevich had imputed to me in his letter had been accepted as evidence of my grave opposition."

Prince Jacob Dolgorukyi, a relative of Prince Vassilii, interceded for him.

"Have mercy, liege Sire," he wrote to the Czar. "Let us not, in our old age, go down to our graves branded as a line of malefactors; that would not only deprive us of our good name, but also cut short the thread of our lives. And again I cry out to thee: have mercy, have mercy, Most Compassionate One!"

The shadow of suspicion fell even upon Prince Jacob himself. Kikin had shown that Jacob Dolgorukyi had counseled the Czarevich not to go to his father in Copenhagen.

Peter did not touch the old man, but so dire were the Czar's threats that Prince Jacob deemed it necessary to remind the Czar of his previous faithful service: "For which, I now hear, a cruel death, through impalement, has been promised me as a reward," he concluded with bitterness.

Once more Peter felt his loneliness. If even the righteous Prince Jacob was a traitor, in whom, then, could he put his trust?

Captain-Lieutenant Grigorii Skorniyakov-Pissarev brought the erstwhile Czaritza Avdothea [or Eudoxia], now the nun Ellena, from Suzdal to Moscow. *En route* she wrote the Czar:

"MOST GRACIOUS LORD!

"Many years ago,—but in just which I remember not,— in accordance with my vow, I took the veil in the Pokrovsky Nunnery at Suzdal, and was given the name of Ellena. And upon taking the veil, I went about in the raiment of a novice for half a year; but, not wishing to be a nun, I did put off the garments of a nun and the nuns' ways, living secretly in that nunnery, apparently a nun, but really as one of the laity. And this my concealment was discovered by Grigorii Pissarev. And now I put my hopes on the humane leniency of Your Majesty. Throwing myself at your feet, I beg for mercy and for forgiveness of my crime, that I might not

die the death before the full course of my years is run. And
I promise to revert to my nunhood, and to remain in nunnish-
ness until my death, and I shall pray to God for thee, my
ᴸiege Lord.

"Your Majesty's lowliest slave,

"Your former wife, AVDOTHEA."

The venerable nun who was bursar to the same nunnery,
Sister Maremiyna, testified:

"We durst not question the Czaritza as to why she had
taken off the habit of a nun. She was wont to say, many's
the time: 'Everything is ours, and pertains to the Sovereign;
and ye know well how the Sovereign repaid the Streltzi for
what they did to his mother. Then, too, my son is out of
his swaddling clothes by now!' And when Major Stepan
Glebov came to Suzdal, to recruit soldiers, the Czaritza would
admit him to her cell; locking themselves up they would talk
together, while I was packed off to my cell to cut out quilted
jackets, and, having been given a silver coin, would be ordered
to chant Te Deums. And since Glebov would demean himself
insolently, I would say to him: 'What art thou putting on
airs for? All the people know about it!' And the Czaritza
would upbraid me therefor: 'Who the devil asked thee? Thou
hast begun to watch even me!' And others would say unto
me: 'Why hast thou angered the Czaritza?' And, besides
that, he, this same Stepan, used to go to her of nights,
which was told to me by the day-laborer and the she-dwarf,
Agatha: 'Glebov goes right past us, yet we durst not as
much as stir. . . .'"

Another venerable nun, Kaptelina, confessed:

"This Glebov used to come of evenings to her, to this
Czaritza-staritza Ellena, and would buss and truss her. At
such times I used to go out of the cell. I used to receive
Glebov's love letters."

Glebov himself testified briefly:

"I did fall in love with her, this erstwhile Czaritza, and
did live with her in wantonness." In everything else he proved
stubborn. Frightful tortures were inflicted upon him,—he
was flogged, seared with red-hot iron, drenched and then
allowed to freeze; his ribs were broken and his flesh torn

with pincers; he was made to sit upon a board studded with nails and to walk barefooted over wooden stakes, so that his feet began to fester. But he endured all tortures and betrayed no one, nor did he confess to anything further.

The erstwhile Czaritza testified:

"On the twenty-first day of February, I, the *staritza* [nun] Ellena, was brought to the General Court, and, being confronted with Stepan Glebov, did testify that I had lived in wantonness with him, pleading guilty thereto. Written in my own hand—Ellena."

It was the Czar's intention to make this confession public to the people later on, in a manifesto.

The Czaritza also testified:

"I did put off my nun's rainment, inasmuch as the Bishop Dositheus, citing voices emanating from images and sundry numerous visions, did prophesy that the wrath of God was coming, that there would be sedition among the people, that the Sovereign would soon die, and that I, the Czaritza, would rule in the future, together with the Czarevich."

Dositheus was seized, stripped of his Archprelate's rank in full conclave, and renamed Demid, the unfrocked monk.

"I alone was caught in this matter," Dositheus had said during the conclave. "But what if ye were to look into the hearts of all? Let men with open ears be sent among the people,—let them report what the people say!"

The unfrocked monk, Demid, was raised on a strappado in the torture-chamber, and questioned:

"Wherefore didst thou desire the death of His Majesty the Czar?"—"I did desire to have the Czarevich Alexei Petrovich ascend to the throne, and to have the state of the people lightened, and the building of St. Peterburgh abate, and then cease," answered Demid.

He implicated Abraham Lopukhin, brother to the Czaritza and uncle to the Czarevich. Lopukhin, too, was seized and tortured, being confronted with Demid. Lopukhin was given fifteen lashes, Demid nineteen. Both confessed that they desired the Sovereign's death, and the Czarevich's accession. Demid also implicated the Czarevna Maria, the Sovereign's sister.

"The Czarevna was wont to say: 'When our Sovereign will

be no more, I shall be glad to help the Czarevich with the people, to the utmost of my power, and to direct the realm!' It was she, too, who said: 'Why do you high-priests not take a stand in the instance of the Sovereign's having married another while his first wife is still alive? He should either take the former Czaritza to him and live with her, or die!'"

And when, after taking his oath of allegiance to the Czarevich Peter Petrovich, he, this unfrocked monk, Demid, had come from the Cathedral to her, the Czarevna Maria, she had said: "'Tis in vain, now, that the Sovereign has so ordained that his elder son is put aside, while his younger is exalted; the latter is only two years old, while the former is already of age.'"

The Czarevna proved contumacious, but, once she was brought to the torture-chamber for confrontation with Demid, she confessed everything.

The inquisition lasted for more than a month. Peter was present almost every day in the torture-chamber, watching the tortures,—occasionally taking a hand himself in the torturing. But, despite all his exertions, he could not find the chief thing which he sought: a real conspiracy, "the root of the vile uprising." Even as in the testimony of the Czarevich, so in the case of all the other witnesses, there was no conspiracy evidenced,—there were merely words, rumors, gossip, the delirium of hysterical and possessed women and little innocents, the whispered gibberish of half-witted dotards and crones in cloister nooks. At times he dimly sensed that it would be better to drop all this, to vent his rheum upon it,— show he despised it and forgive everything. But he no longer could halt, and foresaw that there was but one end to everything: the death of his son.

All this time the Czarevich was living under guard in the Palace of the Transfiguration, alongside of the General Court and the torture-chambers. Day and night he heard (or imagined he heard) the screams of the tortured. He was constantly being taken to confront those on trial. Most dreadful of all had been his meeting with his mother. Rumor had reached the Czarevich that his father had apparently flogged her with a *knout*, with his own hands.

Almost every day, toward evening, Alexei was drunk to

unconsciousness. The royal physician, Areskin, prognosticated brain fever for the Czarevich; but whenever he stopped drinking such weariness of spirit would fall upon him, that he could not bear it, and would again hasten to become drunk. Areskin forewarned the Sovereign also about the illness which was threatening the Czarevich. But Peter replied:

"He will ruin himself through drink and die like a beast,— and serve him right. A dog's death for a dog!"

However, latterly, even vodka was no longer a nepenthes to the Czarevich, but merely supplanted the fearful actuality with still more fearful dreams. He was tortured by visions not only at night, in his sleep, but even in reality, in broad daylight. He was living two lives,—an actual and a phantasmal one; and each life impinged upon the other, became confused, so that he could not distinguish one from the other,—did not know what occurred in his sleep and what in reality.

Now he would dream that his father is flogging his mother in the torture-chamber; he hears the swish of the *knout* in the air, and the abominable, apparently moist slapping of the lashes on the naked body; he sees dark-purple stripes one after the other, appear on the wan,—exceedingly wan,— body; and, responding to the fearful scream of his mother with a scream still more fearful, he falls down dead. . . .

Now (apparently having decided on revenge against his father for his mother, for himself, and for all the others), he wakes at night in bed, gets a razor out from beneath his pillow, gets up, clad in nothing save his night-shirt, and steals along the dark passages of the Palace; after stepping over the orderly sleeping on the threshold, he enters the bed-chamber of his father, and bending over him, groping for his throat, slashes it,—and feels that his father's blood is chill, like the ichor of dead bodies; he drops him in horror, without completing his slashing, and runs without looking around. . . .

Or, again (apparently having recalled the word of the Scriptures anent Judas the betrayer: *He went and hanged himself*),[72] he is stealthily making his way into a cubby-hole under some stairs, where all sorts of lumber is stored; he mounts upon a broken, three-legged chair, having propped it up with an overturned box, takes a lantern-rope off a hook in the ceiling, makes a noose, throws it around his neck, and, prior to kicking the chair away, wants to make the sign of the cross, yet cannot:—his hand refuses to rise,— when suddenly, none knows whence, a huge, black tom-cat leaps under the Czarevich's feet, caressing him, rubbing against him, purring, arching his back, then, getting up on his hind legs, he puts his forepaws on Alexei's shoulders: and this is no longer a tom-cat, but some gigantic beast. And the Czarevich recognizes in the beast's maw a human face,— with broad cheek-bones, and goggle-eyes, the mustache-tips turned upward like those of the fabled Cat—Cattabriss. And the Czarevich is fain to tear himself free from these paws. But the beast, having knocked him down, is playing with him, as a cat does with a mouse,—now seizing, now releasing him, now caressing, now scratching; and suddenly the cat sank its claws into his heart. And the Czarevich recognizes him of whom it is said: "And they worshipped the Beast, saying, Who *is* like unto the Beast? who is able to make war with him?" [73]

IV

On the second of March, which was the Sunday of Ortho-doxy, Theophan Procopovich, the newly-appointed Arch-prelate of Pskov, was performing divine services in the Cathedral of the Assumption. Only those of noble birth, or belonging to officialdom, were admitted. Peter stood near one of the four gigantic pillars supporting the vault, which was covered with ikonographic, dark visages upon dull gold, under a tinted canopy, where the ancient Czars of Muscovy used to pray. Alexei stood by his side.

As he looked at Theophan, the Czarevich recalled what he had heard concerning him.

Theophan had supplanted Fedosska, the Chief Adminis-trator of Spiritual Affairs, who had grown senile, and of late fell more and more frequently into "melancholy." It was this very Theophan who had formulated the *ukase* commanding that crimes against the government, revealed in confessions, be reported. It was he, too, who was compiling the Spiritual Regulations, in accordance with which the Most Holy Synod was to be formed. The Czarevich scrutinized the new head of the Church with curiosity.

A Circassian, born in Little Russia, about thirty-eight years old, full-blooded, with a glossy face, a glossy black beard, and huge, glossy, black mustaches, he resembled an enormous black beetle. When he smiled, he wiggled his mustache as a beetle wiggles its mandibles. By this slight smile alone one could see that he was rather fond of forbidden Latin jests,—that he liked the *Facetiæ of Poggio* no less than he liked fat dumplings, and that he liked keen dialectics no less than he liked good distilled brandy. Despite his sacerdotal pomp, something far too gay, akin to tipsiness, constantly quivered and darted through every little feature of his face,—a something as lively as a minnow: he was drunk with his own intellect, this ruddy-faced Silenus in his Archprelate's cassock. "Oh, thou head, thou head, that hast drunk thy fill of intellect, where wilt thou lay thee down?" he was wont to say in his moments of frankness.

And the Czarevich wondered with a great wonder, as the Apocalypse has it,[74] how this vagabond, this fugitive Uniat who had taken the vows of the Roman Catholic Church, who had been first the disciple of the Jesuits, and then of Protestants and godless philosophers,—perhaps even a godless man himself,—could compose the Spiritual Regulations upon which the destinies of the Russian Church depended.

After the Protodeacon of the Cathedral had pronounced the Anathema specified for the Sunday of Orthodoxy, against all heretics and apostates, from Arius to Grishka Otrepiev and Mazeppa, the Archprelate ascended the ambo and delivered a discourse *Concerning the Power and Honor of the Czar*.

In this discourse he set out to prove that which was to become the corner-stone of the Most Holy Synod: The Sovereign was the head of the Church.

"The Apostle Paul, the teacher of the nations, doth speak with a loud voice: *'For there is no power but of God: the powers that be are ordained of God. Whosoever therefore resisteth the power, resisteth the ordinance of God.'*[75] Truly a thing to marvel at! One might say that Paul had been sent from the rulers themselves to preach, so zealously doth he inculcate, as though he were hammering the point home, repeating again and again: Power is of God,—of God. I pray ye to judge for yourselves; what more could the most faithful minister of a ruler say? Let us apply to this teaching, as though we were crowning it, the names and titles appertaining to the high powers, such as adorn the kings more than robes of purple and diadems. What are these titles? What are these names? Autocrats are called *gods* and *Christs Gods*, because of the power given by God,— that is, they are called the viceroys of God upon earth. The other name, *Christ*,—that is, *The Anointed*,—is derived from the ancient ceremony wherein Czars were anointed with chrism. And Paul the Apostle, sayeth: '*Servants, be obedient to them that are your masters . . . as unto Christ.*' [76] In this instance the Apostle maketh the masters equal with Christ. But that which quite amazes us, and which strengthens this truth as if with an armor of adamants, is a passage we can not overlook: the Scriptures command obedience not only to benevolent authorities, but even to those who are evil, and faithless, and impious. The word of Peter the Apostle is known to every man: '*Fear God. Honor the king. Servants, be subject to your masters with all fear; not only to the good and gentle, but also to the froward.*' [77] And the prophet David, himself a king, doth call King Saul, though rejected of God and impious, the *Christ, or the anointed of the Lord,*—not once, but repeatedly. But ye may say: No matter what Saul was, he was, none the less, anointed to rule through the clear command of God, and for that reason attained that honor. Well and good! But tell me: who was Cyrus of Persia, who was Nebuchadnezzar of Babylon? Yet God himself, through His prophets, names them His Anointed Ones,—that is, according to the word of David, *Christs of the Lord*. Who was Nero, the Roman Cæsar? Still, the Apostle Peter enjoins us to obey even him, this cruel torturer of the Christians, as an Anointed One, a *Christ of the Lord*. One dubiety remains: That not really all men are subject to this obedience to kings, but that certain ones are exempt,—to wit, the clergy and the monks. This is a thorn,—or, rather, a fang,—but the fang of a ser-

pent! This is a most pernicious spirit! For the Clergy
are simply another class among the people, but not another
empire. And even as the military have one pursuit, and the
citizenry another, and the leeches and the merchants and
the master-artisans have their different callings, thus even
the pastors, and all persons of the spiritual calling, have their
own pursuit: to be the servants of God; however, they are
subject to the reigning powers. In the ancient Church the
Levites were subject in all things to the kings of Israel.
And if it be so in the Ancient Testament why should it not
be so in the New? For the law concerning rulers is immutable
and eternal, co-existent with the existence of this world."

And, finally, came the logical conclusion:

"Let all the people of the Russian realm, not only the
secular, but the ecclesiastical as well, revere the name of
their Autocrat, the Most Pious Sovereign Peter Alexeievich,
as their Head and the Father of their Fatherland, and a
Christ of the Lord!"

The last words he uttered in a loud voice, looking the
Czar point-blank in the face, and with his right hand uplifted toward the vault of the Cathedral, where, upon dim
gold, the Visage of Christ showed darkly.

And once more the Czarevich wondered with a great wonder.

If, he reflected, all kings, even if apostates from God,
were *Christs of the Lord,*—who, then, was the last and the
greatest of them, the coming king of the earth,—the Antichrist?

This sacrilege was being uttered by an Archprelate of the
Orthodox Church, in the most ancient Cathedral in Moscow, before the Czar and the people. The earth, it seemed,
ought to yawn open and swallow the blasphemer, or a fire,
coming down from heaven, ought to scorch him. Yet everything was calm. Through the oblique sheaves of sunbeams,
through the blue waves of the smoke of censers, the gigantic
Visage of Christ in the vista of the vault seemed to soar up
from the earth, unattainable.

The Czarevich glanced at his father. The latter, too, was
calm, and was listening with pious attentiveness. Encouraged by this attentiveness, Theophan concluded solemnly:

"Be thou joyous of soul, O Russia! Make thyself great,—proclaim thy glory! May all thy frontiers and towns wax joyous,—inasmuch as upon thy horizon, like to the light-diffusing sun, is rising the glory of the Most Illustrious Son of the Czar, the three-year-old infant, the God-chosen heir, Peter Petrovich! Aye, may he flourish in joy, may he flourish in prosperity,—Peter the Second, Peter the Blessed! Amen."

When Theophan had fallen silent, a voice was heard amid the throng,—not loud, but distinct:

"Oh God, save, preserve, and have mercy upon the only true Heir to the throne of All the Russias,—our Most Pious Lord, the Czarevich Alexei Petrovich!"

The crowd, like one man, shuddered and held its breath from horror. Then it began to hum, to stir:

"Who is this? Who is this?"—"Is it some one half-mad or what?"—"Some hysterical woman, I guess, or some fellow possessed."—"What are the guards about? How did they let him in?"—"They ought to seize him with all speed,—or, like as not, he will slip away, and they won't be able to find him in the crowd. . . ."

In the furthest nooks of the Cathedral, where nothing could be seen or heard, ridiculous rumors were flying about:

"An uprising! An uprising!"—"Fire! The altar has caught on fire!"—"They have caught a man with a knife,—he wanted to assassinate the Czar!"

And the alarm was constantly increasing.

Paying no attention to it, Peter approached the Archprelate, put his lips to the Cross, and, returning to his former place, ordered the man who had shouted "these unseemly words" to be brought to him.

Captain Skorniyakov-Pissarev and two sergeants-at-arms led a somewhat gaunt old man up to the Czar. This little ancient handed a paper to the Czar; it was a printed broadside of the oath of allegiance to the new heir. At the place left blank for the signature something was written in a cramped handwriting, with the curlicues and pot-hooks of a pettifogger. Peter glanced at this paper, and then again at the little old man, and asked:

"Who art thou?"

"A former clerk in the Department of Artillery,—Larion Dokukin."

The Czarevich, standing alongside, glanced at him and immediately recognized him: this was the same Dokukin whom he had met in the spring of the year 1715, in Peterburgh, in the Church of St. Simeon,—the very same who had visited him at home, on the day of the Festival of Venus in the Summer Garden.

He was still the same: an ordinary pettifogger, one of those who are styled inky souls, governmental quill-drivers; all rough, as though petrified, and as dull, as drab, as those papers over which he had pored in his department for thirty years, until he was expelled through an informer's report concerning his bribes. Only in the very depths of his eyes there glimmered, just as it had done three years ago, a single, fixed idea. Dokukin was looking at the Czarevich by stealth, and something darted through the harsh features of the old man which suddenly recalled to the Czarevich how Dokukin had implored him to assert himself for the Christian faith, and had wept and embraced his feet, and called him the hope of Russia.

"Dost thou not want to take the oath?" Peter uttered calmly, as though with wonder.

Dokukin, looking the Czar straight in the eyes, repeated by heart that which was written in his hand on the printed sheet, in the same voice that he had used a short time ago,— not loud, but distinct, so that it could be heard throughout the whole Cathedral:

"Because of the undeserved deprivation of, and expulsion from, the throne of All the Russias of the only true Heir, the God-Preserved Lord, Alexei Petrovich, I do not take the oath, and do not swear thereto upon the Most Holy Evangel, nor kiss the Life-Giving Cross, nor acknowledge the Czarevich Peter Petrovich as the true Heir, even though the Czar's wrath be poured out upon me therefor. Let the will of my Lord God, Jesus Christ, be done. Amen, Amen, Amen."

Peter looked at him with still greater wonder.

"But dost thou know that for such opposition to Our will the punishment is death?"

"I know, Liege Sire. That is just what I have come for,—
to suffer for the Word of Christ," Dokukin answered, simply.

"Well, thou art a brave fellow, old man! But bide a while,
—we'll see if thou wilt strike up the same song when I will
jerk thee up on the strappado! . . ."

Dokukin raised up his hand in silence, and sweepingly
crossed himself.

"Hast thou heard," the Czar continued, "what the Archprelate hath said concerning obedience to those vested with
power? *For there is no power but of God*. . . ."

"I have heard, Liege Sire. All power is of God,—but that
which is not of God is not power. But to style most impious
Czars and Antichrists *Christs of the Lord* is not fitting, and
for such words the tongue of him who uttereth them ought
to be torn out!"

"Come, now, dost thou deem me, too, an Antichrist, like
as not?" asked Peter, with a barely perceptible and almost
kindly smile. "Speak the truth!"

At first the old man was taken back, but immediately
lifted up his eyes and looked straight into the Czar's.

"I deem thee the Most Pious, Orthodox Czar, Autocrat
of All the Russias, and the Anointed of God," he uttered
firmly.

"Well, if such be the case, thou shouldst obey Our will,
and keep silent."

"Czar and Liege Sire,—Your Majesty! E'en if I were
fain to be silent, 'tis a thing impossible,—there is something burning within my belly, like to a searing flame, inasmuch as my conscience gnaws at me,—'tis past my enduring . . . were we to keep silent, the very stones would cry
out!"

He fell at the feet of the Czar.

"My Liege Sire, Peter Alexeievich, Batiushka,—lend ear
to us poor folk, who are crying out to thee! To supplant,
or to change aught, we dare not, but even as thy parents,
and thy parents' parents, and the most holy patriarchs did
attain salvation, so do we, too, long to obtain it, and reach
Jerusalem the Celestial. For the sake of the True God, seek
out the truth! For the sake of the Blood of God, seek out
the truth! For the sake of thy own salvation, seek out the

truth! Make peace in the Holy Church, thy Mother. Judge
us without wrath, and without fury. Have mercy upon thy
people; have mercy upon the Czarevich! . . ."

At first Peter listened with attention, and even with interest, as though trying to understand. But then he turned
away, shrugging his shoulders in boredom.

"There, that will do. Thou wilt never get through, old
man. Evidently I have not executed and hanged enough of
you fools. And why do you put yourselves in the way? What
profit do you find therein? Or dost believe that I revere the
Church of God, and believe in Christ, my Saviour, less
than you do? And who has appointed you slaves to be the
judges between the Czar and God? How dare ye? . . ."

Dokukin got up on his feet and raised his eyes toward
the dark Visage on the vault of the Cathedral. A ray of sunlight falling thence surrounded the hoary head with a radiant nimbus. "How do we dare, Czar?" he uttered in a loud
voice. "Hearken, Your Majesty! The Divine Scripture proclaims: 'What is man, that Thou art mindful of him? or
the son of man, that Thou visitest him? Thou madest him
a little lower than the angels; Thou crownedst him with glory
and honour, and didst set him over the works of Thy hands:
Thou hast put all things in subjection under his feet." [78]
Man is ordained to be self-governed! . . ."

Slowly, as though with an effort, Peter took his eyes from
Dokukin's; as he was going away he turned to Tolstoi,
who was standing nearest to him, and said:

"Take him prisoner,—hold him under close guard until
he is put to the question."

The old man was seized. He resisted and shouted, still
trying to say something. He was bound, lifted up bodily
and carried off.

"Oh ye mystic martyrs, be not horrified, and despair
not!" he kept on shouting, looking at the Czarevich. "Suffer
ye,—suffer ye but a little while more, for the sake of the
Lord! For He shall come, nor tarry in His coming. Yea, come
Thou, Lord Jesus! Amen."

The Czarevich looked on and listened, all pale and trembling.

"That is the way to act,—that is the way to act!" he said

to himself, as though, only now, he had suddenly comprehended all his life, and everything had become overturned,
upset within his soul: that which had been a burthen had
become wings. He knew that he was again falling into faint-
heartedness, despondence, despair; but he also knew that
he would not forget that which he had at last comprehended.
And he, even as Dokukin had done, lifted up his gaze to
the dark Visage on the vault of the Cathedral, and he imagined that amid the oblique rays of the sun, amid the blue
waves of censer-smoke, he saw this gigantic Visage stirring,
—only now no longer retreating from the earth, as it had
been a while ago, but lowering, descending from heaven
upon earth,—and that the Lord Himself was coming.

And with a joy which was like to horror he kept on repeating:

"Yea, come Thou, Lord Jesus! Amen."

v

The inquisitorial investigation at Moscow ended on the
fifteenth day of March. The fate of the accused was decided
by the verdict of the Czar and his ministers, given in the
General Chambers in the Palace of the Transfiguration.

The Czaritza-nun Ellena was to be sent to Old Ladoga, to
a nunnery, and the Czarevna Maria to Schlüsselburg,—both
were to be kept under close guard. Abraham Lopukhin was
to be sent to St. Peterburgh, into the Fortress of SS. Peter
and Paul, until a fresh investigation. Others were to be executed.

On the morning of that same day, on the Red Square, near
the Brow [or Execution] Place, the executions began. The
evening before the iron spikes upon which the heads of
the Streltzi, beheaded in the year of sixteen-hundred-and-
ninety-eight, had stuck for the duration of twenty years,
were cleared, in order that new heads might be stuck upon
them.

Stepan Glebov was impaled. The iron stake came out
through the nape of his neck. There was a wooden perch
below to keep the victim in a sitting position. To prevent
his freezing, so that his agonies might be protracted, fur

garments and a fur cap were put upon him. Three priests stood watch by turns, day and night, on the alert for some new relevation from him before his death. "And from the time that Stepka was stuck upon the stake," one of them reported, "he did not offer any repentance to them, his spiritual preceptors; he did but ask in the night, secretly, of the Archmonk Marcellus, that he supply him with the Holy Communion, if it were in any way possible to bring it to him secretly; and in this state he did give up his soul, toward the morning of the sixteenth of March, in the eighth hour, and in the second quarter thereof."

The Archpriest of Rostov, the unfrocked monk Demid, was broken on the wheel. There was a story current that the Czar's secretary, to whom the execution had been entrusted, had made a slight error: instead of chopping off his head and burning the corpse, he had merely broken the Archpriest on the wheel.

Kikin, too, met the same death as Demid. His agonies were protracted, with pauses between. His arms and legs were broken one after the other, the torture lasting for more than four-and-twenty hours. The most excruciating agony was caused by his being so tightly bound to the wheel that he could not stir a single limb,—he merely moaned and groaned, imploring for death. It was also told that on the second day the Czar, who, it seems, was riding past Kikin, had bent down toward him and asked:

"Alexandre, thou art a clever man,—how, then, didst thou e'er venture on such a deed?"—"The mind is fond of expanding,—whereas thou makest it feel cramped," was Kikin's purported answer.

The third to be broken on the wheel was the Czaritza's spiritual father, Fedor of the Desert, a sacristan, for that he had acted as her go-between with Glebov.

Those who did not receive capital punishment had their noses and tongues slit, and their nostrils torn. Many, who had merely heard about the Czaritza's taking the veil yet had seen her in secular garments, were commanded "to be mercilessly beaten with cudgels."

A quadrangular pillar of white stone, some six ells wide, with iron spikes in its sides, was erected on the Square;

the heads of the executed were stuck upon these spikes; upon the summit of the pillar was a flat broad stone: the corpses were placed thereon; in their midst was Glebov, apparently seated in the center of his circle of accomplices.

The Czarevich had to be present at all these executions.

The last to be broken at the wheel was Larion Dokukin. On the wheel he declared that he had something to reveal to the Sovereign; he was taken off and brought into the Palace of the Transfiguration. When the Czar walked up to him, Dokukin was already in his pre-mortal delirium, babbling something inarticulate about the Coming Christ. Then he seemed to come to for a minute, looked intently into the eyes of the Czar, and said:

"Liege Lord, shouldst thou execute thy son, his blood shall fall upon all thy line, from head to head, unto the last Czar's. Spare the Czarevich,—spare Russia!"

Peter walked away from him in silence and ordered his head to be lopped off.

The day following the executions, on the eve of the Czar's departure for Peterburgh, a "night session" of the Most Drunken Conclave was to take place in the Palace of the Transfiguration. During these ensanguined days, just as at the time of the Streltzi executions, and the blackest days of his life in general, Peter occupied himself more heartily than ever with his All-Fools' Conclave. It was as though he were purposely deafening himself with laughter.

To fill the place of the late Nikita Zotov, a new Prince-Pope [or Lord of Misrule] had recently been chosen,— one Peter Ivannovich Burturlin, a former "Metropolitan of Sanct Peterburgh." The election of the "Bacchus-emulating father" had taken place in Peterburgh; the imposition of hands in Moscow, just before the arrival of the Czarevich.

Now, in the Palace of the Transfiguration, the investment of the newly chosen Pope in his cassocks and miter was to take place,—a buffonade simulacrum of the investment of a Patriarch.

The Czar had found time in the midst of the inquisition at Moscow to compose and write down by himself the entire order of ceremonies.

"The night session" was to take place in a spacious beamed

chamber, lined with lengths of red cloth, and illuminated with large wax candles, adjoining the General Court and the torture chamber. The narrow long tables were disposed in a horse-shoe; in the center was a dais with steps, upon which steps sat the Hierarchs-Cardinals and other members of the Conclave; under a velvet canopy was a throne of kegs, with bottles and small brandy glasses decorating it from top to bottom.

When all had gathered, the Sacristan and the Cardinal-Protodeacon,—the latter was none other than the Czar himself,—led in solemnly, supporting him under his arms, the newly-chosen Pope. Two flasks of "most intoxicating wines" were borne before him,—one was gilt, the other silvered; there were also two platters,—one heaped high with pickled cucumbers, the other with sauerkraut; there were also unseemly ikons of the naked Bacchus. The Prince-Pope, bowing thrice before the Prince-Cæsar and the Cardinals, brought his offerings to His Majesty: the flasks and the platters.

The Archpriest kissed the Pope:

"Wherefore hast thou come, brother, and what dost thou ask for from our Intemperance?"

"I would be invested in the cassocks of Our Father Bacchus," answered the Pope.

"How dost thou keep the law of Bacchus, and what are thy works therein?"

"Yea, Most Drunken Father! Upon arising in the morning, while there is yet darkness, and light hath scarce appeared—and, occasionally, even about midnight,—I do pour out two or three bumpers and drink them off; nor do I waste the rest of the day-time but pass it in the self-same way, filling my belly well, as if it were a barrel, with diverse drinks, so that I e'en carry edibles past my mouth, because of the trembling of my hands, and the mistiness which is before my eyes; and thus do I do always, and promise to teach those entrusted to me to do likewise, inasmuch as I deny all those who would be wise, and do anathematize, though for the barbarians that they are, all those who contend against drunkenness."

The Archpriest proclaimed:

"May the tipsiness of Bacchus, that maketh all things grow dim, and to tremble, and fall down, and wax insane, be with thee all the days of thy life!"

The Cardinals led the Pope up on the ambo, and robed him in his vestments,—a motley simulacrum of the saccos, amophorium, stole and an epigonation with embroidered representations of dice, cards, bottles, tobacco pipes, a naked Venus, and a naked Eremka [Eros]. About his neck, in lieu of a panagia, they placed clay flasks with jingle-bells. They put in his hands a cross made out of pipe-stems and a book that was really a cellarette, with vials of different vodkas. His head was anointed with potent wine, which was also put about his eyes, "in the form of a ring":

"Thus shall thy mind go round and round, and may such rings, of different sorts, appear before thy eyes, from this day hence, for all the days that thou dost draw breath!"

They also anointed both his hands and the four fingers that take hold of a bumper:

"Thus may thy hands tremble all the days of thy life!"

In conclusion, the Archpriest placed upon his head a miter of tin:

"The crown of the mistiness of Bacchus be upon thy head! I, who am drunken, drunken, this fellow who is not sober—

> In the name of all drunkards,
> In the name of all tankards,
> In the name of all loons,
> In the name of all buffoons,
> In the name of all wines,
> In the name of all vines,
> In the name of all casks,
> In the name of all flasks,
> In the name of all tobaccos,
> In the name of all pot-houses—
> Since they be dwellings of Our Father Bacchus,
> Amen!

All present raised up their voices:

"*Axios!* He is worthy!"

They next seated the Pope on his throne of kegs. Over his head was suspended a little silver Bacchus, astride a keg.

By tipping it, the pope could pour the vodka it contained into his glass, or even right into his mouth.

Not only the members of the Conclave, but all the other guests as well, walked up to His Holiness in turn, and, bowing down to his very feet, received in lieu of a blessing, a thump on the head from his pig's bladder, soaked in vodka, and took communion in pepper-brandy from an enormous wooden ladle.

The hierarchs chanted in chorus:

"O most honorable father Bacchus, born of burnt Semele, reared in the bosom of Jupiter,—thou extractor of the wine contained in grapes! We implore thee in the name of all this drunken conclave: Prolong and direct the steps of the Prince-Pope of the universe, for that he followeth in thy tracks. And thou, all-glorious Venus. . . ."

This was followed by indecencies.

Finally they sat down at table. Theophan Procopovich sat down opposite the Prince-Pope, while Peter sat down alongside of Theophan, with Fedosska next to him, and the Czarevich facing him.

The Czar began discussing with Theophan the news, just received, about the self-inflicted burnings of many thousands of the Raskolniki, in the Kerzhensky and Chernoramensky forests beyond the Volga. The drunken songs and the shouts of the Zanies interfered with his conversation. Whereupon, at a sign from the Czar, the priests ceased their chant to Bacchus, all grew quiet, and, in this suddenly fallen silence, the voice of Theophan rang out:

"Oh, the accursed madmen, the frenzied martyrs! With an insatiable lust do they thirst after suffering; of their own will do they give themselves up to be burned; manfully do they fly headlong into the abyss of hell, and thus show the way to others. It awaiteth but little to call such people insane: they constitute a certain evil, the like of which can not be named! Yea, may every one reject them and vent his rheum upon them. . . ."

"What's to be done, then?" asked Peter.

"It should be explained to them, in an admonition, Your Majesty, that not every suffering is pleasing to God, but only such as is lawful. Inasmuch as the Lord doth not say simply: *Blessed* are *they which are persecuted,* but *Blessed* are *they which are persecuted for righteousness' sake.*[79] But such a persecution for righteousness' sake is never to be feared in the Russian realm; inasmuch as it is of the orthodox faith, such a thing is out of the question. . . ."

"Admonitions!" exclaimed the disgraced Fedosska with a malicious sneer. " 'Tis a likely thing, never fear, to get anything through their heads with admonitions! The thing to do is to break the jaws of these apostates! For if it was an ordinance of the church in the Old Testament to kill those who did not submit, it should be followed all the more in the blessed church of the New Testament, inasmuch as there we had but images, while here we have the truth itself. It would be a good thing for heretics themselves to die, and to kill them is benevolence,—the longer they live, the more they sin, inventing an exceedingly great number of all sorts of enticements, debauching an exceedingly great number of people. But whether a sinner be killed by hands or with prayer, 'tis all one."

"Such talk is not becoming," retorted Theophan calmly, without looking at Fedosska. "Through such cruelties the hearts of the tortured are rather inflamed than made submissive. They should be converted to the Holy Church not through fear and compulsion, but through the preachment of straightforward Evangelical love."

"Verily so," concurred Peter. "We do not wish to coerce the conscience of man, and willingly leave each man to care for the good of his soul in his own way. As far as I am concerned, let them believe whatever they wish to, and if they be past conversion through reasoning,—then neither sword nor fire will avail. But as for as being martyrs out of folly,— there shall be no glory accruing to them therefrom, nor any benefit to the realm."

"Soft and easy does the trick,—and, look you, everything is smoothed over," Theophan chimed in. "However," he added in a low voice, bending toward the Czar, "there should be instituted a double tax upon the Raskolniki, so that under pressure of sundry fines it might be more convenient to make the straying ones join the Holy Church. Also, in punishing such people, find, if it be possible, some obvious transgression outside their schismaticalness; such people, after being lashed with the *knout,* and having their nostrils slit, should be sent to the galleys, as the law proscribes, but should there be no obvious cause, they should be dealt with in accordance with a verbal *ukase*. . . ."

Peter nodded his head in silence. The Czar and Archpriest understood each other.

Fedosska wanted to say something, but let it pass in silence; however, his malice distorted his little face,—the muzzle of a bat,—with a caustic sneer, and made him contract, like a coiled snake, and turn green, as if he had become swollen with venom. He understood the meaning of dealing "in accordance with a verbal *ukase*." Bishop Peterin, who had been sent to Kerzhenetz to admonish the Raskolniki, had recently reported to the Czar: "They have been most cruelly tortured and lacerated,—so much that even their inwards could be seen." And the Czar, in his *ukases*, forbade any interference with Father Peterin "in his work, which is equal to that of the apostles." Love,—in words; but in reality, as the Raskolniki complained: "Mute teachers stand near the strappadoes in the torture chambers; instead of enlightening us with the Evangel, they do so with a *knout;* instead of teaching us what the Apostles taught, they teach us with fire." However, this was precisely the "spiritual politics, or dissimulation," which Fedosska himself had preached. But Theophan had proven craftier than he, and he felt that his own song was already sung.

"But then," the Archpriest began again, loudly, so that all might hear, "the wonder is not that the rude *mouzhiks,* who are ignorant in the extreme, are waxing mad, because they have strayed so far from the truth. What is truly a wonder, is that in the high ranks of the petty nobility, amid the very servants of the Czar, there are to be found certain wiseacres, morosely submissive, who are worse than the Raskolniki. Matters have come to such a pass that even the most shiftless make shift to take part in deeds,—and deeds that are, to boot, of the most abominable and provocative sort! Even the lees of our people, the cheapest of souls, people who are born for nothing else save to batten upon the toil of others,—even these have risen up against their

Czar,—even these have risen up against the Christ of the Lord! Why, when ye break bread, ye ought to wonder and say: 'Whence cometh this to us?' 'Tis a renewal of the story of King David, against whom the blind and the halt did rise up in revolt. Our pious monarch, who hath brought such weal to Russia, through whose industry, all have attained glory and security, hath now an opprobrious name and a life beset with many ills. And when, through heavy toil, he doth draw down a premature old age upon himself,—when, for the preservation of his Fatherland, neglecting his health, he seems to be rushing as if at a gallop, toward his death,— the thought has come to certain people that he has lived too long! All sorrow, all shame, to Russia! Let us beware lest there spring up in the world this by-word concerning us: The Czar is worthy of such a Czardom, but the people are not worthy of such a Czar."

When Theophan had fallen silent, Peter began:

"My heart and my conscience are known to God, as well as how much good I desire for my Fatherland. But, demoniacal foes work abominations against me. Hardly any of the princes have ever endured such misfortunes and calamities as I. Foreigners say that I rule over slaves. But English freedom is out of place here,—as useless as bombarding a wall with peas. One must know a people in order to rule them. 'Tis difficult for any one who does not know the whole matter to determine my innocence. God alone sees the truth. He is my Judge. . . ."

No one was listening to the Czar. All were drunk. He fell silent without having finished his say, made a sign, and the priests again struck up their chant to Bacchus; the Zanies raised up a din; a chorus,—supposed to represent *Spring*,—began whistling the various bird-calls, from the nightingale's to robin redbreast's,—so piercingly that the walls threw back the sounds.

Everything was as it had ever been. In the same old way they swilled and guzzled until they were unconscious. Venerable dignitarians fought, tugging one another by the hair, and then, making up their quarrel, would fall together under the table. Prince Shakhovskoy, a Cavalier of the Fools' Order of Judas, let his face be slapped,—at so much per slap. An old *doyarian*, who had refused to drink, had vodka poured into his mouth through a funnel. The Prince-Pope, from the height of his throne, vomited upon the wigs and kaftans of those who sat below. The drunken female fool, the Princess-Abbess Rzhevskaya, danced, pulling up her skirts shamelessly, and sang in a hoarse voice:

> Mince, stump, ye low knaves!
> One, two, and then hop,—
> I would dance and never stop!

The revelers whistled in time to her, and stamped so that the dust rose up in a pillar:

> Ho, burn,—ho, burn!

Everything was as it had ever been. Yet Peter experienced ennui. He purposely drank as much as possible, of the strongest English vodka,—*pepper and brandy*,—that he might become drunk as soon as possible, yet drunkenness would not come to him. The more he drank, the more did his ennui increase. He arose; sat down again; arose once more and took to ambling among the bodies of the drunkards which were strewn over the floor, like corpses slain upon the field of battle, and could find no place for himself. Something was mounting toward his heart with deathly nausea. Oh, to escape, or to make all this riff-raff scatter!

But when the chill light of the winter morning mingled with the malodorous murk and the dim light of the flickering candles, the human faces became still more frightful,—grew to resemble still more the maws of beasts, or monstrous phantoms.

Peter's gaze came to a stop on his son's face.

The Czarevich was drunk. His face was deathly pale; long scandent wisps of hair had stuck to his sweating forehead; his eyes had grown bleary; his lower lip hung down; the fingers with which he held a full goblet, trying not to spill the wine, shook like those of a dipsomaniac.

"Wine is not grain,—if you spill it you won't be able to pick it!" he muttered, carrying the goblet to his mouth. He downed the drink, made a wry face, grunted, and, wishing to chase it down, long and vainly prodded his fork into a slippery pickled mushroom, which eluded him to the end; giving it up, he thrust a bit of black bread into his mouth and fell to chewing it slowly.

"Friend of my heart, am I drunk?—Tell me the truth,—am I drunk?" he kept on pestering Tolstoi, who was sitting alongside of him.

"As drunk as drunk can be," Tolstoi acquiesced.

"There now, that's just it," the Czarevich went on, his tongue refusing to obey him. "But what do I care? Before I taste the first glass, it wouldn't make any difference to me if there were no such thing as drink, at all, at all; but, soon as I've drunk off one glass, I'm just done for: no matter how much you give me, I won't refuse. It's a good thing that I am good-tempered when in my cups. . . ."

He began to snicker and giggle, and suddenly looked at his father.

"Dad,—oh dad! Why art thou so down-hearted? Come hither,—let's drink together. I'll sing a little song for thee. 'Twill be merrier so,—honest!"

He smiled to his father,—and this smile was his erstwhile one: endearing, childlike.

"Altogether a little simpleton, a little innocent! Well,—how can one execute such a fellow?" thought Peter, and suddenly a wild, awful, cruel pity sank its fangs, like some beast, into his heart.

He turned away, and pretended to listen to Theophan, who was telling him about the formation of the Holy Synod. But he heard nothing. Finally he called an orderly and commanded his horses to be got ready at once to go to Peterburgh, and, while waiting, he again took to wandering, weary of spirit, sober amid the intoxicated. Without himself noticing it, as though some force were drawing them to each other, he walked up to the Czarevich, sat down alongside of him at the table, and again turned away from him, pretending to be engrossed in a conversation with Prince Jacob Dolgorukyi.

"Dad, oh dad!" the Czarevich gently touched his father's arm. "Why, what makes thee so down-hearted? Why are you so weary? Or is *he* wronging thee? Put an aspen stake down his throat,—and there's the end on't! . . ."

"Who is *he?*" Peter turned round to his son.

"Why, how should I know who *he* is?" The Czarevich smiled with such a strange smile that Peter felt eerie. "All I know is that now thou art real,—while the devil alone knows who that other fellow is,—a false pretender perhaps, or some accursed beast, or a warlock?"

"What art thou saying?" his father looked at him closely. "Alexei, thou shouldst drink less. . . ."

"If you drink,—you will die, and if you don't drink, you will die; 'tis better to die, yet drink! And 'twill be better for thee also: if I die, thou wilt not have to execute me! . . ." He began to snicker again, altogether like a little fool, and suddenly struck up a song in a low,—most low,—barely audible voice, which seemed to come from afar:

> A young maid, I will wander,
> Over peaceful meads, where broad streams meander,
> Gathering flowerets blue,—
> Cornflowers dear of the deep sky's hue;
> I will plait myself a maiden's wreath,—
> I will hie me to the river's bank,
> And the chaplet cast in the stream beneath,
> Fixing all my thoughts on the one I love . . .

"I had a dream, the other night, dad: methought I saw Aphrosiya sitting on the snow, in an open field, at night,—naked and dreadful, just as if she were dead; she was rocking and lulling a little baby, that also seemed dead, and, as though she were weeping, she sang this same little song:

> My little wreath sinks down,—down!
> Heavy, heavy, is my poor heart grown;
> My little wreath doth sink out of sight,—
> My beloved one hath forgot me quite.

Peter listened,—and pity,—wild, awful, cruel,—was gnawing, like some beast, at his heart. But the Czarevich sang on, and wept. Then he bowed his head to the table, overturning a glass with wine: a red puddle, as if of blood, spread over the tablecloth. He placed one hand under his head, shut his eyes, and fell asleep.

For a long while, Peter regarded his face,—pale, seemingly dead, side by side with the red, seemingly bloody puddle.

The orderly approached the Czar and reported that the horses were ready. Peter arose, for the last time glanced at his son, bent toward him, and kissed his forehead.

The Czarevich, without opening his eyes, smiled to his father in his dream, with the same tender smile as in his childhood, when his father used to take him, a sleepy little boy, into his arms.

The Czar, unnoticed of any, walked out of the chamber where the drinking-bout was still on; he took his seat in the covered cart and was off for Peterburgh.

BOOK TEN

THE RED DEATH

I

In the forest of Vetluga stood a rude cloister of the Raskolniki, called Long Mosses. Impassable morasses had covered all the ways to this cloister. In the summer time people barely managed to get to it over the narrowest of planked paths, through thickets that, even in the daytime, were almost as dark as at night; in the winter they used snow-shoes.

The legend ran that three of the holy ancients from the forests of Olonetz, near the Lake Tolvuy, upon the destruction of the cloisters thereabouts by the Nikonians, had come to this locality, following a miracle-working ikon of the Mother of God which floated ahead of them through the air; they had built a small hovel on the spot where the ikon had descended to earth, and had embarked upon their desert life, delving the soil with a crooked stick, and, clearing the forest along the ridges with fire, sowed under the ashes. A brotherhood gathered about them. The holy ancients, when dying,—all three of them on the same day and in the same hour,—had left their behests to this brotherhood: "Little children, live ye here on this spot which we have blessed; though ye were to go far and seek much, yet will ye ne'er find such another place; the crow and the raven have cooked their porridge here, and there shall be a great cloister here."

The prophecy was fulfilled: a religious refuge sprang up in the depths of the forest and bloomed like unto a lily of Paradise, under the holy mantle of the Mother of God.

"A great miracle!" said those who dwelt in the cloister. "Radiant Russia has lost its light, while somber Vetluga has become radiant; the wilderness has become filled with worthy saints,—they have come flocking like unto the six-winged seraphim."

It was here, after long wanderings through the forests of Kerzhenetz and Chernoramesk, that the holy ancient Kornilii, the preacher of self-burning, had taken up his abode, together with his disciple, Tikhon Zapolsky, the runaway scholar and the son of a Streletz.

On a certain night in June, near the cloister of the Long Mosses, on an abrupt cliff over the Vetluga, a bonfire was blazing. The flame lit up the lower branches of an old pine, to the trunk of which had been nailed an ikon that had been molded of copper upon the shore of some sea. Two people were sitting near the fire,—a young girl serving her novitiate in the cloister, by the name of Sophia, and Tikhon, now also a novice. Sophia had gone to the forest to search for a lost heifer. Tikhon was returning from a certain recluse who dwelt in a distant wilderness, to whom he had carried a missive from the holy ancient. The lad and the girl had met at the crossing of two paths, late at night, when the gates of the cloister were already shut, and had decided to wait together for the morning by the fire.

Sophia, looking into the fire, was singing in a low voice:

> Then Christ Himself, Heaven's King, up and spake:
> Yield ye not, my beloveds all,
> To that Serpent, the Seven-Headed One;
> Fly ye to the hills, to the clefts of the earth,—
> Build ye there fires fierce and great,
> Burning brimstone sprinkling over them,
> And your earthly flesh to the flames give up.
> Suffer for my sake, my beloveds all,
> For my Faith,—for the Faith of Christ.
> And if ye so do, my beloveds all,
> I shall ope to you Heaven's mansions fair,—
> Into Heaven's Kingdom I shall lead ye all
> And shall live with you through Eternity.

"That's the way of it, little brother," concluded the girl, after a protracted look at Tikhon. "He that goeth into the fire shall have the salvation his soul doth desire. It would be a good thing if all were to burn for the love of the Son of God."

He kept silent and, as he watched the moths circling over

the flames, falling into it, and burning up, he recalled the words of the holy ancient, Kornilii: "Like to the gnats or midges, which, the more they are crushed the harder they buzz and dash into your eyes,—so are the dear little people of Russia glad to suffer, thrusting themselves into the fire in whole troops!"

"What art thou thinking about, little brother?" the girl again began. "Or art thou afraid of the fire? Be bold,—spit out upon it,—be not afraid! 'Tis but little one has to endure in the fire here,—in the winking of an eye the soul leaves one's body! Before thou enterest the fire thou mayst have fear thereof,—but as soon as thou hast entered it, everything is forgot. 'Twill flame up,—and thou shalt see Christ and the angelic countenances about Him; they draw the soul out of the body, while Christ, our Hope, Himself blesses it and bestows Divine power upon it. And the soul is no longer heavy then, but as if it were winged; it flies along with the angels, soaring like to a bird,—rejoicing that it has flown out of its prison,—its body. Just before, it had been chanting, weeping: 'Bring my soul out of prison, that I may praise Thy name.' [80] Well, it has gotten all that it has been weeping for. Its prison is blazing in the great fire, while the soul, like to pearls, and like to pure gold, is being offered up to the Lord. . . ."

There was such joy in her eyes as though she were already beholding that which she spoke of.

"Tisha, Tishenka, little darling, can it be thou dost not long for the red death? Or art thou afraid?" she repeated in an ingratiating whisper.

"I am afraid of sin, Sophiushka! Is it the will of the Lord that men throw themselves in the fire? Is that which is within us of God? Come, now,—is it not from the Arch Foe?"

"But where are we to hide ourselves? We are in sore straits!" She wrung her bloodless hands,—thin little hands, altogether like those of a child.

"There is no escaping, there is no concealment from the Serpent,—neither in the mountains, nor in the caverns, nor in the deep places of the earth. He hath envenomed the earth, and the water, and the air with his venom, which is hateful to God. Everything is abominable,—everything is vile!"

The night was calm. The stars twinkled as innocently as

the eyes of babes. The inverted, waning crescent rested upon the black tips of the forest firs. From below, out of the swamp mist, came the sleep-inducing crakes of landrails. The pine grove breathed forth the crisp warmth of the resinous acerose needles. Near the very fire a lilac-hued bluebell, lit up by the red flame, was drooping on its stalk, as though it were nodding its frail and sleepy little head.

And the moths kept on flying, flying into the fire, and fell therein, and were consumed.

Tikhon narrowed his eyes, which were tired from the glare. He recalled a summer noonday; the odor of firs, in which the freshness of apples was mingled with the scent of olibanum; a forest glade; the sun; bees hovering over clover, lungwort, and rosy, sticky ragged-robin; in the midst of the dell stood a decrepit, half-rotted, covered cross,—probably over the grave of some holy hermit. " 'Thou wilderness resplendent, dear mother of mine!' " he had been repeating his favorite canticle. The Lord had at last fulfilled his long-cherished desire,—had brought him to a "haven of benign peace." Tikhon had gotten down on his knees, and, parting the tall grasses, put his lips to the earth, and kissed it, and wept and prayed:

> Wondrous Queen, Mother of God,—
> Thou earth, thou earth, our Mother dank!

And, looking up at the sky, he had kept on repeating:

> The Mother, to Whom all chant praise, shall descend from the Heavens,
> Our Sovereign Mistress, Mother of God!

Both the earth and the sky had been one. In the celestial visage which was like to the sun, in the Visage of the Woman, with eyes of fire and winged with fire,—St. Sophia of the Highest Wisdom of God,—he beheld an earthly visage which he both longed and feared to recognize. Then he had arisen and gone farther into the forest. He could not remember where or how long he walked. At last he caught sight of a lake,—small, circular like a chalice, with steep, fir-covered shores that were reflected as unbroken walls of greenery in the water,

as if in a mirror. The water,—as dense as pitch, as green as
pine-needles,—was so still that it was almost imperceptible,
and seemed merely a rift in a subterranean sky. On a stone,
near the very water, sat Sophia, the girl of the cloister. He
had both recognized her and failed to recognize her. A garland
of white globeflowers was perched upon her loosened braids;
her small, black nun's robe was tucked up; her bare white
feet were dabbling in the water; her eyes were like those of
one in drink. And swaying evenly, looking down at the subterranean sky, she was singing a quiet little song, like to
those songs which are sung during round dances, by the glow
of midsummer bonfires on St. John's Eve, at the ancient
pagan revels:

> Little sun, little sun, red and fair!
> O, gaffer Lado,—O, gaffer Lado!
> Ye flowrets, ye flowrets, dearly loved!
> O, gaffer Lado,—O, gaffer Lado!
> Thou earth, thou earth, our mother dank!

And there was something ancient, wild in this song, resembling the sad plaint of an oriole in the dead calm of a
noon before a storm. "Just like a water-pixie!" he thought,
without daring to stir and holding his breath. A twig crackled
under his foot. The girl turned around, cried out, leapt up
from the stone and ran off into the forest. All that was left
were the slow circles spreading over the water, caused by her
wreath having fallen into the lake. And an eerie feeling fell
upon him, as though he had really witnessed a forest wonder,
a visitation of the fiends. And, recalling the earthly visage in
the Celestial Visage, he recognized Sister Sophia,—and the
prayer to dank Mother Earth appeared to him sacrilegious.

Never, with anybody, had he discussed that which he had
seen at Round Lake, yet he frequently thought about it, and,
no matter how much he struggled with temptation, he could
not overcome it. At times, in his very prayers, he recognized
the earthly visage in the Celestial Visage. . . .

Sophia, still looking into the flames of the fire, with a
fixedly-avid gaze, was singing a canticle about St. Kirik, the
infant martyr, whom the infidel king Maximian had cast into
a red-hot furnace:

Kirik, beloved, in the furnace stands,
Chanting the chants of the Cherubim.
The furnace is floored with a sward of green
And blooming flowerets of an azure sheen.
Among the flowerets the infant plays,
His raiment glowing like the sun's rays.

Tikhon, too, was gazing into the fire, and it seemed to him that in the transparently-blue heart of the fire he was beholding the flowers of Paradise spoken of in the song. Their blue, like to that of the pure sky, held forth the promise of a beatitude that was not of this earth; but one had to pass through red flame—through red death—in order to reach this Heaven.

Suddenly Sophia turned around to him, placed her hand on his, and, drawing her face close to his, so that he felt her breath,—hot, passionate, like a kiss,—she fell to whispering in an ingratiating whisper:

"We'll burn together, together, little brother of mine, my dearest darling, my own little one! 'Tis a dreadful thing for me alone, with thee it would be sweet! We will go together to Christ and His wedding feast!"

And she kept on repeating, like some infinite caress:

"We will burn! We will burn! . . ."

In her pale face, in her dark eyes, which reflected the gleam of the flame, again came the flash of that ancient, wild something which had flashed even there, on Round Lake, in the song of the midsummer fires.

"We will burn, we will burn, Sophiushka," he whispered, in that terror which drew him to her as the fire draws moths.

Steps were heard below, upon the little path which led to the cliff.

"Jesus Christ, Son of God, have mercy upon us sinners!" somebody's voice uttered.

"Amen!" answered Tikhon and Sophia.

These were pilgrims. They had lost their way in the forest, and had been almost bogged in a quagmire; in the end they had caught sight of the bonfire's flame and had somehow or other managed to clamber out. They all seated themselves around the fire.

"Is it far to the cloister, now, my darlings?"

"It is right here, at the base of the mountain," said Tikhon, and, after a close look at the face of the speaker, recognized Vitalia, the same one who "led a bird's life," "soaring" everywhere, and wandering about, and whom he had seen two years ago, upon the floats belonging to the Czarevich Alexei, in Peterburgh, on the Neva, on the night of the Festival of Venus. She, too, recognized Tikhon and rejoiced. With her was her inseparable fellow-wayfarer, Kilikeia, the hysterical; the fugitive recruit, Petka Zhizla of the withered hand that had been branded with the government's brand, the seal of Antichrist; and the old boatman, Ivannushka the simpleton, who every night met Christ, chanting the chant of the Coffin-Liers.

"Whence come ye, ye faithful?" asked Sophia.

"We be wandering folk," answered Vitalia, "we wander the world over, from pillar to post, persecuted, pursued by those of heretical faith; having no city of our own now. We are seeking that of the future. But now we are coming from Kerzhenetz. There the persecution is of the cruelest. Peterim, —a ferocious wolf, a bloodsucker of the church,—has demolished seven and seventy religious shelters, and has done away with the soul-saving way of living in the cenobies ..."

Stories of persecutions began.

One sainted ancient had been beaten in three separate torture chambers,—his ribs had been broken with pincers and his navel had been pulled out; then "in winter time, during a most cruel frost, he was stripped mother-naked, and water so cold that it was mixed with ice was poured over his head, until icicles formed that reached from the beard to the ground, as if they had let roots; in the end he was cast into a fire and thus passed away."

Others were made to languish in yokes of iron,—"the said yokes draw the head, the arms and the legs all into one, from which vilest of tortures the bones of the spine are broken at their joints, and the blood spurts out of the mouth,—out of the nostrils,—out of the eyes,—out of the ears."

Others were made to take communion by force, a gag being put in the mouth. A certain youth had been dragged by the soldiers to church and placed upon a bench. The priest and the deacon came with the chalice, while the sextons stretched him out, pried his mouth open and poured in the sacrament by force. The lad had spat it out. Whereupon the deacon struck his cheek-bones so hard that the lower jaw had broken off. It was from this very injury that the sufferer died.

One woman, in order to escape the persecutors, had made a hole in the ice and, having first pushed her seven children of tender years underneath, had then drowned herself.

A certain pious man had made the sign of the cross over his pregnant wife and his three children, and that same night he himself slit their throats as they slept, and in the morning had gone to the authorities and announced: "I was the torturer of my own kin, and ye will do that office for me; and, even as they suffered at my hands, so shall I suffer at yours, and we shall be martyrs together in the Kingdom of Heaven for the old faith."

Many, flying from the Antichrists, were immolating themselves in the fire.

"And they're doing right. Blessed is this concern for the Lord! Inasmuch as even God doth not help those who fall into the hands of Antichrist; 'tis impossible to stand the tortures,—none can resist them. 'Tis better to go into the earthly fire than the eternal!" concluded Vitalia.

"Through fire and water is the only way out!" confirmed Sophia.

The stars were dimming. Wan streaks, between clouds, stretched along the rim of the sky. The windings of the river through the endless forests gleamed like dull steel in the fog. Below, under the cliffs, near the very Vetluga, the cloister, fenced in with a sharp-pointed palisade of logs, resembling an ancient, enormous forest town, was emerging from the murk. Facing the river were huge gates of logs,—over them was the image of Deijesus. Within the enclosure was a "flock" of log-cabins with raised ground floors, and stoops, entries, passages, secret chambers, small attic-rooms, porches, turrets, watch towers with narrow windows resembling fortress embrasures, and with steep, two-gabled roofs of logs; in addition to the cells of the brotherhood, there were different domestic offices: the smithy, the tailor shop, the tannery, the cobbler shop, the hospital, the school, the workroom where ikons were painted, and a hostel. The chapel dedicated to the Tolvuy Mother of God was also a simple structure of logs, no bigger than the others, with a wooden cross and a cupola of carved shingles; right alongside of it was the belfry, showing black against the wan sky.

A high-pitched, plaintive tolling was heard: summons to morning, struck on gongs made of oak planks; these substitutes for bells were suspended on ropes of twisted ox-sinews, and had a huge, three-sided nail for a clapper; according to tradition, it was with just such tolling that Noah had summoned the animals into the ark. Amid the sensitive forest silence this xylophonic pealing was delectably melancholy and tender.

The pilgrims crossed themselves as they contemplated the holy cenoby,—the last refuge of the persecuted.

"Holy, Holy, Thou New Jerusalem, for the glory of the Lord shineth upon thee!" Kilikeia began to chant, a touching joy lighting up her transparently pale face that had the appearance of wax.

"All the holy refuges have been ruined, but this one they have not touched," remarked Vitalia. " 'Tis to be seen that the Queen of Heaven Herself shields this house with her holy mantle. 'Tis written in Revelation, now: 'And to the woman were given two wings of a great eagle, that she might fly into the wilderness. . . .' " [81]

"Long is the arm of the Czar, yet 'twill not reach as far as here," remarked one of the pilgrims.

"All that is left of Russia is here!" concluded another.

The pealing ceased and all fell silent. It was the hour of the great silence, when, according to tradition, the waters are at rest, and the angels are officiating, and the seraphim beat their wings in holy awe before the throne of the All-Highest.

Ivannushka the simpleton, squatting on his heels, was clasping his knees with his hands, and, as he looked with an immovable gaze at the lightening east, sang his eternal little song:

> A coffin of pine wood
> For me has been hewed;
> Therein I me lay
> To bide Judgment Day.

And again, as at the time when they had been on the float, in Peterburgh, on the night of the Festival of Venus, they began speaking of the world's last days, and of Antichrist.

" 'Twill be soon, soon,—'tis on the very threshold!" Vitalia began. "Now we still contrive to get along somehow; but then, when Antichrist shall have come, we shan't even be able to open our lips,—we may, perhaps, just be able to keep God within our hearts. . . ."

" 'Tis wearisome,—wearisome!" Kilikeia the hysterical was moaning.

"Avilka, a runaway Cossack from the Don, was saying the other day," Vitalia went on, "that a vision did come to him when he was on the steppe: three ancients did walk up to his hut,—all three of them looking alike,—and they spoke in Russian, although somewhat in the manner of the Greeks. 'Whence come ye?' asks he, 'and whither go ye?'—'We are from Jerusalem,' say they, 'from the Sepulcher of the Lord, bound for Sanct Peterburgh, for to see the Antichrist.'— 'Why,' says the Cossack, 'what Antichrist will ye find there?' —'Him whom ye call Czar Peter Alexeievich,' say they, 'he and none other is the Antichrist. 'Tis he who will capture Czargrad [Constantinople], and gather Jews and set out for Jerusalem, and set up his reign there. And the Jews, now, shall recognize him as the real Antichrist. And with him this our age shall end. . . .' "

All again fell silent, as though expecting something. Suddenly, from the forest came a prolonged cry, like the weeping of a child, probably the cry of some night-bird.

"Oh, little brethren, little brethren!" Petka Zhizla began to babble, stammering and sobbing. " 'Tis frightful. . . . We are calling Czar Peter Antichrist,—but what if he should be right here, in the forest? . . . See what confusion there is e'en among us."

"Ye fools, fools,—with no more brains than rams!" suddenly came somebody's voice, resembling the angry growling of a bear.

They turned around and beheld a pilgrim whom they had not noticed before. He must have come right out of the forest while they had been talking, and taken a seat somewhat apart, in the shadow, keeping silent all the while. He was a tall old man, all grown over with red, grizzled hair, with round shoulders and bowed back. His face was almost indistinguishable in the morning murk.

"How could this Czar Peter be ever numbered among the Antichrists,—the tippling, vagabonding, woman-dangling wretch that he is!" the old man went on. "At worst, he is but the leavings of Antichrist. The Last of Devils will go at things far differently, and have far more brains than this same Peter! . . ."

"Abba, Father," Vitalia implored, all aquiver from fear and curiosity, "teach us silly ones,—enlighten us with the light of truth,—impart to us everything in detail: just how will the coming of the Son of Perdition take place?"

The old man began to grunt and stir, and, with great difficulty, got up on his feet at last. There was something ponderous, ursine, heavy-footed about all his enormous person. A boy took his hand and led him up to the fire. Under his stiffened sheepskin short-coat—evidently never taken off—hung a stone harness upon iron chains: one slab in front, the other behind; upon his head was an iron cap; about his waist was an iron belt,—something in the nature of a hoop with a loop.[82] Tikhon recalled the life of an ancient Murom ascetic, Kapiton the Great: a loop served him for a belt, and, with a hook in the ceiling, was likewise his bed: putting the loop over the hook, he would fall asleep, as he hung.

The old man perched himself on a pine-stump and turned his face toward the dawn-glow. It cast its wan light upon him. Where his eyes had been were black depressions, twin sores with bloody whites. The sharp points of the nails driven through the front of his iron cap had sunk into the bone of his skull,—because of that his eyes had leaked out and he had become blind. His whole face was frightful, but his smile was tender, child-like.

He began to speak as if his blind eyes beheld that which he spoke of.

"Oh, my friends, my friends, my poor little ones! Whereof have you become frightened? *He himself*, now, is not yet here, *he* is neither to be seen nor to be heard. Of his forerunners there have been many, and there are many now, and there shall be many hereafter. They are making the path

smooth for him. But when they shall have smoothed out and
cleared everything away, then *He himself* will appear. He will
be born of an unclean virgin, and Satan shall enter into him,
and in everything shall this Dissembler make himself like
unto the Son of God: he will observe chastity, he will keep
fasts, and be meek, and be merciful; he will make the sick
whole, feed the hungry, shelter the homeless, and bestow
peace on them that suffer. And there shall come to him those
who have been bidden and those who have not been bidden,
and make him king over all the nations. And he will gather
together all his forces, from where the sun rises to where it
sets; he will make the sea white with sails, and the fields
black with shields, and he shall say: 'I will grasp all creation
in the palm of my hand like to a nest, and loot it, even as a nest
is looted of the eggs that are left therein!' And he will work
miracles and great portents: he will shift mountains, walk
upon water dry-shod, bring fire down from heaven, and make
fiends seem angels of light, as well as bringing forth his hosts
unincorporeate, which same shall be without number; and
to the sound of trumpets, and voices, and great shouting, and
unbelievably wondrous songs, he shall shine forth like unto
the sun, this chieftain of darkness, and soar up to the sky,
and come down to earth, in great glory. And he will seat
him in the temple of the All-Highest God saying: 'I am
God!' and all shall bow down before him, saying: 'Thou art
God; and there is no other God save thee.' And the abomination that maketh desolate will reign upon the holy place, and
thereupon the earth shall weep and the ocean wail; the sky
will not drop its dew nor the clouds their rain; the sea shall
be filled with stench and vileness; the rivers will dry up,—the
chill springs will be exhausted. Men will die of hunger and of
thirst, and they shall come to the Son of Perdition and say:
'Give us to eat and to drink.' And he will laugh at them and
revile them. And they shall come to know that this is The
Beast. And they shall run, fleeing from his face, yet nowhere
find a place to hide themselves. And a darkness will descend
upon them,—there will be wail upon wail, and woe upon woe.
And men will be as if they were dead to look at, and the comeliness of women shall fade, and there will be no more lust in
men. Gold and silver will be thrown into the dust of the market

places, yet none will stoop to pick them up. And they will die like beasts because of their sorrow, and bite their tongues, and blaspheme against the Living God. And then the heavenly powers will waver, and a sign of the Son of Man shall appear in the sky. He will come. Yea, come Thou, Lord! Amen. Amen. Amen."

He fell silent and fixed his blind eyes on the East, as though he already beheld that which no one else did,—there, on the rim of the heavens, in the piled-up masses of the dark clouds, flooded with blood and gold. Fiery streaks were widening in the sky, like the fiery wings of seraphim, fallen down on their faces before the glory of the coming Lord. Over the black wall of the forest appeared an ember,—white hot, blinding. Its rays, shattering against the pointed summits of the black firs, began to play in a rainbow of many colors. And the glow of the fire grew dim in the glow of the sun. And the earth, and the sky, and the waters, and the leaves, and the birds,—all created things,—and the hearts of men, were exulting with great joy: Yea, come thou, Lord!

Tikhon was experiencing the horror and the joy of the end of the world,—horror and joy familiar to him since childhood.

Sophia, crossing herself as she faced the sun, was invoking the fiery baptism, the eternal sun,—the Red Death.

But Ivannushka the simpleton, squatting upon his heels as before and embracing his knees with his hands, was gently swaying and looking at the East,—the beginning of the day, —as he sang for the eternal West,—the end of all days:

> O ye coffins made out of oak-logs tall,—
> Our eternal homes ye shall be for all!
> Day is over, and the night draws nigh;
> The sun is sinking toward the west,
> And the ax so sharp at the root doth lie,
> And the end of time is about to fall. . . .

II

There was a conclave of the brethren at the cenoby for a council on the disputed writings of Avvacum.[83]

The greatly martyred Archpresbyter had sent to his friend

in Kerzhenetz, the ancient Sergii, certain writings concerning the Holy Trinity, with the inscription: "Receive, Sergii, this eternal evangel, written not by me, but by the finger of God."

In these writings it was affirmed: "The substance of the Holy Trinity is divisible into three co-equal and distinct entities. The Father, the Son and the Holy Ghost have each a separate seat, upon three thrones, as the three Kings of Heaven. Christ sits upon a fourth, separate throne, co-regnant with the Holy Trinity. The Son of God was made flesh in the womb of the Virgin outside of subsistence: merely through grace, and not through hypostasis."

Deacon Fedor accused Avvacum of heresy. The ancient Onuphrii, a disciple of Avvacum, accused Deacon Fedor of the same thing. The followers of Fedor, Con-Substantialists, disparagingly called the Onuphrians Tri-Substantialists, while the latter in their turn derided the Con-Substantialists as addlepates. And there arose a great cleavage, "and, in place of former ardent love, hatred, and defamation, and every sort of malice settled within the brotherhood."

In order to abate the dissension in the Church, a conclave had been convened in the Long Mosses, and Father Ierothei, a disciple of Onuphrii the ancient, and, after his demise, the only head and propounder of Onuphrianism, had been summoned to answer charges.

They gathered in the cell of Mother Golendukha, which stood in a dale in the middle of the forest, outside of the cenoby enclosure. The Onuphrians refused to carry on any discussion in the cenoby itself, being apprehensive of the usual hand-to-hand mêlée, which might end badly for them, inasmuch as there were more of the Con-Substantialists than there were of the Tri-Substantialists.

Tikhon was present at the gathering. But Kornilii, the ancient, did not go.

"What's the use of merely wagging your tongue?" he had said. "We must burn: 'tis in the fire one will come to learn the truth."

The cell,—a spacious hut,—was divided in two: a small side-room, which was the living-chamber, and a large one, used for prayers. All around, along the log walls, were images, placed upon shelves. Lampads and tapers glowed before them. Black-grouse tail-feathers hung upon the candlesticks, by way of snuffers. There were benches along the walls. Upon these lay stout books, in bindings of leather and wood and with clasps of copper, and manuscripts; the most ancient of these were the writings of the great desert fathers, writ upon birch-bark.

It was stuffy and dark within, despite the noonday: the shutters on the windows, with small openings covered over with turbid fish-bladders, were shut against the sun. Only here and there, through the cracks, needles of light had extended, making the flames of the lampads and tapers glow a dull red. There was an odor of wax, leather, sweat, and olibanum. The door leading to the front steps was open,—through it one could see the sun-flooded dale and the dark forest.

The ancients, in black cassocks and cowls, were crowding together about Father Ierothei, who was standing in the middle of the chapel, before a lectern. He had a staid air; his face was as white as a consecrated wafer, and well-fed; his eyes were blue, somewhat wall-eyed, with a different expression in each: one was filled with Christian resignation and the other with "philosophic arrogance." He had a persuasive voice "like to the swallow, harbinger of good tidings." He was rather dandified,—his cassock was of the finest broadcloth, his cowl of velvet, his pectoral cross adorned with balas-rubies. The sweet fragrance of attar of roses was wafted from his aureately-hoary locks. Amid the lowly ancients, the forest mouzhiks, he seemed a veritable *boyarin,* or a Nikonian bishop.

Father Ierothei was a man of learning; "he had absorbed bookish wisdom and reasoning as a sponge absorbs water." But his enemies asserted that his wisdom was not from God. He had, it would seem, two teachings: one obvious, orthodox, for general consumption; the other secret, heretical, for the elect,—people of high station and wealth, for the most part. As for the simple folk and the poor, he seduced them through alms.

From early morn until noon did the Con-Substantialists contend with the Tri-Substantialists, yet arrived at no solution. Father Ierothei was forever wriggling,—"blowing hot and cold." No matter how the ancients beset him, they could not drive him out into the open.

Finally, in the heat of the dispute, a disciple of Father Ierothei, Brother Spiridon,—gimlet-eyed, swarthy-faced, with short love-locks, resembling the ear-locks of the Jews,—suddenly leapt forward and shouted with all his might:

"The Trinity sit alongside of each other,—the Son to the right and the Holy Ghost to the left of the Father. The three Kings of Heaven sit upon different thrones, without any concealment, while Christ sits on a fourth throne, apart from the others!"

"Thou art quadrupling the Trinity!" the fathers cried out in horror.

"But according to the whole lot of you, you must have one Person? Ye lie,—'tis not one but three, three, three!" Father Spiridon brandished his arm as though he were wielding an ax. "Believe in the Tri-Substantial Trinity,—cleave the Uncleavable—never fear, one is not three, while the Subsistence of Christ is the fourth!...."

And he launched forth into an explanation of the difference between Subsistence and Nature: The Subsistence of the Son, now, was inward, while the Nature sat at the feet of the Father.

"Not through Subsistence but through a unique Nature would God become man. Were he to descend as subsistence upon earth, it would have scorched up the whole world and the womb of the Most Pure Mother of God would not have been able to carry the whole of the Divinity,—her womb would simply have been burned up!"

"Oh thou erring and passionate one, examine thy conscience, comprehend God, cast out of thee the root of heresy, —pause, repent, dearest little one!" the ancients strove to convince him. "Whoever told thee, or who has ever seen, that the three Kings of Heaven are sitting separately and without concealment? Even the angels and the archangels may not look upon Him, yet thou hast said: 'They sit without any concealment!' And how is it that the tongue of him who uttered this was not scorched? . . .".

But Spiridon continued to vociferate, his very voice breaking:

"Three, three, three! I will die for the three! Ye could not burn it out of my soul even with fire! ..."

Seeing that nothing could be done with him, they again attacked Father Ierothei himself.

"Why shilly-shally? Speak straight! How dost thou believe,—in the Con-Substantial or the Tri-Substantial Trinity?"

Father Ireothei kept silent and merely smiled squeamishly into his beard. One could see that, from the height of his learning, he looked down upon all these simple fellows, as if they were so many stinking villeins. But the fathers pressed him with ever greater fury,—"butting him as if they were goats."

"Why art thou silent? Or hast thou grown deaf? Thou dost close up thy ears, like to the deaf aspic!"—"Thou hast become hardened and haughty, like to a proud Pharaoh!"—"Thou dost not want to be in council with the Fathers,—hast contemned everybody, hast shattered the love of the Fathers!"—"Thou seditious fellow and confounder of Christianity!"

"Why do ye beset me so?" Father Ierothei finally snarled at them, unable to restrain himself, imperceptibly backing toward the door of the side-room. "Don't crowd me! 'Tis not ye who will have to answer for me. Whether I be saved or whether I be not saved, what affair is that of yours? Live ye your own way,—and we will live ours. You and we have nothing in common. Don't crowd me, I pray you!"

Father Prov, as hoary as a loon, but still a stalwart and thick-set old man, was shaking his cudgel of elm wood before Father Ierothei's very nose:

"Thou most great and insane heretic! Were some secular judge to smooth thy sides with a cudgel like this, thou wouldst find a single faith in thyself fast enough,—either Tri-Substantial or Con-Substantial. But, having had a free rein, thou dost rave on as thy mood moves thee. ..."

"Peace unto ye, brethren in Christ!" came a quiet voice, —but a voice so dissimilar to the others that all heard it; it was the black-robed Father Missail talking, he had come from a distant wilderness, and was a great striver after sainthood,—"young in years, but with the mind of a centenarian."

—"What will be the end of this, beloved Fathers? Is it not the devil who is warring in us, and inflaming us with fratricidal sedition? Yet no one seeks the water of life in order to put out the flame of Satan,—rather, every one seeketh pitch, and tinder wood, and dry faggots, to make the fire worse. Yea, brethren, I have not heard of such fraternal hatred even among the Nikonians! And, should they find out thereof, and begin to torture and to kill us anew, they shall no longer be at fault before God, and to us those tortures shall be the beginning of the pains of eternal tortures."

All fell silent, as though they had suddenly come to their right senses.

Father Missail got down on his knees and bowed down to the very feet, first of the entire gathering, then of Father Ierothei individually.

"Forgive, Fathers! Forgive, Ierotheiushka, dearest little brother of mine! Great is the height of thy wisdom,—there is a fiery mind in thee. Take pity upon us lowly ones, then; put aside the disputed writings, and show us thy love!"

He got up and was about to embrace Ierothei. But the latter would not permit this, himself getting down on his knees and bowing at the feet of Father Missail.

"Forgive me, Father! For who am I? I am no better than a dead hound. And how can I reason better than your holy conclave? There is a fiery mind within me, thou sayest. Yea, thou dost bring great vanity upon my soul! I am but a man, the equal of those creatures that live in foul bogs, which creatures are called frogs. Even as a sow that eateth its young, so do I fill my belly. Were it not for God's help, my soul would scarce escape entering Hell. I do but barely, barely breathe under the lusts which crush me. Woe is me, sinner that I am! As for thee, Missailushka,—may God save thee, for thy admonition. . . ."

Father Missail, with a meek smile, again stretched out his arms to embrace Father Ierothei, but the latter got up on his feet and thrust him away, with a face so distorted, with such pride and malice, that all felt eerie.

"God save thee for thy admonition," he went on in a suddenly changed voice that quivered from fury, "for that thou dost admonish us of little sense and dost point out the way

to us! And yet, my friend, 'twould be a good thing to know
one's mean! Thou soarest high, but beware lest thou tumble
down from that height! From whom didst thou receive thy
teaching title, and who has appointed thee one of the
teachers? All have become teachers now,—yet there is nobody to hear the teachings! Woe is us, and this our time,
and those living therein! Thou art but a young child, yet
thou hast high daring. To tell the truth, we do not even
want to listen to thee. Go and teach them who will follow
thy preachment,—but do, I pray thee, withdraw from us.
What fine teachers! One fellow threatens with a cudgel,
while another attempts to seduce us through love. But what
is there in such a love, when we love for the sake of over-
throwing the truth? Even Satan loves those who are faithful to him. But we, even as we have no glut of love for
Christ, so we have no glut of hatred for His enemies. Even
though God were to will that I die, I would not join with
apostates! Pure am I, and the dust which clings to my feet
I shake off before you, as it is written: One that worketh
the will of God is better than the hosts of the unrighteous!" [84]

And, amid the general confusion, Father Ierothei, his
retreat covered by his acolytes, darted into the door of the
side-room.

Father Missail withdrew to one side and began praying
quietly, to the constant refrain of:

"Misfortune is coming,—misfortune is coming. Have mercy
upon us, Most Pure Mother of God!"

As for the ancients, they again fell to shouting and wran-
gling, worse than ever:

"Spirka, oh Spirka, thou vile fellow, do listen: the Son
sits to the right of the Father on the throne. And 'tis well
thus,—do not displace Him, thou child of madness,—do
not shove him off with thy vile tongue from that kingly throne
to the feet of the Father! . . ."—"Accursed, accursed, accursed! Anathema! Even though an angel were to proclaim
that which is contrary to the Scriptures, let him be anathema!"—"Ye ignoramuses! Ye can not explain the Scriptures. What is the use of wasting breath in talking to you
clodhoppers!"—"God has barred thee out for thy opposi-

tion to truth! Perish thou with thy own kind!"—"Yea, may
we have no dealings with ye, neither in this age nor in that
to come!"

They were all speaking together, and no one listened to
any one else.

Now it was not only the Con-Substantialists who were
ready to rend the throats of the Tri-Substantialists,—the
same held true even of those who were brethren in each belief, yet were eager to do battle over the least trifle: whether
a censer should be swung cross-wise or thrice in a circle;
whether garlic should be eaten on the Day of the Annunciation and on that of the Forty Martyrs; should priests abstain
from onions for a whole day before saying the liturgy?
Concerning the rule against sitting during a fast with the
legs crossed; which was the proper reading: *Forever and aye*
or *Forever and a day?*—there was a battle over every iota,
every comma and every dot in the old books.

"And a small slip of the pen, now, doth create a great
heresy."—"We are willing to die for a single *alpha!*"—"Hold
to that which is written in the old books, and sink thy teeth
into the prayer of Jesus,—and that's all there is to it!"—
"Do comprehend, Fedka,—thou enemy of God, thou dog,
thou whore son, thou hound from hell,—the difference between the cross of Christ and the cross of Peter: the cross
of Christ hath a block for His feet on the *stipes,* while that
of St. Peter hath none," Brother Julian was striving to prove
in a voice grown hoarse,—he was the scholar of Long Mosses,
and always quiet and meek, yet now he seemed to be in
downright frenzy with foam on his lips, the veins on his
temple swollen, and his eyes bloodshot.

"So has St. Peter's,—so has St. Peter's!" Fedka was straining himself.

"It hasn't! It hasn't!" vociferated Brother Julian.

And, coming to his support, Father Triphilii, another
scholarly monk, leapt forward (so the story was told subsequently) "like a ruff out of the water, with a great howl, his
eyes popping out, all aquiver and trembling from his great
zeal; his very bones seemed to contract, his members to
shudder; his beard fairly danced up and down, while his
teeth snapped; his voice was frenzied, like to a camel in

heat; he was unmerciful, untamable, and horrid to behold because of his savageness." He no longer strove anything, but merely cursed with maternal oaths,—being answered in kind. They had begun with benedictions and had ended with maledictions.

"Satan himself has crawled into thy skin! . . ."—"Thou black-frocked knave, thou hast sold thy soul for a flask of wine! . . ."—"Oh, the profanations,—oh, the abominations! Thou swine, accursed and unworthy of being on this earth,—there is none lower to be found in this world! Thou erring beast! . . ."—"There be certain vermin, whose foul bellies belch forth that the Holy Trinity . . ."—"Hearken, —hearken to what is said of the Holy Trinity! . . ."—"Is there anything worth while hearkening to? Nobody can make head or tail out of the tissue of lies thou hast woven, —thou hast woven it like a bast sandal, and cunningly hid the ends thereof. . . ."—" 'Tis given to me to know the mysteries of Heaven!"—"Enough of thy blather! Stuff an old foot-clout down thy maw!"—"Be ye accursed! Be ye accursed! Anathema!"

In this council of mouzhiks in the forests of Vetluga, the disputation was carried on almost precisely as it had been fourteen centuries ago, during the time of Julian the Apostate, at the Ecclesiastical Councils held at the court of the Byzantine Emperors.

Tikhon looked on and listened,—and it seemed to him that these were not men disputing about God, but beasts clawing and gnawing one another, and that the calm of his splendidly beautiful wilderness Mother was forever defiled by these sacrilegious disputes.

Shouts were heard near the windows of the cell. Mother Golendukha, Mother Meropia, and Mother Uleia (the oldest of the lot), looked out of the windows, and the three of them saw that a whole mob was emerging from the forest into the dell,—coming from the direction of the cloister. Thereupon they recalled how once, during just such another gathering of the Brethren at Kerzhenetz, in the Larion clearing, some lay brethren, hired hands and bee-masters, all of whom were bribed, had come to the hut where the gathering was held, armed with blunderbusses, bear-spears and pointed stakes, and had fallen upon the ancients.

Fearing lest, somehow, something of the same sort happen now, the mothers darted into the chapel and bolted the outside door with stout oaken bolts, at the very instant when the crowd was already breaking it down and hammering at the door:

"Open! Open!"

They were shouting other things as well. But Mother Golendukha, who took charge of everything, and was rather hard of hearing, did not make out what they were saying. As for the other Mothers, they merely dashed about and clucked like thoroughly frightened hens: they were deafened, too, by the shouts within the chapel, where the Fathers, paying no attention to anybody, kept on with their dispute. Father Spiridon announced that: "Christ, now, did enter the Virgin through Her ear, and did come out of Her side, in a manner ineffable."

Father Triphilii spat in his face. Father Spiridon seized Father Triphilii by the beard, tore his cowl off, and wanted to strike his bald pate with a copper cross, but the ancient Prov knocked the cross out of Spiridon's hand with his cudgel of elm wood. An Onuphrian scholar, Arkhipka, a most robust fellow, made a dash for Father Prov's temple so hard with his fist that the old man was felled like one dead. A free-for-all began. It was just as though fiends had taken possession of the ancients. In the sultry darkness, barely lit up by the dim light of the lampads and the slender needles of sunlight, one could glimpse a helter-skelter of frightful faces, clenching fists, leather rosaries,—with which the brethren lashed one another over the eyes,—torn books, pewter candle-sticks and burning candles,—which, too, had been requisitioned for weapons. The air was filled with maternal oaths, moans, roars, howling, squealing. . . .

Outside, the hammering and shouting was kept up:

"Open! Open!"

The old hut was shaking from the blows,—they were using an ax to chop a shutter through.

Mother Uleia,—porously plump and as white as flour,—fell down on the floor in an hysterical fit and began to call with such a piercing, hiccoughing voice that all were thrown into a panic.

The shutter splintered and tumbled down, and, through the burst fish-bladder that formed the window, was thrust in the head of the cenoby's harness-maker, Father Mina, with popping eyes and gaping, shouting mouth:

"The soldiers,—the soldiers are coming! Why have ye locked yourselves up, ye fools? Come out as fast as you can!"

They were dumbfounded. Just as they were, standing there with uplifted fists, or with fingers sunk into the hair of some opponent, they stood rooted to the spot, as if they were carved. A dead silence ensued. Father Missail alone kept on weeping and praying:

"Misfortune has come,—misfortune has come! Have mercy upon us, Most Pure Mother of God!"

Coming to their senses at last, they made a dash for the doors, opened them, and scuttled out.

From the throngs that had gathered in the dale they learned fearful news: a company of soldiers, with priests, hired witnesses, and clerks, was making its way into the forest; this company had already demolished the neighboring cenoby at Moroshko, on the River Unzha, and, if not to-day, then to-morrow, it was bound to arrive at Long Mosses.

III

Tikhon caught sight of Kornilii the ancient, surrounded by a crowd of cenobites and *mouzhiks*, country wives, and children, from the hamlets round-about.

"It behooves no believer to lend ear to idle arguments and to hang back," preached the ancient; "come into the fire boldly,—suffer for the sake of the Lord! Step, skip and a jump,—and right into the flames! There now, thou devil, —here's my body; thou hast no concern for my soul! Now our portion at the torturers' consists of fire and faggots, of earth and the ax, of the knife and the gallows, but, over there, the songs of angels, and words of glory, and praise, and joyance await us. When our dead bodies shall be made alive through the Holy Ghost we will again come forth out of our Mother Earth, even as a babe comes forth out of its mother's belly. Prophets and patriarchs shall not 'scape the trial; the countenances of all the saints shall have to face the river of fire; we alone shall be free, for that our trial will have consisted of our having been just burned; our fiery river,—of having gone into the fire of ourselves. We will flare up like candles, as a sacrifice to the Lord! We will be baked, like to sweet bread, for the Holy Trinity! We will die for the love of the Son of God! More beautiful than the sun is the beautiful red death!"

"We shall burn! We shall burn! We shall not give ourselves up to Antichrist!" the crowd fell to roaring with a frenzied roar. The country wives and the children yelled louder than the *mouzhiks*.

"Run, run into the flames! Set yourselves on fire! Flee from the torturers!"

"Now it is the cenobies that burn," went on the ancient, "but later on it will be the villages, and the hamlets, and the towns, that shall be set afire! I myself would take fire and ignite Nizhnii; I would wax joyous were it to burn down from one end to the other! And, being envious of us, even of all Russia, will burn up! ..."

His eyes were blazing with an awesome fire; it seemed that this was the fire of that last conflagration wherein the universe would be destroyed.

When he had ended, the throng scattered over the meadow and the edge of the forest.

Tikhon, for a long time, had been going through the ranks of the crowd, listening closely to all that was being said in the individual knots. It seemed to him that they were all going out of their minds. One *mouzhik* was saying to another:

"The Kingdom of Heaven is falling into thy very lap of itself, yet thou dost keep on putting it off: thy children are so small, now; thy wife is so young; thou dost not want to ruin thyself. But, my soul, hast thou much with them? Maybe a sack and a plack, and, to make it three, the bast sandals on your feet. Yet you, a man, are more foolish than any country wife. Well, now, thou wilt live to see thy wife well-bedded and thy children wedded. But after that, what?

Is it not the grave? Whether thou dost burn or whether thou dost not, death remains thy only lot!"

One novice was striving to convince another:

"Take any sort of penance,—it means ten years of epitimesis! Where are thou going to fast and to pray? But, no sooner dost thou enter the fire, than there's the whole of thy penance,—neither toiling, nor fasts, nor moiling, but that very hour thou art in Heaven rejoicing; the fire, now, will cleanse thee of all thy sins. Just as soon as thou art consumed in the flames, thou art free from everything!"

One gaffer was inviting another:

"Come now, my dearest dear, thou hast lived long enough. The radish, now, has eaten through thy belly. 'Tis time to go to the other world,—even though we'll be of the lesser martyrs!"

The little lads played with the little lasses:

"Let's go into the fire! In the other world our shirts will be of gold, our boots will be of red leather; there will be plenty and to spare of nuts, mead, and apples."

"It would be a good thing if the babes were also to burn," the ancients blessed them, "for they shall not sin when they grow up,—they shall not wed, nor lie in child-bed; but, best of all, their purity shall not be corrupted."

Tales were told of former great self-imposed *autos-da-fé*.

There had been a vision in the cenoby of Paleustrov, where two thousand and seven hundred people had burned themselves together with the holy ancient Ignatii: when the church had caught on fire, Father Ignatii had issued out of its very cupola, amid great smoke, bearing the cross, and, after him, sundry other ancients, and a multitude of people, —all in white garments, amid great glory and radiance,— had marched in ranks up to the sky, and had vanished within the heavenly portals.

While in the hamlet of Pudozh, where some nineteen hundred and twenty souls had burned, the soldiers on guard that night had beheld a pillar of light which descended from heaven, colored with divers colors, like to a rainbow; and from the summit of the said pillar three men had descended in vestments that shone like to the sun, and walked in a file around the fire; one blessed it with a cross, another

sprinkled it with holy water, while the third swung a censer
with frankincense therein, the while all three chanted in
a low voice; and then, having walked around the fire thrice,
they again entered the pillar and mounted up to heaven.
After that, on the eve of high Sabbath-days, many saw, in
the night-time, on the same spot, candles burning, and heard
singing sweet beyond all telling.

And a certain *mouzhik* in Pomorië had had another sort
of vision. He had been lying unconscious in a burning fever,
and had beheld a whirling wheel of fire, and upon that wheel
were men in torment and screaming: "This is the lot of
those who would not burn of themselves, but who dwelt in
frailty and worked for Antichrist; go thou and preach over
all the earth,—that all may throw themselves in the flames!"
And a drop from the wheel had fallen upon his lip. The
mouzhik awoke,—and lo! his lip had rotted away. And he
preached to all the people: " 'Tis a good thing to burn; and
this, now, has been put upon my lip for a sign by those
dead men who had not wanted to burn themselves."

Kilikeia the hysterical, as she sat on the grass, was singing the canticle of the Halleluiah wife.—When the Jews
sent by Herod had been seeking the Infant Christ to slay
him, the Halleluiah wife had concealed him, but had thrown
her own child into the furnace in His stead:

> Then Christ, the Heavenly King, he up and spake:
> Ho, thou, Halleluiah Wife,—thou most merciful!
> Go thou, preach My will unto My lambs all,—
> Unto all the Christians that to Me true are:
> That they cast themselves in the flames for *Me*,—
> That they cast therein all their sinless babies. . . .

But here and there one could already hear voices raised
up against self-burning:

"Dear little fathers of mine," Father Missail was imploring them, " 'tis a good thing to be zealous for God, yet one
should know the mean! Self-willed martyrdom is not pleasing to God. There is but one path to Christ: those who
have not been captured should take to their heels; while
those who have been captured should endure in patience,
but by no means thrust themselves upon martyrdom! Rest
ye from this horror, my poor little ones!"

And even the raging Father Triphilii concurred with the meek Father Missail:

"Ye are no brands, to be burning in vain! Can it be possible that, having huddled together like pigs in a sty, ye will set yourselves afire?"

"What profound ignorance!" Father Ierothei shrugged his shoulders squeamishly.

Mother Golendukha, who had already burnt once, but had not burnt completely,—she had been dragged out and doused with water,—sought to frighten everybody with stories of how bodies in the fire shrivel and squirm, the head and feet being drawn together, as if it were with a rope, while the blood boils and foams just like a stew in a pot. Also how, after a fire, the bodies lie bloated up most mightily, and, having been broiled in the flames, give off an odor of roasted meat; some, however, remain whole,—but, no matter what one pulls them by, that part comes loose. Hounds,—may they be accursed!—prowl about, their muzzles all black, devouring the flesh of the baked bodies. A most oppressive stench arises from the site of such a fire for a long time, so that none can walk by without holding his or her nose. Then, too, during an actual burning, people had seen, above the flames, two black fiends,—something on the manner of Ethiopians, with the wings of bats,—exulting and clapping their hands and crying out: "Ours,—they be ours!" And for many years thereafter voices were heard in that place every night, whispering: "Oh, we have perished,—we have perished!"

At last those opposed to self-burning beset Kornilii the ancient:

"How is it that thou hast never burnt thyself? If it be such a good thing, you, the teachers, ought to be the first to go in! But, as things stand, ye shove your poor followers into the fire, just so's to grow jolly fat bellies for yourselves. All of you who teach self-burning are like that: ' 'tis a good thing, 'tis a good thing,—but for others, and not ourselves.' Fear ye God; ye have burnt enough,—spare those left at least!"

Thereupon, at a sign from the ancient, the lad Kiriukha,

a most ardent incendiary, stepped out, brandishing an ax.
He grunted out in a resonant voice:

"He that will not burn of his own free will, let him come
out with an ax, and we shall fight. And whoever hews the
other down will be in the right. Should he kill me, it means
that self-burning is not pleasing to God; but, should I kill
him,—set yourselves a-fire!"

No one accepted the challenge, and the victory remained
with Kiriukha.

Kornilii the ancient stepped forward and said:

"They that would burn, let them stand to the right; they
that would not,—to the left!"

The crowd parted. One half surrounded the ancient; the
other stepped aside. Of those eager for the flames there
proved to be some eighty souls; of those who were against
burning,—about one hundred. The ancient made the sign
of the cross over those about to die, and, raising his eyes
to the sky, uttered solemnly:

"For Thy sake, Lord, and for Thy faith, and for the love
of the Only Begotten Son of God, do we die. We spare not
ourselves, laying down our souls for Thy sake, nor shall
we violate our baptism, but receive a second baptism,—of
fire; we burn ourselves out of hatred for Antichrist. We die
for Thy Most Pure Love!"

"Burn, burn! Set yourselves afire!" the crowd again began roaring with a frenzied roar. It seemed to Tikhon that,
were he to remain any longer in the midst of this insane
crowd, he himself would go out of his mind.

He ran off into the forest. He ran until the shouts died
away. A narrow little path brought him to the familiar
glade, grown over with tall grasses and surrounded by
slumbrous fir trees, where once upon a time he had prayed
to dank Mother-Earth. Upon the dark summits of the trees
the evening sun was expiring. Golden cloudlets floated in
the sky. The grove breathed forth a resinous freshness. The
quietude was infinite.

He lay face down on the earth, buried himself in the grass,
and again, as at that time on Round Lake, kissed the earth,
—prayed to the earth, as though he knew that the earth

alone could save him from the fiery delirium of the Red Death:

> Wondrous Queen, Mother of God,—
> Thou earth, thou earth, our Mother dank!

Suddenly he felt some one place a hand on his shoulder, he turned around and saw Sophia. She bent over him and was looking into his face,—silently, intently.

He, too, was silent, looking up at her from below,—which made the face of the girl, under its loose black monastic kerchief, stand out sharply against the aureate azure of the sky, like the countenance of some familiar saint upon the gold background of an ikon. Pale with an even sallow pallor,—with lips scarlet and fresh like a flower half-opened, —with eyes child-like and as dark as a still pool,—this face was so splendidly beautiful that his breath was cut short, as if from sudden fright.

"So that's where thou art, little brother!" Sophia uttered at last. "But there's the ancient man a-seeking thee everywhere,—can't think where thou couldst have got to. Well, do get up; let's go,—let's go as fast as we can!"

She was all haste and joy, just as though in a festive mood.

"Nay, Sophia," he uttered calmly and firmly. "I shall not go there any more. There,—I have had enough of it. I have seen and heard enough. I'll go away,—go away from this cloister altogether. . . ."

"And thou wilt not go into the flames?"

"That I won't."

"Wilt thou go off without me?"

He gave her an imploring look:

"Sophiushka, my little dove! Listen not to the madmen. There is no need of burning,—'tis not the will of the Lord! 'Tis a great sin,—a temptation of the Fiend! Let's go away together, my own dear one! . . ."

She bent still lower toward him and, with a sly and tender smile, drew her face close to his face, her lips to his lips, so that he felt her hot breath:

"Thou shalt not go anywhere!" she whispered in a passionate whisper. "I shan't let thee go, my dear little one! . . ."

And suddenly she clasped his head within her arms, and their lips blended together.

"What art thou about,—what art thou about, little sister? . . . Can one do such things? They may see . . ."

"Let them see! Everything is permissible,—the fire will purify everything. Do but say that thou art willing to burn. . . . Dost thou want to?" she asked in a barely audible sigh, nestling up to him ever closer and closer.

Without reflection, without strength, without will, he answered in the same sigh as hers:

"I do want to!"

The last ray of the sun had expired upon the dark firs and the golden cloudlets had turned gray, like ashes. A sweet-smelling humidity was diffused through the air. The forest cast its slumbrous shadow over the two. The earth covered them with its tall grasses.

And it seemed to Tikhon that the forest, and the grass, and the earth, and the air, and the sky,—that all things were aflame with the flames of that last conflagration through which the universe was to be exterminated,—the flames of the Red Death. But he no longer feared,—and believed that the Red Death was fairer than the sun.

IV

The cenoby was deserted. The monks had fled from it like ants out of a trampled-down ant-hill.

The Self-Burners had gathered in a chapel which stood to one side of the cenoby, upon a knoll, so that they could not help but see from afar the approach of any soldiers.

This chapel was a log cabin of very ancient, dry lumber, built in such a manner that none could "drop out" during the holocaust. The windows were like mere cracks. The doors were so narrow that even one man could barely enter. The stoop and stairs had been demolished. The doors were hoarded up securely. Bolts and bars—all of thick beams—were placed over the windows. Then they began laying down the kindling,—heaping up tow, straw, oakum, resin, birch-bark; the walls were smeared with pitch; gunpowder was poured into special grooves running around the entire structure, while several pounds were kept back in reserve, to strew in little paths over the floor at the last minute. Two sentries were placed on the roof, whose duty it was, by turns, to watch day and night for the coming of the persecutors.

All worked joyously, as though preparing for a festival. The children helped the grown-ups,—the grown-ups became like children. And all were merry, as if they were intoxicated. Petka Zhizla was the merriest of all,—he worked for five. His withered hand, with the government brand, the seal of the Beast, was healing and regaining its activity.

Kornilii the ancient ran about, darting here and there like a spider in its web. There were strange spells in his eyes,— so light that it seemed they must glow in the darkness like the pupils of a cat,—with their heavy and caressing gaze: whoever these eyes looked upon was shorn of his or her will and worked the will of the ancient in all things.

"Come now, all together, my little ones!" he jested with those about to die, "I am the old man who can, while ye are the children small who are helpers all: we shall mount right up to the sky, even like unto Elijah the prophet in his chariot of fire!"

When everything was in readiness, they started shutting themselves in. The windows (save one, the narrowest of all), and the entrance-door were battened down. All listened in silence to the strokes of the hammer: it seemed that the coffin-lid was being hammered down over them while they were still alive.

Ivannushka the simpleton alone kept on singing his eternal song:

> A coffin of pine wood
> For me has been hewed;
> Therein I me lay
> To bide Judgment Day.

To those who desired to take the last rites the ancient said:

"Come, now, little children! What have ye to repent of? Ye are now like to angels of God, according to the words of David: *I have said, Ye are gods.*[85] Ye have overcome the Adversary's whole power. Sin hath no more dominion over ye. Ye can no longer sin. And, even though any of you were

to kill his own father, or to sin carnally with his mother,—
even he would be holy and rightous. The fire will purify
everything!"

The ancient ordered Tikhon to read the Revelation of
St. John, which is never read in any church services.

*"And I saw a new heaven and a new earth: for the first
heaven and the first earth were passed away. And he that
sat upon the throne said, Behold, I make all things new. And
he said unto me, Write: for these words are true and faithful. And he said unto me, It is done."* [86]

Tikhon, as he read, experienced the familiar sensation of
the end with such force as he had never experienced before. It seemed to him that the walls of the log cabin were
shutting out all those within from the world, from life, from
time, as the sides of a ship shut out water: there, outside,
time was still going on, but here it had already halted and
the end had come,—it was the consummation.

"I see . . . I see . . . I see . . . Oh, dear fathers of
mine!" Kilikeia began to scream, interrupting the reading,
—all pale, with distorted face and an unmoving stare in her
wide-open eyes.

"What dost thou see, mother?" the ancient asked her.

"I see a great city, the holy Jerusalem, coming down from
heaven, from God, like to precious stones,—like unto crystal
iaspis, and smaragd, and sapphire, and topaz. And its twelve
gates are twelve pearls. And the ways of that city are all of
pure gold, most clear, like unto glass. And there is no sun,—
but the glory of God doth light everything. Oh, 'tis a fearsome thing, 'tis a fearsome thing, my fathers . . . I see
His Countenance,—more radiant than the radiance of the
sun. . . . He is coming to us! . . ."

And to those who heard her it seemed that they were beholding that whereof she spake.

When night fell, candles were lit and, kneeling, they struck
up a troparion:

*"Behold, the Bridegroom cometh at midnight, and blessed
is the servant that shall meet Him waking. Be thou vigilant,
my soul, nor be thou weighed down with slumber, lest thou
be delivered to thy death and the gates of the Kingdom be
barred against thee, but arouse thyself, calling: Holy, holy,*

*holy,—God have mercy upon us, through the mother of God.
Think on that dread day, O my soul, and keep thy vigil, lighting thy taper and burning the light-giving oil, for thou knowest
not when there will come to thee the voice proclaiming:
Behold, the Bridegroom!"*

Sophia, standing by Tikhon's side, was holding his hand.
He felt the pressure of her trembling hand; he saw the smile
of timid joy upon her face,—the smile of the bride to the
bridegroom at their espousal. And a responsive joy filled his
soul. It seemed to him now that his former trepidation had
been a temptation of the Fiend, and that the Red Death
was the will of God: *For whosoever will save his life shall
lose it; but whosoever shall lose his life for My sake and the
Gospel's, the same shall save it.*[87]

They expected the arrival of a detachment of soldiers
that very night. Morning came and, together with it, a
fatigue which resembled the heavy after-effects of much
drinking.

The ancient kept a sharp eye on everybody. To those
who grew despondent or lost heart he gave rolled pills, somewhat resembling berries, made of a fragrant, dark paste,—
probably containing some stupefying herb. Whoever swal-
lowed one of these berries was thrown into an ecstatic fit,
ceased to fear the fire and raved about it as if it were
paradisaical bliss.

In order to bolster up their courage they told tales of the
Hungry Death in crude cabined oubliettes,—a death incom-
parably more fearful, it seemed, than death through self-
burning. These Eternal Fasters, after taking the severest
oaths, were placed in a bare hut which had neither doors nor
windows,—naught save broad sleeping berths near the ceiling. To prevent them from doing away with themselves all
their clothing was taken off,—even their belts and their
crosses. They were let down into the hut through the ceiling and the ceiling was then battened down, so that they
might not "fight their way out." Sentries with cudgels were
posted. Those who had chosen this death suffered three, or
four, or even six days. They wept, they implored: "Give us to
eat!" They gnawed at their own flesh and cursed God.

. On one occasion, twenty people had been placed in a

woodland threshing barn. As soon as they felt unbearably nauseous, they found stones and, knocking a board through, started crawling out. But the watchmen beat them with cudgels over the head, killing two, and after barring the opening, did report the matter to the holy ancient in charge of the affair. What were his orders regarding these people? And the ancient did order straw to be placed about the barn, and fire set thereto.

"Why, the Red Death is far easier: thou wilt just go up in flames and never feel a thing!" the narrators would conclude.

Akulka, a seven-year-old girl, who had all this while been sitting peacefully on a bench and attentively listening, suddenly began to shake all over, jumped up, darted toward her mother, seized her by the hem of her skirt, and began crying, with piercing screams:

"Mother, oh mother! Let's go,—let's go out of here! I don't want to burn! . . ."

Her mother soothed her, but she cried ever louder, ever more frenziedly:

"I don't want to burn! I don't want to burn!"

And there was such animal fear in this cry that all shuddered, as though they had suddenly comprehended the horror of all that which was taking place. The girl was petted, threatened, beaten; but she continued to scream and, finally, turning all blue, gasping from her screaming, she fell down on the floor and began to thresh about in convulsions.

Kornilii the ancient, bending over her, was crossing her, tapping her with his beads, and reading prayers of exorcism.

"Get thee out, get thee out of her soul, thou accursed one!"

But naught availed. Thereupon he took her in his arms, pried her mouth open, and forced her to swallow a berry of the dark paste. Then he fell to stroking her hair most gently and whispering something in her very ear. The girl quieted down little by little, as though she had fallen asleep; but her eyes were open, with the pupils distended and her gaze immovable, as in delirium.

Tikhon listened intently to the whispering of the ancient. The holy man was telling her about the Heavenly Kingdom, about the gardens of Paradise.

"But will there be any raspberries there, uncle dear?" asked Akulka.

"There will be, my own, there will be: so-o-o big, every berry the size of an apple, and fragrant, and sweet,—most sweet."

The little girl was smiling. One could see that her mouth was watering from a foretaste of the paradisaical raspberries. The ancient, meanwhile, continued caressing and lulling her with the tenderness of a mother. Yet Tikhon imagined he saw in his bleak eyes something insane, pitiful, and awful,—something spidery. " 'Tis just as if a spider were sucking away at a fly!" he reflected.

The second night came, but the detachment of soldiers was still not arriving.

In the night-time one holy old woman threw herself out. When all had fallen asleep,—even the watchmen,—she had climbed up to their turret and wanted to let herself down by some kerchiefs knotted together; but her rope breaking, she fell, injuring herself, and for a long time moaned and groaned under the windows. Finally she quieted down,— probably she had crawled off, or some passers-by had picked her up and carried her away.

The chapel was jammed. They slept higgledy-piggledy on the floor,—the brethren on the right side of the hut; the sisters on the left. But, whether it was the vision of sleep, or through fiendish visitation,—stealthy shadows began to flit through the darkness in the middle of the night,—from right to left, and from left to right.

Tikhon awoke and hearkened. A nightingale was singing outside a window, and in its song one could sense the moon-lit night, the freshness of the dew-covered dale, the fragrance of the fir forest and freedom, and languor, and the happiness of the earth. And, as though in answer to the nightingale, one could hear within the chapel strange whispers, rustlings, stirrings, sounds resembling the sighs and kisses of love. Strong, evidently, was the adversary of mankind: not even the fear of death could extinguish the ember of sinful flesh, but rather fanned it.

The ancient slept not. He prayed and neither saw nor

heard aught,—but, if see he did, he, probably, forgave his "poor little children":

"God alone is without sin, whereas man is frail; he falls, like to clay, and rises, like to an angel. It is not wantonness if one go with a maid or a widow; but it is wantonness if one strays in matters of faith. It is not we who stray when we make free with our flesh,—but the church when it holds to heresy."

Tikhon recalled the story of how two holy ancients had led off a certain maid into a forest, for some twenty versts, and, in the midst of the forest, had begun to nag her: "Work the love of Christ upon us, sister."—"What love of Christ's," says she, "am I to work upon you?"—"By coupling with us carnally," say they, "the same being the love of Christ." The maid weeps: "Fear God!" But the ancients console her: "The fire, now, will purify us." The poor thing still holds out, but they frighten her: "If thou dost not obey, thou shalt not receive the heavenly crown!"

Suddenly Tikhon felt that some one was embracing him and snuggling up to him. It was Sophia. Fright fell upon him, but the thought came to him: the fire will purify everything. And feeling through her small, black monastic habit the warmth of her innocent warm body, he put his lips to hers and drank avidly thereof.

And the caresses of these two children in the dark log-cabin, in this common coffin, were just as devoid of sin as, on a time, had been the caresses of the shepherd-lad Daphnis and the shepherd-girl Chloe upon sun-flooded Lesbos.

But Ivannushka the simpleton, squatting on his heels in a corner, with a taper in his hands, and swaying evenly as he awaited the "call of the chanticleer," was singing his eternal little song:

> O ye coffins made out of oak-logs tall,—
> Our eternal homes ye shall be for all!

And the nightingale, too, sang, thrilling about freedom, about languor, about the happiness of the earth, and in this warbling of the nightingale one seemed to hear tender and sly laughter over the funereal song of the simpleton Ivannushka.

And Tikhon recalled a white night, a knot of people on a float upon the smooth expanse of the Neva, between two heavens,—two abysses,—and the soft, languishing music which had been wafted to him across the water from the Summer Garden, like unto kisses and sighs of love from the realm of Venus:

> Thy arrows, Cupido, forego—
> For not a heart here but doth know
> A most delectable, dear woe;
> Not one but that has, to its sorrow,
> Felt of thy barbéd, golden arrow;
> We in submission all bow low.

Before dawn the octogenarian ancient, Minei, also wanted to throw himself out. Kiriukha caught him. They had a scuffle and Minei almost axed Kiriukha. The old man was bound and locked up in a cubby-hole. He kept on shouting from there and cursing the sainted Kornilii with indecent oaths.

When at dawn Tikhon looked out of a little window in order to find out if the detachment of soldiers had yet come, he beheld merely a desolate, sun-flooded dale; the kindly, morose, somnolent firs, and radiant rainbow-hues on the dewdrops. Such a pleasant odor of the freshness of pine-needles was wafted upon him, and such a tender warmth from the rising sun, and such a peaceful calm from the blue sky, that everything which was taking place in the log-cabin again appeared to him mad delirium, or a malefaction.

Another long summer day began its weary course, and the tedium of expectation fell upon all. Starvation threatened. There was but little of water and bread,—only a mat-bag of rye biscuits and two baskets of consecrated wafers. But then, there was a great deal of wine,—church wine, red. It was drunk with avidity. Some one, having drunk his fill, suddenly struck up a gay tavern song. It was more horrible than the wildest scream.

They were beginning to murmur. Gathering in corners, they exchanged whispers and looked at the ancient with eyes that boded no good. And what if the detachment were not to come? Were they to die of hunger, or what? Some demanded that the door be broken through and bread sent for;

but in their eyes one could see their secret thought: flight. Others desired to be set on fire right off, without waiting for the persecutors. Some prayed, but with such an expression on their faces as though they were blaspheming. Some, having eaten their fill of the berries containing the loco weed, which the ancient distributed ever more frequently, were raving,—now laughing, now weeping. One lad, falling into a frenzy, made a rush and seized a candle burning before an image and fell to igniting the kindling. The flame was extinguished with the greatest difficulty. Some sat in silence for hours at a time, in a coma, without daring to look one another in the eye.

Sophia, sitting alongside of Tikhon, who, grown weak from sleepless nights and hunger, was lying on the floor, was humming a dismal little song, which the sect of Lashers sang at their vigils,—a song concerning the great orphanhood of man's soul, which is forsaken in the midst of life, as if in a dark forest, by the Lord Batiushka and Matushka —Who-has-given-birth-to-a-God:

> I felt dreary,—most dearisome.
> I felt dreary,—most drearisome.
> When the heart grows heaviest within my breast
> Then I long to go to Batiushka, for to be his guest.
> I, a maid, shall hie me to my Batiushka.
> But the rapid rivers must have overflown—
> All the bridges have been swept away,—
> All the ferriers must have gone away,—
> And I, a maid, had to wade a ford.
> I have wet my feet on the way to the Lord,—
> I shall dry myself at my Batiushka's.
> When the heart grows heaviest within my breast,
> And the well-spring in my heart runs high,
> Then I long to go to Matushka, for to be her guest,—
> For to see the Most Gentle One,
> For to talk with the Most Gentle One.

And the song ended with a sob:

> Most Holy Mother of God,
> Intercede for us, my Most Beloved;
> For with Thee away, Most Beloved One,
> Many sinners live on earth,—
> Upon the dank earth, that our mother is,—
> That our mistress is, and that feeds us all.

None saw them. Sophia had let her head drop on Tikhon's shoulder, with her cheek pressed against his, and he perceived that she was weeping.

"Oh, I feel sorry for thee,—sorry, Tishenka, my own little one," she was whispering in his ear. "I have sent thy dear soul to perdition, accursed that I am! . . . Wouldst flee? I'll get a rope, or else I'll tell the ancient: there's an underground passage to the forest,—he'll lead thee out. . . ."

Tikhon, in his infinite weariness, kept silent and merely smiled to her with a sleepy, child-like smile. Distant recollections, which were like delirium, were rushing through his mind; the most abstract, mathematical deductions,—for some reason or other he now particularly felt their graceful and severe elegance, their icy clarity and precision, for which old Glück used to compare mathematics with music, —with the crystal music of the spheres. He also recalled Glück's dispute with Jacob Bruce over Newton's *Commentaries on the Apocalypse,* and the dry, harsh, seemingly wooden laughter of Bruce, and his words, which at that time had echoed in Tikhon's soul with such a premonitory horror: "At the same time when Sir Isaac Newton was composing his *Commentaries,*—precisely here, in our midst, in Muscovy, at the other end of the world, those savage fanatics who are called Raskolniki, or Schismatics of the Old Faith, had also composed their own commentaries on the Apocalypse, and had come to well-nigh the same conclusions as Newton. Awaiting from day to day the end of the world and the Second Coming of Christ, some of them lie down in coffins and sing their own requiems; others immolate themselves through fire. . . . This, then, say I, is the most curious thing of all: in these Apocalyptic ravings the extreme West meets with the extreme East, and the greatest enlightenment with the greatest ignorance,—which might, really, inspire the thought that the end of the world is approaching, and that all of us shall shortly go to the devil!"—And a new, sinister meaning was imparted to Newton's prophecy: *"Hypotheses non-fingo!* I do not make up hypotheses! Like a moth flying toward a flame, a comet shall fall on the sun,—and from this fall the heat of the sun will increase to such a degree that everything on earth will be extirpated by fire.

'Tis said in the Scriptures: *the heavens shall pass away with a great noise, and the elements shall melt with fervent heat, the earth also and the works that are therein shall be burned up.* [88] Then will be fulfilled both prophecies: of him who had faith and of him who had knowledge."

There came to his recollection an ancient, mice-nibbled octavo in the library of Bruce, numbered 461, with an illiterate Russian inscription: *Lionardo Davinci's Tractate on Painting, in the German tongue,* and the portrait of Leonardo laid in the book: the face of a Prometheus or a Simon Magus. And, together with this face, he recalled another, just as awesome: the face of a giant in a Dutch skipper's leather jacket, whom he had once come upon in Peterburgh on Trinity Square, near the coffee-house of The Four Frigates, —the face of Peter, at one time so hateful but now suddenly desired. Both faces had something in common, a something seemingly contrastedly similar: Da Vinci's held great contemplation; Peter's, great activity of mind. And from both faces there was waited upon Tikhon the same beatific chill as is wafted from mountain snows upon a traveler fatigued by the sultriness of valleys. "Oh Physics, save me from Metaphysics!" he recalled the saying of Newton, which Glück was fond of repeating whenever he was in his cups. In both of these faces there was to be found the sole salvation from the fiery heaven of the Red Death,—"thou earth, thou earth, our Mother dank."

Then everything became confused and he fell asleep. It appeared to him that he was flying over some fairy city,—it may have been Kitezh Town, or the New Jerusalem, or to Stockholm,—Stekoloë,—like to "the clearest glass and the crystal stone iaspis"; and mathematics constituted the music of this refulgent Town.

Suddenly he awoke. Everybody was bustling, running about and shouting with joyous faces:

"The detachment,—the detachment has come!"

Tikhon looked out of the windows and beheld afar, at the edge of the forest, in the evening dusk, around a blazing bonfire, men in tri-cornered hats and green frock-coats with red lapels and brass buttons: these were the soldiery.

"The detachment, the detachment has come! Come, lads, set yourselves afire! God is with us!"

v

Captain Pirsky had written instructions from the Spiritual Chancellory in Nizhegorod: "The habitation of the Raskolniki is to be reached secretly, in order that they might not set themselves afire. But, should they lock themselves fast in their cœnobium, or in a chapel, a guard is to be placed nigh their shelter, night and day, taking every precaution and surrounding them with a cordon; they are to be watched and safe-guarded closely, nor, under any circumstances, must they be allowed to burn themselves,—rather, they ought to be persuaded to give themselves up and admit their fault, by holding out to them assurances of their being pardoned without any further malice. And, in event of their surrendering, a list of all of them is to be made, and wooden foot-stocks,—or whatever else may come in handily,—are to be put upon their legs, lest they contrive to give leg-bail on the way, and they are to be dispatched to Nizhnii with all their belongings. But if, after all due persuasion, they should refuse to admit their fault, and obstinately prefer to remain shut in, bring pressure to bear upon them, and they are to be captured in any way possible, so that an absolute end might be put to these thieves, and no dissemination of their thievish doctrine allowed,—they are to be taken bodily, or starved out without any bloodshed. But should they set their thievish shelters or their chapel afire, you are to throw water on such shelters, and, chopping down, or breaking through the doors and windows, drag them out alive."

Captain Pirsky, a brave old soldier who had been wounded at Poltava, deemed the abolition of the cenobies an "intriguing invention of the long-maned priestly command," and would rather have led a charge under the severest firing against Swede and Turk than fuss with these Raskolniki. It was all very jolly for them to burn themselves,—but it was he who was held accountable and who received reprimands: "Such irregular actions are to be prohibited to the said captain and to other secular commanders, inasmuch as it is evident that these people gave themselves up to the flames, being in fear from him, the aforesaid captain." He explained that "the Raskolniki were seeking death not out of any fear, but out of sheer ingrained obduracy, inasmuch as they are puffed up with dreadful malice, and hold us to be quite fallen away from piety, and declare that they will keep their stand unto death, nor will they adapt themselves to conform with present-day ways,—so puffed up and confirmed are they in their dissoluteness."

But these explanations were not heeded, and the Spiritual Chancellory demanded:

"Inasmuch as the Raskolniki resort to sham self-burnings, to avoid paying a double tax, but in reality settle in remote places and, having concealed themselves there, freely gave themselves up to their abominable impiety,—the secular commander should therefore count the bodies of those burned, and, having counted them, enter them in a register, since corpses, no matter how great the fire, can not burn to ashes."

But the captain, deeming this sort of thing degrading to one of military rank, did not bother going off to count the corpses,—and received a new reprimand for his remissness.

At Long Mosses he decided to exercise greater caution and do everything possible not to give the Raskolniki an opportunity of burning themselves.

Before the coming of night, having ordered his detachment to withdraw as far as possible from the log cabin, and not to stir from the spot, he walked up to the chapel, alone and unarmed, inspected it thoroughly, and knocked on a window, reciting a prayer after the Raskolniki manner:

"Jesus Christ, Son of God, have mercy upon us!"

No one answered him. The log cabin was as quiet and as dark as a grave. All around was a wilderness. There was a subdued soughing among the tree-tops. A fresh night-breeze was rising. "If they set themselves on fire, there is going to be trouble!" reflected the captain, as he knocked and repeated:

"Jesus Christ, Son of God, have mercy upon us!"

Again silence: save that landrails craked in the swamp, and, somewhere afar, a dog set up a howl. A falling star flashed in a fiery arc through the darkness of the sky and scattered into sparks. He suddenly felt eerie, as though he were really knocking for admittance to the dead in their sepulcher.

"Jesus Christ, Son of God, have mercy upon us!" he pronounced for the third time.

A shutter on a window moved. A feeble light gleamed through a narrow crack. Finally the window slowly opened, and the head of Kornilii, the holy ancient, was thrust out.

"What seek ye? What men are ye, and wherefore have ye come?"

"By ukase of His Majesty, the Sovereign Peter Alexeievich, have we come to reason with ye: ye are to make known your persuasion, your rank, and your families; how long ago you came to the forest; by whose leave ye left your homes, and by what *ukases* and permissions ye abide here. And if ye have any doubts against the Holy Eastern Church and her rites, it behooves ye to state them in writing, and to put forth your preceptors to deliberate the matter with the spiritual authorities, without any fear or malice. . . ."

"We, of the peasantry and commonalty, have all gathered here in the name of Jesus, the dear Christ, and we shall take our wives and our children with us, and put them to rest," answered the ancient, softly and solemnly. "We would die by burning in the fire for the old faith, nor shall we yield ourselves into the hands of you persecutors, inasmuch as yours is the new faith. But if any yearn for salvation, let him come here to us to burn: we are now going off to Christ Himself."

"Come, that will do, little brother!" retorted the captain, kindly. "The Lord be with you,—drop your abominable intent of burning; go ye your ways to your houses,—none shall raise a hand against ye. Live as of old in your villages, with never a care. Ye will have but to pay your impost,— your double tax. . . ."

"Well, captain,—tell things like that to the little babes cutting their teeth; as for us, we know such deceptions from long ago; there's many a slip 'twixt the cup and the lip."

"I take my oath upon mine honor,—I'll let you all go, nor lay a finger on ye!" exclaimed Pirsky. He spoke in all sincerity,—he had really decided to let them go, contrary to the *ukase* and upon his own responsibility, in the event of their yielding. "What's the sense of yelling our lungs out,— we will but get hoarse!" he added with a kind smile. "Thou canst see the windows are high up,—one can not hear well. Tell thee what, oldster: order a strap to be let down; I'll tie it about me and you can hoist me up through the window,—only not this one, but another, a bit wider, or else I shan't be able to crawl through. I am alone, whereas ye are many,—what have ye to fear? We will reason the matter out,—by God's will we may come to an agreement. . . ."

"What's the sense of talking with all of you! What chance have we who are poor and lowly in contending with you?" the ancient smiled sneeringly, evidently taking his sweet fill of dominance and power. "A great abyss is fixed between you and us," he concluded, again solemnly, "so that those who would go hence to you can not, nor can those who would come to us from you do so. . . . As for thee, captain, thou hadst better get thee gone, or else, look thou, first thing thou knowest we shall set ourselves afire!"

The little window slammed to. Again there was silence, save for the soughing of the wind in the tree-tops and the crakes of landrails in the swamp.

Pirsky returned to his soldiers, ordered a tumbler of wine to be distributed to each one, and said:

"We are not going to fight with them. They have but few men, I hear,—mostly women and children. We'll break down their doors and catch them all, bare-handed, without any weapons."

The soldiers got ready ropes, axes, ladders, pails, barrels of water to quench the fire, and *kokoti*,—special long poles tipped with iron hooks, used to drag burning people out of the flames. Finally, when it became quite dark, they set out for the chapel,—at first in a roundabout way, on the edge of the forest; then across the meadow, crawling stealthily through the tall grasses and bushes, just like hunters surrounding game.

Having come right up to the log cabin, they began propping their ladders against it. Within the log cabin all was dark and quiet, as if in a grave. Suddenly a little window opened and the ancient cried out:

"Get back! When the saltpeter and the gunpowder will start exploding you, too, will be killed by the logs!"

"Surrender!" the captain was shouting. "We'll take you in a fight, anyway! You can see we have muskets and pistols."

"Some folks may have pistols, but we have the cudgels of Christ!" somebody's voice retorted from the chapel.

In the rear ranks of the detachment appeared a priest with a cross, and began reading a pastoral exhortation from the Archbishop:

"Should any one inflict an unlawful death upon himself, such a one is the most accursed of all men: he both destroys his temporal life in torment, and escapes not eternal torment. . . ."

The muzzle of an ancient, ancestral arquebuss was thrust out of a window and a blank shot thundered forth,—they were not shooting to kill but merely to frighten their persecutors.

The priest hid himself behind the backs of the soldiers, while the holy ancient, shaking his fist, shouted after them in frenzied fury:

"Ye firebrands of the portals of hell! Ye embers of the fires of Sodom! Ye seed of the confusion of Babel! Give me but time, ye dogs,—ye shall not 'scape me,—I shall set my foot upon the throats of even the best among ye when it comes to Jesus Christ, our Lord! Lo, He cometh soon and will make war against ye with the sword of His lips; and He shall move thrones, and give up your bones to be eaten of hounds, even as He did with Jezebel! We are burning in a fire of this earth,—whereas ye burn in the flames everlasting, both now and in the hereafter! Forge, then, a multitude of swords,—prepare the cruelest of tortures,—invent the most fearful of deaths; for so shall our joy be of the sweetest! . . . Set yourselves afire, lads! God is with us!"

Breeches, women's sleeveless jackets, sheepskin jerkins, shirts, and rustic short-coats came flying through the window:

"Take them for yourselves, ye persecutors! Cast lots for them! No need have we of aught. Naked were we born, and naked shall we arise before the Lord! . . ."

"Ye might at least spare your little children, ye accursed ones!" the captain cried out in despair.

A low chant, as if over a grave, came from the chapel.

"Climb up, lads, and chop them out!" commanded Captain Pirsky.

Everything was in readiness within the log cabin. The kindling was all in place. There were piled-up heaps of tow, hemp, resin, straw, and birch-bark. The wax tapers before the images were so insecure in their holders that they were found to fall from the least jar into the grooves containing gunpowder,—this was always done purposely, so that the self-burning might resemble suicide as little as possible. The adolescent children had been seated upon benches, with their garments nailed down, so that they might not tear themselves loose; their arms and legs were trussed with rope, so that they might not thresh about; their mouths were gagged with kerchiefs, so that they might not scream. Frankincense,—about three pounds of it,—was ignited in a vessel of unbaked clay, so that the children might suffocate before the grown-ups, and not behold the utmost horror of the holocaust.

One pregnant country wife had just been delivered of a girl. She was placed on a bench with the other children, to be baptized with the baptism of fire.

Then, stripping themselves to the skin, they put on new white shifts, which were also shrouds, while upon their heads they put crowns of paper, each with an eight-pointed cross drawn thereon in red ink, and got on their knees in rows, holding candles in their hands, so that they might meet the Bridegroom with burning tapers.

The holy ancient, with uplifted hands, was praying in a loud voice:

"Lord God, look down upon us, thy unworthy slaves! We be frail and weak,—therefore we durst not yield ourselves up into the hands of our persecutors. Take under thy protection this gathered flock which follows thee, Thou Good Shepherd, and flees from the fierce wolf, the Antichrist. Save us and have mercy upon us; make us part of Thy destinies; strengthen and ordain us for the ordeal of fire. Have mercy upon us, O Lord,— have mercy upon us! Knowing not to what account we may be called, we sinners offer up this prayer to Thee, as well as to the Queen of Heaven: Have mercy upon us! We die for Thy most pure love's sake!"

They all repeated the prayer after him in unison,—and this wail, addressed by man to his God, was both pitiful and awesome:

"We die for Thy most pure love's sake!"

At the same time, at a command from Pirsky, the soldiers, having surrounded the chapel on all sides and clambered up their ladders, were chopping away at the thick beams of the log-cabin walls, the bolts and bars on the windows, and the boardings over the doors.

The walls quivered; the candles tumbled down, but all of them missed the grooves filled with gunpowder. Whereupon, at a sign from the ancient, Kiriukha seized a cluster of candles burning before the ikon of the Mother of God, threw them right into the gunpowder, and leapt away. The gunpowder exploded,—the kindling flared up,—waves of fire spread over the walls and rafters. Dense smoke,—at first white, then black,—filled the chapel. The flames were stifling, expiring in the smoke; but long, red tongues here and there struggled free of the smoke, whistling and hissing, like stinging snakes, now drawn toward the people and licking them,—now leaping back as though in playful mood.

Frenzied wails arose. And, through the wails of those burning, through the rumbling of the fire, sounded the chant of joy triumphant:

"Lo, the Bridegroom cometh at midnight!"

From the instant of the fire's flaring up, until Tikhon lost consciousness, only two or three minutes had elapsed,—but he had seen and forever remembered all that was taking place in the chapel.

The ancient seized the newly-born babe, made the sign of the cross over her: "In the name of the Father, the Son and the Holy Ghost!"—and cast her into the fire,—the first sacrifice.

Ivannushka, the simpleton, stretched his arms toward the fire, as though he were greeting the coming Lord, Whom he had awaited all his life long.

The shift of Kilikeia, the hysteric, began to smolder, and her hair blazed up, surrounding her head with a fiery chaplet;

but she, feeling no pain, seemed as if turned to stone, with widely-opened eyes, as though she were beholding in the fire the great City, Holy Jerusalem, coming down from Heaven.

Petka Zhizla dived into the fire, head first, as a gay swimmer dives into water.

To Tikhon, too, there seemed to be something gay, intoxicating, in the fearful glitter of the fire. He recalled the song:

> The furnace is floored with a sward of green
> And blooming flowrets of an azure sheen.

It seemed as if in the transparently blue heart of the fire he was beholding flowers of Paradise. Their blue was like to that of a clear sky, holding forth a promise of a beatitude not of this earth; but it was necessary to pass through the red flame, the Red Death, in order to attain this heaven.

The besiegers knocked out two or three logs. The smoke poured out of the opening. The soldiers, thrusting in their *kokoti,* began to drag out those burning, and to pour water over them. The centenarian mother Theodulla was dragged out by her legs, exposing her virginal pudency. Vitalia, that holy ancient woman, seized hold of her and also crawled out, but immediately gave up her ghost: her body, because of her burns, was like one huge blister. Father Spiridon, when he was dragged out, seized a knife hidden in the bosom of his shirt and slit his throat. He lived on for four hours more, ceaselessly making the two-fingered sign of the cross over himself, reviling the Nikonians, and rejoicing, as the captain's report read, "for that he had been so successful in inflicting a deadly wound upon himself."

Some, after their first burns, darted of their own volition through the opening, falling down, crushing one another, clambering up over the heap of fallen bodies, and shouting to the soldiers:

"We're burning, we're burning! Help us, lads! . . ."

The angelic rapture upon their faces was being supplanted by a bestial horror.

Those remaining strove to hold back the fugitives. Gaffer Mikhei seized the edge of the opening with both hands in order to jump out, but his seventeen-year-old grandson hit him over the hands with a pole-ax, and the gaffer tumbled back into the fire.—A country wife escaped out of the blaze, and her little son started after her,—but his father seized him by the legs, swung him up, and slammed his head against a beam.—An obese cubiculary of the cenoby, having fallen flat on his back into a puddle of burning pitch, was squirming and leaping,—just as though he were dancing: "Like a carp on a frying-pan!" thought Tikhon, with a horrible laugh, and shut his eyes in order not to see.

He was stifling from the heat and the smoke. Dark-lilac bluebells on a field of bloody red began to nod to him, tinkling piteously. He felt Sophia embracing him, snuggling up against him, and through the thinness of her shift-shroud, the freshness of her innocent young body, like that of a night-flower, was the last freshness amid the blazing sultriness.

And the voices of those still living resounded through the wails of the dying:

"Lo, the Bridegroom cometh . . ."

"My Bridegroom, my beloved Christ!" Sophia was whispering in Tikhon's ear. And it seemed to him that the fire burning in his body was stronger than the fire of the Red Death. They sank down together, as though in an embrace; they lay down, bride and groom, upon the bridal couch. The Woman, fiery-eyed, fiery-winged, was bearing him off into an abyss of flames.

The heat was so intense that the soldiers had to retreat. Two were scorched; one fell into the log cabin and was burned. The captain stormed:

"Ah, the little fools,—the little accursed fools! 'Tis easier to battle with the Turk and the Swede than with this riff-raff." But the old soldier's face was paler than it had been when he was lying wounded on the battlefield of Poltava.

Fanned by a raging wind the flame mounted ever higher, and its noise was like thunder. Firebrands flew on the wind like fiery birds. The whole chapel was like a red-hot furnace, and in this furnace, as if in the fire of hell, stirred a heap of fallen, squirming, contorted bodies. The skin upon them was bursting; their blood burbled; their fat seethed. One could smell the stench of scorched flesh.

Suddenly the cross-beams fell down,—the roof caved in.

A pillar of fire soared up to the very sky, like a gigantean torch.

And the earth and the sky were flooded with a red glow, as though this were verily that last conflagration through which the universe was to be destroyed.

Tikhon came to in the forest, upon cool, dewy grass.

Subsequently he learned that at the last instant, when he had lost consciousness, the holy ancient and Kiriukha had caught him up in their arms and made a dash for the altar of the chapel, where, under the communion table, there was a small door, something like a hatchway, leading into a subterranean chamber; they had descended into this secret place, which was known to none of the others, and, through an underground passage, had come out into the densest thicket in the whole forest, where their persecutors could not find them.

Thus did almost all preachers of self-burning act: they burned others while they saved themselves and their nearest disciples for new preachments.

Tikhon did not come to for a long time; long did the ancient and Kiriukha throw water upon him,—they thought he would die. His burns, however, were not serious. Finally, having come to, he asked:

"Where is Sophia?"

The old man glanced at him with his clear and kind gaze:

"Do not fash thyself, little one,—grieve not for the little sister, the little bride! Her most beautiful little soul is in the Kingdom of Heaven, together with saints who have suffered for the Father."

And, having raised his eyes to heaven, he crossed himself with touching joy:

"Eternal memory to the slaves of God, who have burned themselves of their own free will! Dwell there, my dear little ones, until resurrection, and pray for us; and we, too, shall drain the same cup to the Lord when our hour is come. But as yet it has not,—we must yet work for Christ. . . . Thou, too, my child, hast passed through the test of fire," he turned to Tikhon, "thou art dead to this world,—but risen anew for Christ. Strive, then, to live this thy second life not for thyself, but for the Lord! Gird thyself about with the armament of light; attain goodness, be a warrior for the Christ Jesus, a preacher of the Red Death, even as we sinners are!"

And he added, with a cheerfulness that was almost sprightly:

"We'll go on a jaunt to Ocean, to the limits of the Sea's Marge. We'll kindle a fire or two there also. Yea, we will work most bravely; we'll burn as many of our dear little brethren as we can. And, if God grant, it may be that, becoming jealous of us, even all of Russia may burn,—and, after Russia, all of creation!"

Tikhon kept silent, with his eyes shut. The ancient, thinking that he had again fallen into a coma, passed into an earth-hut to prepare certain herbs wherewith he treated burns.

But Tikhon, left alone, turned away from the sky, which was still blazing with a bloody glow, and fell with his face to the earth.

The dampness of the earth abated the pain of his burns, and it seemed to him that the earth had heard his supplication, had saved him from the fiery heaven of the Red Death, and that he was coming out anew from the earth's womb,—like a babe being born, like a dead man coming to a new life. And he embraced it; he kissed it as if it were a living woman, and wept and implored:

> Wondrous Queen, Mother of God,—
> Thou earth, thou earth, our Mother dank!

A few days later, when the ancient was getting ready for the road, Tikhon ran away from him.

He had comprehended that the church of the old faith was no better than the new church, and decided to return into the world, in order to seek the true church until he found it.

BOOK ELEVEN

SON AND FATHER

I

THE Church had ceased to be The Church for the Czarevich since the time of his learning of the Czar's *ukase,* by order of which the secrecy of confessional was violated. If God had permitted such a profanation of the Church, it meant that He had left it, reflected the Czarevich.

At the conclusion of the investigation, on the twenty-fourth of March,—the eve of the Annunciation—Peter returned to Peterburgh. He busied himself so zealously with his Paradise, the building of the fleet, the establishment of governmental departments, and other matters, that to many the investigation seemed definitely ended, and the matter given up to oblivion. The Czarevich, however, was brought to Moscow under guard, together with other convicts, and placed in a separate house adjoining the Winter Palace. Here he was kept as one under arrest: he was not allowed to go anywhere, nor shown to any one. Rumors were current that he had gone out of his mind from excessive drinking.

Passion Week came.

For the first time in his life the Czarevich did not fast. Priests were sent to him to persuade him, but he refused to listen to them: they all seemed spies to him.

Easter fell on the thirteenth of April. Radiant Morning Mass was held in the Cathedral of the Trinity, the foundation of which had been laid at the founding of Peterburgh; a small dark church of logs, resembling a village church. The Sovereign and his Consort attended, as well as all the ministers and senators. The Czarevich had not wanted to go, but, by order of the Czar, was brought there by force.

In the half-dark church, over the representation of the Saviour in His grave, the canon of the Great Sabbath sounded like a funereal chant:

"All that the world holds is upon the Cross, raised up; and every creature weeps aloud; beholding Him hanging in His nakedness. The sun hideth his beams, and the stars put by their light."

The priests performing the holy service came out from behind the altar, still in their black Lenten vestments; raised up the Representation of the Saviour in His cerements, bore it to the altar, and closed the gates of the sanctuary: they had laid the Lord in His sepulcher.

The last Troparion of the Midnight Mass was sung:

"When Thou didst come down to earth to Thy death, Thou Life undying. . . ."

And then came silence.

Suddenly the crowd stirred, moved, as though hurriedly preparing for something. One candle after another kindled with a warm glow. The whole church was illumined with a bright, soft light. And this radiant hush held the expectation of a great joy.

Alexei lit his candle from that of the man next to him,—Peter Andreievich Tolstoi, his Judas the Betrayer. The tender flame reminded the Czarevich of everything that, on a time, he used to feel during the Radiant Morning Mass. But now he was stifling this feeling within him,—he did not desire it and feared it. Gazing, without any thought, at the back of Prince Menshikov, who was standing in front of him, he strove to think only of how to keep the wax of his own candle from dripping on the gold embroidery on this back.

From beyond the gates of the sanctuary came the voice of the deacon:

"Thy resurrection, O Christ Saviour, is hymned forth by angels in Heaven."

The gates opened, and now two voices sang:

"And help us upon earth to glorify Thee with a pure heart."

Those performing the service, now already in light Paschal vestments, came out from behind the altar, and the Procession of the Cross started. The Cathedral bell boomed forth,—it was answered by the bells of other churches; it was followed by the rumbling of cannon-fire in the Fortress of SS. Peter and Paul.

The Procession of the Cross came out of the church. The outer doors were shut, the temple emptied; and everything was once more quiet.

The Czarevich stood without moving, his head downcast, gazing before him as meaningless as before, striving not to see, not to hear, not to feel anything.

Outside was heard the senilely feeble voice of the Metropolitan, Stepan:

"Glory to the Holy and Con-Substantial and Life-Creating and Invisible Trinity, now and forever, throughout all the ages."

And, muffled at first, softly, as though from afar, one could hear:

"Christ hath risen from the dead."

Then, louder,—ever nearer, ever more joyous. Finally the doors of the church opened wide and, together with the noise of the entering throng, the song burst out like a cry of victory, shaking heaven and earth:

"Christ hath risen from the dead, through death having conquered death and bestowed life upon them that are in their graves."

And there was such joy in this pæan that naught could withstand it. It seemed that, at any second, all that which the world had been expecting from its beginning would be fulfilled,—that a miracle would be consummated.

The Czarevich paled; his hands began to shake, almost dropping the candle. He was still resisting. But an unbearable joy was already welling up within his breast, striving to win its way out. All life, all tortures, even death itself seemed insignificant before it.

He burst into unrestrainable tears and, in order to conceal them, walked out of the church, upon the front steps. The April night was quiet and clear. One could smell the thawing snow, the moist bark of trees, and their as yet unopened buds. The church was surrounded by people, and below, upon the dark square, candles glowed warmly like stars, while the stars glimmered like candles up above, in the dark sky. Cloudlets scurried by, light as the wings of angels. Ice was floating on the Neva. The joyous din and crackling of the breaking ice blocks blended with the din of the bells. It seemed as if earth and sky were singing: Christ is risen.

After mass the Czar, going out on the front steps, exchanged greetings with everybody,—not only with the ministers and the senators, but even with all of the court servants, down to the last stoker and cook's-boy.

The Czarevich regarded his father from a distance, without daring to approach. Peter caught sight of his son and himself approached him.

"Christ is risen, Alësha!" said the father, with his kind endearing smile of yore.

"Verily, He is risen, Batiushka!"

And they kissed thrice.

Alexei felt the familiar touch of his father's shaven, plump cheeks, and the soft lips, and the familiar odor. And suddenly, as used to be the case in his childhood, his heart once more began to pound, and his breath was cut short from an insane hope:

"What if he were to forgive, to grant pardon!"

Peter was so tall of stature that, in kissing, he had to bend down in almost every instance. His back and neck began to ache. He hid within the altar enclosure from the besieging throng.

At six in the morning, when it had already become light, everybody passed from the Cathedral to the Senate,—a clay-daubed, rather low, long building, in the nature of a casern,—also right alongside on the square. In the cramped reception halls tables were set with loaves, Paschal cakes, hard-boiled eggs, wines and vodkas, for breaking the fast.

At the front entrance of the Senate, Prince Jacob Dolgorukyi caught up with the Czarevich and whispered in his ear that Aphrosiniya would be in Peterburgh almost any day, now, and that, glory be to God! she was well, save for being in the last days of her pregnancy: she was bound to give birth if not to-day, then to-morrow.

In the entry the Czarevich met the Empress. With the Blue Ribbon of St. Andrew over her shoulder, from which a diamond star depended, in a magnificent *robe-ronde* of white cloth-of-gold, and a two-headed eagle embroidered in the front thereof, in pearls and diamonds, slightly rouged and whitened,—Katenka appeared young and rather pretty. Meeting her guests, she, like a good hostess, smiled to everybody with her unvarying, demure smile. She smiled to the Czarevich as well. He kissed her hand. She exchanged Easter greetings with him, kissed his lips, exchanged eggs, and was just about to step aside, when he suddenly fell at her knees,—so unexpectedly, and looking at her so wildly, that she staggered back.

"My Empress, Matushka, take pity upon me! Beg Batiushka to permit me to marry Aphrosiniya. . . . There is naught I want besides,—God sees there's naught! Nor, methinks, will I live long. . . . If I could but go away from everything,—could but die in peace. . . . Take pity upon me, Matushka, for the sake of the Radiant Holiday! . . ."

And again he looked at her so that she felt eerie. Suddenly her face puckered up,—she began to weep. Katenka both loved, and knew how, to weep: it was not for naught that the Russians were wont to say that her eyes were a wet place; while foreigners said that, when she wept,—even though one knew what it was about,—one nevertheless felt one's self touched, "as at a performance of an Andromache." But this time she was weeping sincerely,—she really did feel sorry for the Czarevich.

She bent toward him and kissed his head. Through the cut of her dress he glimpsed her magnificent white breasts, with the two dark, enticingly-beautiful birth-marks—or were they beauty-marks? And these birth-marks made clearer to him than anything else could that nothing would come of the matter.

"Oh, my poor, poor fellow! Would I not be glad to try for thee, Alëshenka? . . . But wherein is the good? For will *he* listen to me? Like as not, 'twill be still worse in the upshot. . . ."

And, looking quickly over her shoulder,—lest some one overhear,—and drawing her lips to his very ear, she whispered in a hurried whisper:

"Thy affairs are in a bad way, little son,—so bad that, if thou canst flee, drop everything and flee."

Tolstoi entered. The Empress, leaving the Czarevich, imperceptibly dashed some tiny tear-drops away with a lace handkerchief, and, turning around to Tolstoi with her former joyous mien, asked him whether he had seen the Sovereign anywhere,—why did he not come to break his fast?

In the doors of an adjoining chamber appeared a tall, bony German lady, festally and tastelessly arrayed, with the long, narrow, equine face of an old-maid,—the Princess of East Friseland, the head of the late Charlotta's household, who was bringing up her two orphans. She walked with such a resolute, challenging air that all involuntarily made way before her. She was carrying little Petiya on one arm and leading the four-year-old Natasha by the hand.

The Czarevich barely recognized his children,—it was so long since he had seen them.

"Mais, saluez donc Monsieur votre père, mademoiselle!" the Princess was nudging Natasha, who had halted, evidently also not recognizing her father. Petiya at first regarded him in open-eyed curiosity, then, turning away, started beating his little arms and bawling.

"Natasha, Natasha, my own dear little girl!" the Czarevich stretched out his arms toward her.

She lifted up her great, sad, pale blue eyes, altogether like those of her mother, suddenly smiled, and threw herself on his neck.

Peter entered. He glanced at the children and wrathfully said to the Princess in German:

"Why have you brought them here? This is no place for them. Betake yourself off!"

The German looked at the Czar, and indignation flashed in her kindly eyes. She was about to say something, but seeing that the Czarevich had submissively released Natasha from his arms, she shrugged her shoulders, furiously shook Petiya, who was still bawling, just as furiously seized the little girl by her hand, and without a word stalked toward the exit, with the same provoking air with which she had entered.

Natasha, as she was going away, turned around toward her father, and looked at him with a glance which reminded him of Charlotta. In this glance of the child there was the same quiet despair that had been her mother's. The heart of the Czarevich contracted. He felt that he would never behold his children again.

Everybody sat down to table. The Czar sat down between Theophan Prokopovich and Stepan Yavorsky. Opposite them was the Prince-Pope with his All-Fools' Conclave. They had already managed to break their fast, and were beginning to carry on.

It was a double holiday for the Czar: Easter, and the opening of the Neva. As he thought of the launching of new ships he glanced gayly through the window at the white blocks of ice, floating like swans over the blue expanse, in the morning sun.

The conversation veered to matters spiritual.

"But, Father, will our Patriarch be ready soon?" Peter asked Theophan.

"Soon, Czar,—I am putting in the last stitches in his vestments," the latter answered.

"Well, I have his hat ready!" the Czar smiled.

The *Patriarch* was the Holy Synod; the *vestment* was the spiritual code which Prokopovich was composing; the *hat* was the *ukase* in confirmation of the Synod.

When Theophan began speaking of the benefits to be derived from the new collegium, something much too merry began to play, to dart like a tic in every feature of his face, even the smallest: at times it seemed as though he himself were laughing over that which he was saying.

"A collegium hath a greater spirit of freedom than a single director would have. This, too, is a great consideration: that from a collective directorship no uprisings against the Fatherland are to be apprehended. For the common folk do not know how spiritual power differs from autocratic, but, astonished by the honor and glory of the Grand and Supreme Pastor, are under the impression that such a spiritual ruler is a second sovereign, equal to the autocrat,—or even greater than he. And, when one hears of any disagreement among them, all will follow the spiritual, rather than the secular ruler, and will have the courage to fight for him, and will flatter themselves, the accursed ones, that they are fighting for God Himself, and that they are not defiling but consecrating their hands, even though they be intent upon bloodshed. 'Tis difficult to put in words what great calamity this gives rise to. One has but to ponder on the history of Constantinople, subsequent to the times of Justinian, and much of this will become evident. And even the Pope came out on top through no other means than this, and not only did he split the Roman Empire in twain, and usurp a great portion unto himself, but made even other governments totter, well-nigh to their complete ruin. Nor need we recall the like attempts which have taken place in our own land! There is no place for such an evil when spiritual direction is in the hands of a Council. The people shall dwell in submission, and will put aside all hope of aid in their uprisings, from those of spiritual calling. Finally, such a rule by council will constitute something like a school of spiritual government, where any one can conveniently master spiritual policy. And so in Russia, through the help of God, all uncouthness may soon depart from those of spiritual calling, and we may hope for the very best in the future. . . ."

Looking straight into the Czar's eyes, with a fawning smile, which at the same time was so crafty that it seemed almost impertinent, the Archpriest concluded solemnly:

"*Thou art Peter, and upon this rock I will build My church.*" [89]

Silence ensued. The members of the Most Drunken Conclave alone kept up their din, and the righteous Prince Jacob Dolgorukyi was muttering under his breath, so that none could hear him:

"*Render to Cæsar the things that are Cæsar's, and to God the things that are God's.*" [90]

"But what sayest thou, Father?" the Czar turned to Stepan. While Prokopovich had been speaking, Stepan had sat with downcast head, his eyes narrowing as though he were dozing; and his senilely bloodless face seemed that of a dead man. But Peter imagined he saw in his face that which he feared and which he hated above all,—submissive revolt. Hearing the voice of the Czar, the old man came to with a start, as though he were awaking, and uttered softly:

"Who am I to speak on such a matter, Your Majesty! Old am I, and foolish. Let the young speak while we will lend ear. . . ." And letting his head drop still lower, still more softly he added:

"One can not go against the river's current."

"Thou art forever whining, old man,—forever beating

about the bush!" The Czar shrugged his shoulders in vexation. "And whatever dost thou want? If thou wouldst but speak right out!"

Stepan glanced at the Czar, suddenly becoming all hunched up, and with an air in which, by now, one could see only submission, without any revolt, began speaking very rapidly,—most rapidly,—both avidly and piteously, as though hurrying and dreading that the Czar might not hear him out:

"Most Gracious Sire! Do let me go to my rest, let me take a vow of silence. My service and my humble efforts are surely known to the holy God and partly to Your Majesty as well,—through which efforts I have wrecked my strength, my health, and well-nigh my life. My vision has grown dim; my limbs have grown feeble; chiragra has twisted my fingers; gall-stones have well-nigh done me to death. However, in all these misfortunes of mine I have found my sole consolation in my Czar's graciousness and fatherly, benevolent protection, and all my bitternesses have been sweetened thereby, as with sugar. But now I see thy face averted from me, and thy graciousness not as of yore. Oh, Lord, whence cometh this change? . . ."

Peter had ceased listening long ago,—he was taken up with the dancing of the Princess-Abbess Rzhevskaya, who had launched into a squatting dance, to the singing of the drunken buffoons:

> Oh, my club, start in to swirl,
> Oh, my bag-pipes, start in to skirl!

"Let me enter the monastery at Don, or wherever Your Majesty may will and desire," Stepan continued his "sniveling."—"But—

"But shouldst thou have any doubt whatsoever of my retirement, may the Blood of Christ serve for my perdition if I contemplate aught of guile, whether in Peterburgh, or in Moscow, or in Riyazan,—the might of your autocracy is ever over me; for 'tis impossible to hide from it, nor is there aught to hide for. *Whither shall I go from Thy spirit? Or whither shall I flee from thy presence?* . . ."[91]

But all this while the song was going full blast:

Oh, my club, start in to swirl,
Oh, my bag-pipes, start in to skirl!
My man's father fell with a thump
Right behind a big tree-stump;
I'd have been only too glad,
Higher to have made his bed,—
Higher to have made his bed,—
So that he might break his head. . . .

And the Czar was stamping and whistling in time:

Ho burn,—ho burn!

The Czarevich glanced at Stepan. Their eyes met. The old man fell silent, as though he had suddenly recalled himself to his senses and become ashamed. He let his eyes fall and lowered his head, while two small tear-drops rolled down along his senile wrinkles. His face again became like that of a dead man.

But Theophan, a raddle-faced Silenus, was smiling sneeringly. The Czarevich involuntarily compared these two faces. The first expressed the Church's past; the other,—its future.

It was stifling in the low and cramped chambers. Peter ordered the windows to be opened.

On the Neva, as is frequently the case during the breaking-up of the ice, a chill wind had sprung up from the Lake of Ladoga. Spring had suddenly turned into autumn. The cloudlets which at night seemed as light as the wings of angels, had become as heavy, as gray and rugged as field stones; the sun, tenuous and albescent, just as if it were consumptive.

From the drinking places and the pot-houses,—of which there were a multitude in the neighborhood of the Square, in the Hostelry Court, and further on, beyond the Crown Works, upon the Provender Mast and the Flea Fair,—came the din of voices, resembling the roaring of beasts. Somewhere a fight was going on, and someone was vociferating:

"Baste him good and plenty,—he's fat enough, Thoma!"

And the deafening pealing of the bells, rushing in at the windows together with this drunken roaring, also seemed drunken, coarse and insolent.

Before the very Senate, in the middle of the Square, over a dirty puddle on which floated the shells of red Paschal eggs, a *mouzhik* was standing, with nothing on but his shirt, all his other clothing had probably gone for drink; he was swaying, as if contemplating whether or not he should fall into the puddle, and swearing obscenely and loudly, hiccuping so as to be heard all over the Square. Another fellow had already tumbled into a ditch, and his bare legs, sticking out of it, were threshing about helplessly. No matter how severe the police were, on this day they could do nothing with the drunkards. They lay sprawling everywhere on the streets, like the bodies of the slain on a field of battle. The whole city was nothing but one tremendous tavern.

And even the Senate, where the Czar was breaking his fast with his ministers, was no different from this tavern; here, too, in the very same fashion, they were raising a din, and swearing, and brawling.

The scaramouche choir of the Prince-Pope started a dispute with the choristers of the Archpriest, as to who could sing better. The latter began to sing:

"Christ hath risen from the dead."

But the others continued singing:

> Oh, my club, start in to swirl,
> Oh, my bag-pipes, start in to skirl!

The Czarevich recalled the holy night, his holy joy, his touched emotion, his expectation of a miracle,—and it appeared to him that he had fallen from heaven into mire, as the sot outside the windows had fallen into the ditch. Was it worth while to have begun, as he had, only to have everything end thus? There was no miracle of any sort, nor would there ever be; there was only the abomination that maketh desolate in the holy place.

II

Peter loved Peterhof no less than he did the Paradise. Staying in it every summer, he himself supervised the construction of its "pleasure gardens, vegetable enclosures, cascades, and fountains."

"One cascade," the Czar commanded, "is to be made so as to spatter, while another is to have its water flowing as smooth as glass to the very ground; there is also to be a water pyramid, made up of small cascades; in front of the topmost and largest cascade is to be depicted the story of Herakles, contending with a seven-headed reptile, which reptile is styled a hydra, with water spurting out of the said heads; there is also to be a Neptune's chariot, with four sea-horses, with water spouting out of their mouths, and, along the projections, make tritons, the same seeming to be blowing their sea-conches, and these tritons are to be constructed in such a manner as to make the water play, and form many and diverse jets of water. Order each fountain to be designed beforehand, and every other goodly spot in the perspective is to be drawn and laid out, as French and Roman gardens are."

A white May night lay over Peterhof. The sea's marge was as smooth as glass. Against the sky,—green, with a roseate fringe as of mother-of-pearl,—stood out the ebon firs and the lurid walls of the palaces. In the turbid windows of the latter, as in the eyes of the blind, the despondent light of a never-extinguished dawn flickered, and everything in this light seemed wan, faded; the green of the grass and the trees seemed gray like ashes; the flowers seemed wilted. It was quiet and deserted in the gardens. The fountains slept. Only over the mossy steps of the cascades, and from the porous stones over the walls of the grottoes, infrequent drops were dripping, like tears. A fog was rising, and in it the innumerable marble gods, a whole Olympus of resurgent gods, gleamed whitely, like phantoms. Here, upon the ultimate boundaries of the earth, by the Hyperborean Sea, during this white diurnal night, resembling the nocturnal day of Hades, these wan shadows of the shades of dead Hellas were imbued with infinite sadness. It was as though, after having become resurgent, they were again dying,— this time with a second death, from which there was no resurrection.

Over the rather low, clipped garden, near the very sea, stood a small Dutch house of brick,—the Sovereign's palace of Mon Plaisir. Here, too, everything was quiet. Only one window showed a light,—a candle burning in the Czar's office.

Peter and Alexei sat facing one another across a writing table. In the double light of the candle and the dawn their faces, like all things on this night, appeared phantasmally wan.

For the first time since the Czar had returned to Peterburgh, he was questioning his son.

The Czarevich answered calmly, as though he no longer experienced fear before his father, but only weariness and ennui.

"Who, among the secular or the spiritual, knew of your intended opposition, and what words passed between thee and them, or between them and thee?"

"I know nothing more," Alexei answered for the hundredth time.

"Didst thou utter any such words as: 'I will out upon everybody,—as long as the rabble be whole-heartedly for me?'"

" 'Tis possible I may have spoken thus, being in my cups. I can not remember everything. When drunk I always blabbed all sorts of things, and my tongue was ever loose; I could not do without contentious speeches in gatherings, and may have blurted out something of the sort, not mistrusting those about me. Thou thyself knowest, Batiushka,—there isn't a living soul that doesn't drink. . . . But all this is but a trifling matter!"

He looked at his father with such a strange smile that the latter felt eerie, as though he were facing a madman.

Having rummaged among some papers, Peter got out one and showed it to the Czarevich.

"Is this thy handwriting?"

"It is."

This was the rough draft of the letter he had written in Naples to the Archbishops and Senators, supplicating them not to desert him.

"Didst write it of thy own will?"

" 'Twas against my will. I was forced thereto by Kühl, secretary to Count Scheineborn. 'Write this, inasmuch as there has been talk of thy being dead; but, shouldst thou refuse to write it, we will in our turn refuse to keep thee,'—and he did not leave the room until I had written the letter."

Peter indicated with his finger a certain passage in the letter; it consisted of the following words: "I implore you *now* not to leave me *now*." The word *now* was repeated twice, —and was twice crossed out.

"This *now*,—for what reason was it written, and wherefore is it blotted?"

"I can not recall," answered the Czarevich, and grew pale.

He knew that this blotted *now* was the sole key to his most secret thoughts about the revolt,—about the death of his father,—about the latter's possible assassination.

"Was this verily written against thy will?"

"Verily so."

Peter rose, walked out into an adjoining room, summoned an orderly, issued some order to him, returned, again sat down at the table, and began writing down the statements which the Czarevich had just made.

Steps were heard on the other side of the door. The door opened. Alexei cried out faintly, as though he were about to fall into a swoon. On the threshold stood Aphrosiniya.

He had not seen her since he had left Naples. She was no longer pregnant. Probably she had been delivered in the fortress in which she had been placed immediately upon her arrival at Peterburgh, as he had learned from Jacob Dolgorukyi.

"Where is the Silvel One?" thought the Czarevich, and began to quiver, all drawn toward her,—but immediately froze under the intent gaze of his father, merely trying to catch her eye. She was not looking at Alexei, as though she did not see him at all.

Peter addressed her kindly:

"Is it the truth, Fedorovna, as the Czarevich says, that the letter to the Archbishops and Senators was written against his will, through the coercion of the Kaiser's people?"

" 'Tis untrue," she answered calmly. "He alone wrote it, and none of the foreigners were present thereat, there being no one save myself and him, the Czarevich. And he said to me that he was writing the said letters in order that they might be spread secretly throughout Peterburgh, while others were to be submitted to the Archbishops and Senators."

"Aphrosiya, Aphrosiushka, dear little mother of mine!

What art thou about? . . ." the Czarevich began babbling in horror. "She doth not know,—she hath forgotten,—I fear me she has mixed things up," he turned to his father once more, with that strange smile which made one feel eerie. "At the time she speaks of I was secretly dispatching to the Viceroy the plan of the attack on Belgorod,—but never this letter. . . ."

" 'Tis the very same letter, Czarevich. 'Twas right before my eyes that thou didst seal it,—or hast thou forgotten? I saw it," she uttered, just as calmly, and suddenly looked point-blank at him with the same gaze she had used three years ago, in the house of the Viyazemskys, when he, intoxicated, had thrown himself upon her to rape her, and had raised a knife over her.

This gaze was enough to make him comprehend that she had betrayed him.

"Son," said Peter, "methinks thou thyself seest that this matter is of the utmost importance. If thou hast written the letters in question of thine own will, 'tis evident thou didst intend revolt not in thy thoughts alone, but that thou didst plan to carry it out in reality. And, therefore, all that thou didst conceal in thy previous admissions of guilt was so concealed not through faulty memory, but through guile,—evidently for just such other actions and intentions in the future. However, we do not wish to have an unclean conscience before God by believing in information where the informant has not been put to the question. For the last time I ask thee,—is it true that thou didst write this of thy own will?"

The Czarevich kept silent.

"I feel sorry for thee, Fedorovna," said Peter, "but there is no help for it. I shall put thee to the torture."

Alexei glanced at his father, at Aphrosiniya, and realized that she would not escape torture, if he, the Czarevich, were to be stubborn.

" 'Tis true," he uttered, barely audibly, and no sooner had he uttered this than his fear again vanished,—everything again became a matter of indifference to him.

Peter's eyes gleamed with joy.

"With what end in view, then, didst thou write *now?*"

"This,—that the people might side with me more zealously

bearing in mind the printed news concerning the mutiny of the troops in Mecklenburg. But, later on, I thought the word poor and did blot it out. . . ."

"That means thou didst rejoice over the mutiny?"

The Czarevich made no answer.

"And if thou didst rejoice," Peter went on, as though he had caught an inaudible answer, "then, methinks, 'twas not without certain intentions. . . . If this mutiny had been actual, thou wouldst have joined the mutineers?"

"If they had sent for me I would have gone. And I expected the summons would come upon thy death inasmuch as—"

He stopped, paled still more, and finished with an effort:

"Inasmuch as they wanted to slay thee,—for I did not think that they would dethrone thee alive. . . ."

"But what if this were done while I was alive?" Peter asked, hurriedly and softly, looking his son straight in the eyes.

"Had the conspirators been strong enough, I might have come even while thou wert alive," Alexei answered, just as softly.

"Tell everything thou knowest," Peter again turned to Aphrosiniya.

"The Czarevich always desired the succession greatly," she began, rapidly and firmly, as though repeating that which she had learned by heart. "And he went away because thou, Sire, wert supposed to be doing everything to put him out of the way. And when he heard that your younger son, the Czarevich Peter Petrovich, was ailing, he did say to me: 'There, thou seest, Batiushka works in his own way, but God works in His way!' And he did place high hopes in the Senators: 'I, now, shall get rid of all the old ones, and choose new ones for myself, to suit my will.' And whenever he heard of any visions, or read in the gazettes that everything was quiet in Peterburgh, he used to say that the particular vision and the quiet were not in vain: 'Either my father will die, now, or else there'll be an uprising. . . .'"

She spoke on for a long while, recalling certain utterances of his which he himself did not remember,—exposing certain secrets of his heart which he himself had not perceived.

"And when Master Tolstoi arrived in Naples, the Czarevich

wanted to leave the protection of the Kaiser for that of the Pope in Rome,—and I did hold him back," Aphrosiniya concluded.

"Is all this the truth?" Peter asked his son.

"'Tis the truth," answered the Czarevich.

"Well, thou mayest go, Fedorovna!"

The Czar held his hand out to her. She kissed it and turned around to leave.

"Dear mother of mine! Dear mother of mine!" the Czarevich was at once all drawn to her, and fell to babbling as if in a delirium, without himself knowing what he was saying. "Farewell, Aphrosiushka! . . . For we may never see each other again. The Lord be with thee! . . ."

She made no answer, nor did she turn around.

"Why dost thou treat me so?" he added softly, without any reproach,—merely with infinite wonder; he hid his face in his hands, and heard the door close behind her.

Peter, pretending that he was looking through some papers, occasionally eyed his son from under his brows, but stealthily, as though he were expecting something.

It was the quietest hour of the night, and the stillness seemed still more profound because it was as light as day.

Suddenly the Czarevich took his hands away from his face. It was frightful.

"Where is the little babe? . . . The little babe,—where is he? . . ." he began, fixing his unmoving and blazing gaze upon his father. "What have ye done with him? . . ."

"What babe?" Peter could not understand him at first.

The Czarevich indicated the door through which Aphrosiniya had gone.

"He died," said Peter without looking at his son. "It was a still-birth."

"Thou liest!" Alexei shouted, and raised his arms, as though he were threatening his father. "Ye killed him, ye killed him! . . . Ye strangled him, or chucked him in the water, like a puppy! . . . Why have ye done this to him, an innocent infant? . . . 'Twas a boy, was it not?"

"'Twas a boy."

"If it had been God's decree that I rule," Alexei continued thoughtfully, as though speaking to himself, "I would have

made him my successor. . . . I wanted to name him Ivan.
. . . Czar Ioann Alexeievich. . . . The little corpse,—where
is the little corpse, now? . . . Speak! . . ."

Peter kept silent.

The Czarevich clutched his head. His face became distorted,
—it turned purple. He recalled the Czar's usage of bottling
still-born children in spirits, even as he did with other "mon-
strosities," in order to preserve them in his cabinet of curiosities.

"Thou didst put him in a jar,—a jar of spirits! . . . The
heir of the Czars of All the Russias is floating about in
spirits, like some tadpole!" He suddenly burst into such wild
laughter that a shudder ran through Peter's body. He again
reflected: "He is mad!" and experienced that revulsion, like
to unearthly horror, which he always experienced toward
spiders, cockroaches and other vermin.

But at the same instant his horror turned into fury,—it
seemed to him that his son was laughing at him, purposely
"playing the tom-fool," in order to maintain his stubbornness and conceal his malefactions.

"What more hast thou within thee?" he resumed his inter-
rogation, as though not noticing that which was taking place
with the Czarevich. The latter ceased laughing just as suddenly as he had begun, threw his head back against the back
of his chair, and his face blanched, sagged, looking like that
of a dead man. He gazed at his father in silence, with a look
devoid of intelligence.

"When thou hadst hope of the rabble," continued Peter,
raising his voice and trying to make it calm, "didst thou not
send anybody to the rabble, to incite sedition, or didst thou
not hear from anybody that the rabble was eager to rise up
in rebellion?"

Alexei kept silent.

"Answer me!" cried out Peter, and a spasm distorted his
face.

Something quivered in Alexei's face. He opened his lips
with an effort and spoke:

"I have told everything. I am not going to speak any
further."

Peter struck the table with his fist and leapt up.

"How durst thou! . . ."

The Czarevich arose and looked point-blank at his father. They again became like to one another, with a momentary and seemingly spectral resemblance.

"Why dost thou threaten, Batiushka?" Alexei uttered quietly. "I do not fear thee,—I do not fear thee in the least. Thou hast taken everything from me,—both soul and body. There is naught more to take,—save that thou canst slay me. Well, what matters it,—go ahead and slay! 'Tis all one to me!"

And a slow, soft, bitter smile distorted his lips. Peter imagined he saw in this smile an infinite contempt. He burst out roaring like a wounded beast, and, throwing himself upon him son, seizing him by the throat, knocking him down, and fell to strangling him, trampling him underfoot, beating him with a stick,—still with the same inhuman roar.

People awoke in the palace and began to bustle, to run about; but none dared to enter the Czar's room. They merely blanched and crossed themselves as they stole up to the doors and listened to the fearful sounds issuing thence. It seemed as if some beast were rending a man into pieces on the other side of the door.

The Czaritza was sleeping in the Upper Palace. They awakened her. She came running, half-undressed,—but she, too, dared not enter. Only when everything had quieted down did she open the door a little, peek in, and enter on tip-toes, stealing up behind her husband's back.

The Czarevich was lying on the floor unconscious; the Czar was lying in an armchair, almost in a swoon.

The royal physician, Blumentrost, was sent after. He re-assured the Czaritza, who feared that the Czar had killed his son. The Czarevich had been cruelly beaten, but there were no dangerous wounds or fractures. He soon came to, and seemed calm. The Czar was in a worse state than the son. When they led him, almost bearing him in their arms, into his bedchamber, he had such convulsions that Blumentrost feared paralysis. But toward morning he bettered, while in the evening he was already up, and paying no heed to the entreaties of Katenka and the warnings of his physician, he ordered a small sloop to be brought and went off to Peterburgh. The Czarevich was carried alongside in another covered sloop.

On the following day, the fourteenth of May, a second manifesto concerning the Czarevich was published among the people, which proclaimed that the Sovereign had been pleased to promise pardon to his son, "provided he offered a true confession of everything and concealed naught; but inasmuch as he, having contemned such paternal mercy, did conceal his intention of attaining the succession through foreign help, or by force, by the help of rebels, this pardon was no longer to be held a pardon."

On the same day a Supreme Court was appointed to judge the Czarevich as a traitor to the state.

A month later, on the fourteenth of June, he was brought into the garrison of the Fortress of SS. Peter and Paul, and placed under guard in the Trubetzkaya bastion.

III

"To the Most Reverend Metropolitans, and Archbishops, and Bishops, and Others of the Clergy.

"Ye must already have heard enough of Our son's crime against Us, both as his father and his sovereign,—a crime almost unheard of in universal annals,—and, although I have sufficient power over him, both by Divine and civil rights, but particularly through those of Russia (which absolutely deny any judgment between father and children, even among the commonalty), to punish him for his crime according to my will, without the advice of others,—yet I have the fear of God before me, lest I err: inasmuch as it is but natural that people see less clearly in their own affairs than others might; even as is the case with physicians,—even though one of them be the most skillful, yet he will not venture to treat his own ailment, but doth call in others,—and thus do even We, entrusting Our ailment to you, requesting treatment of it, with the fear of death eternal before Us. Were I to treat my malady myself, I might never have known its full malignancy; all the more so since I, swearing by God's Judgment Day, did promise forgiveness to My son in writing, and afterwards did confirm the same by word of mouth: that is, if he did make full and true confession of his transgressions. But even though he did violate the said condition through the concealment of most important matters, and particularly concerning his seditious intentions against Us,—both as his parent and Sovereign,—nevertheless, being mindful of the word of God, which adviseth in such cases that those of ecclesiastical rank are also to be consulted, as is written in the seventeenth chapter of Deuteronomy,[92] Our will is that you, the Archprelates, and all others of spiritual rank, as the propounders of the word of God, will not so much issue any decree concerning this matter, but rather that ye shall seek out and show Us true instruction and reasoning in the Holy Scriptures as to what punishment is merited by this God-detested intention of Our son, the like of which is to be found only in the instance of Absalom; ye are to be guided by the Divine testaments, and other examples and laws, of the Holy Scripture. And this shall be given Us under your signs manual, in the form of a letter, so that We, being guided thereby, might have an unburthened conscience in this matter. In which matter we place Our hopes upon ye, as men worthy of keeping the purity of the testaments of God, and as faithful pastors of the flock of Christ, and well-wishers of your fatherland; and We do adjure ye, by the judgment of God and by your sacred office, that ye act in this matter without any hypocrisy or partiality.

"PETER."

The heads of the church answered:

"This matter appertains particularly to a secular court, and not a spiritual; and Your Most High Power is not subject to the judgment of its subjects, but works whatever it pleases, according to its own discretion, without any advisement of those of lesser degree; however, inasmuch as we have been commanded to do so, we have sought out in the Holy Scriptures that which might be applicable to this terrible and unexemplified matter."

Extracts from the Old Testament and the New followed, and, in conclusion, it was reiterated:

"This matter is not for us to judge; for who has placed us as judges over him in whose power we are? How may the members direct the head, when they themselves are directed and dominated by the head? Furthermore, our spiritual judgment must apply to the spirit, and not to flesh and blood, inasmuch as those of spiritual rank are not vested with the power of the sword of metal, but with the power of the sword of the spirit alone. All of which we submit with due humility to Your Most High Monarchic consideration; and may the Sovereign do that which is most suitable in his own eyes: Should he desire to punish the transgressor according to his misdeeds and the measure of his guilt,—the Sovereign hath before him the examples from the Old Testament; should the sovereign be pleased to be compassionate, he hath before him the example of Christ Himself, who did receive the prodigal son, and who extolled mercy as being greater than sacrifice. Putting the matter briefly: *The king's heart* is *in the hand of the Lord*.[93] And may the Sovereign choose that part to which the hand of the Lord may incline him."

They signed themselves as:

"The most humble Stepan, Metropolitan of Riyazan.

"The most humble Theophan, Bishop of Pskov."

Then followed the signatures of the foremost bishops; two Greek Metropolitans,—of Stavropol and of the Thebaid; four Archimandrites,—Theodosius among their number; and two Arch-monks; all these were future members of the Most Holy Directing Synod.

To the main question of the sovereign,—concerning the vow he had made to his son, to forgive him no matter what happened,—the holy fathers did not reply at all.

Peter, as he read this disquisition, experienced an uncanny emotion: it was just as though that from which he had sought support had fallen through under him, like a rotted tree.

He had attained that which he had himself desired,—had attained it only too well, perhaps: the church had submitted to the Czar to such an extent that it seemed as if it had ceased to exist altogether; he himself constituted the whole church.

As for the Czarevich, he remarked about this disquisition with a bitter smile:

"These humble fellows are more cunning than the devil himself! There is as yet no Spiritual Department,—yet they have already mastered spiritual politics."

Once more he felt that the church had ceased to be the Church to him and he recalled the word of the Lord to him of whom it is said: "Thou art Peter, and upon this rock I will build my church."

Verily, verily, I say unto thee, when thou wast young, thou girdest thyself, and walkest whither thou wouldest: but when thou shalt be old, thou shalt stretch forth thy hands, and another shall gird thee, and carry thee whither thou wouldest not.[94]

IV

The first session of the Supreme Court was set for the seventeenth of June, in the Audience Hall of the Senate. Among the number of the judges were ministers, senators, generals, governors, captains of the guards and of the navy, majors, lieutenants, second lieutenants, ensigns, chief war-commissioners, the members of the new departments and aged *boyars,*—the Czar's own dapifers, and courtiers of the second class; altogether there were one hundred and twenty-seven men, civilian and military: rag, tag and bob-tail, as those of high station complained. Some of these judges were down-right analphabets, so that they could not even sign their names to the verdict.

After a mass to the Holy Ghost at the Cathedral of the Trinity, to implore Divine aid in such a difficult matter, the judges passed from the Cathedral into the Senate.

The doors and windows of the main chamber were open,— not only for the sake of the fresh air (the day was sultry, foreboding a storm), but also to give the trial an appearance of being held before all the people. However, all of the adjacent streets were barred with *chevaux-de-frise* and barricaded, and a whole battalion of life-guards stood upon the Square with shouldered arms, without allowing the "base common folk" to pass through.

The Czarevich was brought from the fortress like a convict, under the guard of four officers with bared swords.

There was a throne in the Audience Hall. But it was not upon this throne that the Czar took his seat, but on a common armchair, at the upper end of an open quadrangle formed by rows of long tables covered with scarlet cloths, at which the judges sat; the Czar sat directly opposite his son, as plaintiff before the defendant.

When the session was pronounced open, Peter arose and spake:

"Gentlemen of the Senate, and ye other Judges!

"I beg of you that you decide this matter in the spirit of truth which it merits without flattery or sycophancy, and putting by all apprehensions that, if this matter be deserving of but a slight punishment, and ye act accordingly, it may be contrary to my wishes,—I swear by God Himself and His Dread Judgment ye need have no fear! Also, do not take into consideration the fact that it is my son ye have to judge, —that is, the son of your Sovereign; but rather, disregarding the person, get at the truth, and send not your souls and mine to perdition, so that our consciences may be clear on the day of the Dread Judgment, and our Fatherland remain in welfare."

The Vice-Chancellor Shaphirov read a lengthy enumeration of all the crimes of the Czarevich: old ones, already published in former admissions of guilt, as well as new ones, which, it was purported, had been concealed during the first investigation.

"Dost thou plead guilty?" Prince Menshikov, who had been appointed President of the assembly, asked the Czarevich.

Everybody expected that the Czarevich would fall on his knees, fall to weeping and imploring for mercy, even as he had done in Moscow, in the Administrative Chambers. But, by the way he rose, and looked over the gathering with a calm gaze, they knew that such would not be the case.

"Whether I am guilty or not, 'tis not for you to judge me, but for God alone," he began,—and immediately silence fell: all listened with bated breath. "And how can you ever mete out righteous judgment without a free voice; for where is your will? Ye are the sovereign's slaves,—ye watch his lips: whatever he wills, that will ye favor. This is a court merely in name, but in reality 'tis lawlessness and most ferocious tyranny! Know ye not the fable of how the wolf judged the lamb? And *this* is the judgment of the wolf. No matter how much in the right I may be, ye will condemn me just the same. But, if it were not you, but all of the people of Russia, who were judging between me and Batiushka, things would be different at such a court from what they are here. I took pity on the people. Great,—most great,—is Peter, yet is he rather heavy: one may not even draw breath under him. How many souls have been done to death,—how much blood has been spilled! The earth is groaning with a most grievous groan. Do ye not see,—do ye not hear? . . . But what avails it to talk! What sort of Senate are ye,—ye are the serfs of the Czar,—louts, louts, every single one of you! . . ."

A murmur of indignation drowned the last words of the Czarevich, but no one ventured to stop him. Every one was looking at the Czar, awaiting what he would say,—but the Czar kept silent. Not a single muscle moved on his immobile face, which seemed turned to stone,—save that the gaze of his blazing, wide-open eyes was fixed upon the eyes of the Czarevich.

"Why art thou silent, Batiushka?" He suddenly turned upon his father with a merciless sneer. "Or is it a rare thing for thee to hear the truth? Thou shouldst simply have ordered my head to be lopped off,—I would not have uttered a word. But since thou hast gotten the idea of going to law, then thou must needs listen, whether thou likest it or not! When thou didst entice me to come to thee, leaving the protection of the Kaiser, didst thou not swear by God and by His Judgment that thou wouldst forgive everything? Where now is thy oath? Thou hast disgraced thyself before all of Europe! The Autocrat of Russia is a perjurer and a liar! . . ."

"Such things can not be listened to! . . . 'Tis *lèse-majesté!* . . . He is out of his mind! . . . Take him out, take him out of here! . . ." A din of voices arose.

Prince Menshikov ran up to the Czar and said something in his ear; but the Czar kept silent as though he neither saw nor heard aught in his lethargy, which was like to catalepsy, while his death-like face was like to the face of a statue.

"Thou shalt be the first to spill upon the headsman's block the blood of thy son,—the blood of the Czars of Russia," the Czarevich resumed, and now it seemed that he was no longer speaking of his own accord: his words sounded like a prophecy. "And this blood shall fall from head to head unto the last Czars, and all our line shall perish in blood. God will punish Russia because of thee! . . ." [95]

Peter stirred slowly, ponderously, with an immeasurable effort, as though trying to rise up from under a fearful weight. Finally he arose, his face becoming distorted with a frenzied spasm. It was as though the face of the statue had become alive. His lips parted, and a stifled rattle escaped from his throat:

"Be still,—be still! . . . I'll curse thee! . . ."

"Thou wilt curse me?" cried out the Czarevich in a frenzy, and, making a dash toward the Czar, raised his hands over his father's head. Everybody was frozen in horror. It seemed as though he would strike his father, or spit in his face. "Thou wilt curse me? . . . I—I shall curse thee myself. . . . Thou evil-doer,—thou murderer,—thou beast, —thou Antichrist! . . . Be thou accursed! Be thou accursed! Be thou accursed! . . ."

Peter fell back in the chair and thrust out his hands, as though to ward off his son.

Everybody leapt up. A confusion, such as takes place during a fire or an assassination, sprang up. Some were shutting the windows and doors; others were running out of the hall; others had surrounded the Czarevich and were dragging him away from his father; others still were rushing to the aid of the Czar. The latter was unwell. He was in the throes of a seizure similar to the one that had overcome him a month ago, in Peterhof. The session was declared closed.

But that same night the Supreme Court again convened, and condemned the Czarevich to be put to the torture.

v

"Order of Procedure in Torturing the Accused:

"For the torture of those accused of crimes, there is a special walled-off place, called the torture chamber, surrounded by a palisade and roofed over, inasmuch as, during the tortures, there are present the judges and their secretary, as well as a clerk to take down the words of the tortured.

"A strappado is built in this torture chamber, the said strappado consisting of three posts, of which two are set into the ground, while the third is placed across the top of the other two.

"And at the time designated the *kat* or executioner must be in the torture chamber with his instruments,—to wit: a yoke lined with wool, with a long rope attached thereto; and sundry *knouts* and straps.

"Upon the arrival of the judges in the torture chamber the executioner shall throw one end of the long rope over the crossbeam of the strappado; then, taking the one condemned to torture, shall twist his arms backward, and, having placed them in the yoke, shall draw them up with the aid of men set there for that purpose, so that he who is tortured will not be able to stand on the ground, and his arms will be thrown back entirely, the condemned hanging by them; next the legs are to be tied with a strap and attached to a pillar, placed in front of the strappado for that particular purpose; after having stretched the condemned in this manner he is to be knouted, at which point the questions concerning his crimes are to be put to him and all that such condemned may say is to be written down."

When, on the morning of the nineteenth of June, the Czarevich was brought into the torture chamber, he did not as yet know about the verdict of the court. Kondrashka Tutun, the Czar's Jack Ketch, approached him and said:

"Strip thyself!"

The Czarevich still did not understand.

Kondrashka placed his hand on the Czarevich's shoulder, —the latter turned round to look at him, and finally comprehended,—but, apparently, did not become frightened. His soul was a void. He felt himself as if in a dream; and in his ears rang the nursery song of his prophetic dream of long ago:

> Fires are lit most hot;
> Water seethes in many a pot;
> Knives sharpened are, of steel:
> 'Tis thee they fain would kill!

"Raise him up!" said Peter to the executioner.

The Czarevich was raised up on the strappado. He was given twenty-five lashes.

Three days later the Czar sent Tolstoi to the Czarevich:

"To-day, after dinner, go thou to him, question him, and write down his answers,—not for the investigation, but for information:

"One: What was his reason for not obeying me, and not doing the least thing to please me,—did he not know that such conduct is not indulged in among men, to say naught of its being sinful and shameful?

"Two: Wherefore was he so fearless, and did not apprehend punishment?

"Three: Why did he seek the succession in a roundabout way and not through submission?"

When Tolstoi entered the prison-cell in the Trubetzkaya bastion, where the Czarevich was incarcerated, he found the latter lying on his berth. Blumentrost was bandaging him, inspecting the wales of the *knout* on his back, taking off the old bandages, and applying new ones, with refreshing compresses. The royal physician had his orders to make him well as soon as possible, so as to prepare him for the next torture.

The Czarevich was in a fever and raving:

"Fedor Franzovich! Fedor Franzovich! Do make it scat,—make it scat, for Christ's sake. . . . There, thou canst see it's purring, the accursed one, rubbing itself against me,—but then 'twill make one leap at my breast, and start strangling me, and scratching my heart with its claws. . . ."

Suddenly he came to his senses and looked at Tolstoi:

"What dost thou want?"

"I come from Batiushka."

"To torture me again? . . ."

"Nay, nay, Petrovich! Be not afraid. This is not for the investigation, but merely for information. . . ."

"I know nothing more,—nothing, nothing!" the Czarevich began to moan and toss about. "Leave me alone! Kill me, but torture me not! But if ye do not want to kill me, give me poison or a razor,—I'll do it myself. . . . Only let it be done speedily,—speedily, speedily! . . ."

"What art thou saying, Czarevich! The Lord be with thee," Tolstoi began in his soft, velvety voice, looking at him with his tender, velvety eyes. "God willing, everything will come out right. After the grain is milled, there'll be flour. Soft and easy does the trick. Smoothly and peacefully, —that's the way to do it. It's all in a lifetime. God's patience was tried and by His example must we abide. Or dost thou think I do not feel sorry for thee, my own? . . ."

He took out his inevitable snuff-box with its Arcadian shepherd lad and shepherd lass, took a pinch of snuff, and brushed away a tiny tear.

"Oh, I feel sorry for thee, our poor ailing fellow,—so sorry that I'd give up my very soul for thee, it seems! . . ." And, stooping over him, he added in a quick whisper: "Believe me or no, but I have ever wished thee weal, and wish it even now. . . ."

Suddenly he stopped short,—he was unable to finish under the gaze of the wide-open, unmoving eyes of the Czarevich, who was slowly lifting himself up from his pillows:

"Judas Betrayer, take that for thy weal!" He spat in Tolstoi's face, and, with a dull moan (probably due to a slipped bandage), slumped flat upon his back.

The royal physician darted to his assistance and shouted at Tolstoi:

"Go away,—leave him in peace, or I shan't be responsible for anything!"

The Czarevich again fell to raving.

"Look how it's gazing at me. . . . Its huge eyes are like candles, while its whiskers turn right up, altogether like those of Batiushka. . . . Scat, scat! . . . Fedor Franzovich,—Fedor Franzovich! Do drive it off, for Christ's sake! . . ."

Blumentrost was giving him spirits to smell, and applying ice to his head. At last the Czarevich came to once more and looked at Tolstoi,—but now without any malice, having apparently forgotten the insult he had inflicted upon him.

"After all, Peter Andreievich, I know that thy heart is kind. Be thou my friend, then,—make me pray God for thee! Beg Batiushka to let me see Aphrosiya. . . ."

Tolstoi solicitously applied his lips to the Czarevich's bandaged hand, and pronounced in a voice that quavered from sincere tears:

"I will,—I will beg that favor for thee, my dear little fellow,—I will do everything for thee! If we could but, somehow or other, answer the questions, point by point. . . . There aren't many of them,—only three little points, all in all . . ."

He read aloud the questions, which had been written down by the Czar's own hand.

The Czarevich closed his eyes in exhaustion.

"Well, what answers am I to make, Andreievich? I have told all,—all, as God is my witness. There are nor words nor thoughts in my head. . . . I've become altogether daft. . . ."

" 'Tis naught, 'tis naught, father of mine!" Tolstoi began to bustle, drawing up a chair and getting paper, quill and ink-pot ready. "I'll dictate to thee,—all thou wilt have to do is write. . . . Will he be able to write?" he turned to the royal physician, and bestowed such a look upon him that the latter perceived in this gaze the indomitable gaze of the Czar.

Blumentrost shrugged his shoulders, muttered "Barbarians!" under his nose, and took the bandage off the Czarevich's right hand.

Tolstoi began to dictate. The Czarevich wrote with difficulty, in sprawling characters; several times he stopped. His head was spinning from weakness,—the quill repeatedly fell out of his fingers. At such times Blumentrost would give him some certain drops that acted as a stimulant; more effective than the drops, however, were the words of Tolstoi:

"Thou wilt see Aphrosiushka. And mayhap he will forgive thee entirely,—will allow thee to marry her! Write on, write on, dear little fellow!"

And the Czarevich would again fall to writing.

"On the 22nd day of June, in the year 1718, I answer, point by point, the questions put to me by Master Tolstoi:

"One: The reason for my disobedience to my father was that from my infancy I lived with my mother and her women,

where I learned naught save indoor amusements; and I
likewise learned bigotry,—to which I was inclined even by
nature. And my father, being concerned that I learn matter
befitting a czar's son, did command me to learn German
and other subjects, which was most hateful to me, and I
went through these studies with great indolence, merely to
kill time, but having no desire thereto. And since my father
at that time was frequently on military campaigns, and for
that reason separated from me, the people who were about
me, seeing my inclination to do naught save indulge in
bigotry and in conversation with priests and black-friars,
visiting them frequently and drinking with them, not only
did not hinder me, but even did the like in my company.
And they did estrange me from my father; and, little by
little, not only my father's military and other affairs, but
even his own person, became most detestable to me.

"Two: As for my having been without fear of my father,
and unapprehensive of any punishment for my disobedience
of him,—that, too, came about only because of my evil
nature, as I myself truly admit; inasmuch as, even though
I had fear of him, 'twas not a filial fear.

"Three: As for my seeking the succession in a roundabout
way, and not through submission,—'tis a matter any one can
easily judge: since I had already strayed altogether from
the strait path, and did not want to follow in my father's
steps in any way, how was I to seek the succession in any
other manner save as I did, wishing to attain my ends
through alien aid? And had matters reached the stage where
the Kaiser would have begun putting into action that which
he had promised me,—his purpose being to obtain for me
the crown of Russia through armed force,—even then, re-
gretting naught, I would have striven for the succession,—
more particularly, had the Kaiser wished for Russian troops
to help him against any adversary of his, or have wished
any great sum of money, I would have carried out everything
in accordance with his will, as well as given great presents
to his ministers and generals. As for the troops which he
might have supplied me for my purpose of obtaining the
crown of Russia,—I would have taken them for maintenance
at my own expense, and, to put the whole thing in a word,

I would have spared naught to carry out my will in this matter.

"ALEXEI."

Having signed the document, he suddenly regained his senses, as though he had come out of his delirium, and with horror comprehended what he was doing. He wanted to cry out that all this was a lie,—he wanted to seize and to tear up the paper. But he was deprived of the use of his tongue and all his members, as are those who are buried alive,—who hear everything, feel everything, yet can not stir in the catalepsy of their deathly sleep. Without motion, without voice, he watched Tolstoi fold the paper and put it away in his pocket.

Upon the basis of this last deposition, read in the presence of the Senate on the 24th of June, the Supreme Court handed down its decision:

"We, the subscribing Ministers, Senators and persons of Military and Civilian ranks, in accordance with our common-sense and our Christian conscience, in accordance with the behests of God in the Old and the New Testaments, in accordance with the sacred writings of the Holy Evangel and of the Apostles, and the canons and rules of the Councils of the Holy Fathers and the Teachers of the Church, in accordance with the Statutes of Roman and Greek Cæsars, and other Christian Sovereigns, as well as the Laws of All the Russias, have unanimously and without any dissent agreed and decided that the Czarevich Alexei,—for his seditious design against his Father and his Sovereign, and for his intrigues and plottings to obtain the Paternal Throne through many years, even during the lifetime of the Sovereign, his Father, not only through rebels, but even through the aid of the alien Kaiser and his outlandish troops, with the subsequent ruin of the entire Realm,—fully merits death."

VI

That same day he was again put to the torture. He was given fifteen lashes, and, without the torture being finished, was taken down from the strappado, inasmuch as Blumentrost declared that the Czarevich was in an exceedingly poor state, and that he might die under the *knout*.

That night his condition became so bad that the officer on guard grew frightened and, hurrying away, reported to the commander of the fortress that the Czarevich was dying, —like as not, he might die without the last rites. The commander dispatched to the Czarevich the garrison chaplain, Father Matthew. The latter at first did not want to go, and implored the commander:

"Excuse me from this, Your Honor! I am not used to such matters as this. This matter is an awesome one, appertaining to the Czar. If I be nabbed and held accountable, there'll be no wriggling out of it. I have a wife and children. . . . Have compassion!"

The commander promised to take all the responsibility upon himself, and Father Matthew screwed up his courage and went.

The Czarevich was lying unconscious,—he was past recognizing anybody, and was raving.

Suddenly he opened his eyes and fixed them upon Father Matthew:

"Who art thou?"

"The garrison chaplain, Father Matthew. I've been sent to shrive thee."

"To shrive me? . . . But why hast thou a calf's head, Father? . . . There, even thy face is all shaggy, and thou hast horns above thy brow. . . ."

Father Matthew was abashed and, in silence, kept his eyes downcast.

"Well, now, my Lord Czarevich,—will it please thee to be shriven?" he finally managed to say, with the timid hope that the Czarevich would refuse.

"But, dost thou know, Priest, that *ukase* of the Czar which commands you, our spiritual Fathers, to report to the Privy-Chancellory any treason or uprising which is revealed to you in confession?"

"I know it, Your Highness."

"And should I reveal anything to thee under the sacred seal of confession wouldst report it?"

"What else is one to do, Czarevich? We are not men who

can work our own will . . . I have a wife and children . . ."
Father Matthew mumbled out, and reflected: "There, it's
beginning!"

"Then get thee gone from me,—get thee gone, get thee
gone, thou calf's head!" the Czarevich cried out in fury.
"Thou serf of the Czar of Russia! Ye are louts,—louts, every
single one of you! Ye were eagles,—but ye have become
yoke-oxen! Ye have sold out the Church to Antichrist! I
shall die impenitent, nor will I accept thy Viaticum! . . .
The Blood of the viper, the Body of Satan! . . ."

Father Matthew staggered back in horror. His hands began to shake so that he almost let drop the chalices with
the Viaticum.

The Czarevich looked at him and repeated the words of
a certain holy ancient among the Raskolniki:

"Dost thou know unto what your Lamb is like? 'Tis like
unto a dead dog cast out upon the ways of the city! No
sooner hath a man partaken of its Body than his life is
ended: so caustic is this Communion of yours that it is even
like to arsenic or corrosive sublimate; it penetrates quickly
through all one's bones and marrow,—and the Cunning One
speeds to one's very soul: rest thou thereafter in the fiery
Gehenna, and moan in the flames of Hell, like unto Cain
the sinner beyond Redemption. . . . Ye would fain poison
me,—but ye shall not succeed!"

Father Matthew fled.

The black were-cat leapt upon the Czarevich's neck and
fell to strangling him, clawing at his heart.

"My God, my God, why hast thou forsaken me?" [96] he
moaned and threshed about in his mortal anguish.

Suddenly he sensed that near his bed, on the very same
place where Father Matthew had just sat, some one else
was sitting now. He opened his eyes and looked.

It was a diminutive, hoary ancient. He had let his head
drop, so that the Czarevich could not see his face distinctly.
The little ancient resembled now Father Ivan, the porter
of the Cathedral of the Annunciation, now a certain centenarian gaffer, a bee-keeper, whom Alexei had once met in the
heart of the Novgorod forests, who was forever sitting in
his apiary, warming himself in the sun,—as hoary as a

bald-kite, and permeated through and through with the odors of honey and wax; he, too, was called Ivan.

"Father Ivan? Or art thou the gaffer?" the Czarevich asked.

"Ivan, Ivan,—that's just who I am!" the old man spoke kindly, with a soft smile, and his voice, too, was soft, like the hum of bees or a distant angelus. This voice put the Czarevich into an awesome and delectable mood. He was all the while striving to see the face of the little ancient, yet could not.

"Be not afraid, be not afraid, my own little one," the ancient uttered still more tenderly and softly. "The Lord Himself hath sent me to thee,—and He Himself will come soon after me."

The little ancient lifted up his head. The Czarevich beheld a face youthful and eternal,—and recognized Ioann, the Son of Thunder.

"Christ is risen, Alëshenka!"

"Verily is He risen!" replied the Czarevich, and a great joy filled his soul,—as at the time of the Radiant Morning Mass to Christ, in the Cathedral of the Trinity.

Ioann held in his hands what seemed to be the sun: this was the chalice with the Body and Blood.

"In the name of the Father, the Son and the Holy Ghost."

He gave the Viaticum to the Czarevich. And the sun entered within him, and he came to feel that there was nor sorrow, nor fear, nor pain, nor death,—but that there was only the life eternal, the sun eternal: Christ.

VII

In the morning, examining the sick man, Blumentrost was amazed: his fever had passed, his wounds were cicatrizing; the improvement was so sudden that it seemed a miracle.

"Well, glory be to God, glory be to God," rejoiced the German, "now everything will heal before the wedding!"

The Czarevich felt himself well the whole day; an expression of quiet joy did not leave his face.

At noon the sentence of death was made known to him.

He heard it to the end, calmly, made the sign of the cross, and asked for what day the execution was set. He was told that the day had not been designated as yet.

His dinner was brought. He ate with relish. Afterward he asked that his window be opened.

The day was fresh and sunlit, as though it were a day in spring. The wind brought an odor of water and grass. Under the very window, out of the crevices in the wall of the fortress, grew yellow dandelions. He gazed for long out of the window; outside swallows skimmed by with joyous cries; through the prison-bars the sky seemed bluer and deeper than it had ever been when he was free.

Toward evening the sun lit up the white wall at the head of the Czarevich's bed, and he imagined that he beheld in the midst of this beam a little ancient, as hoary as a bald-kite, with a youthful face and a soft smile, and with a chalice in his hands which was like to the sun. As he gazed upon him he fell into such a gentle and sweet slumber as he had not enjoyed for a long while.

On the following day,—Thursday, the 26th of June, at eight o'clock in the morning,—the Czar, Menshikov, Tolstoi, Dolgorukyi, Shaphirov, Apraxin, and many other Ministers gathered again in the garrison torture-chamber. The Czarevich was so weak that he was carried in arms from his cell into the torture-chamber.

Again they questioned him: "What else art thou hiding within thee?"—"Hast thou falsified aught, or screened any one?"—but he no longer made any answers.

He was raised up on the strappado. No one knew how many lashes he was given,—they lashed him without keeping any track of the blows.

After the first blows he suddenly grew still, ceased moaning and oh'ing,—only all his members were strained and stretched out, as though they were stiffening. But, most probably, his consciousness was not forsaking him. His gaze was clear, his face calm,—although there was something in this calm which made even those most hardened to witnessing suffering feel eldritch.

"He must not be flogged any more, Your Majesty!" Blumentrost was saying in the Czar's ear. "He can die.

Besides, it's useless. He no longer feels anything,—he is in a catalepsy. . . ."

"What?" The Czar looked at his physician in wonder.

"Catalepsy,—it is a condition which . . ." the latter attempted to explain in German.

"Catalepsy thyself, thou fool," Peter cut him short and turned away. The executioner halted for a moment to catch his breath.

"What art thou lolling for? Lash him!" cried out the Czar.

The executioner fell to his lashing. But it seemed to the Czar that the fellow was purposely decreasing the force of his blows, pitying the Czarevich. Peter imagined he beheld pity and indignation upon the faces of all those surrounding him.

"Lash him,—lash him, now!" he leapt up and stamped his foot in fury. Everybody looked at him in horror: he seemed to have gone out of his mind. "Lash him with all thy strength, I tell thee! Or hast unlearned thy trade?"

"Why, I *am* lashing him for all I'm worth, as it is. How else am I to lash him?" Kondrashka muttered under his nose, and stopped once more. "We lash in the Russian fashion,—not having learned the trade from the Germans. We be of the Orthodox faith. Would it take much to have the sin of murder upon one's soul? 'Twould be no hard matter to lash him even to death. There, see,—he barely breathes, the poor fellow! It isn't as if he were a beast, now,—he, too, is a Christian soul!"

The Czar ran up to the executioner.

"Wait, thou devil's son,—I'll flay thee so that thou wilt learn thy trade!"

"Well, now, Liege Lord, do thou teach me,—thy will be done!" the executioner looked at the Czar morosely from under his brows.

Peter snatched the lash out of the executioner's hand. Everybody dashed toward the Czar, wishing to hold him back, but too late. He swung back and struck his son with all his might. His blows were clumsy, but so terrific that they were capable of breaking the very bones.

The Czarevich turned round and looked at his father, as though about to say something,—and this gaze reminded

Peter of the gaze of the dark Visage in its crown of thorns, in the ancient ikon before which, on a time, he had prayed to the Father, ignoring the Son, and reflecting, as he shuddered from horror: "What is the meaning of Son and Father?" And again, as at that time, an abyss seemed to gape open at his feet, and a chill dread wafted therefrom that made the hair upon his head stand up.

Overcoming his horror he once more lifted up the lash, but, feeling upon his fingers the stickiness of the blood with which the lash was dripping, he threw it from him in disgust. All surrounded the Czarevich, taking him down from the strappado and laying him upon the floor. Peter drew near to his son. The Czarevich was lying with his head thrown back; his lips were half-open as though in a smile, and his face was radiant, pure, youthful,—like that of a fifteen-year-old boy. He was gazing at his father as before, as though he wanted to tell him something.

Peter got down on his knees, bent toward his son, and embraced his head.

" 'Tis naught, 'tis naught, my own!" the Czarevich managed to whisper. "I feel well,—everything's well. Let the Lord's Will be done in all things."

The father applied his lips to those of his son, but the latter had already lost all strength and drooped in his father's arms; his eyes had dimmed,—their gaze had become extinguished.

Peter arose, swaying.

"Is he going to die?" he asked his physician.

"He may live until to-night," the latter replied. Everybody ran up to the Czar and drew him out of the chamber.

Peter had suddenly wilted altogether, had grown weak, quieting down and becoming as submissive as a child. He went wherever they led him; he did whatever they wanted him to do.

In the entry to the torture-chamber Tolstoi, having noticed that the Czar's hands were in blood, ordered a ewer and basin to be brought. The Czar submissively began to wash his hands. The water turned to rosy hue.

He was led out of the fortress, seated in his small sloop, and carried off to the Palace.

Tolstoi and Menshikov did not leave the Czar's side. In order to occupy his mind and distract him they spoke of extraneous matters. He listened calmly and answered intelligently. He issued resolutions and signed papers. But later on he could not remember what he had been doing at this time, as though he had passed through it all in his sleep, or in a swoon. He himself made no reference to his son, as though he had forgotten about him altogether.

Finally, toward six o'clock in the evening, when Tolstoi and Menshikov were informed that the Czarevich was on his death-bed, they had to remind the Sovereign about him. The Czar heard them absent-mindedly, as though he did not grasp what they were talking about. However, he again took his seat in the small sloop and set out for the fortress.

The Czarevich had been carried from the torture-chamber back to his cell, and placed in the same bed. He did not again come to.

The Sovereign and his Ministers entered the room of the dying man. When it was learned that he had not taken the Viaticum, they began to bustle and run about with a distraught air. They sent after the Dean of the Cathedral, Father Giorgii. The latter came on the run, puffing, with the same frightened air as all the others in the room, hurriedly took the reserve Holy Sacrament out of its ostensory, went through a silent confession, mumbled out his prayers of manumission, ordered the head of the dying man to be raised, and brought the chalice and spoon to his very lips. But his lips were set close,—the teeth tightly clenched. The golden spoon struck against them and rang in the trembling hand of Father Giorgii. Drops of the Blood dripped on to the purificatory. Horror pervaded all faces.

Suddenly a wrathful thought flashed across Peter's unemotional face. He approached the priest and said:

"Cease! 'Tis not necessary."

And it seemed to the Czar,—or did he merely imagine it? —that the dying man smiled to him with a last smile.

At the same hour as yesterday, on the very same spot near the head of the Czarevich's bed, the sun lit up the white wall. A little ancient as hoary as a bald-kite stood there, holding in his hand a chalice like to the sun. The sun expired. The Czarevich sighed, as children falling asleep sigh.

The royal physician felt his hand and said something in Menshikov's ear. The latter crossed himself and announced solemnly:

"His Highness the Lord Czarevich, Alexei Petrovich, has ceased this life."

They all sank to their knees,—all save the Czar. He stood motionless. His face seemed more death-like than the face of him who had died.

VIII

"Everything in Russia will some day end in a dreadful uprising, and Autocracy will fall, inasmuch as millions cry out to God against the Czar," Weber, the Hanoverian Resident, wrote from Peterburgh, in reporting the death of the Czarevich.

"The Crown-Prince died from no stroke of apoplexy, as is maintained here, but either from the sword or from the ax," reported Pleier, the Imperial Resident. "On the day of death no one was admitted into the fortress, and, before evening, its gates were locked. A Dutch carpenter who had been working on a new turret of the Cathedral, and had remained there for the night unobserved, had in the evening seen from above, near the torture cell, the heads of some people or other, and had told thereof to his mother-in-law, who is midwife at the house of the Dutch Resident. The body of the Crown-Prince was placed in a common coffin made of the poorest boards; his head was covered to some extent, while his neck was tied with a kerchief in pleats, as if for shaving."

The Dutch Resident, Jacob de Bie, dispatched a report to the States-General to the effect that the Czarevich had died from venesection, and that an uprising was apprehended in Peterburgh.

The letters of the Residents were opened in the Post Office, and brought to the Czar. Jacob de Bie was seized, brought into the Chancellory of Ambassadors, and questioned "with assiduity." The Dutch carpenter who had worked on the spire of the Cathedral of SS. Peter and Paul was also taken under guard, as well as his midwife mother-in-law.

To controvert these rumors, there was sent to the Russian Residents in foreign ports, in the name of the Czar, a report of the death of the Czarevich, composed by Shaphirov, Tolstoi, and Menshikov:

"Upon the pronouncement of the sentence of the Court upon Our son, We, as a father, were torn by a natural impulse of mercy on the one hand, and a due care for the integrity and future safety of Our realm on the other, and could not yet come to a resolution in this most difficult and important matter. But the Almighty God, desiring, through His Own Will and His Righteous Judgment, according to His Mercy, to free Us from such doubts, and Our realm from danger and ignominy, did cut short, yesterday (this is written on the 27th day of June), the life of Our son Alexei, through a serious illness, which in its inception resembled apoplexy, and which overcame him upon the pronouncement of the said sentence and the revealment of his so great crimes against Us and Our entire realm. Nevertheless, he subsequently recovered his full memory, and, as is a Christian's duty, confessed and received the Sacrament, and did request that We come to him,—which We complied with, disregarding all the vexations he had caused Us, coming to him with all Our Ministers and Senators; and he did extend to Us a full confession of all his crimes against us, with many tears of repentance and with remorse, and did beg forgiveness therefor, which We granted him, according to Our duty as a Christian and as a parent. And so did he end his life, in a Christian manner, about six o'clock in the afternoon of the twenty-sixth of June."

The day after the death of the Czarevich, the twenty-seventh of June, which was the ninth anniversary of Poltava, was celebrated as usual. A triumphal standard, yellow, with a black eagle, was raised over the fortress; mass was celebrated in the Cathedral of the Trinity; cannons sent forth their salvos; a feast was held in Post Office Court; while that night, in the Summer Garden, upon the open gallery over the Neva, near the pediment of the Venus of Peterburgh (to quote from a contemporary description), "all waxed rather merry," to the sounds of tender music, resembling the sighs of love from the realm of Venus:

> Thy arrows, Cupido, forego—
> For not a heart here but doth know
> A most delectable, dear woe.

That same night the body of the Czarevich was placed in a coffin and transferred from the prison-cell into certain empty quarters in a wooden building near the house of the commander of the fortress.

In the morning it was carried out to the Cathedral of the Trinity, and "men of all ranks,—whosoever wished to do so,—were allowed to draw near the coffin of the Czarevich, to behold the body and to bid farewell to the same."

On Sunday, the twenty-ninth of June, there was another festival, the Czar's Name-Day. Again mass was celebrated; cannons sent forth their salvos; all the bells were rung, and a dinner was given in the Summer Palace; in the evening the celebrants arrived at the Admiralty, where the launching of a new frigate, *The Old Oak*, was held; the usual drinking-bout took place on board the ship; fireworks were set off at night and again "all waxed rather merry."

Monday, the thirtieth of June, was the day set for the funeral of the Czarevich. The requiem was most solemn. The services were held by Stepan, Metropolitan of Riyazan; Theophan, the Bishop of Pskov; six other Priests of the highest rank; the two Metropolitans of Palestine; several Archimandrites, Deans, Hieromonks, Hierodeacons, and eighteen local priests. Those present included the Sovereign, his consort, Ministers, the Senators,—all those of military or civil rank. Incomputable throngs of people surrounded the church.

The coffin, lined with black velvet, stood upon a small catafalque, under a white cloth-of-gold, and was guarded by a guard of honor, consisting of four sergeants belonging to the Life Guards of the Transfiguration, with their swords drawn.

Many of the dignitaries had splitting heads from the orgies of the day before, and the ribald songs of the buffoons were still ringing in their ears:

Oh, my mother was a-dancing when she gave me birth;
I was christened 'midst the tavern's mirth. . . .

And, on this clear summer day, especially somber seemed
the dull flame of the funeral candles, and the subdued sound
of the chant for the dead:

*"Let the soul of Thy servant, O Christ, rest with the saints,
where there is neither sickness, nor sadness, nor sighing, but
life never-ending."*

And the dismally reiterated ejaculation of the deacon:

*"Once more we pray for the peace of the soul of God's
servant Alexei, who hath gone to his long sleep, and that
every transgression, voluntary or involuntary, may be forgiven him."*

And the dully dying wail of the choir:

*"Lamentations over the grave are wrought into a chant:
Halleluiah!"*

Some one in the crowd suddenly broke into loud sobs,
and a shudder ran through all those in church when the choir
launched into the last canticle:

*"Beholding me voiceless and without the breath of life,
come, all ye that love me, and kiss me with the last kiss."*

The first that drew near to bid the Czarevich an eternal
farewell was the Metropolitan Stepan. The old man could
hardly keep on his legs. Two Protodeacons led him along,
supporting him under his arms. He kissed the Czarevich's
hand and head, then bent over and gazed long into his face.
Stepan was burying together with him all that he loved,—
all the old days of Muscovy, the Patriarchate, the freedom
and grandeur of the Ancient Church; he was burying his last
hope, the "hope of all Russia."

After the clergy the Czar went up the steps of the catafalque. His face was still the same death-mask that it had
been during the last few days. He glanced at his son's face.

It was radiant and young, as though it had grown still
more radiant and youthful after his death. The smile upon
his lips said: All is well,—the Lord's will be done in all
things.

And something began to quiver, to stir, in Peter's unmoving
face, as though something were being revealed with a slow,
frightful effort. Finally it was revealed,—and the Czar's dead

face became animated, radiant, as though it were illuminated by the light from the face of the departed.

Peter bent toward his son and pressed his lips to the latter's chill lips. Then he raised his eyes to Heaven,—all saw that he was weeping,—crossed himself, and said:

"The Lord's will be done in all things."

He now knew that his son would vindicate him before the Eternal Judgment, and that there he would explain to him, his father, that which Peter had not been able to comprehend in this world: the meaning of Son and Father.

IX

It was announced to the people, even as to the foreign courts, that the Czarevich had died from a stroke.

But the people did not believe. Some said that he had died from the beatings given to him by his father, others shook their heads dubiously: "This matter was over rather quickly, somehow or other!" While others asserted, without any hesitancy whatsoever, that, in lieu of the Czarevich, there had been placed in his coffin the body of a certain sergeant in the Life Guards, who had a facial resemblance to the Czarevich; while the Czarevich himself had, so it would seem, run away from his father,—either to the cenobies beyond the Volga, or else to the Cossack stands upon the steppes, "upon the free rivers," and was in hiding there.

A few years later, in the Cossack stand at Yamen, upon the river Buzuluka, a certain Timothy the Toiler appeared, who, to look at him, was a begging vagabond; to the questions: Who art thou, and whence comest thou?—he would answer openly:

"Out of a cloud, out of the air. The beggar's crutch is my father; the beggar's wallet my mother. They call me Toiler, inasmuch as I toil for God, in a great deed."

But secretly he said of himself:

"No *mouzhik* I, nor a *mouzhik's* son; I am an eagle, and the son of an eagle, and 'tis my wish an eagle for to be! I am the Czarevich Alexei Petrovich. I was born with the mark of a cross upon my back, and that of a sword upon my thigh. . . ."

And there were also others who said of him:

"No common man, he; and he is fated to be one because of whom the whole earth will quake! . . ."

And in the surreptitious broadsides which were distributed from his place throughout all the Cossack stands, it was said:

"Blessed is our God! We, the Czarevich Alexei Petrovich, are setting out to seek Our rights, as bequeathed to Us by Our sires and grandsires, and We put Our trust in you, the Cossacks, as in a stone wall, to stand up for the Old Faith and for the common folk, even as ye did in the times of Our sires and grandsires. And ye, who are naked, who tow barges; ye barefooted, shelterless vagabonds,—come ye all to Us in the day and in the night, wherever ye may hear Our voice!"

The Toiler was roaming the steppes and gathering a free band, promising to "discover a great Town, wherein the sign of the Most Holy Mother of God is, and the Evangel, and the Cross, and the Standards of Czar Alexander of Macedonia; and he, the Czarevich Alexei Petrovich, would rule in a manner worthy of those standards; and then the end of time would befall, and Antichrist would come; and he, the Czarevich, would do battle with all the mighty host of the Enemy, and with Antichrist himself."

The Toiler was seized, put to the torture, and had his head lopped off, as a false pretender.

But the people continued to believe that the true Alexei Petrovich, when his time came, would appear, take his seat upon the throne of his father, and execute the *boyars*,—every single one,—but show his favor to the commonalty.

Thus, even after his death, he remained "the hope of all Russia," to his people.

X

Having ended the investigation concerning the Czarevich, Peter, on the eighth of August, left Peterburgh for Reval,—by sea, at the head of a fleet consisting of two-and-twenty warships. The Czar's ship was a new one, recently launched from the Admiralty wharf,—*The Old Oak*, a frigate of ninety guns: the first ship built according to plans drafted by the Czar, without the aid of any foreigners, all of Russian timber, and by Russian master-workmen alone.

One evening, as they were leaving the Gulf of Finland and entering the Baltic Sea, Peter was standing at the helm and steering.

The evening was inclement. Heavy, black clouds seemingly of iron, were piling up, low over the heavy, black crests of the waves,—also seemingly of iron. The ship rocked a great deal. White tatters of sea-foam flickered like pale hands of furiously threatening phantoms. At times the waves lashed over the ship's side and swept with their rain of salty spray all those on deck, but most of all the Czar-helmsman. His clothing had become drenched through and through. An icy dampness pierced his body; an icy wind beat upon his face. But, as always when at sea, he felt himself buoyant, strong, and joyous. He gazed intently into the dark distance and steered with a firm hand. The whole gigantean fabric of the frigate trembled from the onslaught of the waves; but staunch was *The Old Oak,* and, as a goodly steed obeys its bridle, so it obeyed its helm, leaping from wave to wave, and occasionally dipping, as though it were diving into the hoary depths; it seemed as though it would never come up,—yet every time it flew out, triumphant.

Peter was thinking of his son. For the first time he was thinking of everything as in the past,—with great sorrow, but without fear, without torment, without remorse; sentient in this instance, as in his whole life, of the will of the Higher Fates.—"Great, great is Peter, but most heavy,—one may not even breathe under his weight. The earth is groaning with a great groan!" he recalled the words his son had uttered before the Senate.

"How else should it be?" Peter was thinking. "The anvil, too, never fear, groans under the sledge-hammer. He, the Czar, was naught but the sledge-hammer in the hand of the Lord,—the sledge-hammer with which Russia was being forged. He had roused Russia from her sleep with a fearful blow. But, had it not been for him, she would have been sleeping even to this day the sleep of the dead."

And what would have happened if the Czarevich had remained among the living?

Sooner or later he would have come to reign, would have returned the power to the priests, to the holy ancients, to the long-beards,—and that band would have turned from Europe back to Asia, would have extinguished the light of enlightenment,—and Russia would have perished.

"She's comin' on to storm!" the old Dutch skipper remarked, approaching the Czar. The latter made no answer, and kept on gazing intently into the distance.

It was darkening rapidly. The black clouds sank ever lower and lower toward the black waves. Suddenly, upon the very rim of the sky, through a narrow rift underneath the clouds, the sun flashed out, as though blood had spurted out from a wound, and the iron clouds, the iron waves, were encarnadined with blood. And marvelous and fearful was this ensanguined sea.

"Blood! Blood!" thought Peter, and recalled the prophecy of his son:

"Thou shalt be the first to spill upon the headsman's block the blood of thy son,—the blood of the Czars of Russia,—and this blood shall fall from head to head, unto the last Czars, and all our line shall perish in blood. God will punish Russia because of thee!"

"Nay, O Lord!" again, as at that time before the old ikon with the dark Visage in its crown of thorns, Peter, ignoring the Son, prayed to the Father who had sacrificed His Son. "May this never befall! His blood is upon me,—me alone! Punish me, God,—but spare Russia!"

"She's comin' on to storm!" the old skipper repeated, thinking the Czar had not heard him before. "I told Your Majesty a while ago 'twould be better to turn back. . . ."

"Have no fear," Peter answered with a smile. "Staunch is this new ship of ours,—it can weather the storm. God is with us!"

And with a firm hand the helmsman steered over the iron and ensanguined waves toward the unknown, the distant.

The sun sank, darkness fell, and the storm began to howl.

EPILOGUE

THE COMING CHRIST

I

"Our faith is not the true faith,—and there is e'en naught to stand up for. Oh, were I to find the true faith itself, I would let my flesh be made into mince-meat for its sake!"

Tikhon, in his long wanderings after his flight from the Red Death in the forests of Vetluga, frequently recalled these words of a certain pilgrim who had passed through all faiths,—and accepted not a single one.

One day in late autumn, in the Pecherskaya Cloister of Nizhegorod, where he had stopped for a rest, and where he was working as a book-scribe, one of the monks, Father Nikodim, when the two of them were discussing faith, said:

"I know what thou hast need of, little son. There be some sage folk living in Moscow. They have a certain living water; having once drunk of this water, one will never thirst again, through all eternity. Go thou to them. If thou art found worthy they shall reveal a great mystery to thee. . . ."

"What mystery?" Tikhon asked eagerly.

"Be not in such haste, my little dove," retorted the monk, sternly yet kindly; "don't go off half-cocked. If thou dost truly desire to partake of that mystery, thou must undergo the ordeal of silence. No matter what thou mayest see, no matter what thou mayest hear,—know but one thing: be silent and say nothing. *I will not impart thy secret to thine enemies, nor give thee the kiss of Judas.* Dost understand?"

"I understand, Father! I shall be e'en as voiceless as one dead. . . ."

"There, 'tis well," Father Nikodim went on. "I shall give thee a bit of writing to Parthen Paramonych, the merchant

Saphiyannikov, who trades in flour in Moscow. Go thou to him, and bring him my greetings, and a bit of a present,—a small keg of preserved Kerzhen claudberries. We two be gossips from of old. He will take thee into his place. Thou hast quite a head for ciphering, while he hath need for such a goodly lad in his shop. . . . Art thou setting out right now, or wilt thou wait until spring? 'Twill be winter-time soon, now,—whereas thy clothing is but so-so. Wilt thou not freeze to death?"

"Right now, Father,—right now!"

"Well, go, and God be with thee, little son!"

Father Nikodim blessed Tikhon on the way, and gave him the bit of writing he had promised him, which he permitted him to read:

"To our beloved brother in Christ, Parthen Paramonych,—greetings and joyance.

"The bearer of this is the youth Tikhon. Stale bread doth not fill him,—he hath a craving for soft and sweet pastries. Feed him who is hungry. Peace unto all of ye, and joy in the Lord.

"Humbly thine,
"FATHER NIKODIM."

Tikhon set out for Moscow over the first road beaten through the winter snows, accompanying the Makiriev cart-caravan of fish.

The flour stores of Saphiyannikov were situated on the corner of the Third Street of the Commoners and the Little Sukhareva Square.

Here, despite Father Nikodim's letter, Tikhon was received suspiciously. To test him he was placed as assistant to the porter, for the hardest sort of work. But, seeing that he was a sober lad, hard-working, and well-skilled in figures, he was transferred into the shop and seated at the account-books.

The shop was like any other shop. There were purchases; there were sales; there was talk of profits and losses. Only occasionally were there whispered discussions about something or other, held in nooks and corners.

On one occasion Mitka the porter,—a simple-hearted,

splay-footed giant, all powdered over with white flour-dust, —began singing a strange song in Tikhon's presence, lugging tremendous flour sacks on his shoulders at the same time:

> In our Russia, holy Russia, this thing did befall,
> In our glorious Mother Moscow, that is builded of stones,—
> In the Third Street of the Commoners,—
> Two friends met with exceeding joy,
> They so radiant were one might think them suns.
> Ivan Timotheievich, he bows low before
> His guest rich and dear, Danilo Philipovich:
> Thou didst well, dear friend, for to call on Me
> In My kingly palace, in My lordly halls,
> For to partake of my poor bread and salt;
> And full glad am I for to hear Thee speak
> Of the End thou bringest to all days and time,
> And of Thy Great Day,—God's Dread Judgment Day. . . .

"Mitiya,—I say, Mitiya,—who are these fellows: this Danilo Philipovich and this Ivan Timotheievich?" asked Tikhon.

Mitka, caught off his guard, halted, bending under the weight of an enormous sack, and his eyes popping out from amazement:

"Why, canst thou not recognize the God Sabaoth and Christ?"

"But how can the God Sabaoth and Christos be on the Third Street of the Commoners? . . ." Tikhon looked at him with still greater amazement.

But the other had already regained his wits, and, as he walked off, muttered glumly:

"If thou wilt know a great deal, thou wilt age before thy time. . . ."

Shortly thereafter Mitka was taken with lumbago,—he had probably strained himself lugging sacks. He lay in his cellar cubby-hole for days, groaning and oh'ing. Tikhon visited the sick man, drenching him with a decoction of sage, and rubbing him down with spirits of camphor and other medicaments procured from a friendly German apothecary; and, since it was damp in the cellar, he transferred Mitka to his own chamber,—warm and light, on the second floor over the main ambry. Mitka was a good-hearted fellow. He became attached to Tikhon, and began to be more open in their conversations.

From these conversations, as well as from the songs which Mitka used to sing in his presence, Tikhon learned that at the beginning of Czar Alexei Mikhailovich's reign the Lord God Sabaoth Himself, with his Angels and Archangels, with his Cherubim and Seraphim, had come "a-rollin' down" from the sky in a chariot of fire before a great concourse of people, upon the Gorodina Mountain, near the villages of Mikhailitza and Bobynina, in the parish of Egoriev, which is in the Old Oak district, which is in the Mouromsk region. The Angels had soared up to the sky, but the Lord had remained on earth, entering the most pure flesh of one Danilo Philipovich, a runaway soldier, at the same time proclaiming a certain bond-*mouzhik*, by the name of Ivan Timotheievich, as His Only Begotten Son, Jesus the Christ. And, in the guise of beggars, they set out for to roam the earth.

Fleeing from those who persecuted them, they endured cold and hunger; they sought shelter in pig-sties,—in pits wherein dead animals are cast,—in hay-ricks. Once a country wife had hidden them under the floor-boards of a cattleshed. A calf standing above them had let go,—"the urine sluiced down under the flooring: Danilo Philipovich, upon beholding the same, spake unto Ivan Timotheievich: "Thou wilt get a wetting!" But the latter answered: "No matter,—if but the 'King escape getting one!'"

Their latter years were spent in Moscow, on the Third Street of the Commoners, in a special house called the House of Sion, where both passed away and mounted up to the heavens in glory.

After Ivan Timotheievich, even as before him, many Christs had been "revealed,"—inasmuch as the Lord doth not wish for any more pleasant dwelling-place than the most pure flesh of man, according to the saying: *For ye are the temple of the living God.*[97] God gives birth to Christ when everything is dying. Christ ended His Work in the flesh of one man, and begins it again in the flesh of others.

"Then that means there are many Christs?" Tikhon asked.

"The spirit is one,—the bodies are many," Mitka made answer.

"And it is so even now?" went on Tikhon, whose heart suddenly stood still from the premonition of a mystery.

Mitka nodded his head in silence.

"Where is He then?"

"Do not question me. It may not be told. Thou wilt see for thyself, if thou be found worthy. . . ." And Mitka fell silent, as though he had filled his mouth with water.

"*I will not impart Thy secret to Thine enemies,*" recalled Tikhon.

A few days later, in the evening, he was sitting in the shop, working at his account-books. It was a Sabbath eve. Trade was already over. But a new shipment had driven up, and stevedores were lugging the sacks from the carts. Whenever the door opened, swirls of frost-engendered steam would burst into the room, together with the crunching of snow and the pealing of the evening angelus. The snow-covered white roofs of the small, black log-houses of the Third Street of the Commoners gleamed with a steady and even rosy light against the clear, aureately-lilac sky. It was dark in the shop, save for a lampad glowing in its very depths, amid the flour sacks piled up to the very ceiling, before an image of Nikola the Miracle-Worker.

Parthen Paramonych Saphiyannikov,—a white-bearded, red-nosed old man, who resembled Grandfather Frost, and his head-clerk, Emelian Retivoy [the Zealous],—a squat, red-haired, bald-headed fellow, with a hideous and clever face that recalled an ancient mask of Faunus,—were drinking a delectable hot concoction of water, honey and spices, and listening to Tikhon's stories about the life of the holy ancients beyond the Volga.

"But what is thy opinion, Emelian Ivannovich,—should one seek salvation in accordance with the old or the new books?" asked Tikhon.

"Once upon a time there lived a man in Russia by the name of Danilo Philipovich," said Emelian, with a sly smile. "He read books, and he read them, until he read them all through,—yet he saw that there was but little sense in them;—so, putting them all together in a sack, he chucked them into the Volga. Neither in the old books nor in the new is there any salvation; there is but one need——

> The Book of Gold,
> The Book of Life,
> The Book of the Dove,—
> The Holy Ghost, the Lord Himself!"

The last words he chanted in the same way as Mitka used to chant his strange songs.

"But where is this book?" Tikhon persisted, timidly and eagerly.

"Why, there,—look!" he indicated the sky to him through the open door. "There's the book for thee! With the little sun for His golden quill the Lord God Himself writes in it the words of the Life Eternal. As soon as thou hast read them thou shalt fathom all the mystery of heaven and all the mystery of earth. . . ."

Emelian looked at him fixedly,—and from this gaze Tikhon suddenly felt eerie, as though he had peered into bottomlessly-transparent, dark water.

But Emelian, having exchanged winks with the master, suddenly fell silent.

"There is, then, no salvation, neither in the Old Church nor the New?" Tikhon hurriedly began once more, fearing lest Emelian fall altogether silent, even as Mitka had recently done.

"What are your churches?" Emelian shrugged his shoulders in contempt. "Ant-hills, synagogues falling into ruins; the flea-fairs of the Jews! The timbers whereof they were built were chopped down by thieves and carted by oxen. The blessedness of these churches of yours has turned to stone. This blessedness once consisted of spirit and fire; it has now turned into the precious stones and gold upon your ikons and upon the vestments of your priests. The word of God has turned stale, has turned into stale crusts,— one could never chew it, but would merely break his teeth thereon."

And, bending toward Tikhon, he added in a whisper:

"There *is* a true church,—new, secret, a beautiful chamber of light, builded of cypress, of barberry and anise-wood, —a mansion of Sion. It has none of the stale crusts,— pastries hot and sweet and soft are eaten therein, taken right out of the oven: living words from the lips of prophets;

there one finds the joys of Paradise, the joys of Heaven, and the spiritual ale whereof the church sings: *Come ye, drink of the new drink, from the well-spring of incorruption, from the tomb of the reviving Christ!* [98]

"There, that's the drink for thee! Man doth not thereof with his lips partake, yet it doth his whole life tipsy make," exclaimed Parthen Paramonych and, suddenly rolling his eyes up to the ceiling, began singing softly, in an unexpectedly high falsetto:

> God Himself that ale did brew,
> And the Holy Ghost prepared the mash. . . .

And Retivoy and Mitka hummed in chorus, harmonizing with him, stamping their feet in time, jerking their shoulders as if they were simply itching to whirl off into a dance. And the eyes of all the three grew tipsy.

> God Himself that ale did brew,
> And the Holy Ghost prepared the mash;
> The Holy Mother of God skimmed it off Herself,
> Swinging with the Lord, turn and turn about;
> The holy Angels bore it,—
> The Cherubim did pour it.

It seemed to Tikhon that a stamping of countless feet was reaching him,—an echo of a tempestuous dance; and there was in this song something inebriate, savage, frightful, which made one's breath stop short,—and which one longed to listen to: to listen to without an end.

But all at once, just as suddenly as they had begun, all three fell silent. Emelian started looking through the account-books: Mitka lifted up the sack he had thrown down and carried it farther; while Parthen Paramonych passed his hand over his face, as though wiping something off it, got up and yawned, and, lazily stretching himself the while, made the sign of the cross over his mouth and let drop in his usual proprietorial voice, such as he used every evening:

"Well, lads, go to your supper! The stew and the porridge will get cold."

And again the shop became like any other shop, just as though nothing had ever happened.

Tikhon pulled himself together and also got up,—but

suddenly, as though some force had thrown him to the floor, he fell on his knees, and, all a-tremble and pale, stretched out his hands and cried out:

"Fathers of mine! Take pity upon me,—be gracious! There is no more strength in me,—my soul is weary from longing to enter the courts of God! Take me into your sacred communion,—reveal unto me your great mystery! . . ."

"Look ye, what an eager fellow!" Emelian eyed him with his crafty smile. "A fairy-tale is soon told, brother, but a task is not so fast done. One must at first ask Batiushka. Perhaps thou mayst e'en be found worthy. But in the meanwhile eat thy mushroom pie but hold thy tongue close by,— know but one thing,—keep silent and say nothing."

And they all went off to supper, just as though there were nothing out of the way.

Neither on that day nor in the days that followed was there any talk of any mysteries. When Tikhon himself would broach such subjects, all kept silent and eyed him suspiciously. It was just as though some curtain had lifted up before him, only at once to fall again. But he could no longer forget that which he had glimpsed. He was not himself; he walked about like a lost soul; he listened yet did not understand; he answered at haphazard; he became confused in his accounts. The master upbraided him. Tikhon feared lest he be driven out of the shop entirely.

But on Saturday, just a week later, as Tikhon was sitting alone in his room late in the evening, Mitka entered.

"Let's go!" the latter announced, hurriedly and joyously.

"Whither?"

"To Batiushka, for a visit."

Without daring to question him Tikhon dressed hurriedly, went downstairs, and saw the master's sleigh near the front steps. Emelian and Parthen Paramonych, the latter muffled up in a great fur coat, were sitting in the sleigh. Tikhon nestled down at their feet, Mitka took the driver's seat, and they whirled off through the nocturnal, deserted streets. The night was calm, light. The moon wore a coat of mail, made up of tiny, nacreous clouds. They crossed Moscow River over the ice, and for a long while wove in and out of the deserted by-lanes of Moscow-Beyond-the-River. Finally, through the lunar haze, in the midst of a field of snow, came the gleam of the turbidly-pink walls of the Donskoy Monastery, with its white battlements and turrets.

At the corner of Donskaya and Shabelskaya Streets they got out of the sleigh. Mitka drove into a courtyard and, leaving the sleigh with the horses there, came back. They continued their way on foot, keeping close to old, ramshackle, snowed-under fences. They turned into a cul-de-sac, where they sank in snow up to their knees. Walking up to a double gate with iron hinges they knocked on the wicket. It was not opened to them immediately,—they were asked first who they were and whence they came. Beyond the wicket was a big court with many out-houses, but save for the old man who was gate-keeper, there was never a soul around, nor any gleam of light, nor as much as the bark of a dog,— just as if everything had died out. The court came to an end, and they again began making their way through an exceedingly narrow, much-trampled path, between high drifts of snow, over some back-yards or other,—one could not tell whether they were waste lands or truck-gardens.

Having passed through a second set of gates, the wicket of which was no longer shut, they found themselves in an orchard, where the apple and cherry trees showed whitely in their coverings of snow, as if abloom with vernal blossoms. The stillness was as intense as if the nearest dwelling-place were thousands of versts away. At the end of the garden one could glimpse a big, wooden house. They went up on the front steps, knocked once more, and were once more challenged from within. The door was opened by a morose fellow in a calotte and a long-skirted *kaftan,* who resembled one of the lesser brethren of a monastery. A great deal of upper clothing, masculine and feminine,—simple sheepskin short-coats, coats of rich furs, old-fashioned Russian hats, new-fashioned cock-hats and monastic cowls,—hung upon the walls or lay upon the chests and benches in the spacious entry.

When the arrivals had taken off their fur coats, Retivoy asked Tikhon thrice:

"Wouldst thou partake of the mystery of God, my son?"

And Tikhon answered thrice:

"I would."

Emelian blindfolded him with a handkerchief and taking his hand, led him off.

They walked for a long while through endless passages,—now ascending steps, now descending them.

Halting at last, Emelian ordered Tikhon to strip himself to the skin, and then clad him in a long linen shift, putting cotton stockings on his feet, but leaving off his boots, as he pronounced the words of the Revelation:

"He that overcometh, the same shall be clothed in white raiment." [99]

They then went on. The last staircase was so steep that Tikhon had to hold on with both hands to the shoulders of Mitka, who was walking ahead, in order not to miss a step, since he was as one blind.

An earthy dampness was wafted upon him, as though from some cellar or underground place. The last door opened, and they entered an over-heated chamber, where, to judge from the whispering, and from the shuffling of feet, there were a great many people. Emelian bade Tikhon get down on his knees, bow thrice to the earth, and utter after him the words which he was uttering in his ear:

"I swear by my soul, by God, and by His Dread Judgment, to suffer the *knout*, and the fire, and the ax, and the headsman's block, and every sort of torture and death, yet never abjure the holy faith, or impart to any that which I may behold or hear,—not even to my father in the flesh, nor to my spiritual father. *I will not impart Thy secret to Thine enemies, nor give Thee the kiss of Judas.* Amen."

When he had finished, they seated him on a bench and took the blindfold off his eyes.

He saw a big, low room; there were holy images in one corner, with a great many candles burning before them; upon the white plaster of the walls were large blotches of damp, here and there rivulets of water actually trickled down from the ceiling, seeping through the crevices between the black, tarred boards. It was as stifling as in a bath. There was steam in the air, surrounding the flames of the candles with misty rainbows. The men sat on one side, upon benches along the walls; the women sat on the other; both were clad in uniform white shifts, evidently put right over the naked body, and in cotton stockings, but without any foot-gear.

"The Czaritza! The Czaritza!" an awed murmur sped through the room.

A door opened, and a tall, graceful woman entered, clad in black raiment and with a white kerchief on her head. All rose and made a deep obeisance before her.

"'Tis Akulina Makeëvna, our Matushka, the Queen of Heaven!" Mitka whispered to Tikhon.

The woman made her way to the holy images and took her seat beneath them, herself like an image. All began approaching her in turn, bowing down to her feet and kissing her knee, as though they were applying their lips to a holy image.

Emelian led Tikhon up to her and said:

"May it please Thee to baptize him, Matushka! He is a catechumen. . . ."

Tikhon got down on his knees and lifted his eyes up to her: she was swarthy, no longer young,—about forty,—with fine wrinkles around her eyelids, as dark as if they were touched up with charcoal, with thick, black eyebrows that seemed grown together, and faint black down on her upper lip,—"Just like a Gypsy or a Circassienne," the lad reflected. But when she looked at him with her great, dull-black eyes, he suddenly realized how comely she was.

The Matushka made the sign of the cross over him thrice, with a candle, the flame almost touching his forehead, his breast, and his shoulders:

"In the name of the Father, and the Son, and the Holy Ghost, the slave of God, Tikhon, is baptized through the Holy Ghost and the fire!"

Then, with an easy and rapid movement, evidently one of long usage, she threw open her raiment, and he caught sight of her splendidly beautiful body, as youthful as that of a seventeen-year-old girl, aureately-swarthy, as though it were carved out of ivory.

Retivoy was nudging him from behind and whispering in his ear:

"Kiss the most sacred belly and the most pure paps!"

Tikhon cast down his eyes in confusion.

"Be not afraid, little child!" uttered Akulina, with such kindliness that he imagined he heard the voice of mother, sister and beloved, all in one. And he recalled how, in the impenetrable forest, near Round Lake, he had kissed the ground and looked up at the sky, and had felt that the earth and the sky were one, and had wept and prayed:

> Wondrous Queen, Mother of God,—
> Thou earth, thou earth, our Mother dank!

With reverence he kissed thrice this splendidly beautiful body, as if it were an image. A most sinister odor was wafted upon him; a sly smile flitted across his lips,—and because of this odor, because of this smile, an eldritch feeling came over him.

But her raiment was now drawn together, and once more she was sitting before him,—majestic, austere, holy,—an ikon amid ikons.

When Tikhon and Emelian returned to their former places, all began singing in chorus, in churchly fashion, dismally and protractedly:

> Give us, O Lord, Jesus Christ,
> Give us, O Sire, the Son of God,
> And the Holy Ghost, our Consoler!

They fell silent for a minute; then they began anew, but this time in a different chant, gay, rapid, like that of a dance, stamping their feet and clapping their palms in time,—and the eyes of all grew tipsy:

> The Saviour Himself
> Dwells in our houses on the Don,
> With His Angels,
> And Archangels,
> With His Cherubim, O Sire,
> And His Seraphim
> And with all the Host of Heaven. . . .

Suddenly an old man of benign and comely mien, the mien of St. Sergii of Radonezh, as he is limned on ikons, leapt up from his bench, ran out into the middle of the chamber, and began whirling, round and round.

He was followed by a girl of some fourteen years,—almost a child but already pregnant, as small and slender as a reed, with a neck as long as a flower stalk; she, too, leapt up and started dancing in a circle, statelily, like a swan.

" 'Tis Mariushka, a little innocent," Emelian pointed her out to Tikhon, "she's mute and can not speak,—she doth but low; yet, when the Ghost comes upon her, she sings like any nightingale!"

The girl was singing in a child's voice that tinkled like silver:

> Come, my birdlets, sit no more
> Time has come for us to soar,—
> Out of prisons and dark cells,
> Out of dungeons deep as wells!

And she fluttered the sleeves of her shift, as if they were white pinions.

Parthen Paramonych tore loose from the bench, as though he had been caught up by a whirlwind, ran up to Mariushka, took her by the hands, and began circling with her, like a white polar bear dancing with a Little Snow-White. Tikhon would never have believed that this ponderous carcass could dance with such ætherial buoyancy. Spinning like a humming top, he trilled, singing in his high falsetto:

> Up in Heaven,—the Seventh Heaven,—
> The Saviour Himself 'gan dancing,—
> And his dancing never ends;
> Oh, my friends, my friends, my friends!
> Of morocco Christ's shoon be,
> Stitched most fitly, daintily!

One after another joined the round dance. A chap with a wooden peg instead of a leg was also dancing, in no way worse than the others,—as Tikhon found out subsequently, he was a retired captain by the name of Smurighin, who had been wounded at the storming of Azov.

A squat little, round little auntie, with venerable gray ringlets, the Princess Khovanskay, was whirling like a ball, while next to her hopped Yashka Burdaev,—a lanky master shoemaker, flinging his arms and legs high, grimacing and squirming like that enormous, sluggish gnat called *karamora* [or daddy-long-legs], and kept on crying out:

> As we dance and as we burn
> Ever to Mount Sion we turn! . . .

. By now almost everybody was dancing,—not only in "singles" and "grappling" [in couples], but even in whole rows, forming "a little wall," "a little corner," "a little cross," "the ship of David," and "little flowers and little ribands."

"By these diverse whirlings," Emelian explained to Tikhon, "are figured forth the heavenly dances of the Angels and Archangels, soaring about the throne of God; and by the waving of arms is figured forth the fluttering of Angels' wings. The sky and the earth are but one: that which is upon the summit of Heaven is upon the earth below also."

The dance was becoming ever more impulsive, so that a whirlwind filled the chamber, and it seemed that they were not dancing of themselves, but that some force was whirling them about, with such rapidity that the faces could not be distinguished, while the hair upon their heads stood up on end, while their shifts, billowing, became trumpet-shaped, and the human being was transformed into a white, whirling pillar.

As they circled some whistled or hissed; while others gabbled, shouting frenziedly, and it also seemed as though it were not they themselves who were shouting, but that some being was doing so through their throats:

> He has rolled up! He has rolled up!
> Holy Ghost,—Holy!
> Roll up,—roll up! *Ho!*

And they fell to the floor in convulsions, foaming at their mouths like those possessed of devils, and prophesied,—for the most part incoherently. Others stopped in exhaustion, with faces as red as calico or as white as a sheet; sweat ran from them in streams, and was wiped off with towels; they wrung out their shifts, which were so sopping that pools of sweat formed on the floor; this sweating was called "the bath of the second life." And, having had barely time enough to catch their breath, they again whirled off into the dance.

Suddenly all stopped simultaneously and fell flat on their faces. A dead silence ensued,—and then, just as recently, at the entrance of the Czaritza, an awed murmur sped through the room:

"The Czar! The Czar!"

A man of some thirty years entered, clad in long white raiment of semi-transparent stuff, so that his body could be glimpsed through it; he had a muliebrile face, just as un-Russian as that of Akulina Makeëvna, but of still more alien and extraordinary charm and beauty than hers.

"Who is this?" Tikhon asked Mitka, who was prostrated next to him.

"Christos Batiushka!"

Tikhon learned subsequently that this was a runaway Cossack, Averiyanka the Fingerless, the son of a Cossack from beyond the Volga and a captured Greek woman.

Batiushka walked up to Matushka, who rose before him respectfully, and "bussed" her,—embracing and kissing her lips thrice.

After this he came out into the middle of the chamber and mounted a small round elevation of boards, somewhat like those lids which are used to cover the mouths of wells.

All burst into song,—thunderously yet solemnly:

> The Seventh Heaven opened wide,
> The wheels of gold forth did ride,—
> Wheels of gold, and eke of fire;
> 'Tis the Holy Ghost that rides,—Our Sire;
> And no common steed is His:
> Its very tail of pearls is;
> Fire do its nostrils breathe,—
> Its eyes are stones of margarite.
> He has rolled up! He has rolled up!
> Holy Ghost,—Holy!
> Roll up,—roll up! *Ho!*

The Batiushka bestowed his blessing upon his children, and again the circling began,—still more frenzied, between two fixed points: the Matushka at the very outside of the orbit of the whirling circles, and the Batiushka at their very pivot. The Batiushka, at infrequent intervals, would slowly wave his arms, and at every wave the dance went faster. One heard inhuman cries:

"*Evà-Evò! Evà-Evò!*"

Tikhon recalled having read in the old Latin commentaries to Pausanias that the ancient Bacchants and Bacchantes were reputed to have greeted the god Dionysos with shouts that had almost the same sound: "*Evà-Evò!*" Through what miracle had these mysteries of a dead god penetrated, just as though they had seeped through together with underground waters, from the summits of Kythæron into the subcellars of the back-yards of Moscow-Beyond-the-River.

He looked upon the circling, white water-spout of the dance, and there were moments when he lost consciousness. Time had stopped. All things vanished. All colors had blended into uniform whiteness,—white birds, it seemed, were flying into a white abyss. And nothing existed,—he himself did not exist. There was only a white abyss,—a white death.

He came to when Emelian took him by the hand and said: "Let's go!"

Although the light of day did not penetrate the underground place, Tikhon sensed the morning. The guttering candles were emitting soot. The stifling air was unbearable,—it stank. The puddles of sweat upon the floor were being mopped up with old rags. The Vigil of Joy was at an end. The Czar and Czaritza had gone. Some, making their way to the exit, swayed and hugged the walls, crawling along like sleepy flies. Others, having slumped to the floor, were in a dead sleep, resembling a swoon. Others still were sitting upon the benches with their heads drooping, their faces like those of drunkards who are feeling qualmish. It was as though the white birds had fallen to the ground and smashed themselves to death.

II

From this day on Tikhon began attending all the Vigils of Joy. Mitka taught him how to dance. At first he felt ashamed, but then he became accustomed, and developed such a passion for dancing that he could not live without it.

One new mystery after another was being revealed to him at these Vigils. Yet at times it seemed to him that the most important and awesome mystery of all was being concealed from him. From that which he saw and heard he surmised that the brethren and sisters lived in carnal knowledge of each other.

"We be celibate cherubim, living in fiery chastity," they were wont to say. " 'Tis no lechery when brother and sister live in the love of Christ,—the true love; but that which is lechery and abomination is marriage as solemnized by the church. Before God 'tis abomination, before man, a profanation. Husband and wife—'tis the devil's own strife; they are but accursed nest-makers, while their children are merely shards and vile puppies!"

Those children who were born from husbands not of their sect, were abandoned by their mothers in public baths, or else the mothers killed them with their own hands.

One day Mitka, in all simplicity of heart, announced that he was living with two of his own sisters,—nuns in the New Convent of the Virgin; while Emelian Ivannovich, the prophet and teacher, lived with thirteen women and wenches.

"Whichever one seeks his spiritual counsel, the same one lives with him."

Tikhon was confounded by this admission and, for several days thereafter avoided Retivoy, not daring to look him in the eye. The latter, noting this confusion, one day when he happened to be alone with him, began in a kindly tone:

"Hearken now, my little child,—I shall reveal a great mystery to thee! If thou wouldst live, thou must mortify, for the sake of the Lord, not only thy flesh but even thy soul, and thy mind, and thy very conscience. Strip thyself of all laws and rules, of all virtues, all fasting, all abstinence, all chastity. Strip thyself of holiness itself. Descend into thyself as if into a grave. Thereupon thou, a mystic dead man, shalt be resurrected and the Holy Ghost will enter into thee, and thou shalt nevermore be deprived of It, no matter how thou mayst live and no matter what thou mayst do. . . ."

The hideous face of Retivoy,—the mask of Faunus,—was illuminated by such audacity and such craftiness that fear fell upon Tikhon: he could not decide who was before him: a prophet or one possessed of devils?

"Or art thou distraught," the other resumed, still more kindly, "because we indulge in lechery, as men say about us? We know that many of our deeds are not to be reconciled with your human righteousness. But what are we to do? We have no will of our own. The spirit works upon us and the very indecencies of our life are an inscrutable path laid down by the Providence of God. I'll say this of myself: When I have coitus with virgins and women, my conscience doth not at all bother me because of it,—but, rather, an inexpressible joy and delectation seethe within my heart. Were an angel to come down from heaven then and say: 'Thy ways of life are not the right ways, Emelian,'—even then I would not listen. My God hath acquitted me,—and who are ye to judge? My sin ye know, but the graciousness of God toward me ye know not. Ye will say: 'Repent,'—but I will say to you: 'There is naught to repent of.' He who hath come to his journey's end hath no need to know what roads he has traversed. What need have we of your righteousness? Send us to hell,—even there we find salvation; place us in paradise,—and even there we shall come upon no greater joy. We are sinking in the deep waters of the Spirit even like to a stone in the midst of the sea. But we keep ourselves secret from the outsiders,—for that very reason, now, do we play the fool, that they might not learn everything. . . . That's the way of things, my dear little one!"

Emelian was gazing into Tikhon's eyes, smiling ambiguously while the latter experienced from these words of the teacher the same emotion as from the whirling of the dance: as though he were flying, yet knew not whether he were flying upward or downward, to God or to the Devil.

On one occasion the Matushka, at the conclusion of the Vigil of Joy, during Palm Week, distributed bunches of pussy-willow twigs to every one, and sacred little scourges, of rolled-up narrow towels. The brethren let down their shifts to their waists; the sisters also let them down to the waist, but only in the back, going no lower in front, than their breasts; and both brethren and sisters started off in a circle, scourging themselves with the twigs and the sacred scourges,—some launching into a loud song:

> Be vigilant for God,
> Spare neither flesh nor rod!
> Ye must serve God with zeal,
> Nor care for Martha's weal!

Others were softly sibilant:

> Lash quick, lash quick,—
> 'Tis Christ I seek!

They also beat themselves with iron balls wrapped up in rags,—implements somewhat like slings; they lacerated themselves with knives, so that blood flowed, and, gazing at Batiushka, squealed hysterically:

"*Evà-Evò! Evà-Evò!*"

Tikhon was flogging himself with one of the small scourges; and, under the kind gaze of Akulina Makeëvna (who, it seemed to him, was gazing at him,—at him alone), the more excruciating the pain of his blows became, the more delectable was his sensation. His whole body was melting from delectation, as wax melts from a flame, and he would fain have melted away, have guttered away to the very end before Matushka, like a taper before an image.

Suddenly the candles began to go out, one after another, as though they were extinguished by the whirlwind of the dance. At last all of them went out, and darkness fell, and, —just as at the time in the log-cabin of the devotees of self-burning, on the night before the Red Death,—one could hear whisperings, rustlings, stirrings, kisses and sighs of love. Bodies entwined with bodies, as though a single many-limbed gigantean body were squirming in the darkness. Somebody's eager, tenacious hands were extended to Tikhon, —they seized him and threw him down.

"Tishenka, Tishenka! My darling, my little bridegroom, my little beloved Christ!" he heard a passionate whisper, and recognized it as Matushka's.

It seemed to him that some enormous insects or other, male and female spiders, say, were devouring one another in a monstrous lust, having entwined themselves into a ball.

He thrust Matushka away and, jumping up, sought to escape. But at every step he trod upon naked bodies, crushing them; he slipped,—he stumbled,—he fell time and again, only to regain his feet and go on. But the eager, tenacious hands clutched at him,—sought to catch him,—caressed him with shameless caresses. And he weakened, and felt that at any moment he would become altogether weak, would fall into this fearful, communal body, as into warm, dark slime,—and that suddenly everything would be overturned: that which had been uppermost would become the bottommost; while that which had been at the bottom would become uppermost; and this ultimate horror would constitute the ultimate rapture.

With a desperate effort he gave a tug, made his way to the door, seized the handle of the lock,—and could not open it; the key was turned in the door. He sank to the floor in exhaustion. Here the bodies were fewer than in the center of the chamber, and for a minute he was left in peace.

Suddenly somebody's thin, small hands, seemingly like those of a child, touched him once more. He heard the tongue-tied babble of Mariushka the little innocent, who was trying to say something, but could not. Finally he made out a few words.

"Leth's go, leth's go. . . . I'll leave thee out. . . ." she was babbling, and tugging at his hand. He felt the key in hers, and went after her.

Hugging the walls (where there was more room), she guided him to the corner with the images. Here she bent down, and compelled him to stoop also; lifting up a cloth-of-gold pall which hung before the image of Emmanuel, she groped for a little door, something in the nature of a cellar trap door, unlocked it, darted into the opening, as nimbly as a lizard, and helped him to crawl through as well. Through an underground passage they emerged upon a staircase with which Tikhon was familiar. Ascending it, they entered a large chamber which served as a cloak-room. The moon was peeping in through the windows. Along the walls hung the white shifts used in the Vigils of Joy, resembling phantoms in the light of the moon.

When Tikhon had gulped in a breath of fresh air, had

glimpsed through the window the blue sparkling stars, such joy filled his soul that for a long while he could not gain control of himself, merely squeezing the thin, childlike hands of Mariushka.

Only now did he observe that she was no longer pregnant, and recalled that Mitka had told him within the last few days that she was supposed to have given birth to a boy, who had been proclaimed the Infant Christ, inasmuch as he had been conceived from Batiushka himself, through the instigation of the Ghost: "Not of the blood, now, not of the desires of the flesh, nor of the desires of man,—but it was of God that he had been born."

Mariushka made Tikhon sit down on a bench, seated herself by his side, and again, with an immeasurable effort, attempted to tell him something. But, in lieu of words, she emitted mere muttering, a lowing of which, no matter how hard he listened, he could make nothing. Finally, having become convinced that he would never understand her, she fell silent and burst into tears. He embraced her, placed her head upon his breast, and fell to stroking her hair most gently,—by the light of a moon-beam it was as soft and light as flax. She was all aquiver, and it seemed to him that a captive bird was fluttering in his hands.

Finally she looked up at him with her large, humid eyes, dark blue, like dew-covered cornflowers; smiling to him through her tears, she became exceedingly alert, as though she were listening to something, stretching out her neck,—long, slender, like the stalk of a flower,—and suddenly, in a child-like little voice, as clear as silver,—the same voice she had sung with at the Vigils of Joy,—began half-whispering, half-chanting into his ear. And immediately she ceased stammering,—her words became articulate in this half-chant, half-whisper:

"Oh Tishenka,—oh Tishenka, my brave,—save us from the grave! They will slay him,—they will slay Ivan-nushka! . . ."

"What Ivannushka? . . ."

"Why, my little son, now,—my poor little boy. . . ."

"Why should they slay him?" doubtingly asked Tikhon, to whom her words sounded like raving.

"So that they may take communion in living blood," Mariushka whispered, nestling to him with illimitable horror. " 'That,' say they, 'is what such a Little Christ, a lamb without a stain, is born for,—in order to be slain, and given as sacred food to the faithful.' 'Tis no living infant, they claim, but a mere vision, a holy little ikon, and flesh incorruptible,—he can neither suffer nor die. . . . But they all lie, the accursed ones! I know, Tishenka,—my boy is a living little baby, and he's no Little Christ but Ivannushka. . . . My own little son! I'll perish myself, but I shan't give him up. . . . Tishenka, my brave,—save us from the grave! . . ."

Once more her speech became incoherent. At last she fell silent; she let her head drop on her shoulder, and went off into a daze,—or was it a doze? . . .

Morning was coming on. Steps were heard beyond the door. Mariushka came to with a start, ready to flee. They made their farewells and crossed each other, while Tikhon gave her his promise that he would defend Ivannushka.

"The little simpleton!" he was reassuring himself. "She knows not herself what she is saying. Probably she has imagined all this."

A Vigil of Joy was set for Passion Thursday. Through dim hints Tikhon surmised that at this Vigil a great mystery was to be consummated,—"Come, was it not that of which Mariushka had spoken?"—he pondered with horror. He sought her, wishing to take counsel as to what was to be done, but she had vanished. They may have hidden her deliberately. A lethargy, as of delirium, took possession of him. He could hardly think of that which was to take place. Had it not been for Mariushka, he would have resorted to immediate flight. On Passion Thursday, toward midnight— the usual time,—they set out for the Vigil of Joy.

When Tikhon entered the Chamber of Sion and looked over the gathering, it seemed to him that all were in the grasp of the same horror and catalepsy as he. They seemed to be doing that which they did not of their own will.

The Matushka was not present.

The Batiushka entered. His face,—deathly pale, extraordinarily beautiful,—reminded Tikhon of the god Bacchus-

Dionysos, as he had seen him depicted upon engraved stones and cameos in Jacob Bruce's collection of antiquities.

The Vigil of Joy began. Never before had the white water-spout of the dance whirled as madly as now. White birds, it seemed, driven by horror, were flying into a white abyss.

In order not to arouse any suspicions Tikhon, too, danced; but he tried his best not to yield to the intoxication of the dance. He frequently left the circle, taking a seat on a bench, as though to rest, watching everybody and thinking of Ivannushka.

The dancers were already attaining frenzy; no longer in their own voices, they emitted occasional shouts of:

"The Ghost has rolled up!"

Tikhon, no matter how hard he struggled, felt that he was weakening, losing his self-control. As he sat on a bench he convulsively grasped it with his hands, in order not to tear loose and fly off in this mad waterspout, that whirled faster, faster,—ever faster. Suddenly he, too, cried out in a voice which was not his own, and the Ghost filled him as well,—lifting him up, carrying him off, whirling him away.

There was a last fearful, general wail:

"Evà-Evò!"

And suddenly they all halted and fell down on their faces, as if stricken by a thunderbolt, screening their faces with their hands, their white shifts covered the floor, like white pinions.

"Lo, the Lamb without Sin is coming, to be sacrificed and to be given as sacred food for the faithful," the voice of Matushka broke the stillness, issuing from under the floor,—muffled and mysterious, as though "the Earth,—the Earth, our Mother dank" were speaking herself.

The Czaritza came out from thence, holding in her arms a silver bason, something in the nature of a small font, with a naked infant cradled therein upon folded, white swaddling-clothes. He slept: probably he had been given some soporific herb to drink. There was a multitude of burning wax candles placed upon a thin wooden hoop, fastened by spokes to the base of the font, so that the flames reached almost to the level of the bason's rim, and lit up the infant with a bright light. He seemed to be lying within a baptismal font, surrounded with a wreath of fire.

The Czaritza brought the font up to the Czar, proclaiming: *"That which is of Thee, I bring to Thee, as vicarious atonement for all men and all things."*

The Czar made the sign of the cross thrice over the infant: *"In the name of the Father, and the Son, and the Holy Ghost."*

Then, taking him in his arms, he raised a knife over him.

Tikhon, like all the others, was lying prostrate, his face covered with his hands, but he was stealthily peeping with one eye through his fingers, and saw everything. It seemed to him that the body of the Infant was glowing like to the sun, and that this was not Ivannushka but the Mystic Lamb, pledged from the beginning of the world, and that the face of him who had raised the knife over him was like the face of God. And he waited with immeasurable horror, and longed with immeasurable longing, for this knife to plunge into the white body, and for the scarlet blood to be spilt. Then everything would be fulfilled, everything would be overturned,—and this ultimate horror would contain the ultimate rapture.

Suddenly the infant began to cry. The Batiushka smiled, —and, from this smile, the face of a god was transformed into the face of a beast.

"Beast,—Devil,—Antichrist! . . ." flashed through Tikhon's mind. And a sudden, fearful, unearthly anguish constricted his heart. But in that same instant,—just as though some one had jolted him awake,—he came out of his delirium. Leaping up he threw himself upon Averiyanka the Fingerless, seized his hand, and arrested the blow.

All leapt up and made a rush for Tikhon and, had they not heard a thunderous pounding at the door, would have rent him in pieces. It was being battered in from the other side. Both halves yielded and crashed down, and Mariushka ran into the room, followed by men in green *kaftans* and cocked hats, with their swords bared,—they were soldiers. To Tikhon they seemed the angels of God.

Everything grew dark before his eyes. He felt something pressing down on his shoulder, raised his hand up to it, and felt something warm, sticky: it was blood,—probably, in the set-to, he had been wounded by a knife.

He closed his eyes and beheld the red flame of a blazing log-cabin,—the Red Death. . . . White birds were flying amid the red flames. The thought came to him: "More fearful than the Red Death is the White,"—and lost consciousness.

III

The affair of these heretics was investigated by the newly founded Holy Synod.

By sentence of this court the runaway Cossack, Averiyanka the Fingerless, and his sister Akulina, were broken on the wheel. All the others partook of the cat-o'-nine-tails, or had their nostrils slit; the men were sent into penal servitude,— the women into weaving factories and convent prisons.

Tikhon, who almost died from his wound in a prison hospital, was saved by his former patron, General Jacob Williamovich Bruce. He took Tikhon into his house, nursed him back to health, and interceded for him with the Prelate of Novgorod, Theophan Prokopovich. Theophan took an interest in Tikhon, his desire being to evince in this instance that pastoral compassion toward stray sheep which he was always preaching: "One must act with moderation and reason in the case of the Church's enemies, and not, as now, with harsh words and alienation." He also wanted Tikhon's rejection of heresy, and his acceptance into the bosom of the Orthodox Church, to serve as an example to other heretics and Raskolniki.

Theophan delivered him from the cat-o'-nine-tails and from penal servitude, taking him to do penance, under his own eye, and carried him off to Peterburgh. The Prelate's Peterburgh domicile was located on Apothecary Island, upon the small river Karpathka, in the heart of a thick forest. The library was located on the ground floor of the house. Noticing Tikhon's love for books, Theophan entrusted him with putting the library into order. The library windows, looking out directly upon the forest, were frequently open, inasmuch as it was the time of sultry summer days, and the stillness of the forest blended with the stillness of the book-treasury,—the rustling of its leaves with the rustling of pages. One could hear the tapping of a woodpecker, and the silly call of the cuckoo, or see a tower-antlered elk and his doe emerging upon a forest glade,—they had been driven here from the Petrovsky Island, at that time altogether a wilderness. A greenish twilight filled the room. It was cool and comfortable. Tikhon passed whole days here, moping among the old books. It seemed to him that he was back again in the library of Jacob Bruce, and that all these four years of wanderings were nothing but a dream.

Theophan treated him with kindness. He did not hurry his return into the bosom of the Orthodox Church,—he merely indicated for reading (since a Russian Catechism was not available) several German theologians, and, when he had leisure, discussed with Tikhon what the latter had read, correcting the errors of the Protestants to reconcile them with the teaching of the Græco-Russian Church. For the rest he gave him full liberty to occupy himself with whatever he pleased.

Tikhon again took to mathematics. Amid the iciness of reason he rested from the fire of madness, from the delirium of the Red Death and the White.

He was also re-reading the philosophers,—Descartes, Leibnitz, Spinoza. He recalled the words of Pastor Glück: "True philosophy, if one but merely sip of it, leads one away from God; but, if one draw deeply therefrom, it brings one to Him."

God for Descartes was the Prime Mover of prime matter. The universe was a machine. There was no love, no mystery, no life,—there was nothing save reason, which is reflected in all the universe, as light is reflected in transparent crystals of ice. Tikhon was inspired with fear by this dead God.

"Nature is full of life," affirmed Leibnitz in his *Monadology*. "I will prove that the cause of every motion is spirit, while spirit is a living monad, consisting of ideas, even as a center consists of angles." The monads are joined into a single whole through a harmony foreordained of God. "The universe is the watch of God,—*Horologium Dei*."—"Again, in lieu of life, there was a machine; instead of God there were mechanics," reflected Tikhon, and again fear fell upon him.

But the most fearful of all, inasmuch as he was the most lucid of all, was Spinoza. He said to the end that which the others had not the courage to say. "To affirm the embodiment of God in man is just as absurd as to affirm that a circle has taken on the nature of a triangle or a square. *The word became flesh* is an Oriental turn of speech which can have no significance to reason. Christianity is distinguished from other professions of faith not by faith, not by love, not by any other gifts of the Holy Ghost, but merely that it takes for its basis a miracle,—in other words, ignorance, which is the source of every evil; and in this manner it transforms faith itself into superstition." Spinoza had revealed the secret thought of all the new philosophers: One had to be either with Christ against reason, or with reason against Christ.

On one occasion Tikhon began speaking of Spinoza with Theophan.

"The foundation of that philosophy is shown to be most silly," declared the Prelate with a contemptuous sneer, "inasmuch as Spinoza has woven his cogitations solely out of miserable contradictions, and has covered his silliness only by beautiful, fine-sounding words. . . ."

These revilements neither convinced Tikhon nor set him at rest. Nor did he find any help in the works of foreign theologians, who controverted all philosophers, the old as well as the new, and that with the same ease as the Prelate had controverted Spinoza.

At times Theophan gave Tikhon for transcription papers dealing with the affairs of the Holy Synod. In the oath of the Ecclesiastical Regulations he was struck by the words: "I profess, under oath, that the Supreme Judge of this Spiritual Collegium is the Monarch of All the Russias Himself, Our Most Gracious Sovereign." The Sovereign was the head of the Church; the Sovereign,—in Christ's stead.

"*Magnus ille Leviathan, quæ Civitas appelatur, officium artis est et Homo artificialis*. This great Leviathan, which is called the State, is a product of artifice, and an artificial Man," he recalled the words from *Leviathan*, a book of the English philosopher Hobbes, who also asserted that the church must be a part of the state, a limb of the great Leviathan, the Titanic Automaton. Was this not that very *ikon of the Beast,* created in the image and likeness of the god-beast himself, as it is spoken of in the Apocalypse?[100]

The chill of reason which was wafted upon Tikhon from this dead church of a dead God, was becoming just as murderous as the fire of madness, the fire of the Red Death and the White.

The day had already been set for the rite of anointing Tikhon as a mark of his returning into the bosom of the Orthodox Church, which rite was to take place in the Cathedral of the Trinity. On the eve of this day, guests gathered for supper at the house on the Karpathka.

This was one of those gatherings which Theophan in his Latin epistles styled *noctes atticæ*,—Attic nights. Wetting the salted and smoked delicacies of the Prelate with the famous ale of Father Gherasim, the house-manager, they conversed upon philosophy, upon "matters of substance" and "laws of nature," for the most part in a liberal spirit,—but, according to the opinion of some, even in an atheistical one.

Tikhon, as he stood in the glass-enclosed corridor which linked the library with the refectory, heard their conversation from afar:

"Disputes about faith cannot take place between clever people, inasmuch as clever men do not touch upon the faith of one another, and 'tis all the same to them whether a man be a Lutheran or a Calvinist, or a pagan,—inasmuch as they do not regard faith, but actions and morals," Bruce was saying.

"*Uti boni vini non est quærenda regio, sic nec boni viri religio et patria.* One should no more question a worthy man about his faith and his fatherland, than the origin of good wine," Theophan supported him.

"Those who forbid philosophy are either the greatest of ignoramuses or evil and crafty priests," remarked Vassilii Nikitich Tatishchev, the President of the Department of Mines.

The learned Hieromonk Marcellus was proving that many of the lives of the saints showed up but poorly when it came down to the truth.

"There is a great deal of knavery done,—a great deal of

knavery!" he kept on repeating a famous saying of Rhedosska's.

"There are no miracles in these our times," Dr. Blumentrost concurred with the Hieromonk.

"Within the last few days," Peter Andreievich Tolstoi began with a subtle smile, "I happened to be at the house of a certain friend of mine, where I saw two corporals of the Guards. They were carrying on a great dispute between them: one maintained, while the other denied, the existence of God; the man who denied it was shouting: 'Stop talking bosh,— there's no God, no matter what you say.' I joined the conversation and asked: 'But whoever told thee that there is no God?'—'Why, Second Lieutenant Ivannov, only yesterday, in Hostelry Court!'—'What a place thou hast found, to be sure!' . . ."

They were all laughing,—all merry. But Tikhon had an eerie feeling.

He felt that these people had set foot upon a path which could not but be traversed to the end, and that sooner or later they would reach the same goal in Russia as had already been reached in Europe: One had to be either with Christ against reason, or with reason against Christ.

He returned to the library, took his seat at a window next to a wall lined with even rows of books uniformly bound in leather and parchment, looked up at the nocturnal, void, dead, fearful sky, white above the black firs, and recalled the words of Spinoza:

Between God and man there is just as little in common as there is between the Constellation of The Dog, and a dog, the barking animal. Man is capable of loving God, but God is not capable of loving man.

It seemed that there, in this dead sky, was a dead God who was not capable of love. It would be better even to know that there was no God at all. "But,—perhaps there even is not?" he reflected, and experienced that same horror as when Ivannushka the babe had begun crying, while Averiyanka had lifted up a knife over him and smiled.

Tikhon fell on his knees and began praying, looking up at the sky and repeating only one word:

"Lord! Lord! Lord! . . ."

But there was silence in the sky, and silence in his heart. An illimitable silence,—an illimitable horror.

Suddenly, out of the utmost depth of silence, Some One answered,—told him what he had to do.

Tikhon got up, went to his cell, dragged out from under his bed his kit, took out from it his old pilgrim's cassock, his leather belt, his beads, calotte, and a little image of St. Sophia of the Highest Wisdom of God,—a present from Sophia; he took off his *kaftan* and all the rest of his German-made clothing, put on that which he had taken out of the kit, tied a knapsack over his shoulder, took his stick in his hand, made the sign of the cross, and, unnoticed of any, walked out of the house and into the forest.

On the following morning, when it was time to go to church for the rite of anointment, they began to search for Tikhon. They sought him a long time but could not find him. He vanished without a trace, just like a stone thrown into water.

IV

Legend has it that Andrew, the First-Called of the Apostles, when he arrived from Kiev at Novgorod, had come in a boat to Balaam Island, upon the Lake of Ladoga, and had there raised up a cross of stone. Long before the Christianization of Russia, two most saintly friars Sergii and Herman, having come to Russia from Eastern lands, had built a holy cloister upon Balaam Island.

Since that time the faith of Christ has glowed in the savage North, like a lampad in the darkness of midnight.

The Swedes, having gained possession of the Lake of Ladoga, had demolished the Balaam cloister many times. In the year sixteen-hundred-and-eleven they had demolished it to such an extent that not one stone was left standing upon another. For a whole century the island was left desolate. But in the year seventeen-hundred-and-fifteen, Czar Peter issued an *ukase* about the restoration of the ancient cloister. A tiny wooden church was erected, in the name of the Transfiguration of the Lord, over the holy remains of the miracle-workers, SS. Sergii and Herman, as well as several lowly cells, to which were transferred certain friars from the Kyrillo-

White Lake thebaid. The lampad of the faith of Christ began to glow anew and there was a prophecy that it would no more be extinguished until the Second Coming.

Tikhon had fled from Peterburgh with a certain holy ancient belonging to the sect of The Runners.

The Runners taught that those of Orthodox faith, in order to save themselves from Antichrist, must run from town to town, from hamlet to hamlet, unto the very ends of the earth. The ancient was enticing Tikhon to some unknown Kingdom of Oppon, upon the Seventy Islands of White Waters, where, in one hundred and seventy-nine churches of the Assyrian tongue, the Old Faith was supposed to be preserved inviolate; this kingdom was located beyond Gog and Magog, upon the very rim of the world, whence the run rises.

"And if God helps us, we shall reach it in ten years," the ancient encouraged him.

Tikhon believed but little in this Kingdom of Oppon, but he went off with the Runner inasmuch as it mattered not to him where he went, or with whom.

They reached Ladoga by floats. Here they changed to a *soima*,—a frail, wretched lake vessel which was going to Serdobol. A storm overtook them upon the lake. For a long while they were dashed over the waves and almost perished. Finally they entered the Cenoby Haven of the Balaam cloister. Toward morning the tempest subsided, but the *soima* had to be repaired.

Tikhon set off to roam the island.

The island was all of granite. The banks rose over the water in sheer crags. Tree-roots could not secure a firm hold in the shallow top-soil of the granite, and the forest was rather stunted. But, on the other hand, moss grew here splendidly,—it veiled the firs as if with cobwebs; it hung upon the trunks of the pines in long elf-locks.

The day was sultry, hazy. The sky was milky-white, with a misty azure barely peeping through. The water of the mirror-smooth lake blended with the sky, so that one could not distinguish where the water ended and the earth began; the sky appeared to be the lake,—the lake, the sky. The stillness was breathless; the very birds were silent. And a silence not of this earth, an eternal quietude was wafted upon the soul by this sacred wilderness, this austere and tender midnight Paradise.

Tikhon recalled the song which he used to sing in the forest of the Long Mosses:

> Thou wilderness resplendent, dear mother of mine!
> I shall wander through forests and through marish lands,
> I shall wander over hills and through caverns deep. . . .

He also recalled that which one of the friars of Balaam had told him:

"What a blessed lot is ours! Though thou wert to remain for three days in the forest, thou wouldst not come upon any wild beast or any evil man; there is but God and thou,— thou and God!"

He walked for a long while, left the cloister far behind him, and, in the end, lost his way.

Evening came on. He was afraid that the *soima* would sail away without him.

In order to get the lay of the land he ascended a high hill. Its slopes were grown over with pines, growing close to one another. Upon the summit was a round glade, with lilac-rosy heather in bloom. In the center stood a pillar-like black stone.

Tikhon had become tired. At the edge of the glade, by the firs, he caught sight of a depression in the crag, just like a cradle of soft moss; he lay down therein,—fell asleep.

When he awoke, it was night. It was almost as light as if it were day. But still quieter. The shores of the island were reflected distinctly in the mirror of the lake, down to the last little cross of the sharp-pointed fir tips, so that it seemed that there, below, there was another island, re-sembling perfectly the upper one, but merely inverted,— and that these islands were suspended between two heavens. Upon the stone in the middle of the glade, Tikhon saw a kneeling ancient whom he did not know,—probably a holy man who lived in this wilderness. His black profile against the aureately-rosy sky was unmoving, as though it were carved out of the same stone upon which he knelt. And upon his face was such a rapture of prayer as Tikhon had never yet beheld on the face of man. It seemed to him that there was such silence encompassing everything about because of this prayer, and that it was also because of it that the sweet odor of the lilac-rosy heather rose up to the aureately-rosy sky, like to smoke out of a censer.

Daring neither to breathe nor to stir, he gazed for long upon the praying man and prayed together with him; and, in the infinite sweetness of prayer, as though he had lost consciousness, he fell asleep again.

He awoke at the rising of the sun.

There was no longer anybody upon the stone. Tikhon approached it, perceived among the thick heather a barely noticeable path, and descended it into a crag-encircled valley. Below was a grove of birches. In the middle of the grove was a dell grown over with tall grass. An invisible stream babbled there with the babbling of a child.

In this dell stood the holy man,—the same whom Tikhon had seen that night, and he was feeding bread out of his hands to a moose-cow with her small, absurd nursling.

Tikhon looked, and could not believe his eyes. He knew how timid moose were, especially cows who had recently calved. It seemed to him that he had managed to spy the eternal mystery of those days when man and beast had dwelt side by side in Paradise.

Having consumed the bread, the moose-cow began licking the ancient's hand. He made the sign of the cross over her, kissed her shaggy brow, and said with gentle kindliness:

"The Lord be with thee, Matushka!"

Suddenly she looked back wildly, staggered to one side, and was off at a run, seeking the depths of a ravine. All one could hear was a crackling and a rumbling sweeping through the forest. She had probably caught scent of Tikhon.

He drew near to the ancient:

"Bless me, Father!"

The ancient made the sign of the cross over him with the same gentle kindliness as just now in the case of the beast.

"The Lord be with thee, little child! What do they call thee, now?"

"Tikhon."

"Tishenka,—'tis a *quiet* sort of name," he innocently

punned upon his name. "Whence has God brought thee? This is a forest place, a desert place, but little trod by the children of the world,—'tis but rarely that we see the little pilgrims of God."

"We were sailing to Serdobol from Ladoga," answered Tikhon; "the *soima* was driven to the island by storm. Yesterday I went off into the forest, but lost my way."

"And was it in the forest you passed the night?"

"Aye,—in the forest."

"But hast thou as much as a bit of bread about thee? Thou art hungry, like as not?"

The slice of bread which Tikhon had taken along with him he had finished the night before, and now he was indeed feeling hungry.

"Well, let us go to my cell, Tishenka,—I'll feed thee with whatever God hath sent us."

Father Sergii (such was the name of the holy man), to judge by the many gray hairs among the black, was past fifty; but his walk and his movements were as quick and buoyant as those of a twenty-year-old youth; his face was dry, rather Lenten, but also youthful; his brown, somewhat near-sighted eyes were constantly puckered up, as though they were smiling with an unrestrainable, and almost mischievous, and just a wee bit sly smile,—he seemed to be keeping to himself something exceedingly jolly, which other people did not know,—he might impart at any moment, and then everybody would feel jolly. But, at the same time, there was also in this gayety that calm which Tikhon had beheld on his face during his night-prayer.

They walked up to a perpendicular granite crag. Beyond a decrepit, crooked wattle-fence vegetable beds were laid out. A crevice in the crag formed a natural cell: three walls were of stone, while the fourth consisted of logs, with a small window and a door; over the latter was a small ikon, grown black from time, of the miracle-workers of the Balaam, the SS. Sergii and Herman; the roof was of earth, topped with moss and birch-bark, and bearing a wooden, eight-pointed cross. The opening of the valley, facing the lake, ended in a shoal of earth and pebbles, brought down by the stream which flowed at the bottom of the valley and fell into the lake. Small trammel nets and ordinary ones were drying ashore, stretched out on poles, and, right here, another ancient,—barefooted, up to his knees in water, squat, broad-shouldered, with a wind-beaten face and remnants of gray hair around his bald skull ("a veritable Peter the Fisher," reflected Tikhon),—was repairing and tarring the bottom of an overturned boat. There was an odor of pine-shavings, of water, of fish, and of pitch.

"Larivonushka!" Father Sergii called to him.

The old man looked over his shoulder, immediately dropped his work, approached them, and bowed to Tikhon's very feet in silence.

"Have no fear, my little child," Father Sergii reassured the confused Tikhon, smiling with his mischievous smile, " 'tis not to thee alone, but to everybody that he bows to the very feet,—even to the smallest children. That's the kind of a meek little fellow he is! Come, Larivonushka,—prepare a repast for to feed a little pilgrim of God."

Getting up from his knees, Father Hilarion looked at Tikhon with a meek and austere glance. *Love all men and flee all men,*—one could read in this glance the saying of that great hermit of the Thebaid, the most holy Abba Arsenius.

The cell consisted of two unequal parts,—one, diminutive, like a chimneyless hut; the other, a cave in the solid rock of the crag, with holy images upon the walls which were just as jolly as Father Sergii himself,—the Mother of God in Joyance, Our Lady of Mercy, the Flower of Fragrance, the Blessed Womb, the Life-Giver, the Joy Unknown,—before this last one, which was especially beloved by Father Sergii, a lampad glowed. In the cave itself, which was as dark and cramped as a grave, stood two coffins, with stones in lieu of pillows. It was in these coffins that the holy ancients reposed.

They sat down to their repast,—their table consisted of a bare board placed upon a moss-covered pine-stump.

Father Hilarion brought bread, salt, and wooden bowls containing chopped pickled cabbage, salted cucumbers, mushroom stew, and a concentrated soup made out of certain fragrant forest herbs.

Father Sergii and Tikhon partook of their food in silence, Father Hilarion reading aloud from the Psalms:

"These wait all upon Thee; that Thou mayest give them their meat in due season." [101]

After the repast, Father Hilarion went back to his tarring of the boat. As for Father Sergii and Tikhon, they sat down on the stone steps near the entrance to the cell. Before them spread out the lake, still as quiet, as smooth and wanly-blue as ever, with big, white, round clouds reflected therein,—as though it were another, nether heaven, altogether similar to the upper one.

"Art thou taking a pilgrimage to fulfill a vow, my little child?" asked Father Sergii. Tikhon glanced at him, and felt an urge to tell him the whole truth.

"In accordance with a great vow: I am seeking the true Church. . . ."

And he told him all his life, beginning with his first flight from the fear of Antichrist and ending with his last rejection of the dead Church.

When he had ended, Father Sergii was silent for a long while, his face covered with his hands; then he got up, placed his hand upon Tikhon's head, and uttered:

"The Lord saith: *And him that cometh to Me I will in no wise cast out.*[102] Go thou to the Lord then in peace, my child. Be not afraid,—be not afraid, dear little fellow,— thou shalt be in the Church, thou shalt be in the Church, thou shalt be in the True Church!"

There was such prophetic force and might in these words of Father Sergii that it seemed as if he were not talking of his own volition.

"Be compassionate, Father!" exclaimed Tikhon, embracing his feet. "Take me as thy novice,—bless me for a life in the wilderness with both of you!"

"Thou mayst live here, little one,—thou mayst live here, with God's blessing!" Father Sergii embraced him and kissed him. "Tishenka,—*my quiet little fellow,* thou shalt not disrupt our quiet life," he added, by this time with his usual jolly smile.

It was thus that Tikhon came to remain in the wilderness, and began his life with these two holy ancients.

Father Hilarion was a great keeper of fasts. At times he did not partake of bread for weeks at a time. He peeled the bark from the great pines, dried it, pounded it in a mortar, and baked it together with flour,—and that was all his meat; as for his drink,—it consisted of water purposely taken out of puddles,—tepid and scummy. In winter he prayed standing up to his knees in snow. In summer he stood naked in a swamp, giving up his body to be food for gnats. He never washed, quoting the words of the most saintly Isaac Sirin: "Bare not a one of thy members, but, shouldst thou feel the need of scratching, wrap thy hand with an old rag or a foot-clout, and scratch away thus; but never, never put thy hand on thy bare flesh, nor look in any manner upon thy secrets, even though they may rot away."

Father Hilarion told Tikhon about his former teacher, a friar from the Kyrillo-White Lake thebaid, a certain Father Tryphon, styled The Filthy,—"inasmuch as, through his beatified filthiness, he attained the power of foreseeing the future."—"This Tryphon never let water touch his head or his feet during the whole of his life, yet he was not lousy, which he did bewail greatly, deeming that in the other world, now, he would have lice as big as mice. It was this same Tryphon who sent up a prayer to Jesus by day and by night, and his lips had so formed themselves through this habit of praying, that they moved by themselves all the time, without any control; upon his forehead, from his ceaselessly making the sign of the cross, there was a black and blue bruise and a sore; whether he was saying his Hours, or chanting the morning mass or the evening, he wept so that he would fall into unconsciousness from his great sobbing. Before his death he lay for seven full days and nights in a most excruciating state, yet he never moaned nor groaned, nor asked for a drink; but, if any came to visit him and would ask: 'Batiushka, art thou in very great pain?' he would answer: 'All is well.'"

On one occasion Father Hilarion had approached him softly, so that he might not hear, and saw him smacking his lips just the least wee bit, while he himself was softly whispering: "If I could but drink my fill!"—"Wouldst drink, Batiushka?" Father Hilarion had asked him, but Father

Tryphon answered: "Nay,—I would not." And this made Father Hilarion comprehend that Father Tryphon was tortured by a great thirst, but that he was enduring it,—that he was fasting his last fast.

Despite all these fasts, these toilings and great deeds, salvation—as one could perceive from Father Hilarion's words—was well-nigh impossible to man. According to the vision of a certain saint, out of thirty thousand dead souls only two had entered Paradise, while all the others had gone plumb to Hell.

"Strong is the Devil,—oh, but He is strong!" he would at times sigh, with such despondence that it seemed it was still uncertain which was stronger and which would conquer the other: God or the Devil. At times it seemed to Tikhon as well, that, were Father Hilarion to bring his thoughts to their logical conclusion, he would arrive at the same one the proponents of the Red Death had arrived at.

Father Sergii was a contrast in all things to Father Hilarion. "An immoderate and unreasoning abstinence," he taught, "bringeth greater harm than eating unto repletion. Let every man set a mean unto himself in the matter of food. Of all viands, even of the sweet ones, one should take a little, for to the pure all things are pure, and every creature of God is goodly, and naught is rejected."

He supposed salvation to consist not of the outward tasks of the body, but of an inward "reasoned action." Every night he prayed upon the stone, standing immovably like a statue, but Tikhon imagined that he perceived in this immobility a more impetuous winged flight than in the insane dance of the Flagellants.

"How should one pray?" he once asked Father Sergii.

"Keep silent in thought," the other replied, "and gaze ever into the depths of thy heart, and say: *Lord Jesus Christ, Son of God, have mercy upon me!*—And pray thus in thy standing, and thy sitting, and thy lying down; and lock up thy reason within thy breast, and hold thy breath as much as thou canst, breathing but rarely. And at first thou shalt find within thee a great darkness, a harshness, and thou shalt come to know a certain obstacle in thy outward prayer, like a brazen wall between thee and God. Yet despond not,

—pray most zealously, and the wall of brass shall fall, and thou shalt behold within thy heart a Light which is beyond words. Then words shall become silent; and prayers, and sighs, and genuflexions, and the supplications of thy heart, and most delectable outcries,—all shall cease. Then there is a great silence. Then there is a great trance, and man no longer knows whether he be in his body or without a body. Then there is great awe and a visioning of God. Then man and God are one. Then is consummated the word of prophecy: *God is made one with God and made known through God.*[103] *That* is praying in one's mind, my little child!"

Tikhon noticed that Father Sergii's eyes as he said this were just as tipsy as those of Averiyanka's "little children of God," save that there the tipsiness was brief, riotous, while here it was perpetual: a calm and a seemingly sober tipsiness.

Father Hilarion and Father Sergii were so different in spirit that apparently they should not have agreed in anything, and yet agree they did.

"Father Sergii is a chosen vessel!" Father Hilarion used to say. "God hath chosen him for a pure use, while me He hath chosen for a lowly one; he is made out of white ivory, whereas I am made of black; to him everything shall be forgiven, whereas of me an account for everything shall be demanded; he flieth like to an eagle, whereas I crawl like to an ant. He is already saved of a certainty,—whereas whether I will save myself, or whether I will not, God alone knows. But when I shall be perishing, I shall seize hold of Father Sergii's coat-tail, and he will pull me out!"

"Father Hilarion is a most firm little rock,—a pillar of righteousness,—a wall indestructible," Father Sergii would say, "whereas I am but a leaf swayed by the wind; without him I would have perished long since, would have forsaken the traditions of the Fathers. 'Tis he alone that is my anchor. I am at peace in his shadow, as if I were within the bosom of Christ's dear raiment!"

Father Sergii said nothing to Father Hilarion about his first talk with Tikhon. But Father Hilarion surmised everything, scenting a heretic even as a sheep scents a wolf. On one occasion Tikhon accidentally overheard him conversing with Father Sergii.

"Endure a while, Larivonushka!" Father Sergii implored him. "Endure him a while, for the sake of Christ! Let there be peace and love. . . ."

"What peace can there be with a heretic?" Father Hilarion retorted. "One ought to struggle with such unto death, without yielding to his perverted reason. 'Love thine enemy,'—but not God's! Flee from a heretic, and speak not to him about the true faith, but spit out upon him. Yea, even worse than any dog or swine is a heretic! May he be accursed! Anathema!"

"Endure awhile, Larivonushka! . . ." Father Sergii kept on reiterating, with a prayer infinite, yet impotent, as though even he himself doubted his being in the right.

Tikhon walked away. He suddenly comprehended that he was waiting in vain for aid from Father Sergii, and that this great saint, as mighty as an angel before the Lord, was before men as weak as a child.

After a few days Tikhon was again sitting with Father Sergii upon the stone steps leading to the cell, just as he had done on the first day. They were alone. Father Hilarion had gone out in his boat to fish.

It was a sultry white night, but darkening because of thunder clouds. During the last few days the storm had been constantly gathering, but could not get to the point of bursting. There was a dead stillness upon the earth; in the sky, however, stormy, rapid clouds, also as soundless as the earth, were scurrying along,—as though mute giants were rushing to battle. Occasionally one heard subdued, distant thunder, apparently subterranean, resembling the growling of a sleepy beast. Pale heat-lightnings flared up now and then. All the outlines of the island stood out against the glow of their white flames, down to the last little cross of the pointed fir tips,—distinctly, sharp-cut,—and were reflected in the water, as though, far below, there were another island, altogether similar to the upper one, but merely inverted, and as though these two islands were suspended between two heavens. This summer lightning died out,—and everything would again be plunged into murk, into silence,—save that one heard the growling as of a sleepy beast.

Tikhon kept silent, while Father Sergii gazed into the

dark sinister distance and sang an acathistus to Jesus, the Most Delectable. And the subdued words of the prayer blended with the sounds of the subdued thunder:

Jesus,—Thou strength invincible,—
Jesus,—Thou mercy infinite,—
Jesus,—Thou beauty most radiant,—
Jesus,—Thou love past all utterance,—
Jesus,—Thou Son of the living God,—
Jesus,—take compassion upon me, a sinner.

Tikhon sensed that Father Sergii wanted to tell him something, but could not find the resolution to do so. Tikhon could not see his face in the gloom, but, whenever he glanced at it in the brief flash of the summer lightning, it seemed to him more sorrowful than it had ever been before.

"Father," Tikhon finally began first, "I shall soon go away from ye. . . ."

"Whither wilt thou go, my little child?"

"I know not, Father. 'Tis all one. I shall go wherever my eyes lead me. . . ."

Father Sergii took his hand, and Tikhon caught his fluttering, kindly whisper:

"Return, return, my little child! . . ."

"Whither?" Tikhon asked, and suddenly felt afraid, without himself knowing why.

"Into the dear church, into the dear church!" whispered Father Sergii, even more kindly, even more flutteringly.

"Into what church, Father?"

"Oh, 'tis a temptation, 'tis a temptation!" sighed Father Sergii and concluded with an effort: "Into the Sole, Holy, Cathedral, Apostolic Church. . . ."

But there was such dead heaviness and such stammering in these words that it seemed it was not of his own will he was uttering them, but that some other was compelling him to utter them.

"But where is that church?" Tikhon moaned with inexpressible torment.

"Oh, my poor little fellow, my poor little fellow! How can one live without a church, now? . . ." Father Sergii began whispering again, with a responsive and equal torment, through which Tikhon sensed that the ancient understood everything.

A heat-lightning flared up. He saw the face of the old man,—his lips, tremulous with a helpless smile,—his wide-open eyes, filled with tears,—and Tikhon understood why he felt frightened: the frightful thing was that this face could be pitiful.

Tikhon sank to his knees and stretched out his hands to Father Sergii,—in final hope, in final despair.

"Save me, help me, intercede for me! Canst thou not see? The Church is perishing,—faith is perishing,—all Christianity is perishing! The mystery of unrighteousness is already being wrought; the abomination that maketh desolate has already come upon the holy place, and Antichrist is already fain to come. Rise up, Father, to a great exploit. Go out into the world and do battle with Antichrist! . . ."

"What art thou saying,—what art thou saying, little child? How can I, sinner that I am, do so? . . ." Father Sergii began to babble with resigned horror.

And Tikhon comprehended that his prayers were in vain, that Father Sergii had forever withdrawn from the world, even as the dead withdraw from the living. *Love all men and flee all men,*—Tikhon recalled the fearful saying.—"But what if this be verily so?" he thought in mortal agony. "What if one must choose one of two things: either God without the world, or the world without God?" He fell with his face to the ground, and lay there for a long while without moving, without feeling the ancient embracing him and consoling him.

When he came to, Father Sergii was no longer with him. He must have gone up the mountain to pray.

Tikhon arose, entered the cell, put on his traveling clothes, tied his knapsack over his shoulders, and put about his neck the image of St. Sophia of the Highest Wisdom of God, took his staff in hand, crossed himself, and walked out into the forest to resume his eternal pilgrimage.

He wanted to go away without saying farewell, because he felt that a farewell would be too oppressive, both to him and to Father Sergii.

But, in order to catch a glimpse of Father Sergii for the

last time, even though from afar, he went up the mountain. There, as always, in the middle of the dale, kneeling on the stone, the ancient was praying.

Tikhon sought out the depression in the crag, the cradle of soft moss, where he had passed his first night; he lay down and for a long while contemplated the motionless form of the praying man, the blinding white flame of the heat-lightnings, and the soundlessly-flying, tempestuous clouds.

Finally he fell into that sleep which the disciples of the Lord had slept while their Teacher prayed a stone's throw away, and, coming back to them, found them asleep, *for that they were heavy with sorrow.*[104]

When he awoke the sun had already risen, and Father Sergii was no longer on the stone. Tikhon approached it and kissed the spot where the feet of the ancient had rested. Then he went down the mountainside and, by overgrown paths, started through the forest thicknesses toward the Balaam Cloister.

After his heavy sleep he felt himself broken and weak, as if after a swoon. It seemed that he was still sleeping,— that he wanted to, but could not, awaken. He was experiencing that dreadful melancholy which always came upon him preceding his spells of epilepsy. His head was turning round. His thoughts were tangling. Through his mind darted snatches of remote recollections. Now it was Pastor Glück repeating Newton's words anent the end of the world: "The comet shall fall upon the sun, and from this fall the heat of the sun will increase to such a degree that everything upon earth shall be consumed by fire. *Hypotheses non fingo!* I do not make up hypotheses!"

Now it would be the dismal song of the Coffin-Liers:

> O ye coffins made out of oak-logs tall,—
> Our eternal homes ye shall be for all. . . .

Or the last wail of those who had chosen to die in the flaming log-cabin: *Lo, the bridegroom cometh at midnight!*

Or else it was the insane white waterspout of the fanatical dance and the piercing cries:

> Evà—Evò! Evà—Evò!

And the low cry of Ivannushka, the Immaculate Lamb, under the knife of Averiyanka the Fingerless.—And the quiet words of Spinoza about "an intellectual love of God —*Amor Dei intellectualis:* Man is capable of loving God, but God is not capable of loving man."—And the oath of the Spiritual Regulations, rendered to the Autocrat of Russia, as if to Christ the Lord.—And the morose submissiveness of Father Hilarion: *"Love all men and flee all men!"*—And the kindly whisper of Father Sergii: "Go back to the dear church, the dear church, my child!"

For a minute he regained his senses. He looked about him. He saw that he had lost his way.

For a long while he sought the path which had vanished amid the heather. Finally he became altogether lost, and started walking at haphazard.

The storm had again retreated. The clouds had scattered. The sun was scorching. He was tortured by thirst. But there was never a drop of moisture in this wilderness of granite and pine-needles,—there were only the dry, gray, spider-mosses, lichens, Iceland mosses, puny, gray dwarfed pines, woven over with moss as if with cobwebs, their excessively slender, frequently broken trunks stretching upward like emaciated, ailing legs and arms with a reddish, inflamed and scaling skin. Between them the air quivered and streamed from sultriness, while over everything was the merciless sky, like brass at white heat. The stillness was the stillness of death, and there was an illimitable horror in this blindingly-sparkling noon-day stillness.

He again looked about him, and recognized a spot where he had frequently been, and through which he had passed only this morning. At the very end of a long aisle,—probably a forest road laid down at some time by the Swedes, but long since abandoned and grown over with heather,—glittered the lake. This spot was not very far from Father Sergii's cell. Probably, having gone astray, he had made a circle and had returned to the spot which he had started from. He felt a deathly fatigue, as though he had covered thousands of versts,—as though he had walked, and would thus walk, forever. He reflected: Whither was he going, and wherefore? —Into the unknown kingdom of Oppon, or the invisible

Kitezh Town,—in both of which he himself no longer believed?

He sank in exhaustion upon the roots of a withered pine, towering in its loneliness over the low, new scrub. It was all one,—there was nowhere to go. If he could but lie thus with his eyes closed, without moving, until death came . . .

He recalled that which had been told him by one of the proponents of a new faith, who were called *Nay-sayers,* because to every *aye* of the Church, they answered with *nay:* "There is no Church,—there is no clergy,—there is no grace,—there are no mystic rites: everything has been taken up to heaven."—"There was naught, there had never been aught, there would never be aught," pondered Tikhon. "There is no God—there is no universe. Everything had perished,—everything was at an end. And there was even no end. All that there was was the infinity of nothingness."

He lay for a long while in a coma. Suddenly he came to, opened his eyes, and saw that an enormous blue-black cloud with whitish blotches (for all the world like suppurating swellings upon a livid and bloated body) had advanced from the East and had already encompassed half the sky. Slowly, slowly, like a titanic spider with a pendulous, fat belly, with shaggy, crooked paws, it crawled up to the sun, just as if it had stalked it, extended one paw,—and the sun began to tremble,—grew dim. Nimble—most nimble—shadows, gray, spidery, began to dart over the ground, and the air turned turbid, viscid, like a cobweb. And there was blown upon him a stifling sultriness, as if out of the maw of some beast.

Tikhon was gasping; the blood was pounding in his temples; everything was growing dark before his eyes; a chill sweat was coming out upon his body from his fearful lassitude, which was like to the nausea of death. He wanted to get up, in order to drag himself somehow or other to the cell of Father Sergii and there die in his presence; but there was no strength in him; he wanted to cry out,—but his voice had gone from him.

Suddenly,—far, far off, at the very end of the aisle,—something upon the blue-black cloud showed whitely, began fluttering, like a white pigeon illuminated by the sun. It grew larger and larger; it was drawing nigh. Tikhon was gazing at it intently, and finally saw that this was a holy little old man, all white, passing down the aisle with rapid little steps, as buoyant as though he were borne upon the air,—going straight toward him.

The old man approached, and sat down alongside of him upon the pine roots. It seemed to Tikhon that he had seen him before,—only he could not recall where and when. The little old man was of the most ordinary sort, apparently one of those pilgrims who go carrying ikons through towns and hamlets, through churches and cloisters, collecting contributions for the erection of some new temple.

"Rejoice, Tishenka,—rejoice!" he uttered with a soft smile, and his voice, too, was soft, like the hum of bees or a distant angelus.

"Who art thou?" asked Tikhon.

"I am Ivannushka,—Ivannushka. Or hast thou not recognized me? The Lord hath sent me to thee, while He Himself will come soon after me."

The little old man placed his hand upon Tikhon's head,— and peace descended upon him, as upon a babe in the arms of its mother.

"Art tired out, my poor little fellow? I have many of you, —many of you little children. Ye roam the world over,— beggared, orphaned; ye endure cold, and hunger, and sorrow, and oppression, and cruel persecution. But be ye not afraid, my little darlings. Bide awhile,—I'll gather all of ye unto the new Church of the Coming Lord. There was an ancient Church of Peter, the steadfast Rock that could not be riven asunder,—there shall be a new Church of Ioann, the Winged Thunder. The thunder shall strike the rock— and the living waters will gush forth. The first Testament was the Old,—the Kingdom of the Father; the second Testament was the New,—the Kingdom of the Son; the third Testament will be the Last—the Kingdom of the Spirit. One is Three and Three are One. Faithful is the Lord Who Promises, Who is, and has been, and Who will come!"

The little old man's face suddenly became youthful, eternal. And Tikhon recognized Ioann, the Son of Thunder.

But the hoary little old man raised his eyes to the black sky, and cried out in a loud voice:

"And the Spirit and the Bride say, Come! And let him that heareth say, Come! . . . He which testifieth these things saith: Surely I come quickly. Amen. Even so, come, Lord Jesus!" [105]

"Even so, come, Lord Jesus!" Tikhon repeated, and also raised his arms up to the sky, with a great joy which was like to great horror.

And the lightnings began to flash, white against the black sky, as though the sky had been rent asunder.

And Tikhon beheld One like unto the Son of Man. His head and his hairs were white like wool, as white as snow; and his eyes were as a flame of fire; and his feet like unto fine brass, as if they burned in a furnace; and his countenance was as the sun shineth in his strength.

And seven thunders uttered their voices:

"Holy, holy, holy, Lord God Almighty, which was, and is, and is to come." [106]

And the thunders were stilled, and there fell a great stillness, and in the stillness was heard a voice which was more still than the stillness itself:

"I am Alpha and Omega, the beginning and the ending, the first and the last. I am he that liveth, and was dead; and, behold, I am alive for evermore. Amen." [107]

"Amen!" repeated Ioann, the Son of Thunder.

"Amen!" repeated Tikhon, the first son of the Church of Thunder. And he fell upon his face as one dead, and lost his speech for ever. . . .

* * *

He awoke in the cell of Father Sergii.

All day long the ancient had yearned for Tikhon, tortured by the premonition that something evil had befallen him. He frequently went out of the cell, roving through the forest, seeking him and calling: "Tishenka! Tishenka!" —but only the wilderness echo responded in the stillness preceding the storm.

When the cloud overcast the sky, it became as dark as

night within the cell. The lampad glowed in the depth of the cavern, where both the ancients were at prayer.

Father Hilarion was chanting a Psalm:

"The voice of the Lord is upon the waters: the God of glory thundereth: the Lord is upon many waters.

The voice of the Lord is *powerful; the voice of the Lord* is *full of majesty."* [108]

Suddenly a blinding white flame filled the cell and a crash so deafening pealed forth that it seemed as if the granite walls between which the cell had been built were falling down.

Both ancients ran out of the cell and saw that the withered pine towering in its loneliness on the edge of the clearing over the low scrub was blazing, like a taper, with a vivid fire against the black sky—it must have been ignited by the lightning.

Father Sergii dashed off at a run, loudly crying: "Tishenka! Tishenka!" Father Hilarion ran after Father Sergii. When they had run up to the pine they found Tikhon lying there, out of his senses, at the very foot of the blazing tree. They lifted him up, carried him over into the cell, and, since there was no other bed, they placed him in one of the coffins in which they themselves slept. They thought at first that he had been killed by a thunderbolt. Father Hilarion was already about to read the prayer for the dead, but Father Sergii forbade him, and began reading the Evangel. When he had read the words: *Verily, verily, I say unto you the hour is coming, and now is, when the dead shall hear the voice of the Son of God: and they that hear shall live,* [109]— Tikhon came to and opened his eyes. Father Hilarion fell to the floor in terror. It seemed to him that Father Sergii had brought a dead man back to life.

Tikhon soon recovered completely, got up, and took a seat on the bench. He recognized Father Sergii and Father Hilarion, and understood everything that was said to him, but did not speak himself, and answered only by signs. Finally they comprehended that he had become mute,— probably having been deprived of speech through fright. Yet his face was radiant,—save that in this radiance there was something awesome, as though he had in reality risen anew from the dead.

They sat down to their meal. Tikhon drank and ate. After the meal they made their prayers. Father Hilarion was praying for the first time together with Tikhon as though he had forgotten that the latter was an heretic, and evidently felt a reverence toward him, not unmixed with horror.

Then they lay down to sleep,—the ancients, as always, in their coffins within the cave; while Tikhon lay in the hut-part of the cave, on a sleeping shelf over the oven.

The storm raged,—the gale blew,—the rain came down in torrents,—the waves of the lake surged noisily,—the thunder pealed without ceasing, and, through the little window came the light of the almost uninterrupted white lightning flashes, blending with the red light of the lampad glowing before the image of the Joy Unknown. But to Tikhon it seemed that these were not lightnings, but a hoary little old man bending over him, speaking to him of the Church of Ioann, the Son of Thunder, and that he was caressing him and lulling him to sleep. To the noise of the tempest he fell asleep, like a babe to the lullaby of its mother.

He awoke early,—long before the rising of the sun. He dressed hurriedly, prepared himself for his journey, approached Father Sergii, who was still resting in his coffin, even as was Father Hilarion, got down on his knees, and softly, trying not to awaken the sleeper, kissed him. Father Sergii opened his eyes, lifted up his head, and uttered: "Tishenka!"—but immediately let his head sink again on the stone which served him as a pillow and fell into a still deeper slumber.

Tikhon walked out of the cell.

The tempest had passed. Again a great stillness had fallen, —save for drops dripping from sodden branches. There was an odor of resinous pine-needles. Over the black, pointed firs, in the aureately-rosy sky, shone the slender sickle of the new crescent.

Tikhon walked along, alert and buoyant, winged by a great joy which was also like to a great horror,—and he knew that he would walk so, in his eternal muteness, until he had traversed all the paths of the earth, until he would set foot in the Church of Ioann, and utter a loud hosanna to the Coming Lord.

In order not to stray, as he had done yesterday, he walked along the high, craggy ridges, whence one could see the shore and the lake. There, upon the rim of the heavens, lay the thunder-cloud, still blue-black, awesome, and screening the rising of the sun. Suddenly the sun's first rays, like keen swords, pierced it, and currents of fire, currents of blood, streamed through it, as though there, amid heavenly portents, was being consummated that last battle wherewith the world would end: *Michael and his Angels fought against the Dragon; and the Dragon fought and his Angels, and prevailed not; neither was their place found any more in heaven. And the great Dragon was cast out, that ancient Serpent.*[110]

The sun was coming out from behind the cloud, shining in its strength and glory, and was like unto the visage of the Coming Lord.

And the sky and the earth, and all created things, sang a soundless pæan to the rising sun:

"Hosanna! The Darkness shall be overcome by Light."

And Tikhon went down the mountainside as though he were flying to meet the sun; all his being was, in its eternal muteness, an eternal pæan to the Coming Lord:

"Hosanna! Antichrist shall be overcome by Christ!"

FINIS

TRANSLATOR'S NOTES

1. Since Tolstoi's version is unrhymed, I preferred to use Nathan Haskell Dole's similar rendering.

2. Psalm CXIX,—1.

3. I am here again indebted to a rendering in *Odes of Anacreon—Anacreontics*, edited [and published] by Nathan Haskell Dole.

4. The first Mock-Dmitrii, pretender to the Czardom of Muscovy, claiming to be the Czarevich Dmitrii, son of Ivan the Terrible; his identity has not been clearly proven to this day. The opinion generally held is that he was Grigorii Otrepiev [The Ragged], a fugitive monk from the Monastery of the Miracle. He was crowned in Moscow in 1605, and next year (after a reign of only eleven months), slain by the *boyars*, under the leadership of Vassilii Shuisky. The rule of this pretender was marked by many beneficial measures; the dissatisfaction of the *boyars* was caused by his independence, the power enjoyed by Poles, the privileges granted to serfs and petty officials, and his opposition to the abuses of the noble *boyars*. There were two other Mock-or False-Dmitriis.

5. Daniel IX,—27; XI,—31; XII,—11.

6. Revelation I,—17.

7. St. Matthew XXVI,—18.

8. St. Matthew XXI,—9.

9. Daniel VII,—7.

10. Isaiah XLVIII,—20. "O my people" is interpolated, to conform to the Russian text.

11. Revelation XIII,—4.

12. Revelation XIII,—13.

13. Revelation XI,—7; XVII,—8.

14. An infallible cure for vampirism.

15. The date of the third—and last—important mutiny of this turbulent military body [The Sharpshooters]. They were first unleashed in 1682, by Sophia, who, in 1689, found them arrayed against her; they made a last, desperate attempt in 1698 against Peter, who extirpated them almost to a man by torture, hanging, and decollation.

16. Psalm XIX,—1.

17. II Peter III,—10.

18. St. Matthew XXIV,—27.

19. *Domra*,—a species of wire-stringed *balalaika*, of Tartar origin, introduced during the Mongolian Tyranny.

20. Job XII,—10.

21. Jeremiah XXII,—11.

22. Psalm XXVII,—3.

23. I John II,—18.

24. St. Mark XI,—9. Also, of similar import: St. Matthew XXI,—9; and St. John XII,—13.

25. An extra syllable is pardonable to one as agitated as the old Czaritza was.

26. The good Fräulein should have qualified "animal" with "two-legged,"—but, since she hasn't, I have followed the text.

27. This blackamoor happens to be an ancestor of the great Push-kin, and is the subject of one of his sketches: *The Blackamoor of Peter the Great*.

28. St. Mark XIV,—54.

29. St. Matthew XXVI,—75; St. Luke XXII,—62.

30. Let us not feel any too superior,—any American bookseller will tell you that the average citizen of these United States has as few books in his home as the average benighted Muscovite had in his, in the days of Peter, and bookshops find it just as hard sledding in to-day's New York as Eudoximov did more than two centuries ago in St. Petersburg. As for the lot of the translator, it is just about the same, save that the publishers are, if anything, even more pernickety than Czar Peter was. . . .

31. St. John XI,—26.

32. Psalm CXLV,—1.

33. The nearest approach to this I have been able to find is at the beginning of the Fourth Chapter of Baruch [The Apocrypha]: "Give not thy glory to another, nor the things that are profitable unto thee to a strange nation." Any better reading will be appreciated.

34. The eighteenth-century Russian could here be rendered almost precisely by the current American expression as "fried." But I have deemed it best to avoid accusations of flippancy.

35. The Czarevich seems to have been influenced by St. Luke XII, —19. Paul [I Corinthians XV,—32] is ironical, and so is that kill-joy Isaiah [XXII,—13]; Ecclesiastes, however, speaks of there being nothing "better for a man," and of such a course of life being "from the hand of God" [II,—24]; in III,—13 it is described as "the gift of God"; V,—18, and VIII,—15 also praise it. . . . Why Epicurus is always the sole one to be condemned for this philosophy has always been beyond me.

36. St. John VI,—37.

37. St. Matthew XXV,—42, 43, 45.

38. I have followed the author's text. St. John XV,—20 reads: "If they have persecuted me, they will also persecute you."

39. I cannot trace this to Nebuchadnezzar. See Ezekiel XXVII,—2, 9.

40. Acts X,—35.

41. Genesis VI,—13, 17.

42. I cannot find any authority in the Bible for this. Any information would be appreciated.

43. Ecclesiastes X,—20. The Russian reads: ". . . in the bed-chamber of thy concubine."

44. Psalm CXLVI,—4.

45. Romans XIII,—1.

46. Revelation XII,—1.

47. Monomach,—the Single Combatant: a title applied to the Byzantine Emperor, Constantine IX, and to Vladimir Vsevolodovich, Grand Duke of Kiev [QPTE-1125]—The Cap (or Crown) of Monomach: there are really two,—Grand Dress and Secondary Dress. The first was used in coronating all the Russian sovereigns up to Ivan and Peter Alexeievich. The second was put on during minor occasions. The Russian saying: "Heavy is the Cap of Monomach!" is equivalent to the English "Uneasy lies the head that wears a crown."

48. St. Matthew IV,—9.

49. St. Luke IV,—5, 6. A little marquetry was necessary here to conform with the Russian.

50. Psalm V,—6.

51. St. Matthew VII,—18.

52. II Thessalonians III,—10. The part about the sluggard seems to have been tossed in by Peter for good measure,—I can find no nearer Biblical authority than Proverbs XV,—10: "And the idle soul shall suffer hunger."

53. Psalm CXVI,—11.

54. St. Luke XII,—1; also St. Matthew XVI,—6 and 11, and St. Mark VIII,—15.

55. Daniel XI,—31; XII,—11.

56. Psalm CIV,—19, 20.

57. An ancient Russian manuscript, composed by the priest Sylvester in the sixteenth century, for the guidance of his son; its sixty-three chapters are crammed with admonitions as to faith and piety, and maxims of moral and worldly wisdom,—especially in matters of domestic economy.

58. Psalm XXII,—1.

59. St. Matthew X,—34, 35.

60. St. Matthew VIII,—20; St. Luke IX,—58.

61. Thus named because the body of Parthenope, a siren who threw herself into the sea because she failed to charm Ulysses, was washed ashore at this spot.

62. This particular Miracle-Worker is St. Nicholas, Bishop of Myra, and should by no means be confused with St. Nicholas of Tolentine, the Confessor; St. Nicholas the Soldier; nor, above all, with St. Nicholas of the Flue, the champion faster of his—and all—time, who went without a morsel of food or a sip of water for 19 years and 6 months. . . .

63. In Russia and, I understand, almost everywhere save in the United States, check must be announced to the queen as well as the king.

64. Condratii Bulavin, a Don Cossack and a fellow conspirator of Mazeppa; shot himself when defeated after a temporary success.

65. Numbers XI,—11, 12, 14, 15.

66. St. Matthew XVIII,—18; also XVI,—19.

67. Psalm LI,—14.

68. Isaiah LXIII,—3.

69. Genesis XXII,—1, 2, 9, 10.

70. St. John III,—16 reads *gave* instead of *spared not.*

71. The passages Peter chose to omit from St. Matthew XVIII,—15, 16, 17 are bracketed: "Moreover if thy brother shall trespass against thee, go and tell him his fault [between thee and him alone; if he shall hear thee, thou hast gained thy brother. But if he will not hear *thee, then* take with thee one or two more, that in the mouth of two or three witnesses every word may be established]. And if he shall neglect to hear them tell *it* unto the church."

72. St. Matthew XXVII,—5.

73. Revelation XIII,—4.

74. Revelation XVII,—6, reads: ". . . wondered with great admiration." *Admiration* is here used in its archaic sense of wonder, surprise, or astonishment.

75. Romans XIII,—1, 2.

76. Ephesians VI,—5, and elsewhere.

77. I Peter II,—17, 18.

78. Hebrews II,—6, 7, 8.

79. St. Matthew V,—10.

80. Psalm CXLII,—7.

81. Revelation XII,—14.

82. Christ, what abominations are committed in thy sweet Name! . . . The present writer remembers, as a boy in Czarist Russia, shortly after the beginning of this century, seeing precisely such a religious maniac. His upper body was enclosed in a sort of cage, made of wrought-iron bars at least three inches broad and one and a half inches in thickness, riveted together. His shoulders (the torso being naked) were suppurating sores where the iron had eaten into them; a huge, ponderous chain was wound several times about his waist; he was seated on the ground and, for some insane reason or other, was tearing calico into long strips. . . . All this with a spring sun at his back, a vivid blue sky over him, and the greenest of grass around him. . . . For other vivid sketches of Russian hagiology and mystical perversion, the reader is referred to *Aglaia* and *I Say Nothing,* in Bunin's *Gentleman from San Francisco* (Borzoi Pocket Classics).

83. Avvacum [Habakkuk] Petrovich: a celebrated schismatic; Archpresbyter of the City of Iuriev-on-the-Volga; noted as a preacher, and a zealot for Russian Orthodoxy; in 1665 rose up against innovations introduced by Nikon [Patriarch of Moscow and All the Russias (1605-1681)], defending the old ritual in many works and epistles; exiled to Siberia; spent fourteen years in the earth-work prison of Pustoversk; indited a dire missive to Czar Fedor Alexeievich; burned at the stake for contumacy in 1681. His autobiography, *The Life of the Archpresbyter Avvacum,* is remarkable as a specimen of apt, forceful, concise Russian.

84. I cannot locate this passage in the Bible. Any help will be welcomed.

85. Psalm LXXXII,—6.

86. Revelation XXI,—1, 5, 6.

87. St. Mark VIII,—35.

88. II Peter III,—10.

89. St. Matthew XVI,—18. St. John I,—42 may elucidate still further this exceedingly feeble bit of paranomasia, which cannot be dignified even as a pun, yet which serves as the sole foundation for an exceedingly strong Church: "And when Jesus beheld him [Peter], he said, Thou art Simon the son of Jona: thou shalt be called Cephas, which is by interpretation, A stone."

90. St. Mark VII,—17.

91. Psalm CXXXIX,—7.

92. More pertinently, Verses 8 to 12, inclusive, of Deuteronomy, Chapter XVII.

93. Proverbs XXI,—1.

94. St. John XXI,—18.

95. It must be remembered that at the time *Peter and Alexis* was written this was really a prophecy. The same applies to other passages in this book, as well as in other writings of Merejkowski.

96. *"Eloi, Eloi, lama sabachthani?"*—Christ, as reported by St. Matthew XXVII,—46, and St. Mark XV,—34, is really echoing Psalm XXII,—2.

97. II Corinthians VI,—16.

98. The nearest Biblical equivalent for this I have been able to find is I Corinthians X,—4: "And did all drink the same spiritual drink: for they drank of that spiritual Rock that followed them: and that Rock was Christ." Suggestions as to better readings will be welcomed.

99. Revelation III,—5.

100. "The beast and his image" are spoken of repeatedly in the Revelation. *The ikon of the Beast* is the precise Russian phrase.

101. Psalm CIV,—27; also CXLV,—15.

102. St. John VI,—37.

103. The nearest authority I have been able to find for this is St. John XIII,—32: "God shall also glorify him in himself, and shall straightway glorify him."

104. St. Matthew XXVI,—44, and St. Mark XIV,—40 are somewhat more blunt: "for their eyes were heavy."

105. Revelation XXII,—17, 20.

106. Revelation I,—13, 14, 15, 16; X,—3; IV,—8.

107. Revelation XXII,—14; I,—18. Also I,—8, 11, 17.

108. Psalm XXIX,—3, 4.

109. St. John V,—25.

110. Revelation XII,—7, 8, 9.

Modern Library of the World's Best Books

COMPLETE LIST OF TITLES IN

THE MODERN LIBRARY

For convenience in ordering
please use number at right of title

MODERN LIBRARY GIANTS

A series of full-sized library editions of books that formerly were available only in cumbersome and expensive sets.

THE TEXTS OF THE "GIANTS" ARE GUARANTEED TO BE COMPLETE AND UNABRIDGED

Many are illustrated and some of them are over 1200 pages long.

G1. TOLSTOY, LEO. War and Peace.

G2. BOSWELL, JAMES. Life of Samuel Johnson.

G3. HUGO, VICTOR. Les Miserables.

G4. THE COMPLETE POEMS OF KEATS AND SHELLEY.

G5. PLUTARCH'S LIVES (The Dryden Translation).

G6. ⎱ GIBBON, EDWARD. The Decline and Fall of
G7. ⎰ the Roman Empire (Complete in two volumes).

G8. THE COMPLETE NOVELS OF JANE AUSTEN.

G9. YOUNG, G. F., The Medici (Illustrated).

G10. TWELVE FAMOUS RESTORATION PLAYS (1660-1820) (Congreve, Wycherley, Gay, Goldsmith, Sheridan, etc.)

G11. THE ESSAYS OF MONTAIGNE (The Florio Translation).

G12. THE MOST POPULAR NOVELS OF SIR WALTER SCOTT (Quentin Durward, Ivanhoe, and Kenilworth).

G13. CARLYLE, THOMAS. The French Revolution (With 16 full-page illustrations).

G14. BULFINCH'S MYTHOLOGY (Illustrated).

G15. CERVANTES. Don Quixote (Illustrated).

G16. WOLFE, THOMAS. Look Homeward, Angel.

G17. THE POEMS AND PLAYS OF ROBERT BROWNING.

G18. ELEVEN PLAYS OF HENRIK IBSEN.

G19. THE COMPLETE WORKS OF HOMER.

G20. ⎱ SYMONDS, JOHN ADDINGTON. Renaissance
G21. ⎰ in Italy (Complete in two volumes).

G22. STRACHEY, JOHN. The Coming Struggle for Power.

G23. TOLSTOY, LEO. Anna Karenina.

G24. LAMB, CHARLES. The Complete Works and Letters of Charles Lamb.

G25. THE COMPLETE PLAYS OF GILBERT AND SULLIVAN.

G26. MARX, KARL. Capital

G27. DARWIN, CHARLES. The Origin of Species and The Descent of Man.

G28. THE COMPLETE WORKS OF LEWIS CARROLL.

G29. PRESCOTT, WILLIAM H. The Conquest of Mexico and The Conquest of Peru.

G30. MYERS, GUSTAVUS. History of the Great American Fortunes.